KT-502-751

A writer of immense gifts, energy, and wit.
— Russell Celyn Jones, *The Times*

Prose of inexhaustible fizz and bite... Novels with the dash, the scope, the prodigal invention and torrential verbal energy of this one come along as rarely as a snowstorm in Manila.
— Boyd Tonkin, *The Independent*

Frighteningly violent as well as beautifully modulated. It is particularly rare for this reviewer to look at an unread block of 300 pages and wish that there were more, but that's what I felt at page 178.
— Nicholas Lezard, *Guardian*

Meditative and high-octane by turns... but consistently engrossing. Almost alone among that band of young English novelists who made their names in the early 1980's he continues to produce hugely entertaining and serious novels that look as if they were based on practical experience of the world beyond the window rather than the odd glance downward from the desk.
— D.J. Taylor, *Spectator*

Mo writes beautifully and in terms of the sheer plenitude of his imagination is astonishing.
— Sam Leith, *Observer*

If a novelist can sink or swim by nothing more than the quality of his fiction, then this is one buoyant writer... a truly international novel by a writer brimming with confidence.
— Martyn Bedford, *New Statesman*

Among the many excitements of this novel is the freshness of its narrative voice. Mo's violent and frequently hilarious odyssey deserves to be read as a well-plotted adventure with its unfailing sense of structure.
— Andrew Biswell, *Literary Review*

Throughout this long, cacophonous, violent, funny novel Timothy Mo asserts a fastidious love of literary order, aligning reprobate themes and characters in military rows... imposing art on life at its most irredeemable. — Rachel Cusk, *Sunday Express*

Renegade
or Halo²

El demonio de las comparaciones…
— José Rizal

Also by Timothy Mo

Renegade or Halo²

TIMOTHY MO

Tim Mo

Cairns — with very
best wishes and
my great gratitude

Elisabeth 21/5 2000

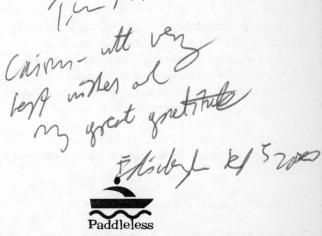

Paddleless

Renegade or Halo²

First published in Great Britain in 1999 by Paddleless Press
This edition published in 2000 by Paddleless Press

Paddleless Press, BCM Paddleless London WC1N 3XX
e-mail: timothymo@eudoramail.com

British Cataloguing in Publication Data.
A catalogue record for this book is available from the British
Library.

ISBN 09524193 35

Printed and bound in Great Britain by Cox & Wyman

CHAPTER I

L OVE YOUR ENEMIES. Far better than your friends, the dolts define you. Isn't the negative always more intriguing than the print?

I'm not too sure who or what my father was, but Ma was the standard slinky Asian Siren, by which I mean she found the A-cup bra a cone as voluminous as Pinatubo's and her shortness became apparent – thanks to God's gift to many Filipinas of comely limbs and perfect proportions – only if you embraced her. Then you looked down on the parting in her hair as if it was the river gleaming in the canyon's blackness. As for me, I was the giant in the pygmy encampment. There was nothing proportional or standard about me. My stature would have drawn stares on any of the world's streets, still less the grimy Lilliputian lanes of Mactan. Before my teens I found I had the strength of at least two of our *barrio's* scrawny watchmen but, more to the point, by ten I was already attracting droves of the prurient as I douched insouciantly by the muddy stand-pipe. Equipment, you see. The Celestial Quartermaster had given me that much more. The calibre of the puny Asian pee-shooter was of no consequence beside the reports of my mighty elephant-gun which had been bruited far and wide.

There I stood, glistening like a bronze of Hercules – me at ten, remember – still as bald and pimply down there as a dressed chicken and as touchingly unselfconscious as the pre-lapsarian Adam, while proud Ma bade me turn this way and that, the better to flaunt my inheritance before the other mothers. She basked in all the vicarious glory of the septuagenarian manager of some world champion; not a mother but wouldn't have shared her glee over Junior's asset, whether she was white or brown, rich or poor, bluestocking or ignoramus and Ma, though she was no simpleton, had the coarse and cheerful honesty of the indigent she was. With the crazed toothbrush she used to scrub our denims she'd lift my tackle to the cackles of her cronies. "Philippine *chorizo* or German prankpurter is more bigger?" she'd ask – like all poor Filipinos they were fond of exercising their imperfect English upon one another: when you all make the same errors, communication becomes flawless – and back would come the response from Auntie Irish or Auntie Lovely-Anne, "Black fudding more longer."

I was careful to keep a face as expressionless as a Chinese poker player, dignity being all we paupers could claim for our own. I would just ladle the water over my shoulders with a tad more deliberation. Once a jeep on its way to the base came to a halt. There were four American servicemen in it. All were black. Their stares converged on my middle zone. None of them said a word to the other. The driver glanced at the Brother by him, and they grinned and shook their heads. It was a moment of perfect mutual telepathy which had me in its compass too.

Without being told, you would be hard put to discern any Malay in my face. Of course, afterwards, you might remark the want of a fold in my eyelid and their lupine form; the height and angle of the ascent to the escarpment of my zygoma. But, unarmed with prior knowledge, you can mistake me for Jamaican, American, even Nigerian. My hair is tight and woolly, or can frizz like any Harlem dude's; my lips, as Father Paul was never to shirk from pointing out, as thick as Othello's. Disproportionately small and delicate, my ears hug a skull which would escape remark in a Dogon graveyard. My unprotuberant nose takes on the joint characteristics of both my races: short, flat, and broad. I remain darker than the lowest Filipino and, of course, next to them vast.

My earliest schoolmates – whose range of cultural reference frequently startled their seniors and social superiors – conspired to call me Frankenstein, that creation of separate parts whose strength was greater than the simple sum of his components. But, really, it didn't suit. Obligingly, I'd lurch around the yard, swinging my arms stiffly by my sides, as fifty brats fled my advance, leaving behind them the discarded rubber slippers which mark the flight of a Philippine mob in the way droppings and shucked tails do that of lizards. My very willingness destroyed the notion of me as monster. Kids are cruel and when they're not that, they're unfair, but nicknames must be accurate or they won't stick. I was too bright and friendly to be Frankenstein's monster.

"What we gonna be da ones to call you, man?" inquired Danton Zarcal, a wizened urchin of my own age but half my inches, whom natural meanness and a slightly greater endowment of brains had made the leader of the pack. He scowled at my chest and picked his nose. I laughed. Man, I've got weapons-grade laughter. You'll see. "Halo-Halo," I replied. Well, this was an inspired witticism at my years but not totally original. However, it was enough to crease my contemporaries, *Halo-Halo*, or *Halo²* in its shorthand form, being the many-hued and multi-textured confection of ice-cream, cereals, neon syrups, crystallised fruits, frosty shavings, leguminous preserves and bloated pulses that you can find under different names all over South Asia. Just one of the region's surprising constants, but at this time I alluded to variety, to delicious hotch-potch and inspired mixing, me as Man Sundae. We all entertained our private notions of this be-jewelled treat, as we might gaze on it in bowl or crystal goblet in the window of Kool Hebin Café or the Ays-Kold Soda Farlour. Our cartoon thought-bubbles must have been almost visible above our heads. *Halo* is what the angel has over his head. What was on our minds looked the same in its spelling – *Halo-halo* – but was pronounced Hallow-Hallow. Our thoughts were surely consecrated to it.

"Sweet," sighed Danton. "Oh, *sarap*, *ka-lami*, mans."

Now I didn't want to go through life being called Mr Ice Cream though it was one better than Bolt-Headed Monster. So I said, "Danton, I'll be called Sugar Rey, *di ba?*"

The small-hearted little thug pondered, and I doubt if he'd have conceded my request. What? Call me after the world's greatest pound-for-pound boxer when he had no inkling that his namesake had been a revolutionary hero? But just then the dynamics of the group swung my way.

"Yay! Boxer! Boxer!" shouted the other slant-eyed ragamuffins, "Nigger Rey! Sugar Rey! Sweet as Sugar!" dancing round me and Danton as if we were neutron and proton, then gathering their slippers and hurling them at me, from a safe distance.

So I, loftily christened Rey Archimedes Blondel Castro, became "Sugar", a common or garden sobriquet distinguished in this case only by its effeminacy, for I never in all my wanderings encountered another man so-named, although half a hundred hospitality girls in our town alone lived by that alias. So who cared? I smiled the smile which was to become my sword and my shield, my buckler and my blade.

Ma was only fourteen years older than me and a mountain-girl from Mindanao: half-lowland Malay, half-highland aboriginal, with a trace of philandering Chinese trader somewhere in the family tree. One more green sago bead and red bean in the *halo-halo*. At fifteen she had already been a veteran of the honky-tonks which stretched down Lapu-Lapu City's main drag, the bikini-ed girls swinging verily from the rafters or tugging at the sleeves of the American airmen with their lugubrious and unambiguous refrains, expressions which were nevertheless superbly succinct:

"Vlow-job?"

"In da ass."

"Hand-job, Joe?"

"Serr, helicoptair?"

I only got glimmerings of that. Ma simply referred to her "work" and cueing on both the mystery and nonchalance in her tone, I was at once accepting and devouringly curious. Around six o'clock she'd begin her primping, just as light was failing. Out to the pump she'd traipse – pressure to the adjoining stand-pipe, theatre of my own morning triumphs, dropping drastically by this hour – to bathe not just in flip-flops but shorts and halter, too. That way you didn't need a screen. Hair first with an expensive shampoo, nape exposed as she bent forward and down, employing the hand that wasn't making the two feet of jet pony's tail squeak and slobber to send the pump's hinged head nodding in a rhythm as professional as any gobbling bar-girl's. I stood ready to take over if suds got into her eye. There was an anonymity about this ablution, face hidden; it could have been any girl in ten Asian countries, akin to the namelessness of the Unknown Urinator, back turned, doodling his Memorial against the side of any tree or fence. She'd hurl her hair away with two hands, then pull out the waist-band of her "city" shorts and pour an entire ladle down the gulch. Back in our seven-foot by seven-foot hooch that slept three, she'd brush her hair through and through, me watching all big-eyed. Then it was the talcum-powder on the cheeks, to blanch rather than to perfume. "Ma, also me," I'd implore. And, "Hoy, Fermanent your ink, Boss," she'd exclaim, with an irritation that was entirely assumed. "Ma-a-a-a," I'd wail before she set off the soft explosion of the powder-puff on my nose, with another minatory "Hoy!"

Then I'd look into our shard of mirror with an eagerness that experience could never dampen to check if some miracle had not taken place. I hoped, you see, not just to view a complexion turned to Snow White's (as was Ma's desire with her own) but straight hair, long nose, and perchance ears like Goofy's. I could have waited longer than the scant seconds before I was pulled, gently, aside to let Ma draw and then mumble her lip-line. She favoured two shades, Mocca, just to be different, and the pale pink which actually suited all Filipinas to perfection. Eye-shadow she didn't often bother with. Manicure and pedicure were at the hands of a neighbouring crone who made her living from the bar-girls at marginal rates. The former service was an indubitable glossy masterpiece whether of scarlet talons or a simple, clear varnish of the dear, childish nails of the Filipina but why the ladies let themselves in for the latter infliction remains a mystery to me. Like many Asian chicks, they tended to be dainty-fingered and sturdy-toed, but for days they'd hobble and slide around in slippers, their cuticles mercilessly gouged, each toe-nail raw and stinging, still edged with the thin pink rime of dried blood and rubbing alcohol. If simple locomotion was painful, dancing on stage in stilletoes must have been akin to the mermaid's penance of walking on knives and forks. And when Ma got back at five a.m., or midday if it hadn't been a short-time guy, I'd be the one to provide the service she truly craved: a finger massage of neck and clavicle, followed by a deep kneading of those minuscule yet long-looking thighs and calves.

THOSE WERE THE EARLY AND MID-SEVENTIES, days so long departed for someone of my age, so fixed and defined in style and history, that when I look back they might as well be the *eighteen* seventies. It was the twilight of R & R. Down south we didn't get too much in the way of grunt and matelot overspill from Olongapo and Angeles, themselves just a brimming-over from the great trough of Bangkok. Once a year an oiler or a still lowlier fleet auxiliary might make its subdued grey presence felt in Mactan harbour (invisible in inverse proportion to the waves its crew were making ashore). Once, just once, a small carrier docked for four days that passed into local legend. The clap-rate quadrupled – an antibiotic-resistant Subic strain that drank ampicillin for breakfast, man – and some of the older bar-girls retired to their barrios on the proceeds. Most of the time, though, it was just the airmen from Mactan Field, serviced by gals like Ma in the clubs, or masseuses like Auntie Monalisa in Plato's Academy, the big parlour in Mandaue, half-way to Cebu, or just plain freelancers and hunting girls like the youngest of Ma's barkada, Auntie Lovely-Anne.

We were pimping for the pum-pum girls by the time we were six or seven. Danton Zarcal even got under the perimeter-wire one baking summer day in April and clinched a deal for Ancient Auntie Iris(h), the washerwoman and duck-egg seller, with the Puerto Rican fitting the drop-tank under, I think, a Phantom. He did her under the shade of the wings, the Sidewinders above them, his own snake up and hooded, and Auntie Irish's spindly legs in the air like inverted undercarriage. We were spying from our bellies in the grass. Auntie Irish was a good-natured old biddy, named after the flower, not the inhabitants of Ireland, but we all found it easier to shut our teeth and say "sh" rather than hiss the ultimate "s" of her name.

Plenty of enlisted men and even some officers had regular live-ins and when their tour was up a tiny handful even married and took their sweethearts home. Mostly they just vanished but, while they were around, a hierarchy existed. "Auntie Monalisa da live-in of First Sergeant Uncle Jimmy, da one to be Loadmaster not da one is Armourer," Ma would explain painstakingly – that inherent desire to regularise the irregular for the young – "but your Ma Ma is not live-in anyone."

"Where's my Fa, Ma? Live-in to you vefore I'm got borned?"

"Your Pa away in America, Blondel. That's all I know. Runaway da *lalaki* from da *babae* when she's fregnant, like all *lalaki*. Why you're not *babae* like your sister?"

"Aw, Ma. I'm *babae* and not *lalaki*, then I will having no big *tin-tin* for show while I'm bathing."

"'*Sus Maria!*" and the expensive Mason and Pearson hair-brush would stop inches short of my butt. Ma's punishments were ingenious but not truly painful: a chilli on the lips for taking the name of Our Lord in vain (she was allowed to) and kneeling on rock-salt with bottles held at arms' length for failing to wash. It was the temporary outcasting which was the infliction, not the mild physical discomfort.

I think Ma enjoyed her work. Some girls did, many didn't, but Ma did. Don't be too surprised. She had that optimistic and cheerful nature which makes courage easy and she enjoyed the society of men. She didn't dredge up the bad memories she couldn't change and she didn't worry about a future she was powerless to control. "Have got mind advance-dirty," she was to say with scorn of Father Paul. Oriental fatalism, something real, not the invention of the West. Even on Ma's official night-off which was the day before her weekly hygiene check, presumably the moment gonococci would have incubated to their most dangerous point – she would still repair to the B-52 Lounge because that pulsing cube of light and sound with its predictable customer-lady dialogues – as dependable as well-oiled machinery – and the totally unforeseeable revelations of the hospitality girls' gossip amongst themselves as they folded paper napkins on a quiet night, was far less boring than home. And when there was a supply cut the Fireball's generator came to the rescue, cheered by the patrons as if its first stuttering piston-strokes were the bugle notes of the US Cav, whereas we only had kerosene lamps which drew even greater swarms of mosquitoes. Going to the bar in her civilian attire, Ma was inhibited by the girls' etiquette from poaching because she held the temporary advantage over them. The guys buzzed round her. In her simple jeans and T-shirt she looked like the girl next door compared to the whores in their cocktail dresses and swimsuits and high heels. The homely cashier got porked three times as often as the most beautiful go-go girls because the customers were under the pitiful illusion that two thousand men hadn't had the same brainwave before them.

I remember Ma with her tough, self-possessed, snub-nosed face, the pugnacious expression that changed instantaneously to laughter. She had character; she had warmth; she was a gift to the men whose value they never realised.

Not many of the girls were locals; most had made their way to the strip from the shanties of mean provincial towns in northern Mindanao or from far-flung fishing barangays on waterless islets nameless save to the thirty families who inhabited them. Most of the bar-girls who'd been born in Mactan or Cebu were themselves the children of bar-girls and, more than likely, customers. In the B-52 and its neighbours the Bomb-bay and the Pistol 'n Holster alone were five black girls about whose proportions and hue there was

15

nothing in the least Filipino, yet whose mothers had been dinkier than even Ma and who when they opened those wide mouths were – oh, boy! – more Visayan than the Visayan. What was it? Not exactly Frankenstein, but a self-perpetuating human production-line for the bars, a compost-heap that produced inexhaustible supplies of yet more compost from within its seared and febrile heart. It was the sustainable growth the politicians are forever wittering about.

Because everyone was a transient or migrant they had no hang-up about their ancient profession. Their children came to the honky-tonks on errands or, like me, accompanied their mothers once in a blue moon on night-off. There was a homeliness about the life, the girls squatting on their hunkers outside, slurping soup-noodles, or snapping sideways at BBQ sticks, with their high-heels kicked off to reveal toes that were either those of a glamour-puss or a torture victim, depending how long since the pedicure.

We were safe with our mothers. There wasn't a lot of paedophilia in Mactan. I did once hear a visiting naval Signalman Second-Class saying, "Oh, yeah, you better believe it. You're a virgin in Olongapo till you've had a nine-year-old," but that was 'longapo and we looked down on those cocksuckers like Gomorrah might have looked down on Sodom.

Another time, when Ma for once was home by the kerosene lamp, she and Auntie Myraflora were discussing Auntie Monalisa, who had just then left the bar to work as a *masahista*. "She taking *pistola* in da hand-bag," Auntie Myraflora, a skinny, short-haired eighteen-year-old from Samar, told Ma.

"So? What so big danger about giving *masahi*?" Ma asked. "You got to massage crocodile? You'll be da one to shake his tail, ha-ha!"

"No, Rowena. Cannot choose customer there, *di ba*? Just sitting behind one-way mirrors, cannot look out, customer choose girl by number badge. So very old or very sadist, you don't know it. Have no system talkings, no lady's drink."

"O."

"So, anyway, massage begin. She always use alcohol, not powder or oil. Kill to all germ. So finish. She wait for da customer to ask, any extra service. He sure want it, yup. OK, half-sensation or hole-sensation, serr? All da way? Hole it gonna be, serr. First, some singalong. His mike deep in her mouth, *di ba*? Customer humming, too. Then he want doggy-style. OK, money down already. Then he changing da itinerary. It's her *koan*, whatsis! Hoy! she say. No way! Birgin hole. Sir, I don't like to dirt-track! No, he's half-way arrive. She can just crawl to her wash-bag, unzip, and get her twenty-two. He's on her back all da time, like riding. Then she point it back right on his nose, but she can't turn her head, only feel. Then she say, quit or I fire gun. No answer. He's concentrate on one thing only. Hoy! Sir, you fire your gun, I'll fire my gun. OK, he say, I fay extra. No! Out! She pull back da hammer. That get da attention. He move back, she turn over. He say I already pay, I want climax. That true, she think. OK, he in again, but all da time she got her twenty-two in his ear. Finish, take shower, all friends. Even tip. Of course, gun never loaded. Real gun, *pero walang bala sa fistola*."

"Niggers man, the customer?"

"No. German tourist. 'Kano is fay up front there."

"Ma, what's dirt-track?"

"That's when you do something from behind, Blondel, you should do it from da front."

"Like back-fighting, Ma? Making *Tsismis* and gossip about da feople?"

"Something like. Get three ice-candy from da store."

"Yay!"

I could still hear them snickering from the other side of the road. The customer's wasn't always the only game in town.

Ma mentioned my sister. Bambi quite clearly had a different father. She looked nothing like me, but was to all intents and purposes a doll-version of Ma. She was three years younger than me and was the product of Ma's short-lived Filipino boyfriend whereas I could have been nothing other than customer progeny. The guy had been short-lived in all senses. I barely remembered him. He'd got hacked to death at a Sunday cock-fight by two guys with specially sharpened *bolos* over a 50 centavos debt that had festered for months. I wouldn't like you to think this was very usual. The trifling sum involved was still a source of amused incredulity in the compound a decade later. Bambi's nickname was *Sincyo*, or small change. We were a family that cried out for grisly aliases. Why couldn't we have been Lofty and Baby, or even one of the cosily doubled-up monickers like Ta Ta and Jin Jin? No such luck.

Bambi was tubercular, and how. Not just a question of emaciation and coughing up blood and sputum. If you sat next to

17

her, you could hear her wheezing and leaking with every breath. Each inflation and deflation was a struggle, a minor victory in a war she was likely to lose. She hated the dope, you see. It really made her feel awful, to the point where cure seemed worse than disease. The bacillus, like clap, had developed resistance to the early medications and poor Bambi was on *halo-halo* multi-drug therapy, which she needed to maintain for two years. She'd have rather taken cyanide the once. Bambi had a little difficulty keeping up with our juvenile games, panting at the rear like a steam engine from a Negros island sugar plantation on shunt. Danton Zarcal was a merciless little thug who was prepared to leave stragglers to fend for themselves on trespassed property – whether it was rich *pinoy's* or Uncle Sam's – or stranded deep on some other ganglet's turf in an adjoining barrio, with his jeers their only farewell. Many the time I was the one to drop back on my mission of Bambi-extraction, retrieving my kid sister across my shoulders in the style of the Marines in the *Halls of Montezuma*. Once, not after a particularly arduous piece of derring-do, when we'd strolled back hand in hand, she wheezed with a smile, "Blondel, maybe I die next year or soon."

I said, "Maybe you die soon, Sis."

This was after we'd been digging for General Yamashita's gold-hoard on a patch of US-leased land. Danton, who was warped but perfectly logical, had made the following connections: the US, the Japanese, and then the US again, had been occupying powers in our country – no one had found Yamashita's gold – it must be on American land because the Americans had beaten the Japs – no one had dug where we were looking – therefore, it must be there. Our hole, and the mound of spoil beside it, had grown with surprising speed, Bambi playing the part of sentry with me as head-digger.

"Sst! *Mannoy*, looking da 'Merikano!" she'd called. I'd put my head over the lip both precipitately and gingerly and seen the guard with arm-band and helmet over at the wire some five hundred metres away. The others were already scrambling out of the pit, Danton, who'd never been in it, already off base land. The guard was unslinging his rifle but I knew that was pure bluff. Uniformed Filipinos would have shot children without a qualm, but not the Yanks, under ordinary conditions. And now that I could see the blackness of the guy's face under the helmet I knew it was gonna be cool. I took Bambi's little hand – with all our differences we had the same shape of thumb-nail as Ma – more for solidarity than help out of the hole. Then we walked nonchalantly to the wire, me pulling Bambi back when she wanted to go too fast. I turned when we were out and waved to the guard. He nodded.

It was when we were heading towards a sullen-looking Danton that Bambi said, "Blondel, maybe I die next year or soon."

Within ten minutes Danton, who felt he had lost face in front of his lieutenants, had me playing coconut pilot, shinning up the palm while I appointed Bambi guardian of my slippers. I didn't mind being fifty feet above ground on what was nothing more than a giant, pliant stalk but I objected to the rats which had their nests in the fronds at the top and, above all, to the snakes which also made their homes there. I'd lobbed three unripe nuts down – the best for Buko juice – when, indeed, I heard a horrible hissing and saw the tiny diamond-shaped head coming towards my face. If I'd been Bugs Bunny I'd have turned round and gone down head-first; as it was I arrived at the bottom with skinned knees in a few seconds, the serpent – I was informed – having abandoned the pursuit half-way down the trunk and slithered sedately back up into his balmy retreat. I didn't mind Danton's hoots too much; like TNT the little fellow was a dangerous but predictable quantity.

CHAPTER II

L IFE CHANGED DRASTICALLY for me at thirteen. Life began when I met Father Boy. Yet we are who we are, aren't we? I've learned to believe in destiny, in the immutability of our natures, in the ultimate victory of essence over context.

Better to say that Father Boy let down a ladder to me – in the analogy of the child's board game of Snakes and Ladders which was one of the first recreations he introduced us to (knowing from experience that the urchin had an instinctive grasp of it as metaphor, while the fact of rules might come as a surprise) – and I scrambled up its rungs with the alacrity of my years and hunger. He saved me several throws of the dice – time measured for one's turn in years rather than seconds – and he preserved me from slithering retrogressively down many a snake's back, but in the end I'd have travelled the same number of squares on life's board.

Later, at Artheneum, Danton said to me he remembered looking round his father's hooch at the age of eight or nine – a cardboard and nipa thatch rabbit-hutch even tinier than ours, and thinking, "Hey, mans, da life ain't for me." He had no experience larger than the barrio, no real comparison, only the utter certainty of this conclusion. He'd be Jesuit, New People's Army hitman, oil-rigger, stick-up artist, or drummer, but he wouldn't accept the lot of his family.

Father Boy was from Palo Alto and as Californian as raisins or sashimi. This could startle Filipinos. His name conjured up some diminutive and bespectacled native cleric with a blink and a little wispy facial hair, once an earnest local seminarian. In fact, you got the six feet plus, two hundred pounds, of Father Boy, blue eyes, fair hair, drawl and all. I do believe he'd adopted the popular local name

– Boy, Bhoy, Boyet, Boywin, take your pick – the better to blend in with the environment in the adaptable way of his Order which, for once, coincided with his own bluff and unassuming inclinations. Typical of Father Boy, the result was the opposite of his intentions. We ourselves, the youthful flock, grew used to observing the hurried internal revisions passing ill-concealed across the countenances of visiting dignitaries and, often enough, their frank dismay at having to cope suddenly with a 'Merikano priest likely to be unreverential of their position. I do believe Father Boy had little idea of the shock waves, or at the very least psychic discomfort, mere use of his name caused on a daily basis in his adoptive country but passed through his avocations in that state of bliss which was also the condition of blind Mr Magoo.

Just a few times in his life he was brought face to face with the consequences of his own actions when these bore an inescapably human shape: in the major instances, Danton's and my own ill-matched forms. 'Viper in the bosom', or 'Double-edged sword', and even 'Frankenstein's Monster' might have been the expressions which crossed his mind, except he was far too forgiving both as man and priest to permit himself to think in these terms. 'Hoist with his own petard,' was but one of the highly esoteric and colourful expressions used by his sidekick Father Paul. I learned later it was a technical expression from medieval siege warfare, referring to the fate of a sapper who'd got blown up by the very charge he'd attached to a castle gate – and perhaps Father Boy might have permitted himself this rueful archaism. To use another Father Paul-ism, Father Boy and Father Paul were as different as chalk and cheese, though sharing in some respects a common history. I guess like Danton and I. Where Father Boy was large, blond, and friendly bear-ish, Father Paul, an upper-class Englishman, was small, dark, and endowed with a tongue that stung like a cone-shell's spur. For priests they were a pair of oddballs, or so I thought at first. But then their generation had fought a major war and the fact that both Father Boy and Father Paul had been tankies was after all not so weird when one considers that Don Inigo Recalde y Loyola suffered that terrible leg-wound at the siege of Pamplona. To fight and not to heed the wounds, *di ba?*

Father Boy had tattoos.

All tattoos are interesting. I venture that proposition with confidence. They fascinate even those who – like me – instinctively consider them vulgar and repellent. Even the veriest visual cliches, rampant dragons, snarling tigers, writhing snakes, recumbent mermaids, command at least a moment's attention. But writing! No, writing on the body is of an entirely different order of imperative, demanding, compelling, extorting the tribute of perusal in the way that the greatest poetry or philosophy on the printed page, the most ancient and pithy of lapidary inscriptions, the sweetest nothings of the loved one on fragrant vellum cannot and never will. *Mom, Dad, Jane. Yea – though we walk through the Valley of the Shadow of Death we shall fear no evil because we are the evillest motherfuckers in the Valley.* Do we not spell these cardinal legends out with sensations of amusement, contempt, or horror, that no tome or broadsheet could ever elicit?

And Father Boy's tattoos – obviously professional handiwork and not adolescent ink-prickings – included messages alphabetically encrypted that defied our intensest efforts to decipher. Nothing in the Latin of the early Fathers, in the Roman tongue it cost our young and pliant brains so much anguish to acquire, nothing in Jerome, in the musings of Aquinas, or in the stronger meat of the Memoirs of St Augustine, was ever scrutinised with greater interest than the bodily stigmata of Father Boy. On his delts, fuzzed with blond hair and still shimmering as the muscle flexed under the marbling of middle-life fat, was what was unanimously agreed to be a unit insignia. We could make it out when he took us for basketball or gymnastics, dressed in *sando pinoy*, Oxford bags, ancient brown sand-shoes, and with his whistle in his mouth. (Father Paul chose to be martyred by heat in formal attire if standing in for his colleague at pommel-horse and spring-board). Under Father Boy's *sando* glimpses of writing could be discerned, whether motto, memento, threat, or proclamation of love it was impossible to discern. Once, purposely misjudging my trajectory off the ancient willows of the spring-board – a kind of giant, inverted mouse-trap – I stumbled on landing. This was at some deliberately contrived peril to both myself and receiver but Father Boy was the only permanent resident of Cebu who could have body-checked my impetus, already as formidable at thirteen as an adult linebacker's, so the only harm done was further pattern alopecia to the coir mat. I was so close to Father Boy I could notice blond hairs in his nostrils that were invisible at two feet and the fact that he didn't consider it un-priestly to use

Odo-ro-no. I looked at his chest rather than his eyes. His grip on my arm, as I thumped down like an Intruder on a carrier, had been formidably powerful but neutral, benevolent. Now it tightened to the point where his finger-marks were still pale on my black skin when I rejoined the line of my staring accomplices.

"What's up, Castro?" he asked, eyes mild, voice even, so it was quite impossible to recollect whether it had been suspicion or solicitude I had heard.

"It says, *ips…* I couldn't read the rest," I hissed as I went past Danton, the next in line. Well, the little monkey was the only one of us who could do a straight-legged through-vault but he was so excited he mis-timed, and even Father Boy couldn't stop him burning his knees on the mat.

"*Ips…* like fucking what, mans?" Danton interrogated me in the shower-room.

"*Ipse* – himself?" I ventured on a scholastic hunch.

"Ipswich," suggested another of the bunch, milling round my locker. "Town in London. Father Paul was showing us the map last month in Geography. He's from Ampleforth, man, the best school in all London. He's gonna get a scholarship there for the best of us, too."

"*Dili,* you misread it, you stupid nigger. It's IB5, mans. Infantry Battalion 5."

"No, Dant. He was a tanker."

"Get under those shower-heads this minute or it'll go very much the worse for the lot of you."

This was Father Paul, with his hands behind his back in the folds of his cassock, for all we knew holding his Buddy, the tawse or strap. I later discovered tawse was a Scottish word, very Protestant, but Father Paul was nothing if not Catholic in his vocabulary. We were under the faucet in seconds, pausing only to don the swimming-trunks which were mandatory for modesty and certainly utterly welcome to me.

That was as far as we ever got with Father Boy's tattoos. The thought that Father Paul might be tattooed didn't even occur to us.

It had been handed down from our predecessors that both priests had fought in armoured units during the Pacific war, and to this extent I believe in the intrinsic accuracy of oral legend. Stories about Father Boy pulling an unconscious and bleeding Father Paul from the turret of a blazing Sherman I set less store by. Father Paul, a

Briton, was unlikely to have encountered the American, Father Boy, unless he'd romantically signed with the Marines in 1941. But Father Paul never did anything in his whole life that was uncalculated. Father Boy, yes. Perhaps it had been touch and go whether it was to be the Jesuits for him or the Legion for a terminal dose of the violence his soul was sick of.

DANTON AND I literally ran into the priest in the black mud and gritty puddles of a wet-season dawn. We'd been looting from the PX: nothing big, confining ourselves to dry-roast peanuts, Hershey Bars, Tootsie rolls, Ritz crackers, and Jack Daniels, eschewing the cameras and electrical equipment which Danton knew would lead to our eventual detection and capture. Dant's uncle, on the lam from the provincial correction and rehabilitation centre where he'd been doing a life stretch for homicide, had given us bolt-cutters, a hacksaw, and a roster, all supplied by a Senior Airman who was in it for six cases of Jack Daniels. It had been one of our more successful forays. Danton himself had wriggled through the gap made by cutting out the centre of a trinity of bars – every now and then he'd lead from the front – and in this case his lack of inches and his agility suited him perfectly for the part. I was outside, receiving the heavy liquor cases, which was only proving taxing because of the awkward position for my elbows against the PX wall. As this was judged solely a boys' operation there was no Bambi on look-out. All went well until, padding along a muddy track, we thought we were in the clear. Then as we turned a corner we ran slap-bang into a Philippine Constabulary patrol, themselves removing an air-con from a Chinese trader's house.

Shhhee-i-i-it! I thought, along with everyone else, PC murderers included.

I had yet to learn the expression *Cave!* from Father Paul, who in his mellower moments would regale us with accounts of his schooldays. These were designed to provide us with boyish examples worthy of emulation or to enhance our vocabularies, preferably with Latin.

The PC had just begun to wear evil smirks when Father Boy materialised from that evanescent, rarely accessible but glorious dimension wherein comic book heroes and the Church's more flamboyantly martyred have their being. On his way to celebrate

Mass in a newly consecrated chapel, he was wearing a shimmering *barong tagalog*. Just at that moment a ray of Brother Sun's fell javelin-like through the strato-cirrus and lit him up in his white and gold. Not so much Captain Marvel; for me, with his blond hair, his air of vulnerable majesty, he was Alan Ladd in his buckskins in the opening shots of *Shane*.

Danton, whose only terrors were supernatural, dropped his box of cookies and exclaimed, "Holy Shit! *Wak-wak*!" or in English "Vampire!" This, I believe, was the moment Father Boy decided it incumbent to claim him for the Church. He'd already clocked me, my mouth agape, with three cases of Jack Daniels held in my stiff, monster arms.

"*Diri na lang*, my lambs," said Father Boy. "Here already now, my lambs. Put it down."

Some Jesuit!

Note, not a falsehood sullied those lips of a casuist. The Constabulary thugs looked at each other with what on other faces would have been consternation but on those dead and soul-less pans was closer to a crocodile's indigestion. And being as obtuse as they were vicious, the subtly implied wasn't enough for them.

"Ha-hah," said the sergeant. "It's yours, *di ba*, this stuff, Father? You know these, these…" The words for youthful scum like us, so much future salvage carrion, eluded him. Father Boy nodded. I think probably in answer to the second question and not the first. I don't believe his conscience would have pricked him at all. "God's children," he said. He then launched into the parable of the sparrows. Danton snickered, inaudibly except to me, and then my nerves made me find it funny too. A Sparrow was a member of a New People's Army urban hit-team, a bird-kneed lad not too much older than ourselves who specialised in firing into the Law's back, appropriating the corpse's service side-arm, and then making flight as unobtrusively as one of the dusty little city birds. It probably acted at the primeval level on the policemen's sub-conscious, for they started to get twitchy, tweaking their holster-fasteners, and looking round all corners of the marshy and hostile maze in which dawn had discovered them.

"Carry this to the officers' vehicle," Father Boy instructed me, his Chosen One, and I did not disappoint him in his assessment of my physical prowess, dumping the liquor and taking the air-conditioner

– a brand-new National – single-handed to their unmarked van. Another nod from the good Father and a case of Bourbon followed it, no doubt creating a new and favourable opinion that I didn't have muscles in my brains either. Father Boy was a big man, too, mind you. We turned and took care to make ourselves busy while the Law slithered their way uphill in second and then back down in first gear, sometimes turning a routinely suspicious glare back upon us. There were no flies on Father Boy, but we weren't dopes either. He'd thrown us a rope but we'd been the ones to tie a bowline in it.

There was something special about Father Boy. The vestments were no flak jacket. Under Martial Law priests disappeared, too. Father Boy could have been thrown backwards with half a dozen .45 rounds in his chest but he had an invisible mantle around him. Yes, he was a 'Merikano but as he stood there in the mud he exuded a more than sacerdotal authority. *"I've led better men than you,"* was the subliminal message to the PC. He was secure as he would have been with an inch and a half of Sherman's plate around him.

Thus it was that Danton and I found ourselves singing our heads off in Father Paul's choir, Cardinal Newman instead of Thunderclap Newman.

I OFTEN WONDERED IF OUR JESUITS hadn't deliberately set up their enterprise in the place where the prognostications were least favourable. In addition to the Base and the Strip our island, Mactan, connected by a bridge to the much larger one of Cebu, was officially celebrated for the monument to Lapu², the native chieftain who'd chopped Magellan up. Since then the island had become more notorious for the local expertise at poisoning. The shrine to the Birhin sa Regla ran a distant last place in real fame and, even here, Ma said the Rule was the woman's monthly.

We were kind of an unofficial junior seminary. Father Boy, Father Paul, and an Irish Monsignor now departed, had started the foundation on a shoestring in '57, the year President Magsaysay had perished in the aircrash. They'd begun as a foundling programme, for the waifs and strays, those kids who were much worse off than myself or Danton. Of course, Father Boy and Father Paul had no intention of wasting their team talents on simple relief work for much the same reason Lenin despised trade-unionism – it was a waste of time, was just a palliative and not a cure, had you forever responding to symptoms rather than effecting a cure (though with the two Fathers it was the cure of souls). I think it had been easier to get money non-denominationally for big-eyed urchins than for an austere Jesuit-staffed theological boot-camp. There was something of the blinkered ruthlessness of the Marxist about my two priests, although both, so dissimilar in appearance and temperament, were united in their detestation of the radical priesthood and its liberation theology. "Purest ego," Father Paul would say in his withering way of those clerics, the ablest all like himself S.J., who'd abandoned their black robes and crucifixes for camos and Garands, Confessions for Interrogations. "Vanity, Pride, the besetting sins of the priest." We couldn't have been more flattered. Father Paul was wilier than the most devious psy-war specialist; in his swannish, donnish hands Colonel Lansdale would have been so much putty at a tropical noon. His remarks, pungent as camphor, were Tiger Balm which stimulated the worst of Philippine instincts: gossip and treachery to the group. Oh, vices for us as sweet and addictive as adultery! So wholly worldly, our two priestly mentors were unabashed elitists with the holy aim of sifting out the best seed-corn, the priests of the future.

Among the most generous contributors to the Foundation of San Ignatio had been the bar-girls. San Ignacio would have been more correct but that happened to be the name of a nearby barrio with a bad name for drug-dealing and low-class native prostitution. Low-class was the problem for Jesuits because our priests, like Bolsheviks, clearly believed ends justified means. They had not scrupled to place their collection-boxes in the B-52 Saloon and the Bomb-bay Bar. And when they weren't Bolsheviki, they were bar-girls themselves. Weren't they a self-recruiting, self-perpetuating body who'd renounced the norms of society, in possession of trade secrets, mysteries of the craft? The Jesuits were cognisant of the magnitude of the Love of God, the girls of how little they cared for the customers who became enamoured of them. The priests were long-versed in all the intellectual misgivings which might trouble the sophisticated; they were masters of the logical riddles which proved beyond disputation the existence of God. Their Order, if not themselves, had been witnesses to the long train of believing and doubting humanity who had gone before. But the girls were also privileged with a jealously guarded knowledge. This was the number of customers they'd had (often as mind-boggling as the astronomical mileages of the heavens). And if the Jesuits had taken the vow of celibacy and the girls that of promiscuity, they were both available to all, scorning none when they lifted Ladies Drink or Communion wine, veterans both of the stranger's inchoate confessions, structured only by their own well-rehearsed and professional responses. They were post-masters and past-mistresses of duplicity. The Oldest Profession? Shit, man, it was wholly vocation.

WE'D ARRIVED A LITTLE LATE FOR FATHER PAUL'S LIKING. He believed in catching them young. He was unlikely to get his hands on the future soldiers of Christ before the classic age of seven, but our lowest grade certainly contained boys as young as nine. Whether Father Paul was susceptible to anything as vulgar as racial prejudice must remain enigmatic, but he did not take an immediate liking to me. Perhaps he just found me, in a favourite word of his, 'uncouth'. Which I don't doubt I was. In the pedagogical debate which was already years out of date outside their own particular circles Father Paul subscribed to the opposite side from Father Boy. Father Paul believed in 'brains' and Father Boy in 'character'.

"Grammar," Father Paul would intone before *mensa, mensa, mensam* and the later more complex verbal tenses and moods on his blackboard, "by which I mean order, law, hierarchy, and precedence in human affairs as well as communications, is that which makes civilisation possible. Without a universally observed system of rules, clear and unambiguous exchange between large groups is impossible. Then without mutual comprehension both cooperation between those living and transmission of knowledge to those unborn could not take place. Grammar is even more important than invention. It is the *sine qua non* not just of development but the safeguarding of what has already been attained."

"Father Paul," asked one of Father Boy's disciples (not me), "it's the Love and Power of Almighty God which creates society and the invented things, *di ba*?"

"Yes," replied Father Paul, who had heard this before, "but syntax was among the first gifts of the Love of God. And that is why we must strive to be perfectly proficient in it."

"Father," I now inquired, "Love may be possible without mutual comprehension? The Love of God passeth all understanding."

"Open your Kennedys. Page 139. Subjunctives."

But while the rest of the class were fumbling through their dog-eared primers he stared at me, and I have to record that from that smarting soul it was not an unfriendly stare. Henceforwards, I was the protege of both Fathers, Father Paul who believed intellect leading to a capacity for ethical discrimination was what made a priest and Father Boy who inclined to heart. Father Paul's interest in me was to be expressed in a particularly virulent sarcasm, in much the same way as his authentic affection for our nation, the only Christian Malays and predominantly Roman Catholics at that, was conveyed in sneers or gibes. For instance, musingly, with hands folded behind head, and chair tipped back on rear legs: "Why are Filipinos so slow thinking? Because they are accustomed to sleeping on wooden floors. A wooden floor is hard, so sleeping on one's back is more comfortable as distributing the weight of the body more widely than on one's side. But this means one snores and draws in less oxygen, thus starving the brain."

We would laugh sycophantically but he didn't shrink from sharing these startling observations with adult Filipinos, reflections which would have been grossly offensive except that they were always, but always, made in Father Paul's totally, but totally, perfect Visayan. (A language wherein his belovedly distinct cases of nominative and accusative could without warning turn into each other for reasons of emphasis and wherein possessive, dative, and ablative could become syntactical *halo-halo*). As regarded me, he made a point of mentioning "colour" in my presence as frequently as he could, whereas with Father Boy it was as if I was transparent. Discussing St Augustine, he informed us that Hippo in North Africa was near Carthage. I'd already been informed and diverted by Father Paul's (unoriginal) theory that Hannibal, whose feat of splitting Alpine boulders with vinegar seemed to us so much more impressive than the use of elephants as cavalry, had been the first great black general.

"And the world had to wait two thousand years before Chaka the Great," Father Paul would add drily. "Now, Castro, you with the unenviable name, can you enlighten us as to this?"

I'd shake my head. Was I embarrassed, humiliated, enraged? No, I was delighted by the attention.

And when Hippo came up, Danton asked, all innocence, "St Augustine a niggers man, too, Father, like Sugar?"

Father Paul replied, "A nigger, Zarcal. Niggers is the plural of that unlovely word. Re-phrase your question grammatically and idiomatically. Castro, help him."

"Yes, Father. Was St Augustine a nigger? Like myself?"

"Bravo, Castro. We'll make a scholar, if not a gentleman of you yet. Now, Zarcal, you have spoken with extreme disrespect of one of the Church's greatest and certainly most complex saints. You may do so in my class – my Order were the opponents of all inquisitions – but do not expect to do so with impunity. Extend your hand."

Many years later, in Pattaya, I watched a (very indifferent) movie about a navy cook's son trying to make it through Officer Training School as an aviator. I'd only gone because the "PI" (Philippine Islands in American military parlance) and specifically Olongapo, had been billed to feature – as it transpired for three minutes in what was obviously not a real location but a studio backdrop. However, the Marine drill sergeant had subjected the officer candidate to an unremitting stream of insult and denigration relating to his humble origins (before, naturally, the cook's son had passed). Anyway, I'd at once made the connection between a priest in his biretta and the black sergeant in his wide-brimmed hat. They had both been at one and the same time testing the aptitude and reinforcing the fortitude of what was their beneficiary rather than their victim. Just like the Navy, the Jesuits wanted a priest purged of personal weakness and tribal traits, a preoccupation with the self. They wanted him wrenched out of his context to be the more loyal to them.

All this was just Father Paul's daily routine. When time came for the annual school play in the first semester of my second year, what was my dismay when I learned it was to be *Othello*. I could see it coming – me getting the starring role at a precocious age not on the grounds of surpassing talent but for reasons that were purely circumstantial. I didn't mind being a blackamoor – no make-up required, as Father Paul pointed out – and certainly having him call me 'Thick Lips' for six months was as water off the duck's back. I dreaded having to get all the lines up. Eventually I did, and with Danton as Desdemona (he'd been more miffed than me with his girl's role when he saw himself as the perfect Iago) we enjoyed a successful one week run before such varied worthies as the Mayors of Mandaue and Mactan, two Assemblymen, a lady Senator, a USN Rear Admiral, a USAF Colonel and Major and (at the dress rehearsal), Ma and Bambi. The plot, I believe, was more easily comprehended by our native groundlings than the foreign elite, sexual jealousy, gossip, intrigue, and the *crime passionel* being so many staples of domestic Philippine life. Wiping tears from her eyes backstage, Bambi struck me on the breast, crying, "Why you don't let Danton explain to all for you vefore you strangles Desiree Mona? Take for while only, *na lang.*" It was at this time, after listening to Father Paul's cautions and plans for myself that Ma had described him as having a "mind advance-dirty", e.g. excessively preoccupied with hypothetical problems of the future.

Our uniform from the age of thirteen – and it was the only one I ever wore – was the seminarian's cassock. Our little ones wore blue shorts and white T-shirts, hand stamped with the San Ignatio motto, *et virtutem et musas.* Filipinos loved to wear uniform, to lose their puniness in a gaggle and, of course, we were all wedded to our ID cards. NO ID, NO UNIFORM, NO ENTRY ran the sign on the San Ignatio gate, as it did at the Police Camp, and at the Department Store staff-entrance. We Filipinos needed our ID cards like we needed to breathe air or drink water. Three hundred years of Torquemada and fifty of Loony Tunes – man, we had no idea who we were anymore. Only in our addiction to our specific vices, if you were to believe Father Paul, were we steadfast and coherent and one in particular of these national failings drove him to distraction. Worse, for dear Father Paul, than the murderous rage of the amok, than gangsterism and cheating in baseball-game or presidential election, was our heinous propensity to bear witness against each other, to inform on friend or enemy for the smallest of pecuniary considerations or even gratis for the sheer, shameful joy of it.

At Ampleforth, that acme and paradigm of juvenile excellence, Father Paul informed us, tale-bearing had been regarded by priests and pupils alike as the worst offence against their unwritten boyish code of honour. Sneaking, Father Paul called it, with a curling lip. "As a Roman Catholic priest, more, one imbued with the tradition of Yorkshire recusancy, I despise such treachery, such looseness." Stories of priest-holes in stately homes and secret Masses in cubbyholes followed, the priests eluding pursuit over hill and winding dale, bell and ornaments safe in their custody. That was the only time I tasted the tawse. In the interval between classes we'd been up to our usual tricks, including the flicking of ink pellets at unpopular boys,

31

one of whom had fled the barrage to the front of the room before, in desperation, hurling the board-rubber at Danton. He'd missed Dant, who, San Ignatian or not, still possessed the reflexes of the street urchin and the rubber had crashed through the window glass just as Father Paul was entering the building. Father Paul found us in an unnatural silence, all absorbed in our fascinating verb tables. No one dared look up, though collective horror was beginning to be replaced by group glee at the trouble the malefactor had got himself into.

"Who is the vandal?" Father Paul demanded. Silence in the classroom greater than at prayers. "Come, come now. Who has done this?" We could hear Father Boy's cheerful voice outside, taking the little ones for rounders, but we were not there. We were with Father Paul in cantankerous mood. "If the malefactor is a man, he will own up to his transgression." Plainly he wasn't. "Ten seconds, or it's detention for the whole class."

I caught Danton glaring at the window-breaker, who was sitting tight.

"It was Robles," I said helpfully. "Bonaparte V. Robles IV," narrowing it down from Demosthenes Robles and Beethoven Robles. I wasn't too worried by the prospect of an hour's detention. I was the only one in the class – which included a future Monsignor and, who knows, maybe yet a Bishop or a Cardinal – who actually enjoyed Latin. I just wanted to be helpful to Father Paul and popular with my classmates.

"Robles."

"Yes, Father?"

"Come to the front."

He got three strokes.

"Castro."

"Father?" Unlike Robles's my surprise and consternation were genuine.

"I do detest an informer with all my heart. His offence is far worse than a vandal's."

I got six and I returned to my desk with my eyes watering, though I was twice Father Paul's size and could, if the truth be known, have hurled him through the window like a board-rubber. It hurt far more than you would think – without remembering all the nerves with which the organs of touch are so plentifully supplied

– but above all my feelings were wounded. Father Paul – and I understand now – felt I had betrayed a comrade and, in particular, his stern Caucasian's code of honour. But though I was a Roman Catholic I was not, for instance, Irish, and I felt Father Paul had betrayed *me*.

SEMESTER CAME AND SEMESTER WENT. By the month it seemed, I became taller, heavier, stronger. The well-tried economy of the good Fathers in which superior class sold its gowns to up-coming year broke down in my case. At sixteen I stood fractionally over six feet and weighed nearly two hundred pounds, none of it flab. There was nothing for it: Father Boy *gave* me two of his cassocks. I liked him the more for not joking about it. He didn't smile and I looked serious as I said my "Thank you, Father." They'd covered his tattoos and I hoped they'd cover my own inadequacies.

In the great game of Snakes and Ladders becoming a San Ignatian was quite clearly one of the longest ladders one could ascend so early in life. But even on this first stretch of squares the tricky serpents abounded: one could flunk an exam too many, one could be expelled, or at the end of one's schooling one might find neither ladder nor snake but just the tedious prospect of life one square at a time.

Danton was more mercurial than me. He gave the good Fathers a headache, but he was the effervescent remedy, too. Father Boy liked me because I was big, like him, and maybe also because I was black and not blond as he was, but best of all he liked Danton because he was a scamp. In moderation, Father Boy preferred the Prodigal. Don Inigo had himself been a wencher, gambler, and duellist before he metamorphosed into Saint Ignatius. On the other hand Father Paul was your archetypal smooth man and, whether I was a 'sneak' or not, he found a kindred ponderer in me. No one else in all his years at San Ignatio had taken Cicero apart and bolted him together again the way his prized black Frankenstein had. Cicero and Atticus the pair, man. I was able to parse Cicero before I could recite the list of Philippine Presidents. Cicero, the vain fuck, collected his own Letters but not those of his correspondent, Atticus. Neither of Atticus's Histories, not a single one of his letters to Cicero, have survived. We know Atticus as an absence, an echo of an echo, defined only by the empty shape around him, much like the forms left behind in the lava by the non-existent Pompeian corpses, whose plaster-casts Father Paul's great-uncle helped to take. All we have to recreate Atticus are Cicero's elegant answers to his long-vanished queries and the latter's complimentary remarks on the former's correspondence. The sound of one hand clapping, *di ba*? There was no *Reply* or *Save Draft* button to click on for the sad fucker. No prizes for guessing how much Father Paul loved and worshipped the paradox inherent in this as much as he adored the mystery of the triune essence, the invisibility and universality of the Holy Ghost. A little spittle lay on his nether lip as he spoke in what for him was tongues.

"My dear boy," he apostrophised me, (and I basked in this address more than the pastoral 'my son'), "the kernel in any book is not its content but what it has left out. A volume of the greatest history or philosophy doesn't recreate the world; it annihilates it as theology does; it dispossesses and destroys it. The greatest art floats on the value and volume of what it has displaced. It takes its shape from what isn't in it."

"Like *Hamlet*, Father?" I asked. "We don't see Rosencrantz and Guildenstern killed, we don't see the Prince of Denmark fighting the pirates? And it's all taking place afloat."

"Bravo again, Castro. Yes, how our contemporary Tagalog film-makers would have relished those scenes. They certainly would not have excluded them."

Glazed, desperate glances from everyone else, while my knuckles whitened on the desk-top with the excitement, the sheer, heady thrill of the intellectual adventure.

Like the sable jackdaw, I collected Father Paul's words for their sheen – his freshly minted original coinages for their glitter, his pithier, folksy hand-me-downs for their ancient patina – though expressions like 'Gormless boy' had, *siguro*, never been uttered on our shores till he gave them currency. Language, Father Paul taught us, was the ladder over the walls that divide us. I thought not everyone could remain aloft on the rungs of his perilous scaling-gear. Still, though he was free with tawse and tongue, he was not bereft of a sense of humour. I recall him weeping with laughter after Danton, screwing up his monkey's face with the mighty effort, guessed an auto-didact, such as me, was "flying dinosaur it winds up, *ba*?" The good Father was a devout adherent to the very English philosophy of 'effortless superiority', a desideratum I fulfilled rather better in the gymnasium than the class-room. I thought we Flips were unrivalled at effortless inferiority but I did my level best to get above my context. You didn't have to learn a string of long words for this. It was in the rhythms of the English language, the repetitions you chose or avoided. We speedily learned the grown-up words 'the former' and 'the latter', substituting for 'the first' and 'the second', but only I made Father Paul start when I employed them in an answer, not a statement. "Are you physically fatigued or merely bored, Castro?" he'd inquired with dangerous mildness when he caught me yawning in class one sweltering afternoon. "The former, Father," I'd replied. His eyebrows rose, but not the hand holding the strap. Another time, after we'd been reading Rudyard Kipling – a favourite of the Father's, if not ours – I referred to Jun Revista, Napoleon Jumao-as, and Melton Duerte, who had been caught with titillating literature – as the Offenders Three. It didn't take too much in the way of effort to invert the word order, *di ba*? You just had to know it could be done and the effect it would produce. The others were cognisant, forgive me, of the former but not the latter. "Incorrigibly" was a favourite adverb of Father Paul's and I quickly learnt that placed before an adjective it doubled its impact and made you sound twice as clever. Here I was not alone. One day Dant used the word as an adjective before a verbal noun, "Da kid is an incorrigibles puck-up, mans." A stylistic trick of higher-class English speech that came absolutely naturally to native Visayan-speakers like ourselves was the pattern of repeating the definite article before two qualifiers, separated by a comma. Thus without too big a vocabulary the simple statement, "Michael is dirty and lazy," could be transformed into the entirely patrician, "Michael, the filthy, the idle." We were used to repetitions, but repetitions that weakened, not strengthened: *init* was hot but *init-init* was luke-warm, *amahan* was father, but *ama-ama* was step-father. When I played aimless pursuit with Bambi as a kid it was running-running; definitely not just running when I could have been after her for sweets or her cherry. And, of course, *halo-halo* was a fun, a dolly-mixture. Thus Father Paul built me up from nothing, circuit by circuit, association by association. Sneer, if you will. I began my ascent from the bottom, as a wind-up dinosaur.

Father Paul was quick on the draw, too, a classicist but smart and savvy with it. When I took a leaf from the notebook of a politician

I'd seen on TV and began, "With respect, Father…" he cut me short with a dry, "That is invariably the harbinger of something disrespectful. Proceed with caution, Castro, great caution."

When he was speaking from the heart one day, he uttered the expression, 'Spartan Christianity.' My brow furrowed. I raised my hand, only to see him smile faintly, and say, "Yes, I know, Flower, I know." That was the day I learned the word oxymoron, a momentous day for anyone, *di ba*?

We read, oh, how we did read. Father Paul was an erudite but maverick mentor. The two novels of Dr Jose Rizal constituted an important part of our national curriculum, Rizal the opthalmologist, writer, and martyr of independence whom the Spanish Friars had shot in 1896. There was no love lost between the Jesuits and the Friars so that wasn't the reason Father Paul despised Rizal. He found him vulgar. In us he implanted the treasonous notion that Rizal was a mediocre novelist, an unthinking imitator of the worst melodrama and contrivances in Hugo and Dumas. We must have been the only Filipinos who approached *El Filibusterismo* and *Noli me Tangere* (translated by an out of earshot Danton as *Don't Puck with Me*) with less than marbled reverence. In one respect only did Father Paul speak commendingly of poor Rizal. In all this secular saint's compendious writings he found but one phrase to approve of. Rizal, an *illustrado* who'd travelled in Europe, wrote of *'el demonio de las comparaciones'*, the restlessness and uncertainty brought on by too wide a knowledge of the world. The indigestion *halo-halo* can bring on, I guess. Rudy, the future Monsignor, then eighteen, asked, "So better not to read Rizal, Father?" Our teacher shook his head. "No, Madrid. Our condition is the modern condition, even if it is the work of the devil. Read, but remember that the antidote to the imp in the bottle is Faith. Faith is truly said to move mountains but it can also hold a feather still in the middle of a typhoon."

Lightweight our intitial reading may have been but Father Paul consecrated it to a weightier purpose. We read *The Jungle Book* early on, followed by *Captains Courageous*, *Stalky and Co*, and my favourite – budding Anglophile that I was – *Puck of Pook's Hill*, though Father Paul remained blissfully unaware of the unwisdom, the terminal unwisdom, of permitting such a title into the Philippine mouth with its friendly lack of discrimination between the consonant values of "*p*" and "*f*". Richmal Crompton rang a bell with Just Danton, while this was followed a semester later by Robert Louis Stevenson, Walter Scott, Captain Marryat, the Smollett of *Feregrine Fickle*, C.S. Forester, *Bevis*, and Father Paul's favourite of all, the Father Brown stories of G.K. Chesterton.

He under-dosed us, I have to say now, with the American boyhood classics. I had to find Mark Twain for myself in the Hong Kong City Hall library some years later, but I can't complain. We had the *Sketchbook of Geoffrey Crayon, Gent.* and most of James Fenimore Cooper. All Amerasians dreamed of the States, thought of it as their spiritual home. For most of us the RP was a way-station, purgatory with palm-trees, while Africa was perhaps hell. All except me. Through Father Paul's unbalanced reading-list I became an ardent anglophile. Nevertheless, the month we spent on the 19th century American frontier was the month I learned something salient, something more relevant, something for the years ahead. Father Paul, *Everyman* in hand – or was it an Oxford classic? – was expatiating on Deerslayer's almost holy reverence for nature and the animal kingdom. My long black arm lagged behind Danton's short one on this occasion.

"Yes, Zarcal?"

"How Hawkeye loves da peathered priends and da deers when all da time he's da one to fop off la longue carabine at thems?"

"That is a conundrum only for the simple of mind, Zarcal. Castro, elucidate."

I shook my head.

Father Paul smiled his thinnest smile. "He loves them, respects their guile, and admires their dappled beauty, even as he hunts them. The skilled and painless despatch is the highest expression of his love for them. Love, Zarcal, *amor Dei*, or profane love too, Duerte, are not simple things. You might say, Love your enemies. Well certainly, dear boy. But that is not an injunction to *like* your enemies. Loving them in Christ's sense is quite another matter."

No one else thought twice about all this, but I went home with my head spinning. I wasn't sure where I was or whither I might be bound but one thing I knew was that it was my aim to sound like a streetwise 230-pound Yorkshire Jesuit with a natural sense of rhythm. When reading brought me no peace, I'd resort to collages, borrowing Tailor Alvin, Military and Executive for Rugged or Civilians Attire, his scissors, to cut Father Paul's body out of the San

Ignatio year-book and surmount it with my own head. Then I'd hold his mug-shot before my own pan in Ma's cracked mirror to see him captain of my craft. Try it. The mirror throws you smaller.

Siguro, I could hardly be Father Paul[2] – his essences were too delicate to be smeared so widely. He was the most fastidious fellow who ever walked Colon. Once I looked at his plate when we accompanied him to the blessing of a Chinese optician's store. Father Paul chose macaroni-salad, some strands of crab-flesh, boiled rice, and a sliver of cold chicken-breast. Everything on his plate was white. I looked in dismay at mine: adobo gravy with peppercorns, squid in its ink, and shrimp-paste lurid as day-glo. That morning Father Paul had sent Washington Alegre out of the class-room for the impropriety, "the uncouth and illiterate practice" of licking his finger-tips before turning the page of a book. Alegre was licking his greasy fingers now but, of course, escaped censure, this being quite different.

Father Paul set down a classic English banquet of the mind before me but I'd be the one to turn it into a buffet. I devoured every Tagalog komik and Batman adventure I could, natch; watched violent local and American rubbish at the Ultravistarama and Belvic with Dant and the rest; and I read Bertrand Russell and Emile Zola. These latter would have caused Father Paul more consternation, had he known it, than any of Duerte's smutty mags. He'd made the mistake of denouncing the notorious French anti-cleric during a discussion of the Dreyfus affair, itself a tangent from his comments on a film about the French penal settlement at Devil's Island that was currently playing in Cebu. Father Paul made some unfavourable remarks about Jews, which I didn't understand as we'd never met any, but I was already planning a trip to the bookstore. There I was struck by a comment of the Frenchman's that I've never forgotten. "Hatred," said Zola, "is holy… if I am worth anything today it is because I stand alone and I know how to hate." Maybe what he meant also was that to hate on behalf of others was the intenser and purer flame. Then it becomes so fierce it is transmuted by alchemy into a sort of love.

Father Paul's mission was to love the sinner and hate his sin, to minister to those he considered his congenital inferiors. Was that why he loved me? He was as excited by the sin, the old Adam in our young souls, as a pervert might be by the odour of shoes on a pretty girl's bare soles.

Twice a year we went for three days to the San Carlos retreat-house on the mountainside. From there we looked down on urban sprawl and the coral-reefs beyond. The first of the retreats of my third year was marked by a fierce electric storm at night. I could sleep through anything and certainly by that age didn't take refuge in Ma's skirts if there was a loud noise in the sky. It wasn't the reverberations of the enormous clap of thunder which woke me but the admonition of a silenter presence. By the flash of the next golden lightning I saw Father Paul's face above me in the dormitory. The long room was darkened by the brownout that was more inevitable after a storm than the flooding. It was the strangest look he bore. Exultation, pride, wonder, fear, tenderness, and awe, fought for supremacy on his face. Darkness came, then the gelid and silent instant of brilliance before an enormous peal, hard upon it, so that I knew we were at the centre of the storm. By that flash I had a mental illumination. Father Paul's regard had changed. He looked down on me now with the affection of proprietorship, as of an owner for a rotweiler dog, an artist for a sculpture, or even of a parent for a child grown huger than himself. The lightning seemed to have seared my brains but I felt galvanised. Shit, it was freaky as the mad scientist's lab. "Father," I murmured, and I didn't know if it was a salutation to a priest or a lament for the family figure I'd never known. When the next fork lit up the dorm Father Paul had gone, whether he was *in loco parentis* or just plain loco.

IN THE END, OF COURSE, I was just too weird a mouthful for Mother Church, if not my Jesuits, to swallow. All the selection and the cramming, the prayers and the spiritual exercises, the cold showers (which were not the penance in our climate that they had been at Ampleforth) and the hot strappings – in short, the ripping-up of young plants from their proper context and then the intensive cross-pollination in the nursery – were to produce priests for the Church. That was what the retreats, the fancy reading-programme, and the sports were all about. I guess I made the short-list a lot more interesting but I was never gonna make the final cut. The fact that I was illegitimate wasn't so much the stumbling-block. That was but a canonical technicality in the eyes of someone so sophisticated as Father Paul. Many a priest from the branch sinister has been ordained. Trouble was I looked out of wedlock. The presumption

39

was against me, whereas it would have been neutral for a standard *pinoy*. In our archipelago, at once so rollicking and so prim, I would have as much audience with the public as a leper. A woman impersonating a man would have had a better chance. Me a priest? No way, José.

Father Boy and Father Paul as well, for all his flights of classroom fancy, were nothing if not realists. I think they discussed me a lot, much more than they did the boys who went on to proceed with vocations. At the bottom of it, I was interesting but inappropriate. I didn't kid myself, man. Father Paul's great gift to me was the ability to be dispassionate about myself, to see things cold-eyed from the outside. The key to the world of logic and learning could have come from someone else. Or, like a thief, maybe I would have picked the lock myself in time. What he gave me, Castro the sneak, the wind-up dinosaur, was a cool heart and a permanent emancipation from tribalism. Funnily enough, the former was the most enigmatic, the most Eastern of all virtues – I should say Buddhist rather than Christian. It was something to prize more than a mere code of silence, which is just an abstention and represents neither a doing nor the enduring fortitude of the true hero. What has a cool heart? *Halo*². I'm still a snitch, too, for who did they choose for the priesthood? Danton.

Chapter III

Galway,
March 1 1982

Hey, "Sugar Mans"!

Shit! I got to get my acts together mans, we gotta get outta dis flace if it's da last ting we eber do girl dere's a vetter life for you and me. Well, to all co-workers thanks returning from me sincerely yours. This place so cold so cold man it's like they putting your "balls" in da ref two days. I don't kidding you mans. Flane journey not so bad. OK long hours in da seat but free da drinks man. Starting with cokes then asking a beers. First da guy won't want to serve me. Ask: "How old you are, sonny?" I say, "Nineteen, sir." He say, "I think fourteen." Well "shit" mans you know I running seventeen next September. So OK I don't blowing my cools. He say, "If you're nineteen, you're a shrimp." I say, "Small but terrible, sir." He laugh man, laugh so much I think maybe *ihi* himself in da briefs. Then bringing me da two beer. I think he's da one to be a *bayut* man. All da three stewards look that way to me man holding their hand, mans, like it da bird wing and they walking like they got their week wage hide up da backside mans. Later I'm going to da CR – tiny place in da flane tail, man, you scare it gonna fall off if you push da flush – he's da one to be waiting outside. Look at me in a certain way, you get da drift. Anyhows, more beer coming. I reckon he da one try to get me drunks. Da chicks da good-looking ones da stewardess mans. But snub me mans. Those kind of chick thinking their "shit" don't stink man. Stop in Vombay, man, I'm really in liquor. Fall to sleep on bench it's da wooden one. Some passengers I hear complaining how hard da wood but it's OK to me. Remembering Fr. Paul his comment da Pilipino sleep on his back. Then I don't hear da announcement. Indian guy with cloth round head is da one to wake me got da old guns but well maintain not armalite, not Garand, bolt da action, but he and da gun together man they look a good team, man. Steward waiting for me at top of metal steps to da flane door.

Arms folded head one-side. I'm 100 per cent he's da one to be a pucking *bayut* now. He say, "Nanny didn't wake you, dear?" I know Nanny now – means in Pilipino Yaya, man. I say, "Puck you, you pucking *bayut*, man." He say, "As Oscar would have been proud to say." Who is Oscar I don't know. I know Mike Nevada Oscar Papa. Rest of flight OK. At da end I'm getting off, got three mini bottles of whisky in my pocket, man, some 4711 cologne from da CR, sachet scented wet napkin, others sundry. Da *bayut* saying bye bye everyone at da door. He see me coming, say, "Here, sir, have a few more to go with da ones in your pocket. With da compliments of da airline and my own." It's four mini-bottles gin tonic, vodka, brandy, whisky, mans.

Well waiting a long time already at da airport for da next plane for operational reasons of fogs man. I'm da one to walk around da transit lounge and see a kid pouring four old coffees half left into one cup make one big one. Look a *pinoy*, man. We looking. He say, *"Pilipino ka ba?"* (I don't know how many time I said that until now, mans, maybe one hundred more and always correct). Reply, "O, mans." Turn out he's going to Galway too but we didn't see each other one on da plane. On purpose of Fathers, I think. He's a little guy called Simeon Limot, real bright, mans, as bright as you maybe, Sugar. Same way of talking. He wait and think, you worry he's tongue-tie, then rat-atat-atat, like you it's coming out like a machine-gun. Always da one to help me with my work and Latin.

Funny, not so much goddam pucking Latin here, but plenty of games. Every other day have football or rugby or hockey. I real good at hockey mans other two don't so much care for. I can whack da Irish boys knees accidental on furpose, mans, ribinge taste sweeter than honey da Frophet say. You glad to run for it's so cold here like I say da inside of da refs. Wind blow from da ocean day long, spoiling your hair-styles except of course no chix here for da chix-killer, me truly. To all for now, Sugar mans. Remember distance is no hindrance of forgetfulness. The Boss man was writing,

Danton.

Hey Sugar

It's me again your old buddy in correspondence always. Now I'm writing from da dorm before in da CR (Common room mans not Comfort Room). I'm in da old folks home detail today. Not such popular job mans. Sometimes can go to da Boys Club or best have da Girls Club here even very young but already noticed da Pilipinos don't get much chance of this. Most time I'm da one to work in da gardens have not just flowers mans but plenty fruit tree vegetable potato you name it man we got it. No manga or coconut, I seen already manga in da shop but big red and green not like Pilipinas and you know how much it cost maybe two hundred pesos mans not five or ten and these more like *basura* manga mans carabao manga mans. I try telling da Irish kids what it taste like but can't. How you can describe flavour of manga? Except delicious *sarap* but sometime make you feel vomit allergic. Plenty pear apple man real cheap and plenty not like apple in Pilipinas man but you know want to describe pear taste in da mouth to you but can't. It grow a small trees man like apple not big like manga man. About eighty per cent da kid in seminary here is local man. Rest is foreigners. Hey mans I a *foreigner* now ha ha! Guess we're all *Halo*[2] here man. *Tsismis* here man – gossip da English word of slang – is it cost each one da foreigner student more than twenty thousand pounds da Fathers spending. Wow! And so far mans only maybe one in fifty go to proceed with their vocation mans. Very disappoint da Fathers *di ba?*

Hey man, I start write this letters to you again mans but now in da Common Room again not dorm. Been da old folks home until now yuks man. Cannot chew man have no teeth but also man *nangihi* and worse in da trouser and briefs man yuks. In da wheelchair spit man come from da mouth man dirty from da nose no wipe yuks. Not happening with us mans like that. Looking after Lolo, Lola in da own house man by da own family man in da Pilipinas. I don't like to be in da pucking wheelchair like that man better dead already, your friend and buddy until now

Danton.

Galway
April 20 1982

Hi Sugar!

How you are? Regarding me I'm fine all things considering. Sure, and I'm never da one to be complainin' old friend. Spent two days in da Sanatorium mans. Really suppering terrible in my life mans from da pain of da bee bites. I'm da one to go and collect da honey and da wax last Sunday. Fathers can sell in da special jar or da special label plenty cashes and da pure white wax worth more than da honeys and da impure brown one nearly. *Sarap* man da honeys on da toast bread. I been da one to do it before wearing special thick glove and apron mans and da hat wide-brim like da Marine also got da voile on it man pucking bees don't get through da net, *di ba*? This time don't use da frotective gear coz I'm da one to see Fr. Aloysius collect da combs have nothing little smoke only already. Oh shit mans and how making da terrible mistake there. I use too much smoke mans burn da bees man and also standing in front block their escape route mans. Bees they got real mad mans buzz buzz go for me even one bite two OK mans but maybe fifty sixty I'm da one to get it in da face and da hands. Running mans jump in da carp-pond bees still wait da surface got to hold breaths get head under da water mans. I so swollen in da face mans I think my own Mama not recognise me. Well they tell me I coulda die if I real allergics *pero suerte ko* mans. Those pucking bee mans like *pinoy* man dangerous in da gang group, small but terrible man. Da other kid man even da *pinoy* think it's real funny mans can't stop laughing and I suspicious even da Fathers man their face. Maybe also you mans don't laughing I kill you motherpucker. Hands sore a little now from da writings. I write soon thanks your letter man. I show Simeon and he say perfect your English man I say Latin 2 mans.

From Dant da one got bite.

Hi Sugar!

I sin not writing you so long old friend sorry mans I freoccupy.
Oh boy have big trouble. They catch me two things mans. I running
da table tennis league pay silber coin can win anudder silber coin if
you going through da League only little ways, have draw who da one
to play who. Look easy mans but depend who you getting to play.
Well da Irish da English kids mans they can't spin da ball man. Hold
da bat man like they got da snake by its neck mans instead of pen
hold grip man we learn from da *insik* pucking Chinese man. So it's
no hassle I win every time excuse I love myself my native land man.
So what happens is I take every time da silber coin like candy from
da baby but show other result on League list no one notice no one
care if they beaten early, *di ba?* So far so goods. Then I looking da
silber coin. I think hey can dip da same size coin da copper fenny in
silber no one know da difference. Learning this one in da chemistry
class. So man I put da fenny in da solution run electric current
through man and you rilly-rilly surprise man. Look just like da silber
coin also man. Slow-slow spending in da "tuck-shop" man (that's not
casa like full of chix is *mga borikat* frostietutes man it's just where you
get snacks mans you feeling hungry OK). Anyhows I spend too fast
or sumpin or da fat lady in da tuck-shop not so stupid as she look
man coz upshot soon they seeing sumpin wrong da *sincilyo* they got
man. Well I'm da one they catch. Well natch man I'm da one to
deny all da charges of moral turfitude, but it's no availing. Da way Fr.
Aloysius look at me mans I know I got no chance. I offended man
his lack of trust coz I pucking starting to believe myself mans. Then
da clincher mans – it's da *pinoy* who da ones to spill da beans on
yours truly. Get together whispering man face holy holy then
choose one to be da Judas Iscariot. Eyes everywhere mans never
know they know already. It's da first time I see what Fr. Paul mean
man – I don't like da pucking informer mans is da lowest of da low
da scums of da earth. I guess I stop being Pilipino man! Irish kids say
nothing mans. Shake their heads man when da Fathers asking about
da table tennis tournament. They look at me mans I know I going
to get it but from them not da Fathers. I have to change into football

short man no brief underneath man rill thin da cloth man. I standing at da front in assembly afterward man and I tinking you pucking eejit Dant. Fr. Aloysius he's big young priest big as you and Fr. Boy but mean man like hell and he's da one to tan me. Oh man! Just so bad as da bee bites only don't get no two days in da San after. My eyes watering man to tell you da truth I crying man then have to shake hands with Fr. Aloysius when man I like to kick da Culchie Mug in da balls or pay da Constabulary or Sparrows to salvage da motherpucker. They're a little bit crazy these 'Merikano Sugar. OK is all for now. Yup I receive all your letter thanks for your memory of your old friend specially da dry strip manga *sarap lami* man and is easy and cheap to slip in da envelope coz thin but heartily given man God bless you.

It's Danton.

Galway
March 12 1983

Dear Sugar,

I'm da one to owe you four letters to be sure but it's never eight months since I wrote? Seems like a few weeks old friend. We went to Achille island it was great crack old friend. We're da ones to ride in da bus da Fathers hire. It's a long way down da coast, man, like from maybe Talisay man until Oslob. It would remind you of home if yourself was da one to be here. Da lighthouse keeper there have a little rifles .22 varmint rifles man. He's da one to hunt da rabbit with it. Never seen so many rabbit Sugar even he's shooting them every day. Would you say da poor rabbits had nothing else to do except you know whats old friend? I got one pop! Maybe twenty yards in da head. It was great crack man and a real good ficnic lunch. I see da Keeper give Fr. Aloysius a Guinness, that's black beer stout. Hey man! Suit you to be sure. I never see a single black guy all my time here to be sure. I real sorry to be a unreliable writer. I got nearly a girlfriends in da town here. She's da one working at da tea-bar, colleen which is chick here she's got red hair old friend. I tell her learning from da Irish kids, "You're da beautiful girl of da world." No response no regard. But I'm also no retreat no surrender. "You move me," I'm da one to say. She say "Here's your tea," but da way she say, "Milk?" then "It's da sugar there," I know she's da one to like they say fancy me. Keep coming your letters for me mans coz I'm not reply don't mean I don't get them.

Your friend, Dant.

Hook Of Holland,
August 19 1983

Jaizus, Sugar! Real trouble, old friend. Maybe I'll be da one to see you before you get this letter not sure how much money da stamp to put on. Catch me in Amsterdam, man, my pants is down and worse man I da one to catch Fr. Aloysius with his pant down. We going to play hockey v. da Dutch seminarians – real big Frotestants there so encourage da Roman co-workers OK – then we miss our train connection in Amsterdam CS (that's Centraal Station spell a little different in da Dutch language but I know old Sugar is da one intelligent to work it out OK mans) and we make a walk thirteen of us eleven player one linesman one reserve in our cassock holding valise and hockey stick and to be sure with Fr. Aloysius and Fr. Padraig (but say it Pawrick) it's net figure fifteen little Injun. We take da wrong turning to be sure old friend we get off da big street call it Damn Rat sumpin over small bridges and river ways a little like I see Tondo and Pasig and hey man it's full of chix and colleens in da house windows. Bold show old friend! It's not night ten a.m. in da morning *na lang* they're not wearing nothings mans even they 'Merikana sumpin telling me da little birdie mans these colleens is frosties man. Open da curtains and show you all – titty, canal, pussy, old friend it's more than Mandaue man where lewd inside no bold show outside. I tell you one minute we're lost all separate. Not on furpose man like they blame me now you believe me I'm telling da truths it's just where our attention was concentrate. Some looking in this window some being da ones to cross da road, some walking full ahead hand over eye, others slow astern watchful mans and some, to be sure old friend, pucking dead already in da water man so nett figure already of just three little Injun near me. I'm in front of one window, da curtain open and shit! Looks just like Filipina. She's da one to wink, real slow and dirty and bend da finger at me man. It's come here sweetheart or this is da way I finger myself? Don't know which. Going in, man. *Pilipino ka ba*? No she's da one to be Thai old friend. Coulda fooled me exactly same, skin, colour, size man. But she's got a buddy and it's Pilipina but just now occupy. She say to me, I give you special frice. Those words, man, are music to my ears. She's going to be da one to give me a hot towel baths – it's free for me – then I hear da door open again. She say OK no problem. Number Three girl will see da customer. Some murmurings – we're only inside a curtain (red velvet) and voice is familiar. I'm wondering who it is. Then I know. Sound like Fr. Aloysius. I know I'm da one to be a stoopid ting but mans I just can't stop myself from being da one to take a feek. Holy Moses! It's young Fr. Aloysius but somehow he found somewhere to change into da tweed jacket and slax but he still got on da white collar eejit. I can't stop myself, my head's coming out more and more like da unwise turtle then he's seen me just my head! Oh Jaizus and all da Saints. I'm through da curtain pull up my briefs under da cassock and going through da door bump I slam into old Fr. Padraig it's just da Irish for Patrick. Now I know he's not da one to be here for funs out of da question man it's a police visit man from him, burn me at da stake. Oh boy! Meanwhile Fr. Aloysius he's da one to be quick to get into my old cubicle with my girl. Fr. Padraig his face man God da father at da Last Judgement old friend. Stern ain't in it mans. Cut da long stories short he's da one pulling me by da ears in da street, we're collecting da other little Injuns one by one, finally appearing Fr. Aloysius in cassock. Where the divil have you been man? Game cancel it's back to ferry great ferry clean da CR not like Pilipinas man.

Anyway old friend I da one to jump from da prying-fan into da fire. Fr. Padraig da one to give me da third-degree treatment. I tink I'll turn state-witness for da amnesty and immunity, mans. You see, I say Fr. Aloysius da one to try to sauce his sosidge too. That's when da shit hit da pan. Fr. Padraig say he gonna give me anudder chance until now was only venial sin but my wicked lie now a cardinal sin.

Looks big froblem old friend. I tink they'll send me home in disgrace.

Have me in your thoughts, Danton.

PS Also your prayer, mans.

CHAPTER IV

EVEN NOW, I'd hesitate to call Attorney Caladong a hypocrite. The little guy had a perfect, a real, reverence for the Law. He'd been steeped in it, to the extent you might say it had pickled his brains. Better than anyone in the Philippines, lawyers knew how useless the Law was: they being the ones who approached His Honour with the bribe and then wrote his judgement for him. They were the ones who'd had all those miraculous escapes when, with a case prospering, flying along pell-mell, they'd had their steed shot from under them. Metaphorically speaking, our Atty Caladongs would pick themselves up, dust off their palms, and mount another but for the steed-client the bullet in the head was a terminal writ. After a while, very sophisticated clients might discover there was little need for the legal preliminaries at all. These throat-clearings, the hoiking previous to the spitting, were a little like the scenes of insult and counter-insult before a set-piece Wars of the Roses battle in Shakespeare. They could be skipped and the business of assassination got on with immediately. After all, the best hired-gun charged a fifth of the worst lawyer's fee.

Man, Atty Caladong had seen it a thousand times, not even the most compulsive and longevitous of litigants could claim that. And yet the Attorney clearly still revered the Law, had anything but contempt for the Court. On the rare occasions when he found his own interests – different from a client's – jeopardised by a more powerful and influential adversary, he displayed the most touching faith in the impartiality and efficiency of the bench, he who of all people should have known better. Thus he had lavished months on the *quo warranto* action and petition to unseat the family foe who had supplanted him in his post of municipal lawyer in the hick-town in

Mindoro from which he had descended to teaching us. It was a hick-town, *siguro*, but a lucrative post (always amazing how much money could be squeezed out of those run-down places – maybe that was why they looked such dumps). Anyhow the family adversary had paid far bigger bucks and his selection was a foregone conclusion. Yet Atty Caladong still spoke in a measured way of according due process, weighed up pro and con – not necessarily in a court-room affair, this could be the merits of clothes-grade bar-soap v. washing-liquid or coffee granules v. coffee powder – with an unhurried deliberation that brooked no interruption. His speech was slow and weighty; he held up each concept, each assumption – powder dissolved better than granules, but on the other hand granules stored better in a tropical climate – with the pedantic meticulousness of a housewife inspecting a papaya or a snapper in the market. Nothing, his manner implied, was so trivial or so high falutin that it could not be subjected to the "lawyer's way of thinking" and the correct, the majestic, verdict given.

Like the wheels of Justice, the cogs of the Attorney's own mental processes ground very slowly, in fact with remorseless cunctation. At some stage in the Attorney's life, if Fr. Paul's dictum is to be believed, he must have passed a great many of his sleeping hours on his back with his brain cells in a chronically anoxic condition. This was by no means peculiar to Atty Caladong – at least half the bar and three-quarters of the Bench grabbed on to solemnity of utterance and graveness of demeanour as if they were the twin flotation pockets of the only intellectual life-preserver which would keep them afloat on the troubled seas of modern thought. It was amazing how Roman Law and 18th century Enlightenment philosophy on, for instance the separation of the civil powers, turned out to be the perfect companions for an ancient native dignity which was too frightened to go faster in case it fell flat on its face. (Fr. Paul was too prudent to comment on this painstakingly turned sentence of mine in his letter to me, a disappointingly bland document, but returned my own missive with a red tick over the sentence and the letters *vg*).

Don't imagine from this diatribe for a moment, please, that the good Attorney was one of our august-looking Filipinos, with a decent paunch, head somewhat heavy and out of proportion to the anatomy below, thick-lipped (I say it) and savouring his own pronouncements with as much slow, lip-smacking relish as if they were so many green mango chips with salt shrimp paste. Atty Caladong, although past forty, was disconcertingly boy-like in appearance. Being five one didn't help a whole lot, but it was also a question of the smooth skin, the plump but small hands, the innocent pride in his toys. Like many men in need of external reinforcement to his virility, he'd hit on a moustache. I used to gaze at this, comparing its sudden, localised bushiness with the puerile, unblemished cheek that was its neighbour, quite innocent of stubble or shadow, and wonder if it wasn't a stick-on.

IN THE UNLIKELY PERSON OF THE LITTLE ATTORNEY, Danton and I had found the second rung of the ladder which might lead to the higher professional strata of our society (the Jesuits the first). It was true we had floundered to it and that it was at best a slippery and rotten point of purchase, treacherous and unreliable to those who might entrust their weight to it, but it was still opportunity in a land where that was scarcer than a chancre on a nun's backside. Like Ferdinand E. Marcos himself, we were to become lawyers. Like the former, we *probinsyanos* might even find ourselves topping the national bar-examination. Of course, in this field snakes abounded as nowhere else and a slithery descent down a serpent's back was quite as possible as a rapid upwards scramble. It was up to us. A very Protestant situation.

We had two places at Artheneum, an exclusive college (though not so exclusive as its rival the Jesuit-run Ateneo de Manila) with its respected law faculty.

I knew damn well Fr. Paul was my benefactor. He was not quite Magwitch, for I believe his expectations of me were greater than mine of him. Why had he done it? It was the motivation which was the mystery; the wherewithal to accomplish it was trifling. I mean, the fees would be impossible for Ma, but for anyone with access to foreign currency it was a bagatelle. Then for our mentors to slip us in among the rich-boys, Danton so obviously the little scavenger-bird on my back, myself the black rhino, was the simplest thing. Man, the Society of Jesus had slipped its backers – among them the most hardened reprobates who ever drew breath: dictators, false-priests, sister-fuckers, father-killers – past the Pearly Gates, so next to that Artheneum was a walk-in. Fr. Paul, *siguro*, felt personal guilt about me which he couldn't sneer away. He'd from my context untimely ripped me, only to leave me nowhere. But, just as certainly, with the priests there had to be the interest of the Church or, better still the Order, in their calculations or they wouldn't add up. Someone like Fr. Paul would scrutinise their motives for the smallest trace of the altruistic, the subjective, then ruthlessly expunge it. They knew the road to a hotter place than the Philippines was paved with good intentions and that the noble-hearted could do far more damage than the mean-spirited.

Danton and I constituted a nuisance, a permanent reproach and potential scandal. Fr. Paul, he of the mind advance-dirty, wanted to salvage us − *pero* canon law, not gun law. *Di ba?* He and Fr. Boy kicked us upstairs, left us masters of our own destinies at the decent remove of Manila.

AND, YOU KNOW, THE PAIR OF US did apply ourselves diligently, in the dutiful, ever-hopeful way of the junior Filipino. "Bright-eyed and bushy-tailed" was but one of the many extraneous Fr. Paul-isms that serendipitously fitted our alien context, a perfect description of us eager-beavers, the on-time, the infinitely accommodating, the super-malleable. Those of us who were already doomed to failure for lack of connections and Papa-aid had about five years before realisation set in. In the meantime, Atty Caladong bull-shitted us mercilessly: responsibility was the hand-maiden of privilege; respect for elders was our instalment-payment now but in the ripeness of time our own fully-discharged due, like life-insurance come to fruition. He counselled the virtue of patience, while loyalty, to the likes of himself, would bring its own reward. He didn't even shrink from sullying the names of Truth and Beauty as they issued from the well-exercised lawyer's organ below his moustache.

Atty Caladong's provincial booty had secured him his Manila pad, representative of the station of the affluent Filipino: a marble and mahogany palace with a galvanised-iron roof. These sub-divisions or housing developments were little colonies of order and prosperity: functioning storm-drains, concrete roads blanched as white as the faces of the householders' wives and mistresses, street-lighting intense as a concentration camp's, and blue-uniformed guards with .38s and 12-gauges at the gate-house. We'd arrive breathless with respect and dizzy with deference, even the rich-boys amongst us, to be admitted at the iron-gate by Atty Caladong's fourteen-year-old maid from Leyte. Mrs Atty Caladong would receive us at the narra-wood entrance, her wrinkled face wreathed in a hospitable smile under the face-powder. *Siguro*, she was thinking there were potential senators, assemblymen, judges, and NBI agents in our number but she was also genuinely welcoming. That was us Filipinos for you, man. There is some good in us, I admit it. Out would come the merienda after quite a long wait by the standards of middle-class English folk or poor Filipinos. That was, *di ba*, the dignified way of our leisured classes but also to make you more grateful for it, that it wasn't to be expected? We'd make short work of the jug of Tang crystals and iced water and the franks 'n spag, while Atty Caladong nodded encouragingly in his rocking-chair. On my second visit the maid bringing the tray tripped over the snapped rubber thong in her slipper and, *ah diay*, everything went: glasses, jug, siu pao buns, and cassava roll. I got to the most indestructible commodity in the freight, the rubbery cassava cake, which would survive a fall from forty as well as it would four feet, with the sideways, rolling dive of the baseball-fielder I've never been, pinching the thick glass plate and the sweetmeats on it between my finger and my thumb about half an inch from impact. Dant dived and was far too late to save a flowered glass. Everyone else just sat still and watched. The teenage maid looked at the destruction around her with an impassivity that fooled neither me nor Danton. At length Atty Caladong broke the silence. "That jug, the glass-set," he mused. "Remember those ones, Mother? We bought them in Singapore or it was Hong Kong?"

"Uy, only Robinson's basement, *siguro*," Mrs Atty Caladong replied without thinking. "Just in Binondo afterwards, we eat Chinese, then taxi home. It was sale-time, ba? Fifty for the set maybe."

Atty Caladong frowned in the way he would at an incompetent witness he had not hitherto deemed hostile. "From Singapore," he reproved his spouse. "Venetian glassware. Costing the whole set one thousand at least."

"Ah," said Mrs Atty Caladong, light breaking. "Well, you were the one to pay."

"Deduction," said Atty Caladong to the maid. I'd always heard this word used by Fr. Paul in its "Elementary, my dear Watson," sense so it took me a while to realise this meant not putting two and two together but a subtraction from the girl's salary. "So, example. I example you. Acquisition value at one thousand. Fair wear and tear, so I allow you three hundred defreciation. It's seven hundred. At thirty per mensem twenty three months."

"Flease, serr. My mens coming fourth da months, not thirty."

Suppressed sniggers which I joined.

"OK, *lang, 'day*," said Mrs Atty Caladong, like the maid, me, and Dant, a Visayan, "See how good is Serr? Not high blood with you. Now clean up this mess."

If any of us had expected additional refreshments to arrive to take the place of what had been dropped, he was going to be sorely disappointed. After half an hour, I figured I deserved a bite of what I'd saved and had a chewy mouthful of cassava. I passed the plate to Dant, he to a rich-boy called Skipper, and within twenty seconds it was bare as a shank of beef dipped into a piranha-tank.

The conversation at Atty's was largely confined to forensic subjects, or was tinged with the language of the court. One of the criminologists Atty also had under his wing ventured the opinion that convictions in a Philippine court were always entirely based on hearsay, from witnesses who could be lying, deranged, or if truthful, later suborned or threatened into withdrawing their testimony. "It's all bullshit, serr," the young fellow told Atty, "like in America you got fingerprinting, DNA comfarison, blood-typing, microscofic analysis of cloth fragments, ballistics, etcetera etcetera. Here, just someone alibi-alibi or give false witness for the fun of it. All we got is the paraffin test that doesn't show from a gun with a good seal anyway."

"Hmm," opined Atty. "The human factor, hah? But then the Bible also thusly. It's testimony, ba? New Testament of Matthew, Mark, Luke, and John. You hear of Christian Witness? Then no jury here in RP – His Honour expert to discriminate the versions, don't worry. It's our way, native style, village denunciation. Don't say it can't be deadly. How efficient is hearsay here? Very. We can measure. Now you remember the rumour from the mill a few years back? Don't shop at Goodprice Department Store. They say every day a shopper goes missing there on the fourth floor. Go in, never to come out."

We nodded. We'd all heard that one. "Well," continued Atty, "The *tsismis* runs like this: one of the Yee family brothers owning the stores is half-snake. They got to feed him a human being every day. Not ordinary snake, hah? Mouses and chicks won't suffice. Tough on the customers, too, *ba*, but it's sale time there?"

We laughed sycophantically.

"So, of course, we educated ones, we're too smart to attach any credences to this, though I catch my Mrs looking over her shoulder when we're there. *Di ba*, Mother? Likely the rumour is mongered by Goodprice's competitors. In fact, not so. I happen to know for certain from my cousin at University of Northern Philippines they were the ones to start it. They want to measure the velocity of rumour, *ba*? They launch the *tsismis* on the third of the month from Baguio, by the tenth it's already reached Iloilo, by the twelfth at General Santos already. Of course, not just speed point to point: has to be local word of mouth to reach saturation-level so the sociologists can measure it. So mean distance to Dadiangas is some 1100 km, taking 216 hours. Velocity of Rumour in the RP until now is… 5:09 kph. They run a control exferiment in Japan, Japs have modern communications, bullet-train etcetera but only manage 2kph. So our *tsismis* is efficient after all."

The young criminologist's face was, as Fr. Paul would say, a picture.

Atty Caladong moved on to Natural Law. I muttered something to Danton. He sniggered.

"What?" asked Atty. We were too old, at least after the initiation, to get detention or the strap on the palm. All Atty could do was destroy our careers and blight our lives.

"Castro say da Laws of Nature is two *lang*, serr," Danton obliged. "Self-freservation and da refroductive urge."

If I'd had a deadly weapon I might have used it then, on Dant or myself. So much for Ireland. I contented myself by shaking my fist at Danton when Atty Caladong stopped staring at me.

But actually, Atty and his Mrs weren't the worst pair. I mean, I saw them clear for what they were, clearer than the rich-boys did and clearer than the respectful, place-knowing poor, the Aunties and Ma, ever could. I was a scholarship-boy and twice over an outsider, and my eye was like a buzzard's. Yet I could never make my mind up, and as soon as I did the balance would swing the other way. My conundrum, as unanswerable as the chicken and the egg or the final value of pi, was this: were the Caladongs kindly but dishonest or dishonest but kindly?

ACADEMICALLY COLLEGE WAS A GREAT DEAL EASIER than Fr. Paul's classroom. Despite the interminable praying at San Ignatio, which I guess was the Jesuits' equivalent of the school ROTC military training and only half as mindless, Fr. Paul wanted us to think for ourselves and not on command. At Artheneum Atty Caladong and the other professors simply expected us to lap up their every pronouncement, to get up the Republic Acts by rote, and learn a little third-rate oratory. Dant was surprisingly good at all this, with a knack for parrotting legal expressions, the more effectively when they were completely out of context. Judges were mostly political appointees and I don't doubt Dant would have, as it were, acquitted himself no worse than some of the hoodlums sitting on the bench. I put this to him. "To be sure, old friend," he replied, "if it's you they arraign I'll have to inhibit myself out of *delicadeza*." He'd acquired the tinge of the brogue in his two years away, much to the amusement of Fr. Boy who still loved a scamp and had forgiven him twice as quickly as Fr. Paul.

"Dili man," I assured him. "No need. No favouritism expected. Just accord me due process."

"Reclusion temporal. I know your man for da rafscallion he is."

I gave him the dirty finger. He pretended to shake soy-sauce on it and sample the result. Dant and I were the staunchest kind of friends by now: unlikely pals who'd begun by disliking each other. Now, to go with the vitalising differences, we had the bond of being poor provincial Visayan boys in this den of spoiled Tagalog kids.

The Fraternity thought it had assimilated us, put us in the tribe, but we knew so much better we didn't even have to voice this sense of apartness to the other. It was better not to: Frats ruled the roost. We had less of it back home, but here the Tags lapped it up. It wasn't just synthetic tribalism, it was synthesised life. It was putting *in vitro* what Dant and I had known in the raw. The idea of the Frat was that it was for adult life, not student days at all. Especially for lawyers, it was the pathway to patronage, kickbacks, elevation. Aquila Legis – I think I'd have got a "vg" with a tick from Fr. Paul if I translate it for you as Legal Eagle – was the most powerful of the Law Frats but Dant and I had gone into Delta Kappa Epsilon. Pain, danger, suffering, hardship, deprivation – I guess these real things held our urchin gang together back home while we were stealing coconuts or shop-breaking. The rich-boys had none of that, they had to re-create it artificially, the blood and guts of it, through their rite of initiation. That was both the bonding and the price, *ba*? I mean, you couldn't just queue up to join, otherwise everyone would have done it, would they not? First of all you had to get your hazing. This was a word Fr. Paul would have loved – certainly of antique marine derivation, like the origins of its sister expression "Letting the cat out of the bag." Of course, the latter now meant snitching but originally it referred to the cat o' nine tails (Fr. Paul doing justice to both meanings when he chastised me for being an informer).

However the practice and nomenclature of hazing had arrived on our shores, the Philippine Frat was a Frankenstein version of the American college fraternity. In our dorm we had a poster of Snoopy as Joe Cool in his shades and Frat T-shirt. Cute notion. What we dudes were was Al Capone in the robes of Julius Caesar. Boy, those rich brats submitted themselves to the mother of all hidings. The chain of punishing hands extended from sophomore to beyond Atty Caladong himself. It was amazing – these pampered milksops replicating voluntarily the shanty-town state of nature which Dant and I were doing our best to leave behind but which like a bad smell on a following wind was continuing to dog us. Danton was obviously surprised by my naivete when he replied, "Da whole world's made up of gangs, man. Way it is. Toughest gang of muddapukkas is called American Senate. If we can join that we join it next day, man. They can cut my legs off and I kneecap your man Atty Whojamaflip in da head for all I care, old friend." Danton spoke somewhat bitterly of the little Attorney who'd given him a hard time at our initiation, Dant in a foetal ball while Atty directed a CFI judge's son to smite him as if he were the Amelekite hip and thigh with the initiation-paddle. We'd been hooded but it was still a cinch to recognise the voices. I hadn't fared so badly. I got the most token of thrashings. That was a reversal of the usual situations in life where the biggest outsiders fare the worst. People seemed embarrassed to clobber me; they'd as soon have lambasted an old and faithful elephant. Belting me as I stood there patiently, twice their size, was in poor taste. It was also, I think, the first time in my life that being black had actually proved an advantage. It was the older men, the lawyers and judges and lecturers, Atty Caladong's cronies, doing the hazing and while being thought a racist would hardly have troubled my contemporaries, it constituted an ancient, half-remembered taboo for these sadistic old Neanderthals from the legal establishment. I came through it with hardly a mark, even bearing in mind my skin didn't show bruising so easily, while Danton and the others carried their shiners for a fortnight after. The rich boys were actually proud of their contusions, luxuriated in their stinging warmth and only regretted they weren't permanent duelling scars. But Danton wore shades over the *Mama's Love* talc I taught him to apply. The sensible fellow took no pride or pleasure at all in having been beaten up. It was a matter of shame for the former gang-leader.

Although the Frat was supposed to be the proving-ground and launch-pad for adult life, it was too much to stick a bunch of rich young Filipinos together, hurt and humiliate, before empowering them, and then expect them not to abuse that power in the here and now. Our brotherhood ran rackets, supported scams, divvied up the dough (peanuts, OK, beside what adult life would offer but nonetheless not to be despised). They – we – also molested girls. Only low-class girls, of course. The most molested girls in the whole wide world – lower-class *pinays*, with fifty times more chance of trouble than the Jennys and Nicolas of this world I would later meet.

On the whole our Frat rumbles didn't involve the use of firearms. That was to say in classical terms, in the pitched battles between massed numbers. Don't ask me why. There was some unspoken collective survival instinct at work here, as well as the desire not to bring adult intervention down. Individual hits were quite another matter. Nothing beat the convenience, the certainty of the pistol here; man, it was a nuisance-queller. One round in the head, one in the back, and off on your motor-bike.

The first task the Brods gave me and Dant was to take the overnight ferry back home and get a basket of proofed *paltik* .38s from Danao.

Danao was a town about twenty miles out from Cebu and they smithed the best home-made guns in the world there, sometimes better than the original pattern. Ingram sub-machine guns, Colts, Smith and Wesson revolvers. *Siguro*, in the nature of things you were better off with a revolver, for if the gunsmith's slide mechanism was as trusty as the sweet-water pump in his backyard the re-loads we all used would have jammed a concrete-mixer or Dirty Harry's piece. The smith showed us his prize exhibit: an *eight*-chambered .357 magnum at one hundred US, with narra-grips. Regretfully, Dant declined. For the same price we took five snub-nosed .38s, a four inch .38, and an eight-chambered .22 magnum on a Brazilian design. The smith, Noy Jesus, had known Dant's uncle as a boy, the one still on the lam from the provincial clink, so he made us drink palm-toddy with him. "Uy," he said, "your Tiyo, Boy Napoleon, was da one until now. No nerves to mention. He was da one sneak in and *gikawat niya ang* bulldozair-vlade."

"Bulldozer-blade?"

"O. Bulldozair-vlade. Da only steel here hab da grade for da pistol-barrel. All other steels to burst. Take a long, long time for him to cut. Come on, drink."

I held my breath as the tuba went down. I'd always hated the fucking brew and so had Dant: we were city urchins not barrio bumpkins. It looked like jissom in the bath-water, smelled like bad eggs, and tasted of fart-aereated gasoline. You always had to take a drink. Refusal caused offence. I could see placid old Noy Jesus running amok, discharging his whole ingenious arsenal in our direction.

"Have you been to Manila lately, 'noy?" I asked, pretty certain he'd never been off the island.

"Huy! Japayuki ko!"

"Hah?"

It was a little difficult to imagine Noy Jesus lighting cigarettes for businessmen in a Tokyo karaoke preparatory to getting screwed.

"Spend already nine years in Yokohama."

"Shit!"

"I da one to make seven hundred eight-three revolver there: double-action, five and six-chamber, also hammerless, but mostly two-inch varrels."

"How that happen, 'noy?" Danton asked with the focussed interest that meant he thought there was a money-making scheme that he could copy.

"*Strikto* already *na lang ang* customs insfection sa Tokyo. All Philippine flight search rigour. All da guns for Yakuza from here – difficult *kaayo* to get gun in Japan. So I arrive at da airfort instead of a case of fistola, ba? No one look at da old man like me – grey da hair already, crooked back, stick to walk. Yaki put me in house, get machine-tool and steels no froblem, import firecracker Cebu *gikan* to empty into cartridge-case make *mga bala nga* .38. Muzzle belocity drop, no exit wound, but still kill. So altogether seven hundred eight-three pistol, not counting spare part cannivalise –

maybe I kill one thousand Japs. More than a Ninja! Da peeble old guys like me! Drink, drink!"

We gulped it down and left before we were invited to join in a game of Russian roulette.

Dant went to press-gang Auntie Irish to be our Red Riding Hood carrying the goodies in her basket on the ferry, I to visit Fr. Paul and Fr. Boy, the last time I would see them for more than seven years. Fr. Paul called me "dear boy" instead of "my son" and said it was good to see me taken away from "vicious habits and depraved influences". Fr. Boy looked at Fr. Paul and I could see him thinking on the lines of, "You can take the boy out of the barrio but not the barrio out of the boy."

BUTCH TAN SY, THE COLLEGE BASKETBALL COACH, understood that perfectly. Butch preferred his baskitboleros a tad sassy, that and tall, *siguro*. Butch, and indeed the whole nation, were basket-case enthusiasts for a game they had no sane reason to take up. Was it our hidden desire to under-achieve, to fail, to self-destruct, that was at play? For how could a short, wiry – fathers and mentors, let me not be mealy-mouthed – teeny-weeny, itsy-bitsy, chronically malnourished, genetically-disadvantaged South-East Asian folk ever have chosen a less appropriate endeavour by which to be measured? Good grief, you just had to look at the hoop on high and at the Filipino below to know the entire handicap at a glance. It was kind of a patriotic penance, like getting crucified at Easter, also high, *di ba*? And yet we Filipinos loved the game, adored it with the deadly and hopeless passion of the doomed suitor nursing his unrequited ardour. All our big companies had their team: San Miguel, Pure Foods, King Kondom (no, joke only) flaunting the firm's logo in the league. No way were the players employees on paid leave but full-time pros who'd never in their lives donned an apron or worn a pair of safety spectacles. Sheer desire had made us the Asian champions two decades back, but we weren't Kings of the Little Guy's League any more. There were huge Northern Chinese, monster Malaysians, towering Thais out there, ready to rub the *pinoy's* nose in his own pee.

No one over five ten was safe from Butch Tan Sy's depredations. And for a black to be at Artheneum – well, Butch had dreamed of this as fervently as a five-year-old with a sweet tooth dreams of liquorice allsorts.

When I jumped the first time at the freshman try-out I'd been summoned to on pain of displeasure, Butch went wobbly at the knees. "Astronaut, *di ba*?" I heard one of the guys in his spindly squad mutter as I came down at last. I landed with a softness that surprised myself, took a step to the side and back again, quite different from the springboard landings with Fr. Boy, for this was just me, no equipment, and the difference was devastating. It was a new experience, the eeriest of sensations: being better than everyone else at something I took no interest in whatsoever. Up, up, I'd gone, never-endingly; it had been like seeing myself in slow motion replay. My hang-time was a devil-given gift. The others, before and after me, had jumped swiftly, by any standard athletically; some had managed to brush the hoop. That had required effort; they'd strained for the height. But I'd gone slow and heavy, with a hint of power held in reserve, like a Saturn rocket lifting off the launch-pad feet at a time before accelerating. It seemed like I'd been up there forever and a day. As I parachute-landed the squeak of my sneaker soles was the protest of the hinges of the door I was shutting, oh, so regretfully, in the faces of my contemporaries' ambitions. And hanging in the air, too, was that unutterable word they were all thinking, the word which explained me and my unasked-for talent, which made my achievement predictable and palatable. *Nigger*. For in that case, it was not surprising that an otherwise raw power was accompanied by a subtle physical deceptiveness. What was difficult, if not impossible, for most to credit was that someone of my size and colour might also have a little intellectual strength and finesse. I couldn't blame them – where others were concerned I held the same prejudice myself. And, it pains me to record that, just like they were, I was right more often than I was wrong. Can we ask for more of any of our touchstones in life?

And yet physical grace and athletic composure were attitudes of mind as well. The other guys were desperate to have the ball, to assert control over it, to adjust bounce and return in the hand, arc it through the air to a praying buddy or send it plummeting through the net. They scrabbled to seize the moment; they were frantic for the opportunity. I, on the other hand, made my own time; I had as long as I wanted; or I lived in a life a second ahead or a second behind everyone else. I swerved, I feinted, I turned, I twisted, I leaped, and all the time I was calm. Part of it was that I truly didn't care; I had no special love for the game and that helped me play it all the better. Out of impossible situations I performed amazing feats of dexterity and balance. I came through it all because I was never wracked by the dread of fluffing my final shot. So what if I did? It was only a game I didn't really care for. I made assists, as well as profited from rebounds. I'll tell you what: my mind wasn't advance-dirty; my cool heart never melted.

Butch Tan Sy saw all this. He saw it clearly because the game was his passion. He shook his head over me as he would have over an errant son-in-law. "If I was you, Castro," he said. "If I was the one to have your talent, I'd be playing for the Magic. You don't appreciate what you've got. It's like you've been given a Lamborghini you don't drive properly."

"Here are the keys, *na lang*, Coach," I joked, pretending to drop them in his hand. But he wasn't amused. The shrewd Chinese eyes behind the spectacles looked mystified and hurt. It was a good analogy he had. It was indeed as if I found myself in the comfortable bucket-seat of some powerful and prodigious piece of modern engineering except it was my own body I was operating. I took no particular pride in it. After all, I was not the manufacturer; I'd won it in a lottery.

Danton came along for the glory of the ride. He'd seen all the possibilities in a flash. "You could have been a frop, man, on da rugby in Galway," he said. "Fathers would have loved you." When we played the other colleges Danton acted as my bag-carrier, rub-down man, and unofficial agent. He brokered interviews, autographs, chicks, and eventually endorsements and a few clumsy attempts at bribes. Endorsements? I did a TV ad, dressed in a grass skirt, holding a spear. Before me was a missionary in a pot. I was weaned from him by a plate of Nang Maria's Chicken Krisplets. A thousand pesos. OK, so I'm a prostie.

My own chassis may have been a Lamborghini's but what the team actually rode around in was a beat-up, glass-less bus with Artheneum All-Stars in fresh black paint on the sides. Butch Tan Sy renewed the legend every month. Neither he nor we ever referred to ourselves as the All-Stars. He called us "Team". Camp-followers and stand-bys weren't meant to ride the bus but Danton had made himself a fixture on the back-seat, leading us in the team tune, *The Impossible Dream*, while we bounced around and regarded Butch's bald patch in the seat next to old Samson, the driver. Somehow or other there was always a crate of beer stashed away under a seat in which on the return trip we'd toast victory or drown our sorrows as, in the words of the song, we vowed to march behind Butch through the gates of Hell. Screwy, but it's the bus-rides back I remember more than the games themselves, the darkness and companionship inside the coach as we rattled past pitch-black rural tree-stands or dim sari-sari stalls on the outskirts of town, rather than jogging out with 11 and Castro on my back into the blazing light of the court to give my little display of solipsistic cool. Never was there devised so selfish or solo a game under the hypocritical guise of team co-operation. It was every man for himself in the agitated free-market of the court, the other guys hustling you for their chance. No, I prefer to remember the generosity of the bus when my black face became more invisible than those of the others and I was just another Tagalog-American voice in the night.

"Hey, beautiful slam-dunk, Ramos."

"Yeah, man, nice. *Bagets ka.*"

"*Guwapo*, man. And Castro's long-bomb, perfick, perfick, *di ba?*"

"Awesome, Brod."

Butch Tan Sy kept to himself on the ride, or would just call up an individual player to the front for a private chat. His moment was the time-out pep-talk. He was superb at these. Sometimes you could hear the other side's adult haranguing his boys and compare your guy's technique with his. Butch never descended to abuse or vituperation. He hadn't been a real player himself, just a messer, but he knew scoldings didn't lift a tired and demoralised side. He could put himself in someone else's boots; more difficult than it sounds. To hear some of the other coaches, they thought a verbal whipping was the next best thing to a shot of dope in the arm. They confused the accurate communication of the state of their own feelings with the correct message or advice their players needed. Sincerity and vehemence were not the desiderata; art (read, insincerity) and empathy were. They consistently stressed the negative. I lost count of how many times I heard the final, throw-away injunction: "And mark the nigger!" Or the real counsel of despair: "Two guys to their nigger!"

Butch didn't know it, but I was judging him by the highest, most classical standards. Not much had changed in two thousand years. There was a limited number of rhetorical devices for a commander of hoplites and legions and fewer still for a Philippine college cagers' coach. But Butch sure knew the tropes. We crossed the Rubicon and the Pasig simultaneously with Butch, burned our boats, metaphorically speaking, on their banks; he'd place his head – i.e. his moderately well-paid job – in our bumbling hands; he'd refer to past victories or drum up a desire for revenge. We were the best team he'd ever had, we were just to go out and do our thing; we were the inheritors of a golden tradition, the vanguard of a glorious ghost army of predecessors. Then next time out, with equal sincerity, he said we were an immortal few, the only good team he had ever coached. Once, like Caesar addressing his legionaries as *Quirites* instead of *milites*, Butch called us "fellers" and not "team". His intention was the opposite of JC's: he wanted to bond with us, not shame us. And as I loped away to the next period with the opposite coach's words still ringing in my ears, I'd think – I assure you without heat – "*O-o*. Sure. Mark this nigger. Mark this nigger, if you can." I meant off-court, *siguro*.

Danton would be operating in the crowd while I was playing. I don't think he bestowed one backward look on the court; he had less interest in the game than even I had. He was searching for his own marks, with a good deal more success than my opponents. My autograph he hawked at five pesos; with a personal inscription by name it would be seven pesos fifty centavos. A photo opportunity with me (supply your own camera, folks) cost ten, with my arm around you twelve fifty. This represented a rising scale of fees, designed to get you to go for value by spending very slightly more for the most expensive service, not unlike the shrewd strategy of Ma's colleagues which steered the customer to "BJ is one hundred but add all da wey only one twenty." Once Danton returned with an offer of a thousand for me to try less than my best. "No way, man," I remonstrated.

"Come on, Sugar, don't be no eejit. Who da ones to notice? They don't even notice you don't try, I mean da ones to pay is. And your man, Coach Tan Sy, he *never* gonna know."

"Then you're underestimating Butch, my friend. Nix, anyway. No deal."

"Aw, to be sure Sugar, old friend, it's a grand for us."

"*Us*? I'm not taking it – it's dirty money – but what makes you think I'd split it with you if I did?"

"OK, old friend, coz it's youse, just ten fer cent for your old friend."

"No. Get lost, crumb-bum."

"OK, I'll ask them for one thousand five."

"NO! Just get lost. Do yourself a favour. Watch the game *na lang*, like everyone else."

"Watch da pucking game? It's a shit game for physical freaks, mans. Get a giraffe on da team."

"To go with the black man, *di ba*? Screw you."

And I'd jog off, laughing. That was the closest I could come to getting het-up around a basketball court.

Why didn't I take the dough? I'm still not sure. Dant had other, and higher, offers to relay at subsequent games, but I was never tempted by them. Not in a million years. I'm no saint, I'm not even Fr. Boy. I guess I did have a final price. I mean, if someone offered you a trillion dollars to miss a penalty in a college basketball game, you wouldn't be virtuous in refusing, you'd be plain stupid. You could do so much good with the money. So it wasn't the principle which registered with me. And certainly if I was to be a Judas-whore, I'd like to think my price would be more than the pesos Dant was holding out for. I guess if I had to assign a final reason for it, if I had to explain myself to a stern St Peter (only the most illustrious of the saints who would have been too stupid to be a Jesuit) I'd simply say, it wouldn't have been cool, Pete, to treat poor earnest Butch Tan Sy like that. The game was his religion, he the minister, we the neophytes, and I'll respect all religions that respect others. It was Grecian; maybe we athletes were the temple-prostitutes whose bodies the public could enjoy for the price of the entrance fee. And prosties, the good ones, have their code of honour as well: to stay with the guy who's been buying them drinks all night long and not leave him for a last minute better bidder.

It was only Danton who irritated me. If someone got past my would-be middleman and tried to stick the fix in direct, I'd just laugh like the big, good-natured *mestizo* boy which was all they could see in me and later they'd realise that "*Hindi po*," the politest of no's, had been their answer. I didn't get snotty about it, that's all. There are lots of different ways of doing the same thing and if you find my attitude a little bendy, why, the trees that survive the typhoon are the ones that bend.

SHORTLY AFTER I HAD MY GREATEST GLORY ON THE COURT – the basketball-court – Atty Caladong invited me and Dant on his Palawan trip. I wasn't really cut from the cloth of the typical Atty Caladong favourite – usually well-connected rich-boys – but my growing fame on the campus as a cager compensated for it. In our last game, against our arch-rivals Ateneo, I set up three subtle scores for my team-mates which went unnoticed by all save Butch Tan Sy, got off the floor after an outrageous challenge from Wenceslao "Cheech" Chong, a pure-blooded Chinese-Filipino as hefty as myself, and threw in the winning hook-shot without remembering a thing about it through my concussion. I was too hot a property at that time for Atty to forego, although heated pennies get as quickly dropped as picked up.

Palawan island. Then as now the most primitive, or least-spoiled, island in the archipelago. (Give me the chance, I'll always take somewhere spoiled, *salamat*). This long, narrow, never more than thirty miles wide, island had it all: jungle, underground rivers, devastating malaria, wild animals unlike any elsewhere in the RP. In terms of nature it was just an extension of Borneo, to which before the ice-melt ended the intra-species global *halo-halo* there had once been a land-bridge. None of the rich-boys had been there. All except for Skipper. His old man had flown their private plane to the leper colony on Culion island, Northern Palawan. "Sorry to say it, but that is not Palawan, Brod," asserted another of our plutocrats as we peered at the map.

"What's your problem, Lazares?" Skipper asked, definitely aggrieved by the doubter. He'd bragged that he'd taken the controls once they were airborne, though he hadn't got his own pilot's ticket yet.

"So you hold da joy-stick quite often, man?" Danton had asked, though most of the rich-boys were too slow for this.

Lazares said, "Look, it's way to the north of the real Palawan island, Brod. It's a separate island."

"Palawan *group*, sucker," said Skipper. "It's part of the Calamian group of islands off Palawan."

"Nope," said the stubborn Lazares. "Negative, Brod. *Real* Palawan is the big thin one to the south. You didn't get malaria *di ba*? Calamian islands is a whole different concept altogether."

"Shit, Brod. I don't have to get malaria to prove I've been to Palawan."

Lazares, who was slightly more of an asshole than fatboy Skipper, looked doubtful. I kept smiling into the middle distance – I figured I was seeing the "lawyer's way of thinking" Atty Caladong was doing his best to inculcate in all of us. Our junior pedants would have gone on disputing until they were at each other's throats had I not intervened.

"What's the provincial capital?" I asked, knowing the answer perfectly well but willing to make a diversion at the cost of being an ignoramus. Blessed are the peacemakers. "Puerto Princesa, dumbo," sneered Skipper. Lazares united with him to put down the black Frankenstein from the basketball team who obviously had muscles where other people kept grey matter. "Hey, man, where have you been? You've gotta be a Tasaday from the lost tribe."

"Ah," I said, giving them no heat. "It's a nice place, *di ba*, PP?"

Cut to our Philippine Airlines 737 circling the said provincial capital, preparatory to a cautious landing, with Skipper's guffaws over "Pee Pee" still in my mind.

Nice Place. Well, for some I guess it was. You could immediately see the difference between this island and the rest of our glorious Republic. However remote or mountainous other spots might be, rugged cordillera or marshy tract, there would be some signs of settlement or at least casual habitation but here the forest extended for miles below us from the Sulu sea on the East coast to the South China Sea on the West, with not a clearing or a hut in sight, not even the grey tendrils of some untended fire. The town was surrounded on the turquoise of the sea side by the densest mangrove I'd ever seen, scarred with red earth tracks going nowhere and on the other by the green ocean of the jungle. It was a pretty big town but the aerial perspective showed it for what it was: arbitrarily inserted, with civilisation stopping dead at the boundaries, clean as an amputation.

Dant, who considered himself a veteran of flights, had warned me about the discomfort of pressure changes on the ears, explained the purpose of the boiled sweets, and kept a watchful eye on the stewards.

"Those guys look straight to me," I'd remonstrated but Danton had said darkly, "Lock da pucking door of da CR, old friend." Skipper, who had been refused a tour of the flight-deck, was at the centre of another little clique at the front of the plane.

Dant's baggage – a stout cardboard container liberally perforated with breathing holes for Atty Caladong's fighting roosters – came off first. It was the birds' second flight, having arrived as eggs from Tennessee in a Jumbo and hatched in the Philippines. What did that make them? 'Merikanos or *pinoy*? I think, confused. I'd checked in the Attorney's golf clubs at the Manila PAL counter. We never saw a course in Palawan, so I assume he'd brought them just to impress. Woods, irons, the two putters, and bag had all successfully made it to Puerto Princesa just like us. Otherwise, Dant and I only had little knap-sacks with one change of pants, briefs, and T-shirt, as well as razor, tooth-brush, and rubber slippers. We were the class of Pilipino who travelled light and, on my frame, the bag looked like a kiddy's satchel. However, Skipper, Lazares, and Skip's cousin were standing woefully by the baggage hatch. Their effects hadn't made the flight.

"Stealing da baggage handlers?" Danton asked in a loud voice, "or take da wrong plane to Los Angeles?"

"Dunno," I said, stringing along for a mild piece of revenge. "Skipper, hope you didn't have your bold mags inside. Think of the scandal, man."

Atty Caladong was unsympathetic. He behaved as if it was their personal fault. He hated to be inconvenienced by other people's troubles. Socially, that was. Business-wise, other people's troubles were his living. "You should have seen your effects on to the plane," he snapped. "Or pushed it under the seat."

"But, hah, Attorney," Lazares stammered, "it exceeded the permitted dimensions, *di ba*, for the cabin baggages?"

"Then talk your way on. Want to be a lawyer?" While his proteges were handing over their baggage tags to the insouciant ground staff, the Attorney collected his pistol, a Czech CZ 75 9mm, which went a long way to re-establishing his street cred with Dant. "Half da frice of da Beretta, man, and twice as reliable." Certainly it looked as if it had seen more use than the virgin golf clubs. I slung these over my shoulder, making it look more difficult than it really was – I didn't want to spend a weekend on loan as a caddy at the Attorney's country club – while the Attorney personally bore his semi-automatic in its locally-made hardwood case. Moments later we were buzzing in the little trisikad down the tree-lined road to town, a mere couple of kilometers away, leaving the baggage-less in the dust of our wake. Atty Caladong alighted with athletic aplomb at the Lodge, then strode off to check-in at reception, leaving the trisikad driver in the characteristic posture of menials who had dealings with the Attorney: regarding the coins in his palm with a disappointment he judged it politic not to display too openly.

Our inn was a pleasant place, even if we students were five to the fan-less room while the Attorney lodged in solitary air-conditioned splendour. The habitations were arranged around a large garden courtyard the size of ten basketball courts which, apart from the broken fountain, was a microcosm of the green, squeaky-clean town.

But if the balmy little town with its islets and unspoiled wilderness could be described as a sight for sore eyes, then what was at the end of its airport runway was an eye-sore. Extending from the concrete strip over the mud and grass to the sea at the end of the peninsula was a shanty town of cardboard, splintered wood, decayed palm thatch, and orange wriggly tin that put even our Mactan hooches into the one-star category. The handful of blackened Quonsett huts around which this fungal growth had proliferated made it look more rather than less makeshift. Barbed wire fences, guard-posts, and armed policemen completed this picture of a tropical Belsen.

It was the Philippine First Asylum Camp. Or Vietnamese refugee camp. Or boat-people's prison.

And it was for this we had come, this was Atty Caladong's purpose.

"Better we check in at da boat-people camp," Dant said, "right near da airport. Those guys brung more luggage than youse, Lazares. On your shoes again, Skipper, your feet stinking da joint out."

Atty Caladong and his cronies had been milking the boat-people's camp since very shortly after its inception. It was yet another occasion when you had to hand it to the little Attorney. Comparatively few people would have seen in these gaunt and apparently famished figures so many cash cows among the lean kine, but then it took genuine acumen to spot any kind of money-making opportunity in our fair land. I wouldn't like to say quite all the attorneys who went there were out, to change the terms of the metaphor, to fleece the poor Viets but many of them were no better than our guy.

Early next morning, very early, Atty Caladong had us walking up the highway to the airport. No sweat for me. It was deliciously cool before daylight and I was accustomed to Butch Tan Sy's pre-dawn plodathons. Skipper and Co were still beer-befuddled but smart, *bagets* they say in Tagalog, in pleated slacks, long-sleeved polos and ties. Atty Caladong was too spry for a man of his age and his class at that time of day; I suspected him of having had a chick in his room from the rustic bar down the road a-ways and of not having slept at all.

"Shit, mans," Danton exclaimed at a safe distance behind the Attorney, "we look like pucking Mormons." We did, too, with books and pens in our hands. That creased all of us.

"Or the Wild Bunch," I suggested, "going to settle their score with El Jefe. Hey, no, The Mild Bunch."

"Like it, Brod, like it," said Lazares enthusiastically.

"Attorney carrying his nine em-em, *di ba*?" Dant inquired and we all giggled. "Da-dum," I went, imitating the drum-roll at the beginning of that movie's final scene, as we all fanned out across the road, swaggering like pistoleros. Mormon pistoleros. Maybe the Attorney had heard; he, too, was rolling his shoulders.

Almost every time we went to the camp we walked instead of piling into one of the trisikads. In Metro Manila the Attorney wouldn't walk above two hundred meters. I guess it was a much pleasanter stroll in Palawan – greenery, sea-breeze, lack of traffic and pollution, no one waiting to serve you a writ or shoot you, and the amenable clients safely behind the wrong side of the wire. But there had to be something else and, in the end, I figured it concerned those footing the bill. Maybe the Attorney wanted to show the barefoot Viets he was just one of them, a humble guy in Florsheims. In particular, I think he wanted to prove that expenses were under control, that the refugees weren't paying through the nose for his time. If he'd had a chick, though, I knew the item would find its way on to his bill of services under a different name, something like *piccolo* or *service uplift*.

Atty Caladong did as total a snow-job on the boat-people as he did on us. Lie followed hard on the heels of outrageous lie. The fact that we were there didn't faze him at all. Surely, I thought, *surely* he can see we might start putting two and two together, comparing his spiel for the boat-people with his outrageous performances before student audiences. But, no, he was quite unselfconscious, quite unflummoxed. I looked at my companions' faces. Without exception they were taking him seriously. Even Danton had indulged him with his willing suspension of disbelief. Had it not occurred to the Attorney, I wondered, in the way that it hadn't to my contemporaries? Or was he simply correct in his assessment of our obtuseness?

"We're still very confident of a successful outcome," he told the refugees, waiting a considerate interval for his Vietnamese interpreter to get the gist across before continuing. I liked the "still". Plainly, our walk-on part came a little way after the curtain had lifted for the first time, but we were still several acts distant from the denouement and climax. Anti-climax, I would have bet it was gonna be for the poor Viets.

"But," continued the little Attorney "as I have to keep telling you, these things take time. There is a lot of bureaucracy. We submit the forms, the forms pend…" (Inspired choice of word, I thought. So short itself and evocative of such a long non-action)… "and then the officials we are dealing with make a decision and come back to us. Sometimes they need more information. Sometimes you filled the forms out incorrectly…" (Shrewd stroke, Attorney, I thought) "… and then we have to begin all over again."

We were standing in the open air, with the refugees around us. There were kids there as well, some of them balancing on one leg, with the sole of the free foot out of its slipper pushed against the inside of the opposite knee. A rooster stance, familiar to Atty Caladong. All the Vietnamese could have passed for *pinoys*, males and females. The chicks were as good-looking as ours, the guys as scrawny. At the time I thought some of the kids looked very young to have survived a journey on the high seas in an open boat and, of course, later found they'd been born in the camp. It was then I also made my first adult misjudgement, similar to all those who misjudged me for a big, gormless – as Fr. Paul liked to say – nigger (as he didn't like to say). I'd assumed the kids were chiefly the ones who couldn't understand English. The hell they were! Most of them were fluent in Tagalog to boot. These were cool, wised-up kids, on their mettle as much as the Mactan street boys. But listening to Atty Caladong not a trace of comprehension or emotion showed on their faces; they'd learned in the hardest of schools.

"The US officials are the ones to be slower than their Philippine counterparts," the Attorney continued. In that case, they must be the world record-holders for tardiness, I thought. "So those of you who are seeking asylum there must expect long delays. If you're the ones to seek entry here, you may find things a little quicker. And we make no promises, but it's a little easier for your Attorney to deal with fellow Filipinos, *di ba*?" Here the Attorney good as winked at his still impassive audience. "Those of you who are Roman Catholics, you know our Bishops and Cardinals are interceding for you. You have the American missionaries, too. We're all Christians, hah? So, my friends, we're setting the ball rolling. Your part is to be patient."

Patient! I looked at the Viets. No trace of understanding, still less resentment, even after the interpreter (a young guy with spectacles, better dressed than the others) had done his stuff. Atty Caladong was telling a people who'd been at war for more than half a century, who'd seen off the Japanese, destroyed the French, demoralised the Americans, lived in tunnels months at a time, endured bombardment, barrage, and Agent Orange – Atty Caladong had the nerve to tell these dudes to be patient. This coming from a man belonging to a nation which didn't even possess the collective self-discipline to form a queue for ferry-tickets. A Filipino, whose fellow-countrymen were notorious as the hottest heads and most luke-warm adherents in all Asia, was telling an icy, crystal-hard people who hadn't melted under the heat and pressure that turned coal into diamond – hey, don't get het up, stay cool! No wonder he had a posse of young guns standing behind him, no wonder he wanted the biggest dude on the basketball team eyeballing the constituency.

The spiel was over; now came the serious, continuing business of the Sting. Multiple pucking bee bites these were. We were after the camp's honey with double the formidable persistence and acumen of bees or Mormons. Atty Caladong couldn't have secured better results if he'd put us on commission (which we weren't). We were young, we were eager to please. Above all we weren't acting. And our sincerity was patent to the Vietnamese marks. They were readier to give us the money than to Atty Caladong about whose performance they were starting, just starting, to develop serious reservations.

Atty Caladong took Lazares and Skipper's cousin with him while Dant, Skip, and I worked as a trio. This was Atty Caladong's favourite number, just as the Trinity was revered by the priests for different reasons. Three in a cell, even if they weren't Filipinos, was an unstable number. They couldn't get together to pilfer in the way two could. One was bound to blab.

Our assignment was a group of huts on the sea-end, which contained old clients with debts to discharge and some potential new clients, undiscouraged by the example of their predecessors. How this could happen was that occasionally (I should imagine quite independently of anything the Philippine lawyers were claiming to do) a genuine political refugee would indeed secure asylum. Atty Caladong would then usurp the credit and the boat people would take fresh heart.

Skipper was the one with the note-book, Dant the spieler, though communication could have been established with a display of fingers: one hundred dollars, three hundred etc. The first hooch we entered contained what appeared to be a family of Mom, Pop, and two snot-nosed kiddies. They were new, virgins, eager to be taken on the Attorney's books after the heartening departure of a neighbour to the US. They had a mere forty dollars to offer: an ancient twenty and two faded tens in even worse plight.

"Shit, no," Skipper exclaimed. "Atty Caladong said it's a minimum of a hundred bucks." He held up his fingers. The Vietnamese guy shook his head, then held out both his empty palms.

"Naw, he's got more, man," Skipper scoffed. "It's under the floor or in the roof. I hear they brought out gold and all kinds of stuff."

Dant and I said nothing. We were looking at the bare earth floor and the San Miguel calendar which was the only decoration. We were home.

Skip said, "More." He rubbed finger and thumb together. The Vietnamese looked appealingly at him. "ARVN," he said.

"Hey!" Skip exclaimed. "He's got a Filipino name. Alvin!"

Danton rolled his eyes. "No, Brod," he said. "He's Army of da Republic of Viet Nam. He fought with da 'Merikanos."

"Didn't get on the last helicopter, did you, Buster," Skip said jovially. "C'mon, feller, pay up." But it was like getting blood from a stone. The guy wouldn't surrender any more. Skip said. "Don't know if we should take it."

Danton replied, "I know da answer to that, old friend. You ever see Atty Caladong give it away? Coz that's what you're doing if you turn it down."

"O-o, Brod. Guess you're right."

"I'm always da one to be right. Right, Sugar?"

"OK. Hey, careful with the dollars, Skip. It's probably been up his *koan*, you know what. So the pirates didn't get it, *di ba*?"

I didn't mean to leave the family on a cheap laugh, but that's what we did.

Next port of call was two Chinese brothers. They wanted nothing to do with us. Atty Caladong had warned us about them. They'd been stung four times already. Certainly, they had the right to wish us dead, but you couldn't have read anything on those empty Chinese faces. Maybe a little extra Chinese flintiness, but we could have been importunate windscreen-rag sellers for all the emotion they showed.

"Fucking *insik*, man," said Skipper. "Too fucking smart for their own good, those fucking Chinese." Danton and I looked at each other. Skipper was mostly Chinese himself. Too fucking smart, sure.

The third hut cheered Skipper up. Inside were three teenaged Vietnamese girls. One was receiving a manicure from the other, while the third swung her sandal from her toes. When she saw us she dropped the shoe and hid her pinkies under her hams as she sat on the plank bed. This appeared to serve all of them. There were no sheets but a woven grass mat. "Hey," said Skipper. "One each." The girls ignored us. As this was exactly what a Filipina would have done under the same circumstances, Skipper, I could see, felt quite at home. The impertinent remark, the failure to hear, the − in fact − total stone deafness to go with the stone face: the *pinay* and evidently the Vietnamese girl imbibed this with Mama's milk.

"What a dump," Skipper said. "These people live like pigs."

I looked at the freshly swept dirt floor, saw the two toothbrushes on hooks over the basin, one new, for three sets of teeth, and one old, for laundering three sets of clothes. The cooking-pots, blackened on the outside by wood-fires, were drying upside-down; the three pink rice-bowls were stacked neatly by them, on top of each other. I knew the white porcelain insides would be glistening. Just the chopsticks were different from what you'd find in the hooches in our compound: Filipinos only used spoons and forks. I said, "The pig is a clean animal. Man makes it live in filth."

Skipper ignored me. Unlike the chicks, I think he really didn't hear. He was too busy ogling them. Skip made the kissing noises with the inside of his lips that denote "Stop the jeepney," or in other places I'd later go, "I wanna fuck you." Wind and current had snagged the girls on the shores of Palawan, which lay opposite the South of their country like a football goal. They had been speedily incarcerated and thus would never have had the opportunity to ride a Philippine jeepney. (Q. How many people can ride on a jeepney? A. One more.) So presumably they could only interpret the sound as a tactic to secure their whole attention. Skipper got it. "America," Skipper said. He pointed at them. "You want to go to America, *di ba*? Attorney is advising you?"

The girl receiving the manicure nodded. "Fees," Skipper said, "not for him. For expenses with telephone, telex, and United Nations High Commission for Refugees. Understand?" The girl looked blank.

"Yeah, you do. You pay, or you lose the money you paid before. Maybe it's only a few months more. Be a man about it and pay up." He snickered at his own witticism.

The girl pouted. I could see she was going to pay, though if we'd been by ourselves I would probably have advised her not to. "How can be sure?" she asked.

"Hey, look at me," Skip said. "Is this a thief's face?"

As she bent to get a cookie tin from under some underwear, the manicurista and the girl on top of the bed burst into rapid Vietnamese. The other girl was clearly the leader, maybe she was the oldest sister. They'd probably all decided some while before our arrival to continue shelling out the legal fees, but they couldn't stop themselves expostulating. Maybe the big girl wanted them to. Giving away money like that – it probably took as much resolution as cutting the forearm with a knife and watching the blood come.

"How can trust?" she asked Skipper.

"Ah, you can. You can," he said. I was expecting him to ask her how much for a jump, but he surprised me by heading for the door with the money. He and Danton were already in the alley when I turned back and said in as friendly a voice as I could, pointing at the girl on the bed, who now had her fingers laced between her toes, "Hand manicure is OK but be careful of pedicure. Ouch!" Unlike the others, she was dressed in the flowing, loose-legged, tight-assed, taut-bodiced Vietnamese trouser suit with the slits up the side and her sandals were clumpily high. The carefree *pinay* wore shorts, but girls in this gear had to abominate mud-splashes. She stared at me, then spat on the floor. The manicurista said something loudly to the girl with the money-tin, who nodded. She came out with a flurry of contemptuous invective, which needed no translating. I had obviously just heard the Vietnamese for "nigger", whatever it was.

I stared at them for a few seconds, not aggressively, but because I wanted to remember it all. Then I walked away.

"Hey," said Skipper, "did you make us a date?"

"No," I said.

"You won't need precautions, Brod. They're all on the pill. Had to be – they've all been raped ten times on the crossing. You won't make any little bastards."

"Big ones, Skip," I said. "Like me. I had no father I knew, either."

"Oh, yeah. OK. Sorry, Brod. I'm not thinking."

"It's cool, Skip. It's cool, Brod."

We rejoined the others at the camp restaurant. This was a cosy place which the Viets had made a skilful attempt to soften and romanticise with what came to hand. It was the welcome in their hearts which no amount of carpentry or decoration could change. We sat down to a repast which was considerably more appetising, and far cheaper, than anything the eateries of the town could offer. "Oh, man, *sarap*," exclaimed Lazares. "Did you ever taste anything so good?" He waved a segment of peeled boiled sugar-cane on which minced prawn had been moulded, giving it the appearance of a giant blond matchstick or albino chicken drum-stick. "I dig these spring-rolls, Brod," Skipper contributed, "ten times better than lumpia, man."

"Wrap the lettuce-leaf round. Now dip in the sweet sauce. Aha. Thusly." This was Atty Caladong, obviously a regular customer at the restaurant.

I ate more circumspectly. I was worried they'd poison us. No particular attempt was made to give me a selected portion of anything, nor Atty Caladong, so I figured we were OK. I'd decided by now that they hated black faces because of the war when, in fact, as I later learned from Michael, they just hated blacks. I hadn't taken it personally; it hadn't spoiled my appetite.

Atty Caladong was breaking bread, to my ex-seminarian's eye like Jesus among the Apostles. "This bread, boys," he said, "Look at. Perfect French bread. OK, a little shorter and fatter than a baguette, a little darker the crust maybe, but basically fine French bread. Just so good as I got with my Mrs in France. You can't get a product like this anywhere in the Philippines except here. Look at. Savour the aroma, the crust it's so crispy, and the bread – ah, soft and chewy, too. And you know where they bake it? Look at, in half an oil-drum there, just outside the wire." We followed his finger, murmuring in appreciation and surprise. "Don't say these people aren't ingenious."

I figured it already took ingenuity to bribe your way out of Vietnam, avoid shipwreck on those rickety craft, festooned with humanity like a tenement drying-line; survive multiple rape and being hit over the head with boat-irons by Thai and Cambodian fishermen, followed by machine-gunning by the Malaysian Navy, and finally dodging us land-pirates.

But it was great bread, too. We studes didn't tire of it, even though, stuffed with pork, leaves, and chillis, the loaves from the town's stalls were going to be our nightly sustenance for the duration.

Atty Caladong waved a few pesos at the waiter, which were declined with a minimal show of resistance from the Attorney. He then burped complacently and told us we were going. This time he flagged down a trisikad. Skipper and his cousin were able to share the ride, but Dant, Lazares, and I were left with the walk. There was no way the bike-engine was coping with my weight, anyhow, though in general trisikads took you surprising distances at astounding speed for a trifling fare. "Sorry, Dant, Brod," I said. "You could have hitched a lift – you're no extra weight."

"Yeah," said Lazares informatively, "did you know the guys are calling you two Gorilla and *Unggoy*?"

Danton scowled. He really hated remarks about his size, though I was privileged to make them. "I didn't," I said equably. "Gorillas have no tail, *di ba*? But monkeys have one, Dant."

"Shut da puck up, especially it means you, Lazares, eejit."

At this moment we were passing the oil-drums at the side of the highway. Several Vietnamese guys and girls were standing around two drums which were in operation as ovens. The girls were not in national dress, just dirty shorts and rubber slippers.

"This camp's kinda, uh, porous," said Lazares. I turned to him in appreciation, not bad for a rich-boy.

"Like da whole pucking fenal system," Danton said optimistically, probably thinking of his uncle absconding seven years already. Then from another oven rose a face we were at one in imagining to be ludicrously soot-blackened. Despite this – and Dant and I at least knew the horror with which squatters or refugees would greet the prospect of contamination of person or clothing by retentive substances like oil or carbon – it was an unmistakably cheerful face. A poor Asian, dirty but content – what a contradiction in terms that was. His hair also gave him the appearance of either having received a cartoon-style electric shock or having had the curls set in engine grease. Danton was quicker than me. "Shit, it's a niggers, man!"

In that instant Michael's features rearranged themselves for me. I'd been looking at an Asian or a Caucasian face daubed with a cosmetic, or anti-cosmetic, overlay instead of regarding the African asserting itself from, as it were, the core below. Since then, many the time I've stared too long at an Afro-American face – that particular blend of black and white – and thought for a moment it was a white man who'd stained his face. I guess I need a context to place and fix what I see; I'm not too good on the individual in isolation. At that time in my life I hadn't seen too many other black faces, and those few had mostly been female. Dant and my other friends held the advantage over me: they'd been accustomed to seeing a black face daily – mine. And then, at that exact moment, strolling down the pleasant highway in Puerto Princesa, about the last thing in the world I expected to see was another black man.

The other's face no longer looked cheerful: he looked as startled as me. But it was not long before the jolly grin came back on to it. That was Michael for you. His companion, however, continued to stare at me with a gloomy fascination he obviously felt no need to conceal. He was Barney Rubble to my new black friend's Fred Flintstone, while Danton was Booboo to my Yogi Bear. We all started to laugh, tickled by the notion of our tandem friendships, which we'd always assumed to be unique: black giant and street-wise little Asian. Gorilla and Monkey. Here were Gorilla and *Unggoy* MkII.

The black spoke to me in Vietnamese. I shook my head. My inclination, too, had been to speak to him in my native language. I was able to digest the implications of his appearance now and scrutinise the more intriguing aspects a second time more closely; then I saw he was slyly doing the same and again we both burst out laughing. I touched my chest. "Sugar," I said. He nodded. Then smacked his lips. "Soo-gar," he repeated. "Right," I confirmed. He pointed to himself: "Michael." I looked as surprised as Danton and

Skipper. I'd expected one of the (to us) comic-sounding monosyllables that passed for Vietnamese names. "Papa is Michael two," he said. "OK," I said, "your father was also called Michael." I thought, that's more than I know about myself. Michael pointed to the runway and extended both arms like wings. "Bye bye, Papa," he said. He grinned broadly. I knew what was coming. He pointed to me. I extended my arms. "Bye bye, Papa," I said. We both burst into laughter a third time. Dant was looking at me as if I was a half-wit. He'd never made any concessions to anyone in his whole short, hard little life.

Michael was a little younger than me, slightly smaller, but still massive by local standards. He had far less of the gook in his appearance than me. Even the second look didn't bring up any typical characteristics. That little narrowing of the eyes at the corners that marks me was absent from Michael, as was the slight elevation of my cheek-bones. He said something in Vietnamese and guffawed. I caught a few of the words the girls in the hooch had used on me. "Yeah, Michael," I said. "I know. The first words I learned in your language." This he didn't understand, but it wasn't important. It was like we could read the other's feelings when it mattered. Danton was giving Michael's companion a circumspect once-over. He didn't have quite the air of the juvenile delinquent about him that Danton could never shake off, even in a cassock. The guy was actually much older than he looked at first sight, about ten years older than the rest of us. He had a well-healed white scar running from the side of his right eye down to his chin. Now he caught me speculating about it, and grinned. Cool guy.

Michael beckoned me to him. They'd been preparing to fire up the makeshift oven. "Match? Sorry," I said. "I don't smoke, Michael." Lazares did the honours with the camo-pattern Zippo that had been Atty Caladong's birthday gift to him. I knew Lazares didn't smoke either. A girl in her early teens separated from the group we'd seen earlier and came to us with a tray – just a sheet of GI, galvanised iron – on which were the white slugs of unbaked dough. These were a good deal less interesting than the girl herself. She was very fair, with skin that had barely darkened under exposure on an open boat and the patchy shelter of a refugee camp. As she came nearer, the softness of her pale-brown hair, then her blue eyes became evident. There were a few like her in Mactan, though her good looks would have been special anywhere. She made a point of ignoring me. Michael pointed to her then placed both his index fingers side by side. "She's your girl-friend?" Puzzled look from Michael. I pointed to them both, then tapped my heart. He shook his head. "Mama," he said. Then made to hold up two fingers. "Ah, right, Brod, she's your sister." I couldn't hide the instant thought in my eyes: different fathers, both Americans, white and black – they'd been her customers. He nodded, more telepathy. She came back from the oven, pale face flushed with heat in the way no Filipina's or Vietnamese's would have been. It would be a while before there were embers and the bread could go in. I decided to wait with them. "Don't let me hold you up," I told Lazares and Danton.

"Er, no, Brod, I like the chick," Lazares said.

"Get da puck outta here, Lazares. I'll be da one to wait with Sugar. Go on, youse."

"You shouldn't call him, Brod," was Lazares' parting shot. "He's not in the Fraternity."

As Lazares was going, Michael's little Vietnamese sidekick asked: "Eye eff-eff?"

"What?"

He repeated the incomprehensible question.

"Sorry, I don't understand," I said. He looked amused, though as he was the one failing to make communication in a foreign language he shouldn't have been looking so wiseass.

"What-is-your-name?" I enunciated slowly. Unfortunately with my deep voice I sounded like a Speak Your Weight machine or The Mummy.

"Hot Dang Man," the little Vietnamese grimaced.

"Ah, Hot," I said. "Pleased to meet you, man. This here is Danton Zarcal."

"Shit, you stupid asshole, cain't you speak American?" the little guy ejaculated wrathfully.

Dant and I looked at each other in stupefaction. That didn't happen often.

"Hot dang, man, y'all gone out to lunch or what? It sure was hot judgin' by your skins the day you and Mikey was born but mah name ain't Hot. It's Nguyen."

Sometimes I startle and disconcert people when I open my mouth. I don't do this with my accent, which remains obdurately

Pepe Pinoy's – our "r"'s rolling like logs in a river, my trip and pause when uttering "be-ing" and "see-ing" typical of one brought up with the glottal stop, that Claymore-wire set in our throats. No, I surprise with my vocab, my phrasing, the ordering of my thoughts. Big black men aren't supposed to be clever. But, man, were the tables turned on me this time. If there was a prize for having a voice that didn't go with your face Hot Dang Man/Nguyen would walk away with it against all contenders.

"Cat got your tongue, coloured boy? I done asked you for Identification Friend or Foe. Like, is that guy with you or what?" He nodded in the direction of the retreating Lazares.

"A bit of both," I replied. "He's a dickhead but we're with him, right or wrong."

"Know the feeling, man, know the feeling."

Dant and I had been watching little Nguyen with growing wariness, much like an experienced King Cobra would have kept an eye on Rikki-Tikki-Tavi. We'd have felt relaxed if Hot Dang Man's words had been issuing from a head six feet above the ground, surmounted with blond hair, or short and curly like mine.

Nguyen took pity on us. "Aw, I ain't pissed with you, Bubba. I'm kinda ornery coz you're runnin' round free as hound-dogs after a possum while here Mikey and me is, three years and a half in what's no better than the caboose. It's a goddamned jail, man, no two ways, 'cept we've done nuthin' wrong 'cept done what you woulda done in our shoes."

Nguyen had met Michael in the camp. They'd been on different boats, Nguyen washing up there eighteen months earlier. Earlier because he was even more of an eyesore to the communist regime than Michael. He'd been a combat interpreter. When I questioned him it became apparent that he thought he spoke standard American English, because all the Americans he worked with spoke like that – the guys in the spotter-planes and the Forward Observers. I guess the lazy Deep Southern drawl was not the voice of panic, *di ba*? It was self-selecting.

All three of them, Nguyen, Michael, and his sister, wore crucifixes round their necks. Michael caught my glance and held the cross toward me with a smile.

"Plenty of Catholics in Saigon, man," said Nguyen. "We ain't too popular with the Ho Chi Minhs."

"Uh-huh."

Michael pointed to his sister. "Em."

"Pleased to meet you, Em," I said. She acknowledged me, but not Danton.

Michael said, "Amerasian."

"I know the word," I said drily. Then Michael picked up a handful of the dusty Palawan earth. He pointed at Em, me, and himself, then at the dust, before he indicated the sky and threw the fistful of dirt to the winds.

"I couldn't have put it better myself," I said.

"Hey, mans, he's da one to call you guys Dirt of Heaven!"

"Something approximating," I said.

Michael put his right arm round me. With the other he touched my curls, then pushed in my flat nose with his thumb to make it even flatter. No one, especially not Fr. Paul, had ever permitted themselves such a liberty, although I like to think I could have found it in me to tolerate the familiarity. From him it was different.

Dant scowled. "You gonna be da ones to suck each other's dicks, *di ba?*"

"Cool down, Dant. He's an OK guy. Maybe he can tell us something useful."

"Like how much to puck his sister?"

"Hey, Danton."

"Boom boom?" inquired Hot Dang Man helpfully. "No sweat. Tell me which. But not Em."

"No, no, " I said. "Misunderstanding. Change topic."

A very pleasant aroma, that of bread baking, was filling the air. Boiling-rice is nothing so evocative. I moved over to the oven. "My sister," I told Michael and Em, "is small, like you. But one hundred per cent Filipina. Looks like them." I pointed to the Vietnamese chicks at the other ovens.

"Sister – not…" Michael used the uncomplimentary Vietnamese words I'd heard in the hooch again. "No," I shook my head. "She's pure Filipina. Like pure orange juice, no additives, no preservatives."

"So your mother…"

"Right," I said, "right, you got it in one. And my sister has TB." I pointed to my chest, and coughed and hawked.

"That's bad," said Em, speaking for the first time, in Tagalog. "I am sorry."

"*Bahala na,*" I said. Kismet, Hardy, *che sera sera*, it's cool.

In terms of time measured on the clock, I didn't spend long with Michael and Em. But that never tells the whole story. And if I'd been a prisoner like them, three months of shared captivity with its stresses and strains on the character would have been worth a lifetime's knowledge of a person on the outside. However much you try to understand someone, to sympathise or empathise with them, nothing works like being the same as them, or having shared an experience. Michael and I were from the same tribe, a small tribe, and if Fr. Paul had taught me to despise anything as much as a blabbermouth it had been tribalism. But there we were. Dust to Dust.

Away from the uncomfortable heat of the oil-drum, we swung our heels as we sat on a low-hanging bough. I learned about the flocks of Amerasian street-children abandoned in Saigon, the scorn and contempt in which the Viets held them: not just the black ones, whom Filipinas also found, on the whole, ugly – whom I also found, on the whole, ugly, not excluding the spectacle of myself in the mirror – but also the white mestizos and mestizas whom Filipinos were at one in regarding as, on the whole, the most beautiful, the most fortunately endowed among us. "No like?" I asked, pointing at Em, for the average Filipino – not to mention Australian or European sex-tourist – the most ravishing of nymphets. Em shook her head vehemently. She picked up a stone and made to throw it. "For Em," she said, "from Vietnamese."

"And here?"

Em smiled. "Not here, but sometimes for Michael, if no can see behind." Michael guffawed. "If I can see better had run. How about you?"

"No," I said. "Filipinos have many things wrong with them but we are a friendly people."

"Yes, friendly people," Michael said. Em said nothing.

"Very friendly," Danton piped up. He'd been spoiling his good pants sitting on the ground. "Maybe she got a bun in da own oven, *di ba*?" I didn't get the point of this, but I could see he was pissed. He didn't like to be outside a group; all his life that had spelled danger.

"Take it easy, Dant," I said. "They're cool."

"OK," he said. "I'll be da one to just join Lazares, *na lang*."

This didn't disturb my composure. The best way to deal with other people's tantrums is not to have any of your own. Don't react. Gold doesn't; it's a noble metal, *di ba*?

We discussed corruption. Worse, Nguyen assured me, than in the Philippines. I found this hard to believe. Nguyen had bought his way out with jewellery belonging to his grandmother who'd been a Caodaist, part of the sect who worshipped Victor Hugo as a god. (I could just imagine Fr. Paul's hair-raising comments). Nguyen's boat had been stopped by marauding Thai fishermen, the girls taken off to an island in the haze, the men – unusually – left alive in the boat. Nguyen hated the North Vietnamese and said some of the surviving VC did, too. Em and Michael had been luckier, no pirates. Em, aged eleven, had been on contraceptive pills. Michael had been terribly sea-sick. The Malaysian Navy had towed them out of territorial waters. They'd drifted another week and hit Palawan.

I asked if I could get anything for them. Michael shook his head. I sniffed. "Burning?"

Em shrieked and ran for the oven. Out came the loaves, only a little carbonised on the bottom. Michael said, "No one like black." His face was absolutely straight. Then the grin came. "Not even blacks," I said. "OK, I better go. See you next time."

"Y'all come back now," called Nguyen.

I was still smiling when I arrived at our Lodge. Only Skipper was there. Atty Caladong had taken the others to the beach at high noon for some plinking with the Czech pistol. Definitely, I thought, quite definitely the guy's been up all night. "Attorney's in a good mood," Skipper said. "We cleaned up in that camp, Brod. Have a beer. Attorney said just to sign for anything."

Well, why not? I had a San Miguel on the Attorney and then another. I looked up at the verandahs of the rooms. "Skipper," I said, "have you thought this looks a little like the motel where Dr King met his end?"

"Who?"

"Martin Luther King."

"Never heard of the guy, man. Oh, yeah. Protestant, *di ba*?"

Atty Caladong came back from target practice, alive, with no casualties registered among *protegés* or stand-bys. Danton winked at me cockily. He'd learned this in Ireland. The wink was unknown in our archipelago, except when aiming.

That evening Atty Caladong took his dinner in town with civic dignitaries of his acquaintance, while we *bagets* had *baguettes* at the stalls. It was Saturday night and bustling. All the national chains were there, two miles from the primeval jungle: Mercury Drugs, remarked by Lazares, and a Kodak developing machine churning out its prints in a shop-window.

We wound up at a disco. Not one of the purpose-built Manila light and throb boxes but a Chinese restaurant at the top of a five-storey concrete tomb where they cleared back the tables and chairs at 10 p.m. and turned on the sound-system. We city-slickers stood in a disparaging group, making patronising comments about the bumpkins around us, fuelled by San Miguels and the fact that it was we sophisticates who were the chick-less. As the joint then proceeded to close at quarter past midnight we were spared a long ordeal. Skipper could talk about nothing else on the trisikad back to the Lodge. "Twelve *fifteen*, Brods! This is the Stone Age here. What do they do for recreation?"

"What time does Mars close back home?" Lazares asked. "Two, three?"

"Four," said Skipper.

"No, old friend," Dant said. "Until da suffly lasts, da beer and da customer both."

"Yeah, Brod. Hoo-hoo-hoo!" Lazares whooped into the rushing darkness. If he'd had a pistol he'd have fired it into the night. As we came up to a well-lit portion of the highway that turned out to be the parking-lot of the Island Playgirl go-go bar, I saw Atty Caladong – disappointingly girl-less – talking to the security guard. Even Dr King, I thought, had permitted himself the odd lady-friend. Beside him, the Attorney was a paragon of virtue. And how boring virtue can be.

Sunday was cockers' day. The Attorney had sold his American bantams to a senior local policeman and was sufficiently confident in their pedigree to be around when their mettle was tested. His trust was not misplaced. On the whole, my experience was that the less prepossessing a rooster, the more formidable. The smaller, scruffier birds often prevailed over the heavier, well-plumaged cocks, as Danton lost no opportunity in lecturing Skipper and Lazares. In my opinion this was not nature but art, for the law of the natural world, red in tooth and claw, is that the spoils go to the biggest, fastest, and strongest – and the law of nature is not easily flouted. It was the art of the confidence trickster, a betting-ploy. After stuffing the birds with steroids and vitamins for months, the cockers forced themselves to distress and dirty their pride and joys before displaying them to the crowd. I noted that Atty Caladong only stuck his bet on after the rival birds had been allowed a peck at each other, the handlers only taking care to cover the rooster's eyes with their hand. In went the kicks, up jumped the birds. Quicker than the eye could break it down, the beaks jabbed in, the spurs flashed backwards, and a local bird was lying on its side in a pool of gore, its legs pedalling spasmodically. The cocks were armed with the deadly Malay blade, the one which ended the affrays quickest and, in succession, our birds earned back their price in less than fifteen minutes. His pocket fat with bank-notes dirty as only the notes at a cock-fight could be, Attorney preened with pride and satisfaction. He'd made an honest sale and profited by putting his wallet where his mouth was. We, who would have had to act as bodyguards if the deal had gone sour, were also jubilant. The bets were too big for us to place individually but by pooling our resources we were able to get some action, and the winnings compounded spectacularly. Back in the courtyard of the Lodge we were ready to fall at the little guy's Florsheims and worship him. His stock had never been higher. That night, greatly daring, we held a mock-trial of Benigno Aquino and acquitted him. It was the last of our civilised evenings in the wilderness. The next morning we were due to return to the metropolis.

We got to the airport good and early. We were as solid as you could be: checked-in and holding our boarding-cards. The waiting area gradually filled up. From the total silence, broken only by bird-song, the snarl of the trisikads in the horseshoe approach-road built up to a continuous snarl as of so many sick lions. You could see the character of the passengers changing: the paranoaics and the provident-ants succeeded by Mr and Mrs Average, themselves replaced by the cool deadliners, followed by the feckless, the reckless, the compulsively tardy, and finally the influential. Lord Acton, whom Fr. Paul was magnanimous enough to call a great Protestant historian, remarked that all power corrupts and absolute power corrupts absolutely. In Asia, power makes unpunctual and absolute power results in a no-show.

Our jet, startlingly big, had already screamed down the runway from Manila, heartening every homeward-bound passenger in the terminal, when a personal jeep drew up, without any convincing impression of last-minute haste. Four or five men, two women, and a young girl of around our own age got down. They remained noticeably immune from the ragged porters' importunate attentions. The check-in clerk had a sickly smile on his face. Tickets were confidently produced. From gesture and posture we could see news of the re-allocation of their seats being imparted and the subdued reaction. The calmness, the coolness, with which this unwelcome intelligence was received boded poorly for the airline employees.

Atty Caladong transferred his attention from the Manila newspaper he'd found on the seat beside him to the scene behind us in the ticketing hall; it was certainly too low-key to be called a commotion. His case was full of the papers of the Vietnamese we'd been interviewing, but I doubt if he had been planning to open it on the flight even before the chance of fruitful conversation with congenial fellow-passengers had presented itself. I saw his face brighten. His mental processes often seemed snail-like to me but what he'd done now, at the level of instinct, was glimpse an opportunity and at this level the Attorney's reflexes were as fast as those of a kicking rooster. He pushed past the security guards and presented himself to the unanimated VIP's. Hands were shaken, heads nodded. Attorney appeared to know one of the group much better than the others. Through the glass of the departure lounge we heard a gust of laughter. We studes smiled collaboratively, no doubt Attorney being witty and charming. He turned, gestured to us to come out. Skipper, who regarded himself as Attorney's favourite, pointed to himself. Attorney shook his head – all of us. Looking faintly disappointed, Skip led the way. His strut was that of the promising scion about to be introduced to seniors who might be useful.

"These are the boys," Atty Caladong said.

I swear Lazares had been smarming back his thick black hair as he brought up the rear. Our rich boys smiled sycophantically; Danton scowled as only he knew how, like he was up-sizing the ladies for a bag-snatching. Me, I hoped I wore an expression of accessible reserve, of temperate dignity; I hoped I looked modest but not lickspittle.

"Ah," said the taller of the ladies, fragrant, white-skinned Pilipino aristocrats to the tips of their un-enamelled nails. "The boys you were mentioning."

By now Lazares and Skipper would have had their tongues hanging out of their mouths to floor-level of the terminal – as pristine an area as any in squeaky-clean PP – if they hadn't also been afflicted by terminal *hiya*: the becoming modesty, reticence, shyness of the junior before the senior. Those tongues formed the Philippine red carpet. The boys were salivating before privilege and power, greater than that of their own families.

The younger and shorter of the ladies, the one to look like Imelda's kid sister, snapped her patent-leather bag open. Skipper, his cousin, and Lazares were on the point of coming in their pants. Out came a pen.

Atty Caladong said, "Give Mum your boarding cards."

Skipper said, "What?"

Atty Caladong repeated himself with an edge to his voice that we hadn't heard so far on the trip, "Give the lady your boarding cards."

"Here," I said, "this is mine in the name of Castro, A.B. You are very welcome to it."

"Thank you," said Imelda Jr. Long practice enabled her to pack a wealth of meaning into those two words: e.g to communicate the fact that she really was sincerely grateful but I'd be deceiving myself if I was to imagine she'd ever repay the favour. I smiled a wan and gracious agreement. One by one my contemporaries followed suit, Danton last, handing his card over in two pieces, the stationery having detached along the perforations. I could see he took a certain pleasure in this. The lady I'd given my card to was writing their names on the passes.

"Hold it," her consort said. He was a very tall, dark guy only a couple of inches under me but slim, wearing a gold Rolex loosely on his bony wrist and masticating gum as if his life depended on it. "There are five tickets they're giving you but only three of you are going."

"So there are," said the other lady. "There's two spare."

There was a pause. This was the class of Pilipino who believed in pulling the ladder up after themselves. On principle they did no favours. They regarded the boarding-passes as already their own entailable property.

"Ramon was the one to say something about going to Manila when we were at the Rotarians," the tall guy with the Rolex said.

"I can see him already in the departure lounge," said Imelda Jr.

"Also me," said the other lady, by now betraying some small signs of impatience as the passengers were starting to board.

"Auction them, *di ba*?" asked Rolex. I don't think he was joking. "But no, Councillor," said his wife. "We'll be the ones to return them to the young men." She meant Skipper and his cousin whom she had immediately spotted as the best-heeled among us. She handed him the cards. "*Salamat po*, Mum," said Skipper, left with the final impression that he was the one to be done a favour and stand indebted. "Ah, but it's Sugar's."

"Never mind," said Atty Caladong. "You'll be the one. Mum chose you."

While this was going on we'd all been staring, discreetly, at the teenage girl in this illustrious party. Rolex was clearly her Daddy, you could see it in the face but that magical transformation had occurred where his features had become beautiful and what taut wrathfulness and greed were in him had failed to cross the membrane to her. Only super-rich girls wore no jewellery at all and deceptively simple black dresses, whose price only other girls could guess. She was a princess, Snow White, and we were the fucking dwarves. She was untouchable by the likes of even our rich-boys.

"We'll just board already," said Atty Caladong.

"Miss, I'll carry your bag," Skipper offered.

"No, me," said another, to be rewarded with a smile to kill for from Snow White. The party proceeded to the departure-lounge with the ground-staff in their train, bearing their hold-baggage as cabin effects.

After the pair of tickets came back to our group, it became plain Lazares was going to be marooned with Danton and me.

"Ah, Attorney," Lazares coughed. "You're forgetting something, *di ba*?"

Atty Caladong pulled a few small denomination notes from his pocket and put them in Lazares' hand. "Use your winnings," he said, and was gone.

The VIP's send-off party drove off in their empty service without another glance at us, but we went outside to sit under a tree and watch the take-off. None of us, I believe, was so small-minded as to hope to see it crash. Afterwards, the three of us walked the couple of miles to the port, as much to collect our thoughts as to preserve our small-change. There was a boat to Manila in five days time, via Lubang island, taking thirty hours; another to Mindoro via Cuyo islands in three days time, taking twenty-four hours but leaving us hundreds of miles south of home; and one that night, a special, non-scheduled, to an obscure port way down in Mindanao, taking twenty hours, but with an immediate connection on the same shipping line to Manila forty-eight hours distant. We went for the last. I analysed it: though it was the longest mileage it got us home sooner and by sleeping on the boat it would work out cheaper. It was also less hassle – no bus and jeepney switches by land with the age-long waits.

"Sugar, old friend, you are a pucking genius," Danton said effusively. "Next time, how about you're da one to organise da Pope visit? No froblem, mans, get da Holy Fapa to Tacloblan and back." Lazares laughed. I started to think he wasn't such a snotty son of a gun after all. Despite the unwelcome start, it was beginning to turn into an OK day. Truth to tell, even Lazares welcomed getting out from under Atty Caladong's wing. We bought bottled water, crackers, some tins of tuna, and cookies at a supermarket which brazenly surpassed Manila prices – freightage costs, Lazares explained to me – then had BBQ stix and hanging-rice out of plaited leaves as the sun went down on the dock.

Hinterlanders, heading back for the deep South, passed by our stall with intent and abstracted air, a psychic removal as complete as if they were inhabiting a private dimension. We'd accommodated ourselves to a limited insurgency; they were embroiled in a full-scale civil war.

Next to our special lay the regular tub to Mindoro, via Cuyo islands. It was delayed by repairs but the company was allowing the passengers to sleep on board. Our own vessel looked more or less ship-like but this craft with its galleon-sides, multi-tiered passenger-decks, and cage-like bars to prevent sleepers being rolled out of their cots into the waves, resembled Noah's Ark. We would certainly rather have embarked on her, two by two, than our craft – had they been bound for the same destination – for she was laden with girls, returning for the half-term holiday to their remote little archipelago in the middle of the Sulu Sea, girls in loose T-shirts adorned with cheeky slogans and in the tightest of counterfeit Levis and Wranglers. We, on the other hand, were about to spend twenty penitential hours on a boat where the only females were covered head to toe in fabric that was at once gaudy and grubby. I could see we were all thinking the same. However, we put off the depressing prospect by looking at the girls as long as we could. One thing about a provincial ship departure was that you didn't have to be a senator in order to stroll up the gangway as you saw the deck-hands getting ready to pull it up.

"PAL or Nike, serr?" asked the crone running the BBQ-stall, holding up a charred wing and a scrawny claw. "Hoy, hindi," Lazares grimaced, nearly falling off his rickety stool. The difference between Lazares and us was that he was probably still capable of contracting hepatitis or amoebiasis.

"Wow!" exclaimed Dant. "Colleens! Amerikanas! On da boat, mans! Look at!"

"Where, man?" I was scanning the upper decks where tourists were more likely to be found.

"There."

"Where? I still can't see them."

"To be sure, you're da vlind one now."

Then I saw them: three children aged between eight and ten, sitting patiently on the lowest deck a few feet above the water-line. They had the blondest of blond hair and skins paler than any whitening soap could effect.

"Where's da Mama and Fapa, mans?"

"Yeah, they wouldn't be travelling by themselves, Dant. No, they're talking to the Filipina next to them."

"Maybe da Ya Ya, mans."

"Mmm." There was something about it that didn't quite fit: the lack of curiosity about the white children on the deck around them, the ease, more, the bored matter-of-factness with which the little angels – *non Angli sed Angeli* – were themselves sitting, the way they twiddled their toes in their slippers.

"Here comes more talent," said Lazares, "just about legal already, *di ba?*" A couple of blonde girls of about Em's or Bambi's age were alighting from a trisikad at the gates of the port and, moreover, paying the correct coins as if they'd done it a hundred times before.

As the young blondes passed by our stall to reach the Cuyo boat I heard them speaking Pilipino to each other. The whole context was wrong. "I think their parents are missionaries," I said.

"But not da ones to be Roman Catholics," Dant interjected slyly. We sniggered at the thought of blond Fr. Boy fathering a brood of blonde kiddies – out of the question entirely: apart from the faith we had in his priestly integrity, that tough tankie already had it out of his system before he ever became a soldier of Christ. Lazares made kissing sounds to the girls. They didn't so much ignore the noise as blank him out of existence; he might as well have been a ghost. Their toe-nails had been nippered to the quick. The oldest girl limped. There were the tell-tale pink stains on her toes and nails. My own eyes narrowed as I noted that her eyes were slitty. Cheekbones a trifle pronounced... "Shit, Brod," I exclaimed. "They're Filipinas."

"Hah?"

"Just look, *di ba*? Look at them, OK? Now pretend the chicks have got black hair, OK, and imagine the skin is black already, *di ba*?"

"Shucks!" exclaimed Lazares. "You're right!" and in that same instant Danton said, "O-o, mans. You got it."

"They are albinos," I said.

"That's da word, Brod. To be sure it is."

Then in the shadows of the lower-deck I made out some older albino boys, very poorly dressed, like fishermen's sons.

"They're plenty of them," I said. "That's why we missed it. Just one, and you'd see they were a freak, *di ba*? It's the context."

"Hah?"

We looked at them with new eyes; they slotted into place. No more mystery, no more romance. "Serr," said a voice at my side, "I am not a freaks."

"Sorry," I said.

"OK, *na lang*, serr."

We waited, then Lazares said, "They look like people on a film until developed, *di ba*?"

"Printed," I corrected him. "Yeah, their hair and their eyebrows are like that. But, hey, everyone including them, has a black face on the neg."

"What about you, old friend?"

"Never looked."

The sun was setting, even more spectacularly than over Manila Bay. We walked the inconsiderable length of the peaceful little dock, then decided to go on board earlier than planned to secure our cots. There were, indeed, two men in our string bunks and no less than three women in the third bed. I showed them our ticket numbers and they departed without a murmur, cloth bundles and all. Putting Dant's knapsack for him on the bunk above me, I said smugly, "There's no need to get heavy, Brod. A pleasant smile works wonders."

Dant looked at me quizzically. "Old friend," he said, "to be sure, who da puck, who da puck in their right mind, is gonna argue da toss with a two hundred thirty pound gorilla like yourself is?" He and Lazares indulged in some low sniggering. I stretched myself out on the lower bunk, my feet projecting well in to the walk-way between the rows of beds. It was still comfortable enough and, with the pure air coming in over the open deck, who needed air-con? It was healthier here than in the First Class cabin and certainly pleasanter if anyone was going to throw up. I had brought to Palawan Charles Dickens's *A Tale of Two Cities* – unsurpassable symmetry from the opening lines onwards, though *Great Expectations* had more to say to me. I was soon lost to the Palawan present. I concentrated hard on a book; it wasn't like loping on to the court and going on to auto-pilot. You withheld your commitment from an opponent, existed in a different time as a wraith, but the commitment to the word was absolute and you had to inhabit its present, otherwise you remembered nothing from it. Coming to much later, I found it dark on the dock, just a few rags flaring in kerosene bottles. My companions' cots were empty. The ship was lurching decisively to port. The other passengers were smoking and chewing at the railings. I judged it better not to contribute my weight there. The ropes securing us to the dock bollards were already squeaking like mice. I couldn't see Dant or Lazares at the railings.

"Comfort Rooms, mans," said a returning Danton. They hadn't been at the railings but at the stern.

"If you can call it that," Lazares said. "Phew!"

"O-o," agreed Dant, "go now, man. Lazares said this is the time – like early, before they get blocked."

When I returned, I said, "You weren't kidding."

"Ah, to be sure, we'll just piss over da side – just not into da wind."

At 11 p.m., three hours after the advertised time, we felt the metal deck tremble beneath us. A laconic Pilipino voice announced over the p.a., "Crew, stand by for undocking manoeuvre, stand by for undocking manoeuvre, stand by for undocking manoeuvre." It was fifteen minutes before we were under way and another half an hour before I realised that the rate we were going at was not an appropriately prudent speed for clearing port but our tub's maximum. I would estimate it at about six knots. I'd been waiting for the unspectacular white eddies sent spinning along the plates by the boat's less than ardent bows to recede a little more boisterously. "Shit! That's it," I said in disbelief to Lazares. "Man, we better start rowing. It's gonna be a week to Mindanao. How much water did we bring?"

"Well, at least we won't be pissing if we're dehydrated. Let's tell Brother Danton."

Just then the engines appeared to cut out altogether. "Ay!" I exclaimed, "at least they can tow us back to port from here. French sandwiches again. *Bahala na.*"

"*Bahala na*, Brod," Lazares said. He slapped palms with me lazily, "uppeer" we called it, high-fiving, that overhand *pinoy* swat of self-congratulation.

But the crew were dropping a cable ladder down to the water and shortly after a policeman came over the side, not navy, not coastguard, but a khaki land constabulary.

"Shit!" Dant exclaimed. "They're looking for gun-runners, just the same as County Kerry!"

"No way," I pointed out. "There are just two PC, and they've only got sidearms. They wouldn't be going after gun-runners like that."

The PC joined the boat's ticket-checkers, a trio of over-qualified young dudes in snowy long-sleeved shirts who'd never pulled on a hawser in their lives.

"Guys," I announced, "I've got a serious problem – another leak. Send out search parties if I don't return in a week."

Pepsi worked on me nearly as badly as a beer. It had been my intention to urinate through the railings at the stern but I decided not to give officialdom the chance to squeeze me for a few pesos. I entered the chamber, which had become appreciably dirtier in the short time. Debris filled two cubicles. I didn't feel like putting my stream on top. I was going to kick the third door open but restrained myself and checked first. Easy for me – I just looked over the top of the door. Squatting there, trousers up, shirt tucked in at the waistband, clothing adjusted and in no disarray at all, was a large man with curly black hair. For a moment I thought of Dant's gay airline stewards. Then the guy looked up. It was Michael. He was as stunned as I was.

Despite myself, I began to smile. Then I just burst out laughing. Michael held a finger to his lips. It wasn't quite as funny for him as it was for me, *di ba*?

I nodded. "Is Em with you?" I asked. He shook his head vigorously. "Stay behind."

"I see. Can I take it that you've escaped?"

"Escape."

"Gee, brother, we were only talking to you the other day. Why didn't you ask us for help? Didn't you trust me?"

"Trust. Don't angry Michael. Nguyen want to ask your help. I say, Sugar is my brother. I don't use him."

"I understand. I hate to use people too. But next time, don't even think of not asking."

"Sorry."

"Are you by yourself?"

"With Nguyen. He bought the ticket us."

"That's Hot Dang Man?"

"Hah?"

"Small guy, small like my friend? Very good English."

"Yes."

I was starting to think, not like a native who'd slept on his back all his life. More like a Jesuitical poisoner with a dead Pope on his hands. "You can't stay in here." I was thinking out loud for both our benefits. "It's the obvious place. They'll triple-check in here." The look of trust on Michael's face was absolute. It even remained when I proceeded to contradict myself. "OK. For a while. Stay here."

Danton had transferred to my berth when I got back. Lazares was in the canteen. "I like it here, Gorilla," Dant greeted me. "Gonna be da one to throw me out? You make da wanking back there? Long time already."

"Listen up good and listen up quick. Michael's in the CR and his little pal's on the boat, too."

Dant was as quick as I could have hoped. "Black Michael da Vietnamese niggers? Gotta be them da cops is looking for, old friend."

"For sure."

"What we gonna do?"

"Help. If you're up for it."

"Hey, all for da one and one for da all, mans. Father Padraig in Galway also been da one to help da boys in his youth. Da IRAs. Get what I mean? Gun-runners and da sundry fugitive."

"I don't, but shut the fuck up, Dant, and start thinking."

"They got tickets, man?"

"Yes, but they're gonna pick Michael up. As soon as he opens his mouth, man. Hot Dang Man doesn't exactly sound like a *pinoy* either."

"So Michael don't open his mouth."

I decided Danton was not being a lot of help. It was going to be all down to me. That was not the first time I'd under-estimated Dant. "OK, mans. I got da wizard wheeze. They can't be da ones to speak coz they is mutes. *Dili* – for a while, better injured da mouths."

"Yeah. Right." If I didn't give Danton full and immediate credit for his "wizard wheeze", it was because it was so good and so simple, though blatantly obvious once the idea had come, that it sparked my own thinking and left me abstracted. We'd pass Michael and Nguyen off as me and Dant. The police wouldn't think they were seeing double. We'd become one in their minds. The ruse was as old as Sydney Carton and as contemporary as Hanna-Barbera. I rummaged in my bag for my spare Artheneum All-Stars sando, with Castro 11 emblazoned on the back.

"Dant, have you got the team cap I gave you? The duck-bill brim. O-o. Ace, man. OK, stay here. Thank you, Lord, for the Free Size Adjustable Strap."

Poor Michael peered over the cubicle door at me like Kilroy but lit up when he saw the duplicate of the sando I was wearing. He could see somewhere the seeds of a successful plan. "You wear the cap, too, Michael, same as the one I'm wearing now. OK? Pull the brim over your eyes. Oh, yeah, we're brothers. Now give me your polo shirt – too *bagets*, man, for a black guy here. Lousy disguise – you look like an attorney. I'll be the one to stay here now. You go out and get Hot Dang Man, Nguyen. Bring him to Danton, Cot E47, and you come back here. Chop-chop, brother."

Michael was back swiftly. "OK, man. Musical chairs, *di ba*? Stay in the cubicle. I'll go to Nguyen and Danton."

Danton had Nguyen tucked up on the lower-bunk, blocked in by the back of a neighbouring cot.

I hissed to Danton, "Look, just one with the bust jaw, OK? Two is too much to swallow, even if they rolled over in the same jeep."

"Da great minds thinking alike, old friend. Look at."

"Shit, what the fuck have you done to him?"

"It's da pages from your book, man. I mean in balls, man, for da wadding in da cheek and tooths, Sugar."

"I'm *reading* that book, you asshole! I'm nearly at the end."

"Tough shit, King Kongs."

It was fantastic what Danton had contrived. It really looked like Hot Dang Man had monstrous dental abscesses or mangled mandibles. Dant pulled out his spare briefs from his knapsack, then hooked one leg opening under Nguyen's chin and twisted the elasticated waist round before knotting it on top of the head. "He look like da pucking flum fudding da Fathers give us Christmas Days in Galway, man."

"No, it's gonna work. Looks just like a cartoon bandage. How about your bandage? They've got to be identical."

"I'll just be da one to take my vriefs off and wear them."

"Jeez, he's the lucky one, *di ba*?" I put Nguyen in Dant's cot, with instructions to limit his speech to O-o, Boss, it hurts, and salamat.

Danton was tearing out the pages of my novel with a glee he made no effort to disguise.

"Could you take them from the front, the pages I've read?"

"Reserving those one you already fingered for other purpose, old friend, at da other end of me, not my mouth." He went off to the CR to take off his briefs and to reinforce instructions to Michael that he should stay put until we fetched him and, above all, to say nothing.

The ticket-inspectors and the PC had worked half-way down the boat towards us by the time Dant returned, with a thumbs-up signal. "Don't do that again," I said. "No one with a face like that can be cheerful." He looked the very picture of woe, only eyes and nose differentiating him from the bandage-swathed Invisible Man. I lay on my side, curled up, facing the wall. At length the checkers arrived.

"Tickets, please." I handed over mine backwards, my face still turned away. I got a shove on the butt. It was the older PC. "This is him," he said. "Get up."

"You're going back now," he said. "You seem to like boats. Is that why they call you boat-people?" In fact, he didn't look too mad; I guess they hadn't called him on the evening he reserved for his mistress. Nguyen had told us the previous day that we *pinoys* had the reputation for giving the Viets the best treatment in Asia. I said in Tagalog, "Sorry, sir, I don't understand. We're on our way to Mindanao, then we'll ride the boat to Manila. We came from there last week. We're first year law students at Artheneum, came here with Atty Caladong."

"You learned Pilipino, hah?"

"I am a Pilipino."

"It must have been a hot day when you were born."

"My father was a US serviceman. I'm from Mactan, if you know it."

"I don't."

"You, what's wrong with you?" the other officer asked Dant.

"Fell off a motorbike," he said in muffled tones. "I got da worst of it *sapagkat* fillion *ako pero* Sugar's been pissing blood for days."

"ID," the senior said. We produced it. They conferred, while the ticket-collectors very civilly authenticated our tickets. "It's them," the senior said. "How many niggers in Palawan?"

"They're speaking Pilipino like Pilipinos," the other one said.

"They can do that. Been here long enough."

"I play on the All-Stars," I said. "Sugar Rey Castro. Maybe you've seen me on TV? Or maybe you saw the ad for Nang Maria's Chicken Krisplets? I was the African chief."

"*Iwan ko*. I wouldn't know," the senior PC said. We weren't getting any change from this guy.

"OK, get on your feet. You're coming with us."

Now all this was totally unanticipated. We had the inconvenience of having our journey interrupted but, on the other hand, it was a cheap price to pay for getting Michael and Nguyen to Mindanao. Danton had been showing ingrained resistance to the police – second-nature with us – but I could tell he also was starting to see the welcome possibilities. It was a far, far better thing we were gonna do, man, than we had ever done before.

"You're making a mistake, sir," I said for the sake of it, swinging my feet off the bunk.

"I don't think so. And if I am, I don't care."

The other cop whispered in his ear. What the guy heard made him look both more cheerful and more mean.

"Where's your money?" he asked.

"*Walang kwarta*," Dant mumbled through his underpants and wadding. "No money, boss."

"Toothache, *di ba*?" the cop mocked him.

"O-o."

"Maybe we can do something about that for you."

Dant had the sense to shut the fuck up, rather than give him the wise-ass repartee he'd have done five years ago.

"OK, you can come up with five thousand and continue your sea-journey or you can come back with us now."

I could see the glint in Dant's eye through the Y-fronts of his briefs. He was going to kill the two birds with one stone: keep his cockfight winnings and take the heat off Mikey and Hot Dang Man. But then I started to re-consider. Fr. Paul had made me nothing if not mind advance-dirty. Experience and instinct – normally known as prejudice – taught me that Dant's way-outs were usually the wrong ones. And maybe we were panicking too early in the game. If Dant and I got sent off, who'd be there to help Nguyen and Michael on a boatful of taciturn Southerners? Or coach them right in a port full of hill-folk and sea-gypsies? Dant's face, what could be seen of it, looked for the first time truly woebegone as I delved in my pocket for the banknotes. He was unable to restrain a genuine groan of anguish, causing the cops to take a second look at him. At that moment Lazares returned from the canteen.

"What the fuck happened to your face, Danton?"

The cops scowled at him. "Are you with these *comegiante*?"

"Yeah. Why?"

"We'll be the ones to ask questions. You sit down there."

But the cops' disappointment was patent. Lazares validated us. You couldn't fake the guy – his air of assurance, as if he was walking around the jungle that was the RP in a portable private sanctuary to which the clawed and fanged could not gain ingress. He was unmistakably the genuine article – a rich Filipino. The only illegal immigration he'd ever been implicated in was the arrival of his Spanish and Chinese ancestors five centuries ago. "I'm a police asset," he announced. "Here's the copy of the mission order."

"You're a bit young for that, sonny?" the older cop sneered.

"My uncle's a Major in Batangas," Lazares said. "He issued it."

"Are you packing?" the cop asked, with cautious belligerence.

"No," Lazares admitted. "I don't bother with a gun."

"Well, your mission order's expired and it's not valid here," the cop said. "This is Palawan."

I could see they'd given it up; it was just a matter of face.

"Ah, look, Inspector," I said, which was much like calling Fr. Paul Your Eminence, "we're the ones to regret all the trouble we've caused. Can we give something for the boys?"

"What's this?" the young one asked indignantly.

"Sorry," I said, the one hundred peso note peeping from my fist. The cops stalked off. A minute later the younger one was sent back. "You're fined one hundred," he said curtly and took the bank-note from me.

"C'mon, Dant," I said "CR."

The toilet was still filthier than the last time I'd been in it. Michael and Nguyen were sharing a cubicle.

Dant asked, "It hurting the one taking it, *ba*?"

Nguyen said, "Only when I laugh, Bubba."

"OK, cut it, guys," I said. "I'll take you to Dant's cot, Nguyen. Stay in it, turn your face to the wall, and don't wake up even for the Archangel Gabriel. I'll come back here. Then I'll be the one to stay in the cubicle and Dant will escort Michael to his sleeping place. After that, Dant, you come back here and pretend you're taking a shit next to me. When the cops come – and they will – they'll see it's only us again and they won't check the cots. Been there already, *di ba*?"

"Roger that," said Nguyen, skipping out of his stinking compartment.

All went well on the exchange-trips. Most of the passengers were already asleep. Dant and I had only been in the shit-house for a few minutes when we felt the engines start again.

"I tink so, old friend, I tink so."

We high-fived again.

At the cots, where at first Nguyen and Michael kept their backs resolutely turned to us – that was their discipline for you, man – I said, "Turn and turn about, *di ba*? They'll take first shift in the CR and we'll have the cots two hours."

Dant scoffed at the notion. "Just let them find spare cots and we'll be da ones to zizz."

"What if the ticket-collectors come back?"

"Jaizus, old friend, never you mind them. They don't care tuffence. All da wiseguys gonna change veds to da more expensive class after they pinished da checking, even into da air-condition cabins. They know da score. I never seen *any* ticket-collector ever come back after da first check on any ferry I ever been on. More suspicious if da Biets is da ones to stay all da time in da CR, mans."

I gave in to his arguments. We fetched Michael and Nguyen out of their noisome hole. Then we installed them into undesirable berths on the windward side – still infinitely preferable to their previous situation. As we passed below the bridge, Danton signalled to me.

"No, you crazy fuck!" I hissed but it was too late. The monkey was already swarming up the companionway. He beckoned me to join him. I peered through the salt-streaked glass. The wheel was unmanned, its spokes turning aimlessly to starboard and back to port as if steered by a ghost. Empty beer bottles rolled this way and that on the deck, clinking with violent threats of breaking but never actually doing so. Four or five uniformed figures lurched around without purpose, a couple of them still holding brown bottles. As we watched, a flimsy curtain parted at the rear and the Captain came out in rubber slippers, Y-front briefs, and gold-braided cap. I waited for words of reproof, even a mere command for someone to hold the wheel, but he simply rubbed his flabby tit, yawned, and turned in again.

"Jesus!" I breathed.

"O-o. I impress, too," Danton admitted. "I tink time for da Lord's Frayer. C'mon, old friend, let's go down. Porty winks and then see to our friends again. Everyone else safe asleep."

Lazares was sleeping like a baby. Dant took his own briefs off his head and put them on Lazares' face before climbing into his cot. When I woke up Lazares still had the briefs over his face but Dant was gone.

I found him in conversation with the Viets, the three of them sitting on Michael's cot. Dant was concluding some tale about his time in Ireland with the Fathers, our two fugitives guffawing at its conclusion. I didn't know whether to be irritated by the attention they might have drawn to themselves or gratified by the protective screen of laughter around them. Are runaway asylum-seekers, on the whole, mirthful folk?

"Funny life," Michael said, pointing to Danton. "All different pieces not same."

"Look who's talking," I said. "But where will you go? Have you got a plan?" His broad smile said it: "*Bahala na,*" in any language. Michael said, "Maybe lucky, maybe not so lucky. God knowing. I pray America, that's our real home, you and me, Sugar, but from camp my cousin to Germany, girls are three sisters to Mexico…"

"*Mexico?*"

"Yes. Some lucky Canada, but I go anywhere. Anywhere – except Vietnam again." He laughed, this time the unmirthful laugh of the Orient.

"Well, wherever you go, you'll need money."

"Puck, Sugar, what you're doing?"

"It's only the cock-fight winnings."

"Shit, you don't give mine, Brod." Danton snatched the cash out of my hand and counted out his cut, two thousand one hundred and seventy three pesos, then gave the rest to Nguyen. "Jaizus, be generous with your own da next time, Sugar."

I couldn't help laughing, the Viets pretending to be mystified by all this. They tried refusing but then took it.

"I never forget," said Michael. "Never. And you, Danton, my brother."

"Yeah, yeah, old friend. Da Vest of Vritish to you, man, too."

I took Nguyen with me to buy a couple of orange-sodas – mix up the pairings, I thought, and confuse everyone who's half-awake. The tribals were still out to the world. We couldn't have got away with it on a boat full of prying, gossiping Visayans.

Dant took the lukewarm can and swirled it moodily. "Here we are, old friend, fleased as funch for them. But you tink about it, man. Everybody in da Philippines who can get da puck out of here doing it, man. You name it: doctor to Alabama, man, domestic help to Singapore or Hong Kong, tailor to Jeddah, even frostie girl to Japan. Here these stupid pucks are, man, trying to get in to da country."

I looked mitigatingly at the Viets but I guess Nguyen was pretending not to understand what he rather wouldn't hear.

"Freedom," I said mildly to Dant. "We're as poor as they are but a little freer, even with Ferdie and Imelda."

"Preedom, man?" he responded hotly. "Preedom's just annuder word for nuttin' left to lose." I was struck dumb with admiration for this pithy piece of eloquence, until with dawn breaking, I realised where I'd heard it before. Kris Kristofferson, *di ba*, and Janis Joplin?

We were all too frayed now, young as we were, to have much to say to each other. I held Michael's hand a while. At last we came into port. The same laconic Pilipino voice gave the reverse command: "Crew, stand by for docking manoeuvre, stand by for docking manoeuvre, stand by for docking manoeuvre."

I thought of Lazares by himself. "We'd better go back," I said. "You guys be the first ones to get off – we'll be the ones to field any inquiries, like are we all twins. Good luck, guys." I kept it unemotional, I kept it cool. Michael, too, just nodded. I guess they had a right to be more nervous than us. On the way back Danton, nevertheless, fiddled at an imaginary violin. He said, "Farting is such sweet sorrow, man. Why you're laughing?" He knew perfectly well; he was just trying to cheer me up.

Lazares said, "Very funny, whoever the comedian is. I threw the briefs over the side."

We didn't see Michael and Nguyen when we got off, so assumed the best. We transferred to the Manila ferry and were home without further incident less than forty-eight hours later.

As a postscript, I had to satisfy my curiosity about the large number of blond children we'd seen on the Cuyo ferry. I could find nothing in any of the ethnographical works in our library but one of my team-mates put me in touch with his biology professor, who told me a recessive gene in the isolated island population was very likely responsible. "There's a good paper in that," he said.

I thought they'd find some long scientific words for what I'd put differently. Too many white haricot beans in the *Halo*[2] and not enough violet-yam jam.

CHAPTER V

IT HAPPENED JUST A COUPLE OF WEEKS after we got back from Palawan. Since before my days the Gamma Alpha Omega crowd had been muscling in on our shabu distribution network. Recently they had grown from a nuisance into a threat. Distribution was the key to the whole money-making system. So-called Drug Lords, that was senators and Chinese businessmen, imported it by the container-load. The police wholesaled it as a lucrative adjunct to the kidnapping and numbers rackets, and creeps like us retailed it and acted as scapegoats when a bust was needed. Shabu was what we called the white crystals but we knew it was sold as ice in the US. By whatever name, metamphetamine hydrochloride was one of the great up-ers. It was made in gangster labs in Taiwan and South China and mostly came through Hong Kong. This was a piece of general knowledge amongst college youth, more widely disseminated, say, than the sources of the Blue and White Niles which had so exercised Fr. Paul in geography class. I happened also to know that shabu was the first of the designer drugs; the Japs had invented it for the kamikaze pilots. Most forms of Speed improve your reflexes, so it was the perfect drug for doomed guys, no older than us, dodging the fighters and flak in their leather-helmets and goggles. As long as there was a titre of the drug in the blood-stream it also fostered a sense of euphoric optimism and control over circumstances which could overcome any amount of contrary evidence. This poor man's cocaine gave you the impression that you were accomplishing great things until you came off it and saw you'd achieved fuck-all. This disillusionment was a stage the kamikaze pilots hadn't reached, of course. The fact that shabu also produces an unquenchable desire to talk non-stop might seem a disadvantage until one remembers that by that stage of the war the Japs could no longer fit their planes with radio. Sometimes I wished I was in a radio-less Zero or soundproof booth when I had to listen to three stoned morons at the same time.

But, oh, yeah, it was a cool smoke. You sucked it up through a straw held instinctively with both hands so you didn't lose any as the fumes spiralled off the scorching foil. Then *whoosh*, it was straight up in the elevator to cool heaven. I took some the once, so as not to be the odd one out in the group. Yes, it was a good feeling. I'd have felt omnipotent as I crashed my munitions-laden plane through anyone's flight-deck. But it wasn't an experience I'd have cared to repeat. "Oh, yeah, not this time, guys," I'd say, smiling tolerantly as the paraphernalia came out and somehow I managed to give everyone except Danton the impression that this abstinence was the exception rather than the rule for me. Butch Tan Sy would have flipped his lid at the thought of any of his athletes polluting their systems with naughty substances – plenty did, of course – but that wasn't what stopped me. I didn't need their thrill. I was cheerful enough. My smile was genuine. They were artificially inducing what I felt for free every time I stepped out on to the basketball court. You couldn't get any higher than I jumped. Or feel a rush as powerful as my approach and swoop. And their buzz-saw monologues – as memorable as so much wood-dust on the wind – were no speedier than my own mental processes. Perhaps they should have legalised shabu and used it medicinally like morphine, only not to assuage the pain of the terminally ill but to cure the mentally afflicted. If Fr. Paul's diagnosis of our national slowness was as correct as it was simple, shabu should have been prescribed to the entire country.

WHEN THE BRODS WEREN'T SPEEDING THEY WERE TORPID and never more so than when they were recuperating from a hyper-high. Seven of us were laying back in chairs, me because my legs were woolly from Butch's weight-training special, three hundred pounds of discs on the sledge, plus him on top of the discs, and the others because that was the way the wastrels were, when a pair of Brods arrived, breathless with the import and outrage of their tidings. "It's the Gamma crowd. Down by the park. When Rolfram and Celestino came by, they jumped them. Five or six of them, 'Tino says. Took their stock and kicked the shit out of them." The news spread as if the Frat House was an ant-hill; about the one thing

Filipinos were efficient at mongering was rumour. If gossip and tales were commodities the country would have no trade deficit. Within a minute and a half soldier-ants were heading towards the scene of the crime with whatever crude tools came to hand. We found the two Brods nursing their cut lip and bleeding nose on a park-bench. Rolfram, who was Lazares' third cousin, had his T-shirt ripped nearly in half. I thought they could consider themselves lucky; I'd seen much worse suffered by accident in training. However, I kept this temperate opinion to myself as the crowd whipped up its sense of injury inflicted upon its collective self. In the end you might have thought our two heroes had been burned alive.

The Frat held a war-council. Not about whether we should retaliate, a foregone conclusion, so much as when, where, and how hard. The first two, time and place, were easily decided: on their turf, soon. Revenge, they say, is a dish that tastes best cold but we were only hothead kids. What we needed to decide was how far we dared to go. There was inflammatory talk of grenades and armalites.

We went to get Atty Caladong's words of wisdom. That great man, the contemporary Solomon, faintly disappointed those under his sway when he barked: "Institute appropriate counter-measures," and departed into the middle distance.

You might wonder why I trouble to recount these trivial histories, always puerile and now ancient as well. The answer and my extenuation is that these were no insignificant delinquencies of disadvantaged youth. These were the gristly issues on which the leaders of my smiling land – judges, tycoons, ambassadors, generals, congressmen, mayors, senators, maybe even future presidents – cut their teeth.

In the end, just as our predecessors, now numbered among the elite of the land, also had, we plumped for blunt weapons, to be employed in a mass attack, rather than a sneak reprisal with the lone bullet or the single blade. The sophisticated visual aids the good Fathers had never scorned – the overhead projectors, the laser-pointer, the chinagraph pens, the fluorescent cardboard – all these came out for our planning and briefings. Despite himself – he was mightily pissed not to be given a general's role on the council – Danton was impressed. "Not so bad, hah, for da eejit rich-boys, Sugar? Sure, and it's da same plan as da Sige[2] Juniors use on da Sputnikettes in Tondo, mans, way back when in '71. I tink also da same as da lads use on da Prods apprentice boys in Derry Bogside, man, in da youth of Fr. Padraig, man."

"Brod, I hate to disillusion you – the strategy's two thousand years old at least. Don't you remember Fr. Paul's diagram on the blackboard he made up from Livius of the battle of Lake Trasimene?"

"Shut da puck up, you big nigger know-alls. Have no lake in Q.C., man, just da campus swimming-fool."

The strategy was a good deal simpler than any of Butch Tan Sy's elaborate playmakers – had to be with a huge team of non-athletes on a playing-field with infinitely stretchable boundaries. Twelve of our nimblest guys were to go in to an eatery popular with the Gamma crew, whup whoever they found in there on the head, hopefully with their siupao buns and forkfuls of pancit Canton halfway to their mouths, let a few escape, take their time before scooting, put up token resistance to the avenging Gamma hordes, then flee, leading the suckers down a narrow lane to a small open space in the fetid alleyways off the highway – in fact, nothing more nor less than an impromptu basketball court with just the one net for both teams to score into – around which about a hundred of us would be lurking ready to pounce. Killing-ground? Man, we thought it would be an abattoir.

Dant drew the dangerous detail: being bait. "Sure, and I'm da frivileged one," he told Lazares, who was the council member who acquainted him with his selection. Lazares wasn't sure how to take this. He said, "O, Brod," and cleared off. Lazares was a little awkward with us since Palawan.

Once a plan like this was made it had to be executed instantly. A secret couldn't be kept by so many. Accordingly, the next morning, the Frat was ready to rumble. Baseball bats, poles, timber two-by-twos, lengths of lead pipe for those who really knew what they were about, rice-flails, purloined seven- and nine-irons, you name it, we had it. Also, cloth hoods with eye slits and mouth holes and gloves or mittens.

There was a further refinement of tactics on the day. There was to be a reserve, a shock-force to be committed only at a critical moment either of dire emergency when the day looked all but lost or as a coup de grace to administer the final crushing blow as the Gammas wavered. The biggest, the toughest, the meanest, were in this Praetorian elite. And, inevitably, it included the towering basketball guard. For my contemporaries my notability was brawn. Frankenstein was being unleashed.

We all took different paths to our assembly points, some groups actually doubling back on their jeepney routes. We monsters went last by a direct route.

Well, so far from having a bird's eye view of what happened, I was hidden away initially in an obscure corner. And once into the open I saw mere chaos, so I am reduced to piecing together partial and suspect accounts from my better-placed but inherently untrustworthy contemporaries. Danton, principally, for what happened first in the eatery and others for later. Don't ever say Fr. Paul was culpable of burdening us with an irrelevant and outmoded education, those few of us who were capable of grasping his classical torch, for am I not treading in the footsteps of the exile Polybius and the metropolitan Livy, sniffing, sifting as we go for the truffle of truth, discounting the stale, discarding the tainted, and disdaining the pretensions of mere mushrooms? When it was contemporary was the assassination of Cæsar not simply a squalid stabbing? Who knows what sordid horrors grace of language and clarity of thought cannot redeem?

Led by the Frat Treasurer, the youngest son of a Visayan Governor, Danton's group donned their hoods and gloves as their jeepney drew to a halt right outside the carenderia, the obliging driver, who had no intimation whatsoever of the clandestine wardrobing behind him, alerted to stop by the merry "*ding!*" of Dant's coin on the grab-rail. Our Dirty Dozen were in like so many rats down a drain and belabouring the Gamma boys before they knew what they were about. "Like I'm da one to be in a dream, Brod," Danton told me later with wonder. "Slow-slow, mans, but really it's happening past-past like anyting." My own experience of the court told me this wasn't simply the effect of the Kamikaze Koktel they'd all smoked. Swatting flies would have been more difficult. There were only eight Gammas in there – Dant took the trouble to count the bodies on the floor, with one on his back across the table bleeding into the soup puddle. He, as we were later to learn, was one Eleuterio G. Ayayay III. Eleuterio III had been the one to get it on top of his head appropriately enough three times with the thirteen inches of Exhibit A. This was the lead pipe carried by a guy called Brabazon, the leader of Dant's Dirty Dozen. There was nothing particularly spiteful or pre-planned about this special treatment. Eleuterio III had simply been the boy nearest Brabazon, who was first in. And he got hit three times because the first blow with the heavy pipe recommended of yore by Brabazon's older brother, now a high-flyer in the Foreign Service, had been sufficient to knock him spark out and leave him there on his face just asking for the next two knocks, while the others, hit with less useful clubs, had been able to move away or defend themselves with their arms, fractured forearms being preferable to broken skulls.

Unfortunately, this initial assault had proved all too successful. It had been meant as a provocation and a lure – but not one of its victims had been able to get away and raise the alarm.

This inconvenient fact began to dawn on the mega-brains in our Dirty Dozen, Danton by no means the last. Breathless with nerves rather than the small exertion of wielding their homely instruments, they looked on each other amid the savoury aromas of the little place. It was not a spectacle calculated to reassure. Instead of the faces of familiar comrades they gazed upon a sable version of the Klu Klux Klan, so many hooded executioners or hanging vigilantes confronted themselves with the prospect of imminent termination, the loose cloth bags around their faces quivering and puffing with every breath like the inhalations and deflations of the condemned man within his mask as he waits with a halter around his neck. It was twelve minds with but one thought: *"What the hell are we gonna do next?"* Danton confessed to me later, "I not so frighten about any more da Gammas coming, man. We be da ones to deal with that. I'm tinking of youse guys all waiting and how we gonna be da ones to catch it hot from you if we puck up."

"Scapegoat is the word you're looking for."

"Scrape-goat stew is what they was cooking in da carenderia, man. I could smell it real good."

Brabazon instinctively resorted to the final expedient of the Philippine elite in a crisis: boot the helpless around some more. The hapless Eleuterio III, as the Gamma most profoundly unconscious and least likely to be difficult, was taken outside and given yet more stick in plain view. This was unfortunate in that he may still have been alive at that point and doubly so in that it took his Fraternity brothers so long to notice. At length shouts and commotion told the Dirty Dozen they'd been remarked. Only pausing to give Eleuterio III a few personalised, flamboyant, but nevertheless relatively innocuous kicks in the ribs, Brabazon ordered the retreat but found himself upstaged by Danton who dropped his pants and gave their pursuers the moon. Gammas were starting to descend like bluebottles on a dog-turd. In the literal sense Dant now found himself bringing up the rear. Sweat trickled into his eyes. The capacious hood, which he'd filched from me, started to work its way round to the back of his head. Instead of following the others down the two foot wide opening of the alley leading to the playground he continued thirty yards to an exposed corner, realised his mistake, doubled back, and, still moving in dream time, found that three Gammas were going to reach the alley before him. Euclid had never been his strong point, as he was always the first to concede at San Ignatio, but his calculation proved correct this time. Skidding to a halt, he found a strapping Gamma – "I tink maybe on da cagers team, mans," – blocking his way and another pair closing in fast. "Shit, mans, I feelings just like da hunted animals, man, like da hare-coursing or da vadger-vaiting with da dogs. I never torment da poor dumb animal again, Brod."

Dant realised he had but the one chance and a few bare seconds to take it in. Pulling the hood off, he fixed the impressive specimen of native youth before him with a ferocious glare – I knew just how crazy the little snake could look – and, without once taking his transfixing eyes off the bigger guy's face, struck his knees with the water-pipe and bend-connector that was his preferred weapon. "Never pails, Brod." With a muted shriek the big boy dropped straight into a praying posture, whereupon Dant found his own arms in the perfect position to come back and jab him between the eyes with the pool-player's stroke. As the two other Gammas arrived he was just in time to position himself at the mouth of the alleyway, an unlikely Horatius defending the bridge. "If that big guy was a cager he most probably had bad knees to start with," I pointed out. Danton grimaced at this implied slight to his warrior prowess. He'd slashed twice at the Gammas, describing an X with his weapon, then intercepted a pick-axe shaft aimed at his own head by grasping the water-pipe at both ends and raising his hands as if in the gesture of surrender. "I'm da one to peel that, man. Bibrating right down to my feet soles, man. Well, I make da air hum, Brod, when I hit back. Then I turn and run, don't even look back. They're so close I tink I can feel their breath."

More, thus, by accident than design, Danton was the one to lead the Gammas in hot pursuit straight into, pardon my colourful language, the jaws of our crudely laid trap. Unfortunately, or fortunately as I look back on it now, the projected scene of mass slaughter failed to eventuate. Our plan worked all too well. Within a couple of minutes the little square was so choked with combatants, Gammas the crushed peanut and desiccated coconut at the core of the dumpling and we the soft rice-flour envelope, that it was impossible to move one's arms, let alone strike a full-blooded blow. I saw now why Caesar's legionaries were equipped with the very short-bladed stabbing sword. Mortal enemies rubbed shoulders as if they were on the dance floor of a jam-packed Saturday night disco or at a fifty per cent off sale in Shoemart. More Gammas, falling over each other to force their way down the blocked alley, and our own reserves – myself included – doing their best to get in on the action prematurely, further complicated matters. The gridlock was total. I couldn't work out whether we were doing the ambushing or the ones getting counter-ambushed. Brabazon's group had taken so much longer to get back than expected – and for us waiting the seconds had seemed like minutes – that double-cross had started to prey on our minds. Then, as the square filled up, it was quite impossible to tell who was who with the masks on. I was looking for Dant all the time with a degree of anxiety that surprised me even while I was at it, but he wasn't quite so pint-sized as to be easily remarkable in a mob. The same could not be said for me. I did have the advantage of standing a head above everyone else and of, therefore, enjoying an unrestricted view but it was an excellent view of a meaningless scrimmage. How long we would all have gone on swaying and shoving is anyone's guess, though the intended fracas appeared to be degenerating, or improving, depending which way you looked at it, from an occasion of supposed blood-letting into a social affair. Unable to clunk each other over the head with clubs, pressed tit to tit and shoulder to shoulder, our youthful antagonists started to exchange sarcastic barbs, then found themselves laughing at the enemy's witticisms; eventually discovering they had rather a lot in common. They just happened to be in different Fraternities. Now they were fraternising in no-man's-land. Whether, if the police had arrived that bit later, or if the crowd had thinned out to the point where a swing could be taken, the situation would have heated up again I can't say; I doubt it. It's difficult to batter over the head a person you've established social, not to say eye, contact with: even through slits in a hood. Perhaps, as Fr. Paul had explained the tactics used against the claymore-wielding Roman Catholic Highlanders at Culloden, we'd have lashed out diagonally at the guy opposite the comrade next to us. But not me. What had I noticed but that I had a strange effect on those nearest my person.

My Brods were drawn to me like nomads to a fire. Under ordinary circumstances I'd never experienced such popularity. Conversely, I just couldn't get near the Gammas. I had no overwhelming desire to close in and fell the foe, rather the reverse, but after a while I amused myself by pretending to be making big efforts to tag particular Gammas. They melted before me. I might as well have been a sizzling barbecue stick plunged into a *halo-halo*'s ice shavings. At the best of times people gave me a respectful berth but in the hood and gloves I was a lumbering monster, worse than Frankenstein, a Golem.

A siren concentrated all our minds. Quite quickly the throng started to thin, those on the edges jumping walls, scrambling over roofs in their eagerness to get away. Gammas found themselves extending a hand to our guys below, while we gave our erstwhile enemies a bunk-up under their boot-soles as they attempted to scale obstacles that for me weren't high at all. I looked rapidly round for Dant in the circle of disappearing humanity but saw him nowhere.

"That not surfrising, man, coz I da one to be nine inches up da world's asshole, man, in da thick of it. I pirst in, Sugar, if you not ferflex to remember it, man, coz I da one da Gammas is chasing in."

At the time it was everyone for himself, but I still threw the last Gamma over the wall like a Scotsman does a caber, doing it, though, with gentle power: a rapid take-off with his momentum ending as he came to eye-level with the parapet. As he escaped, he turned and looked at me with impressed gratitude. The next time I'd do that, for different reasons, would be to a frail old woman in Mumbai. Then I was over and away myself.

I discovered Danton already ensconced in the Frat House, having a Pepsi.

Well, if it had ended there it would – would it not? – have been a positive, a learning experience: one that could with a little understanding, perhaps some bending of circumstances, have been integrated into Fr. Paul's canon of Ampleforth scrapes, comparable to stealing apples from an orchard. Stalky & Co. But it didn't end happily or conveniently, there were malignant *sequelae*. And we, the subjects, the protagonists, who were at once patient and disease, came to hear the prognosis at third hand.

Skipper had the habit of reading newspapers. He entertained some ambitions towards becoming a journalist, or better, proprietor himself in due course. Two days later he came in with his preferred rag, a Manila daily with negligible provincial distribution called *Ang Bayan*, The Nation, that was written in a mix of Hemingwayese and a Tagalog they sometimes forgot to italicise.

"He's dead, Brods. The Gamma that got whacked in the carenderia. And you know what? He's an Assemblyman's son. Big trouble, Brods." We crowded round. Philippine newspapers would have enjoyed healthier circulations if they'd found a way for eyes to strip print. Dant, I saw, looked very grave. In fact, he looked sick to his stomach, probably as sick as when he was waiting for the burly young Fr. Aloysius to "tan" him.

"The only good Gamma," contributed Lazares, "is a dead Gamma."

There were a few other queasy faces in the circle round Skipper. It wasn't a question of social class. Brab looked even more dismayed than Danton. It was the Dirty Dozen who'd done the dirty business at the carenderia who looked most anxious; everyone else was more or less in the clear.

After a while I began to find the sustained high spirits of the others a little artificial, the smiles too bright, the banter of even lower quality than usual.

So the letter Butch Tan Sy handed me at training that afternoon came as a cloud doubly black.

Philippine First Asylum Camp
Puerto Princesa, Palawan

Howdy-doody Sugar,

D'y'all copy there? Guess you're gonna be kinda disappointed in this but don't take it too hard cause we're still keepin' the sunny side up. After Mikey and I left you on the boat in Mindanao (and we appreciated the quick farewell cause we've had too many of those in our lives) we got out OK from the port and into the town. That was escape, Bubba, but as you'll see evasion was a downright different matter entirely.

114

It was pretty cheap eating in the market and we had us a snooze in the waiting-shed. Mikey then had the bright idea of dressing up as locals. Yeah. Well, looking back on it we must have been loco only we didn't know that then. Cloth in the market was about as cheap as mud in the Delta. We got ourselves covered up pretty good. Next thing you know we're caught up in a big crowd. Man, we was surfin' straight into some rally or such-like, though just like without rice a meal ain't a meal for us slanty-eyes, back in Saigon in the old days we didn't consider a protest had been recognised as such 'less we got a tear-gassing and there weren't a whiff of that in the air here. Some of the signs being in English — and I gotta say you folks are ahead of us here — I was able to tell Mikey we was lending ourselves in support of a demonstration against some logging company or other that was throwing some tribals off their home-patch to get at those trees that was standing to attention on it, just waiting to be cut down. Well, we was doing of our level best to go along but we must have done something wrong or been dressed up like the wrong minority cause next thing there's mutters, funny looks, and before we know it we're surrounded worse than Khe Sanh. I got the cloth pulled from my face but that was nuthin' to the palaver when they saw what they had was Michael. Well, we're on our knees like ketched VC and they're a-tyin' of my hands behind my back. To be honest with you, at that partickler point in time, I didn't think our chances were worth diddley. They'd already started whuppin' me from just shovin' and pushin' when Michael stood up like Samson in the temple when his crew-cut grew out. He picks me up with one hand and then he's headin' the way we come in, with the dang Montagnards hangin' on all over. Shoot, it was like he was Silver fording the Rio Grande and I was Kemo Sabe hangin' on. Mikey's big and strong but he only just made it through the door. In the market-place we ran into an army patrol which we wasn't too sorry about under the circumstances. They slapped us around a bit to placate the Injuns but gave us cigarettes and food while we was waiting for the Law to fetch us back. They as good as told us if we hadn't made the disturbance there and set everyone on the war-path they wasn't interested in where we went or what we did. So there you are.

OK, Bub that's it.
      Your buddy, Nguyen

I showed the letter to Danton. He said, "I pucking glad I had da vrains to keep my winnings, man. Not like some people I know is da mega-vrain but still stupid."

BEING BUTCH'S STAR WAS SOME CONSOLATION. I was popular round the campus, out of the Fraternity. People would point me out to the newcomers who had replaced us as freshmen. They only saw me as an athlete, of course; probably imagined I had difficulty reading about myself in the college newsletter. However, Butch himself had decided I wasn't just a jumping-machine; he told me he respected my calls and my character-judgements. I was deeply flattered. The possibility of me being team-captain next year was floated with porcelain Chinese delicacy, so that afterwards I couldn't recall how it had been broached, or whether I had, in fact, been made a firm promise.

Butch didn't like giving, uh, financial inducements but he was sponsoring me for driving-lessons. I enjoyed these. My instructor, Noy Demosthenes, a grey-haired, half-blind old dude of past sixty, had been a great *palaquero* or ladies man in his youth. So he told me. He still wore his hair in a floppy fifties quiff and would pass comments on the female talent we passed around Quezon Memorial Circle at the funereal pace of fifteen miles an hour. I drove sedately, you see. It was hard, temperamentally, for me to do anything else. I had no aggression in me at all – and the thought of dashing ahead to grab space in front of another car, or overtake blind on a bend or on the inside, or shoot an amber light, were anathema to my prudent soul. Mind advance-dirty, you see. Butch would have been amazed at me, who loved nothing better than to steal a ball from someone's very hands, Castro the flashing pass-interceptor, the dasher who still got penalised for the rookies' over-enthusiasm of "travelling", e.g. failing to bounce the ball as I moved. All my physical boldness, my assets of strength and nimbleness, vanished once I was behind machinery. I became four six and ninety pounds.

"Look at you," Noy Demosthenes would breathe in despair. "I mean, boss, just look at you." He touched my swelling biceps, the size of a good guava and as hard, the edge of my triceps, as clearly cut as *sushi*. "You're a monster and you drive like grandma, like Lola."

I told Danton about this, thinking he'd laugh. I didn't mind telling a joke against myself. But Dant was deadly serious. "Da real pros, da real gunmen is careful round weapons," he said. "It's only da stupid pucks and cowboys like I don't mention da specific names of da rich-boys who shoot themselfs in da foot. None of da IRA gunmen do that. Meticulous, man, and cautious. And when you stops to tink about it, a car's da best weapon."

"Bit difficult to pack in the hip-pocket, *di ba*?"

"Stupid puck. I trying to have a serious conversation with you. Look, it's lethal, man. Heavy saloon travelling at hundred miles an hour got more kinetic energy than a 30mm cannon shell, *di ba*? And it don't arouse suspicion – it's not a weapon, *di ba*, just a vehicle. You hit someone with that, da dick-sucker's ultra double-dead, man, forget even a .50 cal. Then you just drive away, not like holding a .44 magnum smoking in your hand. Wash da car-fender, beat out da dent, it's not like they can trace a bullet to your barrel-grooves, *di ba*, da rifling."

"They couldn't do that if it was a shot-gun blast. Or if you used a semi-automatic pistol and switched barrels."

"*Siguro*. But a lot easier to say you had an accident with a car, than a gun. Don't forget it, man, those are my words of wisdom."

We had this conversation, one I'll never forget, in an indiscreet place, the carenderia near the college-gate. This was the best of those places: always clean, food fresh, non-ripoff prices, and pleasant service. Dant was sweet on a waitress called Haydee, a kid of our own age from Maasin, Southern Leyte, like us a Cebuano-speaker. Basically, Dant would have liked all and sundry to believe he was above such a thing as a crush. The first girl he'd fucked was his eleven-year-old sister when he was thirteen and it had been downhill since then. But I noticed him taking the trouble to ask Haydee's name, what her papa did (he fished from a canoe), and generally modulating his abrasiveness around her. He saw my grin and scowled, the way Just William would. "Hi Danton, hi Rey," Haydee would greet us on our own, instead of clamming up like she did when the rich Tags were around. You didn't even bother to speculate if she was a virgin. For a poor *pinay* she was tall, around five four, and she was, needless to say, pretty. You could see the goodness in her face: straight-forward, kindly, no falseness. I don't know if it's because I'm a Filipino but I find the faces of my countrywomen an open book beside those of foreign females. The opposite of Haydee's was the face with the over-bright eyes and the cheeks brazen as a pair of bare buttocks, like Babyjane's, though I had yet to meet her. Anyhow, Haydee was a particularly sweet kid, neat in her dress, with the restricted horizons that the devil hates. *"Tamis nga dalaga,"* I'd say to Dant because the words for sweet kid sounded less corny in dialect. He'd raise his eyebrows, the coolest of assents.

RICH BOYS AT PLAY, IT HAD DAWNED ON BOTH OF US, belatedly, were a lot worse than poor boys in earnest. The Brabazons and Skippers of this world had been spoiled all their lives. A wet behind the ears Danton had felt the wind of circumstance raise the goose-pimples on him. So had I. But the rich-boys, in urgent need of having the cold water of reality thrown upon them, had enjoyed the dubious advantage of doting parents who were banking up so many fires.

That made it hard for them to cope the first time they got out of their depth. Brabazon was running scared. He'd knocked off an Assemblyman's son. The problem wasn't with the Law; it was with DIY freelance justice. He was having bad dreams about the shot in the head he wouldn't hear as he stepped out of his front-door or booted up the computer in the café.

One thing led to another. Brabazon would sit for hours at a time in his rattan chair, his face flushed with beer and Tanduay chasers, only stirring himself to go pee, which he did outside against the wall of the Frat House as if scared of immurement in the CR. I felt sorry for the guy, rich-boy or not. I decided to give him my sympathy and solidarity. That was what Fraternity was all about, *di ba*? I put my hand on his shoulder, not so heavily. I knew I wasn't bouncing a ball, but he leaped straight out of his chair. His face contorted in anger when he saw who it was. "You stupid dumb animal, don't you ever do that again."

"Hey, hey! It's OK, Brab. Love and peace, man. I'm your brother."

"*You*?"

"Me, Brod. Can I get another beer to replace the one you knocked over?"

"I didn't knock it over, you did. No, I don't want a beer from you. Do me a favour and buzz off."

"Sure. Just ask me if you need me, Brod."

Brab, I guess, felt he'd drawn the short straw. He'd ended up on the lone mission none of the other council members had wanted and it looked like he'd be the one to draw the flak. It was all running away from him towards an incendiary conclusion. He felt out of control. Sounds familiar? Brab was going through the plethora of emotions hitherto experienced by suicide pilots. And what was he gonna prescribe for himself? A Kamikaze Koktel.

After that I went to discuss some plays with Butch, following which I returned to have a nap on the sofa. I decided I'd let Danton lick me at table-tennis when he arrived. I could usually beat him 21-17 or something like that. He played soft drop shots to me, thinking I was too big and lumbering to cope with delicacy, but that suited me dandy. I dropped off. Butch's dawn runs took a lot out of even healthy nineteen-year-olds. I awoke to find three of what I regarded as the meaner spirits in the Frat tickling my toes and nostrils. I felt like Gulliver. "Hey, hey, guys, cut it out," I remonstrated. "Was I snoring that loud?" I got unfocussed grins back, the *pinoy* kind which negate your presence. One of them was humming "Pretty Baby", the others jiving to it with jerky movements that were much too fast for the tempo. I realised they'd been smoking.

"Brod Brab and the others request your attendance, man," said the hummer.

"What for?"

"At the festivities, Brod." They all snickered a bit with that suppressed little explosion at the end like a stifled sneeze which characterises the mirth of drug-users, whether they're on Mary Jane or shabu.

That comes from their vain desire to hide the fact that they're stoned, but it only sends them into a further chain-reaction of giggles, sat-upon atchoos of mirth, and yet more snickers. I waited tolerantly for it all to subside. It took a long while. At length I said, "Yeah, Brods, I'm a little fatigued. You know I like nothing better than a good smoke, but not tonight."

That sobered them up.

They started to wear the expressions of weasels. "No, Castro, you don't understand. Compulsory attendance, man. Participation in the festivities, man." This set them all off again.

"OK." I looked serious about it but not in the way of bad will. As we set off into the night, I asked, "Is Brother Danton there?" This triggered guffaws in which I was unable to share. We boarded a trisikad at the campus gates; then swiftly changed to another ten minutes later, the Brods making the new driver go at once without waiting for other fares. He didn't protest. Sometimes Filipinos weren't as dim-witted as Fr. Paul made out. I'd like to think it wasn't Dant's two hundred thirty pound gorilla which intimidated him so much as his summing up of a trio of shabu-crazed rich-boys. We seemed to go for miles. Then we got off in the middle of nowhere and walked a distance that seemed infinite. Part of being an athlete was feeling much more tired than other people: I'd left my legs in the gymnasium. At length we arrived before a modestly affluent residence. This was neither the seven by seven hovel Ma, Bambi, and I had lived in – the kind Danton had instinctively rejected before he could read – nor the vulgarian's palace in which Atty Caladong resided but something in between: three or four rooms and a "dirty kitchen" for wood-burning cooking outdoors, hollow-block walls, a well-painted sheet-metal roof, with some narra-wood facings under the eaves. An OK place.

There was some whispering at the gate, then the Brod on guard let us in.

There were Brods sprawled all over the sala and more empty beer bottles on its floor than there had been on the bridge of the ferry to Mindanao. Straws and silver-foil were strewn on a low table. Well, I knew they hadn't been drinking chocolate milk and eating fairy cakes. The whole crew were flying kites. "Where's Dant?"

"At the festivities, Brod."

"Yeah, you're invited, too."

It didn't sound like an invitation to me, more of a threat. I was propelled by the speed-enlivened Lilliputians to the bedroom. This contained a double-bed, Danton at last, and five other Brods including Brabazon and Skipper, but they weren't the most noticeable detail, which was a naked girl. She was over by the built-in clothes wardrobe. I took the scene in somewhat less coolly than I would a throng of muscular boys blocking my advent at the hoop.

Was the girl going to the wardrobe to fetch clothes for herself? A logical supposition in any culture, still less ours with its premium on female demureness. No. I discarded this idea. She wasn't opening the wardrobe door but using it for support. Then I saw the way she was standing, one knee collapsed against the other, leaning away from everyone as far as she could, with her long black hair falling forward to screen her face. She reminded me of Ma and, like Ma, the concealing hair was some last grasp at modesty. Dejection and wretchedness were all over her.

Brabazon yanked her head back by the hair. Then he punched her on the nose. Blood speckled the white of the wardrobe door, as if it had been there hours, not one second. The girl uttered a stifled cry, so weak and so despairing that it was clear it was not the first blow she had suffered. She rested her head in the corner, probably grateful for even a moment's respite. Brabazon let out a peal of fake laughter – like the mechanically simulated cackling from a fairground ghoul – which turned into real hoots as the sound of his own ingenuity began to tickle him. His pupils were unnatural. He hit the girl again, this time with a stagey karate punch, shouting "Kiya!" as his first two knuckles drove against her spine. Then he booted her playfully up the cleft of her backside, leaving a black mark, this time shouting "Ee-ha!" like a cowboy riding into a cattle stampede. The girl half-turned, then slid down the wardrobe door to a squatting position, raising her forearms to protect herself from prospective kicks. "Hey!" I said. "That's enough, Brod. Whatever she's done, man, that's enough."

"She ain't done nothing," Brabazon said. "We're the ones to do something, haw-haw." The others joined in the braying. I looked for Danton, but he shook his head infinitesimally and dropped his eyes.

"You're the one to do nothing, too," Brabazon said, abruptly, breaking off his amusement. "Yeah," said Skipper. I saw his carefully greased hair was mussed and that he had dried blood – his own – on his ear-lobe, probably from the girl's nails.

Brab grabbed her by the elbow and as he swung her towards the bed her curtain of hair floated up and I saw that it was Haydee, but with one eye already bloated and a closed and swollen upper lip. One of the Brods said, "That eye looks like a pussy, man."

"O-o," said Brabazon, "you can fuck that next." When the giggling had subsided, Brab said, "No, you're on next, Castro, and it ain't gonna be the eye, Brod."

I didn't look at Brabazon – you wouldn't get much that was sensible out of a diving kamikaze – but at Dant.

"Yeah," said Skipper, "your little sidekick dipped his tiny wick as well."

Haydee had pulled the coverlet of the bed up towards her neck, drawing her knees to her chin. During the time I had been in the room she had not wept or sobbed. However, now she began, with her one eye, to take a concealed interest in what was going on around her. She sensed it was something new and unpleasant, rather than a continuation of the ordeal as it had been.

"I want no part of this," I said. The words jumped out of my mouth; I hadn't meant to sound so intransigent, to disassociate myself so clearly from my Brods. "Sorry, Brab, sorry, Skip."

121

"*Hindi*, Brod," Skipper said, "you don't understand. This is a compulsory session, man. You'll be in contempt, Brod."

At this moment Haydee let out a barely audible sob but it was enough to bring attention down on her again. Her poor little attempt at modesty, at concealing her nakedness, had been enough to turn her from a raw and relatively undesirable lump of meat into a girl again. Her hunched posture on the bed, chin resting on knees, was also by some grotesque coincidence plausibly that of lover or coquette, the lassie waiting for lover-boy to rinse his dick under the tap before he comes back for more. Well, Haydee did shriek and she did cross her arms over her breasts, though there was no pretending about it. Unfortunately, this was throwing gasoline on a bed of half-dead embers because it inflamed the Brods again. The whoops of glee from the bedroom brought the others in from the sala. They'd mellowed out on Mary Jane after the first time they'd used her and then another shabu session had been going on while I was in the bedroom. Brab and Skipper had Haydee under her armpits, then they nodded to each other and flipped her over in unison. They might have been landing a large tuna. The others cheered and applauded. All had beer bottles in their hands and the hard, bright pupils that alcohol alone could not produce.

"Part her fucking cheeks, man," said a Brod I'd last seen sidling to get near me at the basketball-court ambush. "Aw, shit, no," said another Brod in disgust. "No, I'm serious, man," said the first. "I wanna see."

"OK," said Brab, "here you are, Brod, your first view of the Grand Canyon." The whooping rose to a crescendo. The Brod unbuttoned his pants and then dropped them to the knee, doing the same with his briefs. He started to rub his dick; he was having a little difficulty getting it hard. "I'll get Haydee to suck it," he said struck by a bright idea. "You're good at that, *di ba*, Haydee?"

"No, for a while," Skipper said. "Give her a smoke."

"What?"

"O, Brod. Nothing like it for a getting a chick horny. Come on, gimme the gear." Brab got the white powder smouldering away on the foil, then changed his plans and chased the swirling smoke himself. "Hoy! Hoy!" the Brods remonstrated.

"A-a-a-h," breathed Brabazon ecstatically, drawing himself up to his full height, his eyes starting from his head. With his hair tufted in two horns, he looked like the djinn coming out of his cave. "The chick, Brod, the chick," Skipper reminded him. Brab put a straw between Haydee's lips; they were so swollen she had difficulty retaining it. "Suck it, *guwapa*," he said. "Hey, man!" Skipper exclaimed. "She's done it before!" Whether she had or not, the prone position Haydee found herself in – with her head pulled back by the hair – obviously affected her throat because she started to choke and splutter on the acrid fumes. "Now suck on this," said the Brod with the dropped pants and limp dick. "Oh, yeah, *sarap*."

"You ever do it," asked another, "after the girl had ice-cubes in her mouth, or she'd had a cone or some *halo-halo*? That's the way, man." He received no answer. The other boys were getting hot watching. One by one, they unzipped their flies or dropped their trousers, jerking off in an almost solemn rhythm. The guy getting the blow-job pulled out and trotted round the back to the same kind of whistles and catcalls as I got from the bench during dribbling practice. Haydee had cooperated – she knew what was in store if she didn't – but her blank expression turned to a grimace as the guy with the stiff dick mounted her from behind. "Wet your finger, man," someone advised him. "Yeah, Brod, or go down on her."

"Chocolate ice-cream, man."

They laughed so much over that I thought they were going to lose their hard-ons. But the boy doing the business was getting pissed. "Can't get it in, man," he said, "it slides out or what d'you call it, *koan*, ricochet, man." Brab stepped forward, carefully measured Haydee with his left hand and struck her a ferocious blow just under her eye. The cheek burst like fruit-skin. "Don't goof off on us," he said. Well, it was a mercy in a way, for it put the poor girl out. The inept Brod was pulled off and Brab came back to me. I'd been hoping he'd forgotten.

"Let's see what you've got, man. I heard the rumours from the shower-room." Muted sniggers.

"No."

"I told you to do it, Brod. I'm your senior in the Fraternity."

"Anything except."

"You don't understand, Brod. You got to do it – or else."

"Or else – what?"

"Don't push me, Brod."

"I'm not, Brab. I'd never do that, but you respect my choice, too." His eyes locked on to mine. I returned his gaze, without trying to turn it into a staring match. He was way out of it, so spaced out on the shabu he couldn't have kept his eyes on the Second Coming; that stuff, it made you darty; you jumped from concern to concern. Muttering ominously in Tagalog rather than English, he walked with short, chopping strides to the sala.

Although Haydee was drifting in and out of consciousness, the guys hadn't lost interest in her. One of them got her legs up under his arms, as if he was doing Butch Tan Sy's wheelbarrow relay, and was able to penetrate her. He butted with urgent motions of his loins as if frightened of losing his erection. We could hear the slapping of his balls on where her buttocks joined the backs of her thighs. Haydee's legs looked like a string-puppet's and I saw the underneath of her feet, perhaps the most helpless and foolish part of any human being's anatomy, the balls of the curled toes as ludicrous on Jesus Christ as Mr Universe, on Marilyn Monroe as the Virgin Mary.

"Hey, hey, Brod," the guy who'd failed said, "my turn." He got into her in the same position. "Ah, yeah, man, you greased her up nicely."

"Naw, that's Skip's jissom, man."

Unfortunately, Haydee started to come to, probably thinking it was still the same guy continuing his thing, and he began to lose it. He could only manage a girl who was completely out of it.

Brabazon came back. In his hand was a large black revolver. He said, "Get your one out."

"I'm not in the habit of walking round armed, Brod," I replied.

"That's not what I meant. Get it out and screw that girl."

"*Hindi po.*"

Brab cocked the gun which, by the way, neither he nor I knew at the time wasn't loaded. Well, the impossible had happened. I had become more interesting to the Brods than a naked girl. I mean, they couldn't go on masturbating, not with what Brother Brabazon had in his hand.

"I think this is a little excessive, *di ba*, Brod?" I said, speaking as calmly as I could. At the best of times, looking down a gun barrel is an unpleasant experience. When the holder has eyes like Brab did it's, well, positively life-threatening. Skipper, who wasn't flying as high as the others, or had come down just a little, said, "Sugar's OK, Brab. He was a good Brod in Palawan. I think you better put it down, man."

"You – fuck – her – or – I – pull – the – trigger," Brabazon enunciated through his teeth. I shook my head. I would like you to know that I'm not stupid and I'm insufficiently self-centred to aspire to the martyr's crown, those ecclesiastical heroes I suspect Fr. Paul regarded as trouble-makers, Liberationists before there were Liberationists. It was just that I wasn't intimidated by a little punk like Brabazon. He could have been pointing a bazooka at me and I wouldn't have been scared of him. Not scared enough to give in.

Click.

The stupid little fuck had pulled the trigger.

I just looked at him in amazement. That was all I could do. Danton shot across, pulled the revolver by the barrel out of Brabazon's grasp – it was one of Noy Jesus' four-inch .38s we'd brought back, talk of hoist with your own petard – and slapped him resoundingly. Brabazon just stood there. I guess he couldn't have felt it. Flak wounds didn't stop a high kamikaze. He had the stupidest grin on his face. I mean, the guy was a world-class donkey. "Cool it, Dant," I said. Then in his ear, "Thanks, man."

"O."

I decided the best thing was for us to go into the sala. Dant tucked the revolver into his waist-band for safe-keeping, and we left them to it. I swept the smoking paraphernalia off the glass coffee-table and put my feet on it. Uncouth, I know.

"How did this happen, man? And how the fuck did you get up for this?"

"Aw, Sugar, mans, not my seeking. I have to tell you that? Brab's da one to talk to Haydee outside da past-pood. You know he's always admire her from a distance, man. Offer lift home but she refuse. Then Brab – he's already high, man, but not like a vird like now – force her in his Mama's Corolla and bring her here. He's da one to vust her cherry, man, then da others."

"And you, Mr Horny?"

"They make me, man. OK, don't vlame me I'm not da one to be seven feet tall, you know."

"You're telling me you screwed that girl? Just like those animals? They've got more dollars than sense, but you?"

"Shit, man, who you tink you are, Father Voy? I do it coz I had to, man. And for your informations, it's not up, I just touch da lips of her pussy but da snake it's dead. Man, you tink I could do Haydee? I *know* her, man, she's a good girl. OK, I drunk and know no better, I as high as a kite, maybe I can do it to a strange girl. Maybe. But, to be sure, I can't be da one to do it, not to Haydee. I from Mactan, man, same as you, Brother. I can't do it to a foor girl like that, man. I tink of Ma, man. I can't do it. It's like I do it to Ma, man. She's da one to do it with da guys to put vread in my mouth, man. Just like your Ma, man."

"OK, OK. You don't have to tell me that."

"I tell you, mother-pucker. I tell you. I tink maybe you on da way to porget who you are, man, and what you came from. You learn all those vig long word, man, change you in da head. In da heart, Sugar, it's no different. You da same one we flay Prankenstein with, man."

I conceded the justice of his reproach. "OK, Danton," I said, "I haven't forgotten who my real friends are, and you just showed me twice in five minutes. Thanks."

We'd been alone for the duration of this conversation. Now a couple of Brods came in, hitching up their pants in business-like fashion. They made a bee-line for the coffee-table and the decks of dope I'd refrained from sweeping on to the floor. Quick as you like, I got my feet off the table, vaulted over between them and the shabu, and poured it into a tumblerful of what was likelier to have been rum and coke than coke alone. "Enough ice for you, guys?" I asked. Well, they got pretty mad, mad as a guy of five five can get with a guy of six two. I'd poured thousands of pesos of shabu away, probably most of the Frat's dealing stock. High as they were, they still jabbered away and waved their arms but going for me was a poor idea and they knew it. "Or maybe it was sugar," I said. "Hope it's sweet to your tastes, Brods."

Brabazon now came out of the bedroom and passed through the sala to the "dirty kitchen", then retraced his steps with a folded newspaper under his arm. I wondered if I shouldn't check if he wasn't getting ammunition or had another gun stashed away, then thought, "Fuck him."

An anguished cry came from Haydee in the bedroom, different in its pain and desperation from anything that had come before. "Oh, shet," Danton muttered. The Brods at the entry to the bedroom made no attempt to impede us, other than it was difficult to get by them because they were anxious to remain by the door. I couldn't see Haydee. There was a long sigh from the bathroom, which was not Brabazon. I peered round the door and saw nothing. Then there was a tinkle from behind the shower-curtain. I drew it. Haydee was sitting on the tiles, her legs straight out with her back against the shower taps. Her injured eye had swollen more since I last saw it, while the good one was about a quarter open with the rolled-up white showing. She had a wound just under her breasts in the centre. The floor of the shower was rapidly being concealed under as much blood as if someone was douching with a blocked drain-hole. The drain-hole, in fact, actually was blocked. The blood was welling out of the wound distinctly less profusely within the few seconds since I'd arrived. It was, as I'd see in the mortuary photograph in *Ang Bayan*, an insignificant-looking slit an inch wide, the blade of a fruit-knife not being broad at all, but of course the situation of the wound – right over the heart, nothing wrong with Brab's knowledge of anatomy – and its depth – the five inches to the handle – made it deadly. That was if you just looked at only one wound in the photo, took it out of its context where it was not singular at all.

I think Haydee had died a second or so before I came in.

I looked at Brab. Those goddamned eyes. The knife was half-submerged in blood where he'd dropped it to fiddle with the taps behind Haydee. I was surprised he'd left it at one thrust; everyone knew shabu druggies killed in a frenzy.

"Stupid faucet's bust," he remarked conversationally. You'd never have thought that ten minutes earlier he'd pulled not only a gun on me but its trigger. "Let me see if I can help," I said. I did have this ability to unscrew the flash-lights, unjam the stop-cocks, and loosen the jar lids that no one else could (of which jars those gas-pressurised by the fermenting ingredients of *halo-halo* preserves were notoriously the most stubborn). "No, it's not connected, Brod. It's never worked."

He digested the implications of this in silence. I could see he wanted to wash the blood away. We left the bathroom together. The others looked at him not with disgust, or revulsion, or horror, but a kind of awe, as if he'd just set a new record in an inter-collegiate meet. He'd certainly taken them beyond their personal worsts. Their eyes followed him round the room. Dant mouthed silently, "*Patay?*" or "Killed?" I nodded. Brab instructed him: "Get the bucket."

"Get it yourself," Danton said. Skipper put his hand on Dant's shoulder. "We're all in this together, Brod," he said quietly, "we have to pull together, man. I know I can rely on you, Brod."

"Rags, mops, wipe all the surfaces down," Brab said, "especially the glass table." Dant came back with a brimming bucket. "Holy Shet," I heard him say from the bath-room. The water splashed resoundingly on the tiles as if Dant had thrown it all down in a hurry. "Hoy, careful, dork," Brabazon said. "You'll get blood on the curtain."

"You don't call me that name, or you get da vucket on your head, you crazy eejit puck."

"OK, OK, cool it, Brods," Skipper intervened. "C'mon, let's get the show on the road."

I began to wonder how high Skipper and Brabazon really were; they were starting to sound fairly level-headed to me.

"OK," said Skipper. "There's just one, uh, formality." He conferred with Brabazon. "Yeah. OK, Brods. This way." Skip led us into the bathroom. Some intakes of breath, stoned or not. It wasn't a pretty sight. The water had made it worse.

I heard commotion behind me. "Grab him, Brod. Oh, shit." There was the clunk of a head hitting tiles. "Lazares just fainted away, man. Ah, Gee, *his* blood's all over the floor too now."

"Just get him out of here, he'll be OK. Scalp wounds bleed a lot but they're only small surface vessels. Yeah, yeah, my sis is doing med tech, man."

Brab picked up the knife. "OK, Brods. Listen up. Yeah, look at, look at all you like. She's *patay* now, she's gonna be no trouble if we all keep our nerve. Now, each one of us is gonna stick the knife in little Haydee, just like we all stuck something else in her, *di ba*?"

"Consider it," said Skipper, "like being your signature as witness to the transfer. *Ako na lang*. Me first."

We could have been lining up to kiss the Pope's toe. Haydee, of course, didn't even quiver as Skipper stuck the knife in her. Dant looked at me. I raised eyebrows, meaning, yes, do it. The others laughed nervously as their turns came, made facetious comments to break the tension. Lazares, looking very sheepish after his fainting fit, with an egg rising on the back of his head, stabbed the body three times to recoup some face. Dant, stone-visaged, went up, stuck the dead girl viciously, and came back without saying a word. "Good, Brod, good," Skipper said. Danton muttered. I half-caught it. I think it was, "I rather stab you, you motherpucker."

"Sugar."

I took the knife from Skip and did it. There was no more resistance or drama than there would have been stabbing a foam-cushion.

Skipper nodded to Brabazon. All over. We could go in small groups at staggered intervals. Dant was despatched with Lazares and Brab's younger brother, but Skipper kept me behind to clean up with him and Brab. Whether because he thought I was inherently more reliable than the others or simply because I was neither drunk nor stoned, I'll never know. I do know he and Brab seemed mighty capable. They even picked up blood speckles on the sofa I'd missed, but then I hadn't the advantage of being there when they were porking Haydee on the cushions, had I? We rolled her body up in a plastic raincoat with shopping bags over the feet and head and dumped it on waste-ground. Not a light anywhere.

Back at the Frat House, Skipper organised transport for everyone. "Stick together," he impressed on all of us again. "It's the same story for everyone. They can't shake a group alibi. There's too many of us for that. We were here all night. Safety in numbers, man. If anything happens, which it won't, exercise your right to silence." He packed most of the Brods into a couple of cars. Dant, I, and five others squeezed into a Pajero. They sang the Frat song, *My Brother Right or Wrong*, whistled, crowed, reminisced, the events already taking on the patina of a legendary victory. "Hey, you see the way Roger did her, man? He got her ankles by his ears, man."

"Awesome, Brod, awesome."

"And Michael, man, just the mouth, sing-along, *di ba*?"

"But it was perfick, Brod, perfick."

"Hey, *guwapo*, you going out tonight?"

"The Bagets gonna stay with Mama, man. Ee-ha!"

NOTHING EVER KEPT ME FROM MY SLEEP. I hit the sack at eleven p.m. At five a.m. I found Skipper shaking me awake.

Dant was already out of bed. He was glaring at me. "How you can do it, mans?" he asked. "How can? You sleeping da sleep of da just. I wanna put da fillow on your face and asphyxiates you."

"You'd have done me a favour."

"OK," Skipper said. He looked fairly fresh, too. "No recriminating."

"We weren't," I retorted.

"Whatever. We're gonna take the chick down to Laguna and bury her, the four of us with Brod Lazares. No one'll stop us to check at this time – it's safer than dark. Don't worry."

Lazares was waiting for us in the front-seat.

"You drive," Skipper told me. "I'll go in the back with Brod Danton."

I said nothing and got in. We are powerless against some imperatives, even though we may be fully conscious of them. This was a cultural imperative, man: to keep my trap shut and my face blank, even though I thought the seating arrangements were what Butch would have chosen on his blackboard as the best to mark me and Dant, to pop us with head-shots without warning, to neutralise my dangerous hands.

"Can you drive a little faster?" Lazares asked edgily after fifteen minutes. That was when I smiled. I knew they weren't going to, in Danton's words, "kneecap us in da head." I saw Dant's eye in the mirror. The possibility had also occurred to him.

"What's so funny?" Lazares asked.

"You," I said.

"It's OK." This was Skip. "Rey's cool. We'll take it easy. Left turn, Brod."

"I thought we were going to Laguna."

"We are. We gotta collect the chick first from the dump."

"What?" exclaimed Lazares. "You mean she's not in the trunk already?"

"No."

"Ah, fuck."

Those were pretty well my feelings, too, but I kept them to myself. I parked the car on a small mound to give us a better vantage-point. Everything looked the same, featureless. We'd thrown the body down in the dark. It was already hot and we were sweating when Skipper said, "There. Those plastics where the dogs are."

My heart sank. Not just me. Our joint forebodings were correct. The dump-dogs had pulled off enough of the coverings to get to her. I'll never forget that sight.

"OK, Brod, help Brod Rey pick her up," Skipper ordered.

"No. I'll be the one," Dant said.

"Be my guest," Lazares said. "She's as stiff as my dick was. Aw fuck, the stench, man. Fierce, Brod. Fierce."

Next thing Danton had already bopped him, jumping up to land it on the side of his face. Like most rich-boys, Lazares was tall. He went over more with the surprise than the force. I kicked him three times in the back when he was down, the thuds – I think – music to Danton's ears. Not what a hero did in the story-books from San Ignatio but, satisfying, man, deeply satisfying.

Skipper jumped between us. "OK, OK *lang*. Not here. We'll all go down for this. C'mon." He and Dant carried Haydee. I kept an eye on Lazares in case he jumped Dant. I think he was aware of my vigilance.

Out in the sticks at Laguna in a bamboo-grove I dug as long as we could all endure, not quite the hour. Skipper had a knife with him, different from the one which had been used. He flung it with his gloved hand into nearby grasses, along with Haydee's shoes and the bra and panties I'd never seen her wearing. I drove us back a little more quickly, I admit, than we had come. Skip changed the car-plates just outside Metro. I remembered him telling us at Atty Caladong's he kept four different sets in the trunk as a matter of routine. At his house, he made Dant and Lazares shake hands but he kept Lazares with him when Dant and I went for the jeepney.

I braced myself when I read the papers the next day, and the day after, and the day after that, but there was never anything. It was all Eleuterio III, the kid Brabazon had conked on the head, day after day. They wouldn't drop that and, more importantly, nor would his powerful Daddy.

Four days later, there was a piece on the decomposing remains of a girl that scavenging pigs had found. Nine days after that Haydee's younger brother came up from the provinces and gave a tentative identification. And that was that; it joined the files on the scores of other unsolved Metro rape-slays. They had about as much chance of finding us as reconstituting by chance the day's load of passengers on a bus.

Chapter VI

IF HAYDEE WAS STILL MORE HELPLESS DEAD THAN ALIVE – had her ghost materialised at the Frat House, the Brods would probably have raped it, too – the dead Eleuterio III haunted us more with every passing day.

"Brab looks like fucking Macbeth," I said to Dant.

"Yeah, he's right to. Someone gonna inform on him, mans, to save their own skin, feather their own nest. Affly for state-witness."

"No shortage of rats in this country."

"I don't tink I growing a tail yet."

I pretended to check.

Neither of us were quite so blithe as we made out. I wished Fr. Boy were there to hear my Confession. I instinctively preferred Fr. Boy for this kind of shriving. Fr. Paul, I knew all too well, would confuse me with his subtleties and leave me in still greater need of counsel.

Meanwhile, I applied myself to the law tomes for a little comic relief when I wasn't jumping for Butch Tan Sy's edification. Once, I passed Atty Caladong but was loth to presume on acquaintance. However, he surprised me by saying, "Well done, Castro. I hear you'll be Captain of our cagers next year. Advance congratulations, *di ba*?"

This should have been my warning. Any promise or prophecy from Atty Caladong usually proved the kiss of death. The next afternoon I saw Skipper sitting in back of the spectator's seats at ball practice. We were doing lay-up drills. I flunked this easiest of shots. "That's the first time *lang* I seen you concentrate, Sugar," a surprised team-mate commented. I just grunted. Skip collared me on my way to the locker-room. "It's all over, man," he said. "Just don't take the time to shower. They fingered us. It's Brab's group in the shit but we gotta take care of you coz everyone knows you're the little one's pal and, you don't mind me saying so, you're kinda perspicacious on the street."

"Conspicuous."

"Hah?"

"The first rule, Skip, is don't panic. The second is, then panic."

"Yeah, yeah. OK. OK. Danton's waiting for you. Get your civilian attire; you can change in the car."

Dant was watching TV when I arrived at the safe-house. Lazares had the remote. He was trying to get one of the song and dance shows he particularly liked – all absolutely identical, in fact. "Hey, stay with that channel," I said, as Metro Police Patrol clicked up.

"Aw, you don't wanna watch that, Brod."

"There's nothing I want to watch more." When it was over I said, "Funny how they don't say they got a lead on the Eleuterio III case? You'd think that would be the big one." Skip said, "No, Brod. Would they warn the malefactors? We got it on the best authority – the Frat grapevine. I mean, from the big brods, the CFI judges, *di ba*, and some of our guys in the NBI." He opened the cocktail cabinet which lit up and played *Auld Lang Syne*. "You're in the safe-house now, anyhow. And the drinks are on the house, haw-haw."

"This malepactor, Brod, tink da cocktail cabinet a teeny-weeny vit on da bulgar side, eh, old voys." Dant and I sniggered together, excluding Skipper from our mirth.

"OK, guys, I'll get the others. Hang in there. Uh, there's dope stashed in the cashew-tin if you want it." I just looked at Dant. Man, I just looked at him. When Skip and Lazares had gone we took the tin to the CR and watched the water froth as the sludge flushed away. Skipper was back twenty minutes later with just three Brods, obscure guys from low down in the Frat, whose names I didn't know and had no interest in learning. "Where are the others?" I asked.

"Later, not all at once. You don't want to attract attention, *di ba*? Brab and I'll be the ones to be last, maybe in two days."

"Yeah?"

"O. Now look, the big brods got all kinds of papers for you and more to cover you when you get there."

"Where is there, Brod?"

"Singapore, Sugar."

"Singa-pucking-fore! Jaizus, Mary menstruating, and all da saints. What da hell we gonna do there, Skip?"

"Work, play, sleep, eat, shit. What do you do anywhere, Brod?"

"Well, yeah. But there's just the little matter of rules and regulations. We just walk in through the airport and say, hey, we're the boys from Delta Kappa Epsilon come to join in your economic miracle?"

"Yeah, something. Don't worry, man. This is what the Frat's for. We've got plenty of guys from the Frat passed the Foreign Service exam. They'll just be the ones to wave the magic wand for you. It's no sweat, Brod, really."

Skip let the other Brods stay with us a while for company but they were to sleep in another place "to avoid suspicion". I reckoned it was to stop us comparing notes. Skip kept the TV blaring and when that palled the Brods showed us how to play Monopoly (Dant had a positively Chinese talent for that) and we taught them... Snakes and Ladders. After that, Skip took them off.

The following evening Skip and Lazares showed with our fellow escapees. A little later, a big Brod I'd never seen before came with our dox. He left immediately.

The rich-boys received the papers with the acclaim children reserve for invitations to a birthday party. (Not Dant and me – our Mactan contemporaries sold themselves for money and spent the proceeds on group rugby-sniffing). Still, even Dant was getting very jumpy now, and he grabbed his passport in the way Fr. Boy might have hoped to see us pray the Rosary. I said, "*Salamat po*," but I was reserving my judgement. We had several sets of papers, including two passports each, one ordinary, brown-coloured, the other diplomatic, red-coloured. I decided not to read too much into the colour-coding, but, "Hey, that's my photo off the team calendar," I exclaimed. "Yup," said Skipper proudly. "Well, shit," I remonstrated. "This is a diplomatic passport but in my sando, man, I look like a jeepney driver, not an ambassador." When the others had finished guffawing, Skipper said, "Don't worry. The whole point of a diplomatic passport is that no one's entitled to ask questions. You're a ghost, Brod, at the immigration counter. That one's a high-class fake, but even our passport office couldn't tell, it's so perfect. The ordinary one's no fake."

While Skipper was crowing with the rich-boys over their travel documents I asked Danton quietly, "You happy with this?" He made the doubtful sign, rotating his hand with the palm facing down. "I thought so," I said. "Also me."

"I got more paith, man, if it was da Fenians facilitate my escape, but what da hell, old buddy, in for a fenny, in for a found. *Bahala na*."

Skipper and the others left before midnight, after which Dant, I, and Lazares settled into another hand of cards. We were starting to go stir-crazy, leaving dirty dishes around and old socks on the backs of chairs. By the end of the third day we were ready for an excursion into Hell, so long as it was on a return ticket. That was when Skip came back with the three fugitive rich-boys and told us we'd be taken to a ship the next night.

"When's Brab coming?" I asked. "He's the main culprit."

Skipper and Lazares looked at each other in a funny way.

"Soon," said Skipper. "I'll be the one to take the heat here. I'm better connected than any of you, *di ba*? But Brod Brabazon will follow soon. You and Brod Danton get to be early birds coz – OK I don't mince it, Brod – coz you're kinda conspicuous. Everyone seen the black giant there and Dant's the talk of the town the way he pulled them into the ambush."

"Uh-huh," I said.

"Then you got no pull, no family at all to protect you."

"Except my Brods, Skip," Dant said.

"O-o, Brod. Except the Frat. So we give you the first break coz you're the most vulnerable."

"Is that a fact?"

"*Siguro*, Brod. Always thinking of you."

NIGHTFALL CAME. We drove through the clotted streets of Tondo, rather faster than I would have done. I thought I could smell the Smoky Mountain rubbish-field, a blend of brimstone and corpse, acrid but sweet. "Who da one to part?" Danton asked. We laughed feebly. At the wharf, there was no sign of the boatman Skip claimed to have engaged. It was difficult for me to refrain from joining in the muttering, but I mustered sufficient self-control to do so. The polluted sea slapped against the concrete wall. We were getting the worst of all worlds: wild sewage. Skip vanished into the gloom at the end of the wharf. "I tell you, Sugar," Dant said, "this don't come off, and I'm gonna be da one to salbage da pucker."

"Join the queue."

"No man, da countries that salbage feople by depinition not into da culture of da queue. Only da Irish comvine da two, man. Come to tink of it, I inhivit myself from *delicadeza*, man. It's too personal. You be da one to plug him with a Noy Jesus special."

"Man, I'll cut a dum-dum cross on it."

Skip now came back with a little kid of about ten. From the smiles of relief on his face, we knew it had to be OK now.

"Alright, guys, he was just at the wrong landing-steps." We followed tamely. At the bottom of the mossy steps – it was low water springs in Manila Bay, the month of September – lay a small bum-boat. Its exhaust bubbled as consumptively as Bambi as it rose and fell in the pitch. "Where's the boat guy, Brod?"

"This is him."

"What? You stupid puck."

That summed up my opinion, too.

"Hey, hey," Skip defended himself. "The boat works, I been in it myself to check. And the kid's ace. Had his hands on the tiller since before he could walk. It ain't age, Brods, it's ability. C'mon, there's less heat with him, too. You think of that before you're the ones to scold so quickly, hah?"

Well, I'd heard inventive abuse and bad language in Mactan, but nothing to match the invective the three rich-boys poured on Skipper. Even Dant fell silent. When the rich Brods slipped on the water-steps it wasn't on stairs: they were slithering down a snake's back, and they cursed their fortune and their incompetent facilitator as they went. It was harder for them than it was for me and Dant. We'd never had the expectations of life they'd had. Low down in the boat, we couldn't make out the masts and lights of the vessels we had seen up on the wharf. Skip, whom the Brods had pulled by force into the boat, said the ship was Indonesian, Chinese-owned, (of course), and Liberian-registered. A big Brod who specialised in international maritime law and another who was in the Customs had fixed passage for us. It was all squared, Skipper assured us.

I couldn't see a darned thing. Clouds were obscuring the full moon. We'd been going nearly twenty minutes. The kid looked at Skipper, who ignored him. A horrible suspicion started to come into my mind. Did he know where the fuck we were going? He looked at Skipper again. That did it. I knew it was better to have a word in Skipper's ear than to spill the beans openly. It wouldn't have been a pretty sight. They were panickers to the man.

"O-o, Brod. No froblem. I know the anchorage and the buoy number, just it's dark now, hah?"

"If you say so, Skip." I noticed that in his stress he was transposing like the lowest *pinoy*, which was a bad sign. Next thing you knew, his grammar would start to go. And that had been proof against rape, murder, and pity. As if in answer to the prayer he was surely making, a winking light appeared to port. A minute later, Skipper cried excitedly to the boy, "*Dito, lang.*"

"Yeah, right," I said drily.

It was a hazard buoy, I think, from memory. Then I didn't know. We puttered on. Suddenly it was there. A great black cliff loomed sheer out of the sea. I was amazed by the size, the inhuman scale. You couldn't conceive of men inside controlling it. It intimidated more the closer you got. It obliterated any difference between me and the other ants. You were afraid it would turn over turtle and crush you.

Their generator, then and later, was, I surmise, giving them trouble, for they had been showing no lights as we approached. Skip said, his voice trembling, "This is it, guys." None of us uttered a word. Even the boat-boy seemed stymied. We followed the hull round, moving slower than a man walking. Without being prompted, I stood to fend off. I looked up, saw sister moon's cloud-spattered face, and became so giddy I thought I'd fall onto our thwarts. It wasn't as if I had my feet firmly on planking but as if I was an insect half-way up the wall with my sucker palms skidding and popping on the treacherous rivets. Our passage round was just endless.

"What's da flan, Skip?" I heard Dant whisper.

"There'll be a ladder down for you," Skip replied. "Just gotta find it."

"Can't we call up, *na lang?*" asked one of the rich boys, whom nerves had made amenable. "No," said Skipper in a violent whisper, "The fewer in on it the better. Only the Master and the bosun's mate know. And the skipper's steward. He's a *pinoy.*"

Of course he is, I thought.

There was a roar, and then the dead plates vibrated under my hands. The ship burst into light as if it was the centre-piece of a pyrotechnic display. I cringed, ducking with my hands still on the hull, shoving us off and falling up to my elbows in the water, destroying the expression of surprise on my new-born reflection. Rods of light, solid in the blackness, extended from port-holes in the ship's side as if they were ray-gun discharges which had pierced the metal; the whole castle was fretted in that chilly and silent explosion. Then I heard cheers, just like the customers at Ma's bar, the B-52, when the generator restored their evening to them. We were passing under the stern, the most impressive part so far, the rudder towering above us. Where it entered the water it was twice as thick as I was in the body. I looked up again as we were rounding to the starboard side of the vessel, orange rust streaks over her flanks like the gore on a spurred pony, so that now she was no inanimate light-box but a wounded animal, and descried tantalisingly her name and port but at an impossible angle. I thought I saw the name Odessa and strange characters. "Hey, I thought you said she was an Indon."

"Yeah. Chinese-Indonesian."

"Well, it looks like Cyrillic letters to me. You know, Russkies."

"Naw, man, you're seeing Chinky characters."

"There, Oh, Jesus, there."

I followed the rich-boy's pointing finger. A frayed rope dangled to within about eight feet of the water. As it hung there unenticingly, it appeared slightly lower than the untied strands of the open end of a basketball net.

"That?" queried Danton.

"O-o," said Skipper encouragingly. Our faces must have been something. We didn't want to stay in our little boat, nor did we want to leave it. The situation, I thought, was going to prolong itself indefinitely. "OK, guys," I said. "Now or never. Let's go."

"How da puck we can reach it, 'cept you?" Danton asked hotly. I was glad to see his chilli temper was going to warm his courage.

"Get on Gorilla's shoulders, *unggoy*. Show the others how, man." We could have been scaling a PX wall or a coco palm again. The boat rocked a little but not so we were ever in any danger of taking a bath. Then my shoulders were light again. I shielded my eyes against the glare from above but could only see the dancing rope-end against the spots in my eyes. When it had stopped jerking and was just swinging – one heck of a time, that was – I sent the next one up. He took even longer than the nimble and valiant *unggoy*. After that, one more, and finally the last. Then I nodded to Skipper, ignoring his proffered hand-shake, not out of resentment or a lack of generosity but because – don't ask me why even now – I thought it would be weak and unlucky. Mostly unlucky. I sprang with balance and assurance. The little boat failed to rock but Skip still went sprawling forwards from the recoil. Well, you know I came close to taking a drink of Bay water for though I rose well beyond the rope end, it was laying flat against the hull. I lost a finger-nail on the plates and just caught the last few inches of the rope one-handed. Will you believe me if I say I smiled? I did, I really did. Up, up I went without ever putting my feet on the plates. Three anxious faces peered over the railings as I came hand over hand the last fifteen feet. I looked down, way down, to the black water. That selfish fuck Skipper and the boat were already gone. The fourth, and missing face, was Dant's. He was, as Fr. Paul would have said, keeping *cave* for us.

"What took so pucking long?"

"*Me?*" I got my orientations. We were forward of the bridge, with a lifeboat on its davits sheltering us. I could see it was an old ship with holds, not a container vessel.

"Skip tell you who to ask for? Did he give you a password?"

I just laughed at the rich boy and was dumbfounded when he beat my chest with his fists — like Bambi had after my *Othello* — and then choked back a sob. He was dissolving in the heat of it. Dant asked me — I'd clearly been elected team captain *in absentia* — "Sugar, we gonna make ourselves known? Or what?" Like me, he clearly preferred or what. Although they didn't know it that was the most important decision of their lives. And it was taken in less than three seconds for them by someone else.

"We'll hide," I said, "then it'll be too late for them to throw us off."

"In the lifeboat, Brod," suggested one of the rich-boys. "They don't see us under the, *koan*, tarpaulin."

Dant shook his head vigorously. "*Hindi*. First flace they look, man. Maybe it's even da routine check." I thought it was one of the few sensible remarks Danton had made since embarking on the face of great waters. I led them down towards the bow, away from the living quarters and navigation area and, incidentally, in the opposite direction to which Michael and Nguyen had sought sanctuary. The ship appeared to be loaded with a mixed cargo of copra and a horrible grey powder that put me in mind of cremations. The copra smelt worse. The sour reek comes into my nostrils now. Beyond the agricultural produce was a smaller hold not provided with hatch covers, just a tarpaulin, containing thousands of rubber slippers in transparent sacks. Rungs were welded to the side-wall of this hold. Half-way down this built-in ladder was a small door with a large handle. I had to exert all my strength to depress the lever, causing the door to give with a squeal of rusty hinges which was still not as shrill as the remonstrances of my companions. "Lighten up, guys," I said. "We're way down from the living-quarters." The walk-way in front of the door was only a couple of feet wide, with a straight drop to the floor of the hold, so only I was in a position to look in, with Danton craning to peer over my shoulder from the side. "It's a store-room," I informed my tail of hangers-on, "and, good news, Brods, I can see a cobweb over the door. Some brooms and a shovel here. Not much else." We trooped in as if we were taking sanctuary in the Sistine Chapel. "It's a mess," I said, "but look on the bright side. It means no one comes here."

"Try shutting da door, old friend. And then your pucking mouth," Danton suggested. I did. It was pitch dark. I could feel all our hearts sinking. I let rip with a morale-boosting fart. Groans, remarks about the gas-chamber filled the air which was already fetid enough to overcome any additions. Gradually, dim shapes impressed themselves on my eyeballs as the bodies of my companions.

"I can see to all, but where da puck's Sugar?" I heard Danton say. Unoriginal jokes about my complexion followed.

"I tink I see da white of his teeths."

I let them go on a while. If it made them feel better, it was OK by me. Finally, Jago, the nicest of the rich-boys – though he'd still taken his chance to screw Haydee – said, "I think that's about enough, *di ba*? Maybe Sugar's gonna get riled." In our position you didn't have to be very acute to hear the unspoken addendum, hanging in the stale air, "And, shit, do we ever need him now." Danton said, matter of factly, and it wasn't for my benefit, "No, Brod. Sugar *never* get riled, all da days I known him."

"OK," I cut them short, "look round for hidey-holes or something to get behind." There wasn't a lot: a box or two, a locker with no hinges. Way up above, a whole collection of pipes snaked this way and that, connecting and passing each other at different levels. You had to duck low to get into the store-room from the hold but once in it was lofty. You couldn't make out the ceiling in the gloom.

We settled down against the wall for the night. I put the shovel handle against the door lever, more for the secure feeling than anything. I figured it would help the rich-boys sleep. Sleep took a long while to come. We talked in low voices, stopping frequently to listen for sounds of discovery outside. I jerked to suddenly. Danton's awe-filled, amused voice said in my ear, "For Jaizus sake, man, you snoring loud enough to wake da dead."

"Sorry. How long?"

"My watch not da one to be luminous, man. I tink it's a long time already."

"OK."

Soon, chinks of light came through rust-holes and distortions in the plates. The boat was in fairly bad shape. A little later, we felt the engines start. Time extended itself. Seconds seemed like minutes. You couldn't tell whether we were under way or not. We checked the time: 11 a.m. By the time it was 5 p.m. we decided we must be moving – over a flat calm sea. We were thirsty and hungry. And the hold was smelling a lot worse than before our arrival. But I was adamant no one was to go out yet. At 2 a.m. I cracked. By unspoken accord, Danton was the one selected to do our reconnoitring. I let him out like you would a mongoose to catch pythons. Ten minutes later he was back: we were indeed under way over a flat sea with an unobscured moon. No sign of crew. "Food, Brod," Jago asked. "You see any foods?"

"O," we all chorused. "Even some water, Dant?" I begged him. He shook his head. "Didn't go near da living quarters. Too scare. Pood will be in da kitchen, *koan*, galley, man. But too scared, man."

"No, you did right," I confirmed. "Later."

"When are we gonna announce ourselves?" one of the rich-boys asked. "Maybe they'll feed us then."

"Well, yes," I said slowly. "But maybe let sleeping dogs lie, *di ba*? I mean, why spoil things. Maybe we can just sneak off when we hit port. The passage shouldn't be above three days, another fifty hours, even call it forty-eight."

"Don't think I can stand it, Brod," Jago said. However, to my surprise, the others agreed with me. We sat there, unable to see each other's faces clearly, and told stories to pass the time. We began with our own histories, me and Dant first. The rich boys were genuinely interested, the variety of our experiences made theirs look small. "Jeez," said Jago, "you've had three lives already, Sugar."

"Me pour," said Dant.

"What about you guys?" I asked.

"Ah, nothing exotic, Brod," said Jago. "Typical middle-class *pinoy* family. Pa's an attorney back in Cebu. Yeah, I'm a Visayan, man. Guess I'll go into the family law practice when we get out of this one. All of my friends are back home. I played for Boys' High in Cebu, but nothing like your level, Sugar. The Frat was all I knew in Manila." He said this last with something of a sob. Rich cry-baby, I thought, but probably a regular enough guy under ordinary circumstances. "And you," I said to the second shade in our little metal Hades, "I hate to admit it, Brod, but I've forgotten your name."

"Lyndon," he replied. "I'm from Bicol, Brods..."

"Wow! Vicol Express, man. Super hot! I like some now, neber mind da loose bowels!" Dant alluded to the famous spice dish which sent you speeding for water. Even Lyndon laughed wanly; we were grabbing at straws; morale was dropping by the minute. "Pa's a preacher. We're Pentecostals..."

"Ah, Jaizus. A pucking Frod friest. We're da ones to be doomed, man."

"...My uncle, Pa's older brother, owns a pawnshop in the Visayas. He's an attorney, Brod, our Frat."

"Great," said Jago. "Come down to Sugbu. We'll make a great partnership." They slapped palms in the darkness.

"I'm from a medical family," the third guy, Lando, said, "We're all doctors, except Sis – she's still doing Med Tech – but I was stupid enough to go for the Law."

"Yeah. Look where it got you," Jago said sympathetically. There wasn't a trace of irony in his voice. After a while we stopped talking. Too dejected.

Probably an hour later, Lyndon said, "I can't stand it any longer. One of us has got to go get some food and something to drink. Chocolate milk, Brod, that's what I crave. The one from Magnolia."

"No," I said.

"I'm with Lyndon," Jago said. "I'm so thirsty I'm gonna die."

"Vote," I said. "All those in favour of Dant going out, raise their hands. Shit, I can't see the hands."

It turned out it was three to two in favour of stealing something from the galley – only the guy from the medical dynasty voted with me. "Well, I guess you know best. You're the only one who's been out," I conceded to Dant. "Good luck," I added as I opened the door for him.

Ten minutes later we heard the sound of running feet on the deck-plates, shouting, and a subdued but closer sound at the side of our compartment, which was Danton coming down the rungs with more alacrity than discretion. As I opened the door, I heard a spongy thump followed by prolonged crackling. This was the sound of Dant falling into the rubber sandals and then scrambling over the polythene. "Puck," he gasped as he fell in. "They see me, man. Two guys with flashlights. No one there da last time."

"Alright, Dant. It's not your fault," I said.

"You stupid idiots," the guy from the medical family groaned. "What have you done, what have you got us into?"

"This isn't the time for recriminations," I said. "Later, if you still want to." I had put the shovel against the door. But now I said to the others, "Do we let them in? It's meant to be arranged, according to Skipper. We should just be able to tell them. If they're Indonesians there might be a language problem but we could get by – some of the words are the same."

"They're not da ones to be Indons," Dant said grimly. "Blondie, man. Amerikano but not real 'Merikano."

"Ah, fuck," said Lyndon. "He sold us out."

"Don't jump to conclusions," I said. "Wait and see. Listen, I don't think we can keep them out. Better to let them in without fucking them around. OK?" There was a despondent collective assent.

"OK, then, Brods," I said. "Stand back, don't do anything silly." We retired to the back of our little jail. Dant took the spade from me with a grimace. "You don't need no weapon, Gorilla. Da little one does."

The white-painted door lever began to move down slowly. As it did, I found my knees dipping with it. I don't know what it was. Not – I think – instinct, nor – I hope – craven fear but a well-schooled, if misplaced, reflex. One that was way out of its context. This was no gleaming basketball court with its shallow tiers but a dingy stink-hole on a hell-ship. I looked down, I looked up, I ran a quorum of steps. I jumped. Getting airborne was always my route out of trouble, my method of turning defeat into victory. There was an asbestos-swathed pipe very nearly eleven feet – I would not like to be culpable of exaggeration – overhead. I got it, just. The best jump I ever made, and not on shabu but adrenalin. Once I converted the desperate grip of my fingers to the secure hook of my forearms I had my sanctuary. From there I balanced on the pipe and sprang another eight feet into a concealing maze of metal and hose-work. The door had just swung completely open when I looked down from my vantage point twenty feet up. I think Danton beside me was the only one to notice me go, the others had their attention on the door. The beams of three flashlights probed the room. The Brods were dazzled. I saw them putting their hands over their eyes. The men at the door had baseball bats and crowbars and Dant was right, no way were they Chinese or Indonesians.

Jago tried to speak, then had to try again. "We're the passengers you're taking to Singapore." There were mutterings in a foreign language at the door. I could see the shadows of plenty of other men outside in the hold. The wavering torch beams came up again.

"Stay where you are," the guy from the medical family said. "I've got a pistol." This was news to me but if the sailors knew no other word of English they certainly understood that one, for they stopped dead. One of them called for someone outside. He was somewhat older than the others.

"Speak English?" Jago asked eagerly.

"*Da*," the sailor said, which as a cross between "Yeah" and "Ja," we Filipinos took for an affirmative. He had an accent I'd never heard, not even on the television, slurred, extending the e's by prefacing them with a 'y' sound.

"What you do hyere?" he asked.

"We paid you, your captain, for a trip to Singapore."

The sailor conferred with the flashlight holders.

"No," he said. I never heard a more definite, a deader, flatter, yet more eloquent "no". Mine was an unusual perspective. I was looking straight down on them where they were foreshortened pairs of shoulders. I could see the bald patches, the scabbard bayonet the "interpreter" had stuck into the back of his pants. The flashlights didn't dazzle me.

"Yes, we paid. D-d-d-d-efinitely," stuttered Jago. "O-o," the medical boy backed him up. "No," the sailor said, "you are stowaways." Dant hadn't spoken. He was directly beneath me. For once, he looked not much shorter than everybody else. I knew the fiery little fucker; he wasn't much in inches but he had too much heart. He wasn't gonna lower himself – like he wouldn't have if caught on another gang's home-patch.

The word stowaway was also clearly as universal as pistol, for it brought an angry murmur from the rest of the crew. Someone shouted in a foreign language, the same slurring as the English of the older guy. I didn't know the words but the drift was unambiguous. I heard Dant growl; I hadn't heard him do that since we were twelve.

"Whoa!" Lyndon exclaimed. "We paid, man. We're not trying to cheat you."

"Then why you hiding, stupid cunts?"

"We were scared, man," Jago pleaded. "We paid to go on an Indonesian ship."

"This Ukraine ship."

"Again, sir?"

"Oh, Gee, they're Russians," the medic boy said.

"*Nyet*. Not Russki. Ukraine."

Had it been the San Ignatio geography lesson, I would have made myself unpopular with my classmates by putting my hand up and reeling off the facts. As it was, I lay recumbent on the length of my pipe with my head on my elbow and held my peace.

"I think we're in for a beating-up," Lando said to Jago. "Kick our ass, then put us on bread and water in the lock-up."

"Oh, man," said Jago, "if only. Even some water. I don't think the spanking can be worse than the initiation was, Brod."

The sailors were conferring at the door. Dant had moved himself away from the other three Brods. He could derive no comfort from their nervous exchanges. Like me, he could smell the reality of a situation.

Jago had a brainwave. "Look, maybe if there's a mistake, we don't mind paying you again. Or if we're on the wrong boat we're happy to pay you the same. Right, Brods?"

"Oh, yeah, right on," Lyndon and the medical boy chorused.

The old sailor who spoke English was sending people away with messages to relay, probably to the Captain. He pointed to Jago's and Lyndon's wristwatches. They owned respectively an Omega and a Seiko. "Give."

"Sure, no froblem," said Jago. Without being told, the medic boy handed over his Tag-Heuer. Dant never had a watch in his life, but I don't think he'd have given it away.

A very young kid, much younger than ourselves, came in. He swung over the foot and a half of bulkhead at the bottom of the door by the practised expedient of gripping the recess at the top. I imagined Dant made a note of that, as much as I did. He spoke into the older guy's ear. "How many you are?" the older guy asked. The flashlights played over the screwed-up eyes of my companions, blinding them just as their night-vision was returning. "Er, shit, I don't know," said Jago, "I mean, I never counted. Let's see, Sugar, Dant, me…"

"Pour," said Danton, looking straight into the beam at the same moment as Lyndon said "Five."

"Pour," Dant reiterated, holding up his fingers. "You can see to all."

"Are you Filipinos?"

"O. Filipinos," said Jago winningly.

"Shit country. No money. Ten days loading bird-shit in Isabel. You got moneys?"

"Yes, some."

"OK, you give it all to us. Don't hide some. We'll find out, then it's bad for you. You get it from all places now."

The boys put their hands in their pockets, Lyndon unzipping his fashionable fanny pack.

"Can you leave us just a little?" Jago asked

"Later," said the sailor, "we'll give a little back to you later. Give it all to us now. Get it from where you hide it."

"No, this is what we have, sir. We didn't hide anything."

"Don't worry. We'll go outside five minutes, then you get the rest. Give us any papers you got, too." With that he withdrew, locking the door, and leaving us in darkness again. If we had squirrelled anything away, how the fuck the boys were meant to find it again in the dark I don't know. The notion of us secreting valuables against discovery was absurd; it had never occurred to us. He was crediting us with cunning we didn't have; it told you more about him. That was something I learned later: the morbid obsession of sailors or soldiers for tucking their things away, the universal assumption that their friends were as light-fingered as they.

"We're fucked, guys," Lyndon said.

"Yeah," said the medical boy. "Where's Sugar? I don't see him."

"You're luckier than me," said Jago. "I couldn't see anyone with those lights in my eyes."

"Well, I mean I never heard him. Sugar?"

146

I was on the point of announcing myself when Dant said, "You didn't see him go out with them?"

"No?"

"Yeah, right at da start."

"Sure?"

"O-o. But keef quiets about it, man. Maybe he can cut a deal for us. We pace to pace with da wrong guys now, for sure."

"O."

I lay on my pipe in silence like a treed raccoon.

"What do you think?" Jago asked. The others were silent. "Dant?" No reply. I think Dant had now had enough of the rich-boys. Dignity, as I said at the beginning, was all we paupers could call our own; it was a kind of courage.

"Lando? Shucks, I forget. You really got a pistol, Brod?"

"Give it to me," Dant said quickly.

"*Hindi.* I'm just bull-shitting them, man."

"Well, it worked," Jago congratulated him.

"Yeah, good for you, Brod."

The door opened.

"OK, boys, you got something for us? The more you got, the more the Old Man like you."

"Just passports, sir. Here. But we need them back, sir."

I saw the sailors look at each other. That was the first time I saw those stolid East European faces, those faces equally hard in either sex that I don't think I ever saw broken or enlivened by a smile anywhere in the world, even when they were turning a hefty buck.

"I think you got more, Filipino."

"No, sir. I assure you not."

"We come back."

This time they conferred outside, with the door open. I could see their flashlight beams pointed down into the hold, so that they wouldn't dazzle each other.

"OK, you come now." He lit the medical boy, Lando, with his beam.

"W-what for?"

"The captain interview you private. Come. No fear. No one will hurting your hair."

Lando swallowed. "I don't have a gun," he said. "I was just kidding you." I thought he was a fool if he reckoned this would win him any popularity with them.

"OK," replied the sailor soothingly. I found him more genuine when he'd called us stupid cunts, which was then quite a new expression to me. "Go, man," Jago exhorted Lando. "It's gonna be alright." Oh boy, I thought, what a creep. Did Jago think someone else could carry the can for all of them? Or was postponing trouble for himself for a few minutes all he cared about? I abandoned my recumbent position and contracted my body so I was on hands and knees. I felt bad I was abandoning my friends, who appeared quite unable to look after themselves. Jumping down from on-high like Spiderman or a costumed asshole from a Taiwan movie would, I think, just have gotten us all bludgeoned to death then and there – not that it made any difference in the long run. I half-stood, and, just then, I swear, Danton looked up, pursed his lips and shook his head. Hell! I lowered myself on to the pipe again, with the small hairs on the back of my neck turned into brass wires. Telepathy? No, I don't think so, though I thought so then. It was just, I believe, that Danton knew me very well, better than Ma did, better than Butch Tan Sy, better than Fr. Boy.

"OK," said Lando. "For a while, hah, guys." He stepped out into the flickering jet of the hold, the beams from the deck above like UFO's or the Starship Enterprise.

"I tink God funish us for Haydee," Dant said to Lyndon.

The old sailor smiled what he thought was a sweet smile at the remaining boys, showing us a head full of blue and brown teeth. I had the advantage of seeing the bayonet handle lying on the back of his spine – I could imagine what a nice, secure feeling that must be for him – but there was no hoodwinking sharp little Danton. "Anyone else so clever they da ones to speak English like you?" he snapped.

"You decided to speak, little boy?" the sailor said, grinning widely. "No. Only Nikita sail with Englishski."

"Then who da puck da one to translate to our friend, hah?"

A look of pure malice passed across old Nikita's face. Then he grinned again. "The Old Man. He knows everything, the Old Man."

The very young kid came back with some information for Nikita. "OK," Nikita pointed to Lyndon. "Follow your friend up. Go – there's sausage, also vodka." He translated what he'd said into their own language. Prolonged guffawing ensued, loudest from the young kid, whom I took to be cabin-boy or galley-help. He was wearing a certain kind of smile on his face, to which I would later give a name.

"Go, Filipino," Nikita urged. Lyndon didn't like it. He didn't like it at all. But he went. It was easier to go, the line of least resistance.

"Two little Injan boy," sang Dant. "Hey, Jago, they fick us off one by ones. You wanna do sumpin avout that, Brod?"

"Don't know what you mean, Brod."

"Yeah, you do, Brod. I ready if you are, mans."

Jago bit his lip and shook his head. Those rich-boys. What they needed was a time-out Butch Tan Sy pep-talk. Old Nikita was keeping his mouth shut. I figured he didn't want to let the cat out of the bag again. From the way he looked at Danton he'd clearly marked him down as the most dangerous, now they knew Lando hadn't been carrying a gun. The galley-boy came back, fixed Nikita with a funny look, and nodded. "Mister, your turn," Nikita said to Jago.

"Where are the others?" Jago asked. "Why haven't they come back?" He wasn't being recalcitrant; he was terrified.

"Your friends in a more comfortable place," said Nikita. "We just like to check your story separate, OK? Come."

Out went Jago, like a lamb. This time Nikita followed him. I imagined Jago singing his heart out. I figured it might not be long before they started looking for me. They were gone much longer than before. The galley-boy grinned at Danton and thumped what looked like a broken hatch-lever into his palm. Danton cleared his throat and spat on the floor. Minutes passed. I fantasised about jumping down, slamming the galley-boy's head against the bulk-head, and charging into the crew outside with Danton. Then leaping into a lifeboat and rowing away. Dream on. Suddenly I heard a cry. "*Tulong! Tulong!*" which was "Help!" in Tagalog. It was Jago's voice. Feet came along the deck. There was shouting in the foreign tongue. A smack into the hold, louder than Danton's flight. This was Jago falling all thirty feet from the deck on to the cargo. From where I was, I couldn't see into the bottom of the hold. I think Jago must have had the wind knocked out of him, for there was silence. Dant advanced to the door, but was met by the sailors with baseball bats. The galley-boy smirked. I wouldn't have given much for his chances with Danton by himself, metal-bar or no metal-bar. Catching his breath, Jago shouted: "They've thrown them overboard! The railings are open! There's blood all over the deck!" Danton winced. There came a huge bang, silence, then angry shouts from Nikita. He was still mad when he came in. Dant backed himself against the wall in the shadows, but the flashlights followed him round. A sailor with a long firearm, very much like a shotgun, followed Nikita. Nikita said something to him, which didn't need a lot of flair to be translated as asshole or the new word to me, cunt.

"What's your name?" he asked Dant. I could hear them outside carrying what I surmised to be Jago's body up to the deck.

"Go puck yourself," Dant said.

"Maybe we fuck you," Nikita said. He translated to the galley-boy who sniggered. I got the picture. He was likely Nikita's catamite or maybe the ship's common whore.

"What's your name, honey?" he inquired again. Dant said, "Sugar." In some ways he was a genius. They didn't come any quicker. Nikita looked at the guy with the shotgun, who raised his eyebrows. I think one of the guys, probably Jago, had blurted something out while they were whacking him, head, legs, anywhere. I could picture it from Jago's desperate fragments of warning: the gap in the hinged railings, our guys beaten towards it, or thrown unconscious into the sea, the pools of blood from where their heads had lain on the greasy plates. I swallowed.

Nikita advanced on Danton, pulling the bayonet from the back of his pants. Dant closed his eyes briefly – I think it was out of frustration. He said, "I got my butterfly-knifes still from Mactan, pucker, I make you vleed for it, but I'm da rich-voys now." This meant nothing to Nikita. The old Ukrainian closed in, throwing his bayonet from hand to hand as he did so. Dant was an old enough hand at gang rumbles to be unimpressed – he knew fancy feints and manoeuvres meant nothing, it was the judgement of distance that was critical – but he was against a rock and a hard place, he was only human, he got distracted, and the guy with the shot-gun was able to come by his side and smash the gun-butt against his ear. Down he went – I'd have gone, too. They hauled him up, still doubled over, and Nikita kneed him in the face. I knew if I came down like the avenging angel I would one day be, I could put Danton out of his misery if only for a few moments and, not least, wipe the smirk off the cretinous galley-boy's face. He wore an expression of combined spite and weakness that would not have gone amiss on the worst Filipino. But I stayed. It was harder for me to stay than it would have been to jump.

They threw Danton over the broken locker and pulled down his pants. This was going to be a lot worse than his punishment from Fr. Aloysius. Dropping his own jeans, Nikita started to rub himself up. Although only half-conscious, Danton tried to stand, but they drove a crow-bar into his stomach and knocked all the breath out of him. He couldn't even groan as Nikita got it in. Then slam, slam, slam. It didn't take the old *bakla* long. Even as Nikita grimaced with his climax Danton was going blue in the face. The galley-boy pushed forward and I got the opportunity to learn the Ukrainian for "Me, me." I think as a rule he was the meat on the table in that ship. And, reflecting on it now, perhaps Nikita had also spent his own boyhood as the ship's plug-hole, the old cycle of abused becoming abuser.

The galley-boy took a bit longer, prolonging deliberately his pleasure. Dant was getting his breath back. He opened his mouth to try to speak but he couldn't get the words out, not enough wind to drive them. He gathered himself, then said in jerky gasps, the same rhythm in which he was being sodomised, *"Tago, dong. Ayawg saba."* He was telling me to hide, save myself, and he contrived to make it sound like a plea to his abusers rather than a warning to me. They laughed. One of the younger sailors came to the front of the locker and presented himself to Danton's mouth. Next thing, he was screaming in agony, beating at Dant's head, pulling his hair, and the locker was over. Dant had his arms thrown round the guy's waist. He wouldn't let go with his teeth, he was the Irish terrier, the enraged bee. The others piled in, fists, clubs. He just wouldn't let go. The sailor with the shotgun couldn't stand the sight of it any longer. He placed the barrel in the middle of Danton's back and fired. Bawoom! and they all jumped back. Dant didn't stir. He was gone, man. That was it, like a light going out. My ears sang with the report. I couldn't even hear the screams of the guy Dant had bitten. I wouldn't have been surprised if he had chewed it clean off, Dant the small but terrible. "No one puck with me, mans, and then able to tell da world," I could hear him bragging. *Noli me tangere.*

They dragged his body out by the feet, the cock-less guy doubled-up behind, and they abandoned me to the darkness.

CHAPTER VII

Afternoon tea – The price of smoked salmon – My saintly Smiths: non Angli sunt sed angeli *– Extraction as a Last Resort – Hong Kong Helot*

"MINI-SAUSAGE-ROLLS, OF COURSE. But cress or cucumber sandwiches, Jenny?" asked Mrs Smith.

"Oh, I don't know, Mummy. Does it really matter?"

"Of course it matters, darling. Nine parts of genius is paying painstaking attention to tiny details."

"Well, I don't think it takes genius to give an afternoon tea-party."

"A kind of genius, dear. Or more like a talent, I suppose. You've got to prepare and then conduct it, which requires two quite different skills. It's as big a difference as between jam-making or gardening, dear. Now, cress goes soggy quite quickly, so if we did those we'd have to make them later on and I don't know if I trust the local cress quite as much as I would in Waitrose."

"I'd have said it would be much better. Doesn't everything grow much more luxuriantly here? You were complaining about the garden only the other day."

"Well, yes, darling, but it's what they put on it to *get* it to grow quite so luxuriantly, if you know what I'm getting at. I mean, we do *cook* the vegetables, so *they're* safe, but salads are worse than ice. That's what all the books say. They all say wash thoroughly but if you did to cress what you did to a tomato, you wouldn't have any left at the end."

"Nothing that soaking in Milton wouldn't take care of, Mums."

"Oh, I didn't think of that. But a bit *wasteful*, darling. We could scrub the cucumber with washing-up liquid and water and then peel it but cucumber does repeat on you so."

"Well, it would have been a memorable tea-party then, wouldn't it?"

"I think *thinly* sliced cucumber in white bread with the crust cut off. Then we could have egg and cress in crusty Hovis, or whatever, and it wouldn't matter if the cress was a bit distressed, it would be lost in the egg and the mayonnaise."

"How about smoked salmon, Mum?"

"Darling! We're not Chinese millionaires! Have you seen the price of it in Dairy Farm?"

"We could just do a few and cover the cress sandwiches with them. But look, I'll bake scones. Or do you think rock-cakes?"

"You could do rock-cakes. I've taught Babyjane how to do scones. She still puts in too many sultanas but it is recognisably a scone. They've got scones everywhere in the hotel coffee-shops, so rock-cakes would be more of a novelty for everyone. For our Asian guests, I mean. The Indian Consul was talking about them only the other day."

"Who?"

"The Indian Consul, darling."

"No. Who was he talking about?"

"He was talking about rock-cakes, Jennifer. He remembered the old Lyons corner-houses from his days at the LSE. Really, you don't listen to a word I say. If it was Daddy I'd call it marital deafness."

"Filial deafness, Mums. What about samosas? We don't want to be too Home Counties, do we? I mean we should make *some* concessions to where we are. This is a crossroads of civilisations."

"You sound like a tourist brochure, dear. As far as I'm concerned, Hong Kong is a good deal more antiseptic than Surrey ever was and Singapore was positively sterile. I had my bag snatched in Leatherhead but I could walk down Orchard Road or through Cat Street for a hundred years without it ever happening."

"Well, then they should make Mr Lee Mayor of Leatherhead and bring back the birch, shouldn't they."

"Now, darling, I'm not quite the dinosaur you like to think I am and I refuse to rise to the bait. Why don't you go down to the market now with the driver and you'll be back in time for a Pimms in the garden with Daddy."

"I could just walk, Mums. I'm not ready to be the old Colonial Hand quite yet. Everyone batters on about how suffocatingly small Hong Kong and Singapore are, yet no one seems to be able to manage without a car in either place."

"Post-Colonial Hand, dear. There. I may not have been lucky enough to go to Girton but I do read the odd book. Do take the car, dear, it's so terribly hot. *Rey! Rey!* Would you kindly take Miss Smith to the vegetable market and then pick her up half an hour later."

"Yes, Mum. I'll be the one to pick up Commander Smith before Miss Jenny or after? I remember he said at breakfast he was leaving the surgery early."

"After, thank you, Rey. Thank you for reminding me."

"You are very welcome, Mum."

HOW I LOVED THE SMITHS! I took as much pleasure in their lives as the collector of memorabilia or antiques does in the mint condition of his rarest artefacts. I guarded them with a jealous zeal; they never realised how jealously or zealously. No one was to even breathe on my family of figurines without me buffing the moisture from them and setting them upright again. Until I met the Smiths I hadn't believed human beings could exist in such pristine perfection. Jenny Smith was Eve before the Curse and Commander Smith, her father, an Adam who'd partaken of the fruit of the Tree of Knowledge of Good and Evil without being abashed by his own temerity. The very thought of Commander Smith running to hide his face because he was too scared to face the consequences of his actions was ridiculous.

Compared to virtually everybody I'd known they were adults. Tale-bearing, small-mindedness, cliquism, the taking of silent umbrage ("huffs" as Mrs Smith called it) were anathema to them in the way vindictiveness, envy, finger-pointing, and outrageous transference of blame to other shoulders were second nature to five-year-olds and grey-haired, august Asian politicians.

How did these paragons achieve it? In the sense that it was no effort for them, sainthood without the turmoil, Fr. Paul would probably not have regarded it as particularly praiseworthy. Mostly, I think it was knocked out of them in early childhood. When our rich-boys broke their first radio-controlled toy, then looked indignantly at totally innocent *yaya* or older sibling, they got a hug for their amusing initiative, where the Commander Smiths of this world got a warm backside for their slyness. It was purged from them, while the future Philippine senator or Malay parliamentarian was reinforced in the anti-social behaviour of a five-year-old, which he or she then carried into adult life.

And, most important of all, the Smiths of this world possessed an unshakeable sense of who they were and what they stood for.

Context was immaterial to them; they weren't relativists; they were unprepared to compromise on their sense of right and wrong, to make allowances, to bend the rules out of kindness and friendship to fit the individual case. It made them a little rigid, a little china-brittle; they were a tad aloof, a trifle cold for my personal comfort, but then everything comes at a price. The Smiths' identity was bound up with small things: ransacking the local supermarkets for Shippam's Bloater Paste or Gentleman's Relish (I could have told them pink *bagoong* tasted pretty much the same but I knew they'd have been scared of the lurid colour); Mrs Smith's tips for getting various tenacious substances out of carpeting; Commander Smith's gruff love for his red setter, the way he'd always start his birthday or the Gregorian New Year with the promise to quit puffing his briar pipe, seemingly untutored by the experience that the previous resolutions had never lasted six days. They revelled in their parochialism, but in the spirit of a joke which had yet to reach its punch-line. People probably did laugh at them but in a sense the joke was on the other people. Mrs Smith's intellectual horizons definitely were a little limited – though she'd been a teacher before she met Commander Smith – and she was shockingly naive (to me, anyhow) about real human depravity. But Commander Smith was no one's fool. He'd refused to let Jenny and their youngest daughter, Nicola, go to Krabi, southern Thailand, by themselves, much to their chagrin. "The disappearing *farang* is not an endangered species," he'd said cryptically.

Another time they were discussing their second home in England, the country cottage rather than the city apartment. Mrs Smith and Nicky wanted to inform the police that it was empty, so that they could keep an eye on it. I imagined the avuncular British Bobby shining a cursory flashlight into its recesses as he went about his rounds by bicycle. Mrs Smith had told me about the unarmed British policemen. "We have the finest police force in the world," she had said, with a throb of pride in her voice that would have been alien to any middle-class Filipino talking about our uniformed brigands. If they'd rounded up every cop in the country and dumped them on a leper's island the level of petty crime in the Philippines might have risen but, for sure, serious crimes would have stopped. The police wouldn't have been there to commit them.

But Mrs Smith and Nicky had taken it as a matter of course that they would inform their local Crime Prevention Officer of their absence. However, Commander Smith had said, "Hm. I should say the fewer people who knew about it the better. I think we'll keep the fact that it's empty to ourselves." And no amount of "But Daddy," or "I really don't see the logic in that, dear," could shake him in his resolve, or even draw him on his reasons. I could work out what the reasoning was, but the last thing I wanted to do was pop the bubble of Mrs Smith's innocent, confident world. One thing could lead to another and, as I said, the fragrance of their lives was derived from tiny essences. Most of the shrewd people I ever met were flawed by a certain lack of compassion. Fr. Paul had piercing eyes and a cold heart. Commander Smith contrived that difficult balance: to be both street-wise and kind. I remembered Fr. Paul's story about Saint Gregory roving the market of Rome (not I hope in the spirit of American servicemen roaming round Mactan) and coming across the blue-eyed, blond-haired English slaves. *Non Angli sed angeli*. The real thing, man, not albinos.

In one matter only did Commander Smith resemble an Asian paterfamilias. I think he was disappointed they hadn't had a boy. The Chinese father would have drowned Nicola at birth. When Commander Smith went into the girls' bedroom he said, "Stand by your beds, chaps."

There was nothing military about the decoration of the Smiths' house. A burglar or malicious persons bent on vandalism – had there, as Miss Jenny pointed out, been any bold enough to risk the chastisement of the rattan when they'd been in Singapore – would not have noticed anything about the appointments to differentiate it from those of the other expatriates, except for the truly impeccable taste. There were none of the antique or modern firearms on the wall, model sailing-ships, group photographs, or other mementoes so dear to the military heart that would have graced the walls of, say, a Philippine coast-guard captain or Air Force Colonel. The flowery sofa and armchair covers, the dun silk curtains, the family of ascending mahogany occasional tables which cleverly slid in under one another, the water colours by Mrs Smith's brother of so near professional standard as to be immaterial, and the German porcelain that Babyjane, the forty-six-year-old maid from Agusan del Sur, was forbidden to dust, breathed of an effortless assurance that, in turn, was founded on complete self-certainty. By contrast, Atty Caladong's joint was a monument to vulgarity. The very lack of ostentation in the Smith household was a kind of ostentation in itself. Oh, my saintly Smiths!

Commander Smith was, in fact, a dentist. He'd never been a seaman officer at all in the Royal Navy from which he'd retired nine years ago, though it was a family joke that he had finished ahead of the RN officers in the 12ft class dinghy regatta held in Hong Kong every year by HMS *Tamar*. HMS *Tamar* wasn't a real ship at all, a floating vessel. By another one of those British jokes whose true relish resides in their impermeability to the foreigner, like the way a British public school was really a private school, HMS *Tamar* was a set of office buildings, the navy shore base in Hong Kong. Sailing was the only sport Commander Smith was good at; he was the worst tennis-player and golfer I'd ever seen. After he had been awarded a wooden kitchen-spoon trophy at the nine-hole course in Deep Water Bay, I heard him say to Nicky, "Winning doesn't matter at all, darling. It's taking part. Remember that. Losing well is the thing." I'd never heard anything like it. Butch Tan Sy would have thrown anyone who uttered such seditious nonsense off our coach while it was moving. It wasn't so much un-Asian as un-everyone, including un-American. It was quintessentially British. I didn't think it was creditable. It didn't spring from modesty but a deep, submerged arrogance that was Roman in its completeness and its nihilism, and Japanese in its hypocrisy. It wasn't Jesuitical, for sure; they were hell-bent on being winners.

The Commander was a heck of a good dentist, though. I knew this from Babyjane. He'd taken one look at my set and said, "Congratulations, Rey."

"Sir, why?"

"Because you're an anomaly. If everyone was like you, we dentists would be out of a living. Do you know you don't have any caries at all? That's decay."

"I know the Latin word, sir. It's good to know I don't have dental caries. So you won't be giving me any fillings?"

"You can't treat health, old boy. Twenty years ago I'd put in a filling at a suspect point just to stop the rot in advance. But yours are so good it would be a shame and with what we know now about reversing lesions, we're much more conservative."

"You don't pull teeth that much, sir? That's the way of our quack dentists back home."

"A good dentist tries to save a rotten tooth when he can. A filling if possible. Extraction would be the last resort."

"That's a good general principle for life as well, sir. Mind advance-dirty keeps the world and the mouth clean, my mother would say, and if that fails salvage what you can."

"Have your mother and your siblings got good teeth?"

"Not so much, sir."

"Well, you can't have eaten many sweets as a child."

"That's true, sir. We never had money for it. I had my first ice-candy when I was eleven. I can remember the conversation my mother was having at the time."

"Well, keep it up."

According to herself, Babyjane had owned about the worst set of teeth in the Eastern hemisphere, one of those Philippine mouths that resembled city blocks which have been under intensive shell-fire for a week. Commander Smith had persuaded the apprehensive Filipina – usually an intractable combination – to open her mouth and put herself in his hands. "Serr never hurt me. Can believe that? Just a little fain from da needle and it's no more. He's all da time playing old fashion music in surgery." Now she boasted a bridge and more coronal restorations than she had children, and she was a rural Roman Catholic. The Commander's professional services and the classical music had both come free for Babyjane.

I do believe she'd begun with less faith in Serr than she would have had in the local practitioners, there being for us something peculiarly Chinese about the qualities required for dentistry: the finicky attention to detail, the premium assigned to neatness of handiwork, the pattern of black and white, like dominoes or kung fu shoes and socks, the squint-eyed concentration, the need to work the mine out with not a scrap left behind, the prudence and the occasional going for bust gamble on the part of the dentist.

Back home, most dentists weren't just Chinese, they were *lady* dentists, as their signs took pains to proclaim them. Commander Smith, with his fingers like sausages and the sandy hair on the knuckles, was as far from a Chinese lady dentist as you could get, whilst still remaining human. Jenny and Nicola had been fortunate enough to inherit their elegant figures from Mrs Smith. Their nickname for their father, and I didn't appreciate it until some years later when I saw a jumpy video in the games room of a Philippine club in Plaistow, was Goldfinger.

I once heard Commander Smith explaining, or rather defending, his old naval connection to an American banker (when I also noted that the amiable British philosophy of accepting second-best applied to recreational activities only). "The presumption is that we're a bunch of butchers," Commander Smith said, opening the door of our Honda for his acquaintance before I could get round to the passenger side, "barber-surgeons, amputation without anaesthetic, you know. The whole rum, sodomy, and the lash syndrome, but RN dentistry is second to none. And I think I can be objective about it, Don. The best thing for any young fellow recently qualified would be five years in Portsmouth or Plymouth. You couldn't get a more varied or intensive experience to take into civilian practice from even a teaching hospital."

I saw the smile on the banker's face but Commander Smith had certainly convinced me. As his employee, I had the advantage of knowing him better than even his closest friends. I knew he wasn't a bull-artist, but what he claimed could also be corroborated in its own context by Fr. Paulian analysis. The Navy, more than the Army or Air Force, had to have its men's teeth in perfect shape. How could you do any thing about it on a pitching, rolling sea? And whereas a man with toothache could serve a muzzle-loading cannon with unimpaired efficiency, he was unlikely to be able to do the same gazing into a radar-screen or controlling a guided missile. *Quod erat demonstrandum.* The navy didn't so much get the best fliers, as they said in *Top Gun*; it got the best dentists.

WE WERE FORTUNATE ENOUGH to live in a house with a walled garden in a quiet and minutely elevated corner of the city. Nearly everyone else lived in high-rise apartments, both expatriates and Chinese. The public housing for the less well-off – those whose Chinese acumen had yet to make them millionaires – was of extraordinary quality, superior to what our middle-classes had in Cebu. Even more miraculously to a *pinoy* eye, it was all well maintained. There were no rust, no flaking paint, no rotting wood, and not one graffito anywhere. Ramps, bridges, walkways, and fly-overs as solidly engineered as Olongapo bollards and Clark runways inexorably conducted the Hong Kong belonger in perfect security to his or her front door. Man, it was a real estate agent's artistic impression come to life.

Nevertheless, Mrs Smith worried about her daughters acclimatising. She made them ingest so much fluid it amounted to the water torture. The air-con in the Honda was never off. Jenny and Nicky laughed at her but they all romantically thought of themselves as situated at what Jenny had called a "crossroads of civilisations", and they took what they thought were pains to be culturally acclimatised. Well, the respectful affection in which I held my *halo*ed Smiths wouldn't allow me to laugh at them (too loudly or often) but it was me, the Asian, who was in a state of culture shock. It was easier for the Western expats to adjust.

There were any number of us in Hong Kong, lousing the joint up. Filipinos, I mean. We were the largest group of foreigners in town, just like slaves outnumbered citizens in classical Athens. We were on sufferance as a necessary evil, just as the helots had been in Sparta. On Sundays, the whole of Statue Square and that vast, echoing cavern under the Hong Kong and Shanghai Bank became impassable with picknicking, guitar-strumming *pinays*. So, too, did all the nooks and corners of Central: the smallest paths, alleyways, and cul-de-sacs otherwise deserted at the busiest time on weekdays. As for finding a spare bench on Battery Path, there was no way the average Hong Kong Chinese paterfamilias was going to find a place for his well-tailored rump. We Flips had made it so that the holiday in the business district was the most congested and frenetic day of the week. You'd see *insik* matrons glowering at our sunny-faced girls. If I didn't know *pinays* better, I'd have said they were oblivious to the glares. But of course I knew they weren't. The hatred focussed on them made our girls even happier: what Filipino doesn't like being in a huge group, outnumbering the foe and mocking the type and specimen of the tyrant-employer at home? Man, you could see the furled umbrellas twitching in the old Chinese ladies' hands. Even pouring rain didn't dampen the spirits of our girls as they took cover, screamed as drops found the way down their cute little napes (lucky drops, man), patted and fluffed their recently shampooed and now wet-again manes, and rued the impending damage to their best shoes.

It was for each other we left our dark, our flip-side.

Hong Kong was a city where pretty well everything worked. I mean, it wasn't just a place that was efficient, you could take that for granted with the ruthless Chinese. It was that the Chinese lack of compassion encompassed themselves as well. People didn't sit around bitching if they failed, feeling sorry for themselves and jealous of the successful like we did. They picked themselves up, dusted off their palms, figuratively speaking, and took another shot at climbing up the ladder.

Yet in the shiny steel and glass temple to Mammon that was Hong Kong, there existed a little clump of disorganisation, chaos, and envy. This was the area of *pinoy* shops and money-changers in and around New Cosmos Mansions with their *i-stambi* and notices and placards of pointless, festering feuds and grievances that should long have scabbed over. *No monkey business here, bawal bawal. Shame on you Chinese Bank you making second class citizen of Filipino same rate for everyone. Attorney Chan stop your gambling and fay your emfloyees what you owe them instead.* Smeary shops sold the God-awful food we had no need to eat any longer in Hong Kong of all places and the Marcos pesos I wouldn't have wiped my ass on if I'd had the chance to line my wallet with US and HK dollars. If the Filipinos that hung out in the building weren't smiling when they had nothing to smile about, they were nursing a sour-faced grudge that was equally unjustifiable. Hong Kong was a place where, like I say, the citizenry took their medicine stoically when they had to, but we screamed and struggled like brats when the spoon approached our pursed mouths. That was us, man, and it was no use ignoring it and pretending we weren't like that, the way Atty Caladong and his brood with their heads in the sand got mad with foreigners for criticising them.

ONE OF MY FIRST SUNDAYS IN THE COLONY I found I'd wandered too far West. Funnily enough, it was the so-called Western District which was the old hundred per cent Chinese quarter with all the shop-signs in red and black characters and hardly a roundeye to be seen. I'd got off the main thoroughfare, the Queen's Road West, quite a different creature from Queen's Road Central and Queen's Road East as it faithfully snaked along what had been the old coastline but was now hundreds of metres from the water. What threw me was that Queen's Road West had a different numbering system from the rest of the Queen's Road, starting at No 1 all over again, plus I'd veered off and got lost in the ladder streets on the hillside with their granite rungs set into the pavement to arrest the out of control carts of long ago and not so long ago.

Hopelessly disorientated, I halted, smiled propitiatingly at a scholarly-looking greybeard in a gown and cloth shoes, and as I opened my mouth he was already gone. I tried an old lady who sidestepped me as neatly as Cheech Chong ever had on the basketball-court. Even a beggar with his bowl and exposed stump snubbed me. Then, unprompted, a bespectacled, clerky looking *insik* nonentity sneered as he walked past, *"Hark Gwai."* I didn't need a translation. In my augmenting vocabulary of little-known but frequently used epithets in Asian dialects, I now knew not only the Vietnamese but also the Cantonese for "nigger". Do you blame me if I say I was becoming not so much resentful as bored with this? By way of retaliation I smiled my most brilliant smile – the one with the tungsten carbide edge that was wicked enough to cut – at a group of blue cheongsam-ed schoolgirls. The laggards screamed and raced to catch up with the rest of their barkada of junior xenophobes. This was it, man, the authentic face of Hong Kong hospitality. As I was on the approach, it was as if I was invisible or didn't exist to judge by the blank stares and as my back receded it was, to go by the sniggers over my size and blackness – the veritable buck nigger I was – as if I had abruptly materialised from the thin air over these noisome lanes. I guess if they could have bottled me in the genie's lamp and sold me the fuckers would have done.

Chapter VIII

The Longest Wait – The Voice in my Ear
Painless despatch – Swim-swim

FROM THE HOLD of the Ukrainian freighter to the Smith household had been the shortest of physical distances – less than three miles – but in every other sense the longest. It was easiest to think of it as a parallel universe. Long before the anchor-chain had gone thundering down into the murk of Kowloon Roads and the hawser had captured the mooring-buoy, I'd realised we were arriving in a port from the subdued throbbing of the engines and the greater activity on deck. Unlike human beings the engines are generally the better part of a ship, sound and unfurred when the decayed hull seems only held together by rust, whereas Atty Caladong's dodgy ticker was never betrayed by his natty exterior. As the sounds died, I figured the dangerous part was beginning for me. I was worse than on my own; I had the memories of my dead friends to make me extra-special lonesome. After a while I drew strength from this. I decided I was no longer a free agent or more accurately an individual under the universal impulse of self-preservation. I had an obligation to my friends to live: to remember, to honour them, to seek justice on their behalf if it lay within my powers. Then something strange happened. I heard Dant's voice clear as the period buzzer, man, and the hairs on my forearm bristled like copper plug-wires. That was the first of many times and while maybe the later occasions were mostly just auto-suggestion, this first time I swear was no trick of the senses. I was the one to hear you, Brod. You said, "Hey, Gorilla, when it's tough, the tough gets going."

I lay on my belly, high up in the pipes and ducts, clinging to the asbestos cladding as tenaciously as I ever hugged Ma when it thundered. Then I heard the voice in my head say, "Don't get mad, get even." Yeah, I thought, pay-back time and I pondered also how debt-collectors tended to be more efficient than the actual creditor, because they were, *di ba*, more objective in the importunity, the twisting of arms.

I was a little hungry but I had plenty of water, providentially distilled, dripping from the ceiling as it condensed on the cold surface out of the steam leaks. I'd let the Russkis and the Ukes sozzle themselves in booze. That, too, I was certain, was just a matter of waiting. They didn't have the discipline to be patient.

Those were the longest hours of my life. I reviewed my whole life, OK *lang*? I couldn't see the back of my hands or my arms in the darkness but I could pick up the sickly luminescence of my palms. I imagined myself coming down to this: only a pair of eyeballs and hands, like a crab in its grotto waving its stalks and pincers. I snickered and it became uncontrollable and then it turned to shuddering tears. Shit, I was surprised at myself. I hadn't realised I'd loved Dant so much, still less cared at all for the Brods. Sometimes we are better than we fear we are, though most times worse than we hope. I didn't feel saintly for too long. The pipe I was riding was warm, even through the cladding. It made my balls sweat, then my dick to stir. My most faithful companion, bar none. How had I forgotten he was there. In the darkness, fantasy images were all the more vivid. Haydee's swollen face and slim, naked body swam up before me. My cock got definitively hard. Horribly unbidden, images of the crew joining the Brods in the rape danced before my own eyeballs. I saw the galley-boy bringing out his tool with a queasy smile, blind-siding Haydee as she moaned under Nikita, rubbing it in her ear until Nikita rolled off and nodded OK. I saw Haydee sit up, her wig slipped off, and it was Dant. In one deft movement he unhinged his fan-knife and stuck it up Nikita. My erection went.

There was no night or day in the hold. I remained unsure even of what time we arrived in the harbour. I assumed it was Singapore because that had been Skip's game-plan for us. Even with the possibility of his double-crossing us, I still clung to the idea of Singapore as the peg from which all the rest of the plan might hang.

Probably, I waited more than twenty-four hours, maybe even thirty-six. I had to take a shit at one stage, which I did on the pipe as far away as I could get. I wondered if anyone would ever see my desiccated leavings and put two and two together.

At last, at long last, I felt the moment had come. Now or never – and a panic rose within me at the thought of spending the rest of a short existence in this hole. I dropped down, found I'd underestimated the height, tensed up as I passed what I thought was going to be the moment of impact, with the result that I hit the metal on all-fours with an asteroid-like crash. I fucking thought so, anyhow. I lay there, waiting, determined to get my fingers round preferably Nikita's scrawny throat, but no one came. Up the built-in rungs I went, those hoops my vanished friends had so lately clutched.

What I saw as I came level with the deck was the neon lights of Hong Kong. At the best of times, maybe from first-class on a Boeing, they are an impressive sight but I thought I was looking on the Promised Land. I couldn't stop myself gawping with my body still out only to the waist. My feet drummed as I regarded the emerald, ruby, and sapphire lights and the glow from the skyscrapers. Even the Smiths would exclaim as they saw the sight for the thousandth time. The arrival of my palms on the greasy deck-plate as I overbalanced and fell brought me back to my situation. I rapidly took cover, then looked for a weapon: crowbar, lever, spanner, shit, even a bolt or screw I could use as a brass-knuckle. Nothing. I looked over the side. Usually, staring down, as for instance from the high diving-board of the Artheneum pool, is a giddier, more scrotum-shrinking prospect than looking up, but now it seemed a shorter distance to the water than it had a few days ago looking from our row-boat up the towering hull. I crossed stealthily to the port-side, looking at what I now know as Kowloon. (We were moored to our buoy with the bow to the east). On this side steps with a canvas canopy led to within two feet of the water. It was brilliantly spot-lit, as brightly as if it was an outdoor sports field by night. There was no one around on duty which to me, with the Jesuit-infected mind advance-dirty, bore all the appearances of a trap. It was not a warm night, it was oppressively hot with the south-west monsoon blocked out by the mountains of Hong Kong, 120F as the newspaper told me the next day, but I shivered. The goose-pimples rose on my forearms the way they never had before a game. I knew the reason. I had decided to do what Danton would have wanted me to do for him.

I could have got away without further delay. But everything in me cried for equivalence. I won't dignify it with the name of justice and I won't cheapen it by styling it revenge for I sought it impartially on the behalf of others. Murdering someone in self-defence or in order to escape would, I calculated, have amounted to the greater sin. It was not wrong because I couldn't benefit from it. No self-advantage was involved. I was merely a disc on the scales of justice. It was OK and so what if I would enjoy it.

I could have run into King Kong or my namesake Frankenstein himself and I would have sent them the way of all flesh. At that moment I was Superman saving the world from itself. I was hoping to run into Nikita or the young Slav thug with the shotgun, the piece of shit who'd off-ed Dant, but fate threw me as I peered round and under a wooden hand-rail… the galley-boy. The retarded little cocksucker was tip-toeing along, darting quick glances backwards and sideways with what looked like a small book in his hands. There was no one else in sight and it dawned on me that he as little wanted to be seen as I did, that was why he was in this deserted area amidships.

As he came by I stepped straight out in his path. Like I said, he was a weird-looking little runt with a deformed jaw that was not so much recessive as non-existent but, shit, the scare brought out the light of intelligence in his eyes. Shocked out of his wits, he looked more normal.

I had the advantage of having seen him before. Don't forget, no one in the crew had so much as set eyes on me, let alone had the glimmerings of a suspicion that a survivor from the stowaways that they might have missed was a black man standing a full foot taller and weighing one hundred pounds more than their last victim. I guess black guys weren't too thick on the ground in the Ukraine either.

I put out both arms at once, a very instinctive move for a cager, a wrestler, or a volley-ball player but not for a boxer. I could hear Dant say, "That's how you shoot da puckers too, two-hand Weaver-stance grip, mans." But that's not what I wanted to do, *di ba*? Punching the runt out was not at all my intention, either. I didn't want to do violence to him, inflict pain on him, just eliminate him quickly and cleanly from the face of the earth.

My thumbs pressed the button of his Adam's apple, my left and right index fingers linked on his vertebrae at the back. I squeezed with a smooth but ever-increasing power. I looked into his eyes intently and with curiosity, even solicitude, but without spite. I thought I must look much like Boris Karloff in *The Mummy* rather than *Frankenstein*. I was pretty much under control. The runt wasn't. His eyes were popping as much with terror and shock as the asphyxia. I said, "There's nothing personal about this, my friend. I don't hate you. I'm just collecting the balance for the departed." I hoped saying it made it true. I hoped using a vocabulary and sentiments elevated far beyond the immediate context would magically take me out of that very context. His face was black by now. There was froth around his lips. His eyes rolled back. I guessed mine would also only show white in the circumstances. He gave a little sighing grunt as he went but I kept my grip on him another minute, only dragging him round the corner out of view from the bridge. It was easy as carrying a glove-puppet. When I was sure of him I released the pressure. No doubt about it: I'd sent him to a better place or at least to a deserving destination. I sat him with his back against railings. He was no longer a muppet but a ventriloquist's dummy. On the deck was what he'd been carrying, not a book but a wallet. It was Dant's, with twenty dollars still inside and a photo I never knew he'd carried. It was us after I'd been San Ignatio sports day's Victor Ludorum five years ago. Maybe the galley-boy had received a double-shock when he saw me: a shock of recognition.

I put the wallet in my pocket and wondered what to do. Like, I wanted to make a statement to the evil creeps. I didn't just want to put him over the side. I guess if I'd been wholehearted about it I should have cut his cock off and stuck it in his mouth, but I didn't have that in me. Yet.

After a while I picked him up – he'd now become surprisingly heavy – and draped him over the rail. I lashed his wrists to the bars with his shoelaces, arms spread as if he was about to flap and fly. Then I pulled his pants down round his ankles to expose his bare buns and put his legs through the middle rail and then back in under the bottom one, wedging his loose sneakers in amongst the dust and paint-splashes. There he was, man, ready to take it, like he had all his time on the ship. So much the better if the little fuck stiffened into *rigor mortis* before they found him. As a parting pleasantry, I dipped the rag in his rear-pocket into the grease of a davit and wrote *Noli me tangere* across his back. On the deck I wrote *4-1 Injury Time*.

Instead of going to the bow, I searched first for the rope up which we'd climbed into this death-ship. It was there. I figured it must be for a necessary purpose or they wouldn't leave it out. Not unless they were in the habit of enticing stowaways aboard for their private purposes, which I was still sufficiently unparanoiac to doubt. I was, however, prudent enough to test its hold before entrusting myself to the slimy serpent, looking up every now and then, fully expecting to see Nikita's down-turned face and eye squinting down a revolver barrel at me. I'd had to jump high to get to the end of the rope from the row-boat but, of course, when I hung from the end of it at full arm's reach my toes nearly touched the water. I slipped into the harbour with barely a splash.

Although like most of my physical type I've always been a weak swimmer, I felt safer straight away. Once I was in the darkness beyond the ship's lights I felt much, much better. It was a long swim, more than a mile, but I took it easy. Because I was fit I didn't get tired beyond a certain point: my arms were like lead after ten minutes but never grew any weaker from then. After maybe two hours I came ashore on a sandy beach. I didn't know it then but it was Tuen Mun, a fairly obscure but densely populated place where the last thing they'd expect was a *Tago-ng-Tago*, a TNT. I lay prostrate on the sand a while. I decided I'd simulate death rather than inflict it on anyone who might chance upon my drenched carcass. On the whole people preferred to give a dead body a miss. They were scared of the smell rather than the sight. Although I also didn't know it then, most Hong Kong Chinese would be quite prepared to do nothing at all about a washed-up stranger's body, even saving on the price of an anonymous phone call to the cops. I dug my fingers into what I thought was the clean sand of Singapore. I rolled on to my back. I looked up at the stars and a moon that was beginning the wane. The few tears I shed were lost in the salt water on my cheeks.

CHAPTER IX

Girton Girl – In Front of the Servants – Babyjane
Transubstantiation of Substance – Marooned!: The
Nightwatchman's Tale

MISS NICKY WAS FIFTEEN, seven years younger than Jenny who'd just graduated Arts Bachelor from Girton University, Cambridge. Jenny was wondering what to do and had returned to her family to do the pondering. I could see it starting to get to her. Hong Kong was not the place to be purpose-less. No such indecision affected Nicky. She was having a good time at her school in Hong Kong. Jenny had boarded at a very exclusive school in England. Commander and Mrs Smith still groaned about the fees outside Jenny's hearing. Nicky's Hong Kong fees were nearly as steep as her sister's had been – though I reflected that her parents didn't have the air-fares to find – so parsimony had not been the reason they had kept her with them.

"We lost her growing-up years, darling," Mrs Smith told her husband on the verandah when the girls were out. She spoke in the serious, objective way they had of discussing intimate matters or family mistakes, a tone of voice which was peculiarly theirs, which fell just short of scolding or assigning blame because it was unfocussed on anybody, even themselves. I couldn't have spoken like that; Atty Caladong couldn't have spoken like that; even Fr. Paul though from the same social class and the countryman of the Smiths, couldn't have spoken like that. I guess Butch Tan Sy came the closest: the dispassionate analysis he'd make of our tactical errors during the break, never pointing the finger, so as not to to discourage or divide us.

"Mm," replied Commander Smith.

"I looked round and we'd lost our little girl. She'd come out for the hols once a year…"

"More like twice, dear," corrected Commander Smith.

"Well, some years it wasn't. And even with a gap of six months they change so much, dear, you must admit that…"

"I'm not arguing with you, dear."

"I'd catch up every time and adjust but then one day there was no catching up. She was gone, our Nennifa. There was the Girton Miss standing in front of me instead."

"Mm."

"That's why I'd never grudge the fees here, never mind it's an arm and a leg."

"And the other leg."

"Well, you were quite free to send her elsewhere."

"I'm in complete agreement, dear. It's worth any number of trips to Phuket foregone."

"Although I don't like that accent Nicky's picked up. Not quite American, someone's funny idea of American. Pseudo-American, I suppose. Perhaps that's how they sound in Hawaii."

"Chi-chi is the word you're looking for, I think. She'll grow out of it. There are worse things to pick up than an accent."

"Just a moment. N–I–F–O–T–S. Are you looking for something to do, Rey?"

"Yes, Mum. What is your order, Mum?"

"Just give the car another shine, old chap, will you?"

"Yes, sir."

In all the time I worked as their chauffeur I was never able to work out that little acronymic code of theirs. It remained as enigmatic as the fragment of Fr. Boy's tattoo I saw, coming off the vaulting-horse. What I knew then was that it referred to me and to Babyjane, and was uttered when they were discussing something confidential they'd rather we didn't hear.

As far as the substance of this particular discussion was concerned, I agreed with them. Sending your children away from you was a crazy thing. They'd become strangers – Danton and I could have told anybody that. Unless there was a compelling reason for it, such as the great climb we two had thought we were making, it was like deliberately cutting off the tip of your finger. Certainly, doing it because everybody else in your social set did it was not a good enough reason.

There existed a negative aspect to the Smiths – not the ludicrous, stiff Brits their American friends made affectionate fun of, but something deeper which was the bad sister of their intrinsic goodness. There was a chilly, aloof side to them as well, not dissimilar to Fr. Paul, which could disconcert the Canadian engineer and the New Zealand teacher who were their good friends, as well as a syrupy *Pinoy* like me. Cold fish was their English expression, which nicely encapsulated their frigid English-ness. One of the places they learned this necessary frostiness was at schools like Miss Jenny's or, even worse, the boys' version of them: if you kept emotion at arm's length, people at a distance instead of in a Philippine huddle, social temperature dropped. The plus side was that wounds don't go septic nearly so quickly in a temperate climate. There, necrotic tissue will take longer to corrupt. There, enemies don't need to be put on ice.

The funny thing was that Jenny had taken after her mother, more than Nicky had. Successful marriages often involve the attraction of opposites: strength finding frailty appealing more often than you would think frailty would be drawn to strength. Mrs Smith was a vulnerable person. The more you knew her, the more apparent it became behind the facade of reserve and correctness. It would have been unfair to call her a neurotic but she wasn't so far off it that one could laugh comfortably at the notion. Poor Mrs Smith was a martyr to her fairness. The white skin that Ma and her cohorts sought so vainly and so assiduously through their blanching soaps and blocking lotions left Mrs Smith at the mercy of the tropical sun. That beach and swimsuit were impossible for her, even with a hat, dark-glasses, and sun-screen of the highest factor, was a foregone conclusion, but even leaving her arms bare in a sleeveless frock in the city at midday would result in a penalty. She didn't just get the simple redness of sun-burn and the white tatters of blistering skin to follow but purple blotches, maculations, and ulcers followed by a clear, weeping exudate that hardened into a yellow crust. She looked like a dermatological relief-map of marsh-land and mountain. This had a clear physical cause as did her allergies to chicken and chocolate which could bring about attacks of hives even more spectacular than the sun-burn. What was worse was the rash and the itchy scaling to which no discernible cause could be ascribed. "Psychosomatic," said Jenny, a word new to me which I looked up in the Smith's two-volume Oxford English Dictionary with pleasure, but which caused a spasm of irritation to pass across Mrs Smith's face. Often enough, it's who a remark comes from which is the problem rather than the content itself, and so it was in this instance. If it had been Commander Smith, Mrs Smith would just have inquired with genuine interest, "Do you think that's possible, dear?" From the daughter who'd taken after her, it sounded like a reproach.

Nicky got on much better with her mother. There was no tension at all between them. This was hardly surprising as her parents had a rock-solid marriage and Nicky was merely a young, female equivalent of her father: the same shrewd-eyed steadiness, the cheery nonchalance. When you saw it in Commander Smith it had masculine overtones: never the machismo of the Latin, for he was an intelligent and sensitive man trapped in the Goldfinger body, but there was a distinct whiff of nautical sangfroid under fire, cool hardihood of the "Signals? I see no signals," variety. In the adolescent but unmistakably feminine form of Miss Nicky, purged of whatever portion of male bravado remained in the Commander, it was distilled as pure human essence. "She da one," I could imagine Danton saying, "to be a cool little chick, mans. Cute, too." I can't pin down a particular instance of behaviour or anything she said; it was more in the time she'd take to react to a slight or an unpleasant surprise, the small pause before she'd make a reply or a comment, which was always one notch understated for the particular circumstances. She already had a startlingly deep voice in her petite frame. She was built more like a *pinay* than a 'Merikana and, with our love for nicknames and aliases, ten to one we'd have called her *Dugdug*, "Thunder". This I didn't presume to tell her. Early on, I'd decided never to treat the Smiths with less respect than I would have rich Filipinos simply because I knew I could get away with more. It was my way of thanking them, though they'd never know it.

Mrs Smith called Nicky "a very self-possessed young Miss," to which the young Miss in question would respond with barely discernible amusement. On the other hand, the words which always seemed to be hovering about Mrs Smith's own lips and which defined her best – though in point of fact I believe I only heard her utter them once – were, "Well, I never," a very English expression which she would have deemed equally appropriate to greet an attack by Sumatran pirates during a launch picnic or the discovery of a whole mouse buried in a pork pie.

Our routine called for me to drive Nicky and her father to school and work in the morning, Nicky alighting first. At five in the afternoon I'd take Nicky home, then at seven I'd collect Commander Smith, sometimes later if he had emergency appointments. If they went to a restaurant for what Mrs Smith quaintly called "Chinese chow", I'd be required at nine p.m. On Fridays and Saturdays I could be driving them home from parties as late as two a.m., Mrs Smith endearingly jolly with alcohol and society, Commander Smith merely required to pretend to listen. Even on weekdays Miss Jenny slept in till at least half past eleven a.m. I thought this was a cause as well as a symptom of gradual demoralisation but as usual kept my counsel. It did mean she was spending most of her time with her mother, the most similar and incompatible members of what was nevertheless still always a happy household. Mrs Smith did her best to occupy and divert this twenty-two-year old stranger, who was at least twice as intensively educated and three times better read than herself, in much the same way as eighteen years previously she'd brought out the crayons and colouring-books on rainy afternoons in Portsmouth. The closest they came to what Babyjane called "fighting" was when Mrs Smith momentarily lost patience and told her oldest daughter, "Just buck up, will you, darling," followed by Jenny's indignant, "Mums!" I do believe Babyjane mistook Mrs Smith's seemly exhortation for an exotic variant on that four-letter verb as common in the RP as the Anglo-Saxon countries. After Jenny had gone into the garden with her *Spectator*, Babyjane, who was a born sycophant and informer, commented, "Missy so high blood today, Mum. Why? She's so naughty," only to be rewarded with a terse instruction to clean the French windows she'd polished only three days previously. Watching Mrs Smith handle Babyjane was like seeing antibody absorb antigen.

Babyjane was a thief. Although the value of what she took was trifling, she was a big-time thief. She devoted an extraordinary amount of planning and ingenuity to stealing disproportionately petty amounts of cash or cheap household goods from the Smiths. In a Filipina with wider horizons or greater ambitions, better education and a larger appetite, say Imelda or Atty Caladong's No 2, the same or a lesser amount of wiles and patience would have netted millions. Babyjane was satisfied with a few dollars at a time, a trickle acceptable to her so long as it was constant. She stole in such clever ways that the Smiths were barely aware of it; it was like a sub-symptomatic illness. At the back of their minds, I think they knew something was amiss, certainly the Commander, but they didn't want to admit it to themselves. For them, it wasn't like having rats infesting the house, which one could poison or trap without compunction, it was more like having to put the family pet down. They liked Babyjane and they treated her well. The maid's quirks were to them novel and idiosyncratic, a source of affectionate amusement, as were her quaint ratiocinative processes and vocabulary. Even if they hadn't liked her, they would still have treated her well. They paid her government-set wage a few days early every month, gave her a Christmas bonus, and when Babyjane's father died of a *bagoong* and soya-sauce induced stroke footed her return air-fare to the RP out of the bounty their hearts held. For all this, Babyjane was sincerely grateful. She prayed for the Smiths, she told me. I completely believed her when she said she had spent five pesos buying candles to burn for them in church as intercession for their Protestant souls, so that they should not fry in eternity. When Jenny mentioned her new Girton atheism to her mother, Babyjane rolled her eyes in horror and, revelling in the scandal, hurried away to rattle off a volley of prophylactic rosaries. Being sincerely grateful to the Smiths didn't stop her conspiring with the Filipino travel club to show her benefactors the undiscounted ticket and pocketing the difference. And when she came back, she continued the pilfering.

Stealing from a Caucasian employer was like taking candy from the fist of a sleeping baby. The Filipina would feel a mixture of two opposing sensations: superiority and inferiority. The former for the obtuseness of the foreigner compared to the wiliness of the *pinay*, B'rer rabbit outwitting someone much stronger and more powerful than himself. The second sensation because the victim was, on the whole, more magnanimous, more generous, and larger-souled than they, a difference which was also symbolised by purely physical size, a very basic factor never to be underestimated. Sometimes spiteful children can feel superior to the kindly adults they are bamboozling, or whose property they are vandalising, and so it was with the complacency with which Babyjane pilfered from her indulgent employers.

"I could have sworn there was a spare tube of Colgate in the cupboard," would run the mystified refrain, with permutations on, "another bar of soap," "the old pink towel I had," and – with the beginnings of a threat from Miss Nicky to unilaterally drop the scales from her eyes, "the strap-less bra Jenny brought me from Marks and Sparks."

Babyjane would play the part of concerned spectator, eyes round, lips pursed to make the oo-ing sounds of Philippine assuagement. She didn't fool me. The innocent response from her ilk would have been fatalistic detachment of interest and sympathy. On this occasion, feeling the trail leading uncomfortably closely and warmly to her, Nicky in hot pursuit, Babyjane absented herself to her province of the laundry-room, whence she returned twenty minutes later, brandishing the brassiere in triumph. (I imagined her exercising the superb self-control counting off the inculpating minutes which would have been better employed controlling her klepto's propensity in the first place). Less than five minutes would have amounted to a frank admission of guilt. Thirty provided her with a moral weapon purpose-designed to make little Nicky feel joy at the serendipitous discovery and then guilt for her misplaced suspicions. Once, speaking with great earnestness, Babyjane said, "Mum, Serr, I fray St Anthony."

"St Anthony, Babyjane?"

"O, Serr. He is da fatron saint of da lost objects."

Where cash was concerned Babyjane was a sorcerer, the wizard. She had Commander Smith, who was no slouch, going every which way and I think Mrs Smith never even knew she was leaking her small change. I caught Babyjane putting her hand in the Commander's pants pockets once when the Smiths were out. The Commander had sent me back in a hurry from a Christening to get Miss Nicky's disc camera. I watched Babyjane through the open door of the master bedroom for a good minute unobserved. She was counting what there was, her lips moving with the tally. She shook her head in annoyance, then put the wad back in the pocket. I moved silently away, before loudly banging the front door. When I came back she had returned to the kitchen. Swiftly, I put my hand in the Commander's pocket and counted. It was exactly thirty Hong Kong dollars. I replaced the pants over the back of the chair and bugged out. My heart was beating harder than before a match against Ateneo. It had been a dumb thing to do, but now I was hooked. Better than shabu, it was an intellectual rush. I was Holmes the sleuth on his seven per cent solution, but for me adrenalin not cocaine. Nothing beat the excitement of sneaking into the bedroom or Commander Smith's study and counting what he had. Once, if I'd been a dotard, I could have expired as I retrieved his jacket from the back seat of the car while I was waiting in the multi-storey park and got caught opening his wallet. I nearly puked up my heart as Commander Smith's familiar face appeared at my wound-down window.

"Ticket's in the breast-pocket, Rey," he said kindly. "That bloody machine's an absolute bugger. Stops you for half an hour if you've lost it and never mind the people in the queue behind wanting to throttle you. London's no different."

"Serr," I said wanly. I don't think he was showing ultra-nobility by letting me off the hook or was embarrassed by the prospect of a scene in the way an Asian might be (Atty Caladong doubtless ignoring the transgression at the time and having the goons maul the malefactor later). I think he just didn't even consider the possibility that I'd do anything dishonest to him. And he was right, like he was right about most things, though the fact of being totally innocent and well-intentioned but being armed with such a preposterous explanation that I could never hope to be believed if apprehended was what gave my spot-checks such chilli spice.

What I discovered was that Babyjane worked on rules as strictly self-imposed as those of a system-player at roulette. For instance, she hadn't purloined a cent of the Commander's thirty dollars. She abhorred a round sum, you see. A hundred dollars, a thousand dollars would have remained integral, as immune against Babyjane's depredations as if protected by a warlock's spell. What magic in numerology? Not really. Babyjane knew these were convenient figures for Commander Smith to remember. If she transmuted sixty seven to sixty three it would be difficult to put a finger on it. Or a bold feat of prestidigitation like shaving one thousand four hundred and fifty three down to one thousand three hundred and fifty three could be akin to heroic surgery with a successful outcome. She rarely took money that was left out on dressing-table or cabinet, even haphazardly strewn, usually from clothing and preferably cash that hadn't been collected into a wad. It was less likely to have been counted. Later, I noticed something that gave even me, with my privileged knowledge, second thought. Like the forms of early life on earth, Commander Smith's cash was becoming subject to parturition and division in order to multiply, pullulating like a pile of glowing, necromantic frog spawn, changing colour more rapidly than a magic chameleon, altering physical size at will while remaining exactly the same in essence: four red hundred dollar notes, three blue fifties, five green tens, and six brown fives had been philtred into three red hundreds, five blue fifties, six green tens, and four brown fives.

Soon, came her master-stroke: Commander Smith's pile *increased* from thirty three dollars to thirty five. Man, I was awestruck. This wasn't Philippine guile: it was venture capitalism.

Back home Filipino employers would have taken it in their stride; it was an unspoken part of the agreement. They expected it. They cut the wage to the very minimum; the servant was just putting a little flesh on the bone. And the employer had his own tricks to balance everything up at the end, such as routinely not paying the final month's salary after the maid had put in the labour. I wouldn't like to say all servants stole but it would be a safe assumption that the majority did. Babyjane and the cronies she urban-picknicked with every Sunday earned more than a PAF Colonel but asking them to control themselves was like requesting the scorpion not to sting.

I liked all this probably even less than the Smiths would have done, had they determined to be cognisant of what was going on under their long noses. Sure, I wanted to protect them but, from a self-interested point of view, I didn't want Mrs Smith to take it into her head that I was the one with light fingers. That would have really hurt. As it was, it wasn't a great feeling. I had a more acute sense of the shame which afflicted many Filipinos when they found Caucasian friends for whom they had a real affection surrounded by other Filipinos. It was as if everyone was wearing a badge invisible to the Westerner but to ourselves plain writ, THIEF. One wore one oneself. It was maybe like being the benevolent vampire at the Carnival of the Spectres, riding shot-gun on a much-beloved human. I could see why Fr. Paul's cerebral *pinoy* pals might have found his caustic cynicism rather a relief.

To have denounced Babyjane to the Commander would have gone against the grain, would have done so even before I came under the influence of the San Ignatio fathers, even before Danton went to Ireland, for Babyjane and I were castaways adrift in the same boat. Commander Smith wouldn't have welcomed it and, besides, I was in no position to have my own credentials scrutinised should Babyjane riposte with a counter-denunciation taken outside the household.

Will you believe me if I say I was not once tempted to steal from my benevolent employers? Only I sometimes became angry with them, with an unjustified and misdirected anger which I, nevertheless, could not suppress. Look at it from the employee's point of view: every time the servant refrained from stealing from the master he practised a theft against himself. The money left lying out there did not so much present temptation as a wide-open commercial opportunity. It would have been so easily added to the menial's account, his or her little store in the world. Practising self-denial every time one went past it amounted to a terrible asceticism. One nurtured a grudge against the employer and, in time, came to think of him or her not so much as oppressor but as depriver, robber. That's how Babyjane thought of the benevolent Smiths.

There was only one solution, the extra-judicial one. I became a self-appointed vigilante. I salvaged the Smiths' money with the same enthusiasm that Metro Manila police chiefs might salvage petty criminals, with the difference that they took riff-raff out of currency and dumped their half-naked corpses in privy places, while I put the Smiths' petty cash back in circulation by removing it from under Babyjane's mattress and restoring it to its old haunts in the Commander's clothing.

Balancing accounts on my scales, I felt like God. For this was when I first got on to the path that later led me to extreme courses, to usurping His prerogative of doling out the *halo*es. Meanwhile, Babyjane bought herself a large crucifix. She also got her hands on that potent protective idol – a Visayan Santo Nino, the golden-haired baby Jesus in crown and crimson cloak. These she installed in her room, with a bunch of garlic for good measure. And as she passed about her duties in subdued fashion I saw her from time to time surreptitiously cross herself as she hurried past my holy of holies, the Smith bedroom.

ON THOSE RARE OCCASIONS when things got too much for me with Babyjane (and I couldn't indulge my bent of settling accounts) I'd go and chew the fat with my pal Ah Biu, the dejected Chinese watchman. He was different from your average Hong Kong Chinese for the very good reason that he wasn't one of them, though I'd known him for a long time before he revealed this to me. He was in his fifties but baby-faced, still with a thick head of oily black hair he denied dyeing. When it rained I'd tell him the colour was running and he could never refrain from patting his neck and inspecting his fingers. Biu never retaliated by commenting on my own genuine blackness, which was highly unusual. He took me as he found me and never called me a *hark gwai* but addressed me as *Ah Bun Lo, Pal Pinoy*. Biu loved classical music. It was the great solace of his life, I mean Western music; he would listen to Mozart, Beethoven, and Mahler for hours on his Walkman, greatly reducing his effectiveness as a watchman but enhancing his reputation with the round-eyes whose property he guarded.

I think great sports stars, inspirational teachers, brilliant philosophers are born, not made. But I think nice people are made, not born. My friend Drigo the Cuban would later talk about "the Argentinian that is in all of us," the braggart, the rapist, the gloater. What knocks him out of us faster than anything is misfortune. You have to have been down and out yourself to feel pity for the down and out. Biu didn't give me a hard time because he'd had one himself. He was even on good terms with Babyjane, that was what a tolerant guy he was, and the *pinay* domestic helps in his building would bring him back biscuits and rice-toppings from town on Sundays. Sometimes he'd come and give me a hand as I polished the Smith Honda but more often than not he'd wave me into his cubbyhole. This was the broom-cupboard in the courtyard of the small block of apartments, or flats as they were called in British Hong Kong, that he was charged with guarding. In fact, he had made himself very comfortable in there with a solid wooden bed, a Japanese hi-fi, and electric thermos-flask that boiled and stored water for tea, and nice embroidered covers on the walls and bedside table. It was OK if you were a small person; I tended to fill the space.

But, "It's not so bad," Biu would say in Cantonese. He spoke virtually no English; I spoke almost no Chinese, but we communicated. When one of the helps who spoke fluent Cantonese was there, it was like a summit between heads of state. We got on famously as Fr. Paul would say.

"Hong Kong people," Biu told me, "are cruel and unfeeling because they have never suffered. Look at the way they treat the poor Vietnamese who wash up here in their boats."

I nodded. They did treat them like shit. For all that Michael and Em had endured in Palawan in the way of frustrations and delays, they were far better off being held by Filipinos.

"But you're not like that, Biu," I said.

"I have done bad things," he replied, "but only because I had to, not because I enjoyed it." He smiled at me, a beam of pure happiness illuminating his face. "Mine is the saddest story," he chuckled. "Did you think I was born here or in China because my face looks the same as everybody else's? No, I am from Borneo.

"When I was thirteen, distant relatives took me on holiday to their home village in China…"

I nodded politely to Biu. I had no idea I was going to hear about somebody more hard done-by than my precious self.

"My widowed mother was pleased to acquiesce – they told her my father had some small heirlooms there I could bring out. But these relatives cloaked a sly design! They had a young nephew in the village they wished to take out. It was hard in Communist times. One morning I woke up. They were gone, together with my travel documents and their nephew. They'd switched our identities!

"Altogether I was stuck in China for more than twenty years. I became a Red Guard. I did all kinds of terrible things – pulled the stuffing out of people's Western sofas and then the hair out of their heads before beating them to death. Not because I wanted to but because I had to. I was part of a group and in a group the best come down to the level of the worst.

"I'll probably die in this cubby-hole. It's not so bad."

"Did you ever see your family again?" I asked as softly as I could.

"Never. I think my mother died while I was in China. She never replied to my letters and she would have done had she been alive. Here, have another cup of tea," and with that Ah Biu put his earphones on and smiled with the bliss of his beloved music.

CHAPTER X

THE SMITHS weren't exactly what you'd call Old China Hands but they were by no means greenhorns. After leaving the navy, Commander Smith had bought a practice in Surrey, then, when that had failed to live up to expectations, gone to Singapore. They'd stayed there nearly three years. From what I could piece together the island republic had been more to Mrs Smith's taste than either her husband's or daughters'. They'd lived near Tanglin Road with another Filipina, called Mary-Anne, to wait on them but no chauffeur. Apparently the vehicular tax was already so high a driver as added expense was uncontemplatable. This perhaps saved me embarrassment as my performance could not be compared with any predecessor's. Mary-Anne, whose name still figured frequently, usually in piercing whispers when Babyjane was around, had clearly been a much more satisfactory maid than Babyjane who was always cack-handed (as Fr. Paul would have put it) except when she was thieving. Commander Smith had retained their flat in Singapore as an investment and rented in Hong Kong (when as the subsequent graphical comparisons of Jenny showed, he should have done the very opposite). He had also left their Lexus there, a far superior model of automobile to the Civic I drove round Hong Kong at the Smith beck and call. I was provided with a pager on my belt – the cheapest form of cellular communication – which to avoid anti-social disturbance vibrated instead of sounding. Then I'd look at the messages running across the tiny screen: Pick us up at Dragon Seed Dept Store at 4:11 p.m. Return home to take Nicky to the tennis-club. Go to the surgery and get my Number 5 wood.

After Manila, driving in Hong Kong was a cinch, once I'd adjusted to travelling on the left hand side of the road. The granny-ish approach for which Noy Demosthenes had chided me suited the Smiths just fine. They had no desire to travel at the speed of fright, *di ba*?

The three years they had spent in Singapore meant that they, and thus I, knew a disproportionate number of Singaporeans in Hong Kong. These included Commander Smith's receptionist and dental nurse whom he'd brought with him to the Crown Colony, so impressed had he been with them, as well as these young women's set of compatriots. It was easy for Westerners to befriend Singaporeans. In fact, when I think about it, no other folk in the whole world who lived at the equator were quite so befriendable by Caucasians as Singaporeans. It was as if they'd been put down by Divine oversight in quite the wrong latitude, their true situation belonging many degrees North, like Britain, or South, like New Zealand. In the hot spots of the world physical danger and the language barrier are what usually prevent intercourse between native and foreigner, *di ba*? Neither of these fences circumvallated Singaporeans and Westerners and the latter certainly were in no danger of being eaten by the former. Singaporeans were as close as Asians can get to being small Caucasians with straight hair and slanty eyes. Of course, I mean that it was easy for Hong Kong expatriates like the Smiths to get close to Singaporeans, not for members of the expat underclass like me. Singaporeans had a low opinion of the *pinoy*, even if many of us spoke English as well as they did. We were like wasps without the sting, *di ba*?

Jenny was the Smith most enamoured of the notion of possessing Asian friends, while Nicky was the one who actually had them, a little *barkada* of multi-national teeny-boppers. However, Jenny did have a Malaysian-Chinese admirer. It would have been too much to call him a boyfriend.

Nicola still teased her older sister about Jerome, eliciting a conspiratorial grin from Jenny which inclined me to think she had been trifling with him. In Singapore he'd, apparently, taken her to Newton Circus and the Satay Club a few times; they'd been to Chinese-language cinema, Jerome taking advantage of the opportunity to translate in whispers into Jenny's ear, and they'd eaten curried giant prawns off banana leaves at an Indian Club which was the only memorable thing about poor Jerome for Jenny. She'd enjoyed that, but he'd baulked at *pan* afterwards. She'd had his as well. He still phoned a lot. One thing I knew from the Smiths' tut-tuttings over their HK Telecom bill and the rueful comparisons they drew with their ones in Singapore, was that Singapore had the cheapest phone rates in the world. (Their bill would have been a great deal smaller if Babyjane hadn't been in the habit of phoning the Philippines when they were out, unbeknownst to them as calls were not yet itemised). All the same it must have been costing Jerome a bundle of ringgit and Sing dollars to court Jenny down the wire and, unless his job was bringing him regularly to Hong Kong, even more on the airfare. They'd have long, desultory conversations about nothing much. Jenny would rest the receiver on her shoulder and file her nails or signal to Nicky for the bottle of varnish. Sometimes she'd pick up one of Nicky's teen-zines off the phone-table and flick through it in preference to Jerome's monologue.

He was, I think, too nervous to ask her a direct question. Not, "Will you marry me?" or "Will you sleep with me?" but even, "Do you like me?" in case he met with a direct rebuff. This would have been unlikely as Jenny, whatever the uneasy stage of life she presently discovered herself in, was essentially a kind and gracious girl. She was far more likely to accept a date against her own inclinations than to manufacture some tactful excuse. She'd have done this even for an English boy, but was additionally at pains to cater at all times to the oriental concept of "face". Sometimes when everyone was out I'd be the one to field Jerome's increasingly plaintive calls. I tried to speak kindly and reassuringly to him but don't think I got through; he adopted a distant and impersonal tone when he heard my male voice. Once, I heard him get very short shrift from Babyjane. "No, go out already a long time," she snapped. "Why you always da one to be calling, hah?" He'd made his excuses and hung up before I could get to the receiver. Atheism and boys on the phone, the cocktail of depravity for Babyjane. But Jerome was by no means a typical name for a Malaysian or even a Singaporean. Most of them wore their consonant-heavy monickers like emblems of Chinkiness: Ng Chok Bing, Lim Teck Por. The Romanisation of the Chinese ideograms tended not to correspond with the two conventional academic systems Fr. Paul had explained to us during a discussion of Ezra Pound, one of his favourite writers; so the names of quite conventional human beings often seemed outlandish to me. Had Babyjane been capable of two-step logical thought as well as rapid mental arithmetic she might have deduced there was a high probability of Jerome being a Roman Catholic. In which case Jerome would have found a fifth columnist in Jenny's household: a co-conspirator, willing to advance his suit at every opportunity and relay intelligence about his prospects and any possible rivals. But Jerome languished.

Months later, I was driving Jenny, Nicky, Mrs Smith, and two American currency-traders younger than Jenny, from the "country" club.

"Yeah, the Hong Kong guys are wimps," one of the American boys said *à propos* the perennial topic of discussion amongst expatriates, the shortcomings of the host country and its population. He himself had the anaemic pallor that comes from looking intently into a fourteen-inch monitor ten hours a day. "The guys are kinda lacking in *cojones*. Same with the Penang Chinese and the Singapore fellers. But the Singapore gals are the ones wearing the pants. Go-getters, right, Al?"

"*Aggressive* go-getters," Al corroborated. "Yeah, the guys are mostly wimps."

"Jenny would know about that," Nicky said slyly. Jenny pretended to throttle her younger sister. I drew up at a red light. "That's not really fair, Al," Mrs Smith said. "Their culture is different."

"They're wimps," Nicky said, with tired fifteen-year-old's conviction, as if knowing the score adults would rather not. "Jerome was a wimp. Nice but a wimp. A wimp but nice."

"Would that have been Jerome Chow, the analyst from the Hongkers and Chancres?" asked Al with a lack of concern that certainly didn't fool me. "I thought he was from Hong Kong?"

"No," said Jenny. "This Jerome's a Flight Captain with Goldair. He was in the Air Force before. He was a fighter pilot. He flew F-whatever they are. He's a fifth dan at Tae Kwan Do."

At that moment the light changed to green.

"Goodness me, Rey!" exclaimed Mrs Smith as horns sounded behind us. "It's not like you to stall the car."

SINGAPORE GIRL, as everyone including the Als of this world knew, was an entirely different kettle of fish from *Homo Singaporensis*. Singapore Girl couldn't get away from the likes of me, of course, quickly enough but she latched on to the unattached Caucasian male with a speed and efficiency that were wondrous to behold. And if he happened to be already married so far from being discouraged SG took it as a personal challenge to her mettle.

The White Wife lived in fear and dread of the Asian Chick, of Miss Hong Kong, sometimes, of Miss Philippines somewhat more but primarily of Singapore Girl.

"Oo, how I hate those scheming little bitches," I heard one of Jenny's friends say at the poolside of the club. This cool young married, only three or four years older than Jenny and still svelte as Nicky, spoke with real intensity as one who felt genuinely threatened. There came a whole chorus of agreement, the more raucous from the older ones: "Sly little cows", "Stoop to anything", "They're utterly mercenary, it's only tum they're looking after", "Yes, but that's what gives them the motivation."

Jenny looked embarrassed but didn't argue. She was unlike a well-off Filipina or even American in that the last thing she wanted to do was flaunt her educational advantages. The Smiths would have thought it vulgar. Jenny would have, on principle, liked to contradict the general opinion. I could see one of her red flag words "racist" hovering over her head. But she was one of the few there who'd had a college education, let alone the benefit of an elite institution like Girton U., and she didn't want to give herself airs of superiority. Personally, I didn't like this set. Jenny *was* smarter than they were and shouldn't have been bashful about it. They were affluent, they led pampered, insulated lives through the jobs their husbands had, but they didn't have two brain-cells to rub together. As Fr. Paul liked to say, true wealth was knowledge. Apart from Jenny, there was only one other unattached girl there in the deck-chairs, Deirdre, who taught piano at an international school (not Nicky's). She was the bitterest of all. "Well, it's alright for you lot," she said. "At least you've got men for them to pinch. They don't even look at me, our men, I mean." Another chorus ensued, this time of formulaic contradiction. "No, seriously," Deirdre insisted. "I've no social life at all. I can't remember the last time I had a date. The guys just aren't interested in me. I'm Whisky Tango, I'm White Trash. If you're not five feet tall with long black hair and slitty eyes they just don't want to touch you with a barge-pole."

"And no tits, of course," said the cool young married. This last generated the kind of mirth and comments that wouldn't have been out of place in Butch's locker-room, the Frat, or probably the focsle of a Ukrainian freighter. I never stopped being amazed at how dirty-mouthed the middle-class 'Merikana could be, compared to our girls. Perhaps that was part of the problem.

"*Submissive* schemers," said the sunbather next to Deirdre, a podgy banker's wife. "We should feel sorry for the men, actually. They're the real victims. It's like the Trojan Horse."

"The last thing the little yellow perils use is Trojans," said the cool married to further hilarity. I permitted myself a small smile, which actually blended me in; it made me less conspicuous than a blank face and feigned deafness would have done. I was up for all the servant's tics and tricks by now. The ladies spoke quite freely in front of me because I wasn't a man to them, but a menial. That was the power of thought for you, of social subordination. At twenty-one I was, to say the least, an impressive physical specimen and my colour didn't make me less virile. Ma's little prodigy at the stand-pipe had become as sex-less as *Homo Singaporensis* to these ladies at leisure.

When I was in attendance pool-side it was compulsory for me to remove my shoes and then, as a consequence – but out of personal choice – my socks. I was wimp enough to dread them getting damp. Early on, I'd been given a curt reproof by the Chinese club manager, "You, no shoes allow here," and had to stoop in rapid compliance. He didn't like me, whether it was worse that I was a Filipino or black I don't know. Knowing Hong Kong Chinese, I should say he despised me for the former and feared me for the latter. The pool-side board forbade yayas, amahs, maids, and nannies from remaining within the area but, as Nicky had pointed out to the manager, I was none of these. Like a good Hong Konger, he'd gone by the letter of the law even when unfavourable to him.

Standing fully-dressed barefoot wasn't a great ignominy. The foible of Hong Kong men was to stand round in their under-briefs. For their part, Singaporeans of both sexes whipped off their brogues or their stilletoes, their moccasins or their sandals, followed in short order by ankle-length Argylls or pop-sox. This happened at every opportunity in the non-office context, say, quite staid social gatherings. Anyhow, standing there in my naked feet, listening penitentially to the ladies' opinions, I saw Nicky nudge one of her classmates and the teenagers both giggle. If you'd drawn a line from their eyes, it would have led straight to my feet. I smiled a small smile of baffled tolerance and moved my toes. Don't ask me why, back home we considered it polite to wiggle looked-at piggies.

Perched sideways on the driver's seat of the Smith's car with the door open, dusting off the soles of my feet, I caught Nicky and her school-friend giggling again.

"Miss Nicky," I asked, "maybe I can share your joke?"

Further tittering.

"Maybe something to do with my shoes? Because they're so big?"

"It's your feet, Rey."

Jenny shoved her younger sister, but not jokingly. "That's enough, Nik."

"Please, Miss Nicky, I can take it."

"Well, OK, they *are* big, Rey but, OK, they're so … black. I mean your nails, not the skin. They're completely black, like an animal."

"Nik!"

"I've never seen anything like it. I'm sure other black men haven't got nails like that."

I laughed. "You're right, Miss. I used to play a lot of sport and my feet never recovered. Just from running five miles every day and then the jumping and landing on court, it never hurt but the pounding started blood under the nails, just bruises, and, like I say, it never got back to normal. I guess it would look a lot worse on a white guy, *di ba*?"

"Now, that's very nice of you, Rey," Jenny said. "And you, young lady, keep your NF observations to yourself."

"I'm only six years younger than you, Jens," Nicky said with ominous calm.

I sprang round and opened the doors for them, doing my best to nip this sisterly altercation in the bud. "Funny you noticed it, Miss Nicky," I said. "Back home, I'd look at girls' nails and I'd think, wow, that pedicure must have hurt and, you know, maybe all the time the girls were feeling sorry for me instead."

"Oh?"

"By the way, Miss Jenny, help with me my British idiom. NF is the same as Naff?"

"No, it isn't, Rey."

"Oh yes, it is, Jens."

They both burst out laughing, leaving me none the wiser, but happy to see harmony restored. I hated conflict and, above all, it upset me to see the Smiths argue. We can't live without our illusions, even the worst of us.

MAVIS WONG AND IRENE WOO JUK SAU were respectively Commander Smith's dental nurse and appointments secretary, while Cathy Lim Mai Ling was Jenny's aerobics instructor. Irene at thirty-one was the oldest while Mavis and Cathy were in their mid-twenties. Funnily enough, Irene with her page-boy and round, ingenuous face looked the youngest of the trio. All were single, all were slim, attractive, and vivacious in that special indefinable way of Singapore Girl. I wouldn't, actually, have described any of them as scheming little bitches who'd stoop to anything, but then I was a man, *di ba*, and part of being a man, according to the swimming-pool set, was infinite gullibility in the presence of the slanty-eyed connivers, no? Mavis and Cathy had been at school together, then had parted ways in the Singapore educational system. They'd met again at one of the Smith's Hong Kong lawn parties, four months after my arrival. "M-a-a-a-a-vis, I thought you were still nine, lah," Cathy exclaimed. "She was my best friend," she explained to an indulgent thirty-something diplomat hovering nearby.

"I was?" Mavis joked. She was a capable young woman, dark-skinned with very prominent cheek-bones and slender limbs. I knew Commander Smith liked and respected her; he'd told Mrs Smith she was the best extra pair of hands in the surgery he'd ever had, able to anticipate his requests and with instant recall for where the smallest instruments and accessories were to be found. "She's never held a cross word against me, either," Commander Smith had added, "which was more than you could say of the girls the agency used to send me in Kingston."

"I thought you hated me," Mavis continued. "I was always borrowing your pencil and breaking the lead. Irene's my best friend now." She halted and looked round lugubriously, "Isn't she?" All three laughed, a trio of intelligent, utterly captivating Singapore girls. The diplomat clearly thought so. He said, "Blessed shall be the pencil-sharpeners," and was, I think, pleasantly surprised at the favourable reception for his sally. I could see why guys like him might prefer to be around SG than the swimming-pool set (whom, incidentally, Jenny had judged it better not to invite to this occasion). It was definitely less of a strain for him. Standing with the swimming-pool set in the bar of a place like the yacht club was more like being around other men, with the competitiveness still there but the comradeship removed. Oddly enough, SG was far more likely to buy the Western guys the occasional round back – a shock pleasurably akin to a frank sexual proposition – than the Caucasian females, who for all their talk, still liked to sit around waiting for a free drink. That was especially true of the married ones.

The diplomat moved closer, the girls the black magnets, he the grey iron filings.

"We're the native Asians," Mavis said, "but it took a foreigner to bring us together again. Isn't that strange?"

Irene came into the conversation. She was going to concede the race to the others but was happy to assist as pace-maker. "Native sounds like grass-skirts and, you know, ah, bare boobies. Just Asians is the better word for Singaporeans, isn't it?" There was a pause. Cathy and Mavis exchanged glances. Cathy said, "I haven't seen any bare boobies in Hong Kong recently. Maybe other people have seen bare boobies?" The girls giggled. I interposed myself with a silver tray of highly integrated snacks: sausage *and* Spring rolls, not to mention curry puffs. "Savoury, sir?" I said, doing my best imitation of Rochester from the *Jack Benny Show*, which came after the *Sergeant Bilko* repeats on Fridays. "I can recommend the spring roll, made by Miss Nicky herself. Miss Irene?"

"Thank you, Rey." Irene was one of the few Singaporeans who ever bothered to remember my name; the explanation may have been that she was an appointments secretary, rather than that she was interested in me. "Can I get you a Coke, Miss Irene?"

"No, thanks. Better not have any yourself either, if you want to keep those perfect teeth. He has perfect teeth, Mr… I don't think we've been introduced!"

"Bruce."

The guy completely ignored me. I was a lackey, I didn't take it personally. I lit the room with my smile. I prepared to make myself scarce.

"Mmm," said Irene, "that's a great Spring roll. Where did she learn?"

"School," I said. "There are a lot of rich Chinese kids there." Shit, had I been offensive?

"*Gei ho sik, lah,*" said Cathy, also praising the Spring roll. "First question, Mr, er, Bruce," she said, looking him full in the face and smiling at her own audacity. That was a lovely conversational gambit of hers. This was the first time I heard her use it but even the tenth time it never failed to charm me. I never hung around long enough to know what First Question consisted of, or whether it was the same for everyone, but the hidden agenda was no doubt invariable: *Are you married?* As I passed by five minutes later, she was saying, "Third Question…" and Mavis and Irene were in a separate pairing, talking to each other with diminished vivacity. They took sausage rolls this time, but I didn't disturb Cathy and Bruce.

My personal hunch was that diplomats were not a good choice for Singapore girl. Behind the veneer of probity and correctness they were actually less scrupulous in such personal matters than the ostensibly more raffish financiers and business people. They were more likely to string SG along with promises, spoken or unspoken, of what they could do for her in the future, in the matter of acquiring citizenship or residence rights abroad. It would invariably come to nothing. Their rotations were somewhat shorter than those of the guys in business, so it was very much a pop-up target for the girls. The senior embassy people rode ramrod on the newcomers but if the new people had been in poor Asian or Latin countries previously they were already experienced, dangerous, and wily adversaries, like bulls who'd been in the ring before, quite likely to gore Singapore Girl in her suit of lights of many languages, leave her bleeding from the virgin wound, and trot out of the ring with their nuts intact under their tails at the end of it. At the very basic level, and Singapore Girl was nothing if not practical, the diplomats had less of a disposable income. Where a banker might bestow a Patek or a Rolex on her, she'd be lucky to see a Timex or a Casio from the man with romantic immunity.

I was a man, that was my primary visible tribe, but I was also underdog by birth and by temperament. That was my real tribe, that of the despised outsiders, trying to get in from the cold. How many times, too, had I played on giant-killing teams where we'd defied all the odds to come roaring from behind to trounce the semi-professionals or had slumped in defeat in the dressing-room, too depressed to talk, until Butch Tan Sy came in with words of hope and kindness. My sympathies lay with Singapore Girl, not with the men, just as they had lain with Ma and Auntie Lovely-Anne, even though I was as cock-happy as the next guy on the team.

BUTCH TAN SY USED TO SAY that you only knew a team's true worth in adversity and his first defeat was the moment you appreciated the extent of a champion's real greatness. With Singapore Girl it was the other way round. It was in the moment of victory that she became, as it were, more herself; then that she distilled her faint fragrance into the pungency of essence. It was, to be frank, an unedifying process but there was a heroic blatancy about it, which compared favourably with the desolate pretensions of the Filipina married to the foreigner. Nothing came of Cathy's encounter with the diplomat. She continued to give her classes, clad in the pink leotard and pale-blue warmers which might have interested the guys more than her cocktail-dresses. I'd hear her shrill, impersonal bark – she coached in an American accent – as I waited for a glistening Jenny. At Artheneum I'd often played basketball in my street-clothes or gone for a run by myself. Without the uniform, the company, and the music, I don't think Cathy's class would have done it. The context rated more than the activity.

In the context of victory, in the environment of marriage to a foreigner, girls like Cathy came out in their true colours. The enchanting spunkiness, the parade of aggressiveness, became a full-scale annexation. Singapore Girl and Miss Hong Kong were, on the whole, the ones being done the favour. Like their island homes, they lacked resources, but they were darned if they were going to have to be grateful for the rest of their lives. Both towns had thrived on Western technology and intellectual property without feeling grateful for it and Miss Hong Kong and Singapore Girl were gonna tap into their spouse's capital without feeling grateful for it, either. Singapore Girl's whole behaviour was geared to the goal of proclaiming she was as good as Hubby. She became spiky, but at least the quills weren't venomous, like the poisonous *pinay*'s; the wound didn't fester. She developed a bark that was worse than her bite. So, at dinner at the Smiths one rainy August evening, an occasion when I had to run to the cars under Commander Smith's golfing umbrella to bring the guests in dry, one by one, I heard Ying i Hansen say to her husband, who was in the marine insurance business, "Bullshit, Torben," accentuating the last part of the compound noun. Then she said it again, making the company laugh all the harder. Was there some subliminal unease in the air they were discharging through their guffaws and titters, just as the lightning playing against the windows was discharging the electricity in the clouds? For the Caucasians I think not, though it made me feel uneasy, and as I stacked the dirty plates by the sink Babyjane said to me: "She da bold one da *insik* speak her husband like that in company. I like to spank her face for her."

Running in and out of the kitchen, I got a servant's point of view on the conversation – shards and fragments, though in a way I had a more rounded view because I was at liberty to look at everyone's faces unobserved. It was about Malaysian and Singapore Chinese, their rivalry and differences. To me they seemed the same but they, the protagonists, didn't think so.

"You don't know anything about it, Torben," Ying i told her husband as I returned with the lemon meringue pie baked by Mrs Smith and Nicky's very laudable Gulaman Malacca. "We're not close to the Malaysian Chinese at all. They've got an inferiority complex about us. They think we look down on them because they're from the boonies."

"And do you?" Jenny inquired innocently.

"No," said Ying i, a graduate of the Singapore National University. There then occurred one of those unpredictable events only really likely to happen within a gathering of educated Caucasians, and unforeseeable even with them, a product of group chemistry based on a sequence of unrepeatable social chain reactions which the same gathering of individuals couldn't have repeated the next night: they exploded with laughter, all at the same time and as if it was the funniest thing they'd ever heard in their lives. Ying i looked blank for a moment, then forced herself to smile. The assertiveness, the aggressiveness were for her spouse only.

"Boondocks," said Commander Smith reflectively, "is that a Malay word?"

"It must be," said Ying i quickly. "It certainly sounds like it."

"Of course, you all speak Malay, don't you?" Mrs Smith said.

"More or less," said Ying i modestly. "Actually, my Mandarin is much better than my English or Malay." A rush of expostulations followed from the company as I went back to the kitchen for cream. I'd had to swallow my desire to correct the Singaporean wife. Sometimes it was hard to accept subordination. Not at the personal level because I'm not a proud person with a chip, not a Singaporean or a Malaysian. Boondocks was a Tagalog word or a corruption of it. It went back to the guerrilla war against Roosevelt and his Rough Riders.

But compared to the Filipina, Singapore Girls, the Ying i's and Cathy's at their most mercenary, conducted the guerrilla war of wife against husband according to humane and honourable conventions. Singapore Girl wasn't a rough rider. But, oh my God, the *pinays*: I just pitied the white guys, I really did.

The bachelors in Hong Kong, local or expatriate, had an advantage over foreigners who resorted directly to the Philippines in search of a bride: in Hong Kong the mail-order business didn't flourish. The consumer virtually never bought from a catalogue or, worse, sight unseen, both of which were the case with foreigners shopping for the female commodity in the Philippines from abroad. (Although in both Singapore and the RP there was no guarantee on the goods; you couldn't return a defective wife). In Hong Kong you tapped your computer keys and looked at the screen before you bought it; you listened to your hi-fi; you test-viewed your TV. Why not? The whole place was a giant shop-window. And such was the case with the Filipina at large there. The male on the loose in Hong Kong didn't just have the opportunity to watch and listen to the *pinay* of his choice, not to mention smell the secreted pheromes and budget fragrance wafting off her, he was also likely to encounter her during the ordinary avocations of life, much as he would have done with an Amerikana at home. Thus there existed the possibility of a normal contact, courtship on a conventional schedule. The guy wasn't on a whirlwind fortnight hopping from one provincial town to another in Thailand or the Philippines, interviewing and vetting the talent to see if it corresponded with the lure of the letters. (Often it wouldn't. Auntie Monalisa had been much in demand as a telephone stand-in back home. Because of her fluency in English and relative brashness she was better able to maintain a conversation on the scratchy line than the sweethearts paralysed by bashfulness or enlivened by the desire to be tricksy just for tricksiness' sake. One guy had nineteen half-hour conversations – collect, natch – with Monalisa and for the short duration of the marriage – seven months – and perhaps for the rest of his natural span, imagined that he'd been talking to his wife). In Hong Kong or the Lion City there existed as an academic possibility the chance of a spontaneous meeting engineered without undue artifice. There were a few middle-class Filipinas in both places – tellers working in the remittance centres, diplomats and their wives, the odd journalist –

but most of them were servants. Still, be she ne'er so humble, she was still an expatriate, in the same boat as the Canadian stockbroker or the Australian barrister, only in fourth class. In fact, I think the poverty of the *pinay* was a turn-on for a certain kind of white guy: marrying beneath themselves or rescuing a girl from a bar, if not the dragon's cave, were a contemporary knight-errantry.

Did all this mean that Foreigner-Filipina marriages contracted in Hong Kong or Singapore enjoyed a better survival rate than the notorious eighty per cent breakdown on those unions brokered back home? It assuredly did not.

If Singapore Girl or Miss Hong Kong merely flattered to deceive rather than pulled an absolute confidence-trick, rather than sticking in the full-scale sting, the Filipina was a butterfly that reversed the usual development and became a caterpillar, a venomous one. As mild as the adulterated bleach sold as full-strength in the supermarkets back home, so meek, so obliging before the ring was on her finger, so charmingly direction-less and bereft of focussed ambition, after marriage she underwent a personality change so drastic as to amount to a metamorphosis. She simply forgot who she was, adopting a thousand new airs and graces. And, of course, the astounding arrogance, as always, hid a sense of a deep inferiority. It was objective, it could be measured. The voice she used to address the poor sucker became a couple of octaves shriller; she adopted a lofty, distant tone in the presence of fresh Caucasian acquaintance whom she would have wooed and beguiled in the days of her impoverished spinsterhood and the foreigners that had known her in those forlorn times she snubbed and systematically eliminated from her new avatar. It didn't stop with foreigners. She laid it on us as well, we who knew her intimate vices and foibles as well as she, for they were our own. *Where do you go to, my lovely?* I used to hum as I watched the girls parade past with their catches.

Babyjane had known Erlinda, her townswoman and fellow *probinsyana* from Hicksville, Agusan del Sur, since the latter was so-high. They might even have been distant cousins. Erlinda was some eleven years younger and a lot easier on the eye than Babyjane, whose weathered features habitually bore that expression of brutal impassivity worn by my countrywomen when title is defective to the vacant lot inside the skull. Add a hint of perplexity or imagined discomfort − the thin rectangle of doubled-over handkerchief pressed to the nose against the non-existent dust of a Hong Kong shopping mall – and she resembled – I'm the one to say it – a menstruating gorilla. Where pretty girls were in a ratio of one:five in the wild of the streets of Metro M. and the beautiful in the still remarkable ratio of one:twenty, the domestic helps overseas were almost uniformly ugly, or as Fr. Paul put it, *nec iuvenis nec pulcher*. Subjecting it yet again to the rigours of Fr. Paulian contextual analysis, the reason was clear. The recruitment agencies did not want trouble with the wives of the employers.

Next to Babyjane, Erlinda was comparatively youthful and quite pretty when she put her hair back in the characteristic ribbon-bow of the promenading *pinay*. She and Babyjane used to go mall-ing of a Sunday. They'd don their tightest jeans and a pair of toe-concealing trainers or loafers, stuff Babyjane's Rubber Maid receptacles (which I wondered if she hadn't purloined from a previous employer) with rice and a savoury mess before hitting the trail to Ocean Terminal or one of the new malls. God rested from making the world on the seventh day but the seventh day was the day the Filipina in Singapore or Hong Kong made the world. That was, if you believed what Miss Hong Kong and Singapore Girl had to say about it. Our girls bore an unenviable reputation. I knew what to think when I heard Miss Nicky chewing the fat on the verandah with her classmates Sonika Narayan, Angie Verghese, and Becky Chow. "They *all* do it," Becky had said.

"Not all," countered Sonika, wanting to be contradicted. "All," said Becky firmly.

"Yes," said Angie, whose folks hailed from Goa and who didn't look remotely Portuguese. "Even the ones that you wouldn't think would do it, do it. You know, man, the mousey little ones, or the old ones, or the very ugly ones."

"Or the ones that look like *teachers*," said Sonika, with the gleeful enthusiasm of the converted.

"My Ma says, 'Don't ask your maid what she does on her day-off because you won't like the answer,'" Becky said.

"What even Babyjane?" Nicky queried.

"Yuck!" said Angie.

I used to come across the pair of them, Babyjane and Erlinda, in the Plaza until I learned to vary my routine so that I'd arrive after they had gone. This, I suspect, was with customers. The first time I ran slap-bang into Erlinda and BJ as they were absorbed in guessing the price of a necklace displayed in a jeweller's window. Gold and electronic goods were what principally exercised their imaginations but their staple purchases were T-shirts or shoes at a factory discount. I'd left Babyjane an hour ago but we all greeted each other like castaways from the same shipwreck running into each other on the strand the next morning. Erlinda flashed me a one thousand watts smile which revealed her as the proud possessor of braces that didn't look like Commander Smith's handiwork.

Neither Babyjane nor I alluded to the meeting at home three hours later. In fact, we were more than usually uncommunicative. Two Sundays later I saw them snacking (illegally) with their shoes off in the midst of a bunch of friends. Even if they don't go to Confession, Filipinas are in the habit of baring their soles. You get to know the soles of Filipinas in great detail, every whorl, every callus, all the ridges, on the basis of the most fleeting acquaintance, where you could know a 'Merikana twenty years and never see the underneath of her feet.

Erlinda and Babyjane formulaically raised their plastic bowls and invited me to join them but I declined with my own most dazzling, weapons-grade smile. The next week I caught sight of them on the level down from me. Erlinda was a modest two paces distant from the kind of scruffily-dressed, older, lower-income foreigner who patrolled for *pinays* in places like this, while Babyjane was talking earnestly to him. I think she was pimping for Erlinda. You could see the guys hanging round the edges of the Filipina flocks, looking too edgy to speak to the girls. It was excruciating. I could see why the Samaritan-instinct of the older girls might be to ponce, if the guys were too shy to pounce. The poor guys didn't know what emboldened the most backward Filipino: that we were the friendliest people in the world who would go to any lengths to avoid inflicting a public humiliation on anyone. An attention-drawing rebuff from the girls was out of the question. I, too, didn't want to come to anyone's notice. I ducked swiftly behind a corner and risked the ire of security by availing of the fire-exit steps. From there I proceeded to a different mall.

An interesting thing happened here. I was first mystified by, next intrigued, then flattered, followed by irritated, and finally resigned to, finding myself the subject of the discreet scrutiny of every store detective whose premises I entered. More, they started to follow me out of their own outlets into others and along the esplanades and up and down the escalators. It was like being the Pied Piper of Hamelin, trailing my tail of earnest, fit, law-abiding, alert young Chinese behind me, doing what they did very badly, which was second nature to Filipinos: to wit, deceiving. I was Simon Says as well as the Piper. When I stopped, they halted; when I looked in a window, they did, too; when I picked my nose, they scratched their heads. When I turned round, they froze. Finally, I had enough. I accosted not the nearest, who was male, but the tallest girl as least likely to feel threatened by me. In my gentlest tone, I asked, "Miss, what seems to be the problem?" She put on a look of what I can only describe as aggressive Chinese blankness. I knew it was all up to me whether the situation deteriorated or ameliorated. Frankly, suspicious behaviour in the vicinity of property was by common consent, if not the statute book, construed as a capital crime in Hong Kong. "Look," I said helpfully. "I know what you're thinking, and I don't blame you. You can look in my pockets if you want, I am not a shop-lifter, OK? You want ID or my work-permit? I'm a legal Filipino, not an overstayer…"

The store detective said, "Filipino? *You*?"

"O-o," I said equably. "I mean, yes. My Dad wasn't, if that's what you're wondering about. He was a serviceman. American…"

"Wah, so sorry. So sorry. We thought you were a Nigerian." She turned to the rest of the posse. "Filipino, *m'pa*." And with that they were off, minimising time consumed to no purpose. *M'pa*. That meant don't be scared. I might look like King Fucking Kong but everyone knew Filipinos were a threat to no one.

My sanctuary became the Diamond Bookstore, one particular branch, in one particular mall; the least frequented shop on the quietest floor of the most awkwardly situated shopping-gallery in Hong Kong, but for me an oasis of the spirit. By pure chance, many of the writers I liked had names beginning with M, N, and T, so I found myself habitually stationed before the same ten feet of shelving. Again, there were suspicions to overcome. The deputy manager, a stocky, bespectacled Chinese female, took to passing by me at increasing frequencies; then to coughing less and less discreetly, and finally to re-arranging the volumes directly in front of me with ostentatious bustle. Well, I simply smiled to myself. She didn't know she was dealing with a Filipino, *di ba*? In most respects, Hong Kong was a more tautly run ship than the foundering tub of the Philippines as it was then, but they took for granted certain intellectual indulgences not extended to us. STRICTLY NO FREE READING ran the sign in the shops back home, although, of course, unlike the Hong Kongers we could spit and urinate with impunity in the street. In this situation I possessed an iron nerve: hell, I'd even liberated volumes and magazines from their shrink-wrappings in National Bookstore, methodically taken notes, then surreptitiously re-packaged them again. I'd sat before law-tomes in Dunkin' Donuts, enjoying the air-con, the fragrance of the jam and icing sugar, the cinamon and the baked apple, and above all the low-glare fluorescence, from midnight to four a.m. without any of us so much as consuming a coffee. So when the manager, a turbaned Indian I could recognise from the information in the stock on his own shelves as a Sikh, stood behind me and said, "May I help you, sir?" I could turn, review him benignly, and say, "No, I don't think so." But he persisted: "You seem to be very interested in that volume, sir. I think I have seen you reading it on three successive Sundays. You might be more comfortable purchasing it and reading it sitting down at home."

"It's not the same book," I replied. "This is a different book by the same author as I was perusing last week."

"And who may that author who is so compelling be?"

I showed him. "Ah, Mr. – !" he said in surprise. It was a fellow-countryman of his, or at least a man of similar race. "You like his work?"

"Very much."

"I am an admirer of his as well. He was in here two years ago to do a signing. We sold two copies, I'm sorry to say. When he arrived he told me he hated doing this kind of thing, too. It was a terrible ordeal for both of us. What a shame, lah, you were not here at that time. You could have met him in person, even if you didn't have the wherewithal to purchase his book."

"I don't think I would have liked that, sir."

"Heavens! Why on earth not?"

"Look through you, *di ba*? See your soul and no charity."

"Aiy! Yes. Yes, indeed. Well, browse my friend, browse to your heart's content. There is no hurry, lah, no hurry in the world." He returned to his office. A little later the deputy manageress interrupted my reveries. "Stool. Compliments the manager." She banged it down and stumped off.

It was not for some Sundays, then, that my steps took me back to the Plaza but when they did I found Erlinda and Babyjane in their favourite spot. The food-containers were still in Babyjane's shopping-bag. I noticed Erlinda had a cute new satchel on her back, a Koala bear with a Caesarian zip, and a pair of the brand-name basketball boots Butch Tan Sy would personally present to our Player of the Year, shoes that had got so chunkily over-designed they looked more like *Star Wars* flagships than athletic footwear. Same poor-girl's splayed toes inside, I thought, with the vampire nails; Erlinda couldn't change those. But she looked cute, she looked cute. It seemed as if she and Babyjane had only R-V'd a minute or so before I arrived. Erlinda had a pink airmail envelope in one hand. With the other she was doing "Upper" with Babyjane, slapping palms in jubilation. When Assemblymen do it in private, it means assassination accomplished; when Domestic Helps do it in public, it means a little bit of money has come their way.

"Thank you, Lorrrrd!" exclaimed Erlinda, rolling her eyes.

"Ha, ha, ha!" cackled Babyjane. "We go da money-changer here or somewhere else? Ah, Rey, *ikaw!*" She shared the good news with me: "Erlinda fiance send a dollar. It's one hundred!"

"Wow! Compliments, 'Lin," I said. "Invest, *di ba?*"

"Ka-Joker, Rey!" she said, pulling her thumbs through the straps of her satchel so that they lifted up her breasts. "Snack, *na lang.* I'm the one to invite." Well, I declined politely, but they both got me by the arms and dragged me into a fast-food outlet. We'd all have found a noodle-stall tastier at half the price but this was a celebration. I was touched; I'd had sufficient of Chinese dourness to appreciate Philippine kindness the more when it was transposed outside its native context. I really didn't want Erlinda to break her big note; I knew she was far more likely to fritter it once it was subdivided, but I needn't have worried. She pulled a thick wad of Hong Kong dollars from the Koala bear's entrails. I glanced quickly at Babyjane's blank face. Were we perhaps dining, unbeknown to them, on the munificence of Erlinda's employers? I thought about it. No, I was probably being entertained on immoral earnings, rather than stolen property. As I'd been fed and watered on these until the age of thirteen this should have occasioned me no qualms but it felt different from Ma. At least I'd been able to soothe Ma with a massage. I was just giving Erlinda the benefit of my plastic smile. I politely declined the offer of an ice-cream cone but found the money for three of these pushed down the sphincter my curled thumb and finger made at the top of my fist. I realised they'd been sufficiently unpremeditated to invite me but were now bursting with the desire to take up some piece of gossip anew.

Off I went for the cones. This took some time. We were in the second-most efficient place on earth (Singapore being the first) but Chinese food-mania manifested in the snaking queues before the tills provided the immovable object for the irresistible force of Hong Kong method. When I came back Erlinda and Babyjane bestowed the full focus of their attentions on me. They weren't just being polite; plainly whatever it was they'd had on their chests they'd now got off. I ate as little of my cone as was consonant with politeness, made my excuses, thanked Erlinda effusively, and departed. She gave me her warmest smile again, nothing in the least affected. She sensed I didn't really like her but she was resisting in the best way: by exercising her right not to return the dislike. It was, then, standing on the descending escalator in the crowd – I normally made a point of vaulting up or down three steps at once – that I discovered something for the first time: the tension of being polite to a woman I didn't like had made me low-gear horny. That inclined me to hang round the exit longer than usual – just window-shopping from the twilight, with no serious intention of accosting any of the *pinays* hanging out under the lights – when I saw Erlinda and Babyjane, followed at a discreet distance by two guys. Another eighteen inches further behind and they could have alibi-ed themselves, but they obviously didn't want to lose to the throng what they'd just set up. They were a very old Indian guy with betel-ravaged teeth and an equally ancient black in African costume who could, of course, have been from Texas. Oh, well, I thought, at least our chicks aren't racially prejudiced. I went home and satisfied myself by doing what I could do for myself better than anyone in the whole wide world.

Calm and all passion spent, I stayed out of Babyjane's way when she got home. Didn't want to embarrass her. I thought my knowledge might show on my face like a head-up display.

A few days later, no better in some respects than a monolingual dotard with a bolo in one hand and a bottle of Tanduay in the other,

I inquired of Babyjane, "The fiance of 'Lin, he's Australian, *di ba*?"

"O-o," she corroborated warmly. I waited, certain more *tsismis* would be volunteered, and was not disappointed.

"Vairy, vairy old *pero* aggrisib. Ebery day can make da stain in da bed two time. Have a gold card *ka-suerte si* Erlinda." I wasn't sure if she meant Erlinda was lucky because of her aged swain's purchasing or staying power. Most likely the former.

I'd been celibate myself for longer than I cared to calculate. Counting the months made me wince, worse than the dull ache of the deprivation itself. I stopped trying to work it out.

There did exist a couple of streets in Kowloon in a run-down area called Mong Kok where commercial sex could be had, commercial sex that was cheap by Hong Kong standards but way over the Visayan odds, of course. I'd found out about it from the exposé and thundering denunciation in the local newspaper, which thoughtfully laid out the tariff as well. Most of the action took place in Portland Street, which marked an ancient boundary between Chinese and British territory. I couldn't read Chinese but all you had to do was look for a yellow sign. The working girls weren't Hong Kongers. They were mostly mainland Chinese girls, though there were Thais, Indonesians, and, needless to say, Filipinas among them. Mostly they were illegals: sneak-ins like myself, overstayers, and those engaging in acts a tourist visa was never designed to encompass. The local girls, Chinese teeny-boppers moonlighting from school for the money for designer-brands, preferred to work in karaoke boxes.

The narrow stone stair-cases in Portland Street were clean and litter-free but with iron-gates blocking the way on every flight. You rang a buzzer to summon hard-faced mamasans or sharp-faced Chinese kids with gang written all over them. The whole street was a Triad-monopoly, 14-K mostly. Man, what a purgatory. It was a joyless and, yes, sordid place, squalid in a way Subic, Olongapo, Angeles, Ermita, and Lapu-lapu back home weren't. The guys walked furtively on the way there, by themselves rather than in groups; no one smiled, no one dared to be drunk. Suddenly, I thought of Danton and the other seminarians in Amsterdam and I burst out laughing. I guess Danton would have liked that. After I'd investigated a few staircases and had the Cantonese for nigger reinforced in my memory bank, I gave up.

It was very difficult for me to go with a working girl, to use her like a urinal. Nothing particularly exemplary about me, just a matter of what I'd come from. Anyhow, I'd succeeded in dampening the urge and emerged with a laugh on my lips and money still in my pocket. I decided to regard that as a victory.

After those mean lanes, the mall seemed a place of mirth and innocence, an urban Garden of Eden where discrimination between good and evil was unknown, not that Atty Caladong had failed to drum into us the elementary legal principle around which all systems were predicated: ignorance of the law is no excuse. Gossip, the electricity which ran the machinery of Philippine social life, crackled in the air. The *pinays* giggled together; the *pinoys*, caps back to front, just hung out, some with their arms round a *pinay*. Not as great a feat of courtship as you might think: Filipina workers outnumbered Filipino workers. Of course, the last thing I looked was Filipino. Nigerian shoplifter, Caribbean syphilitic, take your pick. The dwarfish crowd washed around me, as if I was a creosoted pier leg at low water. I smiled at a pair of *pinays*. They were talking in rapid Tagalog about the cost of flights with a particular Travel Club, direct to Manila and Cebu or via Kota Kinabalu. One of them, the older, blanked me out; the pretty one made a grimace at the companion I wasn't interested in. Language was the key that unlocked doors. Some Tagalog from me would have done wonders, but I'd still be working up from lost ground. I looked for *pinays* in pairs, that was the combination that was up for naughtiness. Anything larger than that, even a trio, was fruitless. *Hiya* and *ulaw* – in Fr. Paul's classical lexicon, *pudor* – got the better of them. Sinning didn't perturb the Filipina, being found out by her friends did. And a Filipina on her ownsome on Sunday had something sad, unbalanced, and risky about her, like a rogue elephant or a lioness with a thorn in her paw.

Like a gift from the gods, there was a promising-looking pair of fun-lovers by a trash can. Their jeans were the new kind with very narrow bottoms. In Manila they still wore bell-bottoms with pride, even at rich-girl colleges. These two were also sporting lace-up shoes and tinselly socks, which glittered under the street lighting. It was a propitious moment for fishing: twilight, *di ba*? The girls had to say yes or no quickly, for all of us lackeys had to be home soon. I sidled up to the girls. In life, as on a basketball-court, the most fruitful scoring point was from the flank. *Pilipino ka ba*, I would inquire.

"Good evening, serr. Where you are going?"

"Hah?"

Two strange Filipinas had come out of nowhere, like the way Cheech Chong had once stolen a pass out of my hands.

"Where you are going, serr? Who's your *kasama*?" They half-sang it in our friendly way. And our in-born courtesy to the stranger, our reluctance to snub, inclined me to reply, "Stroll, *na lang*," though I wanted nothing more than to shake off these two plain Janes and get to the chicks in the shiny socks. It was always easy for me to look over the heads in a crowd but as I searched for the girls I wanted to pick up, the two new chicks caught my crafty glance. "You meet your friend here, serr?"

"Ay, no," I said. "*Iring²*, *di ba*?" *Iring* just meant cat. Saying it twice, as I've told you more than once, made it familiar, watered it down, and making water was what this cat was bent on. Perhaps Fr. Paul would have come up with the translation of "Tom-catting." You can see I wanted to shake the young ladies off by being a bit naughty but not wholly obnoxious. Unfortunately, they took it in their stride. "Oh, serr, better you have friend, good friends, than *Iring-Iring*. We can be your friends, serr." Not once had they asked if I was a Filipino, or expressed surprise at the obvious fact that I was one of them from the forms my politeness and my salaciousness had both taken. I looked harder at them. They smiled back with a confidence that was pleasant for its openness. Neither overweight, elderly, nor hideous, just the common or garden *pinay* abroad, they were still, in all honesty, unglamorous girls. I looked for the glittery-socked pair, but the few seconds had been enough to lose them. They were wiped from the face of the earth. Don't know how many times that's happened to girls I've been following. It was physically impossible for them to be more than a block away but it might as well have been Mars.

"*Sama*, serr," the dumpier of the two urged, giving the series of spaced half-inch nods that constitute our girls' sincerest encouragement. "OK, *lang*," I said, doing my best not to sound too resigned, and failing. Even then I knew this: you were much better off having sex with someone ugly but friendly than someone beautiful but hostile.

I looked at the short-legged one's ass. Her figure wasn't as conventionally good as her (slightly) slimmer friend's, but I found the way the seat of her jeans twitched from side to side somewhat more alluring than the friend's staccato steps in her high-heeled clogs. I was now in the process of discovering something else: settling for the silver, or maybe it was even gonna have to be the bronze medal, while thinking all the time of the golden opportunity lost, that also made you low-gear horny.

I was prepared to walk a good distance. None of us liked to waste our change on even public transport. Wages were, of course, much better than home – that's why Filipinos were there. But the higher cost of living ate into the bigger wage-packet. It was like treading water to stay afloat. Only the margin which contract workers could scrimp and save to remit home got magically compounded in its buying power.

My companions stayed quiet. I didn't need to be told why. I thought I understood; communication being by *pinoy* telepathy. They'd been forward, they'd been friendly, in the way of the *pinay*. Now, every action having a reaction, in the way of the *pinay* they were being modest and reticent. Silence was a necessary part in getting to know someone. Who knew? It was not impossible that they, too, were looking forward to a jump.

Our walk turned out much shorter than I expected. Back home this would have had alarm bells ringing in my head. Only full-time hunting-girls or robbers' accomplices would have had a pad so conveniently near. But this was Hong Kong. No one had guns, no one in their right mind would choose me as a mark they had to overpower with their bare hands, or even a blade. And I was sure as hell too smart to drug in a Coke or a soya-dip.

Up steps we went. "We are here," said the taller girl, "Fraise da Lord."

The door flew open, as if someone had been watching through the spy-hole. Dumpy, the one with the swishing-ass, pushed me with surprising force and in I tripped.

"Welcome," intoned a deep male voice, before a jubilant female choir broke into a religious refrain – I wouldn't dignify it with the name of hymn – the burden of which seemed to be the unoriginal notion that Jesus dearly loved a sinner. Even as I stood rooted, aghast – for sure I'd have been cooler if four Ukrainians had pounced on me with clubs – I felt embarrassment for how easy it had been to lure me and indignation at the deception, for such it truly was. And being a *pinoy* through and through, saturated in our ancient tribal values like a wick of cotton-wool in blood and lymph, I fought with every fibre in my body to repress my anger, or at least not to show it. Knowing, and even despising, what has shaped you doesn't stop you being its slave. It just adds helpless self-consciousness to your woes.

They'd seen it a hundred times before, of course: the sickly smile on my face, the wish for a hole in the ground to open and swallow me. You know, I've never liked group singing; it's aggressive and excluding, especially when Filipinos do it. I guess the Born-Agains had good intent but it was still the gang laying it on the outnumbered victim and the worst, most transparent, of them wore the same quiet triumphal smirks that the creeps in the Frat wore at an initiation hazing, or rites of a still greater evil. It was the look the galley-boy had worn. It was the Runt's Smile.

"Come," said the preacher. "You are among friends."

With friends like you, I thought, I prefer my enemies. But what I said was, "I think, a-huh, I have made a mistake. I'm in the wrong place."

"No, you are in the right flace."

"O," corroborated half a hundred female voices. They still had one arm outstretched to heaven, the open palms either reflecting God's glory or telling me to halt just there. The girls who'd brought me nodded to the preacher and departed. I really didn't like that. No time to waste; they might still be able to fetch another convert if they were quick about it. Shit, it was as impersonal as being a fly in a spider's web. "Who are you people?" I asked.

"We are Pentecostals."

"Well, I am a Roman Catholic. In fact," I decided Fr. Paul and Fr. Boy wouldn't mind if I stretched a point, "I nearly had a vocation."

"No froblem," the preacher said. "Plenty of us Catholic until we're seeing the light."

"I'll just go, *na lang*," I said

"No, please, friend. Outside, it's the world, the darkling world, a bad flace, full of temptation for a young man. In here you are with brothers and sisters. Please. Here is a hymn-sheet. I'm the one composed it myself. Please sing with us."

"*Sige. Pero…* for a moment, hah? I'll be the one to phone home first. ET phone home, ha, ha. *Balik ko*. I'll be back."

"*Balik*, hah? Be sure to come back." He didn't look too disappointed. Filipinos never did with that response, even if everyone knew it was always a lie. It was probably a better reaction than he was used to. Any guilt I might have had about hurting decent folks' feelings vanished when I saw the looks of mild amusement or frank distaste on the faces of his choir.

As I reached the bottom of the stairs, they were starting on *All things bright and beautiful*.

The next Sunday I stayed home and read in my room. Half-way through the afternoon came a knock on my door. It was Mrs Smith. "Are you alright, Rey?"

"Yes, Mum."

"Oh, that's good. I'm glad to hear it. Only don't think me nosey…"

"I'd never be the one to think that, Mum."

"Oh, good. Thank you. Only you normally go out on your day off. I was wondering if you felt unwell."

"Very well, Mum, thank you. You want me to go out and give you privacy?"

"Oh, no. Certainly not. I wouldn't want to give you the wrong impression. Do what you want, it's your spare time, after all. Only… it seems a waste. And you're such a, well, *vigorous* young man."

"Ah, thank you, Mum. I'll just continue with my book."

"Yes, carry on."

I guess the Smiths sometimes found Babyjane and obviously from this last exchange, me, difficult to fathom, but I also often couldn't work out what the Smiths wanted to say. Was Mrs Smith really worried about the fluctuating day to day health of a servant? Or did she want me out of the way after all? I'd have said the former, but then she had finished by saying what a feisty, bouncy specimen I was. Americans were relatively direct; in some respects, the Brits were Orientals.

Anyhow, I decided to stay but did the minimum moving about.

This went on for some weekends. Then one Sunday I found Babyjane looking listless in the kitchen when I went to drink the tapwater the Smiths eschewed. "What happen, Jane?" I inquired. "You're not the ones to be wow-ing the town with 'Lin?"

She scowled malevolently. "No wey with that one. Snub. She's da one to be so *arte* now she got husband."

"Back-fighting you two?"

"*Dili*. I don't do anything. She's da one to think she's Imelda Marcos already."

"She was seeming such a nice girl when she treat us to snacks before. Very kind of her and generous."

"Generous, ha! She is a *puta. Bori na*, that one."

I feigned consternation. "Jane, Jane! Don't say the words like that! You making my ears hot! Please, you don't say like that!" I was fighting to keep a straight face and just succeeding. It was somehow more difficult when I was speaking the Taglish of any native joker.

"Y-e-e-e-s, I know already what she is," Babyjane screeched. "She a no-good frostietute, hunting all da time for da customers is old, dirty, poor, niggers man, all da same for her if they have da money in da focket and later she forget on furpose to fay da one is da helfer of her always."

I turned away, helpless with laughter.

"Ay!" I exclaimed. "*Ka*-hypocrite *siya*! Now I know what she's really like, I don't like her any more!"

"O!" said Babyjane more complacently. "I'm da one to ofen your eyes, otherwise she trick you, too."

"OK, Jane. Thanks. I'll just take the water to my room and continue my work, *na lang*."

I had discarded Hobbes' *Leviathan* and was writing one of my rare letters to Ma and Bambi, which would have its postmark and stamps removed by the third party it was going to, when there was a knock on the door, more assertive than Mrs Smith's. Babyjane was there in her Sunday T-shirt, the one which said 'Pure Pinoy' on the front and '100%' on the back. She wore it once a week and in time would change it for one with a new and probably cheekier message, the meaning of which would also elude her. Unusually, Babyjane was wearing foundation on her face and lipstick. It aged her at least ten years. "*Kasama, lang*," she said. "We're da ones to take a walk." I accepted with more alacrity than you might think. Babyjane never bored me. Who'd be bored by a constitutional with Mandrake the Magician, who could make things vanish and reappear at will? I had no illusions to lose.

We went past Jenny and her mother at the front gate, who all but nudged each other. We were as intense an object of regard to them and as fruitful a source of gossip as they were to us, though it could be an effort for a servant to see that. Babyjane giggled, not omitting to cover her mouth as she put her arm through mine in the street. "*Bana ko*," she said, "my husband."

"Hoy! *Bana*[2]," I replied, entering into the spirit of things. "*Bana-bana mo*, your half-husband, *di ba*? *Dili ako* mister *mo*." I could see the way that we were going to brake the development of our queer and accidental intimacy was with a series of relentlessly jokey exchanges. It was a reversal of the usual social sequence: man and woman in large group engaging in saucy banter leave the crowd to find themselves shyer than strangers, an inhibiting pall descending as their voices drop. In company Babyjane and I probably would have sobered up. As we went on our rollicking way, fused into one crab, the odd couple, middle-aged BJ coming up to the striation below my pectorals, I don't know who thought they were condescending more to whom, but I know this: I enjoyed having her on my arm. She made me feel more of a man for it, that withered klepto crone, and I revelled in the stares of those we passed.

We took the tram, then in Causeway Bay she bought me barbecued fish balls outside the mall. Responding to her spontaneous generosity, I got a covert hard-on. How are the mighty fallen, I thought. This was me, The Most Valuable Player 1984, who had never been short of a date if Danton or Butch Tan Sy had anything to do with it, getting excited over light-fingered Lola here, grabby grandma.

As we rode the escalator to the second-floor – which in British Hong Kong they confusingly called the first floor – Babyjane grabbed my arm hard enough to hurt. "Ay! I see her! She's over there, da no good *puta*! I going to be da one to make *ulaw* for her." Nothing, it seemed, could make Babyjane's English deteriorate more rapidly than sincerity of emotion and the rage which now possessed her on sight or even mention of Erlinda's name was one of the few genuine things about her Sunday *persona*. I saw why I'd been brought along, not so much as security – though all my life my endowment of stature had proved useful to those who wanted to be my friends – so much as an electrical contact for the torture of excruciating embarrassment to be visited on Erlinda. It wouldn't work, you see, unless there was present another contact of 'Lin's, someone who knew her even slightly, just as the tiniest filament of wire trapped under the nut would be sufficient to conduct a massive charge to the victim of the Philippine Constabulary. With impressive agility,

Babyjane was away, leaving me in futile pursuit. I was proof against *ulaw*, embarrassment, but I was not too happy about the prospect of drawing public attention to myself and maybe getting arrested in the bargain. Coming off the escalator on to the less congested floor, I saw Erlinda for the first time. She was in a frock, the cut and pattern of which were similar to Mrs Smith's everyday wear but which looked quite dramatic on the Filipina. With her sparkling 18-K gold necklace, shinily faceted as only Singapore gold can be, her earrings, charm-bracelets, and rings, she looked like a Christmas tree. Her hair was no longer tied back in the ribbon-bow but cascaded down her back and shoulders. No more Koala bear but a high-quality Gucci fake – ten to one from Temple Street market – which matched her loafers with their green and red cloth and gilt buckles. And, final accessory for the well-finished Filipina, equivalent to a fox-fur, the hairy arm round her shoulders of a bald Caucasian with a paunch.

Babyjane looked upon her with awe as much as malice. Erlinda hadn't yet spotted us; her attention was bestowed upon a display of leather wallets. She's going to find one of those useful, I thought. The guy pulled her on. He'd had enough shopping for that day. As it was early days for the marriage itself, Erlinda went without demurral. I could see the rings on the fourth finger of her left hand. She was fifteen yards out – many the long-bomb I'd sunk from that range – and had still to spot us. I looked at Babyjane – the fight was visibly going out of her. At ten yards and a seven o'clock angle, Erlinda finally got lock-on. A hurt and distant look appeared on her face, until then so engrossed in the moment and the offerings of the world bazaar. She appeared to be disassociating herself from, generally, the context of contaminating surroundings and, specifically, us. Even her short and business-like stride became a kind of floating forwards, not involving leg movement. Butch would have loved it. Without stopping, she looked from Babyjane to me and back to Babyjane. She seemed to apprehend no disturbance, still less potential embarrassment from our quarter. Her attitude and comportment were those of an honest citizen coming face to face with a pair of malefactors whom she knows to be wanted for some particularly sordid crime but whom, out of pity and old acquaintance, she chooses not to denounce. As she glided by, I made some inarticulate sound in my throat.

"Sorry, hah?" said Erlinda, without turning, "we da ones in a hurry, *na lang*."

CHAPTER XI

Mactan,
Easter Day 1985

Hi darling Bebe Blondel,

It's me sister Bambi, your loving sister. *Kumostaka, 'be?* Concerning me, I'm fine hope you are too. Yesterday four day ago I'm da one to cough up flenty bloods. I'm too scared. Also Ma. Run to hospital coz they say it's hemoaridge. I still take da medicines brother so many it's like salad fruit cocktail I don't get better still try, *di ba?* Maybe I autopsy have Streptomycin tattoo inside my chest. I sending this via Fraternity address they say you is in Brunei and all going so well in *trabajo mo* and in flay-time, I real happy for you at least one is doing well from our pamily.

I see Fr. Voy last sometime month. He ask how's Sugar he's not a bad boy misguided by wrong company but can redeem himself. Regards from Fr. Voy and he got me to fay one peso only join Squirettes of Columbus that's like junior Knights of Columbus but is just chicks OK he say Regards Sugar be sure to tell so I say it again two times OK I not gone old age early repeat myself *balik-balik* OK. I don't believe stuff they write you and Danton in newspaper is shit *tae.* Say *mga tsismoso dinhi* that no smoke without fire but Ma git mad. Then know what someone da one to say, "Dat boy's non-comvustivle." It's Auntie MonaLisa, da masahista *duna siyay pistola sa* handbag against da customer frevention *kayat* in dirty flace namely small hole. She say, "Cool? He's da ice-vox." Ma crying then, also me. I know how you sweet your nature, brother. Never hurt anyone you so strong but so gentle never a bully all your life until now. That's only da truth everyone to all know concerning you, *'be.* Life's not so easy here now. Fireball fire Ma guess coz she's gitting old now very young da girls there now younger than me even. She's da one giving massage now but not so many da customer. Choosing young chicks, *di ba?* You got some moneys to send we sure could be da ones to use it even small it's heartily given

I know Sugar. Otherwise you can't it's still OK brother I understand it's life's ferflexities. So, regard Ma – she say you run ewey like your Fa. Joke only. I finish writing now – it's 1-3-4 look like I-L-Y means I Love You, your loving sister, Bam-Bam. PS My *guwapo* brother got girl-friend da steady one yet or is still vutterfly da flayboy? Hahaha. He's da chicks-slayer. I fray God watch over us all. Bam². PPs. Hey I got fin-fal!

Maryknoll Retreat House,
Guam
July 31 1985

My Son,

You will note from the heading that I am on a self-given sabbatical. I am reversing Magellan's journey – Cebu to the Marianas. Fr. Mark (Fr. Boy) was kind enough to assume my teaching and pastoral duties in addition to his own and I had no hesitation in placing the burden on those broad shoulders. I am more in need of mental refreshment than physical rest, whereas I imagine the case is the reverse with you.

The world is replete with injustice but I have never felt indignation was a panacea so much as an indulgence. Try not to be bitter. I am aware of your nickname among your contemporaries and it is, for me, a fair summation of your nature.

Mark and I have decided that he is better situated to commence what remedies may still be instituted at this stage and he is, I understand, already making inquiries and intercessions on your behalf. We make no promises. The fact Mark is a Jesuit is more a hindrance than a help – our Order has some detractors among the local clergy, although His Eminence has never been less than supple and gracious. Your contemporary, Madrid, is now attached to the Cardinal's office – for the life of me I cannot call it a Palace – and is a great favourite. So you have friends, and a young one, at court.

I will not weary you with perplexities but merely enclose a trifle which Fr. Boy has requested me to send. To give, dear boy, and not to count the cost. A bank can cash it without identification. Today is the Feast Day of Saint Ignatius. I have been applying myself to the Spiritual Exercises.

The guidance of Christ be ever with you,

Fr. Paul

To: No 11
From: Coach
Date: Today's

OK, boychik, you're in a tight corner. But if you're half the guy I think you are, you ain't gonna lose it, right? Know whadd I mean? When the going gets tough, that's when the tough get going. I guess you got well and truly set-up, *ba*? Well and maybe not so truly. Still, you didn't get sent off to sit out time and I hear that was a great L-cut when you gave them all the slip.

I'm the one to talk in circles. I haven't forgotten you, Castro. Keep your chin up.

B. T-S

FROM THE OFFICES OF J.C.CALADONG JR., Attorney-at law
Victoria Plaza, Makati, MM.

Date: October 3 1985
Our ref: MAC/1139834/b/#25409/9/18/83 (Pending)
Your ref:

Dear Younger Brod,

We hear you are well and doing us proud. Here we are working on your case as fast as we can but these things go slowly and we ask you to exercise the virtue of patience while for our part every day we will be consulting your file and updating the matter.

Forbes Park
Metro Manila

October 3 1985

Dear Brod,

Good to hear from you and I really mean that, man. No, you got on the wrong ship entirely. We had the captain and crew of a Norwegian ship all straightened out for you: Panamanian-registered but Norwegian captain and, most important, Brod, an all-*pinoy* crew. You would have been better among friends, Brod, you would have been among your own kind. At least, man, the others would have been. That's just to look at, Brod, I know you're one hundred per cent pure Filipino inside and no one would know the difference once you open your mouth or, better still, you're on the other end of the telephone and they can hear but not see you.

Don't be so surprised the big Brod in Hong Kong helped you with your papers and deep background. That's friends, man, that's your brodder right or wrong. Only surprised I have to tell another Filipino that, man. Shame your diplomatic passport got drenched in the harbour, man. That was real difficult to get you that, man. Hilarious you thought you were in Singapore until you picked up the newspaper in the CR of McDo. You were reading or gonna use it as a wipe? Joke only, Brod. Let's not lose our sense of humour.

I'll tell the Frat to use your PO Box no and we'll be the ones to forward anything for you to that, no problem, man. I'm real glad Dant survived with you. You two were the best of the bunch. How about giving me his address, too? Then the Frat and me can give him what he deserves. If he doesn't want to, then you just secretly pass it on to me in his own interests. Like I say, we want to keep tabs on everyone we got an obligation to. He's a suspicious son of a bitch to say he's scared we'll rub you out if we know where both of you are. For the hundredth time, we are Brods, man.

Glad you like your employers. Stay with them as long as you can. Your contract and paperwork's all OK, man, and authentic all the deep background. Shit, the genuine thing, man, even your driving licence. The network fixed that, too. You got no worries about being a Tago ng Tago now. Hear they call a TNT an I.I. in Hong Kong short for Illegal Immigrant (or Aye-Aye, Skipper, *di ba*?) which you ain't, Brod.

Brab's Dad was real mad but he told him he's his son, right or wrong, he's his son and blood is thicker than water. No way he's gonna give him up and as his old man is connected and Uncle's in Congress he's well looked after. No need to leave the country like you.

Only one last thing, Brod, and I mention it only in passing. I'm real hurt about your hint in your letter. No way, man. I'm your Brod. Maybe I read it the wrong way, *di ba*? Tell Dant he's the one to be paranoiac. We will do all we owe when he contacts us.

Forget it, *na lang*.

Always your Brod, man,

Skipper

CHAPTER XII

Travel Plans – Nine-Tenths of the Iceberg – My Yorkshire "a's"
Shattered Tusker

B Y THIS TIME I had as Butch Tan Sy would have put it, somewhat "mellowed out". Even the pricks and kicks, the little frustrations of my humble and mundane existence, had contributed to this smoothing process. They were the counter-irritations known to Mrs Smith's quack acupuncturist. I was taking my life in Hong Kong for granted. I worried about extradition as abstractly as I did about eternal perdition. I relaxed; I behaved tribally.

So when Commander Smith gave permission for Nicky and her friends, chaperoned by Jenny, to go up to Thailand in their vacation via Singapore and Malaysia, I didn't panic as I might have done a year back. Going in and out of immigration was not too dangerous. Indeed it would add another layer to my history and cover my tracks.

Since before my arrival Nicky had been badgering her parents for permission to go on an independent holiday but had always met with a firm and joint refusal from the Commander and Mrs Smith. It was still hardly a solo trip, with Sonika, Angie, and Becky, not to mention Jenny, riding shotgun and me holding the reins of the Toyota Lexus but Nicky had whooped and flung her arms round the Commander. He'd melted before this demonstration of daughterly affection but then collected himself, unfastened her hands from around his neck, and struck the appropriate note of cautious reproof. "We're trusting you, Nicola," he said, "so don't let anyone down." This was very English: scolding or losing your temper with someone you loved, in advance.

We were going to fly to Changi, el cheapo, of course, on a charter flight. Then we would stay at Becky's folks a few days or so in Singapore – she was preceding us by a day on Cathay Pacific Marco Polo class. From there I would drive them on in the Commander's car over the causeway and up into Thailand. On the way back I was to hand the luxury Jap saloon with keys and logbook

217

to an Englishman also by the name of Smith in Hat Yai. It was only as I was letting a little pressure out of the tyres in the garage in Singapore that it occurred to me that the Commander might only be sending us all because it suited his purposes. He wanted to get the Lexus off his hands. The fact that he was flouting three, maybe four, Asian bureaucracies from a safe distance kind of made me his fall guy, *di ba*? If so, what was the difference between him and Atty Caladong? Man, after all my experiences I did hate to be used, tricked, and duped. But the situation of being patsy is emotionally felt, not intellectually perceived. Resentment throbbed in your gut, not your head. And I felt nothing for Commander Smith but my invariable liking and respect.

"Nah," I said to myself, wiping my hands needlessly, for the rubber of the tyre, in contact with the spotless metal of Singapore was surprisingly clean. "The only ones getting taken for a ride are the girls." I figured, too, Jenny could take any heat for me, whether her father wanted her to or not.

Babyjane and I had eavesdropped as per usual on the family palavers, so long before the Smiths had decided to let me in on their plans, we knew what the score was. In fact, so did the next door DH with whom, like any self-respecting Filipina, BJ did a brisk trade in juicier intelligence like pregnancies and quarrels. While the Smiths were making their plans, Babyjane washed dishes with the kitchen-hatch open and chose the best moments to clean the ornaments in the sala. As the Smith pow-wow approached its climax, Babyjane patrolled the room behind them, scowling at imaginary specks, the feather-duster in her hand employed more frequently as a signalling-flag to me through the French windows than as cleaner.

"No, I don't actually," Commander Smith was saying, "I'd regard him as being completely trustworthy."

"Then what do you mean," asked Jenny, the Girton interlocutor, "when you say that there's more to him than meets the eye?"

"Just that, sweetie. You only see one-tenth of the iceberg, the remaining nine-tenths is under water. He's the same. I mean, for a start he's infinitely better educated than he lets on. Have you *seen* his little library? And that's not his natural way of speaking that he uses to us, you know. When he forgets himself, his diction's distinctly superior. Cultured English, I'd say, with the odd Americanism. Call me crazy, but I can swear I hear a suppressed flat Yorkshire 'a' sometimes as well, the way Uncle Brindley – who was a pretentious old b_____ in my opinion – said it, and then on the other hand sometimes he brays like Burlington Bertie before he sounds like a Filipino again."

"It's your imagination, dear," I heard Mrs Smith's voice, from my station by the door. She was obviously enjoying the unusual sensation of being the down to earth, stabilising partner of the union. "He's a very nice young man, but perfectly ordinary once you get used to his rather intimidating appearance."

"With respect, my dear, just about the last thing he is is perfectly ordinary. He's about as ordinary as caviare on vanilla ice-cream."

"I can't say I've tried that."

"In any case, he's not the problem. I've complete faith, as I say, in his character."

"Yes, so have I."

"In that case, not for the first time and I suspect not the last in this always rewarding and stimulating marriage, have I been wasting my breath?"

"Hey, we come into it as well, Dad. It's me and Nicky he's driving."

"Sorry, darling. How do you feel about it?"

"Same as you," Jenny said.

"Nicky?"

"He's cool, Dad."

"I surmise that means you approve?" Laughter from all.

"We'd better warn him in good time, I suppose. Where is he by the way? He was bagging those bloody poinsettias a moment ago."

"Language in front of the children! You only just remembered yourself with your schoolmaster uncle from Keighley. Don't think I didn't notice."

"Language in front of young ladies, please, Mum. Not children."

I went through the kitchen-door to the hallway, then banged the front door loudly before calling, "Serr, flower bagged *pero* front wheel nuts of da car is lacking one."

"Oh, Rey," Commander Smith said, "just a moment, if you would."

"Serr," I said. I also seriously considered saying, "I'm at your disposal, Master Bertie," but decided it would be unfair as well as unwise.

"We were thinking of a trip, which you might care to accompany the girls and their friends on. Before I go on, just say no if the notion bothers you."

"More, serr."

"It would only be about five days…"

"*Dad!*"

"Say a week or ten days at most. We'd pay for your accommodation and food, it goes without saying. Or, perhaps it doesn't go without saying. Anyhow, I can tell you that's something you needn't worry about. Babyjane can cover for your other duties, obviously except for driving, while you're gone. I'm sure she won't mind…"

At that precise juncture there came a huge crash behind us in the *sala*. "Hell's bells, what in Christ's name has she done this time?" exclaimed Commander Smith, and went totally unrebuked. We all trooped into the hallway, as unbidden as witnesses to a traffic accident. The shards of a large Chiang Rai glazed porcelain elephant lay on the parquet. On her knees, Babyjane was pushing the fragments into a heap, while keeping her grip on the bamboo handle of the feather duster and also seeming to retain something in the palm of her other hand, so that she was handicapped by performing all three tasks with closed fists. Mrs Smith let out a wail of pure dismay. "Oh, no, you clumsy old…" I knew what Mrs Smith was about to say, wanted to say, a moment of pure telepathy. It was a very British idiom, though I did later hear an East German deck-hand call a Cuban ice-vendor, *"Du dumme Kuh,"* but it was the inherent power of alliteration which let me into the thought bubble over Mrs Smith's head. "… *woman,*" she concluded, after a tiny pause. Babyjane remained immobile on her hands and knees still, her face more than usually expressionless. The Smiths might have thought it was shock but I had begun to realise it was more than that. When I looked hard and, believe me, in these things Mactan urchins had eyes better than a bird of prey hunting for rodents, I could see the tail end of a bunch of low denomination bank-notes in Babyjane's fist.

Expressionlessly, Nicky said, "That's my mood-stone ring from Selfridge's on the floor."

"So it is!" Mrs Smith exclaimed. "And there's your cuff-links from HMS *Dolphin*, darling."

"Mm," said Commander Smith as grimly as he could, which was not very.

"I get da dust-fan and vrush," Babyjane said swiftly, and vanished. I was left with the baffled Smiths which was good in that it physically put me in their camp but not-so in that it marooned me there at the scene of the misdemeanour to be tarred by association.

"Serr," I half-spoke, half-coughed discreetly, "know I always trying to look out for your interest, *pero…*"

"What?" said Commander Smith with absent-minded exasperation. He wasn't looking at me but frowning at the pieces of Tusker on the floor. I was *pinoy* enough to be squirming at the prospect of watching Babyjane confronted *in flagrante delicto*. Every instinct in me rose up at the thought of witnessing the embarrassment of angry words and recrimination. Shit, give me a quick bullet in the head. Whether it made me co-culprit or not, or at the very best lumped me in the same context as BJ (and I knew how darn difficult it was, even for the Commander Smiths of this world, to refrain from reducing everyone to the tribal pattern, to allow their individuality and distinctness from the rest of the offending gang) I was gonna be drawing some fire.

"I never liked that elephant," Jenny said levelly.

"Yeah. Bit V____, wasn't it?" Nicky said. "I think Mums was having an abar-what? that day."

"Aberration. She probably was."

If they'd been countrywomen of mine I'd have sworn they were as alive to the context, as quick to it as I was, and making common cause, traitorous faction, with me. But they were Smiths so it was impossible.

Babyjane was too smart and too scared to re-appear and she hadn't been re-summoned. Every moment that passed was distancing the event. I decided it would be best to withdraw. At the back of my mind was the ridiculous supposition that the Smith girls might be covering for me and BJ. I resumed bagging the poinsettia (to fool it into flowering unseasonally earlier) and after that planned to find the front-wheel nut which had never been missing. As I went back past the verandah fifteen minutes later Mrs Smith was saying to Jenny, "But do they have jackdaws and magpies in Hong Kong?"

"They've got them *everywhere*," Jenny said firmly. "In fact, they're classified as vermin. Those big black birds near the harbour yesterday were crows or ravens and they're attracted by bright objects as well."

"No, they weren't. They were buzzards, surely. And I think it's grey squirrels which are classified as vermin when you don't expect the cute little things to be."

"They squirrel things away, don't they," contributed Nicky, in rare alliance with her bluestocking older sister, and drawing groans.

"I think you'd better apologise to Babyjane, you know, Mums," said Jenny. "She hasn't come back; she's probably sulking in her room."

"Oh, dear. I did fly off the handle a bit, didn't I?"

"Calling her a clumsy old cow certainly qualifies as that."

"Now, don't exaggerate, Jennifer. I never did that."

"You as good as, Mums."

"As good as isn't the same as actually doing it, Nicola." Mrs Smith saw me hovering. "Call Babyjane, could you, Rey?"

"Mum."

Babyjane was in her room. To look white-faced was as much her ambition as it was every lower-class Filipina's but not, I think, in this way, and it wasn't the broken elephant she was worried about. "Keep your mouth shut," I urged her, "and don't panic, and then everything will be OK. *Di ba*?" She nodded. As if she needed coaching – deny everything, no matter how overwhelming the evidence. She'd taken that in with mother's milk. Mrs Smith said, "Babyjane, I have to apologise to you. I'm sorry I got upset with you just now over the elephant and I want to take back unreservedly what I said to you." She paused. "The girls and I hope you can accept my apology."

Babyjane's eyes flew round the company. Commander Smith was the only one not looking at her. He was looking out of the French window at the poinsettia which bore an uncanny resemblance to an *auto de fe* penitent or a Klu Klux Klanner. Babyjane said with quiet dignity, "Mum, I accept your apology." Then she turned her back and returned to her room.

What next? Was Mrs Smith going to commit ritual suicide on the rug in front of us?

I decided to put another bag on the "bloody poinsettia". When I came back Commander Smith had rejoined his female family. Jenny was saying, "Why won't it be covered? You're paying fortunes on the premium. I've seen the DD's on Daddy's bank statements and that's just the monthly figure."

"Yes, dear," said Mrs Smith, who appeared dangerously sane, "we claimed for the Waterford set the Spanish girl broke in Kingston, even though after the Pru applied the excess it wasn't very much."

"Yes," said Commander Smith, managing to sound both brisk and valiantly patient, "but that was the Platinum Policy and included, *inter alia*, I quote, accidental damage, damage by frost, water-pipes freezing and bursting and consequential damage to fixtures and fittings by aggressive water. Assuming that we were unlikely to encounter sub-zero temperatures at the equator, I decided – I might add in consultation with you, mother – to go for a cheaper policy which excluded accidental damage to glass, decorations, porcelain, mirrors, toiletware, and glass fixed in furniture. On the other hand, it included damage to clothing by moth, which the English one didn't, and damage by malicious persons for which we weren't covered while the tenants were in No 38, by the way."

"Let's just say malicious persons broke the elephant," suggested Nicky.

Well, my ears went up like Bugs Bunny's. The foregoing conversation hadn't been altogether incomprehensible to me – I knew, for instance, what an "excess" was when used as a technical term – not because I'd ever possessed anything worth insuring – but because I'd taken classes on Bottomry and another on Actuarism.

I awaited with keen interest Commander Smith's response to this incitement to defraud. Fr. Boy had always been the softer option to confess dishonesty to but not impurity, whereas Fr. Paul had been relatively lenient with such minor sexual peccadilloes as we might commit but a Tartar with theft or fraud. Now Commander Smith said mildly, "There's no shortage of malice here, but your actual vandal is a bit thin on the ground in Hong Kong, dear. They had the rattan here until comparatively recently, just like your hero Mr Lee. I don't think it would look at all convincing on the claim-form."

"Oh, come on, Dad," Jenny said. "Everyone fiddles their insurance or bumps up their claim because they know the company's going to whittle it down, however truthful they're being."

"Well, that happens to be true, but then the companies wouldn't haggle in the first place, if everyone was honest with their claims."

"So are you saying honesty is the best policy, Dad?" They all laughed, Commander Smith the loudest. He caught sight of me.

"Didn't I ask you to sort that nut out, Rey? It's not like you to swing the lead. Let's get it sorted out *now*, before it goes when you're in the back of beyond."

"Serr." I went off with his quiet words of dissatisfaction, the strongest of reproofs from Commander Smith, tingling. Not just with the case of the non-missing nut, I'd somehow made the rod for my own back, with BJ martyress of the hour and me cast as malingering Pepe. I decided I'd behave out of context: I *wouldn't* hold a grudge against Babyjane.

CHAPTER XIII

The Dumb Ones – Taxi: Becky's Tale – Bus: Angie's Tale
Badminton with Rocks – Cool Heart – Dirty Hands:
Semporn's Tale – Chinese Boxes: Ah Lim's Tale – A Fine Place

"*WE'RE ALL going on a boring trip away,*" sang Sonika Narayan and Becky Chow in reedy unison in the backseat of the Toyota Lexus.

"*We're going where the rain pours daily,*" I replied, not taking my hands off the wheel or my eyes off the palm-lined highway.

"*We're going where the s-e-e-ea is grey,*" contributed Jenny beside me in the front seat, with assistance from Nicky behind.

We were one hundred and thirty kilometres ex-Singapore, long over the Causeway and out of the Malay state of Johore by now as well. It was, indeed, pouring unseasonally. When it hadn't been slashing down, the sky had been a lowering slate, but our spirits were soaring. The girls were drunk with liberty, and so was I.

"I'm surprised you know the song," Sonika commented. "I didn't realise it had got out to the Philippines."

"I'm surprised *you* know the words," I countered. "Shucks, I wasn't born but you guys weren't even *thought* of."

"Oh, the melody has a certain kitsch notoriety," Jenny said. There was a pause. I thought she was worrying if the remark had been over my head, so I smiled encouragingly at the windscreen-wipers.

"I saw the movie on satellite," Becky Chow said. "It was a *hoot.*"

"Eurgh," said Angie Verghese. "He's a God-squadder."

"He may be but they still gave him gyp at Changi because his hair was too long."

"What, *Cliff?*" ejaculated Nicky.

"U-huh."

"Wow," I said, and I meant it. Becky was silent. She was the only Singaporean. Jenny and I, who were nearly the same age, had made common cause so far on the trip. We often found ourselves thinking on the same lines. Now we both spoke simultaneously.

"Go ahead, Rey."

"No, you first, Miss Jenny."

"No. You. It wasn't anything important."

"Nor was what I had to say."

But we'd succeeded in changing the subject. We didn't want to embarrass Singaporean Becky. Especially after the royal time she had shown the girls in her home-town. I liked Jenny a lot, without any complications of sexual attraction. For that, she wasn't my type at all, but I found in the unlikely figure of this well-brought up Caucasian girl a sister under the skin. On the exterior she looked even more unlike me, if possible, than Bambi, but in addition to our taste for books and, more importantly, our capacity as sponges – our thirst for information (mine admittedly the greater capacity because like all auto-didacts I valued learning more highly than those to whom it had been a birthright) – we were both a little out of context. Round pegs in square holes, as Fr. Paul would have said. There was the teeniest hint of fragmentation about her, the hair-line cracks in the personality that time would weather and widen; she had the potential, not always a happy one, for eclecticism. Right now, she was, to use her father's happy expression, as ordinary as vanilla ice-cream, but I could see the possibility of melt and blur, of $Halo^2$ for her children, if not for her.

"Anyone need a comfort-stop?" I asked. "Just say the word. Otherwise Camp Fortescue's at least three hours away." I referred to the old hill-station where we were to spend our first night on the road by its colonial name, rather than the Malay one with its string of consonants like firecrackers. As an Asian, I found the English name more evocatively romantic. Those Westerners educated enough to have a sense of the past probably did, too. The young ladies declined the invitation, with some talk of snakes lurking in the undergrowth. Their innocence of the fundamental cliches of Freudian symbolism seemed so incredible I thought I was the butt of a joke until I saw Jenny's smile of complicity with me. She shook her head slightly. Jeez – thousands of dollars a semester. In Asia a Jesuit education was still the best, whether the recipients were high or low.

My freight of boppers in the Lexus were as flighty and temperamental as race-horses in their box. The singing soon palled. My attempts to render and still worse, teach, them the words of *I've been working on the railroad all the live-long day*, so successful when taught to us by Fr. Boy at San Ignatio, further dampened their girlish spirits.

"Well, look," I said, "who knows a good ghost story?" To judge by the glum silence, no one did.

"Miss Jenny?"

She shook her head. "But why don't you tell us about the Philippines, Rey? About yourself, I mean."

"Not an interesting topic, Miss Jenny, I think."

"It's very interesting," Sonika and Nicky chorused.

"Yes," said Jenny, "I've never met anyone like you. What kind of friends did you have?"

"Nobody you would take to, Miss Jenny, I can assure you of that."

"Don't judge people too quickly," Jenny replied shortly.

I think she was mad because she thought I'd called her stuck-up.

Angie Verghese, bless her Asian dislike of personal disputation, said, "I'm glad we're with Rey. It makes me feel safe."

"What?" scoffed Caucasian Nicky.

"Oh, yes," said Becky Chow. "Things can happen here. I mean Indonesia's spookier. It's terrible for Chinese there, but things happen here, too."

"Like what?" Nicky inquired sceptically.

"All kinds of things happen in Indonesia and Malaysia that don't happen in Hong Kong and Singapore," Becky said.

"Do they speak different languages, Becky? I mean the Indonesians and Malaysians?" Jenny asked

I thought this was an interesting question, too.

"Not really. I mean Malay's more refined-sounding but they understand each other. That's Bahasa Indonesia which they speak all over the archipelago. Singaporeans will understand that, just like they speak Malay. But then there are all kinds of local dialects in Indonesia which people don't understand unless they live in the area, it's such a huge country."

"Have you been lots?"

"Just twice. Dad's got business there with his cousins. He goes all the time but he won't take us to Jakarta, it's too dangerous, and as for Medan, forget it. Like I said, all kinds of things can happen to you and no one will find out."

"Go on then, what?"

"Well, you'd probably be OK, Nicky, because you stand out. They could rob you but they couldn't take you away. It's worse for Chinese: we stick out but we don't stick out, if you see what I mean and even if you're careful they're very tricky."

"Tell me about tricky. I'm interested in tricky." This was me.

"Well, Rey, we had friends go to Jakarta from home. They knew not to go to some places after dark or accept food from strangers in case it was drugged, but they had to get into a taxi to go somewhere in broad daylight in Jakarta. The taxi broke down after a mile and the driver told the husband to get out and push to re-start it. Well, he did and just as he put his hands on the trunk to push, the taxi roared off with his wife in the back still."

"Oh, my God!" exclaimed Jenny. "Did they catch the driver?"

"No. And they never saw the Singaporean girl again either."

"Oh goodness, what did they *do* to her?" asked Angie.

"Made her work in a brothel, I expect," said Nicky.

"Yuk!"

"They don't kidnap you like that in India, not foreigners, I mean," said Angie, "but you can't just go around like you do in Goa. It's almost worse. They do it *publicly*. Everyone's in on it."

"Now don't exaggerate," Jenny said.

"I'm not. Honestly. There were two Swedish girls from the Upper Sixth who went to Calcutta and they got on to a bus with their rucksacks. I mean, how stupid can you get. I could have told them they were asking for it. They were at the front – it was Bretta and Marianne, you know them, Nicks, when they found themselves getting separated from their bags. They said it was like being in the sea and getting moved away from the boat by the wind and the current little by little with you having no control over it."

"I know exactly what you mean, Miss Verghese," I said. "Go on."

"Well, they were half-way down the bus before they realised it was deliberate. The other passengers were doing it, you know, wiggling their hips, turning, nudging them with their shoulders and backsides. Bretta said it was like surfing on a human wave and she said the amazing thing about it was that it wasn't tearaways or young kids doing it, it was perfectly respectable people, women as well. No one said anything, either. It was all done in perfect silence, like a conspiracy by telepathy. But they were all in on it. Well, at the back of the bus the *badmashes* actually *were* waiting for them. It was all men. There were hands everywhere, it was like fighting an octopus. Their clothes were coming off. Marianne's blouse got ripped. Bretta lost her belt, you know that Mexican one with the turquoises everyone wanted to buy from her. Zips, everything. Those Indian men got their hands, their fingers in. It was getting more and more every moment. They were having everything done to them, short of getting raped up completely, and *that* was only a matter of time. They were fighting back all the time – they're quite big girls, those two – and Marianne managed to bite one old guy's ear and he yelled. That was the only sound anyone ever made. The bus jammed on its brakes at a stop, the door opened, and Bretta and Marianne half-struggled, half-fell into the road. They lost their packs and a lot of money but they didn't care."

"Did they report it to the police?" Jenny asked.

"Oh, no. Entering a police station is more dangerous than getting on a bus. Bretta's uncle is in the diplomatic service – he phoned a friend there and he picked them up."

A silence fell upon us. Young people are on the whole not optimistic folk when in a group. They like to spook each other, *di ba*? Especially those who lead the softest lives. I'd made a mistake trying to be master of ceremonies and I decided to leave well alone in future. We arrived through the evening mists at our overnight stop in a hungry silence.

At the rest-house, they put a sensational meal on the formica tables of the empty refectory just for us. This came from the simplest of kitchens comprising just a wood-fire and two pans. There were no concessions with the chilli, rice-flour noodles with egg, shrimp, crunchy sambal, and the most piquant peanut sauce with the satay. The Malays got the vital variety in the mouth, the *halo*[2] effect, with texture rather than clash of tastes. One thing about backwoods Asia: you ate well, however primitive and filthy the surroundings. It was the complete opposite of back home. In the Philippines we were the Sick Man of Asia gastronomically as well as economically. We'd expired of food-boredom but didn't know it. At BBQ stand or five-star hotel, it was the same over-salted and predictable shit, except you were more likely to get salmonella at the five-star than at proud Nanay's stall.

The food here was dirt-cheap by Hong Kong and Singapore standards, which was good because Mrs Smith and the Commander had us on the tightest of budgets. Jenny laughed about it over the orange crush she was washing the fiery *char kway teow* down with, but Nicky's groans and shaking of the head were not assumed. It occurred to me that their parents didn't want them away for too long but then I disabused myself of that notion. The Smiths definitely were mean, no question about it, Mrs Smith a world-class Scrooge. You could have made an excuse and said the way they showed love to their children was by not spoiling them, but the kids themselves certainly thought their parents were a pair of incorrigible misers.

Anyhow, when I got back from a comfort-call, the CR as stupendously filthy as the meal was stupendous to the taste-buds, I found a one and a half litre bottle of beer by my plate. Jenny, who had a few pennies of her own, and Becky Chow whose father was a billionaire, not a millionaire, in US and not in Singapore dollars, and was at least as mean as the Smiths, had clubbed together to buy it for me.

"It'll help you relax and sleep, Rey," said Jenny. "It must be very tiring concentrating on the road all the time." There was a chorus of assent and appreciation from the girls. I was so touched, I felt my eyes prick. OK, I'm a big softie. When I had my hand-job that night, I thought of Becky kneeling in front of me, with her purple Chinese lips wrapped round the head of my dick, while I embraced and kissed Erlinda, protein-stunted 'Lin, whose head came up to my own nipples, as she squashed her small breasts against my abs, wearing only her Koala bear on her back and her brand-name Italian loafers without socks. Then, unbidden, just as I shot, I had a vision of Haydee on her back, blood trickling from her nose, her splayed legs, the waving soles of her feet and the bulbs of her toes, sending the signals of a drowning victim. I grimaced, but there was nothing wrong with my orgasm.

In the morning cock-crow woke me, the city-boy who knew that call well from the champion birds raised by our neighbours for the betting-pit. It was *krepok* crackers, coffee like black ink, and fried rice at breakfast, the shrimpy scent of the crackers leaving your hands as if you'd just fingered a girl. That little tease Angie Verghese smirked as she caught me surreptitiously sniffing them. I wondered if there was time for another hand-job before team-manager Jenny had us hitting the road, then pondered with some desperation how I was gonna get through the trip sane. It was like there was another gear-stick thrusting up between my legs and the steering-wheel. As it turned out, that wasn't a problem. The longer the trip went, the higher the figures clocking up on the milometer, the lower my libido. I luxuriated in the feminine camaraderie. At the age I was then, the better I got to know a woman the less I wanted to fuck her; she became a friend, not pussy on legs. It was like being down at the bar with Ma and her co-workers, as unthinkable as screwing Auntie Lovely-Anne or Auntie Monalisa. I must have been one of the few guys in the RP constitutionally incapable of doing it with a bar-girl and my freight of, for all I knew, middle-class virgins became as untouchable as bar-fined prosties to me.

We were giving the tourist sights of old world Malacca and Penang island on the West Coast a miss as my Misses had seen them before. Instead, we were going up the East Coast.

In retrospect, this probably wasn't such a bright idea but it had borne a compelling logic back in Hong Kong as Commander Smith pored over the map with me. "You can take a detour here," he had said, stabbing the map with those incongruously porky fingers that looked incapable of doing the delicate work they'd done in mouths scattered over all the waters of the world. "That's the real Malaya," he'd said, "*kampong* Malaya, not the Johnny Come Latelys in the cities or the grab-it-while-you-can pols. The traditional values are still intact there in the village, *adat*, the customary law, and the writ of the headman. We couldn't filch it from them, Rey, the British, I mean, and it can't be stolen from them now."

"I admire the way you can talk about the British from outside, Serr, I like it. I like to do the same myself about Filipinos."

"Mmm. Well, I did forget to say Malaysia."

At lunch-time, the sun beating down and the rains yesterday's impossibility, I made my own discovery: the Malays had a drink called *es cendol*, which was a slippery *Halo*[2] more nearly approaching the condition of liquid, though in fact still sludgy, concocted on a more austere palette for the palate of three colours only: white (coconut cream), green (sago-beads), and red (beans). My neutral and objective opinion on this was that it was a masterpiece. Jenny had a studenty discussion with me about the symbolism of the colours: colonialists, Muslims, and Chinese Communists.

As we drove on, I was looking for a place for them to bathe, but it was uncompromising mangrove where we found ourselves. From

Fr. Boy's natural history class I knew the mangrove was the indispensable plant: no mangrove swamp, no coral reef offshore, no fish, no protein for Pepe. On the other hand, in the real world, finding the coral sustained by the mangrove-swamp was no easy task. Adjuvant, yes, adjacent, no. Finally, after the road had curved us inland out of sight of the sea for nearly an hour we came back to a more promising foreshore. Not the beaches of the Malaysian tourist department we saw in brochure and commercial in Singapore but definitely sand, grubby where it wasn't bilious, but nevertheless no longer illimitable tracts of black mud. Away in the distance was a collection of shanties on stilts, the *kampong*. I continued a while before cutting the motor and letting us glide to a halt, like a boat, without braking. Complete silence, which none of us, not even bumptious Angie, broke. The peace was indescribable. We sat in the Lexus, the hot bonnet starting to creak and crack now. Jenny unwound the window, letting in the real air, which cosseted us in its blanket folds. I've never liked air-con. "Oh, God, how marvellous," she groaned. "Why do human beings live in cities?"

"Who's for a dip?" Nicky asked.

It was a great time of day for a swim, the light no longer brutal but golden and yet to wane. They all latched on to the proposal. This was the first time I noticed something that subsequent experiences would confirm: Caucasian, and even Westernised Asian girls, were more up for a dare or fun than the boys were. I pretended to take a leak in the bamboos while the girls took turns to change behind an open car-door. They ran, shrieking, down the sand to the water but the effect and sensation of diving into the waves was denied them. Either it was low water or a very shallow beach for even fifty metres out it came only as deep as their ankles. They stood in a line − if they'd been *pinays* they'd have held hands − looking at the shapes of the islands. Jenny was the only one wearing a bikini. I gathered bikinis, which seemed the last word in modernity and boldness to me as well, though I was more used to seeing them on go-go dancers, were deemed yesterday's attire by Nicky and her contemporaries who all sported monos. I should say these made the two-piece, on the face of it more revealing, look staid. Sonika Narayan's was the most conservative, but even this sleek film of black, poured around the curves and bumps of her young body, gave a more unambiguous indication of what lay underneath than Jenny's generous triangular spinnakers at front and rear. As for what Nicky, Becky, and especially Angie had on, the strategically placed perforations, lattice-work, holes, buckles, laces, and windows were more provocative than nudity. As she came back to the Lexus, through the port-hole sized aperture in the Lycra on Angie's midriff, I could see the hairs around her navel which were somehow more intimate than the pubic curls escaping from the V of her crotch. Was I the lucky guy, or what?

Clunk! a rock smacked into the virgin navy-blue side-panel of Commander Smith's Toyota. *Chok*! and another one, before a third made a grittier impact against a window. Three very young boys emerged from the bamboos, holding more rocks in their muddy hands. I figured at first that this was just rustic juvenile delinquency, occurring in despite of the famous *adat*. But then a very representative age cross-section of the *kampong* rose from behind the canes. Uh-oh, I thought. Wrong place, wrong time. And a moment later as a pair of head-shawled crones advanced on me, shaking their outstretched hands, I got it: wrong dress-code, too. One thing was the same: none of the young men were at all eager to get very near me. For their part, the kids and old women behaved as if I wasn't going to go for them, an assumption which was unfortunately correct. One of the hags came close enough to spit. She missed. Her copious mouthful ran down the car-window. I looked at her sadly. It was difficult to get me angry at the worst of times. I hadn't got mad when Bong Ibanez of University of Mindanao had hit me full in the face with the frothy, lactic saliva of a stressed circulatory system, but then Bong's spit was likely superbly healthy compared to this diseased witch's.

Jenny and the younger girls were hiding behind the open door of the Lexus. Jenny was holding Nicky from behind, both arms protectively round her younger sister's neck, though Nicky looked the least perturbed of them all. Becky Chow was the most scared. In fact, she looked terrified. As a Chinese, she had reason to be before a Malay mob. I felt a small prick of anger on behalf of those I was supposed to be escorting.

"Girls," I said, "this is all managable, if we don't lose our heads. So let's not lose our heads." This was, I admit, a borrowed Butch Tan Sy-ism. Original to our pickle, I added, "Just get your clothes from inside the car and put them on. Put them on over your costumes, don't take off your costumes. Not too fast, don't show you're scared."

"Why should we?" Nicky asked with commendable spirit, except in my opinion it wasn't a great time and place to be belligerent. "It's a free country."

"I don't think it is, Miss Nicky. Just get dressed, please, and we'll discuss it later."

"Do what Rey says, Nicks."

I gasped as a heavy rock took me in the chest. Things were deteriorating. They could have swung any way: a slap in the face of one of the boys or a few friendly words in the Malay none of us, except Becky Chow, possessed, might have halted the slide, and stopped it decisively in our favour. But the way it had swung was downhill, and that had momentum. I stepped towards the biggest of the mature guys. He was at least eighteen inches shorter than me, and he ran backwards five steps without taking his eyes off my face. Quite difficult in a *sarong*. I stepped back, as I'd planned, and even as another rock bounced off the roof still calculated we could get out of it with our dignity ruffled and some dents in our pride as well as the Lexus. Joining the girls in the car, I pressed the button for the central locking and then switched on the ignition. As I slowly moved off, the palms beating on the trunk and bonnet rose to a crescendo.

Then there were a whiz and a roar and suddenly two motorbikes were among us. The riders, in green overalls and two in crash-helmets, dismounted quickly. The pillion-rider of the first bike grabbed a cane from an old man. As three small stones sailed towards him (guess they'd run out of heavy ammo from the river-bed) he smacked two of the pebbles square-on, one after the other, forehand and backhand, sending them whirring, rattling, and rebounding, twice as fast as they had come, through the bamboos. The third projectile, aimed at the Lexus directly behind us, he jumped up and drove with an overhand smash straight into a tree trunk where it embedded itself into the bark like David's slingshot in Goliath's forehead.

Man, we were as shell-shocked as the villagers.

It didn't stop there. The guy took off his helmet and pushed one of the old crones on the shoulder with what I thought was a perfectly measured amount of force, about as much as you'd need to sink a twenty-yarder, as beautifully done in its way as the volleying away of the stones. Some harsh Malay words followed. His companions now got into the act. He himself was clearly of Chinese extraction but his two friends were equally clearly Malay: dark and curly-haired. They aimed kicks which missed widely, as planned, but sent the villagers scurrying away. One of the crowd stopped a moment to glare behind her spectacles at me, with an expression which specifically said she had no sympathy for the Negro. I didn't like her, either. With her better-quality head scarf, the spectacles, the round complacent face of half-baked urban bigotry, she reminded me of the ignorant nuns whom Fr. Paul so fervently despised – almost more than he did the Liberation Theologians.

The Chinese guy tossed the splintered cane away. As he got near us, he said in surprise, "Jenny Smith!"

Well, did that ever get everybody's interest, the focus of it shifting from Sir Lancelot to our own damsel in distress and a bikini halter.

"Jerome!" she exclaimed, through the slid-down window. I moved away politely, to give them a little privacy and to practise not behaving like a Filipino. Now I could see the guys' green overalls were a uniform or flying-suits of some kind.

I played back in my mind's eye what I'd just witnessed. It had just been perfectly, surgically done: the immaculate timing and accuracy with which the guy had swiped the stones away, not to say the ferocity; if he hadn't struck the rocks so perfectly the whole example would have been lost. No one got hurt but the message was clear: you, too, can get whacked with consummate timing. Then the hard but innocuous shove to the old woman, not the sturdy male I'd chosen: that said, you're dealing with ruthless people; people untrammelled by chivalry or compunction. And, in the way Malaysians knew far better than to mess with their own police, they'd decided not to meddle with these uniforms, whatever they were.

"I think you can continue without problems," the guy was saying to Jenny. "But we'll ride cover for you till KT."

"Oh, gosh, thanks, would you, Jerome," Jenny said.

"Sure."

"Thanks so much."

"You're very welcome, lah, Miss Smith. Follow me." He nodded civilly to me. I couldn't stop saluting him which was very stupid because I had no right to do it but it was the same thing we did as kids to the officers at Mactan Field. He nodded again, then got on the pillion-seat of the bike and donned his helmet. The Malay driving it wasn't wearing one. I started the Lexus, no damage to anything other than bodywork, and did my best to drive no faster than usual.

The topic of the next hour was, of course, nothing except what had just happened.

"Where *did* they come from?" Angie squeaked.

"They'd crossed from the Butterworth side," Jenny explained. "They'd finished exercises with the Australian Mirage group there and were going to the resort near KT to swim and spend the night with the other reservists."

"Oh, just like us," Sonika giggled. We all had a hysterical laugh to get it out of our systems.

"How could he hit the stones like that?" Angie asked. "Is it like firing missiles? They played volley-ball in *Top Gun*."

More hysteria.

"Actually, Jerome's played badminton in the SEA Games," Jenny said modestly. "That was before he took up Tae Kwan Do."

"I wonder," Nicky mused, "if that was a crash-helmet or his bone-dome?"

Everyone groaned, and Jenny and I looked at each other. One to go with the Freudian snakes. As we quietened down, the enveloping darkness outside continued as a reassurance to us, even after the bikes had accelerated away, with a last cheerful wave. Ten minutes later I couldn't resist saying, "I didn't think Jerome was very wimpish, Nicky." But she was already asleep.

In the one-horse Malaysian seaside town where we halted we made it early to retire and early to rise. Nicky wasn't the only tired one. I thought it was nervous exhaustion; they'd hardly walked four hundred metres all day long. After they'd ascended the stained concrete stairs with the time-honoured injunction not to bring *durians* into the hotel, past the rusty fire-extinguishers, and into the two rooms whose doors didn't lock – but who was complaining at twenty five ringgit a night – I went for a stroll. Personally, I couldn't have slept without a little exercise. The aura of faint-hearted seediness clung to town as well as hotel; it didn't just afflict transients like us, it was pandemic. The architecture and municipal layout were typical: lanes made up of rows of three-storey tenements, with flights of stairs leading up from ground-level to long open walkways where you could peer over the stone balustrades into the empty street you'd just vacated and find it still deserted. The ground-floor businesses were coffee-shops with spittoons and grubby mosaic floors, Halal restaurants, roti-shops, the odd Chinese noodlery, pharmacies.

Second floor contained travel agents, barber-shops with the twirling red and white poles (which I can vouch are symbols as internationally comprehended as maritime Flag "A") and the odd Klinik or dentist (*Syd* or *Lon*). The top storey was residential. Without leaving the fucking building, you could fill your belly, buy a ticket the hell out, take a shave, have your blood-pressure monitored, and if all else failed, jump from the top floor. It was — how can I put it? — antiseptic but unwholesome, like corpse pickling in brandy-butt. It stifled, it numbed. Looking round you, you felt there should have been a smell in the air, that it wasn't absent but merely overlaid temporarily. The barber shops, with the wary white faces of the Chinese chicks peering through the blinds, hard girls who gave muscular shampoos and snipped amateurishly, had the look of police-harassed but municipally-tolerated brothel about them. The whole town was a wound forgotten because there was no longer any feeling in it. I smelled joylessness and hypocrisy and random and arbitrary punishments and pleasure taken in corners. I preferred back home. We were fucked up but knew it and wore a smile on our faces. Here they didn't even know they were dead. Returning to the hotel along the identical street at the back, I heard Visayan spoken — *dili* for "no" instead of *hindi*. It was two illegal-looking Filipinas, selling cigarettes with faces as miserable as the locals. They didn't smile when I bought cigarettes which I still never smoked even a thousand miles away from Butch, and I didn't startle my fellow Filipinos by speaking Pilipino. I thought they were probably sick of being screwed by the law.

Crossing the border into Southern Thailand the next day wasn't the tonic change I was hoping for. I had this TV-fostered image of the place as one giant Phuket: waterfalls, orchids, sumptuous buffets, chicks even lovelier than the *pinay*, long-tailed boats navigating the limestone pinnacles of *Goldfinger*. Well, we weren't just on the wrong coast for all that. Watching the odd, lying tourist plug for the Republic of the Philippines hadn't wised me up. It was the same hick towns as Northern Malaysia, the concrete boxes even plainer than on the other side of the border, dust, and women covered head to toe, and halal restaurants. It was the southern Thailand of mosque and minaret rather than the North of wat and Buddha. I could even see the Chinese on this side of the border regarding the Muslims with the same stony, implacable faces as the Malaysian Chinese had.

On the other side they were hereditary enemies, OK, but here they were today's enemies. Only the flesh-trade was more open. The reason for existence of the inland town we halted at for early lunch was servicing the Malaysian men who came over the frontier, principally at weekends, to get laid on the cheap by Thai girls who were on the young side. It was less surreptitious than Malaysia, in fact quite open, but done with equal joylessness, a production-line. The girls might have been sticking electrical components into a socket. That would certainly have been better paid.

After our curried duck, on the way out, we drove past a ruined but still forbidding building, a flash of gold surviving on a bulbous tower. Becky Chow said, "I think Chinese broke that many years ago. It's a Mohammedan temple." Saying, "I think," was her way of saying, "I know."

Jenny said, "Otherwise known as a mosque. Religious bigotry is a terrible thing."

I thought silently, "Unless it's each other the dickhead fanatics are whacking." We passed another mosque recently renovated. The Chinese had built a temple, particularly garish even for a modern Chinese temple, so close it was shoulder to shoulder, like guard marking netter. Any self-respecting coach would have screamed foul.

On I drove, ever northwards. I filled with more gas than I really wanted at a ramshackle station flaunting a famous logo – I couldn't get out of the parsimonious *pinoy* habit of a few drops of gas at frequent intervals – because I'd spent most of the small notes lubricating frontier bureaucracy, greasing in garage or border post always a dirty business, and I only had a 500 *baht* note left which the gas station pretended they couldn't change. Jenny noticed my face. "What's wrong, Rey?" she asked. I told her. Nicky said from the back, her head in Angie's lap and her feet sticking out of the open door, "What's the difference? We'll still use the petrol later."

"Maybe someone will suck it out of the tank, Miss Nicky."

"Goodness me," exclaimed Jenny, "that's paranoiac."

"Old habits die hardest," I said apologetically. What was I worrying about? Was it my gas, my money? I'll tell you something: the loyal retainer guards the employer's property *more* jealously than if it was his own.

At last we arrived at the old, out of the way resort town one of Commander Smith's patients, a Thai airline manager, had recommended to him as safe, tranquil, beautiful, and still cheap. An industry tip if ever there was one. This place was so good it felt illicit; it was like having a fix on a game. We meant to stay a couple of days before crossing to Krabi on the West Coast but never got any further. It was the cutest, dinkiest little beach I ever set bare foot on, ten yards wide at low water and just five at high, the sand a warm gold, firm underfoot whatever the tide with groves of scrubby conifers and acacias giving shade further back. The sea itself was as transparent as the export-strength Gordon's gin Commander Smith preferred; when you looked down at your submerged legs it was like gazing into a crystal ball. With all this, it was a working beach, the fishing boats drawn up on the strand by day, going out at night with the kerosene lamps pumped and pressurised to the point of incandescence. All my life there's one thing Pilipino I've never lost: the habit of early rising. I'd see the boats, garlanded with the bow-wave, heading in as I paced the dark beach at four thirty. It would be some time before you could hear the meaty beat of the little engines; they tended to have Jap makes, rather than the ubiquitous Briggs and Strattons and Kohlers of back home. For me it was cold when it was "Oh, lovely and cool," for the Smiths, and I'd shiver in the half-light, listening to the lazy broom-sweep of the sea every ten seconds. Placid enough, but I'd get to thinking about Michael and Em and Hot Dang Man and their companions on the slow drift to Palawan. This was the stretch of water so many of them had died on and the young Thai guys I was buying red snapper from for a few coins were the type who'd been raping the girls on the islands they'd dragged them to and batting and stabbing at the Vietnamese boys' heads in the water. Maybe some of the very guys who'd refrained from bargaining with me with such hardy cheerfulness and who saluted Becky Chow with such faultless courtesy. Then I'd think, fuck, it could happen to anybody, wrong company, wrong time, a haywire context. The pirates were less cold-blooded than the governments and navies who'd towed the boats out of territorial waters and riddled the already rotten hulls with .50 cal till they were floating colanders. My depressive moods vanished with the half-light: it was more difficult to free yourself from an immediate context of weather or minor ailment than a whole upbringing or an entire culture, it really was. I've met Professors and Monsignors born in poverty whose Pa's were truck-drivers and street-sweepers but never anyone who looked cheerful when it was raining on vacation or who were boisterous in a dentist's waiting-room.

I would set the charcoal brickets on fire and by the time Jenny was rubbing her eyes coming down the short walk into the sea, the snapper would be spitting and sizzling for their breakfast, with rice-balls the size of bull's testicles plaited into hygienic banana-leaf jackets and four kinds of Thai dip, purchased from what I would have called a sari-sari store. Somehow, without visible electrical supply, the store-keeper managed to have ice-cold drinks always available, the ten-year-old daughter salting our cokes with no timid hand as if it went without saying, like providing a straw. The Thais were heavily into taste-clash, kick-boxing on the palate. I don't think Nicky & Co noticed the soft-drink tasted less sweet than elsewhere. Jenny didn't want any at breakfast until I pointed out it was as potent a caffeine-shot as Nescafé and that, if she desired, it could be served boiling-hot in the lower-class Chinese way – my first drink in Tun Muen, with the sand still on me. At that point she surrendered and was content to have it cold.

I've never owned a swimming-costume in my life – still don't – but the voluminous shorts that were just starting to become fashionable answered my purpose perfectly. I saw them as team apparel rather than cool street-wear and, in fact, they were equipment as well as clothing for me. I was a terrible swimmer, negatively buoyant, and the trapped air helped keep me afloat at the cost of looking like a farter. Floundering parallel to shore, I'd watch the girls head straight out, much too far I thought, then back in to harass me. As I easily stood in a depth where they had to tread water I wasn't too handicapped. The gentle giant. OK, I was happy with that.

Everyone was happy, in fact, but Jenny and I were in heaven. For the younger of the party it was just a great beach holiday, untrammelled by adult supervision; for me and Jenny it was the chance to be an evolved person, the first opportunity we'd had to practise being adults ourselves. All my life I'd been someone's pupil or protege, in a society where getting to old age was regarded as an achievement in itself. Jenny, I knew, felt cooped in an extended childhood because she was still living at home. This vacation, with its responsibilities, was like an unconsummated marriage to me, the Beast. It was enough for us to get wet, soak up the sun, and feel our age for once.

So when Angie and Sonika discovered there was a "scene" at a town twelve kilometres north, our joint inclination was to say "no", more for the sake of it than any good reason. Angie and Sonika kept smiling, Nicky blew her top, totally unusual for Miss Cool. "Just who do you think you are, Jens, anyway? You're not my guardian, you know. You're just a… a square."

"Goodness me! What an outdated piece of slang. Just saying it makes *you* 'square' yourself."

Sonika, Angie, and Becky burst out laughing, which did nothing to make Nicky feel less pissed.

"Come on Jens, it's only eight miles. We'll walk it if you don't let us."

"What happens at these things?" I asked.

"Don't ask," Angie giggled.

"Well, that certainly makes me more inclined to let you go, doesn't it," Jenny said.

"It's a general *rave*," Sonika told her, the Indian accent coming through more strongly than usual, so it sounded like "reeve". Becky, our Singaporean, said informatively, "Music, silly. Reggae. Rap. Heavy metal. No Cliff. Dancing till you drop. Free food. Free drink stirred in a big drum," much as if she was reeling off the ingredients on a bottle of shampoo.

"Boys," said Jenny. "Alcohol. Brawling. Drugs, probably. No. *Non. Nein. Nyet.* I can't imagine why you'd want to go, Nicks. I doubt you'll be able to hear yourself think. It's for the brain-dead."

"Come off it. Don't tell me you never went clubbing when you were at that crammer's in London because I know you did."

"It's the full moon tomorrow," Becky said. "I remember Andy in Class Six saying that's when they hold the big party."

There was really going to be a full moon, too. The great yellow orb had been swelling in the sky every night. Our juniors worked on Jenny in their different ways: direct Caucasian, indirect Oriental, manipulative Indian, dissembling Eurasian, you name it. Jenny's resolve started to melt. Who wants to be thought past it at the age of twenty-two? She called me in for some back-up. I did my Pontius Pilate bit. I came from a place where if someone really wanted to do something, you sweetly said "O," and acquiesced even if you really didn't like the idea at all. And, in actuality, I had plenty of reservations.

Going the whole hog in the end, Jenny planned to remain behind while I drove the teenies and then waited. But Sonika, Angie, and Becky wouldn't have it. They insisted she should come. I think the three other girls didn't want to hurt Jenny's feelings; Nicky didn't care if she did.

We got there at ten p.m. to find nothing had started. Of course it hadn't. Were we the Hicks from Hicksville or what? Our little teeny-boppers were chagrined but tried to preserve their cool, pretended they knew already. Jenny and I left them at the venue, out on the rocks, ringed by oil-drums, and killed time with a snack. The only thing available that night at the Travellers' Café were fruit-shakes and mushroom omelette. We split the latter and Jenny had a green mango-shake, a novel experience for her. As we were finishing, a girl and two guys came to the only free of the four tables. To say the girl was interesting to me would be to say the Mona Lisa is a painting. She was one of the Lost Tribe of Amerasians: lighter-skinned than most but with the tell-tale skull that even surmounted with blonde hair *à la Cubana* can never be anything else. Her hair was braided in locks and bunched into an unsubdued pony-tail at the side, fetching and original, too. Same Golden Horde cheekbones as me and eyes slantier than even Ma's. Man, she was a perfect specimen of us to look at, but something arrogant in her step, a hint of aggressiveness that Michael and every black girl I knew in Mactan, and also myself, didn't have. She got me in the same glance as I got her, and we both quickly looked away. The guys with her were Asians.

"Those mushrooms are a bit bitter," Jenny said.

"Yeah, for me also. I think the eggs were OK, though, Miss Jenny."

"Do just call me Jenny, Rey."

The Amerasian girl passed us deliberately close on the way to put in their order; the service was self-effacing to the point of non-existent. As she came back, I said, "Hello, Miss, where are you from?" I half-expected her not to understand, or to reply in Michael's pidgin English. She could, after all, have been African, not American. I tried English in the spirit of St Paul, the Roman citizen, laying Latin on a new batch of sceptical pagans in whatever hick town in Asia Minor he found himself preaching because English is, after all, the Latin of our day and Sport our Mithras-cult. *Di ba,* folks? Besides, I didn't yet know anything other than Pilipino. Being with Jenny absolved me from being fresh. To my great surprise, the black girl replied in English as perfect, or imperfect, but certainly as idiomatic, as any Motown star's: "I don't know any more, but not from here, for sure. That's a very direct question, Brother. Where are *you* from?"

"Cebu," I said. "Know it?"

She shook her head. "No, but don't tell me. It's a US navy port, right?"

"Nearly. Airfield. Subic is the Navy."

"OK. I'm from Khorat. Nakhon Ratchasima. Or I was born there. There's an airbase there, too."

"US?"

"I don't think they were Martians, though they might as well have been 'cause no one's seen them since '75."

"Bases for bombing Viet Nam, right?"

"Affirmative."

"Shit! I thought Thailand was an independent, neutral country."

"Yeah, and weren't you?"

"OK," I said, "good net."

"We had it worse, or better, depending on your point of view. Seven bases in Thailand. Does that make me Snow White?"

"Wow!"

"So there are plenty of you and me. Yeah, seven."

"Sounds like witchcraft," Jenny said. We both looked at her. "You know necromantic figure. Not just Happy, Grumpy, Dopey, and Co. Seven Deadly Sins and all that."

"Seven Samurai," I said. "The Magnificent Seven." I looked at Jenny. Her eyes seemed very black and very focussed. The remark had been unlike her, with her exaggerated fear of offending the susceptibilities of races whom at bottom she probably considered inferior.

"OK," said our new friend. "I'm DeLorna by the way."

"Call me Sugar," I said. "And this is my employer, Miss Jenny."

"Jenny Smith. Hi. I'm his employer's daughter, actually. I didn't know you were called Sugar, Rey."

"Ah, it's just what my friends call me. Ay! That sounds terrible. Sorry, Jenny."

She started to laugh and I caught the urge, too. We snickered together. Jenny was no giggler and though I could guffaw with the crudest in the team I didn't normally whinny like a horse. We got caught up on the wave and couldn't stop ourselves for a good minute. DeLorna smiled sympathetically at us, catching her two companions' eyes briefly. When Jenny and I had controlled ourselves she said, "These are Ah Lim and Semporn."

I said, "Hi," and they nodded affably. "Don't speak English? It's no problem. It's my fault for not speaking Thai."

Jenny and I giggled. We thought I'd been very witty.

"They're Cambodians," DeLorna said. "Semporn's pure Khmer but Ah Lim's Chinese. Ah Lim can't speak Thai too good, so the fact that you don't speak it isn't the question." She sounded as if she faintly regretted having begun our conversation. I had the feeling that Jenny and I were behaving like drunken boors, boring drunks. "Apologies," I said. "I didn't mean to sound rude."

A young Thai boy of about eleven or twelve came up with a basket of peanuts. As we all ignored him, he touched the older Cambodian guy, Semporn's, elbow with the edge of the basket. Just the gentlest, politest of gestures. Semporn, who was a refined-looking, bespectacled guy in his late forties with the jet black hair Asian guys of his age didn't think twice about dyeing, turned, saw who it was, and with an exclamation back-handed the kid in the face.

The sickly schoolgirl grin came off Jenny's own face. I was shocked, too. Could have been Dant or me at the same age selling peanuts to sailors. DeLorna smiled faintly now. "Semporn hates young boys," she said. To the Thai kid, she said, "*Jai yen, jai yen*," and gave him a dirty banknote. "What's that?" I asked.

"Twenty baht."

"No. What you said."

"*Jai yen*. Cool heart. It's a Thai expression."

"Oh, man, I like that. Like it."

Jenny was regarding Semporn with a look of fixed aggression, really quite disconcerting even to a guy who liked belting eleven-year-olds in the kisser. Her pupils were scary. "Yeah, *jai yen*, Jens," I said with the liberty the situation allowed.

Semporn said something. DeLorna translated, "He says he just doesn't trust young boys any more. Sorry. He can't stand the sight of them." There was only one reply to this: "Why?"

Before I could speak, Jenny, who hadn't taken her eyes off Semporn's face asked, "*Parlez-vous Français, Monsieur?*"

"Mais, oui, Mademoiselle," and his face lit up. He and Jenny exchanged a few pleasantries that sounded right out of Jenny's old school text-books. Semporn spoke hesitantly, with many pauses, but then with growing enthusiasm as if he had a lot to get off his chest. Which, brother, he had. Jenny complimented him on his French – some Western social conventions were as much lying bullshit as ours. Semporn smiled wryly. *"Je suis d'un certain âge,"* he explained, *"et les gens en Camboge de ce generation parlaient la langue de leurs mâitres mais, comprenez-vous, pas bien, et maintenant c'est… trente ans que je n'ai jamais parlé le Francais. Pour les langues je manque talent. Je suis Professeur de Math, des Mathématiques."*

Jenny turned to me, trying not to look proud of that unusual accomplishment in the native speaker of English – those arrogant and insular souls – a second language. "He speaks French because he grew up in the colonial times but he hasn't spoken it in twenty years. He says he was rotten at languages anyway…"

"… because he was a Math Prof. And I thought it was thirty years."

"How did you know that? Do you know French as well?"

"Nope, but the Jesuits taught me Latin and how to piece together a context. Pilipino's very Spanish *na lang* as well. *Trenta* is what we say for thirty. Go on, Jenny."

"I'm not sure I can, my French isn't as rusty as his, but it's certainly a lot dodgier."

"That doesn't matter, Miss Jenny. It's like *pinoys* speaking English to each other. It's incorrect but Taglish works perfectly because they understand what the other means."

"I don't think we're making the same mistakes. Anyway…"

Semporn was looking from Jenny's face to mine. "Please," I said, "continue." He certainly understood that.

"I hate young boys," he said through Jenny, "because they are completely amoral. There is nothing of which they are not capable. *Je ne crois pas qu'existe l'innocence. Les Khmers Rouges pour la plupart étaient très jeunes*. The average age of the Khmer Rouge with the gun or the whip was fifteen, many as young as twelve, as young as that boy there. *Je ne suis pas seul*. There are many who share my prejudice."

"Mais vous vivez encore, Monsieur," Jenny said. "You are educated, cultivated, distinguished. It is all in your appearance." I understood all the adjectives. "And you speak French. You wear spectacles. How did you survive?"

Semporn laughed. "You saw that film, too? That's a very good film, very accurate in its portrayal. And those other films, the ones of Vietnam, are not at all accurate. But they underestimated the cretinism of the murderers. Look at my hands." He held them out. They didn't go with his face: scarred, dirt ingrained in the calluses that you didn't get from a few seasons in the fields, the nails down to the quick with grime no manicure would ever remove. They were barrio hands.

"That's not from agriculture," he said, "not from the fields of death. *Je suis empassioné de la horticulture, du jardin.* Gardening was my hobby. I loved it. The whole family thought I was crazy. My father was a middle-ranking *fonctionnaire.* People like that would rather die than get their hands dirty. The Khmer Rouge brats didn't look at our faces, they inspected our hands. They'd been told to do that and they obeyed commands to the letter. Absolute obedience or death – that was Angka.

"We stood in a line and rotated our hands, like dinner inspection in a school line-up, except it was the other way round, the kids were the ones doing it."

All of us, including Semporn, laughed. Jenny and I couldn't stop; we were out of control, snorting and exploding. "Apologise to him, Miss Jenny, for us. We shouldn't be laughing at his story."

Semporn replied, *"Mais non, Monsieur, rire c'est de l'antiseptique.* It is a medicine and an act of courage."

I bowed my head. "Ask him if it was as bad as we think."

Back came the reply, laconic, understated as anything from Fr. Paul: *"Monsieur, c'était misérable."* He left it at that. A *pinoy* would have given us the whole catalogue. He only added, *"Pas de la viande.* No rice, no bread, no meat, no fish. Only soup. Soup three times a day."

"And they never suspected you were a mathematician?" Jenny asked.

"Because I knew geometry I knew when I ran for the Border that the shortest distance between two points was a straight line. Because I knew arithmetic I understood the Year Zero. Because I knew subtraction I could count how many of my family died – from nine only two left, so seven dead. I saw my brother taken away. No, I didn't show I was a mathematician."

"Your brother, he didn't denounce you?" I asked Jenny to ask.

"No." His eyes slid away. He didn't want this wound probed. Maybe they'd tortured his brother in front of him, and the brother hadn't cracked. I could understand why he might feel bad or guilty about him. Don't tell me about that.

Jenny asked finally, I think she was sensitive enough to want to get away from the topic: "And Pol Pot is still alive, of course."

"*Oui. Il habite près de la frontiere avec Thailand au nord-ouest.* He has a compound there. The Thais protect him for their own reasons, just like the Chinese and the Americans do, too, to play him off against the Viets."

"So was he mad or just wicked?"

"*Mademoiselle. Cet homme était fou et méchant.*"

We all paused. Jenny said, "Rey, is it my imagination or is the moon brighter than usual?"

"Same old moon, Miss Jenny," I replied.

"That's queer. It's so silvery it hurts my eyes to look at it. And I feel quite dizzy."

"*O-o.* I also feel. But not the dizziness."

"Yes, it's quite exhilarating, really."

"So what gives with you guys?" I asked DeLorna. "You're on vacation like us?"

"No. I work with the Cambodian refugees in the camps up north. Semporn's on the way to take up a post at a school near Hat Yai, the deep south to us, the North to you."

"How bizarre. I mean how inappropriate for a man who hates kids – I can't say I blame him, in his position I would too – and he's a Cambodian, how can he teach in a Thai school?"

"It's not that bizarre, Jenny," I interjected. "The best teacher I ever had was a priest who hated Filipinos *and* kids, I think. He was one sarcastic son of a bitch – sorry – but, boy, he could help you up the ladder if you had it in you, *di ba*, if you were the one who could climb."

DeLorna said, "It's a danger posting. No sane Thai wants it. The Muslim secessionists are assassinating the teachers the government sends down from Bangkok. Semporn speaks OK Thai now, I guess it's no worse than his French, and numbers are numbers on the blackboard. Yeah, he isn't a Thai citizen but I don't think they're too worried about that, in the circumstances."

"So this deep South is worse than the American Deep South," I quipped. Very feeble. But, man, Jenny laughed so much, she was gasping when she quit. "And you, DeLorna," I asked, "how do you fit into the cocktail? You speak Thai, your English is like the *Cosby Show*…". Something had loosened my tongue. I had the *pinoy*'s, the Asian's, natural inquisitiveness which we thought nothing of, as natural as urinating in the open, but I wouldn't normally have been so nosey with another *Halo*[2] so soon after Hallo. I knew we guys didn't like it, *di ba*? We were sensitive that way. But DeLorna was cool about it. She said civilly, "I'm here to spook the gooks, right? Nothing the Viets or the Cambodians hate worse than a nigger. You should see the faces when the Viets or Hun Sen's guys find they're dealing with me. I work for the UN, not the Thais." She took pity on me. "I'm not a Thai subject, I'm a US citizen."

"Wow!" I did keep saying this, not really part of my natural vocabulary, but it kept me politely deferential.

"You're not, I take it. No, my natural father recognised me. That's no problem: the citizenship comes automatically with recognition. You should get yours to do the same."

"DeLorna, I don't even know who my father was."

"Right. Sorry, Sugar. Mine was Hedgemon Williams and his mother was a DeLorna."

"Ah, Hedgemon, like *Jefe*. Hegemony?"

"No, the absolute opposite, Sugar. It was a slave name, after his great-grandfather."

Jenny made a big effort to pull herself together. She began a French sentence to the Cambodian Chinese, Ah Lim – I saw her moulding it in her head first – but DeLorna shook her head.

"Sorry, Jane. Ah Lim speaks Khmer, Vietnamese, Mandarin, and Cantonese, and that's it."

"That's not bad," I said, "when 'that's it' is four languages. By the way it's Jenny, not Jane. Is Ah Lim going to teach as well?"

Now it was DeLorna's turn to laugh. "No. Ah Lim's on the run, in a manner of speaking. A fugitive from injustice."

"That," I said, "is a whole lot worse than being a fugitive from justice. What happened?"

"Chinese boxes," said DeLorna. "That's what." She spoke to Ah Lim, who shook his head wryly as if he could just about still appreciate a sick joke at his own expense. He was younger than Semporn and a lot paler than the Khmer who was darker even than the southern Thais. He was the kind of Asian guy who carried pens in the breast-pocket of his shirt as compulsively as a soldier would bullets and wore a Casio on the wrist that doubled as a calculator. With heavy black spectacles and a three-inch long nail on his left little finger, he had all the distinguishing characteristics of a member of the professional classes, which I surmised was once more what Cambodians aspired to resemble. "I'm from Phnom Penh," he said through DeLorna, who translated from Cambodian into English with an ease that made intelligent Jenny look like what she was, an amateur interpreter.

"And as you can see, I'm Chinese with all that entails in a country where Chinese are hated." He and Semporn, the pure Khmer, smiled radiantly at each other.

"Well, don't put the Chinese down too much because we've brought Phnom Penh back from the dead. It was a ghost town when the Khmer Rouge left in '79, and look at it now! Building everywhere! All kinds of Chinese money: hot money from Taiwan, laundry-funds from Hong Kong. Some fat-cats from Beijing even wanted to build a new-town big as Phnom Penh again right next to it.

"My part in all this was selling apartments to overseas Chinese: Macau gangsters, PLA generals, Singapore professionals, Malaysian casino-operators, all that mattered was the colour of their money.

"A year ago I sold a Communist General an apartment next to some Hong Kong triads − flashy young thugs they were. They'd bought a few weeks back but had returned to Hong Kong to run their protection-rackets. The General had builders in to re-decorate, his own guys from China, probably PLA engineers. Well, he went back to Beijing and the gangsters came back to fool around in the karaokes with the Vietnamese girls and buy guns in the market.

"As soon as they got into the apartment they had an uncomfortable feeling. It wasn't at all how they remembered it. Not at all as nice. An oppressive feeling. It was meaner than they remembered. They began to regret having parted with their dollars so quickly.

"They didn't waste any time getting me up there. I thought it was strange, too, but couldn't put my finger on it. Well, they got very unpleasant, pushing me around. They asked for plans, turned them this way and that, couldn't see anything wrong. Still three bedrooms, bathroom, kitchen and lounge. Then after the brothel, they brought the Chinese tailor up to size them for suits, much cheaper than Hong Kong also. That's when they used his tape-measure and found the apartment was three feet narrower than it should have been. Was it a deviation from the plans by the contractor? A misprint? Shortage of materials? No. Because it had been OK last time they were there. What had happened was this. The PLA general had knocked down the party wall, taken in three feet of the Hong Kong triads' apartment, annexed it to his own, and re-erected the wall, plaster and all, so you couldn't tell the difference! All done behind their closed door.

"Well, it was do your grandma this and do your grandmother that. They had me up there again and beat me black and blue. Nothing I could say would convince them I wasn't in on it.

"What could I do? The PLA general was even more dangerous than the gangsters. I heard they put a fifty dollar contract, a premium contract, on me and I ran for Thailand.

"That's my story. Laugh all you want."

Which we all did – Asian laughter, hiding embarrassment and the condescension of pity and, sometimes, as Semporn said, it was the antiseptic of courage.

"Oh, dear," gasped Jenny finally. "I don't know what's wrong with me. Back to the fourth form tonight."

"I'll be the one to cure you with the strap," I said, and we were off again. I knew what I'd said wasn't remotely funny, but I simply couldn't stop myself having hysterics.

"Well, guys," said DeLorna, "we've been on the bus four hours out of Chumphon, and eight out of Bangkok the night before, so we're not at our best. You'll have to excuse us." She scraped back her chair on the gravel and paid their chit. The two Cambodians smiled at us, ever friendly and courteous, and they were gone. I gave DeLorna my address while I rocked and giggled with Jenny. What DeLorna must have thought of me, I hate to think.

We'd been talking for nearly three hours, so the sounds of music on the headland had only dimly registered with us.

"What beautiful lights!" Jenny exclaimed. I, too, found them glorious. It was the strobe and decorations at the rustic disco on the headland.

"They're... like jewels, rubies and emeralds," I said unoriginally. "Y-e-e-e-s," breathed Jenny. She swayed against me, so her bare arm brushed mine. I could smell the Imperial Leather soap Becky Chow's mother had taken the precaution of pressing on her daughter and which she would have been horrified to know we were all sharing. Jenny had only just convinced her I was safe. The soap did smell differently on me.

"Better check on the young ones, *di ba?*"

"Oh, I suppose so, I feel so lazy." It was true; all my sense of obligation and responsibility had gone, too. I lived only in the present. For me, the table-top, the small stones underfoot, the jewel-lights in the distance, had a momentous but unquantifiable and unstoppable significance as if I was the only person in the world who could decipher the message they were vibrating on a private frequency. The table-top bulged and swelled like a doughnut. Then it deflated again. "Wow," I said for the n-th time that night, but genuinely for the first time.

Jenny smiled dreamily, vaguely. She looked like the Sphinx, like the Mona Lisa. I felt I was about to penetrate a great artistic secret, like the Golden Mean or perspective. The ineffable, the serene inscrutability of both these antique wonders depended on the number of degrees the corners of the lips curled – about one point eight from the horizontal, just like my companion's. "Jenny," I said, "I've got something I'd like to break to you…" She listened to my nonsense; I listened to hers with the same indulgence.

The music stopped. There were no more jewels. We were in the grey pre-dawn. It was Butch's plod time. My imagination had long ceased to skip and fly. I felt exhausted and depressed.

Behind me Nicky said, "Jeepers creepers, Jens. Have you been here all night?"

Jenny turned a bleary face to her sister. For a brief second, in that light and as her features sagged, I saw how she might look like her mother's twin in twenty years time.

"Where've *you* been?" Jenny asked. She spoke not interrogatively, as a surrogate guardian, but as a voyager returned from the lengthiest and most arduous of trips, might address the unchanged stay-at-homes.

"Reeving it up," Sonika said. Amazing. They'd been going all night and looked as fresh as sand after the ebb. That was teenyboppers for you.

Jenny and I had a great disinclination now to stay where we were, so we moved to another Traveller's café serving world food: fried rice for me with gouts of the chilli sauce I suddenly craved, ham 'n' eggs for everyone else, including Sonika who spurned curried noodles. "Ooh, I needed that," Jenny declared, as she put a dangling flap of egg-white away with some iced-coffee. "Those mushrooms weren't very nice at all." Our companions gave each other funny looks.

When we got back to our own beach, I had a shave after which, instead of continuing the day, I promptly went to sleep until two p.m.

The remaining few days were pleasant but uneventful. Some Thai boys let me in on their game of *takraw*, a sport I'd never seen before but which had definitely the highest technical entry threshold of any game in the world. Bar none. You played with a perforated rattan-ball over a badminton net. The object, with the co-operation of your team-mates, was to keep the ball off the ground and then land it on the other side, using every part of your body except your hands. In other words, it was volleyball without hands. I never saw anything like it. Just batting it round to each other by kicking with inside of foot or back of heel was simple enough, but to send it over the net with a realistic chance of scoring required a leaping backward somersault in the air, with the legs straight, to deliver a downward smash while you were upside-down. Your legs turned like the hands of a speeded-up clock as you landed upright again. Gee, it wasn't a recreation, it was an on-going miracle. And everyone was the same build, just like Butch's cagers were, but these were medium-height boys whose legs were remarkable not so much for their great length, which was prodigious, as their extreme straightness. Legs like mine, in fact, only paler and not so heavily developed around the quads. After a few sessions of the standard game, we played another: you had to form a hoop with your arms behind you and kick the ball through that. Yup. Then when that palled we warmed down by standing in front of a real basketball net and helped each other score as many times as we could before the next team came on and tried to outdo us in prolificity. All the time I was intoning in my head, "Boy, I can't wait to tell Butch about this, Boy, I can't wait to tell Butch about this. We'll give up baskitbol, man, throw it out the window like a board-rubber." Some hand-shakes and back-slapping – all the athletes I ever met were touchers to the man and the more so with *takraw* which was a rare team sport with no physical contact at all – and I was off to supervise my young charges. So I thought. They'd been watching from a mound fifty metres away. Nicky opened her mouth but Jenny pinched her arm.

"It's innate," I said breezily, continuing on to sit in the shallows with my shorts ballooning round my hips like a salvor's lifting bags.

Next day we began the run south. Without anything being said, I took us West, the only noticeable reaction being the lifting of a certain tension in the back seat and the enhanced volubility of the three wise monkeys there. However, this left us with some hours driving to the border through inland areas not usually frequented by tourists. Jungly, hilly terrain, not unlike Palawan, and which like Palawan had once also been the preserve of negritos and guerillas. The minor roads were as bad as the Philippines. I liked the Thai main roads, however. They were built to Singapore specifications and they drove on the left, like Hong Kong. Coming at a sedate thirty kph through the outskirts of a large town, our way was blocked by a crowd – still Thais but in sarong and headscarf indistinguishable from their co-religionists over the border. Jenny pushed her door-lock down, also doing the same for the door behind. Becky followed suit with hers. I left mine, but tooted the horn gently. The crowd, unlike the Red Sea, failed to part. Becky cringed in the back. It was quite obvious to me the mob had not the smallest interest in us, still less the desire to threaten anyone. It was just an Asian crowd – they could have been Filipinos or Chinese – being its inquisitive self and glad of some free street entertainment to enliven the monotonous day. Its cheerful callousness at, for instance, the traffic accident this appeared to be, was not completely discreditable for any of its number could be providing the fodder for entertainment on the morrow and, indeed, the victim had herself or himself probably assisted as spectator at innumerable previous happenings. I barped lightly three times, to no obvious effect, then half-opened the car-door and leaned out. I, or rather my blackness, my largeness, my ever-eloquent pecs and delts, secured some respect, a little leeway which I exploited with some gingery clutch-work. Gradually, I prised a gap in the throng. In the middle of all the massed full-body clothing, and with the limited perspective afforded by being at car-seat level, it was like nothing so much as pushing through the racks of garments in a bazaar. I got us up to six kph and the bodies started to jump out of the way more smartly.

"Ooh! Look a sign!" squeaked Sonika.

"Yes, it says school in Malay," Becky informed her in a flat voice.

"What a dump!" Angie said. "It makes our…"

"Christ, there's blood," Jenny exclaimed. "Look, it's running down the camber. Oh, God, there's someone lying in the middle!"

I brought us to a sharp halt, just short of running over the body. The onlookers had parted and there was no one tending the casualty, there hadn't been any warning or buffer-zone. I reversed, actually banging someone at one kph, then turned the wheel fully to the right. As we edged past I saw the victim was a man. A pair of black spectacles, absolutely intact, lay by his head. This was not at all intact. The hair at the back was matted with blood, but most of the flow seemed to have come from the front, which was not visible, as he was lying face down. One well-burnished shoe was off. His right hand lay on top of two sturdily bound books, which he'd obviously been carrying but the sheaf of paper which accompanied them had spilled all over the road. Most had been trodden underfoot, many bearing black shoe imprints, while others were stained red, the cheap, fibrous pulp having soaked up the blood thirstily. It looked like the quality of paper on which we dashed off test questions at San Ignatio and received back in no time with Fr. Boy's well-formed hand-writing or Fr. Paul's crabbed, acerbic comments. The mark would be recorded on the lustrous vellum of the record book but the test sheets themselves were throw-aways. I saw the papers in the road had algebraic notations and geometric diagrams drawn on them, the crude, uneven scrawl of pupils, quite unlike that of a teacher. We were out of the crowd now.

"Rey," Jenny said in a small voice. "I have a horrible feeling about that."

"So do I, Jenny."

"What?" asked Angie.

"Nothing," I said. "Wrong place, wrong time, wrong number on the dice, and back down the small snake when you missed all the big snakes before. Statistics. *Bahala na.*" I spoke more vehemently than a chauffeur should but that, I think, wasn't why the girls kept quiet.

"*Bahala na,*" said Jenny after a while. "That must be the Filipino for Cool Heart."

The rest of the car-journey passed without incident. Jenny found the guy in Hat Yai we were to hand the Lexus to. She gave him the logbook and some other papers and her signature, so if there was gonna be any heat, she'd be the one taking it. When she came back I could tell she wasn't carrying money – she looked too relaxed, only

Flips like Dant could look cool when they had enough money on their persons to make it worth killing them – so it clearly hadn't been a cash transaction. Amerikanos like the Smiths trusted each other: he'd probably paid the Smiths before delivery or they'd trust him to pay later. He hadn't seemed to mind about the dents from the rocks.

We rode a share-taxi across the Border into Malaysia, Sonika and Angie's knees jammed against mine rather more tightly, I think, than the lack of space warranted. I had a boner the whole time officialdom was eyeballing me, the sex-crazed nigger. Man, they were right to suspect me. Then it was the train, fetching noodles for the girls, helping Jenny with a cross-word puzzle as we rattled along by the palms and hutches, and before we knew it, we were at the causeway, crossing the moat into Castle Singapore.

OUR FLIGHT WAS CANCELLED, so we had to wait six days for another charter. That was no hardship for any of us. Becky's folks had the girls lodged again in a splendour that made Malacañang Palace look like a condo, while I had a space once more in the *amahs'* quarters. They were Filipinas, of course, one from Dumaguete City where they spoke Cebuano like me. That helped, boy, did it help. If Liesl-Evangeline Dinolan shut her eyes she could pretend I was five three with slanty eyes. If she opened them she saw liquorice rock. She was thirty-eight and an assiduous remitter but, to coin a phrase, nothing to write home about. I did her twice a night and in the mornings closed my eyes and pretended it was Becky.

I had the whole day to myself, Becky taking the girls on girly expeditions, only once inviting me to accompany them for midnight *laksa* at Peranakan Place, so before the week had passed I knew enough of the Lion City for a lifetime.

The city was famed for its cleanliness. Justly famed. Trees and lawns abounded, even in the placeless centre-divisions and nameless verges of the highways. Not a leaf of newspaper or a polythene bag remained at the liberty of the winds. It had always been second nature to hurl my unwanted wrapper, to spit the lactic froth of Butch's runs, to take a leak against a post whenever the need arose, secure against interruptions to thread of urine or thought. To commit such a trespass in the streets or parks of the Lion City was to guarantee retribution as instant and impersonal as that meted out to the space invaders on a computer game.

The beautiful Sunday morning two days after our return from peninsular Malaysia, I found myself sneezing helplessly as I entered the Lucky Plaza shopping mall. I was allergic to some constituent of the Singapore atmosphere whether it was building dust, pollen, mites, or merely the absence of pollutants. I had to retire whence I'd come. Blinking, squinting, and snuffling, I was black Moley emerging into daylight. As I sneezed, then felt a helpless sequence of atchoos commencing, each of which promised but failed to deliver an end to my discomfort, I shielded my face with cupped hands. A product, after all, of a priestly education, I wished to spare society my germs and the sight of my contorting face. Unfortunately, I was left in a double predicament, with a runny nose and fluid in my mouth. Blowing my nose with my fingers and preparing to spit my inoffensive mouthful, I was on the point of accomplishing all with discretion. My snot was on my fingers, ready to be flicked, my expectoration lying placidly on my palate – the innocuous mucus of the fit young person I was then – when I became aware I was under scrutiny. A Singaporean some ten years older than me, in his early thirties, dressed in black trousers and white shirt, was regarding me with a kind of neutral intensity. He quite definitely wore civilian and not official attire, but I regarded black pants and epauletted shirts as the uniform of the incorrigibly officious. I was already familiar with the notorious urban ordinances. Who wasn't? Singapore was a fine place; they fined you for a whole variety of transgressions. PP had nothing on this place. I stood, dripping. I wasn't presently violating any by-laws; I was just in an uncomfortable fix. But if I flicked or spat, I became a criminal on the spot. I looked at the guy. He looked back at me. Quite a lot of aggressive staring went on in Singapore behind the law-abidingness and it could lead to trouble. A little mind-reading went on. Not very difficult. My options were severely circumscribed. The simplest was, as it were, the least palatable. The Singapore penguin nodded: do it, lah. I swallowed. My fingers were still a mess. I wiped them behind the knees of my pants. The penguin nodded again. Welcome to Singapore.

Not littering, refraining from committing nuisances – these externals were easy once you'd got into the habit of them. Whose ambition is it to live in filth and die in squalor? If they'd taken some of my little store of money as penalty, I could hardly have objected on principle. The fact that it applied to everyone made it worthwhile. You were part of an entire context. It wasn't like, say, waiting your turn back home. If you'd observed the rules of propriety and precedence there – been grammatical about it – you'd never have got anywhere, you couldn't have survived on a daily basis. To make it work, everyone has to abide by a system.

The real culture shock for an Asian was that the external, visible lack of dirt mirrored an unseen, internal, cleanliness.

Singaporeans weren't corrupt.

How did I know? I had antennae for officialdom's signals, man. It was as strong as the invisible pressure-changes hurting my ears in an aircraft. I could read it in the leer of Thai police and Malaysian officials, in the crooked backs and darting eyes of the brigands at our own NAIA. But it was absent here.

I knew the Smiths and their ilk took it for granted. That was part of being them. But I wandered round shell-shocked. It was the negation of everything I'd known. Asians were the slowest sprinters, the lowest jumpers, the shortest throwers. Their unimpressive physiques allowed them the slimmest of chances in any world athletics contest. But at one activity we excelled. If there was an Olympics in the technique of the back-hander, with a round at squeeze, Asians would not just have captured every colour of medal, we would have monopolised all the finals. At corruption we were the world champions: Marcos was just the most flagrant, the crudest. The Indonesians, Malaysians, Cambodians, Thais, Vietnamese, not to mention the Chinese and the Indians, were more subtle; they could have given master-classes; they could have supplied coaches to the Africans and the Latins.

But I had yet to know this. At the time, wandering the sterile streets of Singapore like a bacterium in search of a host, I made a more pointed contrast for, in truth, we Filipinos were the absolute opposite of the Singaporeans. Where they (to make a Ciceronian list) were purposeful, disciplined, cohesive, industrious, meticulous and also petty, mean-minded, sour, fearful, timid to the point of cringing before constituted authority and (squaring the circle) arrogant with it, we were aimless, feckless, factional, mutterers, idle, irresponsible and also open-handed, sunny, forgiving, optimistic without reason, independent, generous with our indignation and concern, and self-effacing with it. They had the worst case of mind advance-dirty in Asia, yet with some justification. They were an island of Chinese thrift and order caught between three seas of Malay disorder and dishonesty: us, the Indonesians, and the Malaysians. They were resource-less, while we had everything, or at least copra, gold, the first tricklings of oil, sugar, pineapples, you name it. What they sold was an intangible, an attitude of mind, the quality of their human being, their ability to surmount: so that they had the most efficient airline and airport in the world, the best hospitals and doctors for thousands of miles. The Singaporeans refined oil, reproduced computer chips. Their towering hotels veritably hummed with the joy of satisfying their guests' every need. And yet all they had were a surfeit of certain virtues underated elsewhere and an unrivalled geographical position. No wonder they were paranoiac. Their food, their water came down the causeway from a land on the slippery slope of religious hysteria, controlled by a people who were the hereditary enemies of their race. It was like dining at a wonderful banquet with someone's dirty hand very loosely wrapped round your throat. Singaporeans themselves were the first to say they were a nation with full stomachs and empty heads but there was a further price to pay for satiation. Under such circumstances indigestion was sure to follow.

How different we were! We *pinoys* whose stomachs grumbled and whose heads were full of dreams, even as we trudged through the mire. With our syrupy natures, we were the caries-creating sugar in the *Halo*², the tart Singaporeans the palate-scouring citric acids. Our strengths and weaknesses complemented each other. Put together – if we hadn't curdled – what a knickerbocker glory we would have been.

The fact that their civic virtues weren't natural for them but a hairshirt voluntarily worn inclined me to respect them more rather than less. It wasn't easy for them, in the way being responsible citizens and good friends was for the Smiths as instinctive and simple as drawing breath. The Singaporeans had pulled themselves up by their boot-straps. They'd wrenched themselves out of context. If violence was as American as cherry-pie, filth and corruption, a polluted environment and dirty money, were as Chinese as a smoking bowl of breakfast congee. Spitting, littering, dumping, the greased palm, were their inclination as much as ours. They were forever looking for their souls, the cultural birthright they'd sold for a mess of pottage. They were on a forlorn quest for the Holy Grail of their identity but corruption and dirt were as vital a part of their inheritance as bloater paste and putting correct change into the honesty box were for the Smiths. The Singaporeans had lobotomised themselves; that was why they didn't know who they were. I didn't think that the fruits of this sacrifice would last forever. The prosperity was precarious. One day we might overtake them. They were a petty people, fanatical about detail, but there was also something doomed and magnificent about them. I cursed them sometimes but I never stopped admiring them. They were the Filipino on ice in a restraint jacket.

After I'd conquered my allergic syndrome at Lucky Plaza, I found I'd lost my bearings. I innocently accosted a Singaporean family for directions. What they saw bearing down on them was a gorilla capable of speech. "Sorry, hah?" said Dad sidestepping smartly enough to get by the basketball star. "We are strangers ourselves, lah."

Erlinda hadn't done it better.

CHAPTER XIV

*Halo Squared — Same shit, different flies — Nicky's Diary
I embark on a new career — Andy is my first job*

MRS SMITH AND THE COMMANDER were in jovial moods, Mrs Smith so heartily unlike herself I wondered if she was about to sprout a beard. They hadn't been at home to field Jenny's warning phone call that we'd be back late. We learned the reason for this on our arrival: they'd taken a trip to, of all places, Manila. The Sunday I'd been parading the malls in Singapore they'd been checking out the Spanish fortifications at Intramuros. They'd only got back the day before us. So in other words they were suffering from the not uncommon psychological affliction that we hadn't been away at all. It was them who'd done all the being away, *di ba*?

"Quite by chance, chaps," the Commander said. "We didn't plan to get you out of the way, honestly. Roger Addison told Charlie Northrop we were here in HK. I thought Charlie was still with Shell in Port Harcourt but they moved him to Brunei. Wherever they drill oil, Charlie drills teeth. Anyway, they were taking a holiday in the Philippines, it was his fiftieth by the way, and we, your mother and I, thought it's only an hour and a half away and we went for it."

"How unpremeditated of you," Jenny said, with Nicky looking on as severely as her older sister.

"Fifty," reflected Mrs Smith, "a much more significant milestone, I feel, than twenty-one, Jennifer." It was intended as a put-down for the kids but it cleared my furrowed brow. I'd been wondering how the fuck anyone could or would spend fifty holidays in the Philippines.

"Had some of your *Halo* squared, Rey," Commander Smith confided to me. "Bit more to the Western taste than ice Kuching, I thought."

"*What*? I mean, again, sir."

"*Halo* Squared."

"Ah, sir. You say it like this…" and I said it. "Think of it as an ecstatic experience, sir: *Hallow-Hallow*."

"Mmm. Well, it was distinctly improved when Charlie Northrop added a dash of Tanduay rum to and flambéd it. I suppose that would be the devil's cocktail, not the angel's."

"Priests reserve that for themselves, sir. But your friend is a genius. A *Halo*^{2} is a whole bunch of ingredients that shouldn't belong together but work when you combine them. Some sour, some sweet, some stale, some new. Yeah, I'm just the one to imagine it on the tongue now. Candied napalm, *di ba*?"

"You've got a distinctive turn of phrase there, Rey. I've often thought so."

"Thank you, serr. I'll just be the one to see to the dent Mrs Smith made in the car while I was away." I went off quickly. I had nothing to fear from Commander Smith – from a man who was certain to have cut his teeth on the no-sneaking code? You have to be kidding – but it was better not to let the mouth run away with itself. When I came back, wiping my hands on a clean chamois Mrs Smith had picked up half-price in Divisoria – she seemed to think it the greatest coup – Commander Smith was saying to Jenny, "I don't think there'll be trouble just for the moment in Malaya. They can keep a lid on the fundamentalism, that comes from below. There's no real friction between the Chinese elite in Singapore and the Malays over the water – they're old chums, they all went to Raffles School there under the British. And Singapore certainly isn't a sanctuary for the disaffected Chinese in Malaysia. They're scrupulous about that."

"Well, it was ugly, Daddy. There was a definite feeling in the air. Once the old school-chums drop off the perch, I wouldn't like to say what might happen."

"Well, you're a pessimist, like your mother, darling. I try to look on the bright side when I can."

THAT WAS THE YEAR OF EDSA, the most optimistic event ever, the demonstrations against Marcos on E de Los Santos Avenue, which eventually led to the downfall of the dictator. At the time I was as excited as every other *pinoy* in Hong Kong. I watched the TV, even bought newspapers instead of waiting for Commander Smith to give me his in the evening. Excitement was in the air.

I feel ashamed of myself now when I think back on it, my gullibility as great as any other baying plebeian at the Circus. And if

I confine myself to these few lines now, I can be said to be making a restitution to my rationality. Fr. Paul would have been sorely disappointed in me. It wasn't just that the system remained unchanged, so did the personnel. In time the cronies crept back – that was to be expected – but, shit, the worst torturers and thieves didn't just escape punishment, they got advancement. We threw Ferdie out but we couldn't give ourselves a dialysis of the soul. There was a little bit of him and Meldy in all of us. People Power, *ba*? People are stupid, never more so than in a bunch.

WE'D BEEN BACK SOME TEN DAYS from our vacation – it had seemed like ten years and none of us, including the adult Smiths, now felt we'd ever been away at all. That was when Babyjane came to me, bug-eyed and bursting. She would undoubtedly have preferred to be running down to the barrio pump with the news that a vampire had sucked all the blood out of a baby in the next shanty but she had to content herself with this.

"It's Miss Nicky," she hissed, as she got me by the arm. "I pind out her secret. She da little flay-girl. *Adis-adis pod*. It's all in da diaries."

Just at this moment Nicky herself came in to the kitchen, a markedly cheerful Nicky, the picture of radiant young womanhood. She helped herself to some chocolate milk from the ref, smiled at me as a friend and not a servant, and departed. Babyjane's eyes were as round as the Honda's headlamps. I tried to stop laughing and said, "I'm not the one to be interested in *tsismis* about the family, Babyjane." She was not taken in by this hypocrisy. For her, a secret without a sharer was like a *balut* egg without salt.

"Look at. You can be da one to advise them."

OK. It never pays to underestimate even those of the meanest capacities. Babyjane was shrewder than I gave her credit for. Nothing would puff me up more than the thought of being an *adviser*, for fuck's sake, to the Smiths. Shit, it was better than Tom Hagen being *consigliere* to the Corleones in the *Godfather*.

BJ had found Nicky's diary inside a hollowed-out *Famous Five*. I was reminded how Danton had cut six half-inch deep notches into a volume of *Table Etiquette* at San Ignatio to conceal his stash of .38 Special shells. Like Nicky, he'd selected the volume least likely to be picked up.

"Read, *na lang*," urged Babjane.

"Ayaw," I protested feebly. "Private, Babyjane."

But she'd already levered the little notebook out of its grave and licked her finger to turn the pages. "Afril Pourteen," she said triumphantly. "I'm da one to remember that date. Read."

Refraining would have required more will-power than I possessed. And I have to record that perusing Nicky's journal was a better read, so far as I was concerned at that moment, than Dumas, Rizal, or William Shakespeare himself, and certainly Enid Blyton. I mean, how many times do you appear as a character in what you read?

The book itself, as an artefact, was not the dedicated kind, with the year 1986 in tooled gold on the leatherette cover, and conversion tables from Imperial to Metric inside, nor even the kind of engagements and appointments book, apportioning the months and the days of the week with discrete demarcation, that socialites might employ for parties or a secretary like Irene might maintain for her boss to avoid his being late. Or girls like Erlinda use to see which man had made them late. Nicky had used an old-fashioned accounts book with marbled covers and thin blue columnar lines and boxes on the pages. I think she hadn't so much chosen it to hide the fact that it was a diary (no sane Filipino would have kept such a dangerous item even in an armour-plated safe with a seven-figure combination) as to savour the adolescent individuality. Just having it in an ordinary notebook would have made it feel less original. I remembered the pleasure of writing teenage notes and reflections in an old graph-book: the sensation of working against the grain, the joy of idiosyncracy, so that the most banal adolescent reflection seemed profoundly original to the inscriber. Boring horizontal lines just weren't the same.

Although Nicky had given private nicknames to the other household members, it was easy to work out who was who from the context. Jenny had the most aliases bestowed upon her: Old Frump Face, Squaresville, Jenibore, Bottleblonde, and Girton Girl, as in: *Caught old Jenibores having a blub in her room. Think Over-achievement is getting to our high-flier* or: *Girton Girl got into a paddy about me borrowing her ceramic nibber for art-class with Hutch. Talk about storm in a tea-cup. She hasn't even got Dame Skinflint's excuse of the menorpause.*

Dame Skinflint was Mrs Smith, aka Flibbertigibbs, Mrs Panic, and occasionally when Nicky couldn't be bothered or when what she was putting down held such interest for her that she forgot about the codenames, just Mums. Commander Smith, whom I was looking to find as Lord Skinflint, was nearly always Dad, or once or twice Goldfinger. The Smiths were a happy and united family, as I said right at the beginning, and whatever fault lines existed really only served to bring them closer but such conflict as there was occurred between Jenny and her mother and Nicky and Jenny. In the diary I was at first surprised how much rivalry and dislike there appeared to be between the sisters, then reflected that it was in the nature of committing feelings to paper. You put things under a magnifying glass and fissures became ravines. Too much light, too much focus and you burned what you scrutinised, scorched the page. When you thought, shaped, and scribbled, you were distilling, you got essence; and it burned like witch-hazel. People you liked or loved got distorted. I mean, I'd loved Danton like the brother I didn't have, but he wouldn't have thought it from some of the observations I could have formulated about him. In short what Nicky had were negatives. In these dark little portraits I was amused to see myself referred to as Man Mountain, less so as BBG or Bottleblonde's Black Giggerlo, and was flabbergasted when I saw her call me Frankenstein just like Dant had.

Dad was going on about Rey, she wrote in another entry, *as he likes to when he hasn't got anything else to inflict on his doting family. He reckons now he (Rey) might have been a soldier of fortune, as he put it (Dad). He said, he's a very gentle lad but not because he's had a soft time, more like someone who's sick of the things he's seen. Mrs Panic said, Goodness me. Do you think he's safe to have in the house. Goldfinger said, very patiently, well, that's what I just intimated, dear. Jenibore said, do you think Africa somewhere, Dad, that's where most mercenaries work, isn't it. I said, he wouldn't stand out there so much as he does here and Girton Girl got into a self-induced bate, just winding herself up because she feels she ought to. She didn't like it when I said self-induced, that's one of her Cantab. expressions.*

I smiled. Babyjane was breathing heavily by me, her exhalation tickling my ear. Her breath smelled of shrimp-paste.

I got to more recent entries: *What had been a great hol has just gone sour on us. Frumpface is throwing her weight around, aided by Frankenstein. They were trying to stop us going to the rave until I got heavy about it. Stupid Angie nearly buggered it all up again, just as I was getting Squaresville to change her mind. I had some grass before the rave really got going but I took the E too late and it never worked. The others wimped out anyway. Shame. Anyhow, talk about hilarious, we came down after the rave was over and found Girton Girl stoned out of her tiny mind! Frankenstein and her had gobbled two omelets full of magic mushrooms. Rey wasn't too bad. I think it would take as much dope to lift him as it would to tranquillise a rhino, but Girton Girl didn't know who she was or where. What a hoot! The bish to end all bishes! We didn't tell her.*

Next day, Rey was fantastic playing that weird game with some Thai guys so the mushrooms can't have done much harm to him. He was amazing, the Thai boys couldn't believe it, including the guy Sonika was snogging with at the rave.

Came back OK, no hassle with the Mozzies like before, though there was a nasty traffic accident in one town, loads of people standing and watching. Ugh! They're not like us at all, even Becky sometimes.

"Here, here," said Babyjane stabbing the page.

Andy, Angie, Rupert, and me went to see a really awful old film with John Wayne in it (eurgh!) and then on to have tea at the Peak Café. Andy paid, I don't know where he gets his money from he never seems short of it. After that we strolled a bit. Andy showed off some of his Tae Kwan Do kicks in the street. It was called a sidekick, e.g. pal which I thought was spastic but Andy wasn't amused especially after he was pretending to kick a traffic meter, then got it wrong, and really hit it. We all ran which on top of the Peak Café's Black Forest and iced Milo definitely was not a good idea.

At McDo we saw the Johnson twins. Andy went off to the loo with the oldest and they came back bombed out of their heads. Then we went to Rupert's place. His old man was there but left us alone. We listened to some of his CD's. Then Andy turned the lights out and lit some pongy joss-sticks. Rupert and I snogged a bit. I let him take my bra off, the one Babyjane tried to steal, then pushed his hand away four times when he tried to put it in my knickers but let him do it the fourth time. It tickled. Craig Hope told everyone in his class he'd fingered Heidi Pfeidwengeler and if that word wasn't horrible enough said he hadn't washed it and let all the boys sniff it. I wish boys weren't quite so ghastly. I didn't touch his thing and I hope he doesn't lie to everyone about it because I'll kill him if he does.

Then Andy brought out his prize exhibit from the stash under the parquet tile. He had some Thai grass and what I'd never seen before, a bag of ice. Even Angie wasn't stupid enough to buy anything and bring it back from Thailand. I didn't want to smoke any ice but Rupert and Andy said there was enough there to get him hanged if he was caught taking it to KL when he went to see his stepfather next week because he wasn't going to waste any by flushing it down the loo. I really didn't want to have any but the guys got really heavy when I said I didn't and said they'd thought I was the coollest girl in the class until now. Well, I did have a few puffs, more than that actually, and Andy was pleased and said now they couldn't hang him if they caught him. I was really spaced out, it was cool and I was in charge and didn't care about anything but I was glad I'd helped Andy. I just couldn't stop talking and when I looked in the mirror my eyes were all funny. I felt there was nothing I couldn't or wouldn't do. I didn't care about people anymore or any consequences. Afterwards Andy took all the money I had in my purse, which I thought was a bit thick, and told me to give the rest to Rupert next week. I'm blowed if I will, as Goldfinger says.

We didn't go disco-ing in the end but went down to Johnston Mess and had some keema and nan. Then to Panda Disco. Same old new-wavers and punks there. Why do the Chinese ravers think it's so cool to wear black all the time? It must be the coolie instinct.

Reading this didn't exactly make me sick to the stomach but it would be fair to say I was disturbed. Babyjane had been looking intently at my face rather than Nicky's rounded handwriting. Now she pounced gleefully. "Ha, what you say now? Da little jinx *ka-maldita siya*. Go with da voys, *adis adis na*. And, you velieve it, she da one to make da palse accusations against da innocent feoples. I like to spank her face for her, naughty little Miss Nicky. She so bad as Erlinda."

I let BJ have it full-blast with a 150-megawatt smile. It wasn't a good idea for her to think she had something over Nicky in particular and the Smiths in general. "Minx is what you mean, not jinx," I said. "It's just like young girls, always making up *mga historia*. Fantasy *lang*. Delusion *lang*. It's their little dream world, like someone who's *loko-loko* only they grow out of it."

"N-o-o-o-o," said Babyjane, eyes widening in sincere conviction. "I don't think so. I think she got da pinger pucking and try da drugs. What's da ice?"

"Ice, Babyjane? You know from the fridge. *Yalo* in Tagalog. The cold stuff you put in, er, Coke."

"I think it a slang words for drugs," she said. Babyjane could be difficult to shift; it was harder to alter her opinions than those of the opposite team at Atty Caladong's forensic debates.

"I think it's something to do with the boy's karate," I said, "for a muscle strain." It was all I could think of to say at the time.

Babyjane ignored this. "How about we be da ones to tell Mum?" she asked eagerly.

"I'm not sure that's such a good idea, Babyjane," I said slowly and consideredly, but without displaying the hesitation that might encourage her. I knew she was too chicken to confront Nicky or go to Mr and Mrs Smith by herself, or she'd have done it already, most easily while we were still away. "But you go ahead and do it, if you feel it's the right thing."

"Aiy! *Ikaw na lang.* You only, Rey. You're da pavourite, Commander always da one to listen to you."

"Ah, later *na lang.*"

The Babyjanes of this world have never caused me anxiety; it would be ludicrous if they did. Babyjane weighed less than my right leg; her IQ was probably half mine. But on the other hand, I was starting to get the glimmerings of a worldly truth: that the strong, the generous, the noble, and the large could quite easily be brought down by the machinations of the weak, the mean, the spiteful, and the petty, and that, on the whole, in dealing with the dregs of Creation it was safer and more efficacious in both attack and defence to come down to their level right from the start.

It was thorny. What was I to do? Of course, I wanted to do the best by the Smiths. But what was that? Snitching, sneaking on Nicky was clearly perceived as dishonourable; even I, the *pinoy*, thought that. It was doubly so in that it had involved snooping in her personal effects. What were we doing there: nosey-parkering, pilfering on the off-chance? I could just imagine the thought occurring to Mrs Smith after the first shock wore off. And I felt closer to Nicky after our trip together. I couldn't rat on her.

Still, she was clearly running with the wrong crowd; she was sure to get herself into trouble. Don't tell me about that.

In the back of the diary were some addresses. Oddly enough, no boys' at all, so I drew a blank there. The only name with the intial "A" was Verghese, Angie Verghese, in fact.

"OK, leave it with me, Babyjane," I said.

When there was no one around, I telephoned the Verghese number. A Tagalog voice told me the family were out. Running my finger down the addresses, I saw a C.-A. Brown. That was Cherry-Anne, Nicky's tennis-partner, a red-haired freckly girl who could do overhead serves. I gathered myself, mentally that was. The paradox was that an American accent was easier for me to sustain than a British, despite my years of Fr. Paul. I could get away with it on the other end of a phone for half a minute. I dialled and hoped I'd get Cherry-Anne herself. I did.

"Hi. I'm trying to get hold of Andy. There's a change to the schedule of the Tang Soo Do class. Have you got his number?"

"Yes, sure. It's 231296."

"That's still Kennedy Road?"

"No, Repulse Bay."

"Can you give me the address? I need to send a circular if he's not there."

"OK. Hang on. Yup, have you got a pen?"

It was Thursday. I waited the two days till Sunday. Early in the morning I crossed the harbour then caught the No 6 bus in front of the City Hall.

The bus was comfortable, fast, air-conditioned, cheap as anything back home, anonymous, and easy. Parking in Repulse Bay on a weekend could be murder, *di ba*? But you may be surprised to hear I wished I was behind the wheel of a car. Public transport has its conveniences, but sometimes you want to make more of an impact, *di ba*?

Andy's folks lived on the way to Middle Bay. I had a pair of white cotton chauffeur's gloves in my pocket, like the ones Chinese police wear at executions, a long-sleeve shirt on, and in my back-pocket, a cloth-hood exactly like the ones we used at Frat Initiations or Rumbles.

I settled on a bench for a long wait. To pass the time, I had the *Autobiography of Benvenuto Cellini* with me, a dangerous dude, contemporary as rock 'n' roll or jet-engines. It was so engrossing I nearly missed Andy. He was coming down the corkscrew car-ramp doing his kicks. Stupid fuck. I thought of Brabazon leaving the mark of his trainer on Haydee's butt.

It wasn't gonna be difficult. "Ays-Kold, Gorilla," said my shoulder-imp. "Cool and calm does it, mans."

I followed Andy round the corner. I had a sock holding a polythene bag full of beach gravel. I swung short and sweet, taking him on the bone behind the ear. He staggered. I came round and booted him full in the face. It sounded like a fruit thrown against a wall. I emptied the sand from the sock. Then I picked his head up by the hair and bounced it on a trash-can like a basketball. He was still conscious as I kicked him methodically in the upper body, not bothering to make each kick very hard, trusting in the quantity of them to do the work. "Don't deal dope," I said, "especially to little girls." I was surprised how out of breath I was. I said it again, put in some more kicks, then left him. Round the corner I took my mask off. It was still early enough that there were no bus queues.

I felt pretty pleased with myself, you can assume. I liked being an avenging angel, the impartiality, the anonymity; most of all the latter. There was no connection between me and him. I never lost any sleep over it.

But I figured I still had to put Commander and Mrs in the picture. There was always another punk like Andy coming over the skyline, no shortage of creeps in the world. Chop down as many as you like, they were a renewable resource. But how could I snitch on Nicky, for whom I'd done all this? Then I had, if I say so myself, a great idea. If I hadn't spanked Andy I probably wouldn't have had it. It was by association: being an invisible adjuster of accounts. I'd simply leave the diary out in a place where Commander Smith could find it for himself and make his own discoveries.

I duly tossed this time-bomb on to the back-seat of the Honda shortly before I arrived at the surgery to collect the Commander. That was the perfect place and the perfect time. There was just him and me, no chance of someone like Nicky or Jenny picking it up, and time for him to compose himself and even consult me if he felt like it. There was only one problem. Commander Smith was the soul of honour. He scorned to read his daughter's diary. I was careful to use the rear-mirror no more than usual, but I was able to see the old-fashioned little book with its up to date delinquencies in his fingers of a labourer. Alas, those crude hands belonged to the perfect English gentleman and model paterfamilias. He obviously saw what it was, immediately stopped reading and closed it. I saw him rapping the spine absent-mindedly against his ginger-haired knuckles while he looked at Hong Kong flitting by, and I despaired of his goodness.

At home luck took a hand. Neither Nicky nor Mrs Smith were at home when we arrived, only Jenny who was in Frumpface mode to the extent that she might actually have been pre-menstrual. I think even if she'd been in the (rare) bubbly Bottleblonde mode, she'd have acted the same.

Commander Smith said, "I think your younger sister left this in the car, Jennifer."

Jenny who had nothing better to do than paint her toe-nails, something she'd probably neither had time nor inclination for at college, didn't even look at what her father put down on the nest of sliding tables. I got out of the way, fast. I thought it was a grenade with the pin pulled, and I was right. Ten minutes later (I knew Jenny to be as fast if not as retentive a reader as myself) I saw her through the french window, heading for her father's study, diary in hand. Some time after that, Jenny went upstairs to fetch her mother. The pow-wow was still going on when I went to collect Nicky from tennis at the country club. I went straight out without informing or asking permission from my employers, for why would I be cognisant of anything going on out of the ordinary?

Kicking a lone, disorderly pebble outside the club-house at the point of her Fila sports shoe, the last thing Nicky looked was your typical *adis-adis*, to wit, sallow, drawn, jerky. In her whites, with her hair in a pony-tail, she looked extraordinarily wholesome. I opened the door for her, thinking, "Boy, are you in trouble, Missy." Back at the house, I didn't have the heart to go in with her, so pretended to busy myself with a repair to the vehicle. That was a great glitch-free piece of Jap technology. I'd buy one myself with an easy mind. But from what he used to hear of it from me Commander Smith would not have been able to give it a good reference. I heard about Nicky's fate from Babyjane, who threw all caution to the north-east monsoon and pressed her ear flat against the door of Commander Smith's study. She needed to do that. None of the Smiths – not even Mrs – raised their voices much in argument. I should say I regard that as the infallible outward mark of a cultured person, its negative imprint. I have always striven to follow that example, whether in focsle or Jesuit's study.

"Whoooo!" oyster-eyed Babyjane told me. "They all gang uf on Miss Nicky. Miss Jenny, she's da one to scold her very hot. Then Commander Smith, I hear him saying: 'We're very disappointed, Nicola.' That's when I think she start da weefing, coz I don't hear her voice no more, you know you speak all da time so deef and steady *pariha lalaki* almost, you under da imfression she's da voy. Da hard words of Jenny don't hurt her but I know she lub and respick her fa-fa." Babyjane spoke her last

270

words with something akin to religious awe. The whole affair was something of an *auto de fe* for her, with Nicky in penitent's hood and us servants as the crowd.

Nicky was now upstairs in her room, Jenny outside in the garden. Commander Smith would have appreciated advice – in his position I'd have liked it, too – but I had a hunch Mrs Smith didn't want Girton Girl sitting in judgement on her favourite daughter. The door opened. Mrs Smith came out, looking as grim as the Queen of England always did on satellite TV. Babyjane and I quailed. We weren't normally scared of her. We spoke to each other in hushed voices about the price of fish per catty in morning market. We crept about the kitchen, wincing as the utensils clattered but also finding silence excruciating. I felt I was the one who'd been sampling naughty substances.

Mrs Smith ordered supper for Nicky. Jenny was the one to take it up on a tray. Next morning Commander Smith instructed me to go to school as usual.

"Serr," I complied, like the military automaton he thought I'd been. He and Nicky didn't exchange a word on the drive in. As they got out, I asked, "I'll just be the one to await you, sir?"

"No," he said curtly. "I'll find my own way to the surgery."

He was back home at lunch-time, with Nicky. This was completely unusual. Babyjane and I exchanged glances of consternation. Like I said, small, silent things with the Smiths took the place of arm-waving and yapping expostulation. After a terrible half-hour at the table, guaranteed I should have thought to give them all indigestion, Commander Smith said to me, "After coffee, drive us to the police-station, Rey."

Babyjane dropped the sugar-basin. This was fortunately of silver and contained, even more fortunately, rather than granulated sugar, the cubes Commander Smith preferred but which the rest of the family considered "naff" (Nicky) and "vulgar" (Mrs Smith). Babyjane's mouth dropped open, in the semi-genuine stage-shock of real-life Philippine shenanigans, which ensuing excesses could reinforce as the one hundred per cent article. "Go upstairs and change out of your school uniform," Commander Smith added. Meekly, Nicky obeyed.

"Serr, serr," Babyjane shrieked. "Do not do, do not do! Miss Nicky your own daughter, serr!"

Had their maid pulled out a pistol and shot down the chandelier (Chinese landlord's fitting which the English tenants were unable to remove) the Smiths could not have looked more astounded. Nicky regarded Babyjane, who was pulling on her arm, in the way she might Candy, the red setter, had Candy suddenly gone rabid and started tugging on her shin. Of course, Babyjane was trying to protect, not savage her. Mrs Smith looked even more amazed than her husband and youngest daughter but Jenny seemed to be struggling not to laugh. I could see she was standing outside it all, like I was starting to. I gently encircled Babyjane's broomstick wrist with my thumb and forefinger. She had both arms outstretched and was leaning backwards with such body weight as she had, but Nicky was still able to hold her own with just one arm.

"OK *na*, Jane," I urged her. "Commander is knowing what's best," although, to tell the truth, I also thought he'd taken leave of his senses. Freeing herself by her own efforts, Nicky headed upstairs to change without further comment. Babyjane stood there with tears rolling down her withered cheeks, beating her temples with her palms. This was to find her hands something to do in stressful moment, much as suspect might gratefully cup his hands around the cigarette interrogator bestows upon him. Jenny rose precipitately, was just able to arrest the back of her chair as it teetered, then fled the room with a hand over her face and shoulders shaking. She'd excuse herself to her mother later by saying something had gone down the wrong way, which in a manner of speaking it had.

In the end, Commander Smith drove himself and Nicky to the police station, while I remained at home. I watched him. He remembered to indicate left-turn at the top of the road. That was the first tumbril Honda ever made.

To cut a long story short, nothing drastic happened to Nicky. I mean no death-sentence, no juvenile offenders home, no probation. She wasn't expelled from school; she didn't even miss a single class the next day. That's what comes from having a great Pop like Commander Smith.

Nicky was, of course, subdued for the next fortnight, but then she always was a quiet girl, not the vixen she appeared in her diary. I did hear her say to her mother, "I'm really sorry, Mums," and saw Mrs Smith hug her, quickly.

As for Babyjane she shook her head in a terrible wonder and asked, "What kind of da Fa-Fa? What kind of Fa-Fa vetray his daughter to da Folice?"

CHAPTER XV

BACK HOME THERE WAS A SPECIAL FIRECRACKER, much beloved of the urchin. Unlike the rockets and golden fountains which marked anniversaries or fiestas at other times, this made its appearance only at the end of the year. Its unusual feature was not so much its deafening noise and stupendous power, sufficient to excavate a hole in the dirt or to blow off a hand, but the extraordinary duration of the fuse's burn-time. At least five minutes, sometimes as much as fifteen. Once lit, it smouldered undetectably inside the twist of blue paper. Not a spark, not a curl of smoke, advertised the fact that it was patiently, inexorably consuming itself. That was when people, sometimes the setter, who should have known better, picked it up and got their fingers taken off. Amputation was the least of it – those wounds nearly always got infected by tetanus spores. As I think of it in retrospect, the inordinate delay could have had but one reason: time for the urchin to make good his escape. They – which was to say Danton, myself, and the rest of the gang – would set match to touch-paper before concealing a Super Lolo or Authentic Thor under leaves, newspaper, or can. Long, long after our urchinly presence was a ghostly memory, the chunky firecracker would explode, causing dogs to flee, babies to cry, and strong men to flinch and curse, while the cool kids grinned. Or sometimes an Atomic Thunder would detonate without a soul in sight; we wouldn't know. Part of the relish of the joke was you never knew. Atty Caladong hated the firecrackers. He never went out on December 24 or 31. To him it sounded just like a client or enemy taking a large-calibre pot-shot at him.

Such a slow match smouldered under Babyjane and myself during our last days with the Smiths. Neither of us menials were aware of the fuse fizzing away under our placid existences, the touch-paper ignited by the steady, responsible, and quite unurchin-like hand of Commander Smith.

In a manner of speaking, the Smiths were going to desert.

The Commander had received an excellent offer from a multi-national petroleum company requiring a dentist in what I thought of then as an obscure Sheikhdom on the Arabian peninsula. They were, of course, under no obligation, contractual or moral, to let us in on their decision, none at all – *di ba*? But this did not make it the less disconcerting to hear the news. I guess it was an instance of rumour travelling at supersonic velocity, for even Babyjane hadn't heard it.

Commander Smith hauled us in to his study on a Saturday at 2.45 p.m., Babyjane already all large-eyed innocence before hearing any specific accusation.

"I think this is the appropriate moment to fill you in, Rey and Babyjane, on our future plans…" began Commander Smith at his kindliest and most imperturbable and then proceeded to dig a hole before our very feet rather than fill it in. When he'd finished, Babyjane asked in a croaking whisper, "What haffen to us, Serr?" This was undeniably more dramatic than the wails and ululations I'd expected from her. Once again, never underestimate the uneducated. Commander Smith said in his kindest voice, "Well, I've just told you in great detail, Babyjane. The contract will still have four months to run at the time we go and, of course, we'll honour its terms and pay you salary in lieu. We'll give you your ticket home, as we're obliged to, and I shouldn't be surprised if there was a small gratuity as well, if Mrs Smith has her way."

"What haffen to us, serr?"

"Rey, please explain to Babyjane. I don't think I can really make it any clearer in English than I already have."

"Very clear, sir. OK. But I think she already understands."

"Oh, Rey, Rey. What going to vecome of us? We lose Serr and Mum is da vest emfloyers in da world. Oh, voo-hoo."

Commander Smith and I shared a glance of amusement which wasn't that of employer and man-servant. I was glad because I'd replied to him more tersely than I meant or felt. Babyjane headed for the door, shaking her head and pretending to blow her nose on her sleeve.

"Just a moment, if you would, Rey."

"Serr?"

He put a hand on my shoulder. "I've a suggestion, a proposition, to which I hope you might be amenable. Say no at once, if you don't like the idea. That's perfectly alright, too. We regard you as very special, Rey, and we'd like to bring you on my next posting. I think it could definitely be arranged, no problem with that, leave it to us, Charlie Northrop…" He halted. The look of pure joy on my face said it all. I grabbed his hand and I squeezed it. He was a large man, nearly as tall as Fr. Boy, but he winced.

"Thank you, sir, thank you so much."

"Alright then. Glad you're agreeable. But mum's the word. You know, Babyjane…"

"She'd get jealous, sir. That's the way we are. You know it, too, OK."

"Good. Ah…" He cleared his throat just as I was at the door. "Pay. Ah, we may not be able to match what you get now because of the allowance there…"

"Oh Gee, sir. No problem. You pay me what you want." I admit if I had known Commander and Mrs Smith were going to cut my remuneration by a third I might not have sounded so blithe, but I certainly wouldn't have descended to haggling about it. The Smiths were as honest as the day was long but cheese-paring was one of their little foibles which you had to tolerate, like smoking in a great friend.

Time now went quickly. I was excited. I was, in another Fr. Paulism, having my cake and eating it. I had the prospect of change and variety, not to mention putting a third kink in my escape trail, combined with security and a reassuring familiarity. Someone else had thrown the dice again for me to climb a ladder.

Six weeks before Babyjane's termination of service, she received a nice cash bonus of an extra month's wages: not extravagant, but a welcome addition to her nest-egg. Was I jealous? No, and I was flattered the Commander didn't try to hide it from me. It meant he didn't consider me part of the alien tribe. I may be looking for mean motives where none existed, but I wonder if Commander Smith didn't look on the gratuity in the light of an insurance premium: to stop Babyjane taking anything that wasn't nailed down when she left. I know Nicky presented her with *two* brassieres and matching panties.

"Very Christian of Miss Nicky," I told Babyjane and left it at that.

THE AIRBUS WHICH CARRIED US TO BOHAIDEN, a miracle of technology made prosaic only by the imaginative as well as physical indolence of the travelling public, was in all respects a Time Machine as well as annihilator of geographical distance. Perhaps a flying carpet fulfils both functions. Going from Hong Kong to Bohaiden was like losing three centuries of human endeavour. This was more apparent in the intangible context of ideas and of notions of what was honourable and what was not, but to a far smaller extent also the material world. Wandering the conundrum of alleys, gulches, steps, and ravines that composed the Old Town of Bohaiden, some of these features man-made but immemorial, some temporary accommodations with nature, the more precipitous being frank abdications to indomitable terrain, there to lose oneself and to look up after midday from the lowest level of the sump formed by sheer rock cliffs and the blank walls of mud habitations and to see the moon and the stars by broad day, with the anticipation of the sun's scimitar stroke at the top of the flight as reward for escape, was to know desolation. It was doing Atty Caladong's *reclusion temporal* in an eternal night before last. That there existed parts of the capital and, indeed, areas of our own new town that looked like the mirage's faithful re-creation of Hong Kong or Singapore only made the darkness at noon the more profound. Burning bank-notes before one's private demon, one's desert djinn, only makes him, *di ba*, more insatiable of control? Paying foreigners to build skyscrapers was not the answer to the riddle of the past, the solution to the maze of the muse.

We lived in a port at some significant distance from the capital, even in the age of modern transport systems. The Czechs and the Chinese had built the Arabs a railway-line and the Japanese constructed a splendid motorway with a toll-gate that had never been operational. Even so, in most other countries the cost of fuel would have raised freightage to prohibitive levels. Here there was more oil than water. Otherwise it would have been simpler to have abandoned the old capital and re-built it somewhat nearer the sea. The Smiths had a house in one of the surrounding suburbs that formed a modern quadrilateral frame for the New and Old Towns. I thought of the Old Town as the negative from which they'd developed the print of the New or as a self-portrait taken by clockwork time-delay as Benjie Bedou ran back and re-arranged his hindering robes just in time for flash-exposure. The town had started as a humble fishing-village, not one of the trading emporia of that great Arab medieval expansion. The Bohaidenese had traded salted snapper, instead of frankincense, gold, and myrrh. There were no sea-monsters, just the odd giant tuna. Fishermen still landed reduced catches at the beach north-east of the Old Town. And pearl-diving continued, the very young boys engaged in this having hair burnt colourless as straw by the sun but backs turned to ebony. It was unexpected as the Palawan albinos, and they too looked like the precursors of a photograph, or shadow-relics of nuclear blast. Dhows still docked at the wharf below the Old Town – in fact they had a thriving traditional manufactory of these, hardly using any metal in the construction of the billowing, curvaceous hundred-foot monsters. Ironically, as the Arab world languished and recuperated from its ancient achievements, trade had at last sprung up in the backwater of Bohaiden: a contraband outward traffic in Saudi gold to India, and return cargoes of Afghan hashish and heroin, cloned Kalashnikovs and Makarov pistols almost as good as the illegal *paltik* guns of our own Visayan smiths, and wiry pre-pubescent Pakistani boys who though ten-years-old and under, tough-looking and reliable as a lightly-oiled revolver, did not seem perfumed catamites. They weren't destined for the sex-trade at all: they were to be jockeys in the dangerous but lucrative spectacle of camel-racing. Dant with his daring, his tininess, his love of the fix – he'd missed his *métier* here.

I had as much respect for the motorised dhow as I had for the junior jockeys. If the camel was the ship of the desert, the dhow was the camel of the sea. Humped, cantankerous with wind, uncomfortable but utterly unbroachable, the lack of nails probably kept it off those radar screens that had not been greased to stop, rather than continue, turning. The dhow beat the bangka outta sight.

As for the ship of the desert, green is what comes to my mind when I recall Bohaiden, which may surprise those habituated to images of the salt and pepper wastes of sand and rock comprising Arabia deserta. I don't retain a black and white negative. My souvenir is Fujicolor, with its veridian hue always preferable to the moody blues of Kodak.

As the Airbus banked that day of arrival I saw the sea was green in all directions, not the dominant royal blue and turquoises of home. This was from slave class in the rear where the airline clerks had put me well away from my employers, though Commander Smith assured me in transit in Delhi our tickets had cost the same.

MONTHS LATER IN THE DESERT, with the Smiths thousands of miles distant across two oceans, I'd see that vast expanse as another sea of green, extending as far as the eye could reach, its rolling dunes as much creations of the wind as waves were. After even the most trivial pricks of rain, not so much drops as dampness with attitude, the desert's aridity was transformed with a magic brush. Out of every nook and flaw, from between the grains themselves, tiny blades and shoots sprouted with cartoon miraculousness. It was instant as pot noodles. The eyeballs veritably ached with the vibrancy of the colour; the wilderness throbbed.

When in the wilds it is, on the whole, better not to stand waxing fanciful as if one was in a class-room. At the time these reflections struck me, I was in a wadi, though I didn't realise it was a river-bed until too late, fertilising the gravel with the contents of my bowels. I was on the way to a job near Northern Saudi while my co-labourers waited in the open truck (standing room only for a journey three times as protracted as the flight with the Smiths). Hep, polio, cholera, typhoid, my cast-iron pauper's gut had known, absorbed, and repelled them all but the scummy lamb-stew and rancid yellow rice the sub-contractor had fed us obviously contained an organism both novel and obnoxious to my intestinal security fauna. I listened to the grumbling within myself, interspersed by the odd hiss and splattering, and at first mistook it for the real forces of nature. With a great rumble and rattling of boulders and gravel and the kitcheny roar of water making a seething landing on a scorching surface, the flood was upon me. I just had time to get to a semi-crouch, make an unavailing grab for my pants, change my mind and spring for a tree growing out of the bank at the horizontal, before the water swept me off my feet. I hung there, minus the pants which the torrent had stripped off my ankles in the instant, with the "R" for Rey motif on the handsome buckle of the reptile skin-belt which had been Jenny Smith's parting gift to me branded into my palm and its thirty-eight inch length swinging before my eyes as if it was Moses' rod come to serpent life before Pharaoh. My reflex was always to let go after jumping, rather than wrecking the hoop, and, alas, as my grip instinctively weakened so the belt dropped into the boisterous water and was carried away much as a real snake would have been. I imagined a party of nomads coming upon it. As quickly as it had come, the torrent was gone. I looked up. I saw a ring of Filipino faces looking down on me from the bank, some concerned, some only curious. I scratched my armpit like a gorilla, hanging one-handed for some cheap laughs – Jeez, we needed it, that truck was a Calvary vehicle – then dropped lightly onto the already drying gravel.

"Come from nowhere, *di ba*?" commented one of the labourers, unskilled like myself, an Ilonggo with a BA in Commerce and Business Administration. "Just a few drops of rain, *na lang*."

"That's the way it is in the desert," said the foreman, a crew-cut thug from Laguna who sported the biblical but un-Fr. Boy-like motto *Vengeance is mine, saith the Lord* tattooed on his left biceps. "*Sige lang*, OK, mount up, guys. You flushed, *na*, flush-flood, boss." As he was the foreman I judged it politic to laugh.

The carpet of green started to look threadbare after only a few hours, the underlay of sand shining whitely through the coloured but wilting pile. I remained pant-less in the throng, on the promise of a pair of shorts from the next biggest guy. Meanwhile, as the truck lurched over a rock or dropped into a hole, I'd be pressed into the guy in front, who was one of those compulsive humorists who shrieked in dismay every time I brushed against his buttocks and loudest when I hadn't. When this palled, he got bigger laughs, including one extorted from me, when he groaned in deep pleasure. Credit me, you don't get anywhere by showing out as cleverer or more sophisticated than your fellows.

We were heading North all the time, an instinct corroborated by a couple of my co-workers who'd been mariners. Other than it was construction-clearance, we didn't know – or care – what we were supposed to be doing when we got there. The drive extended and extended itself. There was no way of communicating with the driver, an elderly Arab, who was probably as poor as he looked, from one of the minority tribes oppressed on a hereditary basis by the royal house of Bohaiden. Many of the *pinoys*, not just the foreman, possessed an excellent command of Arabic but we couldn't get into the cab from where we were. I don't doubt this fact had occurred to our despatchers. We slept leaning against each other; at least I could, the talent I never forfeited and which used to irk Danton so. At length, in pitch darkness, we pulled up at what the driver's lantern revealed as a mountain of jerry-cans (the headlamps had gone a couple of hours back). We helped him re-fuel. Asked where we were going, he said we were bound… there. There. He just extended the goatee on his chin into the blackness. It was a typical Philippine answer, too. We couldn't complain. The others went with it; any qualms I had were eclipsed as I squeezed myself into skimpy shorts that would have been a tent on my benefactor. The stupid fuck I was, it boosted my morale as much as strapping on a gun.

Dawn came, then day, and day was terrible. Although the night was very cold we'd been packed together, so that our body warmth was a comfort. Now the tattered awning offered scant protection from the sun. We stopped for shade by a group of large rocks. Absolutely no one pissed; we were too dehydrated. The sailors, who'd also done a lot of work in the desert, explained to us that high ground, even the slightest of deviations from the level, and barren boulders like these, acted as significant landmarks for navigation in these featureless tracts and were as jealously prized and bitterly contested in a war as the islands in the ocean that are the tops of submerged mountain-ranges and giant extinct volcanoes. These insignificant desert carbuncles were the Iwo Jimas, Guadalcanals, and Leytes of the past and would be again as long as there was Man.

Two hours later we drew up at some drooping barbed wire and sign-posts so blistered an archaeologist could not have deciphered them. I should say they were about two years old. This was also the number of frontiers we had to cross. "What is mine-field in Israeli, *ba*?" asked the wag in front of me, and got a gale of nervous laughter from the entire truck. The foreman translated the Tagalog into Arabic for the benefit of the driver, who took it seriously.

From one benighted despotism, we entered into another, and crossed into the third, all in darkness without anyone ever knowing: one ruled by a fat emir shortly to be poisoned by his brother, the second by bloodthirsty priests, and the third by a military dictator who called himself a secular President but persecuted the minority sect with vindictiveness a zealot could not have surpassed. For us, for anyone, it was the same expanse of unremarkable waste ground, sterile once more after the rain.

We made our destination shortly before daybreak. This by rights ought to have been as joyous an occasion as landfall for parched, scurvy-ridden mariners, or at the very least a source of relief to us with our stiff backs, burnt necks, and knees stiff as antique hinges, but we descended in a silence none of us had the heart to break, even the joker in front of me. I couldn't put my finger on it at the time; I reckoned I was just hungry, sleepy, and disorientated, which was enough to put a saint out of sorts. But after recuperation flat on my back – sheer gratification no matter the ground was unyielding and stone-strewn – and what I had to concede was a good breakfast of black coffee, unleavened bread, eggs, and salt fish, the feeling hadn't gone. We all had it.

It was a low-key foreboding. It was the surroundings. It was finding ourselves somewhere we didn't belong with nobody who cared for us being any the wiser. It was Limbo.

Being lost to the world in the desert wasn't really an eerie experience. It was the opposite of depressing; it was exhilarating. Of course. Such had been the condition of the Old Testament Prophets, spurning the tawdry life of the towns, existing as we just had in a cauldron of rock, thorn, and sand, but without the benefit of gasoline. They hadn't been on a downer: they'd emerged wild-eyed and charged with the voltage of their own revelation.

But we were no longer in the purity of the wilderness. We were up the fundamental end of nowhere in a back of beyond that had human contamination about it. It wasn't one thing or the other; it was neither civilisation nor nature. It was desolate but banal, like a municipal garbage-heap.

In the middle distance were what seemed to be melon-fields and a system of irrigation canals that looked at once complex and inept. Beyond that stood a group of structures, clearly the work of man, and equally obviously huge for us to be able to make them out at more than thirty miles, but whether they were the tanks and towers of a refinery looming out of its clouds of visible pollution or even a nuclear power installation clear-cut in its mantle of transparent airs it was impossible to discern with the naked eye on flat ground. And beyond even those vast and ambiguous forms were the tiny grey cones and white teats, almost invisible, of mighty mountains. Borne on the thin desert airs we heard a dog's bark, followed by a bell's tinkle, and a goat's bleat. Closer inspection of the ground revealed goat's droppings rather than scatter-gun pellets softened in the heat. The main unfamiliarity for South East Asians like ourselves was the gaps, the thinness of the populations. We, too, had uninhabited rain forests and mountain but anywhere remotely habitable was no longer remote. Barrio would have been rubbing shoulder with barrio. I told myself to show some grace, some fortitude, the Cambodian Semporn's antiseptic of courage, to wit a surviving sense of humour. This nascent discernment of what might be amusing in the bleakest situation did not survive the information that a long, low row of roofed concrete stalls were to be our living-quarters on the site. Less than a metre high, so the size of a luxurious kennel or proper sty, these were covered, floor and walls, with grey cement dust. My fellow-workers were as dismayed as I was by the prospect of inhabiting these cells, which offered no protection from animals wild or domestic and, little short of ovens, an augmentation of heat rather than protection from the sun, but they were incurious as to their purpose. That was to say, they were of the class of men who could complain and object but never essentially queried their lot.

When I looked at the constructions it was obvious that they were not designed for the purpose of human accommodation. It wasn't so much that they were physically too low – too cramped, too mean – for I judged our employers capable of any cruelty towards us whether it was by negligence or by design but that the specification was too high. It was first-class concrete, good as anything in Hong Kong or Singapore; in fact, I estimated it superior. Civilian contractors in the Crown Colony or island republic were not in the habit of building hardened bunkers. What the hell were these sturdy little hutches? Oracle cubicles? Eternal Wayfarers' Comfort Rooms? Mini-SAM silos?

"I don't put our dog back home name of Jinggoy in dat, man," observed one of the skilled fitters.

"O-o. High-blood dog dat one," concurred the wag. "Go bite you if de accoms not up to par."

What little effervescence there was to be found in these exchanges grew flat when we were directed to bug out with our shovels and picks south-east. Although the foreman had a prismatic compass, we didn't seem to be heading towards anything either particular or significant. The wag started to whistle the Seven Dwarves song. I'd changed my opinion of the guy – something we should always be ready to do: only the dead are unable to modify a judgement – and was starting to think him worth his weight in gold.

I was latching on to small things to remain cheerful, but the growing brightness of the day was not working its usual transformation. Something extra, something subliminal was making me extra uneasy. It grew stronger. I recognised it as an aroma, one I knew but couldn't place. We arrived at an area of recently disturbed earth, the red and yellow spoil of the lower strata obstinately visible through the dusty grey top-soil which had been half-heartedly strewn over it, leaving the patterned ground like a scrap of flamboyantly striped but grubby clothing, say a coat of many colours.

"'*Sus Maria*," exclaimed our comedian. He bent over as if to pick up something interesting or valuable, maybe a gold coin or ring, then collapsed. I chuckled dutifully, but the joke went on rather longer than warranted. He lay there on his face, the rise and fall of the respiration attesting that he was alive much like an on-court casualty surrounded by the rest of the team. I turned the guy over; it was authentic syncope, man. His face was greyer than the dust now powdering his hair. There was something even greyer which the very soil was extruding: a human hand, wrist, and forearm. Our joker was clasping the fingers in a handshake he had never contemplated when he bent over. I recognised the odour around us now: decomposing bodies. Fierce. Guys all round me were crossing themselves not once but several times. Muttered "'*Sus Maria*s" filled the air and the odd "Aw, puck, man," with one idiot uttering the imprecation while he made the sign of the Cross. Leaning on my pick handle, I took the deep, calming breath Butch Tan Sy had taught us and then regretted it. Widening my stance, I noticed the prolificity of insect-life, both earth-bound and winged. Some yards away the foreman looked paler than whitening-soap could have made him. He clearly hadn't been let in on what awaited us. He was probably worse shocked than us – we hadn't had preconceptions to be shattered. He got a grip on himself and I wondered if he wasn't ex-AFP, used to salvaging and corpses.

"OK, OK," he said. *"Hindi kayo barkada ng madre."* I thought that if we had been a gaggle of nuns, we'd have taken it more in our stride.

"Dig them ups and lay them out in a straight line, what's left of them. Our instructions to clear da site of ovstacles and disfose of all garbages, *na lang*." I imagined those were the very letter of the orders he'd received. Boy, what a joke on someone's part. At least the bodies weren't buried very deep. The mass grave they occupied was so shallow it inclined you to think they'd scratched the hard ground just deep enough to get past the dust, then perfunctorily sprinkled the rainbow sands and black pebbles over the corpses like salt and peppercorns over marinating pork. I'm no expert on stiffs but I think they were recent. I'd say they'd still been breathing men a month ago. Liquefaction hadn't set in yet but then the dryness, the parching heat, the baking sand, likely all had an embalming effect. It wasn't as awful a job as I'd feared; I mean, it was grisly, but I didn't have to fight the urge to puke. We hadn't gloves, aprons, disposable bags – nothing in the way of what you might call specialist equipment for the body detail. One of us had to hold the corpses by their wrists with bare hands, the other the legs. There was plenty of unstated competition to hold the boots, I can tell you. These, I noticed when I finally managed to out-manoeuvre my buddy, were steel-toed safety shoes much like the ones the sub-contractor had issued to us (the inflated cost of which would later be deducted, among other things, including food priced at five star hotel rates, from our pay). All the bodies were male. Most had been placed face-down in the way the witch doctors of our own Siquijor island laid out enemies after they'd been voodooed to shit nails and expire. I had a feeling this was the same with the Arabs, too. Another thing: these dead dudes were all fit young guys, yet they bore no visible injuries or wounds. How had they died? And how come no one was wearing a watch or jewellery?

The head came off the next corpse, straight into my hands, as I tried to show some belated respect by cradling it while my buddy unceremoniously swung it by the ankles. There I was, holding it like a basketball, a deeply undesired pass.

Now, in order to accomplish their tasks, sometimes gruesome, always tedious, and not infrequently dangerous, the rude soldiery – as Fr. Paul once translated a phrase from Caesar's Gallic Wars – which I extend to include riggers, merchant seamen, and labourers like ourselves – these rough men often alleviate their solitude and deal with their horror by employing a humour as rough as themselves. It's a cruel humour, like the best humour always is, with the redeeming factor that yours could be the body cut in half by the snapped hawser flying across the dock tomorrow. The most efficacious antiseptics sting. So, as I stood rooted, working to quell the shock, my partner shouted, "Hoy, guys, look, look!" Catcalls and whistles filled the air, the loudest from the wag who'd fainted. "*Fotbol, na!*", "Tonight, Bulalo soup!", "*Um-um,*" came the derisive cries, the last an onomatopeiac expression for anything long filling the mouth, just short of triggering the gag-reflex, whether ice-popsicle or something warmer and saltier. Like a BBQ hot-dog, *di ba*?

"*Hindi, baskitbol,*" I replied and made to lob the head to the wag. Blow me (so to speak), in the lingo of Captain Marryat and Stevenson, if he didn't pass out again, without the catch ever leaving my hands. Best fake-out I ever made, a testimony to the efficacy of Butch's training methods. "Melon, *lang*, boss," said the oldest guy in the party, an electrician whose distinguished bush of grey hairs belied the fact that he was as skittish as the rest of us. I looked more closely at what I held. "This, guys," I said slowly, my stomach fluttering again as I absorbed the implications, "was a *pinoy*. It's a Filipino face. *Di ba?* The nose short enough for you? Look at the eyes, man, even they're closed it's not a 'Merikano or a 'Rabo. The hair," I dusted the top, changing it from an 18th century wig to the prolific black Asian poll, "is just like yours, Noli, or yours, Edmond. *Di ba?*" The work-force gathered round me. I have to say the rapidity of their mental processes might have caused Fr. Paul to revise his severe judgement on my fellow-countrymen, but then there's nothing like the sense of self-preservation for a stimulus. We were all quiet. Of course, what we were all thinking hung over our heads like a cloud of poison gas. A binary gas: 1. These guys were just like us. 2. Will what happened to them happen to us?

After that it was but a short step to ponder the next implication. If we were to tidy up and hide or eliminate all signs of whatever had happened – I didn't like to use the word "evidence" even to myself – were we going to get eliminated and hidden, too?

Negative, I thought, no more quickly than my colleagues who had not had the benefit of the Jesuits – because otherwise it would go on for ever, liquidation squad mopping up liquidation squad, like the Khmer Rouge.

We continued our task in silence, working at least half as fast again as we had before. I laid down my head, face to the sun, with as much reverence as I could summon, doing my best to locate exactly the right position at the top of the spinal cord. "*Fotbol,*" said the wag, not wanting to let a good gag go, making to place it at the feet, but took one look at my face and desisted. Altogether there were thirty-seven bodies, fifteen more than us. We were all counting in the hope that there weren't twenty-two corpses.

Well before dusk we traipsed back to our blast-proof kennels and, in fact, made our cooking-fire in one of them. Smoky for the cook but serving not to betray our presence in all directions of the night. Even I didn't sleep well, though the watches the mariners divided us into made us all feel a little better.

No one lingered in their bags at dawn. A perfunctory breakfast was followed by a fast march to the burial site where we finished off yesterday's work, tidying up and laying heavy stones on the dirt to keep animals from digging up the remains. The foreman instructed us not to make these look like gravestones or even cairns. That was OK, it looked like the Jap garden of memory I'd seen at a famous battle-site back home but though the guys complied, they wanted something more. There were mutters. Someone said, "These guys were Filipinos. They were probably Roman Catholics like most of us. Someone has to say *koan*, a few words only." A murmur of assent passed around the group, so like the rude men they were: always irresponsible, sometimes callous, but never less than superstitious.

"You're the foreman, Gonzalo," the wag suggested – I'd found out the night before he was the foreman's gay cousin – but Gonzalo shook his head and spat. He had the brittle words of command and criticism but not the lapidary ones of memorial required now. I spoke, causing all heads to turn:

"My fellow-workers, these men, who were men just like ourselves, probably our fellow countrymen, met a strange and unnatural death here in the desert. We don't know their names. They were unknown to us and must lie here unknown for eternity, save to God, with their names and their ages and their origins unrecorded. However, we know they must have had Mamas, Papas, Brothers, Sisters, and maybe sweehearts and wives and children, too, who loved them. They travelled far, like ourselves, in search of a livelihood and to provide a better life for those they left at home. Let us honour their sacrifice but let us not shed too many tears for them, for they were poor men like ourselves, strangers in a strange land, and it is not graceful to pity yourself too much. They were *pinoys* like us, who laughed in life, even when it was hard, maybe most when it was hard, and who knew how to laugh at death, too. We will remember and honour them by living our lives as they

287

would have liked to have lived their own, if they had been given the opportunity. As for their care now and the consequences for those whose cruelty or carelessness brought about their deaths, we leave that to you, Lord."

"Amen," said the wag, looking at me strangely, as for the first time, and twenty other voices followed in solemn but ragged refrain. As I marched behind the foreman, pick on my shoulder like an honour guard, I heard someone say, "Dat guy must be freachers," and someone else reply, "But he is a niggers," and a third supply synthesis to thesis and antithesis with, "Hab got niggers freachers, too, man. You didn't hear already?"

Spirits rose, measurably, with the kilometres we put between us and the site. As we crossed the first border the foreman actually smiled and when we got to the second we all followed the wag's example as we traversed the putative minefield, using both feet to jump like kangaroos and yelling "Boom!" as we landed. By the time we reached the outskirts of Bohaiden the wag and his cronies were pretending to be in rigor mortis as they stood upright in the truck with glassy eyes. The sub-contractor paid us on the spot, which was unusual, and without another word among ourselves we dispersed.

YEAH, I NO LONGER WORKED FOR THE SMITHS. Five months after first arriving on the Arabian peninsula they'd departed. Nicky had only stayed six weeks. Her parents had found a school for her in England. That was the best thing for young Missy. Her parents and older sister were in accord on this. So was I, though I wasn't consulted and, no doubt, Nicky too would have agreed it was in her own best interests. I drove the family to the airport and was told to park and meet them in the cafeteria. That was nice, really nice, of my saintly Smiths, to let me see Nicky off like one of the family, or at least as a friend. It was a cool, matter-of-fact goodbye from the rest of the family – quite unlike the excesses of a Philippine *despedida* – loving but unsentimental, no breast-beating or tears, though they certainly weren't giving the black sheep a chilly send-off. I was the most demonstrative. It was permitted. Wasn't I the open, sunny Filipino, the one who sings his emotions to the world, whether they're real or not? The adult Smiths smiled indulgently as I bestowed upon Nicky the instant sunshine of my beam, then embraced her. I guess it might have been why I was there, as the supplier of surrogate emotion to the reserved British with their emotional inhibitions. Anyhow, recovering from my bear-hug, Miss Kool stepped back and shook my paw with her own dry little hand.

"Cheers, Rey," she said. "Bye Mum, Dad. See you, Jens," and she was off through the passport channel without a backward glance.

COMMANDER SMITH HAD MADE AN ENEMY in the first month of their stay. This was his Middle Eastern colleague. I was rather brusque with the Commander when he made to translate the term *locum* for me. Funny, you could slap my face, call me a nigger, but I was the one to get miffed if you impugned my Latinity. Mr Al-Elvis – as I called him because of his outrageous hair-quiff – had, in my opinion, been plotting against whoever would be coming since well before Commander Smith's arrival. It hadn't started as a matter of personal animus, though it ended that way. Mr Al-Elvis was as highly paid as my employer – for much less of a work-load than Irene had shoehorned into the Commander's appointments book back in Hong Kong.

Mr Al-Elvis had spent so many years in Karachi that he was widely regarded as a Pakistani by the Bohaiden Pakistanis. Certainly he spoke Urdu as fluently as he did Arabic and English. But he was actually a *Halo-halo*. One of his parents had been a Libyan from Malta, the other a Jordanian from Cyprus, with some genuine Indian blood from a generation back thrown in for good measure, like the green cherry a-top the Kool Hebin Speshul.

Putting Mr Al-Elvis and Commander Smith together was like placing the box of matches next to the can of gasoline and hoping there wouldn't be a fire or the bulldog next to the jackal and trusting that fur wouldn't fly. The Commander was but dimly aware of what was going on behind his back. That was part of being Commander Smith; it was of the essence of the man. Nobility of nature implies a certain everyday obtuseness, *di ba*? He didn't want to stoop from his great elevation to see what was going on at the pettier level; he refused to step out of his own context into one for which he had an instinctive distaste. But, like I said, to deal with the sly, the weak, the spiteful, the selfish, you have to come down to their level, or the effect of your abstention is simply to grant them impunity. And that emboldens them to further spite. In fact, in the end, it turns out to be not such a noble abstention.

Mr Al-Elvis didn't look like a snake, still less a worm. A man of distinguished appearance who took pains to present himself as stylishly as he could in the fashion of the Westernised Arabs, he was actually a far more prepossessing figure than Commander Smith. I was *pinoy* enough to wish, sometimes, that my employer wasn't quite so simple, so understated. Mr Al-Elvis favoured navy blue or beige safari suits, with the classic slash and pleat in the back and the half-belt and single-vent that showed his long, lean − I was going to say Indian − legs to best advantage. I dare say he would have looked the same as Commander Smith while operating in the white tunic but Mr Al-Elvis was at great pains to be well-accessorised: reptile-skin Bally's with paste buckles that made Atty Caladong's Florsheims look like thongs, a beautiful black and gold watch around his elegant, bony wrist with matching ring, cigarette-case which Erlinda could have quickly distinguished as either 18K or 22K but which had to remain ambiguous to me, and a fondness for Givenchy Gentleman, lavishly sprayed. Mr Al-Elvis was under a cloud. He'd had two female patients in Gibraltar make separate complaints about inappropriate behaviour. Nothing was ever proved. He'd been told to have a female nurse present in future before he gave ladies the, one, shot. And not, as Robbie Pryce would say later, a meat-injection.

Nicky, only in Bohaiden a week at that time (the British themselves no slouches at speed of gossip when it was juicy and involved the member of a member of an ethnic minority) said, "When you read about it in the News of the Screws, why's it always a Paki doctor or dentist?"

"Nicky!" exclaimed her mother.

"You little racist," said her older sister.

"Well, it's true," Nicky replied, not at all abashed, "you can't say it isn't. Eight times out of ten it *is* a Pakistani or an Indian name. I'm not going to say it isn't when it is. That's just dishonest. Dad?"

Commander Smith didn't rush into this one; he didn't allow himself to be enlisted by whoever was the first to appeal to him directly − i.e. Nicky − nor did he close ranks against the youngest and most consistently erring member of the family. Either would have been the way of the *pinoy* paterfamilias. He seemed to be thinking out loud to himself and, at the end, having laid out the opposing arguments, he appeared − rather aggravatingly − not to have taken sides. I found this remarkably similar to the anonymous opinion columns in a certain London newspaper, the leaders as Jenny told me they were called, which I would peruse in the club-house lobby while waiting for the Smiths. If Philippine papers were an unbalanced stew of extreme and spicy opinions, this English newspaper was plain chicken. No salt, no pepper. And no guts. The Commander said, "It's not fair to say all Indian or all Pakistani or all Nigerian, or all any other group of anaesthetists or dentists or what-have-you are unethical or incompetent. It would be statistically untrue, darling, and a gross insult to the many good ones. Don't you think it would discourage them from making the effort? On the other hand, you'd have to be blind not to be aware of the fact that the same high codes of professional conduct that prevail in some countries – not necessarily Western ones, Singapore, for instance – aren't observed in many third world countries. And particularly with regard to female patients. But then there is such a thing as female hysteria or plain malice that would result in trumped-up charges against the poor health professional, not to mention old-fashioned racism. The simplest thing all round is just to make sure you conduct all examinations, routine as well as intimate or when the patient's unconscious, with a female nurse in attendance. As for Mr Al-Elvis, I believe we should extend my colleague not so much the benefit of the doubt as the presumption of innocence."

In other words, I believe Commander Smith was saying that essence will always vanquish context and, if it doesn't, we should comport ourselves as if it did. If ever Roman fell on his sword, Commander Smith did.

Impartial review of the evidence suggested Mr Al-Elvis was at best a mediocre dentist; although I admit, with my sound teeth and Commander Smith, I never had to suffer in his chair. From what I could gather, my knowledge of dentistry by now surprisingly extensive, if not profound, built up from chance scraps of monologue and overheard conversation much as my understanding of theology had been, Mr Al-Elvis had contrived the difficult feat of being both inert to the point of negligence and ambitious to the point of over-reaching his competence. He had missed a cavity or a cracked filling in a company wife's molar at her bi-annual check-up which hadn't posed serious problems when Commander Smith dealt with it a month later but which had caused the patient, a vociferous

Scotswoman, to complain. Then in another case he'd omitted to lance an abscess or prescribe antibiotics for it, and the infection had spread to the point where it threatened the eye. Finally, he'd embarked on extracting a pair of difficult impacted wisdom teeth under local anaesthesia which had left the patient aware at the time that the procedure had taken three hours and subsequently with no feeling on both sides of his lower lip. Commander Smith had seen the X-rays. At home he'd said to Mrs Smith, "Can't think what the chap was thinking of. A consultant maxillo-facial surgeon with a fully equipped theatre and an anaesthetist on tap would have gulped before attempting those." Anyhow, there was no ethical dilemma for Commander Smith here. The insurance company which underwrote the professional negligence risk insisted on a code of Sicilian *omerta* where erring colleagues where concerned. The welfare of the public didn't come into the moral equation. This would have otherwise caused agonies of conscience for the Commander, I'm sure, the British prohibition against "sneaking", the solidarity of the profession, and fear of being thought racially prejudiced, lining up against wider social responsibility and natural scorn in a conflict that made the question of coping with Nicky seem to have been transparently simple. The Commander had taken Mr Al-Elvis aside for "a quiet word" rather than the quaint "flea in the ear" and thought everything resolved. I knew better. Or, to be accurate, I knew much worse. A little birdy told me a Pakistani or Arab would react the same way as a *pinoy* to Commander Smith's well-meant words of caution and advice. Shit! Imagine one of Commander Smith's Hong Kong barrister friends taking Atty Caladong aside to tell him he needed to re-apply himself to the text-book on tort or that steady on, old chap, His Honour was asking for a little too much grease-money and could a little bit of it be sticking to the Attorney's own palm? It would have had his little moustache going like a rabbit's nose and his little hand twitching for the reassuring fill of the Czech nine milly in no time at all. I resolved to watch the Commander's back as if he was a team-mate.

This could have been effective if Mr Al-Elvis had been playing the same game as us, even if he'd been playing dirty, but he was laying his moves not only off-court but outside the stadium. It was no good him trying to make trouble within the company compound: there were British, Dutch, Australians there. Even the helicopter pilots were Americans, mostly Vietnam veterans. The riggers were Pakistanis, *pinoys*, Thais, Sri Lankans but they were far out and didn't matter anyway. Mr Al-Elvis decided to make mischief where it mattered — among the Bohaidenese — and, for credible back-up, with the two Filipinas who were the dental nurses. He wooed these insignificant and impressionable girls with an assiduity worthy of a better purpose. They were already scared of him. When they called him "Serr", they did so in a different tone of voice than they used for Commander Smith. They might have been calling the Commander "Uncle". They said "Serr" to Mr Al-Elvis in the same way as they would have to a powerful Filipino: someone highly arbitrary, deeply capricious, ultimately unchivalrous, who was always to be propitiated even when there was nothing to be gained from subservient behaviour. (That was how they could justify crawling to themselves; it became heroic female abnegation). They feared him the way the *puta* fears before she loves the pimp and, indeed, when I saw Mr Al-Elvis in his jewellery and those glittering shoes with the stacked heels he looked the part of a superior ponce.

When I look back on it, Al-Elvis's future — or lack of one — didn't just swing on the one thing. Rarely does it happen that way, *di ba*, whether in the abstruse realm of algebra or on the muddy paths of our dirty world? It takes two sides to balance an equation, two halves of the plutonium football to make the big wham-o, and Mr Al-Elvis committed the pair of transgressions for me. What he did to my *halo*ed Smiths was the substantial part of the offence but often what tips the balance is the smaller thing, the hair on the camel's back, to use an appropriate metaphor. Tit-for-tat is ignoble, but in the disproportionate revenge exists something baronial. For me to be seriously moved, I require pity as well as a sense of anger — chivalrous me — and while I could feel vicarious indignation on the Smiths' behalf it was impossible for me to feel sorry for them. It had to be one of my own. The most terrible atrocities are tribal revenges, *di ba*?

It wasn't much, as I say, really. I saw a girl called Gimma Gonzalez going into Al-Elvis's surgery one weekday at one twenty-five p.m. A little after, to be pedantic. She was a very tiny thing, four eight, maybe four nine, with minute hands and feet but her huge spectacles gave her a grown-up air from the front. From the back, she could look eight. Gimma was in her late twenties, a cut above the ordinary

DH, somewhat better-educated than the Erlindas and Babyjanes of this world. She'd been a secretary back home in a company that sold medical oxygen. I'd seen her go in to the surgery shortly after the two dental nurses went out. I was in the Commander's car waiting for him to finish his post-prandial coffee. The new car was an Opel I didn't like but which did have tinted windows and strong air-con. I was at once suspicious. At six minutes after two Gimma came out the side-door and down the short metal fire-escape. She dabbed her right eye and squinted in the harsh sun-light before coming past me to the car-lot exit. I could see it wasn't a speck in the eye she had. She had the beginnings of a mouse underneath, though indeed tears were also coming from the other eye. She halted by my wing-mirror, unable to see me, and saw to her face. She had what we called a Dako, a Big One, a violet and gold one thousand Bohaiden dinar note in her hand, worth about twenty US dollars. I'd switched the radio off before she reached our car, so she couldn't hear me. Above the soft whoosh of the cooling system I heard her sob a few times. She finished powdering under her eye and turned sharply away, not before re-arranging the crotch of her pantaloons where she was probably sticky. She looked at the note in her hand and threw it down before stamping on it. Forty feet away she turned, came back, picked the money up, and put it in her purse. Three or four minutes after she'd gone Mr Al-Elvis himself also emerged from the side-door, looking satisfied with himself. So much so, in fact, that Fr. Paul's expression "pleased as punch" with reference to the look on Mozart Sandukan's face after he'd got a hundred per cent on irregular verbs but before he'd been caught with the crib, came to mind. As Al-Elvis passed before the bonnet of the Opel my knuckles whitened on the steering-wheel somewhat more than they would have done on Fr. Boy's white hand. I wasn't trying to perform any great feats with the steering – I was stationary, *di ba*? I was just doing my level best to stay that way, to keep my right hand off the gear-shift and my foot off the pedal. It was no foregone conclusion, I tell you. Like I said, parking can be murder sometimes. As Al-Elvis sauntered into the club-house, I caught sight of my forehead and eyes in the rear-mirror. My pupils were focussed like dots of light under a burning lens. I fucking frightened myself, man.

Where the Smiths spent most of their time at the house or the company compound – whether they'd have extended their sphere to the Old Town in time must remain enigmatic, but I think so given the opportunity – Mr Al-Elvis was far more acclimatised. I'd see him at the sidewalk tables of the Lebanese coffee-shops, arm thrown over the back of a nearby chair, gulping the black brew or sipping the cooled smoke of a hookah, holding forth to his local friends. The Bohaidenese, on the whole, despised Pakistanis somewhat less than they did Filipinos (reserving their greatest respect for the Yemenis who comprised the police force) but they made an exception for Mr Al-Elvis which proved the rule. He himself was curter, more arrogant with the Pakistanis who came into his orbit than were the members of his Bohaidenese *barkada*. Mostly, the Pakistanis – the legal stayers, this is – were soldiers: moustached fellows with fierce faces and well-maintained, outmoded firearms that looked more convincing than the armalites in Bohaidenese hands. I didn't doubt their martial valour and they, for their part, no doubt accepted the dentist's haughtiness as part of the expected comportment of the military caste, for Mr Al-Elvis gave no indications of being a dental surgeon. He looked like a Major on a brothel-crawl. As for the Pakistani illegals they fawned on him, burnishing those shoes, scrambling for the coins he flipped. "Damned blackamoors," he said in my hearing.

He knew I was the Smith chauffeur. I saw him nudge his cronies when I went by and I heard the occasional raucous laughter, probably about the length of my dick, not that the 'Rabo, according to Philippine mythology, was as under-endowed as the Japanese. Quite the reverse. On this same occasion, as I dawdled round the vendor of pressed apricots, sold in sheets, Mr Al-Elvis continued with a diatribe against the "old colonial types". He'd been around some, this guy, or he was a better raconteur than he was a dentist. Suez, Aden, Crater, came into play, all serving to illustrate the perfidy and hypocrisy of the British – much worse than the French, who were a civilised nation, in his opinion. "Now in Qatar I had a German colleague, first-class dentist and a jolly good chap all round. Lutz detested the English and made no secret of it." He now launched into Arabic in which I had yet to acquire a working proficiency, though I did hear the English word "Jews". The Bohaidenese listened, the older ones with tolerant amusement, the young ones raptly. More pickled whole peppers and halwa arrived. For a dentist Mr Al-Elvis had a sweet tooth. The hookah was called into service again. I was reminded of the old Playboy cartoon which hung, framed, in the main room of the Clubhouse, showing four sheikhs enjoying their water-pipes among dunes with the chubbiest captioned as saying, "Yes, the sand's always getting in mine, too." It was a source of wonder to me that the expats had got away with it for so long. Perhaps their sense of humour was as indecipherable to our hosts as Arabic script was to the Westerners.

Mr Al-Elvis certainly didn't want all his conversation to be unintelligible to me. He switched into English again. "And quite simply incompetent," he proclaimed. "Have you seen his fingers?" His voice broke high. "Like having a gorilla operate on you." More guffaws. I think someone said something about me this time, in Arabic. The dentist said, "A few bananas every month," then smiled in my direction. I thought he wasn't as smart an operator as he considered himself. Atty Caladong would have run rings round him. Atty knew you didn't treat the friends or servants of your enemy as your enemies too; that way, you only acquired more enemies. You treated them as your friends and turned them against your foe. Especially, you recruited his servants. Mr Al-Elvis had known the *pinay* nurses before we came, so that didn't count. He should have wooed me.

The only other conclusion was that he was much more astute than I feared. That he knew he couldn't turn Uncle Rey, the faithful old retainer.

Few of the Western expats liked the Bohaidenese. And absolutely none of them respected them. They had somewhat less reason to detest them than we Filipinos. A white skin there, as in most parts of the world, still afforded better insurance than a Kevlar vest. They were more or less immune from minor abuse and if one of them died a suspicious death, there was no end to the fuss abroad. Still, there were small inconveniences, tiny mortifications that they only noticed and catalogued because they'd never had to endure any in their lives.

One day Jenny came in fuming. Three local women had steamed towards her in line abreast, for all the world as if they were battleships in the black paint of mourning – I smiled as I envisaged it so easily – their eyes fixed on her through the yashmaks like gun-layers aiming through slits in armour-plate. This had been on the broad sidewalk feeding the consumer towards the contemporary bazaar – a Singapore-style mall in the New Town.

"They did it quite deliberately. There was absolutely no need for it. If they'd wanted, they could have let me pass, there was room for all of us – you know those pavements, Dad. I mean, they were the fattest cows I've ever seen, but there was still room for all of us. I don't know what you're laughing at, by the way, Rey."

"Sorry, Miss Jenny. I'm on your side."

"They didn't even give me time to get out of the way – I'd have done that. I know whose country it is, don't I. Anyhow, they just barged straight into me and knocked me for six. Everyone was looking. I just had to pick myself up. I've broken my Ray-Bans. And the Filipinos they had behind them just walked round me. All the Arab women passing by were lapping it up."

"Excuse me, Miss Jenny. The Filipinas wouldn't have been against you – just scared of their employers."

"Mm."

"Darling," said Mrs Smith. "They don't know any better. Just ignore it. And, if you stop to think about it, they're quite right to distrust Westerners. They've suffered abuse themselves."

"What abuse?" Jenny replied hotly. "They were never colonised. And whatever we or the French did to the Egyptians, or whoever, was fifty times less bad than what they would have done themselves. *They* weren't taken from Africa to be slaves – black people are still entitled to get hot under the collar about that – but the Arabs were crueller slavers than the whites were. They've still *got* slaves if you believe what the old-timers at the Clubhouse say."

A full-scale row was brewing between mother and daughter. To try to intercept it – as you know, I hated to see my Smiths quarrelling – I said brightly and equably, "I'm not the one to get hot under the collar about slavery, Miss Jenny. No one enslaved me. The Jesuits taught me to turn the page. I think a century and a half is enough to absolve posterity of the sins of their ancestors."

But it was no good. Jenny and her mother got angrier and angrier with each other, and both were on the point of tears when it stopped. That was the irony of it – Jenny transferring her decent indignation, her tension and her outrage, on to the mother's innocent head, both making themselves miserable while the real culprits were at home enjoying themselves, probably tormenting their *pinay* helpers.

Commander Smith was feeling annoyed enough about having his afternoon tea spoiled to get it off his chest at the Clubhouse. There were clucks and murmurs from his fellow expats. I have to record that griping and bitching about their hosts, the Bohaidenese, were not so much conversational staples there as obsessions. It would have been graceful to resist it a little more. Where did they think their paychecks were coming from? For me, it was OK for the *halo*ed Smiths to let the steam come out of their ears from time to time: pressure supposes a certain amount of resistance to what is confined. The armchair critics at the Clubhouse didn't even try. However, Commander Smith now said, "Look, judge a civilisation, measure its humanity, if you like, by how it treats its weakest members, or non-members. In my opinion and in this case: animals and female immigrant labour in domestic service. Neither have got a voice – or they can't be heard squeaking outside the household. So how do we compare with the Bohaidenese or the Chinese? And who's worse, the Bohaidenese or the Heathen Chinee?"

"'Nuff said, Doc," remarked a New Zealand geologist in the facing chair who had a plummier accent than the Brits. Commander Smith had imbibed a third gin and tonic, on top of his customary two. This may have done something to his inhibitions, or at least politeness and native caution, for he was about to say something terminally unwise. "Heathen Chinee" also formed no part of his usual stock of expressions which were colourfully antiquated but inoffensive. "The day's coming, old boy," he now said, "when we'll all be too frightened to drive a Pajero in case the tyre-marks leave something rude in Arabic about the Emir in the sand."

This got a good reception. It was a cut above what normally passed for wit in that building (which had been well-constructed by Filipino labour ten years before). Mr Al-Elvis had been sitting by himself reading *Asiaweek* magazine in another part of the room. I saw him smile at the Commander's sally, which I accounted open-minded of him, but then there was no denying he was both an elegant and an intelligent man.

Fr. Paul used to talk about giving us delinquents "enough rope to hang ourselves". In retrospect, this was exactly what Mr Al-Elvis was giving Commander Smith, plus a few imaginative loops and twists all of his own. He could sit there listening with full attention because none of the Western expatriates ever spoke to him as individuals, beyond the unavoidable Good Mornings, Afternoons, and Evenings when they encountered him by themselves, nor did they ever take the trouble to enlist him in group conversations. This was unfriendly of them: for all our faults, middle-class Filipinos would never have behaved so coldly: salvaged him fatally if necessary but salvaged him for the circle of amity first. I guess the Brits and Australians froze him because they thought he was a reptile – he was – but being a "wog" sure didn't help either. Racial prejudice? Yes, I believe it was. But Mr Al-Elvis was still a malign essence in their little community and would have been however kindly they treated him.

Some few months after we'd seen Nicky off, Commander Smith got the summons. It was as unexpected to him as the rest of the household, although I alone refrained from the repeated exclamations of scornful incredulity. It was out of the Smith context but squarely in mine, whether the foul play was made by Pakistani or *pinoy* and I didn't believe in serenading my foe with the added satisfaction of my cries of outrage, as well as pain, as I wriggled on the floor of the court.

The personnel manager was the one to interview my employer with the assistance (read, superintendence) of a pair of officials from the Ministry of Labor.

"Goodness me!" exclaimed Mrs Smith, "It sounds like a court-martial."

"Certainly a Court of Inquiry," Commander Smith said grimly. "The only bloody thing missing was the sword turned to me on the table."

"Scimitar," said Jenny, her usual self, who had yet to be reduced to helpless indignation on her father's behalf by hearing the rest of his account.

Mr Al-Elvis had begun by getting the sweeper, a toothless crone from the wrong tribe but still a citizen of the country, to initiate a complaint against Commander Smith. She received a sinecure for waving a whisk three inches above the ground twice a day: her people laid some ancient claim to the land on which the petroleum admin and residential compound found itself and to the nine-hole sand golf-course next to it, suzerainty to which had been more fiercely contested historically than the land on which the compound stood. The whole sorry saga of vendetta, incest, betrayal, fratricide, parricide, poisoning, intermarriage and barefaced theft, was a microcosm of the history of the entire country. Anyhow, the ruling house passed the burden of what were basically ancient blood-money and maintenance payments to the multi-national, whose accountants reconciled the expenditure on their computers in Austin and Rotterdam. Mr Al-Elvis had put it in the deaf old woman's head that Commander Smith had passed slighting comments about her and hers. She was thus the plaintiff and Mr Al-Elvis a principal witness, with all the authority and neutrality of someone called to testify against an abusive colleague by a conscience which transcended the solidarity of the profession. And for the Bohaidenese authorities it was a splendid opportunity to back a member of the oppressed tribe without alienating their own.

"Well, of course," recounted Commander Smith, "I'd never said anything of the kind to the old biddy and I told them so. 'Aha,' says one of the graybeards on the panel, 'but what did you think of her? What is your opinion of her work?' Well, I told them the truth: she's no bloody use at all: she's lazy, crotchety, half-blind, and should be at home being looked after by her sons and grandchildren. 'Aha,' says Graybeard again, 'so that's your opinion, that's what you think of us.' Just a moment, I said. I didn't say Bohaidenese – I said this particular sweeper. 'But,' says the other one, 'she is a Bohaidenese. Did you know that?' Yes, I said – and they just left it hanging in the air a while. 'And that's your true opinion,' asked Graybeard. Of her, I said, not everyone in the country.

"Well, next we had Marilou and Maribeth Joy. I must say I'm disappointed in those girls."

"I think, sir, it was a case of *et tu, Brute*," I interjected. This was the first and last time Commander Smith ever snubbed me. "When I need your opinion, I'll ask for it," he snapped.

"Sorry, serr," I apologised. "What's the wrong-doing of Marilou and Maribeth Joy?"

Commander Smith ignored me but addressed a by now aghast Mrs Smith and scandalised Jenny. "They're a fairly confused pair," he continued grimly. "In fact, I'd have said they wouldn't know where they were going unless they were being led by the nose, if you take my meaning. There was a lot of um-ing and ah-ing and blowing of noses and dabbing of eyes but the upshot of it was that I've got no respect."

"What *on earth* do they mean by that? Respect for what?"

"Well, Maribeth accused me of having no respect for the poor. I can't see what she meant by that. She's not poor – the company pays her a very good whack. And there aren't very many poor Arabs that I come in contact with – even the sweeper's getting as much as the dental nurses. Can't say I've run into *very* many nomads for me to disrespect that recently." The Smiths all smiled, wanly, but they smiled.

"Anyhow the real bloomer I've made is this: Al-Elvis heard me repeating that crack about the jeep tyres in the club house a few weeks back and he brought it up at this... I don't know what to call it, tribunal or whatever."

"Oh, no, Dad," whispered a pale Jenny. "What have you done?"

"Only he, Al-Elvis, claimed I'd said the tyre tracks would read 'screw the Emir' in Arabic script, which I never said at all, of course. Not my usage at all. But the Graybeard asked if I'd said something like it, and I had to agree I had. Al-Elvis then said, 'You see. He admits it.' I can't say I can make out what damned business of his it was to start with."

I had listened throughout with a growing helplessness that eventually smothered the considerable indignation I felt on the Smiths' behalf. Atty Caladong's bold as brass courtroom prevarications seemed distinctly unsubtle compared to the slight distortion, the double-edged nuances, the red-herrings, unfavourable highlighting and meaningful pauses of the Bohaidenese casuist. They twisted everything. It was a nightmare for the grammarian mind, for my Roman logic. The fuckers took everything out of context.

It was a miserable four weeks while Commander Smith worked out his notice. During this time the "graybeard" brought in his grand-niece for attention to some prodigiously decayed milk teeth. He chose not Mr Al-Elvis but Commander Smith, in complete confidence that the child would not suffer any malice at the Commander's hands. I wondered if he'd had his mind concentrated by the fact that the competent Commander was on distinctly finite availability and that if he didn't get a move on, it would be Mr Al-Elvis's services he'd be availing of. Gratis, of course, courtesy of the petroleum company.

All my employer had had to do was deny having uttered the Pajero remark. That would, I think, have thrown a spanner in the intricate works of Mr Al-Elvis's scheme. The Pakistani's word against his. The whole expat community would have come forth and perjured themselves on the Commander's behalf, I'm sure. But the Commander's own intrinsic honesty, his enlightened decency, were weapons in the hands of opponents who revelled in the irony even as they chuckled over his folly.

As I say, it was a subdued few weeks. For Commander Smith it wasn't a financial disaster in the way it would have been for a *pinoy* OCW sent packing: Commander Smith could always practise his profession at home. But he felt the ignominy keenly; though not as keenly as Jenny who seemed to feel it a stain on the family escutcheon. With twenty-two days left and the topic of Mr Al-Elvis elaborately avoided by all up till then, Mrs Smith's self-restraint snapped at breakfast. She'd clearly passed a sleepless night and maybe the murmurs of her parents had kept Jenny up, too, if the inverted thunder-clouds under her eyes were any indication. "Well, I think it's scandalous it's all been done on the simple say-so of that man," Mrs Smith blurted out as the carbonising bread in the toaster started to send out thin grey smoke. "O-o, Mum," I said, accomplice in best *pinoy*-style, and thank God for a sensible Smith, "I'm gonna get the s.o.b. but good, Mum." Not the distanced, elegiac tones Fr. Paul had instilled in me, but it had Commander Smith thumping the breakfast table with his meaty fist, setting all the crockery vibrating. "That's quite enough of that, Rey! I won't tolerate talk like that!"

But it was too late. For the first time in my life I'd discovered the intoxicating glory in mutiny, the un-Filipino sensation Lucifer must have known, and I persisted and exulted in my insubordination not – please believe me – because soon my employer would have no lien upon my livelihood but because what treason I planned would redound to his benefit. "No, serr. You cannot stop me. I'll fix him but good." Oh, the lines I was giving myself, but that was what was issuing from my mouth, as if I was medium and dear, dead Dant was doing the talking. "We know how to deal with scum like him back in the Philippines. You're too good, serr, you're too good for your own good."

"Well, I think there's something in that, darling," Mrs Smith said. I shot her a grateful glance. Commander Smith was scraping the black off his toast with the blunt side of his table-knife, showering his side-plate with soot but doing little to improve the state of the charred bread. The pair of them would no more throw the spoiled slice into the garbage-can than they would flush bank-notes down the john. Commander Smith, I could see, had decided to dispense with an emulsion layer of margarine and was going to apply a coat of neat lime marmalade. I imagined the rancid taste and grainy texture of his current mouthful, the sugar barely overlaying the sourness of the charcoal, like a mouthful of sand and vinegar puckering the flesh and scraping the enamel. "Yuks!" Babyjane would exclaim on similar occasions, like the adolescent crone she was, "why da rich folks is da most *koripot* in da small thing?" One of Mrs Smith's, or was it the Commander's, *obiter dicta* had been the Queen of England's reputed insistence that the last widget of jelly had to be scraped off the side of the glass before a new pot of condiment appeared before the Royal Family. I could believe it all too well, man; I imagined Her Maj on the throne, crown on head, with knife erect in one fist instead of sceptre, the blade tinkling and scraping as it did its work inside the inverted jar, clutched as jealously as orb, of Frank Cooper's Oxford Thick Cut. But now Commander Smith suddenly said, "Good grief, what's going to happen to you, Rey?"

"Oh, yes," squeaked Mrs Smith. "How self-centred of us! What will *you* do?"

To myself, I thought: I'll become Third Murderer. To the Smiths, I shrugged and smiled the same happy smile as when Danton had proposed I be called Frankenstein. "*Bahala na*, serr. That means, loosely, what will be will be."

"You've never said anything loosely, Rey. Seriously, you're in a bit of a pickle. Your contract with us will be automatically void. You're not allowed to find another employer here. Theoretically, you should go straight back to the Philippines. I'm sorry, Rey. It would have been better if we'd left you in Hong Kong, like Babyjane."

I liked the "theoretically".

I said, somewhat disingenuously, "It's all up to you, serr." Commander Smith smiled. "Hardly," he said. I waited. "Of course," he continued, with the faintest of smiles, akin to that of Fr. Paul admitting a prize pupil to one of the ironies he found so exquisite, "you could become an illegal."

"Oh, yes, why don't you? What a splendid idea!" I have to say I was surprised at Mrs Smith. I mumbled something non-committal. "You could just vanish," Commander Smith said enthusiastically, really starting to warm to the notion. "Disappear from the ken of man or the policeman, at any rate. You certainly wouldn't be the only one."

"Yes, but he can't stay here right up until we go," Jenny suddenly said. "They're quite capable of arresting him at the airport and throwing him in clink once we've gone."

"We could," said Mrs Smith, *"disguise* Rey." She and Jenny began to giggle like schoolgirls. Actually I didn't stick out on the Bohaiden street the way I did at home: there were plenty of Sudanese and Ugandans here.

"Serious suggestions, please, ladies," Commander Smith said, but with a big grin. Not for the first time I found I'd acted as a lightning rod for my beloved English family.

Now they began to discuss in great detail plans for my future, waxing more rosy by the moment. Their cheerful enthusiasm for flouting the law of the land momentarily disconcerted me – the rule-run, the honour-bound Smiths – until I recalled the two ancient movies run again and again – no less than three times already during our fleeting residence to date – to full houses of baying Anglos at the clubhouse: *Bridge over the River Kwai* and *The Great Escape*. In the former, under the sadistic Japanese regime of malnutrition and arbitrary execution, one saw the English competing for food and survival with the desperate cunning of sewer rats or poor Filipinos. In the latter under the comparatively benign German administration, one saw the officers and gentlemen, the equivalents of Commander Smith, taking with gusto and the rodent guile this time of rich Filipinos to forgery of documents, pickpocketing, theft, blackmail, and counterfeiting of banknotes. This kind of prankishness seemed to lie just below the surface of the national middle-class character, ready to be tapped in situations of extremity. Hadn't it survived even in the Jesuit, in Fr. Paul's accounts of Ampleforth japes? Like I said, it was all part of a greater consistency.

At one point Mrs Smith referred to my impending "escape". Commander Smith corrected her. "Rey isn't escaping. He'd be escaping from us, which I trust he doesn't want to do."

"Evasion, Mum," I said helpfully. "Continuing evasion. I'll be the one to be a fugitive, *di ba?*"

It was decided in the end that I would vanish from the household eleven days before my employers were to depart. I'd suggested a week, but Jenny hadn't liked the numerology. "It sounds official," she pointed out, "like a period of notice. They might come and check on Rey about then." I, too, thought that was the way the bureaucratic mind worked, even the Middle Eastern bureaucrat.

"Just one final thing, old boy," Commander Smith said in passing, "I want you to give me your word of honour – of honour, mark you, Rey – that you aren't going to cook up any reprisals for Al-Elvis."

Well, that pulled me up short. Commander Smith didn't miss the look of guilty consternation on my face. "Come on, now, no ifs and buts. A solid, Filipino, gold-plate Roman Catholic promise from you."

"Mr Al-Elvis is… an honourable man," I said carefully. "Bery well, serr, I give you a 14-K Pilipino fromise not to molest him."

CHAPTER XVI

*Sacrificial Lambs – Slash 'n' Crap – Wrong directions
Breaking Glass – The Rescue – Time In*

FAT FROM THE ROASTING LAMBS fell on the Fauds' fire, hopping in blue gouts over the orange incandescence of the charcoal, crackling and spitting and scenting the salty air with the sharper aromas of thyme and rosemary on top of the slightly nauseous ripeness of finishing meat. I now got the point of frankincense and myrrh for dressing a corpse. Every stray dog in the neighbourhood patrolled the fringes of the festivities, kept at bay only by the shrewdly projected stones of paid urchins. In all there were twelve lamb carcasses, immaculately butchered. Mountains of rice, yellow from the stamens of real saffron, lay heaped on brass platters larger than small tables. Quail eggs and chestnuts roasted happily in the same braziers, while indoors three pounds of Iranian caviare reposed on the backs of as many melting ice-swans. "Come, come," roared the head of the house of Faud, "No one is eating. Is it so bad? Is the meat rotten? Do the sturgeon's eggs stink? Eat!"

So far as formulas went, the Arabs had magical ones. They practised a social alchemy. "Peace be upon you," Faud greeted his friends and when they replied, "Upon you peace," they completed an inversion and a symmetry beautiful as the arabesque. Even more lovely was the salutation the first arrivals – sitting in a ring – gave the later guests, as they stood framed in the doorway. "Be one of them," they chorused. Not *us* but *them*. It was a jump out of context, a gracious shift in perspective. I imagined Fr. Paul ravished by it.

Meanwhile, Faud strode round, clicking his beads, occasionally kicking one of the Filipinas in the neutral way Commander Smith might clear newspapers from an armchair for a friend. We weren't part of the symmetry.

"Eat!" Faud's was the most redundant of exhortations. His guests had already ravaged the stacks of raw cucumbers, the fresh lettuce-hearts flown in from South Africa, the carrot-sticks in ice-water, the non-Israeli bell-peppers, the twenty varieties of pickle, sweet, fiery, and sour. They waited only for the lambs' skins to crispen.

Faud spoke formulaically in this, as he did in so much else.

His Filipino labourers roasted the sheep for him. I roasted the sheep for him. The skills of timing and even-handedness required were exactly the same as for barbecuing *lechon*, although the pig was as unknown in these parts as a mammoth. Alcohol was more common. The Bohaidenese weren't as strict as the Saudis on the sumptuary side. As if to re-establish themselves, though, they lopped off the heads and hands of murderers and thieves as if there was no tomorrow and dumped mechanical grab-fuls of boulders on adulteresses. The fact that the neighbouring sultanates and emirates abstained from these practices rather encouraged the Bohaidenese than the reverse.

This feast, for a younger daughter's birthday, was comparatively unmunificent where on previous occasions Faud's victorious hospitality had offered no quarter. To say he didn't stint would be to say Ovid was a scribbler. In this open-handedness lay little of kindliness; it was an act of benevolent aggression, like a UN intervention, and in general the outcome was as unpredictable. The mourning sun would rise on a scene of devastation comparable to a tribal ambush: the recumbent bodies in the abandoned postures of death or deep exhaustion, the congealed white fat and blood on the platters with the deeper pools barely skinned over and trembling in the dawn breeze off the Indian Ocean, the carpets and cushions strewn prodigally over the sand with the odd kicked-over coffee-pot or beaded slipper glinting in the first rays reflected off the sea.

That the minimum outlay for one of these occasions would have run to thousands of dollars made it all the harder to understand why the Fauds would trouble to fleece us little sheep of our accumulated wages. The Fauds were a family construction firm, i.e. the worst kind of employers in Bohaiden, as all soon learned. The big companies paid their unspectacular but contractually stipulated packet on time, the medium-sized concerns a slightly smaller packet regularly in arrears, and, on the whole, family operations like Faud & Sons the promised handsome remuneration not at all. Guys would spend three years toiling for the outfit, their passports held in Faud's huge Austrian safe, the claw feet and script of the manufacturer's logo dating it to the previous century, well before the time of Rizal, without getting a smell of what was owing. My reflex joke that some Faud house debts, judging by the age of the strong-box, ran back a hundred years, failed to raise even a smile from my co-workers. It hung over all of us. Back in Lapu-Lapu we used to notice that servicemen got distinctly more cheerful as they grew "short", that is as their tour of duty drew to a close and the count-down of days began. The irascible became quite approachable while the normal and the sanguine by nature became respectively expansive and ecstatic. If you caught the right guy at the right time you could become urchin-rich with Hershey bars, singlets, soap, and the odd .45 shell. The reverse held true with service in the house of Faud. Those with a few weeks remaining before their return to the Philippines became silent and pensive, with the prospect of three years, five years servitude with nothing to show for it. And you couldn't leave for alternative employment. Faud held your papers. You became an illegal. We never saw what happened at the end; they all hoped to get their cheque or cash dollars even in the airport check-in line. Their ultimate fate was a mystery; they might as well have been abducted by aliens. Only once had a card got through from Manila, with the legend, "I work six year for shit nothing shit why I bothered brother you too." This grubby missive was passed round with as much gloomy reverence as if it was a Dead Sea scroll and we surviving Essenes. I tried to console a guy I liked, the former Business Admin graduate I'd done the body-detail with seven months previously. "Look, friend," I said, "see the bright side. At least Faud isn't gonna screw you in the ass, to boot, the way his boys do the DH's in their house."

"Sugar," said my friend with dreadful earnestness, "if he's the one to pay *puwede na lang.* He can."

I was now an illegal. You could take this two ways. Personally I've always been sceptical of the effect the injunction *Abandon hope all ye who enter here* might have on the resourceful reader. Those truly without hope become very dangerous; they have nothing to lose. *Nos morituri te salutamus Caesare,* but wasn't the revolt of Spartacus the most dangerous Rome ever faced?

Some of our girls had indeed abandoned hope. You could see their dejection not so much on their faces (because they had adopted the veil for protection) but in the slump of their bodies. As illegals, they'd entered the realm of ghosts. They were non-persons.

They possessed no valid proof of their identity; they were even unable to leave the country and go home forfeiting their earnings. Having run away from one abusive employer, they were at the mercy of the next, who had no obligation whatsoever to pay a wage, other than the moral obligation to the human being they were exploiting and – I speak a truth apparent only to those with the experience – the Bohaidenese on the whole lacked that compassion, that honesty, that chivalry. They were shameless about cheating their helpless employees. Years later I watched a TV programme in which a grave and bearded Bohaidenese apologist, aided by a bun-faced female, expatiated on their kindness and tolerance and the protection they extended to womenfolk and strangers. They scored debating-points with an ingenuity which a Jesuit might have envied and we *pinoys* watching laughed hollowly, scornfully, or bitterly as our memories and temperaments took us.

I held several advantages, however. I still possessed my passport, for the Smiths had never taken that precious talisman from me, although I'd told Faud my previous employers were a family from the UAE who still held all my documents. That meant all Faud could do was steal my wages. He couldn't keep me a hostage to fortune. And I was resolved not to surrender my cheerfulness to whatever adversity I might encounter, to keep smiling no matter what. I'd never get pregnant, *di ba*?

I'd found work on the body detail through the illegals' grape-vine at a Lebanese café – all of us on that clandestine trip had been fugitives – and with the Fauds through the foreman, who had been unduly impressed by my graveside speech. My eloquence by now had been reduced to a contemptible little paean of hatred. Every time a Bohaidenese humiliated, abused, or cheated me, I'd repeat it to myself. It was neither original nor elevated but what mantras are? It offered me consolation akin to the gag in the mouth of the prisoner receiving the kiss of the rattan. As variegated locals gave me formal dressing-downs or the benefit of their casual invective in the street, I would intone it for my private solace, trusting my eyes were not the eloquent part of me. And as it rang through my head, I would make a point of smiling my broadest smile.

The Bohaidenese weren't the worst, not by a long way. This was the line the Philippine embassy took with us. Our foreign service personnel were like ship's officers on a life-raft already swamped with wretched humanity, trying to deter the hands of those still in the water from clutching the side-ropes. At any time there'd be a hundred Filipinos seeking refuge in the embassy. By common consent, when notes were compared, the verdict seemed just: the Kuwaitis were by far the worst and the Jordanians, though the poorest, a little bit better than the others. I guess the Bohaidenese fell somewhere in the middle, but it never occurred to us to thank our lucky stars.

SEVERAL GENERATIONS OF FAUDS lived in and around the main compound inhabited by the oldest sons, although this was not particularly the Arab style. Unlike the Chinese, whose cosy way it was to put several generations under one roof, the Faud patriarch did not receive excessive veneration from the grown-up sons. In fact, he lived in a rather mean modern bungalow which contrasted with the splendour in which his eldest son, the man I have dubbed Faud (that was not his real name), the manager of the construction company, lived. Yet it was old, tottering, half-blind Faud senior who'd found the money to educate Faud.

Faud himself was forty-six. He had three wives – under different roofs – and in the main compound, from the chief wife, a pair of teenaged twin boys, who had formerly been nicknamed Chip 'n Dale but whom we had taken to calling Wizz 'n' Crap and sometimes Slash 'n' Crap, or in Pilipino *Ihi* and *Ta-e*, the last to rhyme with "Tarry" with a trilled British "R". Wizz was, uh, the paler of the two. Faud was not noticeably portly but Wizz and Crap, pear-shaped, with hair brilliantined to glossy perfection had been grossly obese since babyhood. I'd seen the photos in the solid silver frames in their *sala*.

Man, those plump, oiled brats were the snappiest dressers I have ever seen. They put our most up-to-date Frat dudes in the shade. Faud preferred traditional Gulf costume with the distinctive head-band of Bohaiden, wearing leathern sandals which exposed hairy, gnarled toes that rivalled mine, if you believed Nicky Smith. But his sons never wore anything except Western clothes. These managed somehow to combine elements of uniform while remaining highly idiosyncratic. Preferring to ring such variations as could be managed on white, sensible in view of the climate, they proved Fr. Paul's contention that the human imagination – like roses or poinsettias –

needs to be cut back, cabined, confined, in short denied and mortified, in order to flourish the more luxuriantly, for Wizz 'n' Crap contrived infinitely more with absence of colour than ghetto bucks could with the full palette. Snowy espadrilles and ducks, double-breasted buttoning shirts, and yachting caps with a hint of gold braid, were a successful perennial, as were dungarees after the same pattern as those of Hoss in *Bonanza* with the difference that Wizz 'n' Crap tailored theirs in double-thickness cream silk and not denim. On the comparatively rare occasions they weren't all in white, down to the belt and patent leather boots, they preferred some combination of navy blue hipsters with khaki shirts which, on the face of it, should have been a fearsome colour incompatability but, in fact, hacked it just as beige beans and violet yam jam did in a *Halo*[2]. I guess it was the kind of colour blindness got away with in the contrasting upper and lower portions of military dress, the blue jodhpurs and olive-green tunic of the well-dressed Cossack and maybe even going back to the Centaurs. So far as Faud's sons went, blue pants had connotations of navy or air-force while khaki was definitely infantry. So maybe what they were wearing was appropriate for hovercraft-borne marines or heli-cavalry.

The boys carried these tight and body-revealing outfits with such aplomb and lack of apology for what they covered that it had you thinking a belly bulbous as a dome, a butt like an Arab mare, and an ass-crack like a wadi, were not only normal but desirable. I got plenty of the rear-view.

Some guys smoke, some chain-smoke. Wizz 'n' Crap combed their hair. This was an activity which never palled. They did it for ten or fifteen minutes a throw an average of seven or eight times a day. If a mirror was unavailable a shiny car-fender would do. The comb would appear by magic, produced as deftly as fan-knife by foot-pad before it was trawled lovingly up across quiff and down through Boston with a flourish of the wrist at the end, repeated more than a hundred times. The Saudi was a sword culture, the Bohaidenese a coiffure culture.

In the lexicon of useless gestures stylishly performed – holding a cigarette and bringing it rakishly to mouth and down, or the minutely contrived actions of the Japanese tea-ceremony – Wizz 'n' Crap's hair fetish merited an extensive entry. They did it easily and rapidly but as if overcoming a slight resistance which was the part which might afford the most gratification. Just as they had me wondering whether the acme of the male physique might not after all be a pair of buttocks soft as pillows and round as the moon, surmounting thighs like a side of bacon, so I – who had combed my hair thousands of times in my lifetime but not, of course, anything to match the occasions of Wizz 'n' Crap – began to think I had missed something. I tried combing my own frizz with the same languid stroke and snappy flick but no such luck, man, it was still a chore. Just the once I caught Crap's eye in the mirror of the outside basin we *pinoy* hands used. It was a dead exchange: his eye empty of all interest in me, neither hostile nor alarmed, neither embarrassed by his own vanity nor resentful of my interest. Not even amused. I could have been stung by a scorpion and fallen writhing on the ground; he'd have gone on combing his hair as I frothed and died.

Wizz (alias Slash) was very slightly the less assiduous comber but there wasn't much in it. He compensated by being the one to carry the breath-fresheners. At first I wondered what the fuck they were popping, like was it dope: uppers, downers, metabolism-enhancers, diet pills. Was it recreational abuse or dire medical need? Then I'd look at the flat, dead eyes, the lack of animation, and know it couldn't be. At length the penny dropped. Wizz carried the tiny white or orange sweets in an antique silver pill-box that may have been an heirloom from the days when their forebears were lean, rangy nomads, stringy and tough as the camels they rode. I wasn't in a position where Wizz 'n' Crap's mouths often got very near my nostrils, so it wasn't a direct discovery. I worked it out. Wizz generally offered the box to his brother when chicks hove in sight. In fact, that was when they'd do a double dose out of the cupped palm. When Crap covered his nose with his hand and exhaled, to test the quality of what was wafting, all became clear to me. Strange. The only way they were gonna get girls was to pay them or rape them, or trick them with a combination of the two, but they spent every moment of their waking lives dandifying themselves and sweetening the breath that would play over the girl's grimacing face. What consideration, what gentlemanliness.

Those boys loved to disco. Not possible in Bohaiden, but a feature of their annual summer visit to London with Faud. They possessed a video of themselves winning a jiving contest at a joint I could dimly make out was called the Valbonne. The blue and pink neon of the Frenchified name was obscured by the gas flame emanating from a giant Roman-style torch above the entrance. The boys were in a uniform I hadn't seen them sport in Bohaiden, part of which comprised black velvet waistcoats sparkling with sequins. Wizz 'n' Crap bounced and whirled on the dance floor, at first in a sea of contestants, latterly with the other finalists, and then by themselves, all smiles, their white teeth flashing under the strobe as much as the spangles. They danced like black guys, beat two negro dudes in red suits and black cowboy hats for the bauble. Rhythm, relaxation, neat, original moves: Wizz 'n' Crap had them all. We *pinoys* stood in the compound yard open-mouthed as Wizz 'n' Crap in an ultimate act of solipsism watched themselves cavort on screen and repeated their steps the while. They got a hand from us afterwards, which they fully deserved, but gave us as little acknowledgement as a proud and haughty champion bestows upon an adoring crowd, only nodding coolly to each other.

At five p.m. it was their custom, in common with virtually everyone else in Bohaiden, to promenade under the palms on the sea-front, holding hands with their boon buddies. That always looked odd to me, not faggy, just odd. Faggy wouldn't have been odd. Not in Bohaiden. Not with a Bohaidenese whose happy bent it was to be nine inches up a Filipino ass of either gender. It beat sheep, *di ba*? Conversely, the first time I saw Wizz 'n' Crap hanging out on the street-corner with their barkada I thought they were on the point of rumbling. Wizz's eyes were popping out of his head, the veins standing from his neck. His voice, from bullhorn, had passed into realms beyond the hoarse. Crap was windmilling his pudgy hands, his face an inch away from another young Arab's. As his voice, unimpaired, competed on equal terms with car-horns and motor-bike engines, I concluded he'd come into the fray later, on his twin's behalf. Only someone with a pocket full of Tic-Tacs can have the confidence to shout full into even an enemy's face, still less a friend's. And friend was what the other guy was. They were debating whether to go to the movies before dinner or after. I had been on the point of intervening. Not whacking the screaming, gesticulating Bohaidenese youth prancing in front of Crap – I wasn't that stupid – but playing the part of peacemaker, as I'd often done on court between hot-heads from the opposing teams and our own homebred Artheneum idiots, interposing my own body and maybe taking a blow or two destined for Wizz or Crap. Boy, what a misconception. Off they'd gone, no longer yelling but holding hands.

I stood there, with a silly grin on my face, as if I was a Martian just got out of his flying-saucer.

At least no one ever knocked me flying off the pavement like the old women had poor Jenny. I noticed early on that my compatriots kept their eyes down and got out of the way when groups of Bohaidenese approached, even at the cost of stepping off the sidewalk into garbage and dog-shit. But I made eye contact. To look confident, at home, fully oriented was half the battle. I had already made the mistake of asking directions from a Bohaidenese barkada which if it wasn't Wizz 'n' Crap's was an indistinguishable simulacrum. This was soon after the Smiths had gone but before I'd made my desert trip. In some ways the young Bohaidenese's noisiness, their exuberant spirits were Philippine. This gave me the encouragement to consult them. Weren't we all young when it was said and done? "Please, which is the way to the roller-skating rink?" I asked in English. I had chosen the youth with the kindest rather than the most knowledgeable face. On the whole the Bohaidenese face wasn't a mild face: that semitic nose that looked like it could wound, the hard and pitiless eye, the thin upper lip. Commander Smith used to say people looked like their dogs, fussy old ladies resembling their poodles, burly ruffians their pit-bulls. The Bohaidenese looked like the hawks they prized so much in the hunt. And I was a rabbit, a black rabbit, scurrying over ground broken and difficult for me but plain to them as they began their stoop.

"The roller-skating rink," repeated one of the youths, not the one I'd addressed, who now smiled at the speaker.

Maybe I looked a half-wit primitive to them, a gorilla in trousers. I have neither the most intelligent nor the most sensitive face in the world but it is, I think, good-natured and, if I looked stupid, here was their chance to set me right. "Yessir," I said to this boy, about four or five years my junior.

"OK. You go straight – see the water-tank?"

"Yes."

"Get there, you making right. Then to the round-about and keep going. Don't stop." He said something in Arabic – laughter. OK, just like *pinoy* boys, just like American boys, just like human boys. Never mind.

When I was nearly out of ear-shot one of them called, "Have a nice day." More shrieks of laughter. Without turning, I raised my arm in acknowledgement.

Forty-five minutes later, I found myself on the outskirts of town, clearly heading into the Empty Quarter. Malice, man, just looking for a focus. I did my best not to take it personally. As I took a deep breath and re-traced my steps, not so easy as following a sand-spoor but at least I hadn't been pointed away from a water-hole, every pace a nail in my coffin, I was able to remark a couple of exemplary new buildings. They were too small for malls, too large for residences. (Only the Emir was allowed a palace). Within the next eight months I was going to acquire functional Arabic, but the script would always be a swirling cypher to me. Thus the green and white legends outside the structures were beyond my immigrant ken and there were no English renderings beneath. You know, I was hot, discouraged, doing my best not to get mad – stay cool, Sugar Man, puck da ignorant sons of vitches, I could hear a dead boy's voice say – and I was about to give up on my curiosity and leave it a minor enigma – when I saw the Green Crescent on the building. Opposite of Red Cross, *di ba*? Both buildings bore insignia, but there were no ambulances to be seen, only some large vans with doors at the rear, cut and hinged so that they broke in the middle and were thus effectively two doors. Inclined ramps led up to them. Outside the smaller building were only private vehicles. Two Arabs got out of a Range Rover. The shorter bore something on his forearm. Bore is perhaps too mean a description. He carried whatever it was with a reverence and a care that a prince of the Church would have done well to emulate when draping over his elbow the napkin the Holy Father employs to dry the feet of the poor. At the distance I found myself, it was an indistinguishable but somehow perfectly proportioned object. Was it archaeological relic, fetish, priceless work of art, or merely expensive table-lamp which it would be vexatiously costly, but not ruinous, to replace? To the uninformed eye and, believe me, mine was, there existed something perfectly wooden in its immobility yet somehow animate about its stiff phallic uprightness on the 'Rabo's arm, much as a voodoo doll might be both dead and vital. At under three feet it was small yet somehow large as well. This was no doubt partly a question of the relative – human arms don't normally balance something even that size – but also a matter of consciousness of its own imposingness. As the hooded head turned towards the sound of a back-firing moped, I recognised it as a falcon. Then a horse walked down the ramp from the big van. It took me just a few seconds. Context, *di ba*?

I was outside hospitals respectively for sick falcons and unhealthy horses.

This was where birds with broken wings came, mares with sprained fetlocks, stallions with intestinal blow-outs. I heard the words of Commander Smith again, "You judge a civilisation by the way it treats its weakest members, animals and domestic servants." I was chewing over that one so much, the Bohaidenese excessively fulfilling one half of the desideratum, while falling lamentably short in the other, that my long walk to the rink – where I was to run into the foreman who gave me work – seemed a few moments rather than the best part of an hour.

I WAS A HOD-CARRIER. Of course. I would have been wasted at anything else. I'd rather have hung round the skilled workers, the plumbers and electricians, picking up the rudiments on the job but I saw Faud take one look at my pecs and biceps – when he should have been studying my delts and trapezius for the movements of hod-work – and he assigned me. I don't blame him. Why assume I might have a flair for the finicky when my strong points were there for all to see? The actual bio-mechanics of the movement were uncannily similar to the first stage of one of Butch Tan Sy's manoeuvres, drive without the fake if you see what I mean. I'd dip a little at the knees, up would shoot my arms, the hod-pole held close to me so as not to jeopardise the "S" of the spine, and the layer would browse amongst the bricks like a bookworm in a stack. Unlike the prompt arrival of a book-order in a library, however, or my one time celerity on a basketball court, the rate at which I worked won me scant credit on the building-sites of Arabia. Trotting back for a re-fill, sometimes, in all my innocent exultation in my own young strength, hurdling a wheel-barrow while supporting the hod for the sheer exuberance of it, I was half-aware of black looks, meaningful hoiking, and complicit glances from which I was excluded. At length, with the same caution as one might beard and then counsel a halitotic, Rowell the sparks asked, "Who you think you are, Boss? Vugs Vunny or da Road-Runner?"

"Why you're the one to ask?" I responded, keeping the grin on my face.

"Coz you're da one to show da rest of us ups. Don't work like that, man. You don't get nothing extras for it. You sweat like a horse and maybe Faud he's da one to wonder why da rest of us isn't doing da same."

"Ay, yeah. Afologies, Brother." I slowed to a walk and, would you know it, that's when I tripped and sent my heavy freight bombing in all directions.

Hoddies are the kings of any construction-site but it was doubly so in Bohaiden. Most dwellings were breeze-block fabricated. Only the mega-rich troubled with the detailing of brick, even as a decorative facade. It was the elite working for the elite. So I put it to myself, with all the pitiful pride of the retainer. Anyhow, I adjusted the level of my enthusiasm, treated it as work not play and accommodated myself to the unofficial union of my fellows.

There was no union, official or unofficial, for the female DH's. The completed home was a more dangerous place than the most hazard-strewn building-site. On the rare occasions Filipinas were allowed out under the supervision of their mistresses, they were safer running the gauntlet of leers in the street than they were in the sala.

I remember two incidents. The first was when I was with the foreman in Faud's office, backing up his inventory of the PVC hollow wire-runs – what the fuck would any of us want to steal the long grey tubes for? – our hard hats held respectfully in our work-dusty hands, Faud being big on hard-hats, wearing one himself over his head-dress, when the distinct sound of breaking glass carried from the residence. The crack of armour-plate shivering under the impact of sabot-round cannot be more blood-chilling than the ring of civilian glass, mirror or window, shattering, and announcing felony, assault, or simple domestic mishap. The latter, in a Bohaidenese household, led ineluctably to the former. To the sounds of blasting and the staccato, tooth-rattling jar of the jack-hammer we were all habituated. Yet the three of us, strapping males who'd suffered hardship and witnessed gory accidents (Faud included) froze in our argument. Some ten seconds of positive silence ensued. Then the scuffle of slippers, one pair in advance, followed by others. By the sound, they were leather, for rubber soles made a sharper slap, and the scuffling was the way the Bohaidenese women moved in their costume.

We all had our heads cocked, with the intensity of the Blind Swordsman marking the assassins creeping around him. Now came a wail of grief, dismay, and rage mixed, of the kind that might rise at the sight of a son's corpse at dawn, mutilated and left in the stained sands by a hereditary tribal enemy. Other voices joined this soloist in a chorus of solidarity, much like the rendition of a patriotic anthem. I heard a cry of pain, unlike the voices in the Arab chorus, then a sharp intake of breath and a smothered groan which, with the experience of the competition of the court and, more arduous still, the Tan Sy training session, I interpreted as self-stifled.

The three of us could have been the outside back-up listening to an assault team going into an embassy building to deal with terrorists, the sounds of combat interlaced in meaningless and unrhythmic pattern with intervals of silence for I was unable to make head nor tail of the bumping, the heavy breathing, the sound of tearing cloth, occasional shrieks of exultation or thwarted rage and, finally, rapidly repeated screams of pure and uncontrollable pain. It was as if someone, the inflicters, were pulling a steam-whistle as rapidly as they pleased, the cries fearfully plural but short, real short, and clean-cut. Prolongation of such agony would have brought about unconsciousness but, I guessed, the tormentors were too shrewd for that.

"I will stop this," Faud said wearily, but to no one in particular. Then the foreman put me in the picture as Faud left the office. "They're stubbing cigarettes out on her," he said.

Faud came back. With no evident emotion and, as if he'd just excused himself to perform a natural and ineluctable function to which allusion would have been vulgar as well as otiose, he said, "Now these pipes. I know how many there are. I ordered them from Singapore myself. Don't let it happen again."

"Yesserr," said the foreman. He knew as well as I did that this was Faud's formula for admitting an error under the guise of absolving us from our own dishonesty or stupidity. "Thank you, serr," I added.

I saw the girl who'd been burned, rubbing Tiger Balm into herself outside. By common unspoken accord we ignored her. That was a lot better for her. But I could see the red weals starting on her. Going outside to the old Bohaidenese who sold homemade popsicles to the workers, I bought a pair of violet lollies. "Ssut," I hissed softly to the burned Filipina, getting her attention away from her woes but startling her with the apparent incongruousness of my gift. "Put these on. Cool the burn. Not the Balm, hah?" I knew from her look I'd wasted the money.

The other occasion was hotter and heavier, by far. For one, it took place in the noonday heat. Even with the sea-breeze of that time of year, good grief, even if the Saudis had paid to air-condition and astro-dome the entire peninsula, midday was a time that warped your brains. Dead of night is the time for fell deeds in temperate climes, even in the RP which lies between Capricorn and Cancer, but Dracula's hours amounted to quality time for the Bohaidenese. The Old Town was swarming with dishdashahs and galabiyyas at three a.m. Broad, blatant daylight was the moment when everyone took shelter from the sun and the brilliant streets became as deserted as if there was a monster on the prowl. If you wanted to do something bad – a bank-robbery or an assassination – this was your moment. No wonder they got a head start in Fr. Paul's Dark Ages, *di ba*?

I was with the Ilonggo Business Admin graduate and Rowell the Sparks at the hospital (people hospital). They'd been in an accident with a cement mixer. We'd emerged in good spirits. The Ilonggo had lost three fingers but they'd shot him up with a tankful of local. Better still, the young Jordanian doc who'd studied his medicine at Velez hospital in Cebu City, Philippines, had told him it was free. Like, *gratis*. You could see our guy wondering if it wouldn't have been clever to lose a leg. We came out of the frigid emergency room into the pale furnace of the car-park, my companions giddy with anaesthetic and loss of blood, my own head spinning from mere dehydration. I let them take the pick-up on to our quarters, while I walked back to the site. The act of a very gallant Christian gentleman, *di ba*? As I trudged back I found myself wishing I'd borrowed the foreman's shades. I didn't have any because I was vain enough to dislike the standard frames which had always been wrong for my cheek-bones – made me look like the Mummy – while the small, round-lensed type which suited me, as they did most black people, conferred upon me an air of kooky ghetto imbecility from which my fastidious – read, snooty – Jesuit's heart flinched. I was squinting in discomfort but in no danger from the traffic, for not one car passed in twenty minutes. I was reflecting that the glare off cold snow and hot sand both blinded when I heard a woman's scream. Man, it was as common in Bohaiden as jeepney tyres braking back home except that the sound of the rubber screeching as it was flayed didn't inevitably presage a casualty. You waited for the bang of an impact which might never come. Here, you knew there'd been a bang and someone had come. Well, I hesitated. Too right, it wasn't like back home. You had no rights at all, less than a prize falcon or a brood mare. It was like an amputee going to the rescue of the blind. But I found my stumps were willing and I was moving with the same fluency as when I'd slam-dunked and was taking the congrats of my team on the lope, but this time towards a female cry. The best part of us is on auto-pilot, *di ba*? It was Life^2, a second chance. Redemption. The worst crime of my life had been a crime of omission.

I was headed back the way I'd come, the sun out of my eyes by a few degrees, thus I could make out the double-storeyed, L-shaped modern building for which I was bound. The windows were smoked glass but the frames bare aluminium so they glittered and flashed and sparkled as if it was a warlock's castle, heliographing menace or SOS to my watering eyes. It was the nurses' home.

An upper floor window was slid open on one of the wings of the "L", the muslin drape billowing out like a rogue veil on the air-con's hot exhaust. Another scream, in a slightly different timbre, inclined me to think there were two in trouble. The lower ledge of the balcony was only ten feet high, not at all daunting for even the un-adrenalised me and, in truth, the hormones were already motoring round my system. Up I flew like Superman in flight, hands extended – there was a Superhero who'd have been more credible black – and my fingers found the sill. There's real life and there's the movies where they never make chumps of themselves. Just as I bounded through the curtain I was assailed by an awful doubt. It didn't last longer than a millisecond, too short to translate into physical hesitancy but my stomach did a flic-flac.

What if I'd got the whole situation wrong again, just as I had with Wizz 'n' Crap's friend? What if I was bursting in upon some mere domestic altercation, perhaps between Filipinas, or even upon a single person bewailing a trifling mishap in the excessive way of a poorly educated female? (Although there was no such thing as a trifling breakage in a Bohaidenese household). All such qualms dissipated as the muslin blindfold flicked from my eyes and I looked upon such a scene as I had witnessed once before. A Bohaidenese, who was of an age to know much better, had a girl down on the bed. She was writhing and kicking with all her clothes still on, although in great disarray. The other Filipina, the one to have done most of the yelling, was still standing, struggling with another Arab. The Bohaidenese male not involved in pinioning *pinays* was standing in room centre with his gown held up in one hand while the other was wrapped round his dick which needed no holding up. He leered at a third, smaller *pinay*, trapped in a corner.

My entrance was disappointing; I failed to impress. I burst in among them in spectacular fashion, yet it was as if I was invisible. Dismaying as the scene was, I felt at first a sense of reassurance. I wanted a rape or a murder to be going on, rather than a loud party. But then the inattention the protagonists of the drama were paying me made me start to wonder if I wasn't hallucinating. Man, it was surreal. The girls were busy defending themselves and were not admitting the prospect of rescue, their assailants were thinking only of getting their dicks into something hot and preferably wet. Perhaps it would have been different if I'd simply walked through the door. Perhaps the Arabs would have dropped their hems in a hurry, then. Perhaps they'd have looked furtive about it, been voluble before beating it. As it was, at one and the same time I failed to shock and was an unwelcome intruder. I wasn't Spiderman or Superboy, just a common or garden gate-crasher. Rabo I, the pock-marked deviant jerking himself off, registered my presence with an imprecation which alerted the others. They looked at me, thought about it, then to a man decided to go about their tasks again. Fr. Paul would have called it "cool hardihood". I wasn't the type of guy you took on lightly, *di ba*? Another little Filipino guy would probably have got himself hanged from the lighting flex.

By the wash-basin the Bohaidenese piece of garbage I will call Rabo IV was holding a tiny person's head down in the overflowing water, with both taps full-on. At first I imagined the victim to be a Filipina but as the head came out of the basin I saw it to be a small boy in a robe. I could see why Rabo IV had dunked him. In between his gasps and retching the kid spat and cursed his tormentor in the filthiest, lowest Arabic, comprising words the filthiest, lowest Filipinos like myself also knew. In went his mop of curls again.

I took Rabo II, the portliest, the one holding the *pinay* on the bed, by the arm and applied a ferocious grip to him, sufficient to make him dance. I've never been a violent person, not easy to provoke, at least, and I knew I mustn't hurt the Bohaidenese or I'd pay with my life in a law-court where they would twist things till your frail old Lola was a cross between the Queen who bathed in Virgins' Blood and Cruella Devil. On the other hand, I knew too little was also perilous. How much force? That's a formula which needs a special genius to calculate correctly, whether for an individual or an army. I knew Jerome and his friends got it right in Malaysia with the mob who stoned me and my boppers in their swimsuits. And me, I was gonna get it neither right nor wrong now, just inconclusive. Which was not bad for me; I'll always settle for a draw or a tie.

As my Rabo writhed and gibbered, the others backed off. Bravery was not a Bohaidenese characteristic I'd ever particularly remarked. I then threw him to his friends, with the objective dismissiveness with which one might pass a basketball. This was a mistake; some extra item of play, like banging his head not too hard on the table edge, would have forestalled what lay in store. His friends interpreted what the Smiths, say, of this world would have thought was clemency and forebearance for the weakness it truly was. They gave me dirty looks and dared to curse me.

The *pinays* began to make some sense of the situation, though it was unlikely their appraisal did full justice. If I'd been five five with straight black hair and slanty eyes they'd at once have realised it was one of their own sticking by them – after all one of the most powerful bonds that tie human beings together, short of mother-love – but the vast black man who had come to their aid was more like a cosmic policeman dealing abstract justice and darting bolts. I set them right. I asked the girl who'd been fighting back on her feet in Tagalog, not Visayan, "OK, *ba*, Miss? The men hurt you already?" She shook her head, a girl of some spirit as I later found out. Her bra had somehow got itself back to front and she tried to sort it out without taking off the now button-less white blouse of her uniform. Aligning myself with the girls was a mistake.

Rabo II, a nondescript piece of lard except for a nose unusually sharp even for a Bohaidenese and close-set eyes which give him the appearance of a myopic falcon, stepped in and took a swing at me which I easily avoided, but not the kick in the shins from the sandal of the masturbator, Rabo I. He might as well have kicked one of the balcony-rails. It gave me no grief but he hopped back, with a yelp and a grimace.

Less of a novice in these things, Rabo III made to slap me with his left, then looped a right at my head. The feint. Ploy more ancient than Alexander and Hannibal and futuristic as Luke Skywalker. Anyhow the dodge failed to work on me. I didn't know which was the deadlier, the left or the right he'd had on his dick. I cracked him across the mug, less than half-force, with my open palm. The hurt and bewildered look of a chastised child appeared on his evil face. A fist, an elbow, or a head, Butch Tan Sy said, concuss. A slap causes the eyes to water and in certain circumstances can be more useful. And, sure enough, his eyes moistened, a drop formed, and welled down his swarthy, unshaven middle-aged cheek. He stood on the spot. I'd steadied him up, sobered him. I was thinking now in overdrive, much as I analysed – Butch said sensed – not only a play but the ramifications working off it. And the real difficulty here was not the situation – I could have spanked the middle-aged Bohaidenese with one hand – but the aftermath. I could see myself ending up in court, with their warped logic, as a rapist. Adulteresses were stoned; thieves had their hands cut off. Context suggested what they'd think of for me.

I looked at the malevolent faces and I thought hard. One solution would be to kill them all. It was certainly feasible and there'd be no lying witness against me. The only hurdle was removing the bodies and concealing them, the first a much harder desideratum than the latter, the hospital lobby a more intimidating place in this instance than thousands of square miles of wonderfully empty desert. And then how could I knock off the very girls I'd come to help?

Could I just let the men go? Would clemency inspire a reciprocal magnanimity in them? Man, what a stupid question. Did a scorpion sting? Did a coconut fall downwards?

Well, this only took a couple of seconds. Their faces were emptying. They had the lost look of the team on the verge of annihilating defeat. There was no more resistance in them. A kick up the butt for the fat one would send them all scampering. Oh, man, it was tempting. Especially for me because the one part urged, "O-o, Dodong. Live for now. Just do it. Get rid of them," while the other part, maybe my best part, maybe my worst part, but certainly the cold, appraising part, the Fr. Paul-planted mind advance-dirty part, admonished me, "Look beyond the jam you're in. Future consequences are as real as present relief." And I knew this was correct. I took a step towards the Bohaidenese with the face of a sick bird but he was too leery for me, the tubby shit, and hopped behind Rabo III. This was OK by me. It was only fair to give him a minor piece of revenge.

I did a perfect little V-cut to the left to get him going over to the right, then came back, found him off-balance and pushed him in the chest with as little conviction as was consonant with realism. He was so demeaned, so supine, he made no attempt at resistance, his features merely contorting in panic. This was not the effect I required, the response I was seeking. I had to blow on the embers of their courage; perhaps they had none behind the invective, the shameless bravado and bullying. But then I wasn't really the one was I, *di ba*, to give them Butch's pep talk? Me, their foe. It would have to be, I schemed, a kind of reverse exhortation. I'd let them do better bit by bit. Taking Rabo II by his beard, I began to slap him very, very lightly. This was uncomfortable enough for him to squirm and then to want to parry and block with his effete palm and wrist. He still wasn't trying to resist, just to minimise what was coming his way. As Fr. Paul used to say, one of his more gnomic utterances for us gazing at him glazedly, "It's no use leading a horse to water if it doesn't want to drink." Rabo II needed encouragement, and once he was encouraged so would the others be. I gave a short gasp of pain, then flapped my hand at face-level for relief from the entirely imaginary dolor of it. Still he didn't take advantage of this most golden opportunity. What lousy, swaggering yellow-bellies they were. I cunningly brushed his hand, as if accidentally, with my own and managed to insert my finger in his palm. Then I yelped and started dancing up and down, much as he had earlier. The Filipinas' faces were a picture. At first Rabo II looked puzzled.

Then a glimmer appeared in his eyes, the look of a man not merely thrown a lifeline when on the brink but a man who has also seen the lengthening of the first shadow of an immense opportunity, who has glimpsed the possibility of a glorious reversal of fortune. He applied some tentative pressure on my finger. I grimaced. He applied more. I sucked in my breath. A little more – in truth it was still feeble. I let out a sibilant breath. Now it was like turning the volume dial of a hi-fi, the further he went round the more I yelled, till I culminated in a roaring that would not have disgraced a Protestant heretic at the stake.

A look of pure delight came across Rabo II's face; he could have been a boy presented with a new toy, the Howling Dancing Nigger Mk I. The others had brightened visibly. Plucking up his nerve, Rabo I pinched my arm. Not the most lethal of martial arts techniques but, oddly enough, my exclamation of surprise and pain was perfectly genuine. There you are. I'd have taken a crack from a baseball-bat like a wooden Indian. Rabo III came to join the fun. He did his best to dead-leg me with his knee, one of the great advantages conferred by the galabiyya being total lower limb mobility. I turned my laugh at the puniness of the blow into a choked snort. This was the signal for them all to lay into me. I became the still centre of a maelstrom of milling fists and flailing feet. I say still because I never really lost my composure, never blew my cool, under this ineffectual assault. I didn't deserve a medal, an Oscar was more like my just deserts. I'd made up my mind only to retaliate should things get out of hand, when I'd do just enough to deflect real harm to myself but in fact not once did I have to retaliate. Individually, they were pathetic, as dangerous as flies I chose not to swat. Collectively, they were even more insignificant. The aggregate of their efforts amounted to less than the combined sum of their individual forces: they cancelled each other out. They got in the way, once or twice even took blows from the others intended for me. And as they got out of breath, which was quickly, they became even wilder and more unco-ordinated. I grunted and gasped but the biggest difficulty I had was not bursting out laughing.

With the Bohaidenese seriously winded, I let them pummel and belabour me without troubling to ride the blows. This probably hurt their hands more than it hurt me but no doubt the impact gave them a sense of achievement. Finally, I sagged into a corner on theatrically rubbery knees. "Mercy," I said, e.g. kindly don't make me hernia myself. A couple more cuffs landed on top of my head. I always had a bone-hard head. Fr. Paul said so.

"Let that," said Rabo III, taking huge gasps of air, "be a lesson to you, you nigger Filipino."

"Yessir," I said. "Please be compassionate. Please do not hurt me any more." I got a few kicks for this. They did love to turn your own words round on you. Some more blows and they began departing. An Arab farewell was a protracted affair at the best of times, compared to the relatively truncated good-byes which were the Smith norm, and this departure was punctuated by abuse, sneers at the girls, and some half-hearted gropes which the nurses met with sufficient angry words and slaps to show they were not meat on the table.

This was the Bohaidenese all over for you. I'd given them the illusion of martial valour, joint participation in combat against a terrible foe – I'm sure I became seven feet tall with flames coming out of my nostrils in the saga they recounted all over Bohaiden – with the chance in the aftermath to exercise some real vindictiveness against the vanquished. That's what the yellow-bellies excelled at: ten of them going door-to-door to drag begging victims out for summary execution. Fr. Paul was always savaging Filipinos. I wonder what he would have made of the Bohaidenese.

My new friends Maribeth, Louise, and Perla were respectively an anaesthetic sister, a midwife, and a general nurse. At thirty-five Maribeth was the oldest. She'd been the one in mid-room still on her feet, giving her assailants pause for thought. Even for *pinays* they were sweet girls. All spoke excellent Arabic. They had a combined work experience in Bohaiden of more than twelve years, enough to know what the Bohaidenese were all about but not enough to leave their door shut against an innocent knock in the early afternoon.

Perla's ward was part of the pediatric wing, specialising in injured camel-jockeys. The typical injury sustained by these fearless ten-year-olds from Sind was a fractured clavicle and forearm as they careened off the loping, cantankerous beasts. I only know of one method of conveyance more dangerous than the motor-bicycle and that is it. The little boy valiantly defending the big girls against their would-be rapists, and getting half-drowned for his pains, was a junior-jockey cared for by Perla who, unusually, was a Bohaidenese himself and not a Pakistani. I could only regard this lapse from context, a far more dangerous fall than from his racing-camel, as unbelievably meritorious. He was a wiry, curly-haired fellow, far smaller than he should have been at his age, with a great grin of the whitest teeth and treacherous green eyes, flecked with what looked like mica. When Maribeth had given me three months of Arabic lessons I also discovered Ali really did have the foulest mouth in

Bohaiden. He reminded me of Danton as a kid, which was why I didn't cuff him round the head too hard whenever I caught him pilfering from the breast-pocket of the shirts I hung on the back of the nurses' chairs. I was his idol, you see, as well as his mark.

With Maribeth, Louise, and Perla it was like we'd known each other fifty-five years already from the first minute we exchanged words. It's experience shared which counts, *di ba*, not just chronology. *Siguro*, it wasn't like sitting in the freighter-hold with Dant, but this time at least it was me with my account in credit which, I tell you, beats being in someone's eternal debt outta sight.

"You are our hero, Rey," Maribeth said simply and truthfully a month later, and the others chorused their "O-o,"s as we sat in the back of the Lebanese café, well-hidden from the street, but still to the agitation of the owner, for it was easier to get away with rape in Bohaiden than ordinary socialising between the sexes. I wallowed in it, man, the adulation of the girls. I hadn't had it since sinking those fifteen-yarders as easily as sticking the plug in a wash-basin. There was no Danton to whisper in my ear as I rolled along in my chariot, only Ali whom I saw out of the corner of my eye trying to steal Halwa when the Lebanese's back was turned.

"Yes, even though there was too many of them for you, you so brave," Louise said, with just a hint of doubtfulness below the surface. I was vain enough to open my mouth to try to explain, then shut it. Anyhow, I knew the girls warmed to me the more for not being almighty and for getting beaten up on their behalf. To love, women need to pity sometimes; you can worship but you can't be affectionate about the omnipotent.

I never let the girls within sight of Faud's. I didn't particularly want to have to bury Wizz 'n' Crap in the desert. The nurses understood that situation without having to have it spelled out to them, so I always played my fixtures with them away. It wasn't home advantage; I got more cheers as the visitor. I think some people even got to thinking I worked at the hospital. They probably hoped they wouldn't get me assigned to them, me the lummox and accidental mercy-killer, the nigger with the qualification. In public I was circumspect. Whatever participations between men and women were considered seemly among the Bohaidenese – they were few enough in all conscience – we undertook between ourselves. Otherwise we mostly fraternised behind closed doors. And even after I have recounted all I have to recount, I persist in saying our relations were such as exist between brothers and sisters.

I had my first sex in nearly two years with Maribeth, Louise and Perla – that was as well as Arabic lessons.

Possibly, the Bohaidenese would have killed me, if they'd known. Was I a hypocrite? I think not. There is a medium-length word, called consent.

Maribeth with the short hair was the toughest and most intelligent as well as oldest of the trio. "We're here, *di ba*, of our own free will," she'd say, as we sat listening to Freddie Aguilar's songs on her Samsung, "so let's not cry about the Arabs. They're cruel, but if they pay…OK."

"Yes," I'd argue, "but some don't remain here of their own free will. They're trapped," to which she'd just shrug her shoulders. Nurse or not, she was a typical *pinay*; she wasn't a carer about other people except it touched her warm Philippine heart in the most general way. Louise, the littlest and thinnest-limbed but the biggest-busted with pendulous breasts that seemed attached to the wrong torso, would giggle and then say with utmost seriousness, "Next year when I have four thousand in BPI, I home-coming Bohol again." In order to accumulate savings at home she had to send through the special women-only sharia bank in Bohaiden, which was marginally less reliable for remittances than the men's.

I didn't do them all at the same time, by the way, nor did we start with the intention that I was eventually going to have them all. It just ended up that way, like Faud counting up his money at the end of the week and finding he had more than he thought.

I was coming to the end of an hour's Arabic conversation with Louise, the giggly one with the unlikely mammaries, when she – more bored than I was – and if you have worked to acquire another language in adulthood you will concede that forty-five minutes, with the best will in the world, is as long as a session may be protracted – tittered and said, "You know what is *Vilat* – in Arabic? The *bastos* word?"

"O?" I replied, with real interest, for we do not have to be either silly little schoolboys or wrinkled lechers to find interesting the words for pussy, *boyo, chucha, cuno, muschi, figa,* or *boto* in alien tongues. "O," said Louise, "and *laguy* is the same as the word for sword in Bohaiden dialect."

"*Olok*," I countered, using an even more vulgar word from our native dialect for the male organ. My own *laguy* was beginning to stir. The question was whether Louise wanted it to. Me, hadn't I always liked vocabulary games? But Louise was not a Jesuit in front of a blackboard, nor did I need lessons at what we were about to do, though I was rather out of practice. She leaned over me to turn the electric fan to its second-strongest setting – we found it cosier without the air-con – and to preserve her balance and, no doubt, to encourage me, put her small, unmanicured nurse's hand on my knee. I tapped her supporting arm away – a foul play – and she fell across my waist on her soft breasts, with the giggle that was the only thing infectious about her. Lifting her under the arms, I kissed her short, brown nose. Louise kissed me straight back on the mouth. "Louise," I murmured.

"O?" she replied.

"Just saying it," I answered.

"Why?" with a giggle. "I think I already know my name."

"Your name is important to me," I said. "We're meat without our names."

For answer, she kissed me on the lips again. I think I had an entirely non-Asiatic tendency to talk too much, generally concerning the wrong things, at such moments. Louise kissed me next with parted lips before putting her tongue a little way in my mouth, the assumed tentativeness with which she did this the only thing *pinay*. That was what got me really hot. When you've been brought up on, "I'm not that kind of girl," and "I'm still a virgin," uttered as demurely by the two dollar Jezebels at the barbecue stalls as by thirteen-year-old convent schoolgirls, the comparative brazenness of the 'Merikana or Hispanic could be either a turn-off or the most potent aphrodisiac to the sober *pinoy*. By way of response, I put my hand on one of those pocket battleships of breasts. It felt now firm and kind of official in the coarse, restraining cloth of the uniform. She pushed my questing mitt away as I tried to get it inside but she didn't the next time. With a sigh she let me tip her on her back. Rucking her skirt up, I also fiddled with my own pants and got them to half-mast. The experience I had with *pinays*, even those on the cager circuit to whom my endowments, dimensions, and proportions were better known than my inter-collegiate score average, was that what I had could cause consternation. I was better off burying Cæsar rapidly than standing him up for praise.

Accordingly, I didn't remove Louise's panties but tweaked the gusset into a thin band on one side before rubbing her till she became oily. Meanwhile, she was entwining her tongue with mine in fancy ways that were innocent rather than lubricious. Teenyboppers are ornate kissers. Serial fornicators aren't. The head of my cock knocked against the groove of Louise's outer pussy, then parted the folds like a curious Alsatian's head poked through salmon drapes. Louise sighed again. I decided to take my time and holding dick between forefinger and thumb rubbed it all over the Indian in the canoe. Louise tittered once more but finished with an intake of breath. Her face grew serious. She closed her eyes. I tried to put the head of my dick inside her but she screwed up her eyelids. This wasn't the first time I'd encountered a maximum headroom problem with the *pinay*, and I'd learned to be both patient and resigned. Trying an alternative ploy, I moved down, sucked her nipples, kissed her navel – a barrio navel tied by the village *hilot* with a protuberant knot, quite unlike the neat, recessed, and striated pit that would have been Louise's own handiwork – and licked the fold between her groin and thighs. She uttered a sound of remonstrance and pulled half-heartedly at my wool but I'd also encountered this terminal *pinay* modesty before and persisted. To my surprise, Louise changed her grip from my hair to my ears – which offered a poor hold to any but her little fingers – and pulled me towards her as greedy legionary might amphora. I obliged her for some long minutes, then thought it time for some self-gratification. But I saw her wince as I got little more than a half-inch past my glans into her. So I sawed backwards and forwards, with most of me on the outside. It wasn't completely satisfactory but I could have come, had Louise not opened her eyes and nodded to me rapidly three times, the infinitisemal, part-conspiratorial, part-hortatory nods of a *pinay* determined to get the answer "yes". I sure knew what this meant. Down I went again. The first time I'd enjoyed it. This time it was much more of a labour, even if a labour of love. Slobbering in a foam of my own saliva and Louise's pussy juices, restraining the desire to pick the *kiki*, the stray pubic hairs, from between my front teeth, the last thing I was thinking about was love-making, the last thing I felt was lust. I found myself conjugating the preterites of Fr. Paul's irregular verbs, absolving them of their deviations from the norm by comparison with the elaborate and flowery archaisms and circumlocutions of the

Arabisms of the past five and forty minutes which I found so congenitally alien and unsympathetic to my make-up. The only thing I liked about Arabic, which I'd picked up from Faud and not Louise, was that without a hint of poetic pretension they called a grenade a pineapple.

"Aah," sighed Louise, pushing her pubic bone hard on to my lips and wriggling. I saw her toes clench and curl. She'd come. I'd gone. My dick was as floppy as boiled jellyfish tentacles. I came up, then made to kiss Louise. She dodged and pulled a face. The fastidious little thing didn't want to taste her own secretions. I smiled at her the best I could. Butch Tan Sy had once rebuked me for looking too happy when we lost to Ateneo in the end of season finale, and I hoped I looked as sincerely gracious to Louise as I did to our college oppos. She pulled her shirt down with wonderfully appealing female hypocrisy, then smoothed the folds. "Don't tell anyone," she said. "*Sa bisag kinsa*. Promise?" I refrained from saying I didn't have much to boast about. "Ah," she exclaimed, as she was patting her short-ish hair in the mirror. "You're not climax yet, Sugar?" The practical midwifely side of her now came out. "*Lo-lo*, OK?" She made the motion of masturbating, but being a girl she did it horizontally as if holding the guy's dick like a bottle from which she was pouring, instead of vertically like a joystick as a boy would. However, as she didn't turn from her primping but looked provocatively at me in the glass, I surmised I was being invited to feel free to do it myself. "No, thanks, *hinigugma*," I said and was glad to find myself laughing. She giggled; I hope not at my unrequited plight.

There would be nothing giggly about my sex with Maribeth. I did it with her frequently, as opposed to the once with Louise and the twice afterwards with Perla. Maribeth and I were alone in the evening on the unpropitiously stony and seaweedy beach that began just outside the old town on what I thought was a brotherly and sisterly walk when she sprang one of the very greatest surprises of my life on me by asking without preamble, "Sex *na lang*, Dong, you like *ba*?" As I looked warily round – the punishment for public lewdness was a lashing – I had to figure Louise had been gossiping. Mind you, she hadn't promised not to. She'd just asked me not to.

We did it inside an old row-boat. Maribeth had none of Louise's reticence. She took my dick out of my trousers herself, got it hard with a few cool, soft caresses of her hand, then squinted at it from arm's length in the way Faud might the angle of a measuring-staff. I lay back against the snapped thwart with a smirk on my face that even a nasty knock from a rusty rowlock couldn't wipe off. One of the sweetest things about *kayat* with our own girls, for me, was the sight of my maleness in their cute hands. To my delight and amazement, Maribeth was going to have no stage-fright about sliding down the cobra. She was wearing jeans, not a long dress, which suggested to me that she hadn't planned our little escapade. Her move had been spontaneous, confounding my expectations of our own girls in general and Maribeth in particular and, perhaps, Beth's own expectations of herself. Still sitting on the bottom of the boat, she wriggled off her jeans without assistance from me, then worked the wrinkled skin of my shaft up and down by clasping it between the soles of her feet. I laughed but she looked at me with hot and serious eyes and I never had occasion to smile again when screwing with Maribeth. It was always earnest but delicious. We never got up to any fancy positions. We didn't need to. It was totally straight, missionary position with Maribeth. I didn't lick her out once, nor did I ever even doggy her. She came, eyes open, almost glaring at me, without any clitty-tickling, just my cock in her hole. It was the hard and lascivious way she looked at me that was such a turn-on, that and the languid insolence with which she thrust her pelvis against my every stroke, her stare boring into me all the time. She made me feel abandoned and depraved, which was crazy, as if we were complicit in some terrible crime – I don't know, like ritual sacrifice – and when I shot my load after twenty minutes humping I felt I was doing something for which I could be jailed, not just in Bohaiden.

Straight after I'd come, Maribeth always much earlier than me, she'd grip my buttocks and grit her teeth, moving spasmodically against me until I cried quarter and begged to slide out. I'd rather run three miles than go on screwing with my flaccid member in the excruciatingly tender post-coital state. After that, she'd roll out from under and dress without a look at me. Did I feel a little used? A toy without batteries? I guess I did a little, but it never put me off when the next chance came.

If Maribeth might have gotten hold of me that first time without the collusion of Louise, Perla for sure had the collaboration of the others. I could sense conspiracy prickling in the air when I entered Perla's room to leave off a tome she'd allegedly requested from 'Beth.

Her TV was on. A Bohaidenese meteorologist in traditional head-dress was giving the weather forecast: forty-two degrees, no prospect of rain. I understood the Arabic but not his facial expression. He read as if surprised. Perhaps this was professionalism, designed to keep the viewer's interest. Perla, unsurprisingly, was in her bare feet. Being in her room, she was also able to wear shorts. The only thing daring about these was their colour, turquoise, for they were voluminous city-shorts cut to make the female thigh – those ever-expanding fat-banks – appear slimmer, even if the cloth was taut in waist and ass. The Bohaidenese women would certainly have stoned her for it. Perla's legs were across her little coffee-table, so that I saw the underneath of her feet. Of all human postures this one surely implies the greatest self-absorption. Those adopting it should always try seeing themselves from a radically different perspective: the beholder's. What Perla saw were her own dear piggies from their most flattering anterior, vertical aspect: the regular, perfectly proportioned nails, neither too large-windowed nor too small, the delicate joints, mini-knuckles, which broke the featureless length, and the smooth skin and delicate veins of the instep. She could be pleased by the prospect of what Fr. Paul said were never to be referred to as the pedal extremities. I thought they were cute, too, when I came round. But what I saw first were the blind, chubby, misshapen bulbs of the underside of her toes, the large toes like most people's appearing ungainly long from under, and the balls of both feet which, unknown to her, were black from tiles she failed to appreciate were so dusty.

"Ah, Sugar," she simpered and, at once, I knew there was something, uh, afoot.

"This is your book back from Maribeth. She was going on duty and said you needed it."

"Oh, yes, the book. Can you give me a hand?" Perla inquired, squinting at me down the line of her leg which she'd raised six inches from the table.

"And you'll give me a foot?"

She tittered, with both hands over her nose and mouth. "O-o. I cannot get proper pedicure here and it's difficult to reach." She looked deprecatingly at her thighs which were as long as my mother's. Perla could have been a dancer if she hadn't been a nurse. "Cannot file my nails."

"I'll be the one," said I jovially, picking up a small emery-board, so well-used it was as smooth as a popsicle-stick. Perla pretended to squirm as I gripped her foot, boldly going where no doubt she'd vouchsafe no man had gone before, but I knew my grip was strong enough not to tickle. This was definitely the more aesthetic aspect. Her nails, clipped straight across, were immaculately filed, the cuticles – those encroaching foreskins – pushed back beyond their proper boundary with the field left clean.

"What cute feet," I said. "*Puwede*? May I?" and put my lips to the serrations between her toes.

"TV, *lang*," said Perla by way of reply, which I thought the strangest of non-sequiturs until with the remote-controller, which she nearly lost her balance in retrieving and brandishing, she extinguished the weather forecast. Then with a phut, a fizz, and a whir she brought on something quite other. This was a blue movie.

"Yuks!" squeaked Perla unconvincingly. "Bold! Someone else flaying when I'm gone." There was a coquettish smile around her full Malay lips, thicker than my own, which in a short while I was to see clamped round my helmet. The bodies on screen assembled, broke, and re-formed in unimaginatively choreographed permutations that any self-respecting high school basketball-coach could have bettered. Someone said something in an unidentifiable North European language which was rendered in sub-titles in another equally unintelligible, probably Scandinavian tongue. Context suggested they must have been mutually incomprehensible. One of the guys was a black dude. Perla snickered. "That boy's thing, it's the one to be real?" An unspoken question hung in the air. I didn't, in the circumstances, take offence. So far Perla had made all the running. Now it was time for me. I said, "His is no big deal." Perla looked slyly at me, then sideways at my crotch. I undid my cheap replacement belt, as slowly as I could, to be both langorous and to give Perla time to yell, "Desist, knave," should she wish to do so. (Actually, I didn't think she would). I brought out what I had.

"Yikes, it's true," she squealed.

"What is true?"

She bit her lip and shook her head. This was one of the few occasions in her life when she wouldn't cheerfully betray the conspiracy in which she was involved.

"Oil," she said suddenly. This caught me as Fr. Paul would say "on the hop". Was she initiating a discussion on Bohaiden's modern life-blood, which had a sulfur content higher even than Saudi crude, corroding pipes and pumps quicker than the men-folk acquired strictures of the urethra? But, no, it was the Johnson's Baby Oil with which she made her hair glossy and heavy. Stretching a point, she extended my organ with one hand and with the other drizzled an amber stream of Johnson's on to what was rising. I believe I had a leer on my face which belied my intrinsic intelligence. All my brains had retired downstairs. Perla rubbed my shiny, slippery shaft with an absent-minded frown, then her face cleared. She licked the bead off the top of my cock. Then she pushed me back, had her city shorts round her ankles before my head had touched the cushion, and leapt out of those cloth hobbles with an admirable nimbleness to land laughing on my quadriceps femoris.

"I'll be the one," she said, "to control *na lang*." Like any Filipino I was happy to acquiesce when someone really wanted to do something. I saw what she meant when she took hold of my knob like a gear-stick, assumed the squat, and guided it expertly to her hole. Gingerly, she sat a few inches down. "Don't move, hah? Fromise?" she admonished me. I nodded and closed my eyes. Perla put me in slowly, moving occasionally with a sideways, grinding motion as well as vertically on, I guess, the same geometrical principles as we'd got an enormous new sofa from Dubai through Faud's front door by standing it upright and rotating it about its own axis at the correct moment. Half-way Perla stopped with a sigh. I could live with that. It was still lovely. Full immersion compared to the toe I'd dipped in the swimming-pool with Louise. Something men know and few women realise: not all vaginas are created equal. Some, in young girls even, are so flaccid as to deprive the man of more than half the sensation. Most, of course, are average. One in a hundred grip so snugly and at such a sweltering temperature that the lucky entrant thinks he has entered the halls of heaven. Such was Perla's. She paused. On the TV screen, as I opened one sneaky eye, a long-haired blonde was jumping up and down on a dick with a good deal less inhibition than Perla. On the other hand, if I say it myself, she had a good deal less reason to exercise caution. With rapt concentration, Perla sat all the way down until her ass-cheeks touched my pubic hair. We both stayed still for half a minute, quietly felicitating ourselves, I with less reason to congratulate myself than Perla. Then she began our proper exercise in conjugation and declension. I didn't last very long but I think she was before me. In any case, she had the presence of mind to dismount forwards and slide off me as I spurted horizontally across my belly, looking back on her hands and knees very much like a dog with her right leg cocked for a better view because as she commented, "Half-way my mens coming already and I'm not taking anti-conception like 'Beth and Louise."

"Ah," I said non-committally.

As I put on my pants, it occurred to me that I had not laid a hand on Perla during our love-making. As Butch would say in one of his best oxymorons, "I prefer players with a very non-physical game, No 11."

CHAPTER XVII

IN THE END Bohaiden didn't have much going for it. The country was best thought of as a giant, arid version of the Puerto Princesa internment centre, with Filipinos now in the position of Vietnamese and the Bohaidenese as free Flips, always of course with the desert instead of rain-forest occluding escape.

"Puck, what a dump, mans," I could hear Dant saying.

I was starting to see how out of sheer boredom the Arab women might prefer to stub their cigarettes out on their servants' flesh instead of an ash-tray. It was a novel channel of martyrdom, man. Naturally, there was more on offer for the men of Bohaiden: as well as raping Filipinas they could go hawking or horse-riding. In the Emirate down the road, three hundred empty miles of it, they were more modern: they raced power-boats. In Qatar they'd gone for a non-playboy sport, for the Emir had passable footballers and better runners; though in the latter and even the former I could see the African genes were more important than the financial endowment which paid for the expensive foreign coaching. Even Dubai and Bahrain at least had bustling international airports where the locals could go gawp. The Bohaidenese lacked all that – even a historic external enemy to give them a scare every now and then with some new piece of Russian or Chinese flying and floating hardware. On the one occasion their larger, but essentially no less pusillanimous, neighbours had rattled their scimitars over a disputed island – more an ambitious reef – in the straits, the ruler of Bohaiden had retaliated by holding the feast to end all feasts. Quails, inside goats, inside camels: Faud's forays into entertainment had nothing on the royal munificence. Each dish under its metal dome, even the platters of saffron-rice, was cheered as if it was a tank in a victory parade.

Elaborately vengeful addresses and speeches, bellicose interventions and replies, oaths, promises, and counter-protestations filled the appetising air. Intoxicated with his own ferocity, an aged vizier kicked in swift succession two members of the minority tribe, a Sri Lankan, and a trio of Filipinas whom he thought, presumably, too slow. A roar of approbation went up from graybeard and princeling alike; you'd have thought he'd established the beach-head single-handed already. We minions in lesser service were privy to all this, as was greater Bohaiden. We watched it on local TV.

TVB, which acronym I rely on you to unravel, was after Hong Kong and Singapore a breathtakingly inept channel. Although they were equipped with the latest and most expensive cameras and mixing equipment, their shots went awry, frames trembled, they'd cut to new scenes and subjects without any sense of grammar at all. It made Philippine TV look professional by comparison. I think one of the cameramen decided to put his Sony down and have a handful (taken with the right) of lamb, currants, and yellow rice, for the shot we got of the last *pinay* being kicked was at ankle-level. That was as aggressive as the Bohaidenese got. They tamely surrendered the island and forgot all about it by the time the next feast came round.

Under these circumstances, street-theatre, of any kind, was a welcome addition to the daily round of life in Bohaiden. The most dramatic, the truest, the most spectacular and exemplary public entertainment in Bohaiden took place in the public square. It had emotion, it had simplicity; it offered that shameful glee in the misfortune of others for which only the German language has a specific word but which is as old as the Greek tragedians Fr. Paul thought it best to give us in small doses and in translation. It offered, additionally, a gratuitous display in the variety of human nature: cravenness, fortitude, defiance, resignation, the paralysis of terror. Catharsis for the audience was always complete. The bullfight had nothing on it. It was also free, gratis as well as exemplary. It was the public executions.

These happened rather less frequently than one might have thought from the rate at which they cropped up in casual conversation. For instance, Jenny Smith complained in the first week of her arrival she'd been regaled with volunteered accounts of these beheadings and amputations by six out of ten of her new acquaintance in the clubhouse. I doubted if these raconteurs were reporting from direct experience. White faces in the square were a very great rarity. I mean non-pigmented as opposed to ashen. I never saw one at any of the four sessions I attended. Filipinos, man, was another matter. They, we, were the greater part of the audience. Could have been a Sharon Cuneta or Freddie Aguilar concert back home, down to the screams and the deliberate unpunctuality of the principals, not to mention their unwillingness to relinquish the stage if there was the glimmering of an encore. Ladies and gentlemen, Elvis has shucked off this mortal coil. In my opinion we came out of it quite well. Presented with the lineaments of the gory demise of the most hardened and pitiless malefactors, rapists, murderers, robbers, our warm Philippine hearts were not so hard that they could not feel the stirrings of pity for those who would have cut our own throats as easily as taking a leak. The Pakistanis in the crowd were another matter. To a man, they revelled in the spectacle of the last agonies, more mental than physical, of the trussed, kneeling, and I strongly suspect, drugged, victims of Bohaidenese justice. They chewed, smoked, spat, sniggered and grinned while pointing out to each other some small detail which might have been missed: the tail of the robe soiled in terror, the victim who had a cast in his eye which led one to believe he was looking shiftily in your direction when in fact all his attention was on the executioners. Not even the circumstance that most of the victims were, if not kith and kin, at least Pakistanis of their own class, sufficed to dampen their derisive glee. If anything, it increased it by conferring a securer sense of identity upon them as invulnerable bystanders. I record that very nearly all the Pakistanis I saw died bravely. Most were drug-smugglers. They walked to their doom, heads held high, haughty expressions on bad faces. Filipinos suffering capital punishment were murderers, of each other, Indians, or much more rarely Bohaidenese. They tended to be less in control of themselves, probably because many of them were innocent, set up by the Arabs who were the perpetrators of the crime. I think, shit, I know, that makes it a lot more difficult to exhibit nonchalance about your fate.

There were worse ways to go. The swordsman always got the head off with one hit and I never saw the torso or legs even jerk. It wasn't weird so much watching heads fall off – I'd seen plenty of coconuts go, being roughly the same size and, yes, weight as a head – as observing them lying there afterwards. Not something you got to witness that often in your life. You wanted to tidy up, to put the missing piece in the jig-saw puzzle. I expected the head to come back and re-join the trunk, under the same inevitable attraction of opposites as refrigerator magnets. I can truthfully record I never saw that happen.

Just the once I saw guys I knew getting punished. This was only a whipping, but was in some respects more sickening at the time than witnessing a decapitation. You heard howls; it was gorier. The relative fortitude of the nationalities was reversed here. The Filipinos endured the lashes as silently as they could, the Pakistanis shrieked shrilly enough to bring the heavens down. And yet the Pakistani miscreants were unquestionably the more mettlesome rascals, innured to hardship, treachery, and blood in a way most of us weren't. There you go.

The guys being flogged were from another construction crew. They were contracted to a big company who actually paid their wages on time but didn't lift a finger to protect them from the Religious Police. The poor fuckers had been running a grape still, just like our pharmacist's, but had been denounced by a Pakistani. I like to think Faud would have protected us, or at least made things warm enough for the informant to discourage it ever happening again, but the *pinoys* suffering in front of us would, to add insult to injury, be deported wage-less after the beating while the Paki fink would get a cash reward.

I wouldn't like to be less than fair to Bohaidenese justice. Alcoholism and petty theft were undeniably rare. Of course, crimes did happen and it couldn't be proved that there would have been more without the deterrents of the sword and the lash but I, and everyone else, knew damn well that there would have been. The next logical step, which surprisingly few people are capable of taking, is to concede that prevention – terminal forestalling, MA-D – is a whole bundle better than punishment.

Women were not countenanced but it wasn't unknown for some to dress up as men to witness the show. Lou, with her short hair, looked boyish under my cap but had to flatten those breasts of hers under a tight towel. It was the only time I saw her serious-faced for more than fifteen minutes. She was used to blood and disgusting smells and sights, including detached limbs, but not in this context. Warned by the top of her head drooping against my elbow, I looked down to check her out and found her grey-faced on the point of syncope. My supporting arm went round her before I knew it – public embraces between the sexes frowned on, between guys, of course, OK – and she was able to sag almost to her knees. I don't think she was putting it on.

"OK, *ba*, Lou?" I inquired with the genuine kindness of friendship rather than the mere display of romantic liaison. "I should not have brought you."

"I will be OK. For a moment, *lang*," said the plaintive little voice below me. We were near the front. An incompetent Thai shop-lifter had just lost his hand, which lay on the dust. I'd expected it to turn an ash colour but it had remained obdurately brown. Louise squeaked suddenly. I looked down into her eyes with concern. "O-o," I said gently, "it's a terrible thing, let's go."

She looked troubled. I cleared the way, the Pakis only making space at the last moment before I'd have mowed them down. They leered at Lou in the way only a guy with a hard-on in a flimsy *galabiyya* can.

"OK, *'be*?" I asked when we were out of the thick. "A glass of water will help you."

"Uy! Sugar! I'm OK, *lang*. Just the guy behind put his finger in my *koan*."

"What, who? Why didn't you tell me?"

"Because I don't want them to cut your head off after you're the one to break his neck."

"*'Sus!* You're right! I'd have murdered the guy!" I wondered if he had worked out it was a chick standing in front of him. No, plump, effeminate boys were more to their taste: cleaner than the raddled harridans of the peninsula.

Louise it was who now steered me to our favourite Lebanese café where the bitter, quite sugar-less little caffeine bombs it never failed to surprise my fellow-Filipinos I'd acquired a taste for, restored me, while a soya-bean milk performed the same office for Lou. The owner shook his head. He really didn't like having her there, even in disguise.

"Phew!" I said. "Will you have bad dreams?"

"Oh, no, Sugar. I have worse experience."

"Of course, yes," I mumbled. I thought she meant the time I'd sprung through their window without introducing myself.

"No, I didn't tell you yet," she reprimanded me. They were great girls and we were good friends but I believe she was pulling rank on me. I was a labourer, she was a hospital-worker who'd read text-books till her head spun. She was re-affirming her professionalism after her weakness in the square. So I thought.

"It was in my first year it happen here, so it's since five years already, *di ba*? We're given the call at 1 p.m. so it's in my siesta, Sugar, I'm the one to work all night, but they have three emergency case, so all hand to the fump *na lang*.

"I go in to scrub up then help the surgeon gown-on, it's Doctor Mike, you don't know him, contract finished here gone home to Melbourne long before you're the one coming here on the scene. Good surgeon *pero palaquero* they call him the Dirty Digger. My God, on the trolley, it's a real Bedou, you know, like desert Arab, not the Bohaiden people like here in the city. He's wearing the robes all black. So at first I don't notice it's soak with blood. He's got a sword, two knifes, pistola, and round the chest two long bullet-belt…"

"Bandoliers."

"*Koan*. You know, whatever. Anyhow he's still breathing. Don't need any special knowledge for that, Sugar. His chest, it's going up and down all the time. Well, we got to cut away the vandolier, can't find the buckle it's on his back somewhere, *ba*? No problem – we got flenty of sharp imflement. I'm the one to lift away – wow, it's heavy all the *balas* shining on the belt…"

"Sounds like MASH, Lou. You watch it?"

"No. Then I see tuck in the belt is a roll of money all bloody. Not local – it's Saudi rial. I go to take the other belt. Then yikes, I jump from my skin. The Bedou he got my hand grip in his, feel like strong as a robot's and his eye now open look in mine. It's like an eagle's eye, *di ba*? Then he give the groan and go unconscious again.

"Dr Mike he's the best thoracic I ever work with, it's a real frivilege even though I know he *iyut* with Fe and fromise to marry her but not do it. The Bedou's got a sucking chest wound – next vest thing to dead, Sugar – with two entry wound, one exit wound. That means one *bala* still in him. It's critical but enough vlood to transfuse him and only one lung's collapse. Dr Mike he's the one to be optimistic. He humming to the classical he got on the cassette. All going well when *woom* the flap door open and shut. Shit! It's another Bedou, look ten feet tall, with dagger, vandolier two also but he's got in his hand his rifle and his eyes burning in his head. We just look at him. Even Dr Mike can't find words. Our wounded Bedou he's lying on the operating table, got drips in him, tubes, he doesn't know anything what's happening in the real world. Maybe he's the one dreaming of stick a knife in the other Bedou. Ku-klunk, that's the Bedou advance on the table putting a *bala* in his old rifle. Well, by now we're not so stupid we don't know what's going to happen. We all step back from the operating table included Dr Mike. The Bedou look down his sights – boom! So loud, Sugar, like the thunder! Ku-klock, that's loading again. First time in the chest, spoil all Dr Mike's work. Next time the head. I see it go right there, plop the eye out. That's when we all know finish, we wasted our time. Then the Bedou put his hand on his chest, come out with money, and throw it on the dead one already. Turn on his heel, he's not wearing sandal by the way, bare feet, and out. We all there like frozen. Then Dr Alan, the other surgeon, he's the one to be a Kiwi, off his mask and cap and say, 'Pull up the stumps, folks. He's declared.' Don't really understand what that means, it wasn't an amfutation or DOA."

"Figure of speech, *'be*. They ever catch the Arabo?"

"Never hear of it again. But the reception, they say he arrived in a Rolls Royce car and leave in it, too."

"Probably cheaper than a racing camel, *di ba*? Shucks, that's quite an experience."

"Only tell you so you're not the one to think I'm coward, *'be*."

"Uy! You're the brave ones, I know that. One more milk for you, it's soothing, and I'll have one, too."

I can't say it was the excess caffeine in the system, then, that gave me a restless night of bizarre dreams, featuring Fr. Boy in priestly soutane and Bohaidenese head-dress shooting holes in the basketballs I was trying to pot in a ship's hold from a lofty crane-cabin, with Danton and Nicky Smith cheering from the jetty. Freaky.

I nearly forgot to say Mr Al-Elvis was already dead by this time. In fact, ultra double-dead. He'd been hit, hit but good, by what I'd call a hit-and-run driver except that this was the normal action following a traffic accident in Bohaiden. The correct amount of blood-money would, naturally, be strewn across the corpse of pedestrian or camel. I picked up the expat news-sheet in the Café Corniche, the Lebanese proprietor bringing over my halwa and thimble-cup unbidden, and scanned it really for details of the aftermath. There was a photo of Mr Al-Elvis, no less groomed and immaculate than when he was not inside a photographer's studio, with some biographical information I hadn't known. Such as he had a wife in Baghdad. The tyre-tracks, the report said, seemed to indicate he had been run over twice, the second time in reverse gear. This was the deduction of the compound's Scottish security manager, who'd been a Glasgow policeman, but the local authorities didn't pursue this line of inquiry. The Scotsman had taken the trouble to photograph the tyre-marks, which loomed emptily but eloquently below the portrait of the victim. Disturbed earth can of itself look sinister, especially by flash. Anyhow, the Arab police didn't take a plaster-cast of the ruts and if a message could have been discerned in the tyre-tracks within a week the text was obliterated by the imprint of less meaningful legends.

I could have told them that much.

HUBERT H. CAME INTO BOHAIDEN and my life as unexpectedly as a sudden cleansing gust will scatter litter and blow stale air to the four corners. To use a more contemporary analogy, Hubert was the air-con kicking in after a brownout in some stifling mall. Literally and figuratively, he was larger than life. Although he was unquestionably the good ol' boy, red of face and neck, too, I always imagined Hubert dressed as a *djinn* or as the Air India rajah-mascot in ragamuffin mode, his belly cascading over his drawers, ruby in his navel, sides of his feet spilling over curly-toed leather slippers, turban on his head, and his tits playing peek-a-boo behind a glittering waistcoat of the Slash 'n' Crap variety. Greatly daring, I did once mention this to him when we were both drunk as skunks on the pharmacist's bootleg hooch at Faud's remote hotel development up the coast. "Plenny of lint in thar, feller," he said. "Never saw a ruby in the tub." Technically, he was my boss, more so than the foreman or Rowell the Sparks had been but while I respected his expertise in the construction industry and, to be frank, the fact that he was a Caucasian, I joshed with him in a way I'd never have deemed suitable with Commander Smith, who was, in fact, about his age. I didn't call him "Serr" but "Mister Hubert". A great practical joker, Mr Hubert could take what he dished out. I won him by laughing when he was watching a black heavyweight from his hometown on satellite TV. Sitting in a caravan, gowned, hands taped, the guy, vaster than me, but I think it's fair to say a little simpler, had solemnly repeated the words of his withered minuscule manager, whom Mr Hubert claimed was a distant cousin of his. This latter, wearing the same red baseball cap as his fighting buck, and indeed Hubert, had spat the product of his quid and then intoned in lugubrious but sententious fashion the reflection, "The niggers is gettin' uppity," an opinion promptly repeated by the black heavyweight who was about to lose his crown, "The niggers is getting' uppity, Mr Johnson." I hooted. Hubert later told me it was a saying so often repeated in his town that it had acquired the status of a motto. Another time we were watching basketball. Hubert took a bite of peanut-butter and Jell-o from his leaf of unleavened bread and said, "That team's over-niggered." I squinted at the snowy screen and said, "No, Mr Hubert. It's fully niggered."

The N-word was not a word which ever stung me. The transposition "Flip" for "Filipino" carried a more negative connotation so far as I was concerned. I reckon Philipino would look a whole lot better than Filipino, a spelling demeaning in itself, while sounding just the same. I mean, you've got Philosophy, Philology, Physiology (and, I admit, Phlegm) as against Fuck, Fart, and Fool. Not getting riled by "nigger" was just a question of where and what I'd come from. Maybe if I'd been born in South Philadelphia or the Bronx instead of Mactan it would've been different. What I would later notice about other black men was this: fully half their sense of themselves was founded on resentment of the white man. They found their identity in grievance, much of it real, albeit historical, and not a little entirely imaginary. I could lose that with a shrug and a smile. It wasn't only me. Later, I saw one of DeLorna's *luk krueng* on Thai TV. I couldn't understand a word of Thai. It might as well have been ancient Assyrian they were speaking. But the guy had a crazy flat-top hair-cut just like the black mestizos on our own Visayan TV and a grin that encompassed his own and everyone else's absurdities just as broad as our own Amerasian *comegiante*. We were *halo-halo* with gelatinous and tooth-decaying sweets in the mixture as taken. Our uninfused, essential brothers outside Asia were just sour juice.

So Mr Hubert took a quick, sideways look at my deadpan mug, then guffawed. "You're OK, man," he said. "Don't take no account of me coz 'part from anythin' else, I'm the biggest lyin' son of a bitch ever drew breath." This was true. Hubert delighted in telling tall stories, the tallest with the straightest face.

"Is that a fact?" I replied in my driest Fr. Paul tones.

Hubert's anecdotes always involved himself, generally in conflict with the elements at their most extreme or in single-handed combat with the larger carnivores, as opposed to the more subtly self-promoting histories of a quite different sort of raconteur, specialising in accounts of momentous events with such vividness that one might almost have supposed him to have been there. Atty Caladong was one of those. In Hubert's preposterous fictions and exaggerations, concluding "… and that there brown baar…" (or permutations of cougar, polar bear, grizzly, or moose) "… done walk away with a whole chunk of me but his nuts musta bin sore for a week after." Hubert was a compulsive slayer of wild-life. "A strong man like me," he'd say, "or you, Rey, with a good knife in his hand can take care of most critturs if he keeps his head."

Hubert preferred the chase with traditional weapons, bow, catapult or spear-gun. From his stories one would have gathered that he regarded nothing as too big or too dangerous to hunt and, from my personal observation, I learned even more swiftly that he regarded nothing as too small or too harmless to slaughter, either. He had a sling-shot that fired ball-bearings through one-inch pine (we tested the manufacturer's claim ourselves on more than one of Faud's planks) and, failing duck, buzzards, vultures, or even rabbits, it was squinting Hubert's happy bent to despatch perching sparrows in exploding puff-balls of blood and feathers. He was also an *aficionado* of spear-fishing, subscribing to a specialist magazine sent from Milan featuring photos of thin young men in rubber suits holding fat fish aloft. "Them Eyetalians is unbeatable with a harpoon," Hubert acknowledged. Hubert hunted not with the rubber-powered launchers I remembered from back home or even a spring-gun but a fancy compressed-air weapon.

I'd be his chosen chum to patrol the shallows during our lunch-break (Hubert punctilious about work-hours even with Faud hundreds of kilometres away) when tiddlers that had barely stopped being fry were not safe from my companion's aim. I was amazed how canny the fish were: as soon as Hubert pointed his rod at them they scattered like Filipinos before the batons of the religous police, curving, arching their supple, spiny bodies, confounding his aim and seemingly anticipating which deflection he'd take and breaking in the safe direction. Half of the time he might as well have been trying to shoot confetti as tropical reef-fish for all the success he had. Eventually we'd kick our way back in-shore with a gaudy flapping bracelet of minuscule angel-fish, butterfly-fish, and the odd underage red snapper in their death throes on Hubert's loop of twine.

My co-workers, as many of them from coastal barrios as the big city and expert shooters of fish for protein not sport, exchanged quiet smiles among themselves, which they were nevertheless too smart to let Mr Hubert see.

Hubert and I would sit on the wettest sand we could find – the dry would have fried our eggs – snacking on raw fish seasoned in vinegar and onions while his sun-burn got worse. We were chocolate and strawberry melting into each other.

Nearly every time Hubert would squint at the imposing bluff to our left then say, "A good man could dominate the whole anchorage from up there. A man who knew what he was doin', with a good cartridge and a good rifle."

"Uh-huh," I'd say. I probably treated Hubert with more respect than he deserved. I always admired a performance rather more than I did the performer whether it was a Jesuit or a streetwise b-s artist like Dant. So instead of telling Hubert to cut it, I thought the way he'd assigned temporal priority in his sentence to the bullet rather than the gun argued more expertise than I at least could muster.

"What cartridge would that be, Mr Hubert?" I asked.

"Waal, the Winchester .30 used to be the only big-game cartridge anyone would wanna use. Stop pretty goddam anything in its tracks. There are plenny good new cartridges, but the Winchester'll do me pretty fine. Why? You a shooter?"

"No. I guess not. But I knew plenty of friends who were. Long time ago."

"Was, huh?"

It was kind of restful being with Hubert. He wasn't over-inquisitive like Filipinos were. He was prepared to let things pass or drop. Maybe he did it because he knew what it was like to be on the receiving end. The poor fucker was married to a Filipina called Apple Jusilynn. She was a long-haired little butterball with tits smaller than Hubert's who never opened her mouth other than to complain what a tightwad and playboy Hubert was. I thought it difficult to be both but she only knew the half of it. In the PI, as Hubert referred to the Philippines, he was a serial father. Little *mestizo* Huberts all over the archipelago. "Cain't lay responsibility for you at mah door, Buddy," he guffawed. "Haw-haw." I smiled thinly, not my usual broad beam, I'm afraid. I wasn't offended, of course. It just didn't do to let Hubert walk all over you all the time. Hubert's chequered past included a short spell in a Saudi jail fifteen years back for "sassing" a security guard at a water-pumping station he was employed at in Jeddah. "Son of a bitch wouldn't let me take my jeep outta the park after I'd been working over-time for the goddamned government. That left me with a long walk, so I thought I'd wipe the big grin off his face. Traded a ten mile walk for ten days in a Saudi jail but that was worth it for leaving the s.o.b out cold."

I believed all this, jail and altercation, but not leaving the over-zealous guard out cold. That was too neat. In order to stretch someone out unconscious you had to know what you were doing – focus your force – as well as just being a "good, strong man". More likely, it had been an ugly, panting stand-off of torn clothes and bleeding noses. That's why Filipinos were so ready for the convenient solutions of gun or knife. Hubert had worked with Filipinos before, of course, having been employed at Tabuk, a US base up in Northern Saudi near Israel that I'd never even heard of. "Bigger than Clark," had been Hubert's terse claim. I decided it was nearly as big as Clark Field. Hubert saw my inward revision and smiled. "No, it ain't just a base more like what you'd call a whole military city up there. Not an A-rab in sight." Hubert pronounced Arab like you would Captain Ahab. "More Filipinos than you seen at a barrio fiesta and, man, it's crawlin' with Americans."

"So when do I get to go?"

"Haw-haw." He also laughed like Bluto.

Hubert was here to, as he put it, show us how "to get it up." My outfit, Faud and his merrie men, built – if we flattered ourselves – high-spec villas for the Bohaiden bourgeoisie, those historic nomads who'd given up banditry and grazing for the more sedentary but yet more lucrative pursuits of the middleman: the commission rather than the camel, though these new plutocrats still rode their BMW's and Rollers as if they were desert beasts of burden. Our houses didn't fall down; they didn't leak. They were also surprisingly elegant, once Faud's landscapers – now nominally led by Wizz 'n' Crap – had blurred the angles of driveways and walls with some strategically placed cacti and drought-resistant creepers. Even we galley-slaves took a pride in our handiwork, sometimes extending our lower-lip outside the garden-railings and murmuring how nice the joint looked. But we didn't have the expertise of going beyond five-storeys.

The most ambitious project Faud had taken on until now was a small mall with a corkscrew ramp to the parking on the roof. Once you got beyond fifteen or twenty metres high, it was a whole different ball-game. All the small assymetries, misalignments, and unevennesses that the eye failed to register on a small scale became magnified as the building rose in just the same way that a navigational error of a second of a minute of angle on a moon-shot would be worse than many degrees of error off-course on an inter-island voyage. There were one or two such buildings in Bohaiden that rivalled the architectural disasters of back home: edges and corners on a concrete building as blunt and irregular as thick icing on a cake, skyscrapers that the most inexpert eye caught shying away from the strictly perpendicular, deformed edifices that made the stranger smile but brought tears of rage and mortification to the proprietor's eye. Faud didn't want any of that.

Hubert and the elite crew he'd brought with him, mostly girder-walking Koreans as nerveless as Siamese cats, would see to it all Faud's right angles met sharp as daggers and his stucco would be smoother than a rosewater pudding. The building would be OK, but I reserved my unstinted admiration for the way Hubert managed Faud. The Bohaidenese, of course, had to treat the American with a great deal more respect than he did the Filipinos, although I was amused to hear from Hubert that he, too, had been a pavement recipient of the knocked-flying welcome just like Jenny Smith. I reckoned it had been a very well-padded Arab lady who had been able to deck Hubert. After all, bears and gorillas had come off second-best.

Hubert called Faud "sir" but then in his super-democratic country that was also how you addressed a waiter. Faud called Hubert "Mr H." on the basis that he was a fat infidel but a useful one. Half the battle with Faud was convincing him that he was getting a better deal than his neighbours or doing a better job than his peers. He was a relativist, not a purist. For once that Arab love of apportioning percentages, that bent of a cracked and dialectically-minded justice that found an innocent foreign bystander already ten per cent guilty just by being in Arabia, worked in the foreigner's favour. So Hubert pointed out this flaw and that piece of misdesign in our competitor's handiwork.

"See them two buildings, sir?" he'd ask as we flew by in Faud's Toyota service vehicle, the rhetorical question as self-serving as any Roman orator's. "All it needs is a bridge between them on the third floor. That pathway they're using now is dead-ground, wasted space. They could use that as a parking-lot." Faud and I couldn't share Hubert's vision at first. Bridge summoned up a prospect of grey steel gantries for us. Hubert explained he meant a covered passageway in the air, linking the two buildings, with plate-glass at the sides and a carpet. Carpet was the magic word for Faud, shrewd and Westernised though he was. It could summon up visions of both modern luxury and tradition, tent and international five star, domestic bliss and adventurous wandering.

"Ah, Mr H.," he murmured. Hubert moved in for the kill. "It could even be a *curved* corridor," he suggested as insidiously as Iago. "Who says the straight line is King? They could make an arch, with steps inside." Faud looked like he was gonna come in his pants.

Once, we were sitting in the Lebanese's café, which as you know I found one of the pleasantest places in town to contemplate my deeds and misdeeds, when Hubert told our boss, "While we're a-fryin' in here all they needed to do was put in another big window in back up at the roof. The wind blows straight in here six months of the year, right? Just cut another opening in back and you'd get a through-draft. No need for air-con. It only needed a little thought." That appealed to Faud, no electricity bill. So what Hubert was saying, the hidden agenda, was he could do a Rolls Royce job for Faud for peanuts. Faud lit up at that. Another time, we were treated to Hubert the artist. We were wandering round the lot adjacent to Faud's clients, who were a family corporation controlled by a minor branch of the royals. Faud's principals had some great beach-front but currently we found ourselves splashing round marsh broken by a few gravel-spits. It had been Hubert's idea. "Don't just buy your own lot, buy the ones in front and next to it as well," was a precept of Hubert's we were all familiar with. "That way they cain't filch your view or lean over on top of you to spit, haw-haw." I don't think this was b-s. It was a sound piece of advice, worth Atty Caladong's entire series of realty and title lectures. However, the salt marsh Hubert was currently causing Faud to stain his robes in was desolate to the point of being sinister. It was safe to say no one would think of filching this particular view.

"Right there," said Hubert, "just where that fresh-water is bubblin' is your perpetual water-supply. No need for a conduit. It's here already." Well, holding the prospect of water before an Arab was to show him flocks, children, wealth, and a whole laughing branch-line descended from Abraham and him flourishing on milk and honey. "Yes?" said Faud, lighting up momentarily before native scepticism asserted itself.

"Yeah," Hubert assured his employer. "We'd just dig a hole only needs a coupla feet deep. Line it up with tiles, ordinary swimming-pool tiles, all the sediment'd clear, crystal-clear."

"But it wouldn't be enough for more than a handful of guests, Mr Hubert," I interjected, participating despite myself in the fantasy, if only in the capacity of doubting Thomas. Privately, I thought it would be lucky if it flushed a row of urinals. "Hell, no," said Hubert, ingenious and optimistic as only he could be. "You're just lookin' at the immediate supply, not the storage capacity. See here, you pump it up to a reservoir tank, don't have to be the largest tank in the world on the dune there, same height as your cabins. That'll hold all you need. Mornin' and night when the demand's at its highest you could have the pump permanently on for two hours. Rest of the time, you just have a fixed level in the tank and when it drops to it that'll be the trigger-level for the pump to kick in. Then it can fill up slow as you please at night when no one's bathin'."

Faud and I looked at the gaseous welling taking place in the khaki water at our feet and imagined it as Hubert's dinky blue catchment pool. At that time and in that place it was a particularly compelling and attractive prospect. Hubert swept us up and on as we traipsed now over gravel to the summit of the sand hillocks. "Plant plenty, sir," Hubert admonished Faud as we looked down at the sterile expanse of stone, sand, and tufted grass insufficiently below us even to be transformed by the romance of height and distance. "It'll give shade and it refreshes the eye, too." Wow, I thought. Hubert must have been reading brochures.

"Flowers?" Faud queried. Hubert shook his head. "Naw. Fruit trees. Yeah, flowers look purty but your tourist appreciates the thought of fruit more. Like, he knows he's gonna see it fresh on the table. And the owner, he might go broke but he ain't gonna go hungry, haw-haw." As Faud, who was known to have a financial headache at the moment, didn't look too amused by this last crack I, the *pinoy* peacemaker who would rather sink into quicksand than witness personal unpleasantness, who would risk a *bolo*-cut or bottle over the head to mediate, interposed with, "What kind of fruit trees, Mr Hubert?"

Hubert replied seriously, "I guess bananas fill the gut best. You kinda appreciate a big hand of bananas a-hangin' there. Plenty of shade and the leaves is handy too for wrappin' rice and such like. Don't take too long to grow. And if it ain't fruitin' that long tendril a-danglin' there is a sight for ladies' sore eyes, haw-haw." He nudged Faud, who like myself, knew what a banana tree's maroon stamen resembled. Hubert had probably eaten it diced for salad in the Philippines and made the common mistake of thinking it meat. Haw-haw.

"Papayas is easy, too. Kinda skinny tree though. Jack-fruit, that's your pig-heavy fruit for you."

"And dates, Mr Hubert? Some date palms?"

Hell, Faud didn't even own the plot but he was already more cheerful when we got back on-site. He needed to be. We were two months behind schedule, though this was due to circumstances beyond Hubert's control. Faud's billionaire principals had bounced a cheque for a large quantity of inferior but cheap Indian steel. This was now rusting on the dock in a place I'd never heard of, called Mumbai, instead of becoming the skeleton of our hotel. Faud was still held to the letter of his contract which penalised him financially for every week of over-shoot. I actually wondered if this wasn't the real reason for dishonouring the cheque because the corporation certainly wasn't short of money. If so, I was mean-minded enough to find a measure of poetic justice in Faud's dilemma.

BIG MEN ACCORDING TO HUBERT were naturally close to each other, with an instinctive understanding. It was like belonging to a tribe who were the reverse of pygmies. That was certainly how I'd felt with Fr. Boy, looking at each other eye-to-eye at refectory line-up or as I thundered down the termite-pocked planks to the vaulting-horse. But then it occurred to me that big men also had an instinctive sympathy with small men; I mean like Butch the Bulldog and Tweety Pie. Dant and I had been famous pals. I put this to Hubert. He said, "Big men and little gals, ya mean, sucker." This was true. Apple Jusilynn was small even for a low-class rural Filipina. At four eight or four nine she came to Hubert's elbow.

"You've got a point there," I admitted. "My Ma's tiny."

"And your Paw was a tall, well set-up feller?"

"Circumstantial evidence suggests it, Mr Hubert." That made Hubert wheeze and go red in the face. He was the only guy in the whole of Bohaiden with a sense of humour remotely similar to mine. Poor bastard.

I knew I was being initiated into Hubert's closest circle of companionship when he brought me to his place, a palace compared to our quarters and in fact much better appointed by Faud than his own joint, to show me his collection of bows. These were his holy of holies, his waxed heart-strings. Framed photographs adorned the walls: Hubert with his foot on recumbent horned and antlered creatures in mountain or grassland settings, Hubert, cap on head, beaming behind some muscular, triangular-eared, tawny carcass still transfixed by his arrow that looked suspiciously like one of the great cats. Sure enough it was. "Yup, that's a cougar, mountain-lion if you like."

"'Sus, Mr Hubert! It's dangerous, that one?"

"Naw, not like a jaguar. Jaguar's a big mother. Never got a shot at one of them. You look at a cougar, it's got big shoulders but a right small head. Might kill a woman or a kid but it'd have trouble gettin' its jaws round you or me. Now this here's a mountain-sheep, one of the biggest pieces of game in North America. That there's wild turkey – the most difficult tricky crittur you could ever try and shoot. White-tail deer, that's what everyone learns on, white-tail." Hubert went to his cabinet. "Y'ever shoot a bow?"

"I held a spear one time in a TV advertisement."

"Yeah, and Apple blows a mean blow-pipe. If you look at history, there was two bad-ass bows, the Turkish bow which was a composite re-curve and your traditional English longbow."

"You ever pulled the long-bow, Mister Hubert?"

"Yup. See here, this is an antique Turkish bow, got it one-time in Damascus. That'd still shoot."

"It's like two parentheses on top of each other."

"Right. That's how it gets its power, two opposites working against each other and there's more flexion on the re-curve."

"Hey, the front's different from the back."

"The belly. You call it the belly of the bow."

I kept a straight face, but noticed the bow was formed of two different materials, different grains and textures and different colours. "That," Hubert explained, "is why it's called a composite bow. It's made of glued strips of leather on the back, so when you pull on the bow-string that stretches; then you got strips of horn on the belly which compress, so they're a-storin' energy on the opposite principle. Release, and pow! You got antagonistic forces working together just for you. That'd shoot half a mile or pierce armour at a hundred feet, you name it. See, it gets its power from putting together a whole assembly of parts that ain't worth diddley on their own."

I hefted this traditional piece of *halo*[2] artisanship with appreciation. "Whoa, whoa, buddy!" exclaimed Hubert as I yanked back on the bow he'd just strung with some effort. I thought of us as Odysseus and Telemachus at the feast of Penelope's suitors. "Don't never dry-fire a bow. Only shoot it with an arrow on the string, or you'll bust it up or split it for sure."

"Sorry. I don't think too many Filipinos could pull that."

"You just drew near on ninety pounds there, boy. Now see this here is a modern compound bow, only invented in sixty six or was it eight? That draws seventy but it don't feel like it when you got it out at full draw and you're holding before the release. See them little wheels at the end of the bow-arms?" I nodded. It was what I'd call a Rambo bow. "Them little wheels, they're called eccentric cams, stores all the energy. You pull first and it's all of seventy pound. Get back three-quarters to your chin and you hit what we call the valley – that's where the pull drops to twenty pound. You can hold it there right lady-like, then you release and it accelerates all the way through seventy. And here you are, this is one for the purist." I looked at the six feet of utterly straight pole-like, rounded bow before me.

"That's the other bad-ass bow. The English long-bow."

"It's just one piece of wood, Mr Hubert."

"Yew wood."

"I would?"

"Haw-haw. No. Y-E-W. Don't grow in tropical parts but it's been the best bow wood for five thousand year. That's a pure simple design but it won the battle of Agincourt if you ever heard of that."

"1415. St Crispin's Day. Why didn't the English make composite bows then?"

"Guess they weren't as mixed up as the Turks. Naw – the Turks inherited a shorter bow for horse-back use…"

"O-o. The Scythian bow, the Parthian shot, *di ba*?"

"…Whatever. And I guess if you look at it from the constructional point of view, a cold, damp climate wouldn't be great for a bow made of different natural materials stuck together with traditional glues. So they seasoned single pieces from the heart of the tree."

"Yeah, I'd guess you'd know where you were OK. What's the craziest hunt you ever made?"

"Oh, boy, I been on some crazy ones. Mebbe it was huntin' baboon in Saudi. Thereby hangs a tale, boy."

"They don't have one, Mister Hubert. I happen to know that. So don't tell me different."

"Boy, they got a tail and they got passports, too."

"You could say the same about Filipinos, Mister Hubert." I waited. At length I cracked. "OK, how come baboons have got passports?"

"Waal, like I said it's got some twists and turns I can't rightly explain, but cut a long story short, there ain't too much to hunt in Saudi, 'less you're into hawkin' like the A-rabs which I ain't. But they got some small mountains outside of the place I was workin' in the centre of the goddamned peninsula and that place, boy, it was known to be infested with baboons. They was particular mean baboons, Rey. Sons of bitches was almost impossible to shoot. Course the A-rabs kept firearms and alcohol outta the reach of foreigners as far as they could, but you could always rent a piece from an obligin' Paki and your sportin' A-rab gentleman would let you have a pop on his Purdey or Bond street double-barrel rifle if you took him up there discreet-like. But there was never any problem with bow-huntin'. Now when you goes bow-huntin' it ain't just how straight you shoot, you gotta get in position for the loose. Your field-craft is more important than your archery skills almost. Gotta dress up in your stalking-suit with your scrim round your face, deck your bow with weeds and such-like. That mountain was purty nigh pure slate which went downright perfect with my Montana Fall-season suit which, if you wanna know, was disruptive pattern greys and blacks. When I went to ground you couldn't tell which was my ass and which was the mountain.

"My companions on this hunt you gotta understand was neophytes in the line, though those sheikhs had hunted tiger in Bengal and lionesses in Ethiopia, all done illegal but, hey, you got the dollars we got the heads. If you believed the talk which I half did, those rich dudes had hunted the most dangerous, intelligent, and illegal game of all. Take my meaning?"

"I think so, yeah. Man."

"So they wasn't complete bone-heads but then a lotta folks with the experience could tell you baboons was a lot wiser than human beings. They probably seen us hit the dirt 'coz all the precautions I took, bringin' us from down-wind, crawlin' along dead-ground and below skylines was all a waste of time and knee-patches. One of the sheikhs taps me on the boot-sole as we was nearin' the top, I look back and the whole pack of them, mom, pop, granmaw, and the babies was followin' us up from below. Soon as they seen us, they started a-hootin' and a-hollerin' and you coulda fooled me if they wasn't laughin' their socks off at us.

"Once they seen we'd cottoned on to them, they was pretty sharp about peelin' away to the side and gettin' the higher ground on a small cliff 'bout forty or fifty feet tall. They just stands there gibberin' and a-screamin' and one or two of them start to pick up rocks and just hold them in their hands. It didn't take too much brains to realise they had enough brains to throw 'em down on us pretty soon. As they already seen me and I felt purty darn stupid on my face, I pulled myself up. That really started 'em goin'. I can't say they gave me the finger and still say I'm tellin' the whole truth and nothin' but, however, Rey, one or two of them turns round and shows me their backsides. Gin'rally speakin' anything with red or blue in it like a rainbow or a flag is a purty sight but their backsides, Rey, wasn't a purty sight.

"I nocked up an arrow, makin' sure I got the cock-feather on the outside, and I drew. Got a mechanical release I use for serious huntin'. Some say it ain't for the purist but I ain't ashamed to use all the help I can get. Right on line, the arrow sails away, but the baboon jumps away behind cover and I can hear my broadhead a-tinklin' as it shatters up like shrapnel on the goddam rocks. That point's a bone-buster, man, but the blades, they're fragile even if you could shave with 'em. Incidentally, I shot at the leader of the pack, biggest, orneriest son of a bitch he was. Then the rocks start comin' down and, man, they're more accurate than me with a bow-sight and a mechanical release. Well, it's a pretty uneven battle. They got longer arms, plus they got gravity goin' for them. I got off a few more arrows, never hit one of them and, additional, the big leader picks up an arrow and shakes it over his head like he knows it's an Easton graphite-cored and worth thirty bucks before he just snaps it in half across his belly. By this time, my two A-rab princelings have taken some near-misses and it's just a matter of time before one of us takes a direct hit on the head…"

"Bet you wished you'd taken up some hard hats off the site."

"You takin' me serious, boy? Anyhow, we beats a retreat and them baboons is purty well pleased with themselves. Just as we reach our Land Cruiser there's a big boom. No whipcrack overhead before that, so I know ain't no one's shootin' at us but I'd know the sound of a big-game rifle anywhere. Down the mountain we go, I got the car in neutral outta habit, don't like to make noise even comin' off a hunt and sure as hell is warm there's no shortage of gas in Saudi but I picked up the conservation habit in the PI with Jusilynn's folks. Round an elbow of mountain we come without a sound 'less it's the moan of the wind and the whine of the rubber when, hey, we come face to face with a big ol' baboon lurchin' up the middle of the road plain as daylight but it ain't ended there – he's wearin' a hunter's vest with cartridges in it an' a big horn-handled huntin' knife hangin' from it, a mesh-cap on his head with a badge on the brim, and a pair of Soviet binns round his neck…"

"How the fuck do you know they were Russian?"

"Whoa, just wait, boy. Now he's reelin' all over the place, otherwise we wouldn't have come within a whisker of him. I brake, pull the bow outta the rack and -tonk!- I get an arrow straight into his gut and the broadhead come plumb out the other side. Well, I got a spinal hit on him there because he goes straight down – arrow don't kill with shock like a full-grain bullet, it kills by laceration, other words you bleeds to death slow. But he's gone, straight off. Inside the vest, there's a passport and that's when I see the binns got Russian on 'em. But the passport don't have the baboon's face on it.

It's a Jap. Now we load up the old 'boon, go down the mountain half a mile a ways and come across another Jeep, Mitsubishi, not so fancy as the sheikhs' but a useful conveyance, boy. Lyin' against the front right-wheel with a hole in his chest and a bigger one in his back and a Mannlicher rifle with a walnut stock about ten feet away from him and a Nikon camera right beside that gun, is the owner of the passport. Recognised him direct from his passport. Well, there's a lot of mutterin' from the A-rabs. They ain't left the desert and the fairy-stories behind them so long ago, never mind the Savile Row suits and the Givenchy Gentleman once they're outta Saudi. Too hot for the suits in Riyadh and they might drink the Givenchy, haw-haw.

"I guess I musta stood there a good ten minutes a-tryin' to guess what went on there while we was preoccupyin' ourselves with the baboons on the cliff, lookin' at the jeep, the position of the rifle, the Jap's body, and such like. What was the same importance was the way the old 'boon was staggerin' up the road when we hit him, like he was drunk which, as we know, is impossible in Saudi even for a 'boon, or he'd been hit glancin'-like by another car just before us. Man, the clues was all there but I was wearin' myself out pretty fast tryin' to decipher them. The most aggravatin' thing about it was that it only occurred a whiles before we arrived on the scene.

"One thing the sheikhs and I was of accord on was leavin' well alone. We didn't want no trouble over the blood-money with the A-rabs sponsorin' the Jap, with the ordinary police, and especially not with the religious police. Who was gonna believe the story? We got outta it pretty fast and the A-rabs took it pretty serious coz I never saw them again from that day on."

"Mister Hubert, is that what the English call a shaggy dog story?"

"It most surely is not. That whole history's as true as the daylight you're lookin' on now. In fact, maybe you can come up with an explanation."

"Well, if you're not setting me up, the explanation's somewhere in context in there."

"I thought on it a lot ever since, y'know, no shit."

"O-o. Anyone would. Say – didn't you mention there was a camera? Did you develop the film?"

"Nope. Takin' it would've been theft. And you know the code the A-rab lives by."

"Ouch. Say no more, Mister Hubert. The only thing I can think of that comes to mind is the policeman they found shot through the head near my hometown, wearing a vest stuffed full of shabu – dope, you know. Then for nearly everyone that confirmed their opinion of the Philippine police – trafficking in substances, right? But we urchins, me and my friends, we knew much better, Mr Hubert. That cop with the vest full of dope, he was the only straight cop in the whole station, the one who'd refused to wholesale it to the street punks, and the others blew him away, then stuffed his vest full of shabu just to piss on his grave."

"That don't surprise me, Rey, 'cept my gorilla didn't have his vest full of shabu even though he was lurchin' round like he smoked a key of it."

"I thought they were baboons."

"They was. Slip of the tongue."

We were quiet a while. I said, "Mister Hubert, you sure you never come up with an explanation? Because I have one. It's the only solution."

Hubert looked injured. "I didn't say I didn't have the glimmerin's of it. What's your explanation?"

I told him: a Fr. Paulian rather than Holmesian analysis based strictly on what had been put before me.

"Well, goddam," he said. "Ain't that just a coincidence? That's just what I came up with, 'cept it took all of three years, not three minutes."

HUBERT AND I were increasingly getting plenty of time to chew the fat. Faud's building just wasn't growing any more. He'd run out of skeleton for us to plump out and, unlike a cup coral, he couldn't grow skeleton himself on the outside. The Indian steel he needed for the inside plainly wasn't going to arrive and he'd bought so much of it after his principals' cheque bounced he couldn't easily afford to go to another source. Those of us he was in the habit of paying started to worry about their next packet. Our foreman mentioned this to Hubert. Interestingly, Hubert behaved just like a Filipino. He looked impassive but too expressionless to be natural. When we were by ourselves he started to sweat, though we were in the air-conditioned portable site-office. The poor fucker: like his building, he came pre-stressed and he left post-tensioned. Funnily enough, the prospect of Faud going bust brought a light to the eyes of some of us. Faud was pretty sure to pull the fast one on us anyhow. So Faud and Sons taking a hit was a most delightful prospect, second only to Faud's daughters being raped by syphilitic Ugandans and a camel crushing him to death, or − still better − a camel raping his daughters and Ugandans trampling him.

"We have," said Faud deprecatingly, "a leel problem." Hubert and I were in the Portakabin with coffee-cups giving off vapour before us. It could have been acid in an alchemist's retorts, for we weren't touching it. That was as far as our independence went. Hubert's face was taut. He looked like Miss Piggy, *pero* focussed. When Faud wheedled instead of barked, man, that was the time to think out your escape routes. "Even with the African monkeys it would be easier," he said. "I never consign to Mombasa without the cash paid first and I never pay until they land the shipment in Dubai. But the Indians! I trusted them. What a fool I am! Singapore! Why wasn't it Singapore?"

Hubert listened stonily. I was a Filipino. I hated personal unpleasantness, didn't I. "Ah, serr," I said, just to fill a silence.

"Then," continued Faud, "I − my family − we are the ones to be working through intermediaries with these Hindus. The intermediaries may be the real problem, so quick to give us the green light," he added more hopefully. Through long association Faud had picked up certain Philippine constructions − "the one to be" − so difficult for even the most cosmopolitan among us to lose, while retaining the semitic saliva-crash and an even stronger "r" than the Filipino in his pronounciation. For some reason − with the Lebanese café proprietor Ahmed as well − the "r" was strongest when he uttered that word of mesmerising significance to Arabs, "green". Even when it was used in the most modern and Western of expressions "green light". So I listened to the reverberations of grrrr-een rattling through the thermally efficient but acoustically permeable walls of the Portaka-office.

"Maybe I should be the one to pay them a visit," Faud mused. "But in my position so difficult. So very difficult. I have my position to think of. Then who can I trust?"

Not your fellow countrymen, for sure, I thought.

"You?" Faud suggested after a long pause during which both Hubert and I had conspicuously failed to propose ourselves.

"Insh' Allah," I intoned dismally.

"No, *bahala na*," said smiling Faud.

Actually, he wanted to make sure of Hubert and me as well. We didn't cross the Arabian Sea by ourselves. Not with Faud's Saudi gold in our keeping. It was easier for me to contrive a water-tight solution to Hubert's history of baboons than to fathom Faud's motives for having us aboard his leaky dhow. The problem with the Bohaidenese – and three parts of the problem was that they didn't know it – was that they thought they were too clever by half. Duplicity, double-dealing, hair-splitting, life as chess, only with rules they made up against the foreigner as it suited them – this gave our masters the advantage, but after a while you could compensate for it. If you expected absolutely everything coming your way to be crooked, if you interpreted everything they said to you as meaning exactly the opposite, took a denial as a confession and a promise as a stark refusal, then you were likely to be right more than half the time, just like the fish breaking the other direction from Hubert's harpoon. And while your slave-master was crowing over his or her own cunning, it was you who was master of how things really stood. I have to say it was mostly a purely intellectual, a Jesuit satisfaction. Just one or two times you got a little practical benefit. As that dubious Catholic, Blaise Pascal, said, if the universe were to fall on a man he would be killed but not destroyed because he would be cognisant of the fact but the universe would not. Knowledge, fellow-toilers, is a hard-hat.

If I had to quantify it, Faud had us there sixty per cent as patsies, thirty per cent as bodyguards, and ten per cent as mules. As a general principle, big men look less furtive than small men. Large Caucasian males in the Orient are like Caesar's wife. Someone like Hubert was so impossible to hide he was as trustworthy as a circus elephant. Only I knew he was a rogue. And, especially, if he was a genial, open fellow like Hubert he was ushered to the head of the line, doors flew open for him.

Gold, I think, was the major part of Faud's solution. Everyone in Bohaiden knew of the need of perfectly respectable middle-class Indians to smuggle currencies and bullion, let alone the Mumbai sharks Faud had got amongst. The rupee was about as useful externally as bartering betel nut. That nut will figure, by the way. Hubert was decked out with more jewellery than Faud's third (and, of course, youngest) wife: chunky signet-ring, medallion not unlike

Atty Caladong's Rotarian's, plus a diamond – and more importantly for an Arab – emerald-encrusted 24-K Rolex Oyster that did not require Tabasco or lemon to make an Asian's mouth water. Do I have to say it didn't make my mouth water? Fr. Paul, that man of thin and bitter essences, had left his mark upon me. The English Gentleman's preference, even were he the most faithful of recusant sons, was for a Protestant plainness, not baroque. I had been taught to detest material ostentation as if it was a loathsome disease of the skin. I loved the intangible. My quest was knowledge, not lucre. I valued the travails but I was prepared to donate the Grail. Under my, I admit, unlikely exterior beat a true snob's heart. So when Hubert said, extending his arm and rotating his hairy wrist, "That's a mighty purty time-piece," my nostril curved and my lip twitched. Man, I'd rather have carried a sun-dial. "You pucking crazy eejit, man," my dead, invisible shoulder-imp remonstrated. "Give it to someone as does affreciate da gift."

Faud at the dhow's cooking-fire in its sand-pit, enclosed by a giant iron-basket, gave us an oily smile. The goddam Bohaidenese. They brought sand on a dhow not just as a fire-precaution but to remind themselves, I think, of what they had come from and were. If Rolex had made a gold and diamond egg-timer they'd have ordered one of those, too. I seized Hubert's wrist. "Surprised your baboon wasn't wearing one of these, too, Mr Hubert," then caught the sun on the glass and flickered the dancing light into Faud's eyes before racing it up and down the mast. Petty, but satisfying. For all the notion Faud had, it might have been an Indian Navy laser. My moral stature, my generosity, was dwindling. I could feel it every day. But it was no good pretending to be Commander Smith when I wasn't. And Commander Smith's virtues, those absolutes I had been disposed to worship, I was starting to see as relatives, as part of my own Philippine family of vices. They were only successful in their own context, in a better society. Standards you could live up to in London or Seattle simply ensured your doom in Bohaiden or Manila or Bombay or Surabaya. The Commander Smiths had to become like us lesser breeds there or just fail to survive. The Commander could denounce his own daughter to the English police, to the Hong Kong police, conceivably to the Singapore police. But to Manila's finest? To the Indians? No way, Jose. Not unless he wanted her raped, kidnapped, or the squeeze put on himself ad infinitum. To be noble, to be large-minded amongst the beady of eye and sharp of tooth, was to ask to share the ultimate fate of the giant, browsing dinosaurs. But didn't I know now that there was one ray of light? For spite on a friend's behalf was no longer spite. Sly revenges became an impartial reckoning. Small-mindedness where no personal advantage can be gained is simply a martyr's attention to detail. "I'll be the one to watch Hubert's back," I said to myself. "Like I did the Commander's." What was I? A benevolent Iago who watched and listened and never snitched.

Out of sight of land and when the captain used his sails as auxiliaries, we could have been the contemporaries of Sinbad. I wouldn't have been surprised to see the Roc flap past instead of the frittering jet wakes of the Air Bohaiden Airbus. Our keel carved through waters that were immemorial trade lanes centuries before Magellan ever set foot on Mactan, perhaps before even the Phoenicians Fr. Paul told us about ran to Cornwall for their cargoes of gold and tin. Hubert, improbably disguised as an Afghan with hennaed sideboards – how many of those guys had Swiss chronometers to go with the Russian assault-rifles? – made his stand with me, the Ugandan *hajji*, by the main-mast. A rag-tag of Bohaidenese merchants and the Gulf's waifs and strays were getting splashed at the bow, but were still immersed in a form of knuckle-bones, played out of a leathern cup. Man, if it wasn't gambling I'd like to have known what it was. Once Mumbai came in sight Hubert and I were to turn without so much as a clash of cymbals or puff of coloured smoke into our true selves. Whatever they were.

Ali, at my instance, was along for this ride. He surprised me by throwing up over the side in the calmer seas of the second day. You would have thought he'd have been proof against any forms of motion sickness after the camel racing. The "little varmint" as Hubert called him, had just six weeks ago arrived at puberty at a horribly precocious age. He was probably nine or ten-years old. Commander Smith could have come up with a forensic estimate of this by peering at his few surviving teeth. I had become aware of recent physical development when I came across him masturbating as ferociously as if he was urging one of his humped mounts to the finishing-line, his soiled gown rucked up around his waist, bare heels drumming the floor and crop-hand employed on himself. Maribeth was with me and she had been less disconcerted than I was. "Let him milk himself, *na lang,"* she'd sighed, "otherwise he is such a nuisance." While exciting himself he'd been poring over Maribeth's College Yearbook as adjuvant literature – 2x2 b&w mugshots of Filipinas in white mortar-boards – which I accounted either the depth of desperation or the height of imagination. On the dhow's short voyage he had continued in the practice of his new hobby with an assiduity that gave indications of it becoming a life-long enthusiasm. Otherwise, he was still the same scrawny, green-eyed little monster with the filthy vocabulary which he now knew the true significance of. "Kid's kinda ornery," Hubert said. "Why in hell did you bring him?"

"*Hindi po*, Mister Hubert," I said, Hubert liking to pretend he could speak Tagalog, though he used to give us, the rude workforce, hernias when he said *Boracay* Captain instead of *Barangay* Captain. "Ali is our back-stop. I trust him. If Faud's gonna poison us or dump us over the side, Ali will warn us."

"Oh, right," said Hubert. As the possessor of an American passport, this possibility had not even occurred to him. Hubert thought of himself as a hunter but, man, he was no carnivore, strictly a lumbering herbivore.

Still, Mumbai began as a walkover. We docked; we were processed; we disembarked. I discovered its older, more familiar name and winced at myself. Only Hubert's bag was searched for that most innocent of palliatives, a bottle of whisky. Then he and I came ashore, Hubert now in blue jeans again, and handed over our jewellery to Faud, Hubert more wistfully than me. After that we accompanied our master to some weird office with frosted glass partitions and ceiling fans the size of ship's propellers. It didn't look like it had changed since 1951. It probably hadn't. Faud told us to leave him in the time-warp, but we took Ali with us. A fat Indian at a typewriter had been glaring at Ali, pretending to be hostile but I had the impression that he wanted to fuck him in the ass, not that Ali wouldn't have done it for the price of a haircut.

Hubert was spooked by the Indian city. This surprised me and made me feel superior until I remembered he was by his own admission used to the wide-open spaces. The Empty Quarter wasn't such a shock after the forests and the mountains but the sheer press of humanity on the street here panicked him. Even I, used to Colon on a wet day, Luneta on a fine, was taken aback. It was worse than our little Trasimene, the frat-fight where we splattered Eleuterio III, the pol's son we'd had to run for, who had started my Odysseyette. The Bombay lanes were humanity in congealed form, moving like treacle, strange ripples running through the crowd. I'd never been on a street so tight-packed. Whole acreages were like this. The city at this time appeared to have two colours – grey and red. Where the overpowering throng thinned, relented, and released you into the wide area of a square or major intersection you felt crushed again, by the space. Humanity was absent here because these were inhuman vastnesses. It was perilous to occupy them because of the bellowing traffic or – I hazarded a guess – where the prospect of being run over was not imminent because it was a forbidden zone, where lingering might bring down the long stick-blows of the law. And here the scheme was a prevailing metal-grey, made up of dust, unpainted walls, drain-water, and the ungiving thoroughfare. A hand-cart full of sharks the shade of steel, but bleeding pink where they'd been gaffed, trundled past, matching the ground, for the unremitting duskiness of the pavement was broken by scarlet splotches at frequent but unpredictable intervals. I had no advantage over Hubert here. At the fourth splash we turned slowly to each other with the same wild but certain surmise.

"Poor fucker's hit but bad," Hubert said. "Bright red, man, it's arterial an' it's pumpin' out – see how far the specks at the edges have sprayed out from the main gout in the centre? Like a goddam aerosol – gotta be the aorta or the femoral artery. An' he's still runnin' real hard."

An air of total normality prevailed: the shops and stalls swarmed with as many onlookers as those of home and concluded a cash sale just as rarely; shoe-repairers, scissor-grinders, watch-menders, beggars chatted nonchalantly with each other. People made no special effort to avoid the pools of blood; they failed to curse or give superstitious exclamations when they did step in them in their bare feet. And that was quite unlike home. Were Hindus so accustomed to slaughter? In the way you do, I'd picked up cues in the half a morning we'd been there: smells, sounds, facial expressions. Many Indians were smilers of the same happy Philippine smile as my compatriots; some were nondescript. But many were otherwise. On the whole they were a fierce-looking set, martial. Especially the guys in the turbans, like the one Dant had seen at the airport en route to the seminary. When I thought of Filipinos, we were just kids losing our tempers – even the wickedest among us – behaving with childish spite but unfortunately with adult hardware easily to hand. But Indians! When I gazed at the faces around us, they seemed pitiless individually, implacable in the mass. They bore the same lack of kindliness on the face as the Bohaidenese, the same unswerving self-interest but without the underlying weakness of the Bohaidenese. These dudes were poorer and tougher one on one but, most of all, I dreaded the prospect of them as a mob. Give me my quietus with a clean gunshot any day, even one of Hubert's polypropylene-flighted bodkins in the mortal spot.

We continued on down the lane, the odours of leather, smoke, incense, and drains sliceable in the air. "Biggest spoor I ever done followed," Hubert commented. "Maybe it ain't a bank-robber, maybe it's a goddamned tiger."

"Yeah," I said. "Where the fuck's Ali?" We'd been neglecting to mark the little runt. This was always a mistake with the small but terrible, as I'd learned with Dant. From left field he appeared, with a limping fat woman in pursuit. I had a feeling she hadn't been limping till she met Ali.

"O you pig's cunt," I addressed him. "Where hast thou been?"

"Behind thy mother, Black One," he answered. My swiping cuff contacted the thinnest air. Ali pulled what looked like an ammonite from a Fr. Boy geology lecture, but both orange and sticky, from his grubby pocket and added it to the mess around his mouth. I flipped the fat woman a few of the coins Faud had given us – quite ignorant of their value but cognisant of the fact that you never bought street-food with notes, however small – and left her swearing, with no doubt the Hindi for "Nigger" ringing in my peaceable ears. I would have thought she'd have been pleased – a sale's a sale.

Big blood patches lay before us, going round the corner, and mysteriously in the middle of the road going in the other direction. "There's two hit?" I queried. Hubert, head bent, one foot on the pavement, one on the street, resembled a huge, lugubrious tracker dog from Disney. At that point an old woman hoiked right by him. Clearly she hadn't been shot through the lungs but she'd still expectorated a bright, frothy mouthful.

"Betel!" Hubert and I chorused.

Knowing it was just saliva, lime, and areca nut didn't make us any less disposed to avoid stepping in it, actually more anxious to avoid contamination. The life-blood of the hearty young man one always assumes to be the most likely recipient of a gunshot wound was innocuous compared to the diseased tubercular mouthful of some old crone.

The poverty here was of a different order and magnitude from back home; I'd got that message in the first ten minutes of landing. The compound of stinks which my pauper's olfactory cells could break down into their separate essences at a speed that defied thought – our Mactan alleys being full of the heavy stench of stale urine but not the lighter, sour reek of human shit prevalent here – the spectacular skin diseases and enormous tumours which matched those in Maribeth's dermatological colour atlas, the swollen bellies of the kids, the stick limbs of the starving elderly: all those told their own story to me. Their bodies and their clothes were filthy as well as their environment, whereas Aunties Irish, Monalisa & Co lived in hovels on miry alleys but dressed in whites as fastidiously self-laundered as those of a princess waited on by an army of servitors. In short, when you were starving to death you didn't give a fuck about appearances. Filipinos lived one notch above that. In times of hardship for the others, we'd always had a cup of rice for them.

A stone, rather than, say, a Winchester .30 slug thumped against Hubert's backside – not the most difficult target in the world. I was in time to catch the local urchin in the posture of classic follow-through, clearly not coached, but serving to prove Butch Tan Sy's theoretical dictum that frequent repetition of any particular action will naturally lead the performer to the most economical and efficient technique. Could've been primitive man on his first hunting forays, but this was lost on Ali who'd been goading the local juveniles with the international signal of right index finger rubbed through the fork of left index and middle finger. Ali now took the missile projected at Hubert as an infringement by proxy on his own space. He pulled from his robes a wicked-looking two-inch hilt-less dagger. I was able to hit him this time, much more solidly than I intended. He dropped like a stricken fighter and I only just got my hand to his curly head in time to stop it slamming on a large stone. Hubert gave me a funny look but didn't say anything. He was a 'Merikano, Hubert, but he was cool. Much as the brutally unchivalrous tactics of Jenny Smith's knight-errant, Jerome, had worked in Malaysia, so my unintentional heavy-handedness now extricated us from an uncomfortable but by no means dangerous situation. No one wanted to get within ten feet of a two-hundred pound nigger who punched out ten-year-olds. I carried little Ali as if he was made from polysterene or balsa.

"This place," pronounced Hubert, in the manner of a philosopher having addressed a knotty problem for some years, "is the fucking pits."

"Well, give it a chance, Mister Hubert," I remonstrated half-heartedly.

"Would they give me one? No. Man, this place makes Smoky Mountain look like Beverley Hills."

"I'm not arguing with that."

We were now striding briskly through a better area on the way back to the sea-front. There were even some palm-trees. Ali had not stirred since I picked him up. Twenty minutes later, I became suspicious. I could have carried him for ever and a day, but on principle I disliked being tricked. I think that was part of being a big guy. Big guys were dumb. Big guys got duped. I smiled. I uttered the formulaic preamble, just to get Ali's attention, then followed up with, "I shall drop this imp into the convenient ordure here, much like that from which his father and mother sprang." With an oath Ali leapt out of my arms and then compounded the first curse with a filthier one when he saw how he had been tricked into dismounting.

"You say you were gonna fart, in Arabic?" Hubert asked.

"Sah," I replied. "You is a low reprobate."

If the tone of our exchanges remained resolutely gutter-bound, our surroundings continued to improve. Unlike the garden- and gate-obsessed affluent of Manila or Cebu, the Bombay bourgeoisie appeared to favour high-rise apartments, not unlike those of Singapore or Hong Kong. What they were like inside I'd never know but from the exterior to an eye less expert than Hubert's, but considerably better schooled than my pre-hoddie days, they looked very slightly lower-spec than Chinese construction.

Bamboo and rattan scaffolding covered the fronts of many of these buildings, materials as tough, lightweight, flexible and adaptable as our own Ali. I knew that from Hong Kong. You could build a staircase to the moon with it. We were plainly in the Mumbai maintenance season. Just then four skeletal dudes in loincloths wriggled through a window like so many snakes and swarmed down the giant rungs of the scaffolding, passing a TV set between them slicker than Artheneum forwards could pass the ball. Hube rolled his eyes. I figured chopping off a hand wouldn't be enough with these guys, more like two legs as well.

Ali had been sulking in the rear. I did feel some contrition, but knew it would be a mistake to show a glimmer. Ali scowled at me before addressing his imprecations to an invisible third party at pavement level. There you were: normally he wouldn't have shrunk from directing them at me. You conversed with people in their own language. There was a lot to be said for brutality used on the brutal, in measured doses.

"See them balconies?" Hubert asked. "Two per apartment? Why don't they join 'em? More space for livin'. They coulda made a kinda Hangin' Gardens of Bombay, haw-haw."

"Mr Hubert," I remonstrated, "it's me, man, not Faud."

"What?"

"You know, cut the b-s."

I was now treated to a spectacle I'd never conceived possible, Hubert looking offended. Or trying to. He might have looked like that when he saw the baboon bust his arrow. By the time we'd reached the sleazier part of the docking-area, Ali had forgiven me, was holding my hand and was wiping his snot-green nose on my slippery forearm, while Hubert sauntered ahead, probably now sufficiently acclimatised to start worrying about the prospect of his pay-packet.

Faud was in a real good mood. Whether this augured well for Hubert was moot. Gone was the Three Wise Men outfit. Our boss was in a blue safari-suit and, yeah, he reeked of after-shave. I could see he wanted to say something, was bursting to take somone into his confidence, but was too smart to be so indiscreet with Hubert and me. Basically, he lacked class and address as a businessman. The wizened, bald little merchants of Hong Kong or Singapore never showed a flicker of emotion, whether they were about to lose their life's savings or close-in on the biggest bonanza of the decade. Even the Lebanese café-owners cum money-changers played a better hand of poker than that. Faud was just a jumped-up Gulfie hard-hat when it came to it.

Anyhow, he sent off for flat bread, savoury vegetable messes, stew and rice, all in stainless steel containers locked on top of each other.

These shiny, sanitary boxes inspired confidence in the consumer of their contents. Man, they'd have conferred hygienic ethos and culinary clout on triple-layer turd nestling in piss for brine. Hubert, who had spent ten years in Saudi, was actually better at eating with his fingers than I was. Did I say he was a neat cook himself? Many the forbidden shell-fish chowder and licit free-range custard-tart I had in his kitchen. I'd unconsciously tried to lose the stereotype that fat men, on the whole, liked food. I put obesity down to glands and genetic accident, rather than over-indulgence. But, hey, plenty of fat men were great cooks. The Jenny Smith way of thinking was insidious; it had infected me, me who thought of himself as a head-case gorilla upstairs – a jumper from convention – as well as physically on a basketball-court.

"Some lime-pickle with your lamb, Mr Hubert?" I asked solicitously and got grunts for no.

"Please," said Faud, gesturing as gracefully as only an Arab dispensing hospitality to the useful could. "Please, it is for you. It is my very great pleasure."

The dhow had emptied. The waifs and strays had scattered. Only we remained. I was uncertain whether this was because Faud was tight on the trip purse-strings, or nervous. Hubert was much more restive than I was. How long we stayed wasn't a big source of concern to me. My time hadn't been my own since I scrambled fifty feet up the side of the freighter in Manila Bay. It was all the same to me. I'd climbed half a hundred feet but descended into another world, that of the international under-class who were the slaves of our century. Hubert, though, was a free man and he thought of his time as valuable. He was lingering; I was having a break from the site. The concept of wasting time just didn't apply to me; it was torture for Hubert.

On the third day Faud returned to the dhow looking both resigned and jumpy, again a difficult act but he managed these incompatibles. "I have a deal," he said, "we have the grrr-eeen light."

"Thank You, Lord," I said.

Faud smiled deprecatingly and patted me on the back. He was under the impression I was calling him Our Lord. "That's great news, sir," Hubert said more moderately. Man, it was no good being moderate with an Arab.

"You resolved the misunderstanding, serr?" I asked. "May I inquire if it was difficult for your family?" This was Faud's own euphemism for prohibitively expensive, as when you asked for wages in arrears only to be informed, "Right now, it's a leel difficult for my family."

"Very," admitted Faud, all the readier to tell us the truth in that it acquainted us with the fact that there was less cake to go round for us. "But everything is not guarrr-anteed yet. You, Mr Hubert, will stay here on the boat tomorrow. You, the nigger, er Rey, accompanying me."

"Yes, serr."

That night I had a few words with Ali, shortly before he curled up in his usual place across the lintel of the round-house prohibiting access to me, who slept as always the sleep of the just. "Guard the Fat One," I instructed Ali, "as if he was Thine Sister." This fulsome exhortation received a growl of assent. There is nothing the untrustworthy like more than a display of trust in them. One of the reasons I could manipulate Ali, where adult Bohaidenese could as soon control a mosquito, was that I, or at least my friends, had been him once. Up to a point, travel and the encounters it forced upon you emphasised the differences between human beings, the contrasts between the Babyjanes and Huberts of this world but, beyond that, you started to remark the similarities as well, the dawning possibility that there might be a Bohaidenese Commander Smith or an American Atty Caladong.

In the pre-dawn darkness Faud and I came off the dhow, still yawning. The crew used to take the gang-plank up for security before turning in, so I had the task, single-handed, of laying it on the jetty again. To my mind, it would have been better to have left this narrow, slippery, unsteady, nail-strewn relic of the True Cross in place as a deadly man-trap. Faud, with an interesting brief-case, very nearly fell off and was glad of my aid. I was surprised how hard his hand still was, considering I'd never seen him so much as pat a hollow-block. Squatting figures were accomplishing their morning unmentionable singly, or to my innocent wonder, communally. Faud's nostrils wrinkled in distaste. Those semitic flanges were well-suited to that expression. Proximity in the dhow had taught me that he was particularly punctilious about performing a certain penile ablution. "Filthy Hounds," I heard him say. The sterility of the desert was still with him. They really weren't city-folk, the Bohaidenese.

We got into a rickshaw, the skinny-shanked, dhoti-clad drawer looking askance at me, the overt agenda my weight, the real issue my darkness. Either way, I thought, Faud was gonna have to find a few paise more. The little guy got into his rhythm – the secret of all physical performance, recreational or combative – and we spanked along. He was fit but not healthy. Faud was healthy but not fit. Lucky me, I was both. We arrived, but not at the office of yesteryear, the one with the cream-painted ceiling-fans. I imagined Jenny Smith rhapsodising over it. She wouldn't have wet her pants over this. We were outside a warren, an area of curving lanes and alleyways more like the mazes of home than Bohaiden. It didn't spook me like it did Faud, but it surely got my dander, put me on my mettle. I was on the *qui vive*, as Fr. Paul liked to say.

"Aiya! I don't like this!" Faud exclaimed.

I put my hand firmly on his shoulder. "We will accomplish what you have come to do, Serr." I strode in, Faud following. I had not the faintest notion whither we were destined, but I knew that Faud would go in eventually but that he'd dither in the uncool Arab way (as opposed to Pepe Pinoy's let's-hang-out-and-see attitude) which would only send the wrong signals to every shark in the vicinity. It was safer to be bold.

Behind me Faud tip-toed through the nuisances, holding his case like a crusader shield. "What's your order, serr?" I asked "You have a street or a number?"

"Nair's coffee-shop," he said. "Exactly where here, I don't know." That, I thought, is just great. I recalled Atty Caladong with a degree of wistfulness that surprised me.

"We'd better ask directions," I said.

This threw Faud into a panic. "But no. People will think we're lost. Then they will rob us." The desert-wayfarer's fear, getting lost, which then led ineluctably to falling among thieves.

"They think we're lost already," I said grimly. "And, you know what, they're right." Already stray phantoms were crossing and re-crossing with suspicious frequency on the periphery of our vision, like the larger finned predators in murky water. Faud's apple of Adam went down and up. I started to hum. I felt blither than I had for some time. I mean, it wasn't my money which ran the risk of being stolen and I didn't think any of the half-dead dudes infesting these stews was gonna find the step-ladder to take a pop at me.

Filipinos weren't the modern Spartans, not by a long way, but irresponsibility is a great emboldener – nuthin' left to lose, as Danton liked to sing – and my size had made neither a bully nor a coward of me. Faud, on the other hand, was coming out in his native colours. The Bohaiden flag should have been brown with a yellow streak. "Wh-a-a-at?" he croaked aggressively at a sly and ragged wallah who made to touch his case. I knew this couldn't be pig's skin, of course, but wondered if cowhide might not have conferred some extra protection here. The rickshaw-puller had been compelled to break his momentum once on the way as he waited for a sacred beast to rise from where it blocked the road, and subsequently his short, harsh breathing told me how lactic he'd got during the respite.

More low-lifers joined the fellow near Faud, detritus, whether sea-borne or wind-gleaned, having the habit of collecting together. As usual, no one came within arm-span of King Kong. It was the weirdest molestation I ever saw, slow, unspoken, but concerted; apparently aimless, but irresistible. But, as usual with a mob, they could pretend that as individuals they were not complicit in what they were perpetrating in the mass. From just a few prowlers on the fringes, Faud was suddenly in the middle of a crowd, their hands sticky, gentle, and insidious as anemone-tentacles tangling in the current. Even I was now an island in the sea of humanity, a humanity with clothes rancid from lack of sun when wet, but both the flesh of the men and their sweat heavy and sweet as raisin-rot in a humid carton. They swayed their trunks, nudged with shoulders, barged with a hip, shoved with the backside, processing us as if we were on a conveyor-belt, and not a word was spoken in their tacit conspiracy. Only there was the sound of subdued breathing in the mass, heavy as the beat of a piston in another sound-proofed chamber. Faud's few squawks at the start had become a silent, dismayed resistance. It was amazing how much stronger a crowd of puny individuals could be than a single powerful person. I'd have had more chance with Hubert's polar bears and baboons than these emaciates. Suddenly I remembered Angie Verghese's story during our drive through Malaysia. I tripped, then just found my balance again by grabbing an arm. Either the guy was perspiring remarkably or he'd oiled himself up, because it was like trying to grab a greased eel. He was away, man. I'd caught my foot on a door-step, for when I looked round again we were in a room as devoid of the signs of human occupation as a natural geological feature. Bare wasn't the operative word, man. It was starker than the Vietnamese girls' hooch in Puerto Princesa. I had the sensation of having been washed up in a rock pool by the tide. This wasn't receding by any means. More Indians were still flooding in. Faud was in a corner on the opposite side of the room. He had his eyes closed, the briefcase still over his abdomen, while his lips moved in what I surmised was a form of prayer as mechanical as the Rosary.

The expressions round us were changing from the pretence of unfocussed, impersonal, and trance-like to deliberate. It was then I saw The Smile. That grin was more than multi-national or cross-cultural, it was pandemic. They all wore it, every third-rate robber and rapist in the world, the weak links in Danton's little Mactan gang and the Frat Brods, Nikita's catamite, the cabin boy, the Arabs I'd seen hassling our girls as they promenaded, the mestizo I would see trying to slip a tourist a drug-laced drink in Cienfuegos, and half a million other assorted punks and molesters. It wasn't a question of sometimes seeing The Smile if they forgot themselves. You always saw The Smile. Such was the nature of the beast. They couldn't stop it spreading like treacle over their mugs, even those with the limited wit to turn their faces away to hide it. It was the smile of the runt, of the idiot; someone who'd always been the slowest and weakest of every group they'd ever belonged to, from whom knowledge and the control that comes with it had always been one step ahead of their grasp, who'd been the butt of every practical joke and half-baked irony they'd floundered to comprehend. And when, at last, the opportunity arrived, that moment when they knew something they thought their prospective victim didn't – the impending crime – a great beam of self-congratulation and fulfilment half-covered the habitual spite on their pans. It was the smile of the congenitally weak and stupid thinking they were being clever at someone else's expense and relishing the novelty and power of it. It was as insuppressible as Louise's giggle or Hubert's booming farts.

Well, I reckoned that was the moment to do something. At least you had the advantage of surprise. I barged my way through to Faud. People wanted to get out of my way but were so pressed together they couldn't. Indians squeezed through my knees, oozed under my armpits; I was treading out the vintage of the betel of wrath, leaving the stains underfoot. "Mr Faud," I inquired politely, "you're having some small change with you?" He didn't look at me as if I was mad or had gone over to the other side, I'll give him that, but nodded, reached into his pants pocket and came up with a confetti of small denomination greenbacks, reals, dinars, rupees, and dirhams. Small-chow, man. I doubt if it would have got him the massage part of the massage in Olongapo or Pattaya. But for the pick-pockets in dhotis around us – where did you keep coins in a loin-cloth? – it was riches beyond avarice.

"Money, folks? How much money you want, folks?" I boomed in my deepest voice, jingling the coins and brandishing the notes. "Have I got money for you." I knew it was like back home; I could speak our Auntie tongue in the furthest flung barrio or village, or in the entrails of the filthiest slums, and still be confident there was someone on hand who could understand English and pass it on to his fellows. It was the same in India.

"OK, folks," I said, winding up my arm as far as I could, "come and get it. I mean, go get," and with that I hurled the cash at the doorway, what coins there were sparkling and glowing in the timely morning sunshine. Shit, I could feel the throb of desire pass through the crowd. It wasn't the most reassuring of feelings, but worth it to see the grins wiped off the faces of the worst. I could immediately feel a relief in the pressure of bodies against us. There was chaos at the door, Indians lying on top of each other, legs waving in the air, many getting trampled in the urgent rush outside. But it needed something more. There were before me a tall, well-set fellow, a small girl of indeterminate age – she could have been anywhere between nine and nineteen – holding a remarkably hairy baby, and a very frail and inoffensive old woman with her head covered by a shawl. I could have knocked the sturdy fellow down with the full-blooded swing I was now in a position to take, throttled the girl and lifted her out of her leather sandals one-handed, swung the baby by its heels and dashed its brains out against the wall, or picked on the little old woman. I did the latter.

Bending down in the hoddie's as well as the point-guard's crouch, I put one hand under her bony gluteus, steadied her with the other on the clavicle and projected her as if she was a witch on an invisible broomstick fifteen feet to the other side of the room. This was accomplished with what I would call smooth ferocity.

Man, she sailed. The crowd was still thick where she landed, so though I'd thrown her to within centimetres of the ceiling she only had to drop to head- or shoulder-height where her fall was broken. She didn't make a sound during her neat trajectory but on landing turned and bestowed upon me an uncategorisable look, what Mrs Smith called "old-fashioned", but the indignation mixed with some gratitude. *"In nomine Patris, Filii, et Spiritui Sancti,"* I intoned, suiting the words with the appropriate gesture. If the old girl appreciated the quality of the cast, those underneath her were not in a position to comprehend it. All they knew was I seemed as indiscriminate as their own *lathi*-wielding police. Those in whom the sense of self-preservation was as lively as their grasp of financial opportunity redoubled their efforts to escape. Soon Faud and I had most of the room to ourselves.

"Shall we, serr?" I murmured and into the alley we proceeded. I stepped with fake purpose towards a group of malingerers in the direction opposite to where we were headed, sending them tumbling and tripping backwards. A couple of boys, caught by surprise when we continued in our real direction, cringed as I passed very close to them. Learning from experience, I seized one by his breeches instead of the arm. "Where's Nair's Coffee-shop?" I demanded, intensifying my glare when no answer was forthcoming. The kid's eyes were glazed with fright. I don't think another Indian and certainly not a white guy or an Oriental – even a Jap or a Korean – could have produced the same impression upon him. I relented, even though he was a victim of his own base prejudices. What did he think? I'd eat him? "You?" I rounded on his pal. He pointed a shaking finger. "OK, kid. Maybe you can flip him a coin, Mr Faud?"

"Already all gone."

I wasn't sure I believed this. Once the crisis was past, Faud was reverting to his old ways. "Let us leave," he said, "while we can now."

"Serr," I said firmly, "we will do what we have come to do. Nair's, now." Who did I think I was, you may well ask? At a pinch I could be a Nigger Jeeves but Faud was one hell of an unlikely Bertie Wooster. I think this was a situation – floundering alone together in the ocean, out of sight of land, snow-bound on Everest – where normal social roles and ties were snapped. And I, the younger, the stronger, the smarter, was not the one to be led. But, of course, I was also hoping to get something out of it for myself afterwards, a tip, a favour, even – silly me – Faud's gratitude.

The aforenamed place of refreshment, Nair's, was incongruously clean and spacious, although in a no less contaminated part of the warren. Faud's contact rose from his table and everything, expression, body language, told me we hadn't been set-up. i.e. the mess we'd got ourselves into had been our own fucking fault. Faud's fazed expression alerted the fat middle-class Indian that something was amiss. "Everything is OK?" he inquired. Of course, he would care. He had a vested interest in the Arab not being robbed. "OK," I said swiftly. The Indian frowned. "Who is this?" he asked in the higher-pitched, querulous tone that is the birth-right of the educated Indian. I had yet to learn it then but Indians and negroes were natural enemies, like dog and cat.

"I am Mr Faud's bodyguard," I said firmly, trying to make it sound like I was licensed to kill. So shut the fuck up, man.

"My right-hand boy," said Faud with restored smoothness. That I liked. Sure as hell, it was better than being an Arabo's left-hand man.

I didn't need to be told I wasn't wanted as listener-in at the table, so I posted myself at the front just in from the street. This was one of those typical Asian establishments which was completely open, no door, with an iron grille drawn across at night. From here I scowled at the assorted urchins, gutter-snipes, and would-be warriors who were beginning to re-gather on the other side of the street. I figured that was OK. It wasn't doing-range, just gawping distance. I figured it was uncool to look back in on Faud. Etiquette of the bodyguard; the heavies didn't do it in any of the movies Dant and I had taken in at the empty, gelid matinees of Mactan and Mandaue. But, of all things, there was a Chinese *fung shui* mirror above the cashier. He had looked pure Indian up till then, if creamy-skinned. Now he got Chinkier and Chinkier. In the hexagon of glass Faud was unbuttoning his safari-tunic and pulling up his shirt as if he was going to expose himself to the fat Indian. I looked out to the front again but the cashier had caught my sideways glance. "You Chinese?" I asked hopefully.

"Nepalese," he answered despondently.

Faud tapped me on the shoulder, visibly lightened: "We'll be the ones to go. The gentleman will show us the way."

"Serr."

As we rounded the corner, there was a shout, obviously a Parthian shot aimed at me. "What's that?" quavered Faud, whose new confidence was skin-deep.

"I think he called me a Nigger, Serr."

"No," volunteered the Fat Indian. "A sister-fucker." His eyes shone behind his spectacles. At the main road he shook Faud's hand and didn't look at me. The same rickshaw was waiting. We returned to the dock at a brisk clip, the slap-slap of the drawer's soles suggestive of either *bastinado* or masturbation, the two things I remembered most from *Midnight Express*, a film which had put both Danton and me off drug-smuggling well before we ever joined a Frat. The rhythm began to make me feel langorous, then sleepy. What with our early start my head lolled and I surrendered to the moment. Minutes later, Faud's hoarse cry woke me from the depths. The couple of seconds it took to focus on our surroundings made it already too late to spot the malefactor who'd snatched Faud's brief-case and then legged it against the grain of the traffic in the other lane, but as my eyes came back from the melee of vehicles and humanity surrounding us – no more or less confused for the momentary agitation of the theft and flight – one thing was plain as the burning day. Our puller had been in on it. The Look told me that. What was more, when he caught my eye he knew I knew.

I waited for Faud to blame me but either he hadn't noticed I'd dropped off or he wasn't quite the old woman I imagined him. Our thighs and shoulders rubbed companionably enough for the remaining fifteen minutes to the dhow.

"Don't pay this guy, Mr Faud," I insisted as we alighted from the rickshaw, a recommendation Faud did his level best to appear reluctant to follow before mincing up the gang-plank, leaving the rickshaw-puller shoving his empty palm at thin air. Half-way up the gang-plank myself, I got a terrific kick in the backside, but weighty like it was from a medium-sized beast of burden. I just kept my balance but nearly lost it again when I tried to turn too quickly to see what had happened. By the time I arrived on the deck, the rickshaw-puller's sinewy but obviously ostrich-strong legs had taken him a good way to the dock-gates, beyond pursuit even had I wished to chase him. Pushing himself up to arms-length on the railings, Ali shrieked abuse. In his seventy-two hours in India he had contrived to learn at least two words of Hindi. I recognised them. They were "sister-fucker".

Faud was greatly amused by the kick I'd taken on his behalf. His good humour was explained when he revealed that his briefcase had been empty from the moment we'd left the dhow. "It was all in my money-belt," he explained. "No sweating, you say, Mr Hubert?"

"Yeah, no sweat, Mr Faud. No sweat, man."

BACK IN BOHAIDEN WE HAD TO RELENT A LITTLE ABOUT FAUD. Looking on it now, I may have painted him, as it were, too black. For me he was always tarred by association with the other Arabs. Out of the context I knew him in, he might have succeeded in being a regular guy.

The girders came; the building continued. I did wonder why Faud bothered. Shortly after our return I read an article in a seven months out of date current affairs magazine in Ahmed, the Lebanese's, coffee-shop. I was an avid reader of this particular mag: prose as lively as the inscription on a tomb-stone but packed with info and great pics. There was an article on Bombay, and I learned how the property prices there were the highest on earth, exceeding those of New York, Tokyo, and even Hong Kong. The totally indifferent blocks Hubert and I had passed were worth three times the Smith's place in Singapore, itself ten times the value of Atty Caladong's galvanised-iron and marble palace in Q.C. The freehold area of twenty uptown betel splashes, I calculated, must amount to more than the entire Philippine OCW population of Bohaiden could remit home in a month. I figured Faud could have avoided giving himself a headache and made a shrewder investment by just buying a pad on Marine Drive. Reckoning he could be a mite sensitive on the subject, I kept this thought to myself.

Lo and behold, Hubert got his reward. What Gulf oil-workers had wet dreams about on the rigs: a week in Pattaya.

"Wow!" I said. "That's great, Mr Hubert," with a beam on my face to match the words. I was really pleased for him. I knew what a horny, sex-starved son of a bitch he was. But his blunt, honest face was clouded.

"What's wrong, Hube?"

"What's wrong? You're what's wrong. How about you?"

"Me? Shucks, Hubert. I don't count. Sitting the game out on the bench, man."

"No, you ain't."

I could see the tic in his plump cheek going; it came when he was being particularly dogged. "Well, don't get Faud riled."

"Riled? Fuck him."

Lo and behold (load and be holed, as it once memorably appeared in Danton's dictation-book), Faud arrived waving his hands, with expressionless Hubert to his rear. "A misunderstanding," he grimaced, "the travel agents misinterpreted my instructions. Of course you are to go with Mr Hubert. Of course. The smallest of recompenses for my great obligation. But of course."

We had three nights of seaside R & R on the Gulf of Thailand, courtesy of Faud, with another night in Bangkok, before it was back to our own oil-rich Gulf which was in every sense, literal and figurative, a less polluted sea. So far as I was concerned, Pattaya with its bar-beers was but the adult equivalent of the funfair in Pinocchio where the naughty boys first find their ears lengthening before they turn completely into jackasses. I put this to Hubert as we had what I think was our sixth Singha beer on Soi 8 (or maybe our eighth Singha on Soi 6). Hubert was ogling the bar-maid, while I hoped the kick-boxers on the video came no larger than 126-pounds. "Haw-haw," laughed Hubert, which seemed to prove my point. The guy was like a vampire in a blood-bank. He did fifteen girls in the time we were there. This reflected well on Hubert's staying-power but like all stats could be massaged into being more flattering than the reality: he was having two or even three girls at a time but ejaculating the once. Pretty well like shish-kebabing three baboons on the same arrow.

As for me, I still couldn't do it with a prostie. No surprise. The girls looked alarmingly like Aunties Lovely-Anne, Monalisa, and Ma. Northern Thai girls resembled southern Philippine girls. The only words of the language I knew were *luk krueng* and *baht* but I had a sixth sense for what the girls were saying and thinking that required no interpretation. I'd seen the looks, the slouches, the significant glances in the mirror they sneaked each other. I'd as soon have fucked corpses and, man, I've had the opportunity but not the inclination for that. I just made sure Hubert got the best prices and no one laced his drinks. I went parascending off the dun beach and, hey, we went to the archery-range ten miles away for some clean fun. I was surprised. Hube was good. Far better than his spear-fishing. He shot a sequence called a London Round well enough to get a bunch of flowers.

In the early hours of the morning while Hubert banged three Laotian girls next door, I dreamed of us in the round-house of the dhow, Hubert an overweight Alan Breck with a bow instead of a rapier and me as an unlikely David Balfour while we defended Faud at his accounts from the mutinous construction-crew. Hube, who could be surprisingly sensitive and gentlemanly, never asked me why I hadn't had a fuck but unnecessarily apologised for his carnal appetites. "Guess, I shoulda learned wisdom a long ways back, Rey, in Taiwan."

"Taiwan?"

"Yeah. First job I took in Asia. Had a 'Merikana for a wife then. You know me, boy. Couldn't keep my hands off them little Chinese gals. The Chinese guys didn't like that too much: dick envy, man, like the Japs. Cut a long story short, I was a-top a little gal in the VIP room of the karaoke when the law busts in. Mean-lookin' Chinese ass-holes in uniform. They throws me in a cell but not before they've stripped me bare-assed. Then they phoned my wife and told her to come get me because they found me with a whore, which she done, introduced to me in my cell buck naked as I was. She never got over that, man. That was it."

"Gee, well, I can tell you, Apple Jusilynn would cut your pecker off but she wouldn't divorce you."

"Too right, but that wasn't the end of it. Look here."

Hubert opened his passport to reveal enormous blood-red Chinese characters stamped across the front-page.

"What's that say?"

"FORNICATOR."

"Shit! At least they didn't tattoo it on your dick."

"Yeah, well it back-fired on them. All the bachelors in town wanted to get that stamp, man. It wasn't a competition, so much as a stampede. I ain't ever forgiven the little yellow fuckers, though."

Hubert's indignation told me the story was almost certainly true and it fitted in with my preconceptions about ancient Chinese bureaucracy and their modern love of the slogan. What would the Indians have done? Stamped it in triplicate?

Hubert continued to make a pig of himself at the bar-beers while I turned down the propositions as gracefully as I could. The girls and the ladyboys weren't in the business of insulting potential customers anyhow, but I detected a change in the status of the *luk krueng*, the once despised Amerasian. In such slight nuances of behaviour can great social changes be detected. They thought of me as amusing, glamorous, rather than a sorry product of miscegenation; in a word, cool. It wasn't a question of me, the individual; it was a matter of me, the type. That was OK by me.

At Bahrain airport, in transit, another omen of change. The joint was crawling with Russian whores, girls with the hardest eyes I'd ever seen. Pebbles were softer. There was utter pitilessness in them, unredeemed by a certain brazen calculation. Most of them had dyed blonde hair, including the natural blondes, and favoured the tinselly look: speckled nail polish, glittering sweaters (you saw these in modern Arabia because the bazaar was no longer a soukh but a frigid mall). They looked like Christmas trees. Oddly enough, this chimed in with Arab taste, as did the ample circumference of most of the chicks. Half the whores in Southern Russia seemed to have descended on the place.

I heard the voices and I had an instant attack of the creeps. My whole arm tautened with goose-pimples. Hubert noticed and said, "Hey, you cold? You wanna put on some more insulation. My undercoat's hundred per cent natural, man, like a seal." I smiled sickly enough for Hubert to ask, "You OK? I didn't hear they had malaria in Pattaya."

"Yeah. Just a blast from the past, Hube. I'll be OK."

The girls were bargaining over electronic gear. They wheeled carts full of VCR's, TV's, CD's, and computers. For once the Arab hucksters seemed to have met their match. The girls didn't smile once during the bargaining, even when they got the price they wanted. Smiling was not a Slavonic characteristic. Not unless they were carrying a hidden sword-bayonet and were planning a ducking after a fucking for you. But Hubert said, "Ten to one the gear don't work when they play it back home. The A-rabs know these broads won't be back in a big hurry from Volgograd or Odessa, or wherever the fuck."

"I wonder how many Arabs plugged into *them*."

"Shit, how many stars are there in heaven? I know I ain't got the cojones for it, man."

We regarded the girls some more, a distinct but new tribe for me. The leader of a group with trolleys still empty was half-way through negotiations with a leering young Arab half her weight. "Hewlett

Packard," he was insisting, "is the best. The best. You get other printers under other brand-name, it's a HP in disguise. They make all the laser printer. All."

"*Nyet,*" persisted the Russian girl, who I was glad to see had also peroxided her moustache, "I know Star Printer the only one can make Cyrillic alphabets. You give Star-ski but very cheaper." Her best friend nudged her. She'd clocked our interest. Whether it was prurient, or a business rival's, or just casual, she didn't like it. Both Hubert and I got the eyeball treatment. We quailed. This was a guy who if you believed him (I didn't) had aimed at polar bears with a draw-hand that didn't shake and a guy, me, who'd sunk crucial free throws in front of baying Manila collegians without so much as grazing the hoop. As we retreated, my ever increasing vocabulary was augmented by the Russian or Ukrainian for "Nigger".

"World's kinda fucked-up," was Hubert's honest summation. "The Russkis was our wakin' and sleepin' nightmare for years. Now look at it. Goddam Japs was all samurais and kamikazes and the Jews was all shop-keepers and pawnbrokers and now the Israelis are the world's warrior-race and the Japs is the traders."

"Uh-huh. I guess you could say the team was fully niggered. C'mon, Hube. I'll buy us our last beers of the trip and never mind it's three times the price of Beach Road 2 and half the fun."

"I'm a bigot but the difference is I know it. I glory in it, man."

FAUD INTERROGATED US CLOSELY ON THE DETAILS OF THE TRIP, then hurried off, probably to give Sayeeda the high hard one on the strength of it. Why he sent us I'll never really know. I figured he was purchasing Hubert's silence – which he didn't need to do. Danton and Fr. Paul would have loved Hube; he was a liar and a big-mouth but discreet in the important things. However, Faud judged others by his own standards. He wanted me and Hubert out of the way when things started to happen out of the India visit. It was also a kind of alibi by proxy for Faud. The three of us had vanished together; he didn't want us all around together. It was incriminating.

Hubert remained for another six weeks after that before he returned to Jeddah, theoretically for a couple of months before coming back again to Bohaiden. Whether he ever did or not, I don't know. Of all the friends I ever made, Hubert should have been the one I was destined not to lose touch with. He was the easiest to retain. English was his first – correction, only – language. He had his freedom: he chose where he went. He didn't bow and accept like the rest of us riff-raff and pariahs. Unlike my other correspondents, Hubert had his own PO Box number; he wasn't c/o anyone. He was the contemporary civis Romanus, an American passport-holder. When I saw him off at Bohaiden airport, there was no sense of a closing of a chapter in my life. We expected to see each other again in a matter of months, if not weeks. He shook my hand with the firmness appropriate for the mighty hunter he wasn't. We nodded; he turned, and was promptly engulfed in the departing dishdashahs and galabiyyas. I never saw or heard of him again from that day to this.

Hube, buddy, click me over an e-mail when you have the time. *Dafugitib@daemon.comp.ph*

CHAPTER XVIII

T. Ali Khan B.A.(Hons, Karachi)
Office Manager
DAK Petroleum (Bohaiden Pty)
GPO Locked Bag 114593

January 1 1988

Esteemed Sir,

I am currently holding pieces of correspondence for your late employer Lt.-Commander Smith but, alas, do not possess forwarding address as the late Smiths left with such rapidity as not to solve such details. I am wondering if you are in a position to rectify this. If so kindly allow me to have receipt and intelligence of their whereabouts. I am writing to you c/o the coffee-shop. You have nothing to apprehend, friend.

Yours faithfully,

T.A.K.

Perth
January 1 1988

Dear Rey,

Thank you very much for providing a contact for the Smiths. I needed to ask the Commander for a reference for the job I am applying for at the hospital here. You don't know it (hee-hee) but I married Lindsey on September 23rd, the year you left Hong Kong. We already had our first anniversary and are looking forward to the second. Would you believe the day came round and I forgot it. It was Lindsey's mother who phoned to congratulate us while we were having breakfast and then I remembered. I hope I would have realised by lunch-time. Don't think you ever met Lindsey. He was the tall, bald one at the Recreation Club. (With the wife and kiddies in tow). Wife and kiddies are in Sydney, we are obviously living in WA or it would be the longest way to commute. You remember Cathy, the aerobics instructor, my friend and coincidentally personal trainer for Jenny? She's gone back home to Singapore. I said, "Cathy, there's always other fish in the sea, na. I can get you a date." She said, "No hurry, lah. But has Lindsey got a brother?"

Well, this is a silly letter. I'll close now, and thanks again. Good luck with your job.

Irene (Commander Smith's Appointments Sec. OK?)

Hi Sugar!

Remember me? I'm the *luk krueng* girl you met in southern Thailand, your soul sister, oh, it's gotta be, more than two years back already. Maybe much more. I was going through my address book and saw your name and then when I was at the computer thought, hey, it'd be nice to give Rey a surprise. I finished work already with the aid agency or they finished with me more accurately a year back and I don't figure on being back in Thailand any time soon. I got a real good job in a law office. I got good news for you. Suddenly it's an advantage being *luk krueng*. I'm down here with my bro and my sis, with our dad. Hawaii is a heck of a lot different from any place in Asia, though it being on the Pacific, you see a lot of Asian faces, Chinese, Japanese, Filipinos like you (or not like you!!) and such like but they don't behave like any folks in Japan or the Philippines. A kid opens his mouth and behind his slanty eyes, he's an American kid.

My kid bro just won a sabre fencing title here, to go with his mainland collegiate crown, and he's real excited coz they say he's gonna train on the Olympic squad. People still sound kinda surprised – it's more of a white guy sport than even tennis – but I say, hey, who's gonna be the world's best fencer. Of course, he's gonna be half-black, with some Thai and some Japanese wouldn't hurt either.

Couldn't make out whether the white chick with you was your girl-friend or really your employer, like you said. (Or maybe both, come to think of it?) What happened to her and the little Chinese and Indian teeny-boppers? Weird evening, Sugar. Were you guys high or what? Ah Lim the Cambodian Chinese guy went back to Battambang and then Phnom Penh and, guess what, he's rich now, making garments and selling them to the good old US of A. Actually, it's a Malaysian Chinese guy making them but he uses Lim's Cambodian quota to get them into America. Real sad news now, Semporn, the Cambodian ethnic Khmer, not Chinese like Ah Lim, got shot a few days after you met him. All those years he survived the Khmer Rouge, only to get blown away in some hick town in the south.

Anyhow, here's my addresss. You ever pass through here, be sure to let me know and you can get the taste of some real home cooking. (Just joking – we'll hit the town).

Love,
DeLorna

Ap Lei Chau
April 13 1988

Dear Rey

Oh, it's terrible now. This is me, Bebegene, ba? I working-working so hard now I think my pingers is going to drop off. Employers now is a Chinese family, not in Kowloon now anymore but Aberdeen already the other side of Hong Kong is the island. Oh, Rey, I'm da one to be on duty eighteen hours da day, scrub-scrub, wash-wash and big scolding for me in Chinese if I don't do quickly. Then getting mad with me because I don't understand Chinese language it's not fair. Have da old Lola she's nearly ninety already blind deaf but for sure she's not dumb cos I git big da invective from her I do something wrong even I don't understand it. She's mother of Mrs Chan. Mr Chan he's got shop selling electric fan. Three da kids. (They are da ones to have dirty minds, Rey. Accuse me I stealing, Rey! I say, Mum, put my hand on my heart I never steal from nobody Mum I am a Christians Mum (I think they da ones to worship sea-goddess statue Aberdeen is fishing-villages before they got da highrises already) not like some feople Mum I ovserbe da Tin Commandments Mum. Well Rey they put da pingers in da ears they is real ignorant not like God Bless da Commander and Mrs Smith and their children is vrats not like Miss Jenny and Miss Nicky is real good girls. After I pinish talking they out their pingers. Then they git foliceman another *insik* like them and his radio is making a vig vig disturvance in da house while he's looking everywhere take notes from what I is saying. He knows a little Inglish like the folice all here. Oh it's very degrading for a debout vorn-agins like me. Then they da ones to deduct from my salary and also when I break a ornamint they charge me Hong Kong dollars one eighty-five and I in da shop I saw it's one twenty-five *lang* all worship Mammon *ang mga insik*.

Please give my regard to Commander and Mrs God Bless their kind heart. And God Vless you too Rey you is God's child too even you're rough and biolent like all young mans. You are one of God's Children even your just a nigro.

It's me it's Bebegene.

PS You need hilf remittance money back home its difficult in Arabia send here I can do from BPI *na lang*.

Ho Chi Minh
(make that SAIGON, man)
May 7 1988

Howdy Sugar Rey!

Don't drop dead with the shock, man. This is Nguyen. I figure that name don't mean too much to you, so how's about if I tell you my call-sign's HOT DANG MAN, aka Huckleberry Hound? Roger that. I say again, the fragged-out ol' ARVN dude you met along with your soul-brother Michael in Palawan, Puerto Princesa, R.P. Hey, that's outta the way! How are y'all? Nope, I sure don't want no dollars from you, boy, so set your mind at rest about that, Bubba. Michael and me fitted in OK at the camp again after we got sent back from Mindanao. There weren't no KP, no tiger cages, no nuthin'. Our guards was a pretty lenient bunch all-round. I gotta give them their due. Between PP and Bataan Michael was running back and forth for the Course on American Culture and Language the Embassy was running for them. I guess he must have been up and down there seven times in all. It weren't worth diddley, Rey. Just to string us along a whiles. The initials of the course was CACL and that was what they were doing behind their hands. The INS kept revoking his visa and as for the others in the camp, the Americans kept saying they was frauds. I love Americans, Rey, but sure as hell don't ever depend on them. You can't trust the government, Rey. They'll leave you high and dry when they're pullin' out. The Orderly Departure Programme was fine on paper, man, but the reality of it was that they made it as difficult as they could for us gooks. Trouble for them with Michael, it was kinda difficult for them to say he was a fake. Know what I mean, man? Kinda like the day he was born it was like extra hot and it made his hair curly. Shucks, I don't have to tell you of all people.

Cut a long story short, Michael's away now. He ain't in Vietnam no more. He got doggone lucky or so it seemed at the time. Now it might be doggone unlucky. If he'd waited on the ODP maybe he coulda been Stateside already, but he got impatient some time back and grabbed what seemed best at the time. See, he did some big cadre a favour. The cadre was an old VC. There ain't too many of them left, Rey, fact they're rarer than a lovebite on a nun's behind coz Hanoi expended as many of those hardcases as they could in '68

Tet. Figured those tough ol' boys might be a nuisance after the victory, coz they always knew they was gonna win like we knew we was always gonna lose. Anyhow, this survivin' high-rankin' hard-case was walkin' out with his young wife and kids when one of their kids fell in the river. Michael learned to swim pretty good in the Camp at Palawan which ain't the case with most of the Saigon folks, besides being a natural regular guy, and he just dove in and got the kid while everyone else was standin' round enjoyin' the spectacle and chewin' the fat. I ain't met the cadre cos I'm kinda apprehensive I mighta met him in the past when he was all wired up to the Tucker telephone for interrogation one time (did that kind of interpretin' too, I'm sorry to say, as well as Lazy Doggin' and Arty). He might have a soft spot for me, though, coz none of us likes the Hanoi folks here, they bein' the ones to have all the business connections and the hotels and such-like. Right now Michael's in Cuba, studying forestry. I say again, Roger that. I figure he got it 1. Coz he's black. 2. Coz it's a finger for the Yanks. Yup. He didn't have the brains for veterinary surgeon or doctor, which is the other things you can train for in Havana. I said, "Bring us a box of them Havana cigars, boy. Colonel Dingbell, my boss, liked one of them Romeo y Julietas. They was illegal as hell being as there was a blockade on Castro but he figured as he was being shot at by the VC on behalf of his country he was entitled to smoke 'em.

Rey, this here's a sprawlin' kinda letter and what I really wanted to say to you kinda got lost thereabouts in the woods but we never got the chance to thank you and Danton, and your other friend, for the help you gave us. I couldn't be too clear in the letter I sent you a few years back – didn't want the truant officer down on you guys, too. You didn't have to do it, Bubba, but we surely do appreciate it. I know you felt Michael was the next best thing to kin but Danton didn't have to put himself in the firing-line. Y'all be sure to thank the little guy. I ain't too much in the religious line myself but my cousin's a Catholic like you guys (Diemist, tough shit for him) and I asked him to say a prayer and light a candle for you boys.

So I'll close here. The best to you two boys. Out.

NGUYEN, HOT DANG MAN.

Lapu-Lapu City
July 17 1988

Vlondel, dear Brother,

I have da rilly-rilly terrivle news. Frepare yourselfs. Are you ready now? Ma dead. Auntie Myraflora, too. They go to Santander hometown of Auntie Irish to sell sweetie and cigarette at da cock-fighting *pero gi-crash ang autobus kay gusto overtake ang driver* and he hit da other bus is bound for Badian town. Dead many, students included to total. I'm da one to identify it's Ma and I do da same Auntie Myraflora. Some bloods their lip and nose and have a black eye *si Ma pero nag-smile siya*. Vlondel, have big trouble difficult with da funeral parlour *tungod kay* they refuse release da body of Ma *hangtod gi-paid ang bill*. *Pero* I don't have moneys at all to meet funeral and miscellaneous charges da other expenses. Brother Vlondel, I know how hard your life but can you see your wey to hilf?

Other news. Auntie Milagrosa marridge to Swiss guy hit da rocks. Honeymoon over. She say she rill unhappy but marry is for only once for Filipina she say even though she's da Fentecostal and not Roman da Catholic.

OK. I stop now. I cry and cry when I heard of Ma's death and so do you I know Brother cos she da only Ma we'll ever have and no matter what she always da one to put rice in our mouths. But it's da will of da Lord witch art in Hibin and we suvmit.

Your Father Voy (not Fr. Paul) da one to pass by here. You know da friests don't offer much in da way of consolations: they not da ones themselves to have family, they see folk dying all da time. In fact more than a folice or Sparrow does. I love you, Brod. Take care.

Bambi.

PS I not cough da sfutum no more. I took all da drugs is cocktail, sick all da time, burn my stomach *pero na wala na ang* TB or is in remission. How I'm da one to live and Ma is dead so young not forty yet?

Quezon City
Date: October 3 1988
To: No 11
From: Coach

Kumusta ka, Lofty? As for me, it only hurts when I laughs. The players come and they go, but the coach he stays. *Sige*: you don't have to tell. If he's unsuccessful coach is the one to go first. I got a few pressures to cope with but I don't trouble you with the details. The best players breathe pressure. People just want the players to throw the ball but some people want the coach to throw the match. Over my dead body. I still don't have a bunch to match your rookie intake, Castro. We already win fifteen from twenty-three games but lost the big one. I don't need to tell you, *di ba*? Ateneo hammer us 123-50. I just don't know what happen to my guys. No fire, no drive. Ateneo always get the rebound, man. It's like Tigers v Mouses. Their new coach substituting Hilton De Pena is a younger guy, Cheech Chong – the goon who put you on your back with the professional foul. I don't think you forgotten that one yet. I seen a redwood tree go over on the TV film but you done better than that, Lofty. Ouch!

A mutual friend came to see me, Castro. I think you'll be the one to be interested by this play. Maybe I don't give the guy all the veneration is his due because I'm Seventh Day Adventist – keep that under your hat, ba, because maybe it can prejudice my position – but even I'm not Roman Catholic I know a good guy when ever I see one. The guy's team-player, man. No names, no pack-drill, huh? Especially because this letter, No 11, is like a backward lob shot from centre court, because I don't know if it's going to reach you. It's not certain slam-dunk, like I pick up the telephone and you're on the other end, *ba*? I'll just give you enough clue when I say the gentleman in question, he's about as vast as you, Castro, *pero 'Merikano* and the old Spanish say *rubio*, he's the one to be blondie you know. His initials at the end SJ, but not Super Jock or Slam Jam. This guy always the one to look on high, you know what I mean, not a big scorer himself, more like on the benches, and he's the one to make the supreme assist when the time comes for you to make the cross-over pass. Got my meaning? The long and the short of it, he's like a coach only the one to wear black.

Well, our mutual friend shows up at my office and he didn't waste no time, Castro, but we get down to discussing our mutual *protegé*. To wit, to you, like the owl call. He said there's another SJ – let's call him Fall or Faul – who's more close to you, the two brains of you pair passing it back and forth, but he – Boy – man, I nearly let it out the bag there – was the one to oversee your character development. That's when I butt in and say (don't know whether to call him Father or Boy), a player's character is far more important than his technical skills. You agree, *ba?* I say Castro had a great character, I marked him down for Captain and that's not a position you can buy in my outfit. I said I never believed the shit about you. Now lately, the rumour has been the exonerating not the incriminating one.

The present state of play is the SJ and yours truly BTS is working hard in the dressing-room trying to change the rules in your favour and give you a level playing-field.

Will keep you abreast of the score and the opposition's state of play. Finally, just remember this, when the going is tough, that's when the tough gets going. Give 'em hell.

Yours,

It's your coach, always supporting you.

Butch Tan Sy

Godalming
Surrey

November 15 1988

Dear Rey,

I trust this finds you well. I've been meaning to write for some time. Thank you for being so efficient and considerate in picking up the debris behind us. The whole family are sincerely grateful to you. While you forwarded all our correspondence to us – and Commander Smith asked me to thank you especially for sending on the suit from the tailor that he didn't have time to pick up when we left – you hardly mention anything about your own circumstances at all. Are you well? Jenny and Nicky especially ask me to send you their good wishes and to be remembered to you. You appear to have become a family legend or at least an item of folk-lore.

Godalming is rather different from both Hong Kong and Bohaiden. We didn't go back to Kingston, Commander Smith didn't feel like going back to the same place after so long abroad and the trouble we had with the tenants soured it for us. There was just too much water under the bridge, which is quite an appropriate expression for Kingston. Commander Smith says his hands and eyes are no longer quick enough, so he isn't practising here. I say he should set up as a tax adviser, he seemed to acquire so much knowledge about being a non-resident but I must be talking Double Dutch to you. Unfortunately I haven't been able to find an acupuncturist in Godalming, but I live in hopes. Do get in touch with us again, if you ever pass through here,

Yours sincerely,

Mrs Smith

Bakakun, Caladong, and Ngilad Law Office

Ref: MAC/113 9834 /6# 25409/10/18/88

Dear Castro,

I still have your case file open while matters are pending. You will notice young Ngilad, "Skipper" as his contempts knew him, is now practising as a lawyer in my firm. That's a young man with a bright future. I can recommend to all to follow his example. I have delegated your case to him and, while I have every confidence in the bright young man, assure you I will continue to supervise the punctual conduct of your affairs with all due diligence. In the last resort, we can get a staying-order from the judge or better affidavit of desistance from complainants *pero* expensive that one, ba?

On this matter I take the opportunity to present you with our interim bill as some time has elapsed since the inception of your case and its perplexities which continue until now. However, I have every confidence in your affairs prospering under our hands but only counsel patience. Remittance in dollars US is as welcome as pesos.

Yours faithfully,

J.C. Caladong

Mactan
November 20 1988

Dear Castro,

It must be some years since we last corresponded. Although I cannot recollect the exact date, a priest's memory can on the whole be relied on. Perhaps this is sometimes a disadvantage as well as an asset. My memories of my charges are too retentive, too fixed. I remember the chrysalis too well to imagine the butterfly it has become. Fly is what you did, my son, although my hope had been that I might have given you wings of a different kind. To soar in the figurative sense is a somewhat greater accomplishment than mere physical flight. This was a notion that I think you readily accepted from your earliest times at San Ignatio though your familiar, Zarcal, was obdurately, one might say invincibly, ignorant as to this distinction. Quite why young Zarcal should have been thought more suited to a vocation than you remains ineluctably baffling to my poor sense still. A superior riddle. *Lucus a non lucendo.* I remember well chastising that young spark for what he thought a riddle impermeable to the priestly intellect. Clothed in the decent obscurity of an unlearned language and not uningenious, it may bear repetition, especially as my answer to *What is the wound that never healed?* would be *The heart that never stopped loving.* I think it was Zarcal's palm which bore the wound which never healed after its acquaintance with the tawse, though I am inclined to believe he had not been referring to the stigmata. Perhaps you would be good enough to convey my kindest regards to the Prodigal.

Father Mark, Father "Boy", recently met a Mr Sy of your acquaintance. I am not clear what transpired between the pair but Father Boy gives favourable indications.

I may perhaps leave you, Castro, with a quaint but essentially sound piece of advice common in the Ridings which would stand better as counsel to the reckless Visayan you are not than many an ecclesiastical homily: Neither borrower nor lender be.

And may the love of Christ ever guide you,

In parentis loco and your friend,

Father Paul

Mactan
December 24 1988

Dear Rey,

I hadn't intended to communicate with you so soon as I decided it would be better to have matters further developed before contacting you. I wanted to avoid giving you false hopes or leaving you in suspense. However, my hand has in some sense been forced as Fr. Paul mentioned to me that he had been in touch with you. I have no idea what Fr. Paul might have written to you either on this specific subject which concerns you directly or on more general matters. As much as we both respect Fr. Paul's intellect besides holding him in great affection, I should caution you that the Father has not been himself recently. In particular, his latest theological pronouncements should be greeted with reservations by the impressionable.

On lighter matters both Mr Tan Sy and myself smiled when we remembered your jumping ability in the gymnasium and on the basketball-court. It's been a long time since anyone vaulted the San Ignatio horse as cleanly as you could. I'll be in touch again but nothing may come of our combined efforts, so don't expect anything. Take life cheerfully, as it comes, I know you will.

Fr. "Boy"

CHAPTER XIX

London Down – Fleeing Faud – The Tramp and the Chancellor: Sylvester's Tale – Kicking Butt – A Night Out – Don't call Us, We'll call you – Kicking Butt 2 – Afloat again

---

S O IMAGINE ME THEN, the mournful pilgrim, his teeth chattering with the cold of his first winter, ploughing furrows through the slush of the Plaistow Road. Old Englishwomen shielded their heads from heaven with scarves knotted under the chin. From their blue wrists dangled shopping-bags that were rather more battered than those of the self-respecting Philippine poor. These middle-aged and elderly seekers of family provender tended, it struck me at once, to go out singly rather than in the pairs and even trios in which Ma, Aunties Irish, Monalisa & Co would hit the supermarkets of back-home, although of course quite frequently these excursions would degenerate into shop-lifting forays where safety lay in the greatest numbers and separate retreats. Nothing could have been further from the minds of the down-at-heel dowagers of East London who, though moving in splendid isolation down the highways, were united in their baleful contempt for the odd hobo whose routine it also was to lurch across the road at about the same unforgiving time of day, a Northern hemisphere eleven a.m. The cold of the physical atmosphere had a lot to do with the prevailing social frigidity, I thought, all of us with the possible exception of the hobos who were warmed by raw spirits but destined for hypothermia, vibrating like robots inside our outer coverings as we tried to retain warmth. The thought of being an *i-stamby*, hanging out with one's *barkada* on these street-corners, was so ludicrous as to make me smile through my trembling misery.

These environs encapsulated a novel kind of poverty for me, who'd only known tropical squalors, and it was strange, real strange, to see white folks clearly in their way hard-up amidst the hard-bake affluence. I'd only been close to Caucasians like the Smiths, the Jesuit Fathers, hunting Hubert, or the gum-bestowing aircraftmen of

Mactan base who it seemed only had to whistle to have a lucky dip in the ever-renewing cornucopia that was the PX. Slavs like Nikita and his Ukrainian pathics, or the agate-eyed whores at Bahrain Duty Free, only went to show that the Seventh Fleet and our own armourers and fly boys had all along been protecting the truly free world and its most dubious beneficiaries, the Filipinos, from a fate worse than death, to wit smile-less Sovietism.

By affluence in a hard-bake form, I mean the brittle but crack-less roads as laugh-line free as a Russian face, the telephone booths, the pillar-boxes, the abundance of road-signs and, miracle of miracles, street name-plates that no one was poor, or enterprising, enough to liberate for other purposes like roofing or fishing-net weights. The vandalism here was more malign – it was purposeless. Danton didn't take us on glass-busting sprees – not least because our *sari-sari* stores didn't have any, just a hole – or drool about shattering porcelain-insulators with shrewdly aimed catapult stones. What, and impose a longer brownout on ourselves as penance? Sure, a rival gang had sprayed graffiti on the Ecclesia sa Ginoog but that was a little dangerous because the Eccs had staked the newly re-whitewashed wall out, nabbed the quartet of thirteen-year-old malefactors and their pedalling heels had been the last seen of them as they were taken inside the ecclesiastical compound until they'd turned up as salvage in the Lahug ravine. No causal connection, could have been coincidence, though it made Fr. Paul's tawse seem tame. Here, however, it was a different society. In the East the placid poor lived in terror of the violent rich. In the West the rich lived in terror of the criminal poor. It was Jenny Smith-ism taken to its logical consequences and, being in the privileged position of seeing it from inside-out, from the outside, from both ends of the spectrum – in fact every which way you fucking liked – I found it by no means a more moral situation.

After the hard-bake, the crust of affluence, I came upon the pie-filling itself. Earlier, I had strolled in awe through the consumer splendours of Safeways, Edgware Road, Sainsbury's, Camden, and Waitrose, Finchley Road. These were names to conjure with, names that exerted a more immediate spell than those of Dickens, Stevenson, or Kipling, though I noticed a range of carton-sealed cakes under the brand-name Mr Kipling's. I could find no immediately obvious cultural reference or link, but then I didn't stay long in front of these relatively prosaic items as I was drawn down the wide lanes by vistas of chill-cabinets packed with day-glo vivid blueberry and cherry cheese-cakes, ice-creams of every hue and flavour in tubs, boxes, and cones, which led insidiously on to their total opposite, the pickles counter like a hospital or mortuary display of green and yellow tumescences and excrescences. When piccalilli palled I progressed to Spreads, Jams, and Preserves where I purchased the first but not last jar of Nutella of my life, followed in short order by the Pharaonic munificence of Cereals and Pulses where I beheld the *halo-halo* of variegated grains known as muesli. Health Food. Man, all food had been healthy to us. It kept you alive. Down the aisle to Toilet Paper and Tissues, the kind of paper – I knew at the Smiths – to be so robust even as single-ply as to constitute a different order of material from even the Philippine triple-ply, which at Atty Caladong's had disconcertingly melted in my palm at the stroke's critical point as if it was snow in the Bohaiden desert. You'd have been better off with Ma's ladleful of water unless, of course, Mrs Attorney had prudentially unwound the roll and peeled away the layers to turn triple into single-ply, much like the multiplication of the loaves and the fishes. A good grasp of home economics told you that this was a futile parsimony in that the dainty simply sandwiched more paper together than they would have in the ordinary course of events. In fact, on this subject, it was astounding to discover that virtually all the groceries were cheaper here than they were at home and luxury toiletries like the Borealis A toothbrush recommended in Commander Smith's practice were half the price in the budget pack of three. No doubt about it, the poor *pinoy* got a bum deal.

Those born into this world took, of course, its wonders for the rule. Expressions on the shoppers' faces, female and male, young and old, ran the small range from bored to uninterested. The first time I'd entered a humbler supermarket in Plaistow, desiring escape from the slush and the wind, I'd received a subtle but powerful intimation of the treasures to come in this take-away of Tutankhamun from the absence rather than the presence of something.

"Sir," I'd inquired, still teacher's pet despite everything life had thrown at me, "where is the Courtesy Counter?" This was where you deposited your bag back home, compulsorily.

I'd asked, as it happened, another black man. I was to notice that my fellows tended to predominate in the unofficial, unarmed security corps, although not the regular London police. I figured the reason was that the youths most prone to stabbing guards were least likely to stab someone who, like themselves, was black. Here co-negritude failed me, as sometimes it did. The guard figured he didn't have to be polite to me. "Fuck off outta here, man," he said. So, feeling more furtive with my bag, which might as well have been marked SWAG in orange fluorescent letters, than I had going through the Gatwick airport customs inspection carrying God knew what on behalf of Slash 'n' Crap, I'd entered the treasure-chamber with all the sensations of a tomb-robber. Thinking on it outside, with the north-easter roughening the skin on my cheeks again, I guessed the brusque guard had a raw spot about Courtesy while Counter might sound like a checker or assessor of politeness Brownie points. Then again he might just have been a surly son of a bitch. Like I say, I was going to be amazed how sour, how aggressive the descendants of the New World slave populations were compared to us sweet, sunny, freshly-created Amerasians.

SHORTLY AFTER HUBERT'S departure Saiyeed Faud had loosened up considerably. He trusted me. This was foolish of him in the extreme. I considered I had no debt of honour or loyalty to Faud, either as a type or an individual. I won't say I'd rather have died than betrayed Commander Smith's confidence in me; I wasn't a half-hearted weakling but that kind of behaviour wasn't modern, *di ba*? Defending the Commander, OK, for as Fr. Paul used to remark of the radical theologians, when people say they are willing to die for a cause they really mean they are prepared to kill for it. Faud, however, could go fuck himself.

There were, as the good Father would say, no flies on Faud but his paranoia worked against him after a certain point. With Faud things didn't just happen naturally or occur because of bad luck. He looked for conspiracy, even when there was none. But this made a sucker of him in the end. Because he was naturally over-suspicious, basing his malign view of human nature on his own knowledge of himself and his cronies, Faud had little experience of taking people as they came, step by step. Once the first barrier had gone and, man, it was a mighty, looming curtain-wall with dark horrors in its shade, Faud had no other defences. He hadn't needed them; nobody had got past his initial, withering distrust. I had the run of the castle.

Then Faud felt he'd done me a favour, rather than the reverse. Judging me by his own standards he considered the sex-tour with Hubert to have been the biggest treat ever. People are more likely to go on being good to you, cutting you slack, if they feel they've already done something to put you in their debt. They'll continue the good deeds to top up your gratitude yet more. It's like depositing in a savings account. Altruism as the ultimate selfishness, philanthropy as mind advance-dirty, M A-D. If people are in your debt – anyone, not just cheapskate Bohaidenese like Faud – they are less likely to do you a good turn. Human nature is not to repay at all, or to defer, or to reimburse the actual amount and no more. Even Chinese, with their fanatical insistence on requiting favours, would say, "OK, guy, we quits now." Faud's universal human feeling – Bohaidenese being human – was specifically reinforced by the local impulse. I was taking the brunt of the ostentatious hospitality of the desert. Faud was showing off; I was half-guest, half-slave. And the fact that I was black made me a Trusty in Faud's medieval dungeons, like the giant Nubians guarding the emir's harem. Hell, I think Faud envisioned me in baggy pants and waistcoat with crossed scimitars in my hands instead of a singlet and a hod.

The upshot of all this was I got to ride along with family and entourage in the Golden Falcon to Gatwick. Faud had just smiled at my wiliness when I admitted I was the possessor of a travel document. He hadn't even tried to appropriate the passport. I was already scheming as I plied my plastic spoon and fork, while Faud and Wife Mark 1 dispensed with cutlery and used their right hands up in Caliph Class. Some little while later I'd share an internal Cubana flight on a YAK III with the Cuban national basketball team – monsters who made me look medium-framed, with the exception of the mulatto and the creole there to ensure the team wasn't, uh, wholly Afro-Caribbean – and knew just what they were thinking. It didn't involve deceptive on-court plays. Their feints were for off-court to throw the guys marking them in their hotel. They weren't thinking of covering, of L-cut, and V-cut, of fake 'n' drives or cross-over dribbles. They were wondering, like I had, whether it would be best to defect instantly or wait for an opportunity.

I'd waited.

Going through the Gatwick immigration channel, I presented my ordinary brown-coloured Philippine passport in the wake of the green and gold and purple Bohaidenese booklets. From Club House gossip and the Commander's Tabletalk, I was aware how easy it was for the servants of rich foreign visitors to gain entry to the Smiths' home country; although it was a question of camels and needles' eyes for the unindentured Philippine wives of those Britons imprudent enough to marry them. So I was the tiniest bit surprised when the uniform-less, relaxed, and smiling female immigration officer halted me after Faud's females, the two maids, and Slash 'n' Crap had processed freely after my employer. Man, I felt like Lot's wife. She tapped my passport with a small smile at the corners of her mouth, a charming scepticism. "This is your passport, sir?" she inquired with barely perceptible emphasis on the verb "to be".

"Yes, Mum."

I got the gist. Fuck, the only fate worse than being a legitimate Filipino was getting mistaken for a Nigerian on a counterfeit passport.

"My father was a US serviceman," I said. Light dawned in those soft eyes. As I passed from the quiet eye of the typhoon through the needle's eye, I saw a row of reflective-glass booths on the other side of Jordan's bank which held out the covenant of interrogation even in the Promised Land. I think Soft Eyes had been quite capable of despatching me there.

Faud had unconsciously arranged his retainers, females, and chattels – meaning their Samsonite suitcases – in a protective ring around himself, much as his forebears must have done to beat off the depredations of desert brigands.

"What?" he asked.

"No froblem, serr. Just being the ones to check me."

"OK. Hurry now. Take Saiyeeda's bags."

Which Saiyeeda, I felt like asking in all innocence but decided not to push it. I single-handedly carried the bags of all the Mrs Fauds, not noticing other passengers had wire-trolleys until we reached the taxi-stand. My master engaged the services of two of these hearses. I remarked the fact that he had not violated the sanctity of the queue. Faud led the way with Wizz 'n' Crap and the two maids; I rode shotgun on the wives in the other cab – or perhaps they were riding shotgun on me – without having to attain the condition of eunuch. The unsuppressible odour of new upholstery and its sheen revealed the fact that the vehicle was all but brand-new, though in appearance it looked contemporary with a tartanilla or stage-coach. It was clearly a redoubtable, solid piece of machinery which would still be running when Atty Caladong's Lancer and Pajero would be so many orange junkyard carcasses. Shrewd re-fits and up-dates, like its computerised LCD meter, had extended its serviceability, just as the guided missiles had on the battleship *Missouri* when Danton and I saw her in Mactan harbour. It nevertheless offered a horribly uncomfortable ride, like the armoured perimeter-defence vehicles we brats had ridden in on the base's Open Day. The deadlock brakes, the hard suspension, the amazing manoeuvrability and tiny turning-circle were triumphs of English engineering but they and, I think, the unmellow aromas of leather, plastic and nylon took their toll on my masked ladies. Faud's first wife threw up before we got to the roundabout, the third as we hit the motorway, and the second as we L-cut onto a minor road as congested as any in Manila or Bangkok.

I don't think the driver realised what horrors were going on behind the glass panel. Unable to figure out how to operate the electric window, I would have been quite happy to have changed my plight for a dusty ride in a dilapidated, open-sided jeepney. Man, it was the gas-chamber. Within minutes the women had changed from crows into gaudily splotched parrots. I'd have challenged Fr. Paul at his most transfigured to sit there unruffled. I fought, I flatter myself, a heroic battle in the gorge holding back the mass as it heaved and thrust to pour through the parched cave of my mouth. Much as with anything else, relaxation was best. If I held my breath I paid the penalty with subsequent deeper inhalations. Shallow regular respiration through the nose answered. (I didn't want raw molecules of vomitus pouring unfiltered down my throat). As we disembarked in the Edgware Road, I figured I had about three minutes endurance left in me. On the pavement Faud took the situation in at a glance.

"Water," he said.

I WENT WITH THE FLOW AS LONG AS I COULD, though I got sicker of my employers' foibles by the day. In the Middle East they'd proved crooks and sadists. In West London they were ridiculous. The women's slippers flapped on the pavements of Marble Arch like fish on dry land. No matter that they'd annexed the neighbourhood, with cafés, restaurants, brick-ovens producing unleavened bread, travel agencies, and indeed full-service banks; no matter that the black-garbed women of the Gulf waddled in line abreast as they did on their own turf, forcing the skinny English teenage street-walkers off the kerb, while the men held hands and leered at the little white-legged tarts; no matter the dancing swirl of Arabic was everywhere on the shop fronts, they were still out of context. The filth and litter they'd made in the street contrasted with the relative cleanliness of the adjoining thoroughfares, while they turned the Highway Code into a meaningless and perilous cryptogram. The lights, the contra-flow lanes for the buses, the designated zebra-crossings, the blinking red and green men, meant as much or as little to them as the constellations in the sky. This was OK when they were in their own context, driving on empty roads. It was fatal when they were somewhere else, as pedestrians.

Early in the Fauds' stay, the second wife – who reigned highest in Faud's affections, being less withered than the first and only half as flighty as the youngest – sent me out for fresh plums and pressed dried apricot sheets at the twenty-four hour Pakistani grocery. I could already have told her Safeways was half the price and open until nearly midnight but the prejudiced creature preferred her own.

As I waited at the corner of Sussex Gardens, just below our serviced apartment, five young kids ranging from ten to mid-teens, belonging to two Abu Dhabi families, came prancing up from the phone-booths. They had, I think, been nuisance-calling prostitutes' numbers from the array of cards blu-tacked to the sides. The three pre-pubescent girls were made up like dollies, crusted with powder and rouge, as they were still allowed to be at their age, while the boys were junior versions of our own Slash 'n' Crap.

They had a bag of tomatoes which they were shying at parked cars. They weren't doing any damage to the vehicles at all, but it was the attitude, man. They'd have liked to be doing permanent damage. They had the spite but not the guts, where Danton had more of the latter than the former. I wanted to say something. Don't ask me why, I've always respected the propriety of cars with their dull gleam of coinage. But I thought better of it.

The two youngest girls whirled on the pavement, sending their braids out stiff from their heads. The oldest, about twelve, though it was difficult to tell with Gulf girls, some of whom had moustaches at nine, stuck her tongue out at me. She'd sixth-sensed my disapproval and didn't like it, particularly coming from a lummox nigger like me. Plucking a tomato from her brother, a real over-ripe beauty (the fruit), she lobbed it high into the air, quite at random, and together with her sister stepped sideways off the pavement. The on-coming double-deck bus just missed them. I could see the driver, who was a black man, blowing his grouchy cool. Man, he looked horrified. It was the closest thing you ever saw. The oldest girl's braids had clacked against the side of the bus.

For the kids a miss was as good as a mile. They ran out again, whooping, got to the island, embraced, sprinted for the other side and got hit half-way across by traffic coming from the left instead of the right. Now, I'd had the opportunity to see one other human being at the moment of impact by a car and I observed now that a female child's body behaved exactly like an adult male's. The two little girls went up, high into the air, and there were the same heavy thumps. Someone hit by a car wasn't thrown flat down, as one might think, by the force of the impact – as, for instance, a tackled football-player might be. Instead they were hurled high in almost vertical line, any horizontal movement an illusion caused by the car's own forward progress. And lace-up Barbie trainers came off, just like laceless Bally mocassins, man.

The older girl with the braids came down on the bonnet with a third thump, her limbs all over like a Buddhist swastika, while her smaller sisters landed head-first on the roof, then slithered off the side, away from their big sister under the front fender. Before the screech of the car's tyres had died away, you knew it was a bad one.

Silence descended over the busy road. Then rose a sound unfamiliar even in this Oasis away from the Gulf: the ululation of the grieving Araba. Others beyond the family took it up, the high-pitched wails sending flocks of the tough, Dantonesque London sparrows wheeling in alarm out of the trees and stepping invulnerably off the roof-gutters. The women didn't do anything to help, just stood there with palms out, letting the world learn of their dismay. I found my own arms folded across my chest, akimbo as Fr. Paul liked to say, a posture I almost never adopt. It's either confrontational or to provide physical reassurance – and I avoid the one and am generally in no need of the latter.

An Arab man burst out of one of the phone booths and ran without regard for the consequences into the middle of the road. Every car on the highway had come to a halt, anyhow. I had to assume this distraught soul was the father because my experience of the Bohaidenese, unrepresentative of other tribes perhaps and certainly warped because it was from my perspective of the oppressed underling, was that they weren't so concerned about other people or other families in the abstract that they'd do anything very impulsive or philanthropic. He carried the oldest daughter, whom I now knew to regard as his favourite (she wouldn't have been mine) under her knees and shoulder-blades to the kerb. Everything dangled. Safeguard the neck, you fool, I wanted to call, but I kept the words back.

The two brothers came to their father's aid when he was half-way back across the road. They all treated the road now, you see, as if it was an alien element, like water, where a moment ago they had behaved as if it was theirs as much as the carpet in their back room or their courtyard.

I walked on. Further up the road, by the bank with the pretty turquoise logo, the wailing merged into the doppler-effect of the car-horns and the hiss of their tyres. Returning to the service apartment with my pressed fruit, I crossed to the other side of the road, passing several dingy stores dealing in electronic goods. I'd rather have taken my chances in Bahrain or Dubai airports, particularly when I saw the owners were Indians.

The oldness, the seediness of London surprised and disconcerted me, though it was all impressively solid even in Plaistow. Call me fool, but I expected metropolitan sheen, glamour: physical surroundings to go with the vigour and independence of the moral culture, the mind-set I'd admired in Fr. Paul, Commander Smith, and even Hubert. But the shininess, the pristine-ness were intangibles. It was dirty, corrupt Asia which had the glossy new hotels and malls. The old empires looked... tired. Perhaps Fr. Paul would have been dismayed, if transported to the classical world in Wells's Time Machine, by the "nuisances" which in all likelihood infested Coliseum and Senate.

The Arabs, those despisers of the gift-bearing West, were as out of place in England as I, the ardent Anglophile.

I said nothing to the Fauds about the accident I'd witnessed. I mean, they wouldn't have actually beheaded me for it, but they wanted nothing to do with other people's misfortunes, even though Faud's three wives would have wailed as shrilly as anyone had they found themselves bystanders.

They had their Sri Lankan maid with them, a decent, thin-shanked old woman in her fifties and Luz, an underage Filipina from General Santos City who, despite her name, was a Muslim. The Sri Lankan was an unpaid retainer of twenty years standing, while Luz was simply terrified. For different reasons, they were both more likely to inform on me than to join in an escape. I, therefore, felt under no obligation to play St George to either of these damsels, the way I would have felt constrained to have given even Babyjane a chance.

One day I just walked out of the apartment and didn't come back. I rose at the uneccentric hour of nine a.m., with the servants and junior wives comatose in the living-room around me (there were only two bedrooms, one for Faud and his first wife, one for Slash 'n' Crap). With the Arabs in London there was no need to flee in the dead of night. That would have been the time to find them alert, up and about, just as mid-afternoon was the most reclusive hour to commit a crime in Bohaiden. Had I sneaked out of the empty flat at two thirty a.m. to catch the night bus, the Fauds would quite likely have come across me at the stop opposite those latter-day Gardens of Babylon, Park West. The Fauds after a night in the juice-bars, ice-cream parlours, and Lebanese eateries around Marble Arch – in Wizz 'n' Crap's case the gigantic, desperately un-cool Hippodrome discotheque in Leicester Square – would slumber on till well past midday.

In blatant daylight I stepped on a No 8 bus with the equanimity of a Jesuit boarding the martyr's waggon and began the interminable journey to the Old Ford terminus. In its way it was a transition as total as passing from Hong Kong or Singapore to Bohaiden and in the post-rush hour traffic took as long as the time zone change, four hours.

At no time did the conductor mention the fare, which nestled as prophylactically in my palm as a talisman. We had plenty of time to talk during our marathon ride. He was a little older than me, twenty-five, with the extra maturity and distinction conferred on a black man by expensive spectacles. He was by origin a Saint Lucian and a graduate in French language and literature. I didn't ask him what he was doing conducting a bus. He'd interlard his homey, easy-going Caribbean drawl with words and whole sentences in a snappy, tense French and then his glasses would glint.

I got a lecture on Racine and Rimbaud, followed by some Logic as austere as any in Fr. Paul's armoury. In between, he'd stick up the other passengers for their fares.

These were like ghosts to us; they had no reality. They briefly haunted the bus and were gone. And like the spectres in any house of phantoms they came from different periods and social classes: the foreigners who boarded us with a question on their faces in Oxford Street and disembarked dangerously in mid-street before Tottenham Court Road; the stripe-suited swells who took even briefer rides in the areas designated WC2 and EC4, the Bengalis and Indians after that, and then what Hubert would uncharitably have called "white trash". Sylvester impartially and objectively charged them all. The bankers and attorneys listened to his monologue with quiet smiles. The old, white, working-class women who came on after Liverpool Street, to whom Hubert, I like to think, would have been unfailingly gallant, offered spoken comment on my friend. I remember it because the same judgement was passed twice by different women. "He must," they confided to each other, "have been something once." Man, I thought he was something else, *then*.

Sylvester remained impressively aloof, behaviour which so far from offending the old ladies reinforced them in their respect for him, or at least what he had "been". I thus learned two things about the English, analysing context in the way that a Yorkshire Jesuit – however alienated – couldn't, only a foreigner. I was seeing his fellow countrymen with the same clear and pitiless eye that Fr. Paul did the Filipino. The English, especially the lower classes, had an ingrained sense of the recessional. They were fascinated by, enamoured with decline and defeat, politely called love of the underdog. They liked nothing better than the notion of the "toff" down on his luck. So far as Sylvester was concerned, they were a great deal more class-conscious than they were racist. The lower-classes tolerated upper-class eccentricity, including the idiosyncracy of personal uncleanliness; loathed and despised lower middle-class conformism. Sylvester wasn't dirty, of course; he was forbiddingly neat in his pressed uniform, white shirt, and speck-less black tie, but he was way out of context and they liked that. It made them feel safer and more content with their own circumscribed lot.

"The English," proclaimed Sylvester in a loud voice, audible on the top deck of the bus, "are the only nation in the world who not only have dukes who look like their gardeners but who revel in that fact." He had a French "r" when he spoke his quaint (to me) and impeccable English. "Robespierre and Saint-Just could never have succeeded in this country. Their old retainers would never have allowed the English aristocracy to be executed *en masse*. But how shabby they would have looked in the tumbrils! Not at all an *aristocratie de l'epée*. In fact, an *aristocratie sans robes* even. I remember when I was at Queen's, the term after I had returned from the Sorbonne, we played *un mauvais tour*, what they call a practical joke on the local constabulary. There was un *ivrogne*, a hopeless, what you call him, alcoholic on the steps of the university administration building. The constable on duty caught him using a Doric pillar as a *pissoir*, a urinal, and *baf!* he gave him a kick in the *cul* to assist him down the steps. We rushed forwards. But what have you done, officer! You just kicked the vice-chancellor of the university down the steps.

"Oh, he was inconsolable that officer! He leaped down the steps two, three at a time to get to that old tramp and brush him down as if he were his valet. I'm so sorry, sir, he kept saying, I had no idea, no idea.

"Now, Rey, my friend, I can tell you in no other country of the world could that little piece of theatre of the actuality have occurred. There was no difficulty convincing the constable. Far from it. Nothing was more natural for him than to believe that the reeling, ragged old man was the administrative head of the whole university."

I alighted in the unfamiliar surroundings of East London with a spring in my step. I was headed for Plaistow. I made initially the same mistake in pronouncing the place-name as middle-class English people, who only knew it as green lettering on the tube-map. They said Place-stow, whereas its inhabitants pronounced it Pl-arse-toe. You might conceive of it as an unlikely destination. But for a Filipino on the run, it was golden Samarkand, it was the sanctuary of sanctuaries, much like some medieval warren of thieves around a great Cathedral or the Walled City in Kowloon. It was a magnet for us "illegals", TNT's. Quite gradually, in the way this kind of thing happened, *pinoys* had taken over this unromantic and undesirable quarter of East London, an area which lacked the historical allure of Limehouse and the other riverine areas. Plaistow had been a *pinoy* preserve for more than ten years, occupied before the natives had even realised it, much like steel-helmeted conquistadores had Cebu, except Filipinos wore Reebok and Nike caps. I found stores selling native vinegar, *lumpia* wrappers, and White Flower embrocation, articles no longer homely but exotic in the context of the Plaistow Road. From first-floor or in-back kitchens arose the forbidden aroma of *adobo*, probably rabbit from the gamey odour. Mere soya-sauce with peppercorns, ginger, and vinegar, could never be productive of an aroma so offensive to the European nostril. I inhaled and I was high.

This was good, as I didn't find my fellow-Filipinos falling over themselves to welcome me. I looked like a West Indian: large, violent, and unfriendly to the *pinoy*: a mugger or a pimp of women, in neither of which activities did the back-home Filipino fear competition or the model-citizen *pinoy* abroad desire involvement. Worse still, most of the Filipinos here were Tagalogs and my command of that dialect was a lot worse than Fr. Paul's. Finally, I found a Visayan-speaking woman from Ormoc who needed a hand. I thought she wanted me to stack crates. In fact, she was fighting fire with fire. A group of black boys was giving her a hard time with their quick hands and foul mouths; that was to say pocketing her fruit and giving her lip in the same bargain. Somehow they'd sensed her papers weren't quite right. They knew she wasn't in a position to complain to the law, a law which I knew, like the law in Hong Kong and Singapore, secured all here from rape and molestation unlike the one-sided charter for ravishment and wage-retention which prevailed in Bohaiden. Unfortunately, if she went to the police, she would effectively be denouncing herself.

When she saw me Marites had flinched, rather than ignored me as everyone else had. That got my interest straight away. There was nothing to be got from the blank Asian faces the others were turning to me. Come to think of it, there was nothing much to be gained from the smiling Filipino face I was bestowing upon them. That was my version of a small guy's glare. *"Na unsa ka day? Unsay ang imong problema?"* I'd asked, instinctively in Visayan, and that shaft (of instant tropical sunlight) had flown through the bars of her confinement and lit up her careworn monkey's face. A flow of explanations and lamentations had followed, the word "nigger", as always used unpejoratively in Cebuano, featuring frequently. I didn't object, me. I took it as a compliment. When they got to know me, folks felt so easy with Sugar, they made me an honorary them.

Marites had a boy of indeterminate age with her whom at first I had assumed to be her son, both showing the same simian, prognathous, beetle-browed Visayan face that Ma and Bambi had. But Philbert was her nephew. 'Tes had come over on a short-time – pardon me, short-term – visa to vacation with her sister, who'd married the usual cranky English geriatric that lifted these Philippine girls out of the frying-pan of barrio or city lodging-house and into the cold fire of Caucasian affluence. Sure as cattle stray out of an open gate, Marites had overstayed and moved on to the prospect of pastures green. At some point her sister had also surrendered to her pre-ordained migratory urge and fled the old eagle's nest. She should have stayed five years to get her new citizenship and passport, but just couldn't stand the guy one minute longer. "John always mashing her breasts," Marites said by way of exculpation. In doing this Marites's sister had deposited sonny Jim, Philbert, with Auntie 'Tes.

I could see straightaway the kid was a problem. He was actually fifteen, an undersized street-punk by home criterion and a midget by English standards. Challenged pint-sizers, like Franco, Deng Hsiao Ping, Napoleon, Hitler and, of course, Danton Zarcal, often respond by picking up the gauntlet, and giving the regular world a smack in the chops, but this urchin lacked Dant's charisma and, most of all, his balls. He was the spoiled Bad Boy, OK, with his earring and spiky hair – so pitiful-looking on the Asian head, like a crown of thorns – but also the Runt.

After the black kids had made their call I wondered if Philbert hadn't been in cahoots with them against his auntie. Man, that was so un-*pinoy* it was like parricide.

That was going to be the Jamaican boys' first and last raid while I was there. They came two days after 'Tes had offered me a roof, a blanket, three meals, and a one-pound coin a day to be her champion. "OK, *lang*, 'Tes," I said cheerfully, hoping I was gonna get a ride on her in the bargain. She was a little forty-year-old butterball but it seemed a long time, a real long time since Maribeth and Co. Rich feasting makes rationing harder to bear than if you had been fasting already. I know the Air Force guys at Mactan – Hube, for that matter, too – used to complain the heat made them horny. The opposite was true for me: the cold would make my balls shrivel painfully until I longed for the heat of another body naked in bed next to me.

The black kids came in round five o'clock, their preferred time, according to Marites. She was jumpy, but doing her best not to show it. I accounted that courageous and considerate. When the gang arrived I was re-arranging stock in the grim, overlooked little backyard. That was the way I wanted it. Having them find me there didn't have half the impact. They might not even come in if they saw me lurking on the premises, which was no use to Marites, as I didn't plan on staying there forever and I wanted to solve her problems, not just give her a respite.

I was wondering what the circle cut into the top of the ancient outside brick-oven might be when I heard the little bell on the shop-door clatter. (I later discovered in the Local History section of the Public Library that the hole was for the cauldron in which whites were boiled by launderesses in the days when Cebu was still a Spanish garrison-town). I took in the scene from the back-door for a while, enjoying the feeling of seeing and not being seen. Marites hadn't been exaggerating her plight. The stupider and weaker of the kids had, of course, The Smile on their faces, always the worst but most reliable of prognostications. Quite by chance I was there on the night when they had something extra planned. What that would have been we would never know, but I knew it was Marites's lucky night. As the leader, a shiny-skinned, merciless-looking sixteen-year-old, sank his teeth into a purloined apple, I stepped into the room. Surprise was total. They didn't like how big I was and I really filled that little room of an era when people were tiny. Then I saw the alarm replaced by complacency as they took in my colour. Well, they were making assumptions and it's never safe to do that. It was Marites who was kith and kin. I had no idea what I was going to say until the moment before I said it. Then I found I knew chapter and verse.

"Get the fuck outta here," I recited, only adding to the security guard's mantra, "you little fucks," as inspired addition.

The malice on five bad little faces only deepened. "'oo the fuck you tink you are, tokin' to us like that?" asked the ringleader. He meant to sound aggressive but the truth came out in the timbre. I heard for the first time the high, querulous, injured tone the West Indian malcontent adopts under pressure, not unlike the Mumbai Babu when he'd told me I'd been called a "sister-fucker". And I knew from all my past experience in other contexts – the skeleton-key to life you gradually assembled – that this weakness should be met with uncompromising force if it were not to turn into bullying bluster which would require even sterner measures.

I selected the biggest, still a few inches under my height, measured him carefully, and hit him with all the weight I had on the point of his chin. Some things appear to take a long time to happen because so much depends on them: the long lob-shot in the dying seconds of a game, the car screeching to a halt in front of a perambulator, the rope thrown to a drowning victim, and this kid seemed to hang on some invisible hook in the air, even as his knees dipped and his torso buckled. It was an uncomfortable moment – I wasn't in the habit of belting people, being the peaceable person nature and nurture have made me – and I knew if he didn't go over spectacularly I was in for a messy time. No such problem. He went down like a city building. The glass in the shop-door vibrated.

"Shit!" squeaked the big eyed ringleader. "What the fuck you do that for, man?"

"The sheer unadulterated pleasure of it," I replied, with the impartiality of a tawse-wielding Jesuit, knowing it would prove more effective now to appear out of context. "Kindly depart and never darken these portals again."

The runtiest of the pack, one of those who'd been wearing The Smile, opened his mouth to give me some crass impertinence or the other and I shut it with a resounding slap that made his eyes water.

"Fuck off, nigger," I said, "and don't get any smart ideas about coming back because my brothers are crazy compared to me."

The ringleader opened his mouth to say something which ten to one would also have been sassy until I lifted him straight off his feet by the lapels of his overcoat and said two inches from his face, "I'm not kidding, man. You wanna get killed, I don't care if I do it."

That swung it. They slunk through the door, the leader only pausing at a distance to threaten, "We'll be back."

I knew I couldn't let him get away with that. I chased after them, caught the slowest runt and kicked him repeatedly against a lamp-post, while the others watched at a safe distance. The kid cursed me while he cowered and took the punishment.

"You fuckin' cunt. What you doin' this for? You ain't one of them."

I grabbed him by his wool and banged his nose and then his temple against the metal until he shut up. "I'm not one of you, either," I said. "Come back and it'll be a knife."

There was a little crowd of Filipinos gathered as I walked back to the shop, sweating despite the chill. Philbert was bug-eyed. "You look after your *Tia*," I warned him, "or I want to know the reason why."

I sat down and found I was trembling.

Marites, too, had big eyes and the muscular effort to keep her feelings from showing on her face had left her cheeks as wiped of expression as a pair of buttocks. Not, credit me, an uncommon back-home face.

"Dey da ones to come back," she said fearfully.

I shook my head. "No way."

That was the risk I'd taken for her, and I was responsible enough to be more prudent on another's behalf than my own, me the on-court assist-king. Jeez, it had been an ugly, debasing incident but I'd taken not just the correct but the only course. They weren't the kind of kids you could take aside for a quiet chat about the mistakes they were making in life. They understood but the language they conversed in, which was physical, and its lesson was that a superior level of violence always prevailed. When you shovelled turds with your bare hands, you got dirty. But if you did it for someone else, your conscience stayed clean and quiet as a changed baby. I figured.

I WAS ALWAYS ON THE PROMISE of a hump with Marites but it never happened. Maybe she was waiting for me to make the first move, but I had qualms. In general, not just with her. I didn't like initiating things with the ladies. I felt awkward about it, like I might be foisting myself on them where my company wasn't required, that my overtures might appear aggressive – for I could see all the courtship – the soft words in the *pinay*'s ear, the promises, the presents – as nothing more nor less than the approach-work for a multiple stabbing which happened to create life rather than destroy it. In short, I had a hang-up about being mistaken for a rapist. If I'd been five feet tall and one hundred twelve pounds instead of two twenty-four I'd very likely have proved less bashful. There you go.

Plaistow without sex was like the desert being without water. It was to be expected, but it didn't make it any easier to bear. In my spare moments from the store I'd wander all the way to Silvertown and back, or over to Whitechapel, or down to Woolwich and the river. An unusually "parky" autumn was turning into a forbidding winter but I never so much as had a drop on the end of my nose. One thing I stood in no danger of contracting at Marites's fruit-store was scurvy: I was getting more Vitamin C than at any time in my life. Silvertown with a streaming nose would have been one of the worst fates I could have devised for the expat *pinoy*, short of domestic service in Kuwait. Such a romantic name, a pirate settlement straight out of Stevenson, with modern overtones of Hollywood, of Tinseltown. And it was nothing like that. Its inhuman distances, spaces, and scales were akin to those of the parched Bohaidenese wastes: chimney-stacks and towers as impersonal as natural geographical features; strange, antiquated industries operating on a physical scale that was uncontemporary. It was an ogre's backyard with the plant and the giant sheds casting their shadow over you, just as the rusty machinery in Marites's backyard – the jammed mangle, the cogs with their broken teeth, the empty coal-bunkers and ovens and the absent cauldron – must have loomed over a scurrying mouse.

The public library was my haven from all this and the gelid, gritted streets. I was, to tell the truth, having some difficulty reconciling the abstract, essential England of my *halo*ed Smiths with the concrete, particular England I was absorbing through my glaciated pores and the soles of my damp feet that with their lack of feeling could have been someone else's. The Library restored my faith. It was amazing what they had in this poor quarter of the city. It was better than the Artheneum college library. And it was free! No matter that the hoboes stunk the newspaper room out with their feet or the best books remained on the shelf while the *basura* never got dusty. The potential was still there. As the melting snow from the umbrellas widened in pools on the floor, so did my knowledge – a thirst which could never be assuaged. I loved the Britannica. I loved it more than I would the Internet. That was information $halo^2$. You could dip into it and come up with a fistful of useful knowledge. I didn't bother with the micropaedia, went straight to the macro-entries. I didn't want to skim, man, I wanted to delve. And I was fast becoming an apostate from Fr. Paul's liberal, if still priestly, belief that all knowledge was equally important, that it didn't matter if you were right or wrong, that learning was a crystal construct all the more beautiful for having no direct application. For me, it mattered – desperately – to be right and it was a basic desideratum that what I took on board should prove utilitarian. In any case, I just couldn't get stultefied. It was the sheer variety. The hours flew.

No one took a damn bit of notice of me, except for other black people. The alkies and the old white folk reading the newspapers in their carpet-slippers; the odd, bright schoolkid; white middle-class men and women who clearly were schoolteachers – missionaries within their home country – none of these found it puzzling that a powerful young black guy should be studying a heavyweight work of reference so intensively. I was allowed to "improve myself". Maybe it wasn't so odd for me to have brains; although I could just hear Fr. Paul chiding me.

"Don't mistake knowing a lot of facts for intelligence, Castro," he'd admonished me in the fifth grade. "It's knowing how to think that's important. You'll only get that from Greats, from the Classics."

It was black people who scowled and gave me indignant, scornful, and jealous looks. What did I do? I bestowed upon them my most open and friendly Philippine smile. That really nixed their day.

An important milestone came round, Marites's thirtieth birthday (she said). This anniversary – the birthday, in general, preceded by any figure you cared to pluck out of the air – occurred with amazing frequency in the bar. Ma and Auntie Monalisa celebrated it three hundred and sixty five days of the year if they could. It was a great way of getting a tip or a lady's drink out of the greener customers. Now, Marites was paying me and not vice versa, so I guess it really was her birthday, though even thirty-nine would have been a kindly estimate. She dangled out the prospect of an evening in West London. "The Gloucester Sporting Club," she said coyly, "afterward, dancing at Mariciano's. Chicks."

I murmured polite surprise that such things were possible in London. "Of course," she added, "da gentleman da one to treat da lady here." It took a second for what she meant to register. I must have looked more dismayed than I felt, for she swiftly said, "Dutch treat. It's OK coz heartily given."

"O-o. That's because you'll be spending it on yourself!"

I couldn't stop liking 'Tes. She represented the best of home and the worst of home. She wasn't above screwing a dime out of someone even poorer than herself but she was also warm-hearted enough to flinch from the thought of inflicting humiliation upon me. Of course, I wasn't such a foolish coxcomb, but she wasn't to know that.

I'd been with her three months and I had thirteen pounds to rattle in my Nutella jar. By now, the Fauds would be long gone. Like all the other Gulf visitors, their sojourn in the Edgware Road was calendar-bound between two religious festivals and, as such, was eminently predictable. Even so, I had a few butterflies in my stomach as our Tube train stuttered through West London from our extra-mural thieves' kitchen like a penitent rogue doing an extended stations of the cross. I don't suppose Faud could have had my villein's nose slit. I think he'd probably have just pretended he hadn't seen me. But I could imagine the wives, abetted – cautiously – by Wizz 'n' Crap, raising an echoing, ululating hue and cry in the subway tunnels. I'd be unlucky to get nabbed by anyone official but the embarrassment of it was the awful prospect. Poor *pinoy* me. Poor Marites.

In the actuality, we disembarked placidly on to the open, musty air of the South Kensington platform before striding off in the direction of the Gloucester Sporting Club.

There's a first time for everything. I'd been dandled on the counter of a go-go bar long before I could walk. I'd toddled innocent-eyed round a frank brothel. Hell, I may have been conceived in a short-time room at De Inn or Fluck da Cherry Drive-in. But one place I'd never in my life frequented was a casino. Never had the dough; more importantly, never had the inclination. Marites had no dough either but she was hooked. On the door were a couple of heavily-built white guys in blue overcoats and cowboy boots, plus a guy even taller than me in a red topcoat and stove-pipe hat. These goons gave me the same look Cheech Chong had, the game after he'd fouled me. It said: it's cool, let's make no grief for each other. I smiled, which in context was aggressive, and got stony looks back. Gulp.

This and the fact that members of the peon-class like 'Tes and myself could gain admission inclined me to believe we were entering a low-roller's den. The *habitués*, a United Nations of uncongenial types, were a good deal seedier than what you might find on an ordinary night in the average liberty-port bar or bordello. I'm not kidding.

It failed to faze 'Tes. Eyes aglow, she headed straight for the nearest table, soft and green as a Bohaidenese shepherd's dream. They slotted her slim fold of bills down a mailing-slot in the table and she got some pretty pink and grey chips in return. Without the least bashfulness she threw the dice and, shit, she won. This happened four out of five times. On the last occasion she flung her arms round my waist and jigged up and down before leaving the ground and swinging from my neck for good measure. We all smiled indulgently, croupiers, overseers, and Rey, the staff with more reason than me, for a winner encouraged the other mugs to bet more boldly. A further three throws saw her return to what she'd started from and another four saw her lose her little all. Just before that, she implored me, "You, *na lang*, Rey. You're da lucky one. You'll be da one to throw for me."

But I was having none of that. "'*be*, the only time I ever throwing a dice was when we play Snakes and Ladders at school. And I was always the one to slide down a snake."

She didn't laugh with me. I never saw anyone look so mournful, though losing can hardly have been a new experience for her. Shucks, it probably was the only experience.

Together we watched the croupier, an attractive, scantily-clad redhead, rake in the stake with consideration, humour, and sympathy equal to that with which I reckoned my lady immigration officer sent third world folks into a year's holding pattern. On a good day our salvage-prone, armed gorillas of back-home were more lenient.

"Rey?" asked Marites timidly, turning her tear-brimming little simian's face up to me.

"Yes? Oh, no. Really. No."

"Please, Rey. I'll be da one to pay you back when we get home. Please."

Jeepers creepers. I was a guy who couldn't say no to weeping women. My pauper's trove appeared, the croupier's discreet smile widened, and the coins rattled and whirred into the bowels of the table.

"'Tes," I asked, "do we have return train tickets?"

"One-way."

"Uh-huh."

She won, she lost again, she won. I took her wrist, perhaps harder than I meant, but then I was facing the prospect of a ten-mile hike with a tearful Filipina who thought one hundred metres was a march of some significance. At the moment, the prospect was very real to me and very distant for her. Maybe because I knew I'd be the one ending up carrying her.

"That's enough. We'll be the ones to quit now, while the going's good."

"But, Rey…"

"No buts." I pulled her away with one hand and scooped the chips with the other as dextrously as if I had been doing it all my life. The smile on the croupier's face vanished.

Outside, I felt much better. We now had twenty-six pounds.

"I think," said Marites, not at all timidly, "that half is mine *na lang.*"

I could see us becoming mortal enemies over this if I demurred, 'Tes cutting off her own nose to spite her face by turning me in to the Home Office, in much the same way as Bambi's Pa had got himself *bolo*ed over fifty centavos. Without saying another word, I counted thirteen coins into her palm. She didn't seem to think this would make me any less friendly.

"Mariciano," she said cheerfully, flagging down a yellow-lit hearse. In my opinion a bus would have been more appropriate to both our general circumstances in life and in the particular dilemma of us being virtually penniless at the present moment. But I smiled and clambered in after Marites. *Jai yen*, as DeLorna said, Cool Heart – it was no easier to attain in frigid London than it was in the sweltering chaos of home.

We turned quickly off the booming four or five lane main highway on which the casino was situated to make the rapid L-cuts and swerves in the network of minor roads for which the unlikely-looking hearses were in fact so well-suited. It was tricky driving: plenty of zebra-crossings, one-way streets, road-narrowings, and a couple of double-backs that would have brought a stallion rearing on its hind legs. As if that wasn't enough, there was a wider road lined with opulent, modern townhouses that had those bumps built into the tarmac which rejoice in the name of sleeping policemen. The cab-driver told me that. He was a genial, bald old buffer with reflexes like a cat and the ungridlike lay-out of the London street-system branded into his memory. He was wasted plying for hire. He should have been wheelie on a bank-heist. We spoke through the sliding window. I don't think he realised I had to strain for his words while the acoustics threw my voice comfortably into the driver's section. "Back home," I said, "if a cop's sleeping at least he can't be committing a crime."

"And where might that be, sir?"

"Philippines."

Marites nudged me in the ribs. She thought I was talking too much, considering we were a pair of TNT's.

"Can't say I know anyone who's been there, sir. Like it here, then?"

"Not so much. Hey, you know, you know these roads like the back of your hand. Back home we have to direct the drivers."

"That, sir, is what we're examined upon. You have to know every street in London. Every one. You can see the drivers going round on mopeds with a clip-board. We call it doing The Knowledge."

"Oh, yeah. Like it, man. That's what I've been doing all my life."

We came now on to a road of older houses which common-sense said should be cheaper simply because they weren't new but which, going on Mumbai anti-logic, were probably the jewels in the crown of some rich-boy property company. I wondered if Chinese dominated their economy like DeLorna's and mine. Then I remembered Fr. Paul's comments. He was a Jew-hater, a difficult infection to transmit to us as we didn't know any in Cebu. Now we came on to a huge roundabout. "Nearly there," whispered Marites in my ear. Just then I was thrown back into my seat as the cab swerved violently. The driver wound his window down and shouted, "Oi! Watch where you're fucking going, you black cunts."

A beat-up old Ford with five or six very useful, as Butch would say, West Indian dudes inside had to take evasive action in its turn as our driver cut them up in retaliation for their anti-social manoeuvre. They had a pair of large yellow fur dice swinging from the driver's mirror, like square leopard's balls. Balls was what our old guy had, I thought. Each one of the black guys could have spanked him left-handed, but I noticed with some curiosity that they didn't seem at all inclined to call him out or mouth him off back. Almost as if he was armed, which I doubt he was beyond the car-jack in the trunk. Edwin would later explain this to me. No one fucked with cabbies. Every taxi in the neighbourhood would stop to help one of their own, black or white. They were among the most migratory and warlike of city tribes. Attacking them was, in the short term, worse than assaulting a cop. That was why the negro guys took the left side of a giant grass isosceles triangle that seemed to be a public park, while we sailed on down the right. Just before a tube-train bridge, Marites tapped on the glass to tell the driver to stop.

"Have a good evening, won't you, sir, and the lady," the driver said, seemingly undisconcerted by the fact that I didn't have the funds to tip him.

In a deserted side-street we found a broken-nosed white guy in the mould of the casino security detail stamping his cowboy boots outside a glass door. I made up my mind to get a pair of these when I had the dough. There was nothing on the other side of the glass, just spiral staircase winding down into the darkness.

"Wrong night, I guess," I said to Marites. "Let's go home while we still can. I think the last train won't have gone yet." She clucked her tongue at me. To the bouncer she said winningly, "Friend of Mariciano's. Free. Also my companion."

"No. All got to pay. But Filipinos men is half. Ladies Night so free for you. Your friend pay full."

"But he's a Filipino."

"No."

"Yes, he is. Tell him, Rey."

"Whoa! Whoa! It's OK, 'Tes. I'll pay."

But 'Tes wouldn't hear of it. Eventually the security guard agreed to let her go down and speak to Mariciano personally, but I'd have to wait outside.

While she was gone, I broke a silence awkward to myself by asking the bouncer where he was from.

"Yugoslavia."

"That's a long way. Are you a boxer?"

He grinned and touched his nose. "So you seen. Yeah. Before."

"Do you have to deal with a lot of trouble here?"

"Sometimes. The young guys always. Got to prove themselves. A little bit of drink and they become monsters."

"Yeah, the same back home. But there it's the old dudes who're really dangerous – you know, with goons and guns."

"Where you from?"

"Philippines. I wasn't kidding.'

"Yeah? You don't look like one, that's for sure."

"Father was a US serviceman."

As always this instantaneously dropped the scales from his eyes. "OK. Go down."

"I'd better wait. Don't want to make trouble."

"No, you go, it's OK. Tell the door I said so. You're OK. I'm just careful of the black guys from here. No offence. I don't like them down in the club. Got to keep my back to the wall, if you know what I mean."

"Yeah. I know what you mean. No offence taken. Thanks."

At the bottom of the stair-well was a *pinay* hopefully holding a roll of numbered tickets with an empty shoe-box in front of her.

I gave her the score in Tagalog. Looking disappointed – it was a terribly empty take – she opened the swing door behind her.

Immediately, the scene changed. The joint was swinging, like Mactan with a destroyer in harbour. A young girl, much better-looking than the beach-perambulating Japanese model on the TV screen behind her, was singing the popular Tagalog melody *Magdalena* with the confidence and strength of the professional she clearly wasn't. This fashionably thin beauty with redundant sun-glasses acting as the Alice band in her jet-black mane was, I later discovered, Mariciano's British-born daughter, who didn't understand a word of what she was singing. Oblivious to her serenade, DH-looking *pinays* gossiped at the tables and snacked on *lumpia shanghai* and *pancit canton*. Empty bottles of San Mig stood by the paper plates. Talk about home from home. The only thing missing was the sign adjuring one and all to check-in their deadly weapons at the door.

I couldn't see 'Tes anywhere at first, but as I got my night-vision spotted her with chicken-wing in hand and beer-bottle in the other, chatting to another middle-aged Filipina near the john. Nothing about her demeanour or present position suggested she had been, was, or would shortly be remonstrating with Mariciano about my predicament outside in the cold. Without a moment's embarrassment, she introduced me to her friend, then gave me chicken-wing and bottle to hold while she repaired to john for leak. It was a goddamned creaky smile I had on my face. 'Tes obviously hadn't mentioned me to her pal because we had to go through the process of her pretending to expire with shock when I asked *kumosta ka*?

Mariciano's daughter stopped singing. I was told who she was and also had her father pointed out to me: a tubby Ilokano who was no exception to the rule that beautiful Philippine girls have ill-favoured dads. Fr. Paul would have approved of her song anyhow, which was an update of the Mary Magdalene legend. With a brief and modest bow she retired to even more modest applause. The audience had obviously heard it many a night before. Disco started up. Pairs of overweight *pinays* took the floor. I wondered why there were so many plump Filipinas abroad: about three times the ratio of back home. Perhaps they were feeding their unhappiness by way of consolation. No one smiled much in Plaistow. They were the most serious Flipilinos I'd ever seen and, come to think of it, the Indians in England were miserable-looking compared to the ones I'd seen flashing teeth all over Bombay when they weren't chasing me. The only jolly immigrants I'd seen were black, although they had an excluding kind of humour.

I stayed on the edge of the floor while 'Tes and her pal gyrated their hips suggestively at each other. They were both wearing satiny, collarless US college jackets, with the sleeves a different colour from the body and a giant number on the back.

A tall Filipino in a waiter's jacket approached me. "That will be ten pounds, serr," he murmured.

"What?" I exclaimed.

"Da beer of da lady and da chicken's wing," he said reproachfully.

"Shit! I'm a Filipino," I remonstrated.

"Next time Filipino price. I already make up da bill."

I gave him ten one-pound coins, not a penny more, and glowered at the dancers, no doubt an exciting spectacle for them. I was beginning to look as gloomy as everyone else.

One thing cold did: you had to take a leak four times as often as at home. I went to the men's, on the other side of the basement. It was very dark, with only one bulb. The customers probably filched the others. As I went to the two urinals – conveniently staggered in height to suit respectively the Filipino and the Caucasian inside leg – I suddenly jumped and recoiled with a gasp from the huge and intimidating figure approaching me with dire purpose. My fists bunched and came up instinctively. I V-cut sideways and forwards, ducking as I did so, and my heart came into my mouth as my assailant also moved with speed and unmistakable athleticism into an identical posture. I wasn't used to competing on equal terms with a real threat. As I stood up again to full height, so did my reflection in the mirror. Man, I looked evil.

It was a perfectly ordinary mirror, which neither magnified nor distorted, so I was getting an accurate reflection of myself. I had no idea how I loomed until then. I got my pecker out and snickered while I relieved myself.

Back in the disco Marites was rocking and rolling with unimpaired enthusiasm. I parked myself near a table of old white guys who were speaking Tagalog to their pick-ups but didn't really look like priests. After twenty minutes, Marites's friend packed it in for the night but 'Tes remained under the strobe shaking everything she had. After another fifteen minutes with 'Tes quite alone on the dance floor now, still going like a dervish, I realised she was one of those obese girls present at every disco and all the parties in the world who believes three hours non-stop dancing will burn off the fat laid down by French fries and no exercise the rest of the week. I recalled Butch's rookie-intake lecture on nutrition and the simple mathematical gap between calorific intake and calorific expenditure. We'd all gone out and sunk peanuts and *halo-halo* afterwards on principle. 'Tes's eyes were glazed when the lights finally came up.

"Take care of her, good luck," said the Yugoslav bouncer as we stepped into the street.

"She's not with me," I said.

Of course, I wasn't such a heel. We strolled past gang after gang of black kids before I forced 'Tes to walk through an echoing, urine-redolent underpass to surface near, of all things, a Hilton hotel. We let one night-bus with a turbaned conductor on it go by before the next one came with a black guy, who returned the coins for Marites's fare to me.

I HAD FOR SOME TIME BEEN PLANNING to get in touch with the Smiths. Ever since I'd landed I'd been dangling the idea in front of myself for the pleasure of deferring the treat. Getting mad with Marites wasn't the cause, but it speeded up my decision to phone them at last.

I recognised Mrs Smith's voice the first time I rang from the call-box at nine forty-five a.m., and it discouraged me sufficiently to hang up. The blend of apprehensiveness, tremulous eagerness, weariness, and complacency that was peculiarly hers brought surprisingly unfavourable memories of my old employer back to me, maybe because I was hearing it in its proper context for the first time. I still often surprised myself when little things got me out of sync in the way danger or major hassle couldn't. I waited four or five days, then tried again at three p.m. with a bunch of coins dragging down my pants. Mrs Smith had shrilly and pedantically recited a series of numbers. Nicky said, "Hallo?" in her pleasantly deep voice that already managed to sound happily surprised though she could have had no idea who was calling. "Nicky?" I asked.

"Yes? Who is this?"

"Miss Nicky?"

"Rey!"

Well, ol' Uncle Tom glowed orange with pride and happiness in his phone-booth.

"Jens! It's Rey!" I heard her shout.

"Where are you?" she inquired into the mouthpiece as an afterthought.

"Plaistow," I confessed without a moment's hesitation.

"Plaistow? Where the heck's that?"

"East London."

"What are you doing there?"

"It's a long story, Nicky."

"I'll look forward to hearing it. Jenny, speak to him."

I knew the unceremonious transfer represented her fealty to my special relationship with her older sister.

"Rey! What a lovely surprise. When can we see you?" That was what I liked so much about Jenny. Even if you were only a servant she could still, at the moment she addressed you, make you feel you were the only person in the world.

"It's all up to you, Miss Jenny," I replied. "Just say the word."

"Are you on holiday?"

"Not exactly."

I heard whispering in the background and the murmur of Mrs Smith's voice.

"In transit?"

"I guess you could say that, kind of."

The line fell totally silent with the completeness that only comes when someone has placed their palm over the mouthpiece. It was important to realise this, as if you thought you had been cut off your exasperated swearing would be audible to the other party. And the last thing I'd want would be to shock Jenny, or even Mrs Smith.

The normal background of the line resumed in my ear.

"Have you got a number we can get you at?"

"No, I don't think so. No, wait. Yes." I gave the number of the cell-phone Marites had lately acquired as "hot" through her nephew at a knockdown price. "Much safer for single womans," she'd informed me, perfectly assuaging her conscience.

"OK," said the masterful young voice at the other end of the line, the deep young voice so confident in itself and in its context, a voice which only a hundred tiny daily certitudes could sustain. It didn't sound like Jenny at all.

"It's Nicky again, by the way. Jens is having a spat with Mummy."

"Oh, really," I heard Mrs Smith's voice in the background. The line went pre-Injun attack quiet again.

I looked round the phone-box. There weren't any prostitutes' numbers here, just kids' scrawlings, those poor souls so uncertain of their hold on life and their place in any context that they had to leave a memento behind them wherever they went.

"Well, look," said Nicky. "We're all a bit tied up at the moment but when things have cleared up a bit we'll give you a ring. Maybe you could come over for lunch."

"That would be nice, Miss Nicky. Just ask for me on that number I gave you and Marites will get me."

"Okey-doke."

The line went dead briefly, then I heard Nicky say, "Yes, I did, you heard," but faintly as if she was talking to someone behind her. Then just as I fed a pound coin into the slot, not wishing to subject Nicky to the pipping, she said more crisply, "Well, it was good to hear from you. I won't waste your money on the phone. I'll pass your regards on to Daddy."

"Yes, Nicky. I'll just wait to hear from you then."

"Yes. We might go away next week but we'll get in touch after that. Don't call us, we'll call you."

"Very good. Goodbye then."

"Bye."

NOT EVERY *PINOY* IN LONDON WAS AN ILLEGAL, but the legals among us congregated in West London, while scum like me got whirled to the Eastern peripheries. It was hardly surprising West London had the highest concentration of legal *pinoys*. It was an affluent area, more than that a family area, and what the well-educated mother of the English middle-class family wanted to complete her freedom was a DH or nanny. And this was exactly what the vast majority of Filipinos abroad were.

The postal districts W11 and W10 had the greatest number of these – the black-haired yayas observable with their fair charges in a certain playground in a certain park – with W2 the transition district on the way to Arab-dominated W1 where the Filipinas slaved for Gulf families. Or as Fr. Paul might have put it, with his love of both acid and classifiers, W2 was the purgatory to the hell of W1 and the heaven of W11.

There was also a little group of independent legals who resided in the run-down West Indian area of W11 behind Notting Hill and further west through Latimer Road to Shepherd's Bush. I never lived there but it would perhaps have provided my perfect camouflage on the two counts, and yet I never felt so much out of context anywhere in the metropolis.

London was a place you could lose yourself in utterly. You could sink without trace, even if you belonged to the tribe of green men with pink polka-dots. The place simply swallowed you up.

It was all the more important, therefore, to possess a few points of reference, if only to be reminded who you were. There were times I felt so liberated of all associations that I wondered if my feet might begin to lose contact with the street, that I'd float up, up, up like a balloon let go in childhood and never be restored to earth.

Marites's sister in her legit, married days had possessed Filipino friends who lived in subsidised council housing near the Portobello Road. The father of this family, Edwin, was employed in the kitchens of a vast hospital on the edges of West London, where he earned as much as Atty Caladong did on one of the Attorney's bad days. Definitely, Ed was one of life's good guys. If I had to choose an example of a Filipino who'd taken his main chance boldly, then turned over a new leaf in a fresh context, by which I mean purged himself of our tribal propensity to lie, gossip, cheat, and appropriate – in short, re-invented himself – it would be Ed. He'd done it without repudiating the best in himself and ourselves as well. He'd turned $Halo^2$ into plum duff, both of which, as Commander Smith had observed, were improved with a judicious dash of rum. Ed and Fe kept open house in their warm hearts as well as their well-heated council flat. They had the mixture right, so far as I was concerned. They were model citizens of the country in which they found themselves, exemplars of its cool, correct virtues, but they hadn't forgotten who they were, either.

They lived in a well-engineered, ruddy-bricked low-rise block, on the ground floor. Despite the unusually good quality of the construction and finish – somewhat better than Faud and Sons – you could tell it was for people low on the scale. The ignorance in the white kids' eyes hanging round the entrance told me that. I hated to see it. I wondered if that was why Fr. Paul was so free with the tawse – to stop the light of knowledge going out in our eyes, even if it was only the spark of pain he was implanting. 'Tes and I – and all the other *pinoy* waifs and strays – didn't have a lot of time for the failures of this affluent society. Man, if you couldn't hack it here, you wouldn't make it anywhere, and it was no good feeling sorry for you.

Both further south near the river bank and on the way to Ed's there was an abundance of sturdy beggars. You started to run this gauntlet from deep down in the bowels of the tube station until just before the council estate. The first time they importuned us I was dumbfounded by their ignorance and their presumption. These requests were cringing before they turned aggressive and then insolent. The whine of Communion transmuted into the hot blood of resentment. I couldn't believe they were so witless as to ask us, we who had nothing! A tiny Filipina in the temperate-zone attire of the *pinay* – bulky pastel windcheater accentuating the smallness of her plump legs in a pair of narrow-cuffed jeans ending one inch above feminized basketball boots – scurried past 'Tes and me as we scaled the miry metal-tipped station steps to win the thin daylight of the late afternoon street. My mouth had opened as a dirty teenage girl approached poor Marites with open palm and contorting face. Our passing *pinay* was sensitive enough to Tes's Philippine presence to catch this. She raised her eyebrows and then we all burst into laughter. Colliding contexts *di ba*? The very basis of humour according to the book on psychology they had in Plaistow public library.

Edwin, on this my first introduction to him, said: "O-o. They have those here, too." Edwin was a man who never resorted to irony or sarcasm. This didn't make him boring; on the contrary, it made his society a particularly easy one to keep. He achieved his resonances another way, by leaving a lot unsaid. He didn't wield Fr. Paul's scalpel but a dousing-rod. So when he said "they" had "those" too "here", you had in turn to read a lot into his simple statement: "they" being the aspiring self-reliant poor as well as the upper and middle classes, "those" being malingering scum as well as hopeless failures beyond any help, and "here" the paradise of universal opportunity, even if not universal affluence, which the British newspapers in the reading-room – one self-appointed sentinel in particular – persisted in denigrating and decrying at every opportunity. They should have been reading what was the staple fare in our papers: police who were kidnappers, bank-robbers, and contract killers in the pay of politicians; judges who auctioned their verdicts; priests who melted down the altar ornaments; teachers who sold examination questions.

We Filipinos just looked at each other. There wasn't one of us who didn't know what Edwin meant, although Ed didn't despise the English for their blindness, like some in the room privately did. I looked on it as a lovable eccentricity, the price of being Achilles.

Edwin's other famous understatement, which he uttered to newcomers every time as if it was the first, was his comment on back home. When the topic came up, he'd purse his lips sagely and say, "Very chaotic, ve-rr-rr-y chaotic," and leave it at that. We all knew what that meant, too: police who were kidnappers, bank-robbers etcetera.

It always seemed to be someone's birthday at Edwin's and if it wasn't that, it was someone's kid's Christening with a hundred brats in their party best rushing round the flat. Fish always featured on the menu in one form or other. And I mean as centre-piece. Big fish, a yard in length, and often exotic species from warm waters such as barracuda or parrot-fish. "Mol-mol," I exclaimed as I came through the door the first time from the drab street, recognising the rainbow-hued, chisel-beaked denizen of our reefs. It was better than seeing God's bow set in the sky.

"You must have some," said Edwin at once.

"Hindi po," I exclaimed even more forcibly than my first ejaculation of surprise. The enormous parrot-fish was still absolutely integral, the crowning-glory of the large spread upon the table: delicacies to gladden the heart of any homesick rover: breaded deep-fried calamares rings beside a sweet and sour dip as orange as a Manila Bay sunset, *lumpia* rolls piled like little logs, BBQ stix of charred crisp pork and – more colourful than the *mol-mol* – a great oval glass bowl of *halo halo*.

"Come on," exhorted Edwin.

"Later *lang*. Just later. You don't even know me, Edwin."

"No! A friend of Marites is a friend of ours. Come on."

"Uy! *na-ulaw ko*. I'm embarrassed. Later please."

"Of course," said Edwin, seeing I really was shy and going into reverse gear just for my sake. "Take your time. You are with friends, ah! Make yourself at home."

'Tes got me a 7-UP in a red paper Coke cup and also exhorted me to eat Edwin's feast in that characteristic usurpation so characteristic of us that – equally characteristically – hosts never minded. In some respects the Arabo showed more propriety, though I always found, as I said, Faud's hospitality to be self-aggrandising. It redounded to the host, not the guest. Mine host – or hostess – in a *pinoy* household was really putting himself or herself out for you, God bless us one and all. In Edwin's house in particular it was Christmas every day and a Christmas by Charles Dickens at that. Why not? Philippines was a century behind in everything else, *di ba*?

Edwin's kids didn't eat fish. This was a small but significant abstention, for fish was as symbolic to us as it was to the Early Christians, those wanderers in an alien world. Tuna, Butch would preach, was the chicken-meat of the seas: lean, mean protein from the can. Edwin wasn't trying to preserve us from coronaries but it was a reminder of our origins in the archipelago. Scraped, gutted, barbecued – brutal trinity – fish formed our childhood staple. Like us, the Brits were islanders, with the heart of England closer to the sea than the landlocked centre of Mindanao. No one needed to tell me, the precocious devourer of Marryat and Smollett, about the great English naval tradition but… the fuckers didn't eat fish. If they sometimes did, it was only if a Greek had disguised it as a potato and embalmed it in vinegar.

When we beheld Ed's fish, we viewed the land of milk and honey and we looked into our souls. He had a special deal, a great deal, going with the fishmonger. Like, he got the trade, the wholesale rate, but it was still a king's ransom. Ed made us guffaw when he cracked, "You can only get this here. They never catch the big fish in the Philippines, they go scot-free."

You could taste the freshness of it. These snappers, jack, lapu-lapu, and black brass had less than a day ago been finning round the Mediterranean, the Caribbean, or the Gulf of Thailand. "Ed," remonstrated one of the recipients of his salty bounty, a Boholana Med Tech from a private VD laboratory straight down the Westway, "why you're making it sweet and sour? Spoil the flavour. So fresh."

We all chorused our hearty remonstrances against our kind host. O-o, man. To drench with syrup the firm white flesh and glistening grey skin of this creature, so devoid of briny tang and off-ness that it might have had lungs and grazed, was verily to hide your light under a bushel. "'*Sus*! Fish is fish," Edwin said dismissively, making his wife Fe – who'd spent half the morning just preparing the pompano and the parrot-fish – smile into her macaroni 'n' raisin salad.

Thus when Ed and Fe's twelve and thirteen-year-olds shook their heads as platters were passed to them, it was an abnegation as significant as their inability to speak Tagalog.

They loved their Dad but they were ashamed of being Filipinos, deeply so. Ed had made the costly mistake of taking them on his and Fe's only visit back home in fifteen years, two airfares which would have been better spent on appliances for their grandparents. Being the great guy and responsible parent he was, Ed had refrained from reproaching his kids over this but it was naturally the first thing that had struck every other Filipino whether over here or over there.

"Never again," had been the unadorned judgement of the boys. "It's filthy, Dad. The place stinks," the oldest boy said, and would be drawn no more. They'd hardly spoken to their Lolo and Lola and snubbed their uncles and cousins with the ruthlessness of extreme youth. I could see how the family's fawning greed might turn the boys' dainty stomachs, which in all respects, including susceptibility to amoebiasis and viral hep, were English stomachs. English kids, even mestizo kids, might have forgiven their relatives for being inferior, but Ed's boys with their cockney accents and pure Asian faces hated their deficiencies in the pitiless way one can only loathe oneself. "Uy! It was difficult for them," Edwin summed it up, and we could all read between the lines.

The kids weren't so much aloof in the sala, or should I say lounge, now as utterly undrawable, turning away conversational openings with polite monosyllables. For me they made a partial exception. Ed didn't lose the chance to congratulate me on this when 'Tes and I left in the late Sunday afternoon darkness. "My kids took to you, Rey. That's good. Come again, they'll like it."

The kids thought I was cool because I was black. This I was prepared to live with. I was still good-natured Sugar to all and sundry.

Unfortunately, the way I annexed Edwin as my good friend wasn't so free and easy. I wouldn't, in the abstract, have predicted I'd have liked him. I liked my pals spicier, with more of a sting to them. Ed was bland compared to Hube or Danton, but I didn't find him the least bit boring. I guess, who knows, I'd matured a little; although inside I still felt as immature as ever, no matter my face was leaner with the shape of the underlying bone structure more prominent in the way mountain soil erodes and reveals the rock below, with deep gullies starting to run from my nose to the corners of my mouth. In the mirror, I figured I'd had an above average hard life. Care-lines, man. Not just my own fixes, but also caring for those I liked and taking care of their business when they were too good to do it themselves. Finishing unfinished business for them; finishing it off for them for good, if I really loved them.

The problem with Ed, and our developing friendship, was Marites. She was jealous. Filipinos could get jealous about anything and anyone. We were the possessive case incarnate. In its way, this was worse than hackneyed sexual jealousy. If I'd been the man of her dreams – I wasn't – playing fast and loose, she'd have only had the one stab of it. With two men she knew involved, me and Edwin, it was multiple wounding. It was laughable to me but the pangs were real to her, so I guess I could have been more considerate instead of doing my best to torment and provoke her but then the only plaster-saints in the world neither breathe nor move, although they might weep blood once a year. "Why you always bisit-bisit to Edwin?" 'Tes asked me crossly. "You two is gays or something?"

"O," I replied equably. "You guessed right, 'be. It show so much?"

"Yuks!" she'd grimace, but with an edge to the banter. I shouldn't have done it. Ed wouldn't have.

'Tes and Edwin had both reached an equilibrium in their lives, Ed rather more happily than 'Tes. They'd stopped rolling, they'd gone past kinetic, while I was still bumping downhill and gathering no moss except on my teeth.

The subject of racial prejudice was not once raised during all the time I ran with 'Tes and Ed's *barkada*. Not once, and 'Tes was without doubt what Nicky Smith called a Moaning Minnie. Filipinos were not obsessed by this subject in the way that black people were so quick to use it to excuse their own failures and shortcomings and Indians to exploit it to gain an advantage. I think our average Filipino was at once too sunny to brood about it and, on the shady side, too imbued with a sense of his or her own worthlessness. We all knew our flip-side. We all knew what a dipshit country we came from. We were prejudiced against each other, trusted a foreigner, more exactly a white foreigner, far more where money was concerned than another Filipino. I also believe the degree to which you discern or suspect prejudice against yourself or your kind is the measure of the prejudice in yourself. Those who inveigh the most vehemently are those who hate the most. Some years later with my friend Robbie Pryce I watched a black American preacher on the Korean-made TV of the games room of a Monrovian-flagged bulk-carrier. I say "black"; he was several shades lighter than me, with straightened hair and an aquiline nose. At one stage in his rant he referred to white people as "devils".

"That cunt's a fucking racist," Robbie said, with more wonder than dislike.

Walking the maze of streets in the public estate around Latimer Road with Ed and Fe, or Marites, the fact that our presence was unwelcome to some was barely perceptible but also inescapable. It was only voiced the once − some scraps of words from a balcony more than ten storeys up, which the wind shredded into incoherence, and which I think I am not being paranoiac in believing were addressed principally to me. But it was the feel of it in the chill air. Looks held too long, faces turned away too quickly, expressions too blank to be natural that might have been contorted into a grimace a second before or a second after when your attention was elsewhere. Once, because I was not the object of mockery, I saw kids pulling up the corners of their eyes one-fingered at Ed and Fe. Chinky eyes, as we happily called it in Mactan. Funnily enough, Filipinos − virtually indistinguishable from Chinese in many cases − didn't think of themselves as having slanty eyes, so even had they seen the insulting gesture my two *pinoys* might well have thought it didn't refer to themselves.

People, on the whole, decided it was best not to give me a hard time. Or at the least that it was wiser not to mouth off in my hearing. They weren't to know what a pussy cat I was. What they saw was two hundred pounds plus of ebony nemesis. And, in general, young black males, even the non-heavyweights, got left alone. The slightly built people I thought of to myself as Indians, but who were in fact Bangladeshis, living North of us in East London, were the ones who got it worst, according to my neutral observation. There was nothing imaginary about the violence and insults heaped on these innocuous Muslims, and I pitied them. I saw it a lot. As always, women were preferred prey but the men, too, were distinctive and easy game. Their very inoffensiveness inflamed the animus against them.

'Tes had developed a fondness for curries and pilaffs, for which we would regularly make pilgrimages to a long lane, lined with Halal eating-houses, the name of which now eludes me. It was always dark and spooky going and returning – though the lane itself was brightly lit – much like inhabiting the frames of one of the M.R. James or Sheridan Le Fanu ghost stories Fr. Paul would read to us twice a week in December. The area had been the scene of celebrated murders a century ago, but whether these had been real or confined to the pages of Sherlock Holmes I was unable to discriminate. Certainly none of the waiters in the curry houses could tell me. Once, in a particularly velvety seven p.m. darkness we came past a row of terraced houses to be confronted by what might once have been the most mundane of sights but at that moment and at that time vied with the skulls of the Killing Fields or a bloated torso on our own salvage grounds in its suggestiveness. It was a plain black waggon with a sable awning in the shape of Omega, an unexceptional if old-fashioned conveyance but sharper than life in silhouette and under that dim light it presented to Filipinos reared on horror films and bucolic vampire legends the most sinister of sights.

"Ah, *di ai*," sighed 'Tes. At that moment a tall figure carrying a black valise stepped out of the carriage. "Jesus Maria, *aswang, wak-wak!*" screamed 'Tes and raced back up the street through the rotting vegetables of the deserted market and didn't stop till the railway station. There we both collapsed with giggles.

Whether we'd stumbled across a film-set, an English eccentric with a fetish for the past, or a time-warp 'Tes and I would never know.

If what we needed at that moment was Fr. Paul with sprinkler and crucifix the other drama we witnessed there required Hubert with firehose and cattle-prod. I was again with 'Tes who'd conceived a desire at three thirty p.m. for spiced chick-peas and a plate of what I called Indian lumpia, namely samosas, followed by candied pumpkin. You could satisfy such exotic desires at any time of day and night in London; there was generally always an establishment open, if you were prepared to travel. It was staple English fare which was unavailable outside normal meal-times. Even if it had been three thirty a.m. I would have escorted Marites to the lanes but I confess I was more relaxed about going there in broad daylight.

We'd just crossed in front of a mouldering Catholic-looking but, in fact, Anglican Church, when from the narrow street we usually took to the Bangladeshi quarter shot three dark-skinned boys in motor-cycle helmets as nippily as if they were pin-balls shooting along the rails of an arcade table. Kids fleeing a gang look the same but anywhere. I knew they were on the run straightaway. I'd done the same myself behind my nimbler buddies. There was something unmistakable about the angles they were instinctively cutting off the street corners that were the hall-mark of urban pursuit. The way they were half-looking back without losing any distance, and in spite of the fact that they were very scared, their relaxed three-quarters speed lope (saving the last burst of pace for when a turn hid them and they could disappear) – all these told me they were used to chasing and being chased.

Sure enough, a whole mob of shaven-headed boys in green jackets followed on their heels. I almost omit the salient fact that they were white, very white actually, pale as maggots, perhaps because it was winter, perhaps because they were too poor and too prejudiced to travel to places where their pallor might be admired as an attribute of loveliness, Mactan for instance by Auntie Monalisa, and too fucking brutish, too. With the exception of black people, the shaven-headed have trouble not looking brutish. We, on the other hand, just look more refined under a dome, even the gorillas amongst us, the cagers and fighters. These specimens of white trash would have looked mean and low even with the full head.

'Tes, bless her heart, went bug-eyed with fascination and horror both. As spectacle, it beat Tagalog videos outta sight, *siguro*, and also she was vibrating with the thrill of possible (unwanted) spectator involvement. Inter-active entertainment, man. She was too stymied even to take the few steps to press her back against a wall to make herself less conspicuous. In all, I'd resist the temptation to exaggerate and I'd say there were around twelve of the little fuckers. On the street, when you're one alone, six or seven seems a legion, and the tendency is to over-estimate, like the fisherman with the one that got away. I say "little", which they were to me, but there were five

437

or six solidly-built older ones, looking even bulkier in the puffy jackets, as they were supposed to. They were too intent on their chase to think of giving us grief, however; although in passing the gang Runt, too out of breath to be wearing The Smile, said in a panting snarl to me: "Coon." I laughed in his face. He was last but one. The laggard was, of course, the pack's fat boy. I looked up the street. The others had turned the corner and were out of sight except The Runt, who would be shortly.

Fat Boy came nigh, his high-lace boots clopping like a donkey's hooves. He had a feet-out-turned waddle and one curl in the centre of his forehead fronting the stubble like a question-mark. I decided I'd extend a leg and send him flying into the gutter, maybe deal him a few shrewdly placed kicks in the ribs and legs for sheer badness' sake. And just as he came level with us he puffed out his fat cheeks and blew his single lock ruefully upwards with the most woebegone of smiles. And I couldn't stop smiling back, only aiming a playful kick at his backside's ample target. Weird moment. There's the group and there are the individuals who compose it; not all are bad but the loyalty has to be to the group and if the pluses and minuses come – in the end – to a negative sum, why, then, the fidelity is to evil, *di ba*? I don't suppose the Fat Boy would have refrained from jumping on my head if his pals had been able to lay me unconscious on the kerb – probably that's what he was kept for, dead weight – but, as it was, our destiny was to share a private joke.

"Where you are going?" asked 'Tes as the human steam-roller at last doubled the corner and was gone.

"Curry," I said.

"Are you crazy? We'll be the ones to go back."

"I don't know about you, 'Tes, but I've developed an appetite. Let's go."

Muttering and making the same little growls of doubt and abdication Auntie Monalisa might have when persuaded against her better judgment into giving a b-j to an aircraftman with a green penile-discharge, Marites put her arm through mine and followed. I flatter myself that she felt very safe in my company. I would personally have felt very safe with another me, so I guess she was right. In the end, it was Marites who made a heartier meal than me, native recklessness asserting itself – *bahala na* – while Butch's boy knew not to go to the prospect of violent exercise on a full stomach.

So, yeah, racial prejudice. What can I say, brethren in Christ? I tried never to let it get the better, or for that matter the worst, of me. It was demeaning to be bound by it, by the expectations of others and your own, and – for sure – one way of being bound by it was to get riled or, even worse, carry a chip everywhere on your shoulder. "The well-balanced athlete," Butch would hector the prima donnas in every year's intake, the sullen Goliaths, "has a chip on *both* shoulders. So stop eyeballing me and get going." It took two to make a conflict: them to give offence and me to take it. If you removed just one half of the equation, the explosion couldn't take place. That was the verballing. The sticks and stones part is different, admittedly, that has to be taken seriously if just for self-defence, but then I'm not a Jesuit, I'm not a vendor of solutions or creeds, just a purveyor of snake-oil. I'm Sugar. And, yeah, *o-o*, too much sweetness cloys and then makes for decay and pain. Then you do M A-D dentistry. Sometimes you have to dislodge, knock off, the plaque of life, man, if you see what I mean. Plaque able to be white, brown, yellow, or black, man, but what I knocked off principally being brown.

The streets of Spitalfields were quiet as Fr. Paul's class-room after the tawse had been employed on the tender portions of the refractory. As we neared the market, I regretted not having made a better meal with 'Tes because it looked like fight or flight was not gonna be part of my early evening agenda. Then my foot kicked against something pale. At first I thought it the crash-helmet of one of the fleeing Bangladeshi boys. But 'Tes bent over with a whoop of joy. "Yay! It's a cauliflower, all."

"'*Sus*, 'day. Filthy."

"How big it is! No, I'll just be the one to wash it."

I looked sceptically at the grimy veggie. "It's too dirty."

"Wash it, peel, and fry for chop suey."

So it was we returned to our part of ancient London town without-the-walls, with 'Tes furtively coddling the cauli on her lap, occasionally casting sly, almost lubricious looks round the rest of the bus-passengers, none of whom gave a damn or found anything unusual in the sight. And she proved right in the important respect. It was the main part of a great chop suey.

I'D SPILLED THE BEANS ABOUT MYSELF TO EDWIN, of course, long ago. "Complicated," he'd murmured, cool but not quite as laid back as

Commander Smith who had been in the habit of commenting, "Interesting," whenever presented with intractable, exasperating, or frankly impossible situations.

"*O-o*, Ed. From day one my life hasn't been the simple one."

"Simple I don't respect. C'mon, you're the one to be with friends just for now."

Next time I saw him, about three weeks later, he asked during the climactic shoot-out in the Tagalog video we were watching (but less corpses than Macbeth), "Anyone looking for you?"

My eyes still on the screen, as were his, I said, "No. It ain't like that, brod. No one looking to rub me out if that's what you mean."

"Good. Because we'd help you."

"It's not come to that yet, Ed. Thank you, Lord, 'cause I don't think they could miss me."

Ed didn't smile at all at this nervous joke. He took my fate seriously, which is a much nicer characteristic in friends than the sparkiest sense of humour. Gallows humour is like a melting popsicle, not for the sharing. Ed really had my best interests at heart, more so than the likelier mentor-figures of Fr. Boy and Butch Tan Sy, for he had no team to sacrifice me to in the last resort.

He changed the topic. "Hey, we had a real-life emergency, murder mystery at the hospital. Creepy. They still the ones to talk about it. Haunted bed. In the intensive care, they had five patients die one after the other in the same bed, in a corner. Nothing strange about it, patients dying in ICU, they do it all the time. But all these pass on a Friday at six thirty a.m. exactly. What the hell, hah? What's going on? They got the serial killer on their hands or a ghost or what?

"Well, they put in a video camera in the ward. And you know what they get on film? Six twenty five a.m. in come the cleaner with the vacuum. She pull out the plug that disconnect the life-support, the ventilator, the dialy what-you-call-it like Marcos had, and plug in the vacuum-cleaner instead. Then she do her job like she's paid, in the corners, by the skirting-board, no skimping. Finish that then she unplug the vacuum and in the life-supports again. Trouble is the patient's dead already."

"Gee!"

"What colour you think she is, the cleaner?"

"I'd rather not know, Ed."

"OK. She is a nigger. Man, she polish the patients off."

I threw a cushion at him.

"I wanted to get Marites a job cleaning there, man – office and hospital cleaning at crack of dawn, no one's to run the check-up on you. No one want that job who's in their right mind. Only TNT and Illegals. But she quit after a week."

We were silent a while.

"Marites is a good girl," he said. "If she's a man she would have been a great cocker? No one to beat her at the cock-pit. Roulette she's not so good, blackjack also. Big loser. I see her crying her eyes out here, have to borrow from Fe." I took this as a discreet warning not to leave any dough lying around.

"They can't help themself, you know," Ed said.

"Who? Vampires or gamblers?"

"Both!"

As I said, Ed was a straight-up guy. No subtleties.

Then the next time I was up West, Ed asked, "You happy here? You going to spend the rest of your natural here?"

"Wow, Ed. I hadn't really given it any thought. Just going with the flow, you know."

"What happens if the authority catch you? You're an illegal, you know. You got no right to be here. They'll defort you straight back home. Make you real unpopular with the emvassy here and back home. You're a burden on the Philippine economy and taxpayer – means less for the politician to steal. Then anything they can pin on you back home, it'll all come in to roost, Rey. Automatic fresumption of guilt."

"Shit, Ed. You'd depress the dead."

"Just speak the truth to a friend. That's what a friend is for."

"First they got to catch me, Ed."

"OK, it's not so easy to find you if they have no help. And they have to be careful how they do it. This isn't a police state, not like Marcos. But you think of this: what happen if a Filipino inform on you? What if you quarrel with 'Tes? Or you owe someone, or worse, someone owe you money and want you gone?"

"Shit, Ed, you really know how to accentuate the negative."

We sat in silence. Everything he said was true. It was, indeed, difficult for them to swoop on you. So many of us were TNT, *Tago ng Tago*, illegals, yet it was unthinkable for them to nab everyone at four p.m. on a certain day on the basis that they had black hair and almond eyes or were black-skinned and frizzy-haired, even if it was subsequently shown that two out of ten shouldn't have been in England. All the Jenny Smiths in the country would have screamed blue murder.

But the other half of Ed's argument was equally valid: it only needed a Filipino to rat on me and, man, were we rodents.

"OK, I'll be the one to stress the positive," Ed resumed. "You're a bright boy. You don't belong cleaning or working in a shop. But that's all you'll ever be able to do here. You'll never be an attorney like you were studying for, that's for sure. Want to wash dishes all your life?"

"No."

"You got to move on. And sometime, you got to go home and straighten things out. Or it'll follow you the rest of your life."

"I've a few well-wishers working on that."

"Including Edwin."

We left it at that. Back at Tes's I stacked some heavy boxes of coconuts I'd advised her to buy, in Brixton, then ran a stock-take, something she'd never done till I arrived. She was always poring over some roulette system or blackjack trigger-number but had never known whether she was turning a profit or a loss on her E13 equivalent of a *sari-sari* store.

The cloned cell-phone went. I was momentarily hopeful it might be Nicky or Jenny Smith, but the first two or three words of what would be Marites's half-hour Tagalog gossip session had the effect on me of bromide on a sex-maniac. I knew it wasn't Commander Smith or Nicky paging me. Turning on the twenty two inch TV with stereo sound that reposed on a throne its own height of old newspapers (if a *pinoy* couldn't have a Rolls-Royce they'd settle for a Sony Trinitron) I indulged myself in the finest news and current affairs programmes in the world.

When Marites came through again, I asked, *"Walang gi-telefono para ko?"*

She shook her head. "You expecting?"

"Maybe."

"Until now nothing."

"Ah. When there's a call just let me know."

"No froblem."

More than that I couldn't say. What was I gonna do? Insult Marites directly by insinuating she wasn't passing calls and messages on to me? Still, it was strange the Smiths hadn't been in touch. When it came to it I considered them more reliable than my friend and fellow-countrywoman.

Some weeks went by. The weather warmed up a little. I got a bad cold. I'd thought I was immune. I was no longer trembling inside my clothes, but I guess the bugs benefitted more from the temperature increase than I did. I taught Tes's creepy little nephew the Visayan for "snot" and he told me the word "bogey" which I'd only known as 1. ghost 2. railway-car. 3. intruder into friendly airspace 4. average player's golf-score. You live and you learn. I spent a fortune on tissue-paper, which only left me with a nose the colour of Santa's. I was middling sick of London. Even Safeways, Waitrose, and Sainsbury's lost their charm when liquid glass was cascading out of your nostrils.

This time Ed came by our place after he'd been attending a Roman Catholic Christening in Plaistow. If no one else liked having us Flips in Plaistow, the priest, a jolly Irishman, did. You'd have thought he was being paid by the head, like an English national health dentist.

Ed was tipsy when he came in. This meant he'd had a glass of wine or a can of pilsener; his threshold was really low. This was OK because he didn't change character when he drank. I've always disliked people who charmed when sober but became offensive when drunk. I despise them more than I do people who are overly aggressive the whole time. At least they have the courage to be what they are. Pie-eyed, Ed was still affable Ed. That was his essence. He was whistling, badly when you considered he was a Filipino, *A Life on the Ocean Wave*.

My surprise and pleasure at seeing him were both genuine. I put him in Marites's only chair, an office swivel off a skip, and made him an Ovaltine ('Tes drank neither tea nor coffee). "Where's Fe?"

Edwin put his finger to his lips. "Don't tell her I've been the one to drink alcohol. She doesn't like it."

"OK, Ed. Once in a blue moon? Everything in moderation, including moderation."

"Hey, I like that one. The Father Faul teach you it, too?"

"That was the fruit of auto-didacticism, Edwin. What's new?"

"Fopeye."

"What?" He treated me to a rendition of Popeye the Sailor Man complete with finale of toot-toot through Popeye's pipe.

443

Actually, Ed oiled was screechier than unlubricated Ed. I decided to get into the spirit of things. If you can't beat 'em, join 'em etc. "I yam what I yam and I duz what I duz," I intoned in my saltiest, most grating voice.

"What?"

"Popeye's song," I explained patiently. I remembered Fr. Paul, having confiscated Beethoven Durano's comic, tossing the chalks in his palm and inviting comment from us on "the ontological significance of Popeye's song." None of us had risen to the challenge – Beethoven smirking uneasily the while, thinking he'd escaped the tawse thanks to Fr. Paul's notorious whimsicality (Beethoven hadn't) – but it was the day I'd learned the word "solipsism". One to rank with "oxymoron".

"Who's gonna be Bluto?" I asked. "And who's my Olive Oyl?"

Ed obviously felt he was getting out of his depth in the allusion game – he hadn't had the benefit in youth of Danton's Komix re-cycling syndicate after all – so he got down to the nitty-gritty of it.

"The way out is by sea," he said. "You ship on-board."

Man, that sent a cold finger down my spine. "Oh, no," I said. "Oh, no. I heard that one before, buddy. And it got me deeper into the shit. I'm lucky to be alive still. No way. Never again."

"Listen to it first before you throw it in the trash-cans. I gone to trouble over this for you, boss. So kindly take the trouble to hear it out." This was the nearest Ed ever got to being mad with me and I figured I had deserved the scolding. One thing my Jesuits had infected me with when they taught me to express myself, this being the ticket-price of the capacity for rapid, rail-bound ratiocination – was the mind advance-dirty. Ed, and many of my fellow *pinoys*, thought me cavalier, rude, but it was just that I saw things by lightning-flash and they by taper-glow.

"I'm sorry, Ed. Pardon me, will you."

"Ah, sure. No offence taken." He belched. "Just thinking of your interest all the time. Now listen to this, you'll be the interested party." He told me how he had "*mga* pals" down at a seaman's home by the East River – that's what he called the Thames, I think Ed had been watching too many episodes of a certain American cop series – who'd put him wise to a "golden opportunity". Brazen was what I'd have called it. A West African seaman resident in the home had died. The guy sounded like Long John Silver's (half-) brother.

Delirium tremens had been the least of this lonely man's afflictions. I think he'd been drinking not just methylated spirits but metal polish and cleaning solvents from the Home's broom-cupboard in the end, for I found them tucked into his bed-springs and neatly taped, with sailorly skill and meticulousness, under the shoe-shelf of the clothes cupboard. Edwin gave me a garbled, third-hand account, none of which I find too reliable in retrospect, for having been told the guy had sailed on the *MV Gambia*, what did I discover when I inherited his Seaman's Book but that he'd been born in The Gambia, e.g. Ed had heard, "he's from the *Gambia*."

Nkwem A____ had fallen into the river when in a greater than usual state of inebriation, floated around six inches under the surface for a few days (which as Dant coolly informed Fr. Paul when we were reading the first chapter of *Our Mutual Friend* is what a stiff always does in fresh or brackish water as opposed to the more buoyant sea) and got his face chewed up by a few propeller-blades in the process. Most of his jaw and teeth had gone, which meant identifying him was that much harder. "So," concluded Ed, having used a lot of words for him, "it came to us that it was your chance." "Excuse me, Ed, but have you been telling all and sundry about me?"

"Not to all. But, look, this is your chance, boss. Switch identity."

I was silent. Ed had summed up my position the last time we'd met pretty accurately, much more objectively than I could have done myself. However much I prided myself on the ability to rise above a context, viewing myself dispassionately and neutrally at all times, it was hard not to soften the truth for one's own consumption sometimes. And, in truth, I was in limbo with the only way down, rather than up.

"What am I supposed to do, glue my photo over his?"

Ed now knew he'd sold his idea. "No, boss. Just leave it. I already seen it. Could be brothers."

"You mean, we all look the same?"

"O! Niggers people all look the same! He was a big guy, too."

I escorted Ed to the bus-stop and saw him safely on. That I considered my bounden duty under any circumstances, whether he was merry or as sober as an English judge. "Ed was here, you just miss him," I informed Marites.

"Yes, I know," she said.

I TOOK UP RESIDENCE in the God-forsaken, echoing Seaman's Home for three weeks, at Ed's insistence. I've blocked out most of that time but I remember the twenty-four hour twilight of the corridors and the dead silence as if we were deep inside the Great Pyramid, broken only by the howls of some suffering madman in an unknown room in the bowels of the tomb. I only saw anyone twice at the reception. The Salvation Army Home down the way in Whitechapel was by comparison the Ritz but, wow, I didn't like the Sally Amy's name. The army that salvaged derelicts.

For my part, I felt more like an animal who had to go through quarantine. This was a reverse quarantine. I was going out into the wild again to be M A-D, crazy, know rage, acquire, bite, and spread my special sickness. Call me mutt, call me faithful Fido. What do dogs know? To bite the only hand that feeds and languish their term in the dog's home while their fickle masters and mistresses forget them.

Ed never came there, only arranged to meet me at a dingy but expensive working-man's café in the Bethnal Green Road where a cup of the disgusting beverage, tea, cost as much as three litre-bottles of San Miguel back home. On our second meeting he had a Filipino and a red-haired white guy with him. These were Gerry, a qualified radio officer and Sven, a deck-hand. I liked the look of Gerry, neat, bright, humorous, a model of the best the Manila lower middle-class could produce. Sven was a surly Scandinavian thug I never had to see again. He'd been the deceased's shipmate and used the word "nigger" in a way that wasn't innocent. I grinned my way through our interview. He was the one I paid. Five hundred pounds of Faud's money. Yeah, I did a Babyjane. Sorry. But he owed me more than that.

"OK," Ed said, "you can go. Gerry will pick you up *Miyerkoles*."

"That's it?"

"It."

"Don't worry," Gerry said. "I'll be there for you."

And he was.

I had a nasty dream Tuesday night, something like *Great Expectations*, with me as Magwitch in the boat at the mouth of the Thames waiting to escape on the steamer, Nicky Smith in boy's clothes rowing. When we capsized it was into brown water that tasted sweet as the stewed tea at the café.

In fact, Gerry took me on the bus to Tilbury where we boarded the *MV Dildunia II* in civilised fashion up a gang plank with an awning. "You're the lucky one," Gerry said, "they almost never go from here any more."

My image of a focsle was, however, faithfully anachronistic. We actually had individual cabins, complete with shower and head. Gerry told me to stay on board, but I breached his injunction the once when I left to telephone 'Tes. She informed me the Smiths hadn't phoned, as they had earlier promised, or replied to the over-obsequious message I'd left on their answering machine. "That's OK, *'be*," I said cheerfully.

The times I'd shared with her and still she lied to me. She'd probably told them they had the wrong number, the little bitch.

CHAPTER XX

All at Sea – Echo: Gerry's Tale – Bone-Jarring: Prycey's Tale
Ground Provisions – I get the point

A REALLY MONSTROUS, not just big, wave smashed into the bow of the Dildunia II every fourth time. This was my first Biscay storm, thirty-six hours out of Tilbury. The regularity, the predictability of the event, never prepared me for the immensity of the shock. It was a rare modern vessel that actually gave the sensation of floating, of skimming the surface of the ocean, of being buoyant, of displacing an amount of sea-water equal to its own volume. It was more like being on a lump of solid lead which would immediately sink if it should lose a fraction of its forward momentum. The waves were like giant guards administering illegal body-checks, or a football team's defensive line, hurtling into us as we ran against the wind, each time just failing to bring us to a dead halt and send us to the bottom of the sea. The tremendous force of the No 4 wave made the whole ship shudder and vibrate. More, there was a huge echoing bang, followed by a rumbling, rolling sound as if there was something loose in the hold – like a field-gun or a wrecking-ball – which terminated in a double crash. I don't think Mac-Mac, the old Scottish master, had lost so much of his seaman's instincts to his cirrhosis that he would have allowed a piece of our own equipment or an item of freight so much opportunity. But I do know it occurred every time we encountered rough weather, though my ship-mates pretended not to know what I was talking about. Modern bulbous-prowed carriers and tankers just aren't in harmony, in the way that a beautiful sailing-ship was, with the element they ride on. If the Dildunia had possessed eyes painted on the bows like Mediterranean or Thai fishing-boats they would have had a broken nose set between them.

I spewed my guts out, our first two days in the Bay and then Finistère. Worse than Faud's *dhow*. As I lay on my back, counting the rivets, I wished myself anywhere, anytime, except in my present circumstances. I'd have traded it for the Ukrainian death-ship we'd sailed on out of Manila Bay, I'd have swapped it for back at Faud's as private miscreant number one. There's nothing like sea-sickness.

Early on, Gerry came in to see me. Gerry was by any standards a fairly puny guy but right then he could have done anything to me. However the ship pitched or rolled, he was used to it. You weren't in the condition to resent even the jokers who revelled openly in their immunity, the ones who called out "carrots" and "greasy bacon" when they saw your ashen face, still less a modest and sympathetic type like Gerry. Hearing a rap on the handsome formica of my door, thoughtfully slat-ventilated at the bottom, I groaned "OK, *lang*," knowing only a Filipino would feel welcome to knock under such circumstances. Gerry stepped neatly over the three-inch threshold that was as deadly as a Scout Ranger's jungle trip-wire to landlubbers, took the two paces in that were safe at that stage of the ship's movement, held the thoughtfully-installed drink-holder mounted on the wall as the ship started to climb and as it attained the top of the monstrous wave I'd never see, advanced to my bed-side.

"*'Sus* what happen to you?"

There was an egg-sized lump on my forehead where I'd timed the roll wrong and fallen. As a compensation for my major sufferings, I was able to consider it as of little account as a gnat's bite. And when a particularly enormous sea hurled me straight out of the bunk and nose-first onto the floor as uncompromisingly as a pancake dropping back into a pan, I simply picked myself up and flopped face-down on to the soft beddings. The two bruises would ache and then sting for a fortnight afterwards, making me shake my head in wonder before the tiny shaving-mirror.

"Leave me alone," I croaked.

"No problem. My number two's covering for me, never mind his Morse not all it should be."

"Oh, God, just let us sink. Forget about SOS."

Gerry smiled kindly. He was an even nicer guy than Edwin in some ways and, of course, much better educated. As radio officer he got to wear epaulettes and, when we were in those parts, a fancy tropical rig of shorts and long white stockings.

"It takes everyone this way," he consoled me. "When I've been ashore a long time it's the same for me. Even for the Old Man, Mac-Mac."

At this moment I retched, producing nothing at all, my stomach long emptied, but sending Gerry out of the cabin. There were limits to his tolerance. Actually, what he said about sea-sickness wasn't true. There were individuals who were quite immune to it, rare but they did exist. They had, on the surface, nothing in common: fat women, small men, big men, young children, decrepit pensioners. Only what you couldn't see defined them as a group: the hidden auditory and balancing organs. They spanned the whole spectrum, but it did seem the dashing, the courageous, the enterprising, and the natural leaders got laid low by it, while the timid, the finks, the failures rose above it. On the other hand what Gerry said was true: the old man on every ship I ever sailed in could never openly succumb to it. He had to sit it out at table while lesser souls grew quiet, then pushed back their chairs and made a break for it, hands over their mouths. It was a point of honour, which was weird because the evidence pointed to the fact that it was not a matter of character or discipline, just the way your inner ear was set-up.

About five days out, with the weather only slightly improved, the seas still huge, the wind — when I ventured on deck — like solid matter in the face, I began to feel better. This recovery first manifested itself when having got to rivet twenty-seven, I wondered who was crewing the ship. Gerry had told me he was one of the few still capable of standing upright. This initial curiosity about the world, tiny anxiety about prolonging rather than shortening my existence, then turned into a feeling of great hunger. Man, I was so ravenous I could have eaten one of Faud's sheep whole (though I still couldn't have faced one of Ed's parrot-fish). Getting to my feet gingerly, I had to hold the wall-bracket but because I was light-headed rather than suffering the abandonment of nausea.

It was an unsociable hour by land in London, but life at sea had a different rhythm. I followed the smell of frying to the mess and the tiny, adjoining galley. The off-coming watch were addressing themselves to a midnight feast which in its essentials was breakfast: scrambled eggs, rashers of bacon, sausages, beans, fried bread and canned tomatoes with gouts of brown sauce and vinegar shaken over a side-dish of fries. Well, cured danggit fish and garlic rice would have been more to my taste, but I fell upon it. My companions, I have to say, were an unprepossessing crowd, worse even than the casino dregs. They made Babyjane, Rowell the Sparks, even Slash 'n'

Crap look like paragons of beauty and intelligence. The least retarded, Cookie, was a fat slob with a greasy brown beard and lank hair that seemed to have absorbed the oil from his own deep-frier. Kev, the blond galley-boy, was frankly sub-normal, the runt of runts, with a chin so recessive it appeared part of his neck. Kev was eighteen and the ship whore. I never saw Cookie without his apron, even the time I stumbled across him sodomising Kev while the heavy cold-room door flapped open and shut on its well-greased hinges, the way Kev's sphincter must have been. I sailed two voyages with Cookie and never found out his name. He was from a seaside town in the North of England called Yarmouth. The other guys I knew only by their first names, just as they called me Ray for Rey (I was fucked if I was gonna be called Nkwem, man). We came together by chance, were intimate in our relaxing and working lives to the extent you wouldn't be even with family ashore (some of us rather more intimate than others), were parted, whirled away on other voyages, on different ships, to alternate hemispheres, sometimes to ship together months or years hence, sometimes never to meet again in our lives, but always to take leave of each other with a casual and indifferent nod.

The officers on every boat we knew by their last names: Mr Levinson the First Mate, Mr Watt the Chief Engineer, Mr Pryce, the Bosun's Mate. This latter's title was another esoteric English mystery to me, like the distinction between private and public school, or calling the second floor the first floor, or nett gross. The Bosun was not an officer but somehow the Bosun's Mate, who was Third Officer, was one.

Our officers were, entirely without exception, a group of steady, calm, responsible, and knowledgeable young men – at least at sea – and every captain I ever sailed under was either eccentric to the point of insanity, chronically befuddled by alcohol, pathologically mean, or an abdicator of his responsibilities who inhabited his cabin like an African dictator might his palace. What happened to the bright, likeable young officers when they became captains? It wasn't a question of The Knowledge. Every one of the first officers I knew already had a Master Mariner's ticket, it didn't matter whether out of Singapore, Hamburg, or London, all were equally competent. Something happened to them when they became the Old Man. Overnight they turned into drunken ogres. It was like the VD clinic

I attended a year and a half later in Rotterdam after two agonising weeks of pissing nails all across the Atlantic from Curacao in the Netherlands Antilles and Barbados. One half of the clinic, skimpily segregated from the other, consisted of demure, white, secretarial-looking girls, the other half – equally almost exclusively – of black men, as large as myself, from the lower reaches of society. Context suggested the bucks and the butter-wouldn't-melt-in-their-mouths brigade were infecting each other but who in the first place was giving it to whom? The tribes of officers and skippers were equally distinct and equally reactive in their effect upon each other.

There were two expressions in vogue during the time I voyaged on the *Dildunia* and, indeed, in wide circulation on the other ships I sailed in. They were: "Do you want a meat injection?" and "When out at night, wear something light." I give them in the order in which I heard them. Kev was the first to ask me about the meat injection. I sensed at once it was a rhetorical question. However, I was unable to refrain from repeating in puzzlement, "Meat injection?" which had everyone at the table smiling The Smile.

The second little saying, being a statement – or in fact a ditty aspiring to the status of a rhyming couplet – couldn't be addressed to anyone specific, like Meat Injection. It was uttered generally in company of at least three, and hung in the air:

> "When out tonight
> Wear something light."

I was slower with this. It took a while to realise it was only said when I was around. When I asked about it, I received the benefit of even slyer Runt Smiles. At length I got it: I ought to wear light colours when abroad in darkness because cars were more likely to hit me as I was black. John Dawson, a pale-skinned Cape Coloured who was a deck-hand on my next ship, confirmed it for me. It was a jingle from an English road safety advertisement run some years ago. You wouldn't have thought they wanted to preserve black people so much.

Finally, I noticed *Ol' Man River* was sung a lot when I was around. This, I have to admit, got on my nerves. When it had happened once too often, I approached Smithie who sang the melody the most often and with the most relish, Smithie of the ample cleavage showing at the back of his low-hung jeans, and sang it with him, three inches from his face, looking him straight in the eyes and drowning him out with my choir-trained voice. The tune immediately became much less popular all over the ship. I admit if I had been five feet five and one hundred pounds, it might not have worked, but Dant would have found the way, too.

And at the end of that First Breakfast in the little mess, with the stars shimmering in the pale darkness outside, the first of many such repasts, I heard another refrain in which I also would learn to join. As Cookie pushed the uneaten, virgin rashers, eggs, and sausages into the swill of the gash-bucket, a plaintive voice said, "Oy, I'll 'ave them for me elevensies," to be rebuked by a Cookie-led chorus of, "Nah, don't save nothing for the company." To watch it day by day, the gulls crossing our wake, the good food wilfully wasted, was a disturbing spectacle for someone trained from childhood by Ma and priests to waste narry a grain of rice nor flake of fish. So the reverence universally felt for the Captain, however incapable and irrational he was practically speaking, was not extended by transference beyond him to the Owners, the impersonal shipping firm. Even the company's agents in the ports to which we resorted, not a few of them MM themselves, were heartily despised. Yet it was an article of pride that we did not break the ship's gear or waste commodities like paint, grease, ropes, cables, or even bulbs and fuses. Neatness, parsimony aboard were as much part of the seaman's code as were riotousness, spendthriftness ashore.

MY FIRST VOYAGE involved carrying agricultural machinery to Limassol, with calls-in at Santander and Gibraltar on the way to drop God knows what. Returning, we paid calls to Piraeus, Valetta, and La Rochelle to load olive oil, some dubious crates ex-Libya, and wine. The Med was calm going in, ferocious going out. I couldn't believe the Aegean could get so damn rough, that enclosed wine-dark sea of Fr. Paul's imagination that was his super-ego and my id. I was OK by now, could admire the beauty and majesty of the storm as well as curse the extra work it made all hands. Mac-Mac the skipper – a Scot, so named by the Filipino crew-members – for all his failings was a first-class mariner. We didn't have the latest electronic nav aids the monster ships I'd later sail on had but Mac-Mac didn't need them. He was a traditionalist and I, the spawn of modernity itself, have always respected classicism, however eccentric its particular incarnation. Mr Pryce, the Bosun's Mate, a strapping, gorilla-hairy young fellow with chest curls sprouting out of his collar, was eager to hone his skills and acquire new – or rather old – knowledge. As we scurried about below, we could see him through the streaky glass, binns around his neck, ancient Mac-Mac's giant familiar. I had a friend in young Pryce. Big man's solidarity, of course, but he sensed something different in me as I sensed the ambition in him. He gave me sympathy where I didn't need it: the relentless daily barrage of jokes and references to my blackness. This had actually been more tolerable before I became part of the group, when I was still on sufferance, when I heard *Ol' Man River* a lot. As I merged into the crew, the quips were no longer intended as excluding insults but as bonds between us: proofs that because we were all mates I could be insulted without offence being given. I was supposed to grin and appreciate the specimens of wit as if it was the first time I'd heard them and not the one hundred and third. Factory floor or focsle, I think it would have been the same, and it was peculiarly English. Quite how tedious it could become could only be appreciated if you were the recipient of this friendly chaff. I don't think even Jenny Smith could have suspected how "boring". But you ignored it, like you learned to ignore the spray and the rain.

The constant reference to meat-injections was another form of exorcism: not to contain the stranger in the tribe this time but to manage the heterosexual majority's fear of homosexuality and such urges as might lie within themselves.

Big-hearted young Pryce was supervising some routine work we were doing with a hatch-cover, taking advantage of the sunny skies and calm seas outside, of all places, La Rochelle when a couple of what I would have to describe as my mates, as well as being my shipmates, gave vent to a remark about the nice sun-tan I'd be getting as we worked with our shirts off. This was water off my (bare) back, but Pryce shot me a look. There'd been an incident in a bar in the French port where I'd been instrumental in getting him and the Second Engineer out of trouble after Gerry and I dived in on hearing the British trigger-words "Fucking Cunt" (not uttered by Pryce). Tiny Gerry had been first in, followed by the bolt-headed monster. Pryce still had a bandage on his arm and a plaster on his spine from the broken bottle. Which was why he had his back against the railings, instead of "mucking" in with us, as was his habit. I didn't return the look. Prycey still had something to learn about what it took as an officer (Fr. Paul being somewhat harder on his favourites than on others) and I didn't think I'd better encourage him in his mistakes. Besides which, I didn't want his goddamned sympathy about this. It was my problem and it was cool. Unwanted concern got me more het up than being called a nigger, which today I hadn't been.

That was the first voyage, anyhow. It was beautiful spring weather in England. We docked in Jersey this time, not for long, before setting off for the Caribbean, taking out agricultural machinery again and returning with a perishable, fruit, and some liquor. Human beings were also perishables, of course.

It was pretty well the same crew, with the exception of Kev who'd had a motorbike accident outside St Helier. The knock-on effect of this was that Cookie got a black eye for making up to a young seaman, Roy, who was emphatically hetero and allergic to getting a meat injection. Roy wasn't averse to giving one to someone else, oddly enough, in extremities of deprivation. "Nah, mate," he told me, "it's not queer if you're fucking laughing."

That was the voyage I got my dose (from a lady) in either Barbados or the ABC's. I was only in both places a total of seventy-two hours but by the time we got home I had a lifelong souvenir stricture. The penicillin and tetracycline we had on board didn't work – the former even in injection form, *siguro*. We went to re-fit in Rotterdam, *Dildunia* and Rey Archimedes Blondel Castro both, then came back on the boat-train from Hook of Holland with a vivid night in between in Amsterdam where I tried vainly to figure out in which lane and which cubicle Dant had kept his faith with his priest. I disobeyed Doctor's orders and dicked a Thai girl, finding the few Filipinas somewhat overblown for my taste. I've never liked voluptuous chicks. I was getting worse, man, and I knew it. The first time with the girl hanging round the dock in Curacao was the breaking of a lifelong inhibition. I think it was a coincidence she was black. It was getting as easy for me to use girls as eat a steak. Prycey liked a girl you could get a good handful of, though. I got him a discount with a jolly Tagalog girl.

Coming bleary-eyed into Harwich in the early autumn chill, I asked myself what the fuck it had all been in aid of when I was now returning to the England I had left. Passport control seemed cursory – time and place everything – but Prycey made a point of talking to me immediately before he went through his channel and then coming to mine and immediately resuming the conversation with suspicious animation for the hour. I wondered if he had some inkling of my general circumstances or just did it "on spec" for all foreign seamen. You couldn't have had a more upstanding alibi and character witness than him. Good on you, Prycey. Where are you now? *Siguro*, fat and skippering a super-tanker. The news-agent was still closed when we boarded the waiting train, so I couldn't get a *Guardian* or a *Daily Telegraph*. I'd missed the English newspapers, that and the television. They put most of the rest of the world to shame. Prycey went to get us two paper cups of coffee from the refreshment stall which was open. While he was gone two respectable-looking middle-aged black men in shabby suits came on. They both had paunches and one was balding. I figured we carried this off much less well than some races. Shortly before the train started moving two policemen in their ridiculous helmets came down the corridor behind the black men. "Good morning, sir," the senior of the two addressed the older also of the black men. For the time of morning he was extraordinarily jovial. Both he and his partner were wearing what I would describe as heavyweight versions of The Smile. The black guy looked as sick as if the bogey was bucking about on the high seas instead of lying dead in the station.

"You should have let us know you were coming, sir," the policeman continued. "We could have made arrangements to welcome you, if you'd given us some advance notice."

The object of these pleasantries muttered something that was inaudible to me. He was pissed as hell but anxious not to annoy the policeman. I knew these policemen were not bank-robbers, kidnappers, drug-wholesalers and guns for hire like the police of guess-where but it's been ingrained in me, I can't help it, I've always disliked and distrusted cops in any country. That was why my sympathies lay with the black guy squirming, not just because he was black. I think Prycey felt that way, too. It was a typical English reaction, to side with the underdog. To my surprise, the police left shortly before the train started to move, the officers saying their farewells with great geniality and courtesy so elaborate it appeared Asian. The black men relaxed. At Liverpool Street Station I half-expected them to be arrested but, after a quick glance down the platform to the ticket-barrier and a chuckle of relief between them, they disappeared into the early rush-hour crowd. I never found out what it had been about.

Pryce took me to a better hostel, from which we transferred to the city of Liverpool two nights later. He had a berth as Second Officer, this time on an old tub plying the Windward Islands route and I was glad to ship with him. Although I'd got in and out of the country without problems, and seemed secure in my new alias, I was loth to press my luck and resolved to remain out of England in future if I could. 'Tes's cell-phone was no longer functional: I got a grating, mechanically-generated voice-reply informing me the number I had dialled was unavailable. I tried the Smiths. The number had been changed; they'd gone ex-directory. They must have been receiving nuisance-calls. I grinned as I imagined myself sorting that out, my way.

Gerry rode the train up north with Prycey and me. Fuck, that would have been a long ride without good company. We had some protracted, unscheduled halts built into it, the train languishing in deepest country like a damsel awaiting her rescuer. I dropped off a couple of times – you know me well enough – and as I came to the second time with Gerry and Prycey down at the buffet-car, I wondered if I was in Dr Zhivago. Movie, *siguro*, not book.

I got a buzz out of being with the officers. Sitting with Prycey and Gerry over a can of beer and a hard liquor chaser in a plastic tumbler wasn't quite as intoxicating to the ego as being admitted to the company of Jesuits over soft drinks, but it was still inebriating. Then came the hangover and the return to reality. I was catching tantalising glimpses of the world I should have been moving in, the person I could be – Third Officer and Radio Officer modest enough ambitions – if I'd been anything other than a Filipino. Even black men in Europe and the Americas could rise from the morass without getting a bullet in the head from some wizened warlord as the price of the impertinence to encroach on their ancient rackets, politely termed monopolies.

Gerry wasn't sailing with us. He had the radio-officer's berth on a passenger-cargo vessel plying the Azores, Sao Tome and Principe, and Cape Town route.

"Passengers," snorted Prycey.

"Well, sure," said smiling Gerry, "*pero* I get my own table in the dining-room. Maybe I'll be the one to meet a rich Amerikana, just widowed *na*."

"You should be so lucky," Prycey retorted. "It'll be some old woofter."

"Yeah," I contributed. "Meat-injection for you."

Gerry sniggered. "You got the money, we got the honey."

It wasn't the most elevated conversation but I remember that five-hour train-ride as vividly as I do the more eventful journeys of my life, certainly better than some of the sea-voyages I made with Robbie Pryce, crossing parallels of latitude in northern and southern hemispheres and the higher-numbered meridians of longitude in storm and sunshine, with dolphins curving across our bows and the gulls screaming in our wake. The newly green English fields and budding trees seemed more exotic to me and the juddering bar-car and the long second-class carriage, with its scandalously dusty upholstery that would have brought indignant squawks from Aunties Irish and Monalisa, seemed more congenial than any first-class saloon or stateroom.

The minutes had wings. I told the officers more about myself than was discreet. Gerry said, "You need all the luck you can get and good friends. By the way, your friend Sven never paid me my share of the money you gave him." He waved his hand and smiled. "No. I'm not saying it to get some more. I just don't care. Glad to be of assistance. Put it there, Rey." We slapped palms. "Just so you know who your real friends are. You got your bright ideas, but you wrong about some people and some things sometimes. Better you know that, too. You're the one to be quite arrogant about ideas and things, even though you're OK. Hope I didn't make an enemy just now."

"Ah, *diay*. No, brother, thanks for your frankness."

Pryce let the Flips speak their minds to each other. Then he asked, "What's the worst call you ever made, then, Gel?"

"Ah, Gee. Er. How about my choice of parents?"

"Yeah, Mr Pryce. Choice of country, too. What about you? Ever got a man killed aboard or injured and you know it was down to your call?"

Pryce was silent, which was a "yes" answer to my nosiness.

"I think the worst when you're not the one to be quite sure," Gerry said. "I relay some Mayday calls from ships in distress, like on fire or collisions, some are big tankers, some just private yachtsmen but I never hear more about it. I'm just the one to pick up and pass on, or no one would hear it. But then once I pick up a call so faint, I wonder afterward if I heard it or not."

"What was that, Gel? Pass them peanuts, Rey."

"Those peanuts, Mr Pryce."

"Fuck you, mate. Call me Prycey. What kind of call?"

"Real panic call, Robbie. Like *we're hit, we're hit*. That's in English. But real faint over the ether, not like normal faint. I hear clear, just like someone whispering in my head but like it's a world away from me. I hear, *we're going down*. Then they give the position. Well, I write that fix down fast, man, it's the training doing it, not me. Then I also hear calls next, faint-faint like the first, coming from some strange place long way away but not long way away. Different language this time, it's German, I know that much. And the talking, it's not standard radio convention. I know that much, even if I know only four words German. I can tell from the way they pitch the voice. They're like talking in code, the frequency isn't special, they're not scrambling the message, or hopping, or sending it super-speeded like it's modern. And I can hear the word wolf a a lot, *Wulf*, and wolf-pack. Numbers not ship-names: U-21, U-337. And still it's coming from like half the world away…"

"A long, long time ago," I intoned, "in a far distant galaxy."

"O-o, Rey. Like it all happened a long time ago, like ghosts. Anyhow, I had the co-ordinates written down if nothing else. That showed I hadn't been dreaming. I take them up to the bridge, the skipper of that ship he was Ulf Wir.."

"Christ, not that old Norwegian piss-artist."

It was plainly a small world, that world of men who ranged far and wide.

"Yes," said Gerry with a smile. "No one who sailed under him ever forgets that crazy. Anyhow, he's dead of his liver abscess, let's not speak badly of the dead. Well, Boss, old Ulf took one look at the Lat and Long I had on my piece of paper and kicked me down the stairs again. We had GPS on that tub and we could get a fix down to a decimal point of a second of Lat, accurate forty feet. The position I had was where we'd passed over five minutes before when I'd intercepted the Mayday call."

"Where was that, then, Gel?"

"More North Atlantic than South," said Gerry, then remembering and giving the co-ordinates with his radio op's perfect recall.

"Ah," said Prycey, "they lost a lot of convoys round there. Me old man was an RA gunner on an armed merchantman. Used to tell us yarns till my hair stood on end."

"What's the weirdest thing that happened to you at sea, then, Mr Pryce, Robbie?"

"I wouldn't know where to start, Rey."

"Robbie's followed the sea a long time, Rey. He's the one to start as galley-boy."

"Ah."

"I didn't take no meat-injections, neither. I could fart to prove it, but I'll spare you that."

When we'd all recovered from this fabulous witticism, Gerry said, "You can see plenty of strange things at sea but it's where and maybe when you see it that can make the big difference, *ba*, in the impact it have on you?"

"O? You mean the context, Gerry?"

"Aha. So you see six guys robbing a bank with bazooka and machine-gun in Southampton, man, it's kinda surprising. See it in downtown Manila, man, it's part of the daily round."

"Manila, now that's one place I've never been."

"You didn't miss anything," Gerry, a Tagalog, said wryly.

"Now Hong Kong, Singapore, I been. What you was just talking about, you two, about where you seen something being as important as what you see, I remember something that surprised me. Of all the places it was Singapore Roads. If it had been Surabaya or Port Moresby I'd have been prepared for it.

"I was working for marine insurers then out of Lloyds – they were the ones picking up the final bill the other companies had re-insured with them. It was a whole ship gone missing…"

"Holy shet!" Gerry exclaimed.

"Yeah, as the pilot said when he grounded on the shoal. You've got to understand it wasn't the kind of old wreck that would just founder in a Force 8. Fifteen years old, Korean-yard, three thousand tonner, twin-screws. Monrovian-registered. Nothing special about her. There were plenty like her. She'd been first-owned by an Indonesian company, Chinks of course. They ran her between Surabaya, Ujang Pandang, and Menado, then on their Perth run. Next thing, they'd flogged her to some Taiwan cousins of theirs who did the Kaohsiung, Guam, and Hong Kong run, and they went and sold her on to Filipinos in Iloilo, all Chinese again of course. They'd found her a bit too good for their inter-island ferry runs…"

"O-o. I expect the heads actually could flush," Gerry commented.

"And they leased her to Malaysians…"

"*Insik* again?" I suggested. "Chinese?"

"Dunno. It was a dummy front company but I'd be surprised if it wasn't. Well, by this time she'd had four owners and six runs. I knew because I had to do the detective-work, all the paper-chasing. She'd been the *Lumba-lumba*, the *Chee Heen*, the *Lan Tao Conveyor*, the *Lady of Our Holy Cross*, the *Sarah Rose*, and the *Ahmed* when she was making the Singapore, Labuan and KK run. She'd vanished as the *Ahmed* in the Gulf of Thailand, last sighted 20 nautical miles off Koh Si Chang.

"The insurers had a tip-off she was in Singapore. That was the last place you'd expect a marine scam then, though the villains are a bit bolder now. Well, to cut a long story short, there was a vessel of her size lying in an obscure part of the roads but completely different paint-scheme, very cleverly done, and she'd gained a dummy funnel and an extra crane and another level on the bridge. Now she was called the *Mykonos III* and flying a Greek flag.

"We went out in a launch, boarded her and found not a living soul on board. We searched high and low. There wasn't a thing on her in the way of personal effects, just the ship's cat. She was still plump, funny enough, just a little thirsty 'coz she'd been drinking the water in the heads and on the life-boat covers. She must have been living off the rats. Well, tabby knew the real story, she must have seen it all and I used to look into her eyes and see my reflection and wonder what other reflections there must have been. If only she could have talked!

"All the cargo was long gone but in the No 3 hold we found a row of big old earthenware jars, like Chink wine-jars. We opened them and in each was a human skeleton. Eighteen wine-jars, eighteen complete sets of bones.

"They examined the bones – and they were all of young men, in their late twenties at most. They could tell by the lack of wear on the knee cartilage and the molars. They got an expert in and he told them sure as he could without a shred of doubt they were East Europeans. Slavonic skulls and cheekbones…"

"Zygoma."

"Whatever. Anyhow that was it. No one was at all interested in following it up. Whose jurisdiction was it? No one knew where the crime, if there had been one, had occurred. The insurers covered some of their expenses by selling her for scrap to the Pakis, that fucking tanker graveyard in Bangladesh – that's the only job worse than what you told me about the Arabs, mate – and that was it, end of story."

"Maybe the fuckers had got what they deserved."

"What?"

"Excuse. Hey, it's my turn *pero wa koy historia*, man. The bank's empty. I didn't lead the eventful life like you characters."

"Nah, you ain't getting away with that. Oy, what's that station?"

"Crewe," I read. "Great name for an inland place."

"Fucking arse end of nowhere. Well, at least we're moving. I've waited longer at Crewe Junction than I have for the canal at Port Said. We've got a couple of more hours if I know British Rail. Come on, let's be having it."

I thought hard. Then I remembered a particularly outrageous story of Hubert's. "OK *lang*. You're the ones to talk about mysteries of the sea, *Marie-Celeste, Flying Dutchman* and all. And Gerry's saying it's the unexpected place, the context topsy-turvy, *ba*, that makes it weird. Here's something that's got all those elements.

"I got this story from an American friend I knew only a short time but I'll never forget him. He was working in oil in Darusallam…"

"Yeah, Brunei. Been there. Not a whore onshore."

"O-o. Got to go to Labuan for that, or Brothelton, sorry, Jessleton. Go on, Rey."

"Well, they had a problem there with drought one time. *El Niño* and all that. I mean, it was a real rainy part of the world. You didn't get all that goddamned rain forest without rain, right? But no rains to mention for at least six months and, Gee, the timber and the creepers and the mulch, it all got bone-dry. It just takes someone careless with a cigarette or some broken-glass magnifying the sun's rays and, pow, you've got a raging forest fire on your hands.

"One thing they had there was plenty of money from the oil. I think the Sultan got more Rolls-Royces than any other human being? Also he's the one to get his hands on the top of the line production models from Pilipinas, *di ba*? So they could get their hands on the latest forest fire fighting equipment: that's water-bombing planes.

"Well, it's not like Indonesia or Brazil. Pretty soon they get everything under control. Their damage-assessment people go into the jungle: feet crunching on charcoal, dead animals everywhere, charred to pieces, legs sticking up in the air, smoke curling up from the ground. The whole place, man, it's just grey and black. Then suddenly someone gives a shout! What the fuck!

"They all gather round. There, lying on the burned-out forest floor, next to a monkey and a barking-deer, is the body of a fully-clothed, fully kitted scuba-diver in a melted wet-suit with two tanks on his back, regulator in his mouth, mask on his face, and his flippers fused together…"

"Fins," corrected Prycey, shaking an unopened can of Heineken with a glint in his eye.

"Yeah, fins, Mr Pryce," I continued. "So what happened? Only explanation is: the plane scooped up the diver when it was skimming the sea-surface, filling the water-tank, then dropped him when it bombed the fire. Ah, shit!"

"That'll damp you down, shipmate. Fucking Aida! Do you think I haven't heard that one?"

THE BANANA BOAT RUN, as Robbie Pryce called it (we never actually carried any or the accompanying spiders: the fruit companies tended to own their own boats) was a restful interlude for me. We used to plough smoothly across the Atlantic, away from the stormiest spots, and by the mid-stage it was often positively balmy. There was none of the in-and-out of Med ports every other day with the hassle and danger of loading (Robbie waxing sombre on the subject of the seaman decapitated by a snapped hawser early in his career, splashing him with as much blood as he had me with beer). It was eleven days of easy passage, followed by hard work in port and then R and R.

I was reminded of home except the fact that everyone looked like me made it not like home. "Puck," I could hear Danton say, wearing his *halo* at a rakish angle, "you da only ferson in da whole wide world that feels outta place with his own kind. You comfies with folks is half your size has slanty eyes and straight da hair, even da fubics. You is Gullivers, man."

463

Each of the islands looked very similar as a land-fall, with the exception of Dominica, while each had its own, often startlingly, robust identity. Ebbiola in the old BWI was our main port of call, I grew to know it well. The time I spent ashore in the Caribbean was small. It was a fraction even of the time I spent in England, let alone Arabia or Hong Kong. But I saw it from a different, familiarising perspective. People didn't treat me as a foreigner, as a tourist or an indentured slave. I was one of them, for once. I walked abroad and it was as if I was invisible. No one looked at me twice. The feeling I had was that I was at the Vampire's Ball, passing for an Undead but when we all looked in the mirror at the end of the dance, mine would be the only reflection in the glass. Was it any surprise it seemed a long time?

The Ebbiolans, I should have said, suffered from a crisis of identity as shaky as the Filipino's. Filipinos imitated Americans assiduously but pretended they didn't like them. Ebbiolans imitated the English assiduously and pretended they did like them. The policemen's uniforms – surmounted admittedly by black faces – the passion for cricket, the lush, manicured lawns and pitches like an English country garden on anabolics: all these spoke of an anglophilia which was as intense as their real anglophobia. The latter was an infection which had been brought back by the returned, their *balikbayans* in fact. At home they had possessed a natural immunity to it. They were as jolly a folk as us and, also like us, violent when the jollity failed them.

I could see the poverty in the roads, the shacks that Auntie Irish could have lived in, and as always, the kids' eyes. And there was the consideration they did extend to the non-native, to the white face, of politeness and honesty. A pretence of civilised, magnanimous behaviour which was their way of saying, look, we're decent folk in our way, as good as you. Between themselves they dropped this facade, spoke in flat, unembellished tones to each other because they knew how bad they were.

Of course, I got this face with the mask off, whereas even a guy like Prycey didn't. I recognised it at once because it was essentially the way Filipinos behaved round a 'Merikano and then among themselves when he was gone. We, too, knew what depths of pettiness and dishonesty we were capable of sinking to. So as just another black face I got to see the hard, unadorned features of island life. I used to eat at a food-stall run by an enormous negress who was as bad-tempered as her stand was spotless. Free with her scolding tongue and formidable head-slaps, she might just have straightened out the black juveniles tormenting Marites in Plaistow had she been set loose on them when they were still eight. As I chewed my "provisions", which was to say, "ground provisions", or stewed tuber vegetables – another interesting living fossil of 18th century marine vocabulary for Fr. Paul to ponder – I'd hear "Marnin, Sah, Mam, how are you. It's a beautiful day now." Followed in short order by, "Get de cans out from under, man, and don't chat no shit about it." On the other hand I wasn't assaulted with the ragged, "You white mothah-fuckahs!" hurled by the local *i-stambys* from some guava trees in the itchy dusk. Well, that evening benison sure made the holiday-makers jump and scurry for the last bus to their resort behind its barbed wire-fence. It was one of those resorts that only took couples, you know. For sure, the island was too dangerous for an unescorted woman to walk round by night, even a black one if she was young and good-looking. And for a lone blonde, daylight wasn't safe either. In their way, my black brethren were as bad as the 'Rabo, except less wily and, of course, itching to rape their social superiors rather than, as with the Bohaidenese, their social inferiors.

I took a back seat, man. Looking in this mirror was in no guise flattering.

We made this run twice. Nothing I saw or experienced the second time contradicted my interpretation of my experiences of the first.

Then Prycey took me to ship on a Greek tub making the run to Martinique out of Rochelle. More of the same. One of the things these fuckers liked to impress on the uncouth, non-Francophone black was that they were not a colony as such but a true province of France. It was true the bread was the same as the long crusty loaves in Rochelle and red wine from Bordeaux was as plentiful as rum if not as cheap, but Em and her sisters in Puerto Princesa had baked the same in oil-drums outside the Vietnamese refugee camp and Palawan sure as hell wasn't a province of France. I thought the place sucked. Blacks with airs and graces, like the courtiers of some King of the Beggars.

"Vous êtes un nègre contumace, Monsieur," an old woman with a red-spotted handkerchief on her head informed me when I caught

her short-changing me on the *tambis* they called pomerac fruit. When Hubert called me an uppity nigger I didn't get riled but this ancient negress irritated me enough that I picked up her *bolo*, known piratically in the Antilles as a cutlass -if you like that – and husked three green coconuts in twenty seconds just to let her know what I came from.

The ship itself was an old tub but Prycey had gone up to First Mate. I guessed that at some stage one stopped going for promotion, stabilised, and started shooting for better ships but the same rank. It may have been my imagination but I seemed to notice Prycey drinking more. Nah, it was my imagination, *di ba*? That was the only thing that got a lot of exercise since I stopped hodding. I was, to tell the truth, getting flabby, losing my lines, meaning the little lines, the cuts, my muscular definition, man, not the general shape as in the lines of a ship. That was still the same, maybe more imposing. I looked OK in clothes. A tailor would always hide my impending late-life deficiencies in the way Fr. Boy looked much more venerable in his cassock or *barong tagalog* than he did in his gym *sando*, whereas there wasn't a chick in the world who'd look at a little plump short guy. Not if he wasn't standing on a thick wallet.

Up till now I'd had no problems with my shipmates. There was always a clique of *pinoys*, even if it was only the captain's steward and the least skilled deckie, who accepted me when they heard my Pilipino vernacular, made even more fluent and pungent for the occasion of bonding. But there were two characters on the *Palamede IV* I couldn't hit it with. One was Jock, an engineer from Glasgow, a miserable, sandy, rat-faced dork who only smiled when it was time to gloat over the misfortunes of others. The other was his side-kick, Jean-Claude, who acted as his eyes and ears topside. Jean-Claude was tall, dark, sinewy, tattooed in an obviously vulgar non-Fr. Boy way on his delts and tris and with a Great Plain of Baldness on his pate from which long lianas of curly hair hung past his tattoos. He looked like Frankenstein's assistant. I heard him call me a *sale macaque* one day, which I troubled to look up when we were in port. It took a while as I phoneticised it as *sarl makark* but context got me there in the end. I hadn't misheard him calling me a "filthy ape". I reckoned this was a whole lot worse than "nigger". Still less pleasing was Jean-Claude's suspicion, voiced to me in his fractured, veering English, "'ow eez eet you got no seekatreeks en you fess?" He gave "face" the same pronounciation as another French word I'd learned from him for "buttocks".

"Wrong tribe," I replied. This was a mistake. Normally I snubbed J.-C. absolutely, pretended I hadn't heard his insults. His face became a mixture of the usual sneer plus a certain fresh glee. "'Ow you don't speaks no Afreekan langue? 'Ow you speek Feel-ee-pinot to de guys from de udder sheep when we in Santo Domeengo? *Merde.* You not no fuckin' Afreekan. You a fuckin' useless seaman too. What you work in at sea before?"

I gave him my broadest grin. "Salvage, that was my speciality, J.-C. You think what you like, man, 'coz I don't fucking care what you think."

J.-C. gave me one of the meanest looks anyone ever bestowed on another human being. I'd made a mistake being aggressive this time. I just hoped that my smile didn't falter, that fucking weapon. My insouciance, a pretty sounding word of French-derivation, was of course totally assumed. I feared and respected Jean-Claude as an enemy because he didn't go off at the mouth too much. That was something to emulate. Loving your enemies didn't mean, as Fr. Paul said, liking them but it meant the capacity to learn from the cocksuckers.

Jock was the guv'nor, as Prycey liked to say, not because he was physically tougher or had a superior endowment of brains but because he had a more fecund and ingenious mind when it came to contriving spite and mischief. On a life-boat Jean-Claude would probably have eaten Jock in the end but aboard the big boat with Jock making sure the engines ran sweetly J.-C. was content to follow his suggestions. I don't think Jock or J.-C. especially disliked black people – certainly not as much as I did – it was just that they had to have a focus for all that malignancy or be consumed by it. I was the most obvious choice in that time and place. By the way, they were the ship queers. This was a word I learned first at sea; I'd never heard it on land until then. Wasn't one of our loan words and Fr. Paul and Fr. Boy were hardly likely to let it sully their lips, though Fr. Paul was known to have used the Visayan word *"bayot"*. I had nothing against Jock and J.-C. on this score at all but it was lucky for me they were the outsiders on the tub, for they were unable to turn my shipmates against me which would have made for a miserable existence, even though I hardly exchanged a sensible sentence with anybody across twenty degrees of latitude.

I used to find notes taped to my door and once – I think it was Jock, sneaking up topside – someone succeeded in locking me into one of the heads on deck for two hours before I could attract anyone's attention. They never stole anything from my cabin. That was a kind of unwritten rule between us all, maybe lingering from the days of the focsle.

Living in close proximity to another man for weeks on end, it was like you were watching him under a microscope while every day the magnification jumped another factor; it was life under the high-power field. You developed a tiny angle of vision in which someone's inoffensive foibles became major irritants: the way they looked into their handkerchief or "snot-rag" after blowing their nose, the sound they made when they chewed an apple. Fr. Paul had a low opinion of Sir Walter Raleigh as, "little less than a pirate, a man of brutal sexual appetites, arrogant in profane knowledge, who was coward enough to murder his best friend by judicial process rather than in the generosity of hot blood." But six weeks afloat in a small craft would have taught my beloved mentor how easy it would be to fall out so badly with Fr. Boy that he would have had him beheaded at first landfall on the earliest available islet. Every hour made J.-C. and Jock hate me more. I did my best to ride above context, but it was no darn use. The thinking part of you could stand above your immediate situation but your feelings – to wit, fear, hate, boredom – were firmly shackled to where and when you were. I shocked myself sometimes, man, with the thoughts I harboured.

While Robbie Pryce was aboard he was a stabilising influence. Things couldn't go too far. There were limits. You could feel that just by looking at the guy. Robbie had by now learned to be on the harsh side afloat but was a fair guy and wouldn't tolerate any shit. By mutual accord, we didn't fraternise at sea but would somehow find ourselves in the same bar in port whence we would proceed to sundry other dives by ourselves. J.-C. and Jock knew I was a friend of the First Officer's. They never actually saw us together on land and we didn't even smile at each other on board but there was nothing you could hide at sea, including having a dose.

Robbie had plans for installing me as bosun on his next tub – I think nature had made me a good bosun or team-captain behind coach and first mate – but it wasn't to be. Robbie had a bad fall in Cap Haitien, the most elementary of accidents when he took a step too far backwards and vanished over the lip of the No 2 hold. We all got there in seconds flat. Prycey was a popular officer but he could have been Judas Iscariot and we'd have gone after him. That was the sea. There were hatreds but there were also bonds. Afterwards you could make cruel and tasteless jokes about the victim. At the time you risked your own life for his. I remember getting insulted by a guy from another ship in a bar in France. Quick as a flash Jock was there, with his blade to the sailor's throat. "He's our fucking coon," Jock growled, "and don't you fucking forget it, you cunt." I tried to smile at Jock back at the ship but he ignored me.

And on this occasion, it was J.-C. who was first down to Prycey.

"It's bad," said J.-C. as I swung down. A girder we'd temporarily placed across the hold had broken Robbie's fall a little. "*Merde*, are you OK, Mr Pryce?"

"Never felt better," said Robbie Pryce and fainted. I could see the snapped bone on the left leg sticking out of the skin where his trousers had torn. By the time Jock had come out of the engine-room J.-C. had rigged up a sling, a stretcher had come down, and Robbie, mercifully still unconscious, was being borne down the gang-plank.

"Prycey copped it, did he?" Jock inquired with a leer. Jean-Claude made the confirmatory quacking noise that means throat-cut or dreadful accident. Jock looked so cheerful it was almost benign; he could just have won a lottery. "Seriously, I hope?"

"*Pardon?*"

"Broke his fucking back did he?"

"No. Leg. Port-side."

A shadow came over Jock's face. "Well, that'll keep him out of the fucking way on the next voyage too." He saw me looking over at him and scowled. He muttered something.

"Talking about me, Jock?" I asked.

Jock looked to his familiar for back-up but didn't get any. We'd been brought together by the assistance we'd rendered the First Officer, J.-C. and myself. We'd never been together before, we'd never be together again, but at that moment we were buddies. Jock headed to the engine-room very pissed indeed.

Prycey got flown home. I remained. My honeymoon with Jean-Claude didn't last long. Jock saw to that, if nothing else. The guy was wasted on a ship; he should have been working for Atty Caladong.

The guy greased engines, greased his dick when he remembered, but what he did for me was strip out such lubrication as eased my passage through the ship. I'd see other vessels all the time – we followed the historic lanes as everyone else did – and made the effort to imagine how they must see us as we saw them. You were just as little to them: bows, wheel-house or bridge, stern, and fading smuts – as they were to you. They looked deserted and insubstantial, not the little world you were, with the too well-known faces, the snug retreats, and the moments of extreme discomfort that made you appreciate the retreats more. What can I say? Happy ships were happy in different ways, *di ba*, but unhappy ships were unhappy in the same way, *siguro*. A hell-ship was identical with other hell-ships whether the skipper was Taiwanese or Latvian. These little units of vice and tyranny floated undramatically past us by night or day, carrying their secrets and dramas that were those familiar to us as well. Commander Smith used to say, just like Fr. Paul did when confronted with events like Hermes Urgello's midnight appendectomy at San Ignatio, "Worse things have happened at sea." I think he meant emergencies were easier to cope with by land, so we must count our blessings, but another way of interpreting it might be that the sea was the place where the most evil side of human nature was most transparently exhibited. Man, I'd go with that. Any day.

WE WERE GETTING SOME GREAT SUNSETS to mark Robbie's departure. There was no supernatural mystery about this. There'd been a volcanic eruption to the south east which had thrown up tons of what I should have liked to describe in one of my schoolboy essays as "particulate matter" but which Fr. Paul would have crossed out and called "dust". Even the most brutish members of the crew (namely Yarko the Rumanian who had been the next best thing to a slave before he strangled the circus-owner and ran away and Ned-oo, a Welsh retardate whom Jock was in the habit of feeding Ex-Lax chocolate and who never made the connection between these Greek gifts and his runs to the head) were impelled to stand at the railings and admire nature while they had a puff.

This many-hued splendour contrasted with the deep night of Jock's machinations. I think he had gone a little crazy down in the engine-room, the beat of the pistons indistinguishable from the roaring in his own ears that never left him even when he was released onto the deck. Robbie's departure didn't satisfy him in the way I hoped it might; it incited him to hope it was in his power to make serious harm happen to me too.

Harry, the galley-boy, or 'Arry as I called him like everyone else (I'd learned not to prefix it with the breathy consonant in order to deny Jock the opportunity to mock me with, "Hullo, H'I'm Mister High and Mighty") was a specimen of the ordinary, thoughtless, heterosexual lad who crewed merchant navy ships. He talked about meat-injections and, "It ain't queer if you're fucking laughing," just like everyone else, replying to wake-up calls with, "Fuck off, I'm wanking," but he had no interest at all in a furtive encounter with Jock or Jean-Claude. All in all, he reminded me of the Artful Dodger in the ancient musical Fr. Paul had shown us one Christmas that had not been the treat he hoped (too much like ordinary gang-life with Dant).

WELL, IT CAME TO ITS HEAD IN MOA. This was an out-of-the-way little port-town in Eastern Cuba with a world-class nickel-refinery, if there was world-class for contamination. The earth for miles was as red as a betel-splash.

Going to Cuba should have been a second homecoming for a Filipino, especially for a black Filipino. Think about it: the Americans had moved in on us both a century ago after spanking the Spanish. We had the benefit of Marcos, they of Batista. Rum and cigars we both produced, seen smouldering as frequently in the mouths of their Fidel as our own Fidel Ramos. Then there were the Joses, our Rizal and their Marti, both martyred and both overrated poets, Marti the author (pity him) of the words to *Guantanamera*, Marti who wanted to die with his face to the sun. At Guantanamo, inappropriately enough, they had their version of our Subic: an American naval base on sovereign soil that, despite Fidel's *rodomontade*, had remained there all through the Revolution, even after we would get rid of the Americans. *Siguro*, I was touching base.

I was snoring away in my cabin when I heard the smallest of bumps. They could have dropped a two-tonne crate with the clap of thunder and a shock that would have registered on the seismic scale without shaking me from my repose. But I had antennae for the stealthy (these were like the cuckold's horns absent from Fr. Paul's Shakespeare productions; they sprouted when sufficient deviousness had been practised upon you). My wide-awake half, which was my unconscious, didn't care for the quality of the noise and one eye opened automatically. There followed a scraping and a shuffling, neither of which are ever reassuring to hear – something intrinsically furtive and malicious about them. I tried to match an image with the sound-track and came up with a corpse in cowboy boots and spurs being dragged out through squeaking saloon doors by the arms. This was not so far from the reality. "Fluke it, Eleven, instinct shot can come off," as Butch Tan Sy remarked. When, taking a page from the notebook of the Stealthy Ones, I peeped under and round the bottom slats of my door, I saw three pairs of feet. Or rather two pairs of shoes and one very large soiled foot, with deltas of encrusted dirt betwen the toes and spectacularly blackened nails: the kind of foot the person it was attached to didn't so much seldom wash as never wash. (Somehow less anti-social, *di ba*? Not neglect or omission of hygiene but a consistent and permanent repudiation of it). The feet and shoes, already ten feet away when I clocked them, disappeared, however much I craned my neck and rolled my eyeballs. I'd already identified Jock's grungy Tiger trainers, an excellent Jap shoe, a little unforgiving so far as impact-absorption for a landing two hundred-pounder went but great at coping with lateral torque suddenly applied and completely wasted on an athletic non-starter like Jock and the surface of engine-room gratings.

I slipped out the door, past the line of closed cabins. It was four thirty p.m. and stiflingly hot. Half the ship was ashore, pissed out of their minds since well before midday with the other half malingering under the life-boat davits or, like me, illicitly having an air-con nap. Like I say, this is the real witching-hour in the tropics. It got very dark at the end of the passageway, with one of the fluorescent strip-lights throbbing on and off like the casual notion in Jock's head, which was why I almost ran over them as they were dragging young Aitch into his cabin.

I flitted back behind the corner, just another shadow. J.-C. and Jock were too much looking forward to the dirty deed to have much thought for detection. As the door was closing, I folded the latest letter from Fr. Boy, nestling in my breast pocket, in half and dropped it on the lintel like a springless wooden clothes-peg. That prevented the door engaging properly. I decided I'd give the pair enough rope to hang themselves, whatever it was they were planning and I had a very confident guess to be getting on with. After determining to count to twenty but cracking at thirteen, I inched the door ajar. I'd had enough of busting doors open for a lifetime.

Jock had his orange overalls concertinaed over his Tigers, straight out of the engine-room wear like a snake with its skin shucked over its tail. He had the high, hard one on already, jutting out of his sparse, sandy pubes past the navel. Aitch was face down, flat out on his bunk. There was a pool of pink puke, pink probably from his diseased gums rather than a blow, where he'd thrown up over the edge of the bunk. He was well out of it, drunk as the skunk. Jean-Claude had pulled the boy's jeans down and was now in the process of freeing one of Aitch's legs from the pants. As habitual rapists know, the assailant can do it with both legs in his trousers, but the raped requires one leg out. Not two, just one. There was seamanlike economy of purpose in all Jean-Claude's actions. Aitch's feet were both monstrously large for a scrawny lad of his height and amazingly filthy, not that this seemed to deter Jock and J.-C. See the soles of someone's feet and feel free to commit any atrocity or heap any indignity upon them.

I didn't much care for Aitch actually. The little smartass used to recite "When out tonight" in my hearing in the perfect conviction of its originality. I let the cabin-door swing to and walked quietly off. I got all of ten feet away, shook my head, said, "Nah, it ain't on," in the accents of Robbie Pryce and turned on my heel as smartly as I ever did on court. The door-handle was going up and down as I arrived. This was Jock, alerted by God knew what seventh sense, trying vainly to close it over the paper-wedge I'd omitted to remove, for I met resistance as I pushed. Jock was no match for my weight and having his pants round his ankles didn't help his balance. I barged through to find him on his back, legs in the air, and cock erect in horizontal plane.

"Special delivery," I said, pocketing my mail.

"Get him," Jock snarled. Jean-Claude made to hold his right out to help his accomplice up, then the sneaky so-and-so quickly swivelled and hit me with it instead. I'd never in all my life got punched so hard, not even by Cheech Chong who stood five inches taller and weighed fifty pounds more than Jean-Claude. My knees dipped as if we'd passed over a monster wave on the high seas and I saw bright heavenly light, man. In fact, so vivid was the sensation I

473

wondered as my head smacked against the metal partition if someone hadn't turned the bulb on and off again. As I was involved in this dizzy speculation, J.-C. hacked me in the knee. Now that hurt, where the concussive blow actually hadn't at all. Jock had clambered up and got his rebel dick inside the overalls. I hopped to the centre of the little cabin.

"Nut the black cunt," Jock ordered. I dropped my hands to protect my balls but Jean-Claude ran in and head-butted me on the bridge of my nose. This blinded me and I guess he was able to wind up his next shot at leisure because that one decked me. Funny, I didn't have the sensation of dropping. The floor came up to me. I must have been out a second or two, for when I came back J.-C. had his belt round my neck and Jock was approaching with his clasp-knife out. Even so, what I was still thinking with bemusement was this: how could a skinny dude like Jean-Claude hit so damned hard? Then Jock made my blood run cold.

"I'll cut his fucking knackers off," he said. Ah, Gee, he might as well have given me a shot of adrenalin or a can of spinach. I jacknifed to my feet like a Cossack dancer, sending J.-C. flying over my head. The horrid gurgle was my own, but no matter, I could wrench the belt off my throat and use the buckle end like a whip to crack Jock over his freckled, gingery knuckles and send the blade clattering into the head. That meant I took my eyes off J.-C. for a moment and, boy, was that always a mistake. Next thing I knew I was staring up at the light fixture, flat on my back, reflecting again on the intensity of the icy stellar explosion inside my skull that may or may not have taken place light-aeons ago. Once again, I had to thank Jock for bringing me back to the relevant context. I found myself sitting up just as he rammed his forearm into my throat simultaneous with punching me in the stomach. It wasn't so much of a blow, barely winding me, but I immediately felt very weak all over. And then I did feel breathless, breathless and dizzy the two. Jock was looking at me with a different expression, more impersonal, less hate-filled than before not as if I was his worst enemy in the world at that present moment but more like I was a piece of recalcitrant machinery to which after hours of dirty-handed labour he had found the engineering solution. I looked down at myself, my clammy, darkening T-shirt.

Jock had stabbed me.

I was... flabbergasted. In retrospect, I appreciate it was an inadequate reaction, a form of mental laziness. Experience should have prepared me rather better for this not entirely unlikely eventuality, considering the life I lived. But it was one thing watching it happen to someone else, quite another where one's own precious hide was concerned.

"You finish the fucker off," Jock instructed J.-C., passing the knife over to his stooge. Jean-Claude's fractional hesitation was my salvation. The brass-knuckles I was now able to see glinting on his hand prevented him from gripping the knife in his palm. I turned on to my side with a groan as I felt pain for the first time, then brought my knees to my hips, holding the foetal position just a second for the comfort. Pain, horror, make babes of us all again. Then the instinct for self-preservation brought me up, my hand grabbing the door-handle. Just as I tripped over the bottom-panelling and fell into the passageway, J.-C. stabbed me left-handed just below the gluts. Ah, Jesus. I scampered on all fours, came up, and lurched down the corridor, cannoning from one wall to the other.

A door opened. It was Yarko, the Rumanian circus freak.

"We caught the dirty fucker bumming wee Aitch," Jock called. "Slipped him a Mickey and then thought he'd shag him." I barely got the gist of this. Yarko didn't stand the first chance of comprehending Jock.

"Nooo," he said. Whether he was giving it as his opinion that I was an unlikely turd-burglar, or that I was to be prohibited from accomplishing my fell designs, or just as an indication of his own general bafflement with life, I'll never know. What I was grateful for at the time was that he simply stood there, scratching his balls, sniffing his finger, and then let me go by. I was bleeding fast and heavy; I could feel it running down the inside of my thighs, making my work-pants stick to me and my socks clammy. Man, I was squelching in my own shoes. I more fell than descended the built-in rungs from bridge to deck. Jock was coming after me. I could see the three-inch blade jutting from his fist, as innocuous as a dull icicle snapped from a Plaistow roof. I staggered on, high-stepping the coils and loops of cables and hawsers with Butch's voice ringing in my ears as if it was one of our old afternoon training sessions. We had the gangway down. The Cuban port authorities had even given the shore-side approach an extended awning. It was a small place and as the only non-Comecon vessel in port we were getting what would have been rolled out for a cruise-ship. They had also imposed an armed guard on us at the dock end of the gangway. These dudes, with bayonets fixed to the end of their Kalashnikovs, had at first watched us as stonily and imperturbably as the Grenadiers at Buckingham Palace – the bear-hatted cocksucker at attention I had once photographed Marites embracing – but as time had gone by the Cuban soldiers had opportunity to warm to us. It was difficult to preserve your distance or be haughty with guys who threw up over your boots or reeled back on board at three a.m., singing, with their arms round guys they would not have been sorry to see lost overboard three days ago. And, let it be said, gave away cartons of Camel to the Cubans like they were going out of fashion.

As luck would have it, it was the black guy on duty that afternoon, though the mulatto always gave me a nod, too. When a negro sees a wounded black man being chased by a white man with a knife, he knows whose side he's gonna be on, *di ba*? As I collapsed on the quayside at Alejandro's feet, Jock was brought skidding to a halt by the hefty clunk of an AK-47 being switched from safe to single and its wicked bayonet pointed straight at his eye. That didn't resemble the lemon popsicle he had in his own fist.

"No," said Alejandro, a Spanish word none of us had any difficulty understanding. Jock showed his terrible teeth. He was one of those unfortunate people who look less ill-aspected scowling than smiling.

"Och, it's a wee misunderstanding," he said. "We'll bring him to the doctor."

"Médecin," Jean-Claude said, which Alejandro probably understood. For answer, he trained his assault-rifle on J.-C.'s chest.

"Adiuve me, amice," I recited, Fr. Paul's tawse proving a life-saver. *"Cognosces qui sunt mali."* The world was starting to whirl around me. There wasn't a soul on the sun-baked quay, or the road, for at least a mile and there was now some activity on our bridge. But Alejandro spoke into his radio and within less than a minute a Russian jeep was skimming down the empty vastness towards us. It was getting very dark, despite the bright sun, and I had the illusion of eclipse. As I was loaded into the back of the jeep, I blacked out.

CHAPTER XXI

Holguin – Wrong Turn – Broken Urn – Maricones – Rafting

THREE TIMES A DAY Enfermera Julaidis Sanchez Rodriguez would come to change the purulent bandages on my thigh wound and three times a day I would hear her soulful interpretation of a Tex-Mex hit popular that season in Cuba. I could compare it with the original which was audible rather more frequently than thrice daily on the radio and find Julaidis's version livelier, sassier, more brazen. Of course. She was una chica Cubana, *di ba*? The afterthought wound Jean-Claude had inflicted on me just below the lower crease of the buttock had ended up causing me greater grief than the thrust from Jock which, just missing my heart, had punctured the left lung and given me a pneumothorax. No infection here but the leg had gone septic in a big way. The Russian penicillin they'd given me initially hadn't worked at all (being as ineffective through manufacturing impurities as the AK was reliable even when full of mud) while the Hungarian ampicillin which would have been effective in the first instance could no longer cope. Now I was being brought back to health by Canadian erythromycin administered via a Cuban needle blunter than their bayonets.

I used to protest as I rolled on my belly to receive it, while Nurse Sanchez kept up a series of mocking exhortations which I got in garbled form as "a big hammer was needed for a big nail". She was a particularly striking mulatta with frizzy brown hair that she knotted back in the hospital, legs and butt skinny but athletic even in the shapeless white trousers, as strong and independent of the top half when she was carrying trays and ward paraphernalia as undercarriage. I felt nothing sexual about the touch of her cool hands on my buttocks (an angry baboon red by all accounts). She contrived to be a flirt and totally assexual at the same time.

Weeks later on the sea-front, I saw her with her boy-friend. He was a married white guy. Not that the wedding contract was worth the paper it was written on. Cubans fucked like rabbits and got divorced with less thought than the time-honoured Bohaidenese triple hand-clap. On the tender loving care front Maribeth, Perla, Louise and Co were probably better for patient-morale, since despite the manic sexuality the Cubans were a very formal people. But Cuban medicine was in a different league from Philippine, or the medical mercenaries in Arabia. They were superb. Forget the flat antibiotics. The Cuban surgeons were fantastic. These white wizards, wielding their scalpels and lasers like a conjuror his wand, excised and exorcised contemporary ailments with methods of the past, present, and future. The guy next to me was having a structural vision-defect corrected by heroic methods pioneered by the institute's leading micro-surgeon. The patient was a Mexican. Next to him, a Venezuelan was having a tumour treated by African herbs transplanted and their essences made more potent in the soil of the New World. (The bark and leaves worked, the Mexican lost the sight of his eye but the surgeon's next patient, a Bulgarian general, had his ocular defect remedied). The hospital was even fuller of foreign interns than foreign patients. The Cuban profs trained most of Latin America. These invariably white heavyweights of medicine and pharmacology were as pre-eminent as the invariably black Cuban pugilists were invincible in the rings of the world.

In addition to the inherent formality of the Spanish language – all of us white-sepulchred as *señor* – I noticed a definite hierarchy in the hospital. Shit, why beat about the bush? What they had was a class system. Nicky and Jenny Smith used to joke with Mavis Wong about playing "Doctors and Nurses", a childhood game of barely sublimated nascent sexuality and, of course, in real life girls like Maribeth and Perla would often marry Australian or English surgeons and anaesthetists on a somewhat likelier rate of probability than lightning-strike. In Cuba, home of the authentic revolution, seat of the insurgent masses, land of free health care and universal higher education, they played "Doctors and Doctors". Nurses married nurses or med techs. Doctors married each other – they didn't want to suffer a dilution of household income. The only illicit affair the poor fucks cherished was with the blackmarket dollar. Under the *bloqueo Yanqui* even doctors and dentists felt hungry. Anyhow, Enfermera Sanchez Rodriguez had about as much hope of marrying a doctor in Holguin Hospital 3 as Maribeth had of becoming a sheikh's seventy-seventh wife.

Within a week there had ceased to be a language-barrier for me in Cuba. I remember Fr. Paul describing Spanish as the easiest vernacular language in the world and English as the most difficult, certainly of the European languages. Besides, there was the special affinity. At least fifteen per cent of our modern Philippine vocabulary comprised Hispanic loan-words. Down in the South, we'd had the first contact but the Tags had got it more intensively later. So Tagalogs now used as their own, without pausing for thought, the words – to take two opposites – *novia* and *puta*, while we Visayans used the native words *oyab* and *borikat* for "girl-friend" and "prostitute" respectively. If you thought about it and, Jeez, I did a lot of thinking on my side and front, corroborating once and for all the Fr. Paul theorem that sleeping on your back inhibited the higher cerebral functions, the occupying imperial power would dominate the economy and thus also cash and clock-keeping; it would monopolise access to firearms and create its own bureaucratic weapons of the census and report. Thus, at the price of pressure-sores on my pelvis and dermatitis from the hospital sheets tattooing my external obliques, I realised why I could already count money, tell the time, and state my age in, admittedly debased, Castilian. Spanish Christian and surnames were second-nature to me; I knew what *fusil*, *bala*, and *pistola* were; I could ask someone their *trabajo*; and I knew words like *gambas* and *merienda* that hadn't passed the poor, starving Cubans' lips for years. Man, I was yakking in Dago well before I could sit on my backside again. And that physical perspective, according with my social level of the retainer and the deckie, gave me fresh insight into old words I'd long taken for granted. When Nurse Julaidis placed my special treat on the table, a glass of iced water, and informed me *"esta sobre la mesa"* I at once understood how the Cebuano for "the table" was *ang lamisa*, the word *ang* being our definite article "the". Thus when we said *ang lamisa* we were effectively saying *the the table*, square-rooting ourselves. *Siguro*, it was easy as pie to see how it had happened. You just had to imagine the Castilian matron, the Mrs Smith of her day, saying to Babyjane's half-wit great-great-grandmother two centuries ago – same bug-eyed Babyjane but costumed in long dress and shawl – *"Saca brillo a la mesa!"* and Babyjane's ancestor hearing the word for table as *Lamesa*.

There you are, a window into a past not so dissimilar from the present.

On the whole, I liked Cuba but I disliked Cubans. This was one better than the Arabian peninsula where I disliked both Bohaiden and the Bohaidenese but a reversal of the situation in Britain where I disliked England but liked the English. The Cubana was the horniest chick in the world, bar none. Both in Oriente and Havana it was the same. Seven-years-old or forty-seven, they strutted their stuff. You could smell the pussy-juice in the air. My hunch was that they had got this from Africa, but even the Creole girls, and there were plenty of whites in Cuba, even if the sports teams were fully-niggered, acted up like they were permanently on heat. This time I surprised myself by finding I didn't actually care for it, when push came to shove: the sight of a strapping mulatta leering at me from her balcony and thrusting her index finger through the hoop formed by thumb and index finger of the other hand. I knew what I liked. I'd been going long enough for that. But what still puzzled me was this: if I liked *pinays* five tall with slanty eyes and the straightest of hair, hair that might have been ironed, did that mean I loved my own? Or did it mean I didn't love my own when I felt myself repelled by bold black girls? Did I have a lien on both *pinay* and negress, or on neither?

I found Cubans were able to be both brassy and sly, where the way of Asia was – oxymoron – a simple slyness. In this they resembled the 'Rabo. Ninety-nine per cent of the time slyness involved, of course, money. I lost count of the times small duplicities were practised upon me, even by the nurses, for the little store of dollars I had been carrying in my pocket. I couldn't get too het up about this as the bottom dollar, as it were, was that my entire course of treatment was free, *gratis*, courtesy of the Cuban government. Negritude here, at the level of political principle, had been no disadvantage at all, whereas at the level of daily existence in Cuba being black was a burden you bore as in any other country. For officialdom, however, and the Jesuits never lost a chance to point out to us that revolutionary bureaucracies are the most rigid, I was a gift: a refugee in reverse, a real case of racial persecution by the capitalist system. Frankly, they would have bought any story I sold or told, but I was content with the simple truth: assault by a pair of *maricones*. Man, that was the secret nightmare of every red-blooded, macho Cuban male, a benison on their primitive souls. I got the run of the place, *siguro*. I was a most valuable player, a team asset for namesake Fidel.

Sitting in the square of Holguin, the capital of the province of which Moa had been a municipality, I felt like a piece on a giant chess-board. It was one of the grandest, most beautiful town squares I ever sat in, far bigger than any of the plazas I would find in the metropolis of Havana. It was about the size of a pair of football fields, with poplar trees, fine stone seats, and a marquetry of splendid stone slabs. The splendour was emphasised rather than spoiled by the meanness of the stores in the streets around, the empty ice-cream parlours, the groceries with their few cans and, not least, by the flocks of brazen teenage *putas*, or *jiniteras*, in local slang who settled soon after dusk. I could sit there unmolested by the locals any hour of day and night. I looked like any other Cuban. Only the better quality of my trainers and the cut and style of my jeans would have given me away but these, soaked in blood, had been replaced by standard Cuban civilian wear. It was one of the few places in the world I could get kitted out off the peg with no problems. Big, athletic guys abounded. Only once was I molested when to our huge mutual embarrassment the police spoke roughly to me. After my foreignness was established *no hay ningun problema, señor*. And from being a loitering nigger I'd turned into *"el señor Africano"* to be left to his own devices.

No one liked Negroes in Cuba, not even the Negroes. Two months later, after quitting Holguin for good, I stood at a corner beer-stall in Vedado, surrounded by street-jockeys who were totally deluded in seeing me as a useful mount. An out of work white telecommunications engineer was taking the cash dollars for the cans of Hatuey and Cristal with a lanky, good-natured black guy mopping up the counter. We had a relationship, Angel the communications engineer and myself. He gave me free coffees sometimes, off the espresso machine's third pressing, and if I insisted on paying (because I knew I was depriving him of a much-needed scam) he made sure I got the first pressing. I didn't even count my change; I knew Angel would never short-change me. One morning, worrying for me no doubt on the Havana streets – twenty times safer than even the English streets – he tapped his flanged nose (he had Lebanese blood) and said, *"Rey, no tiene confianza en los negros."*

Guillermo, the black guy, overheard this. *"Si, si,"* he corroborated. *"No tiene confianza en los negros. Todos son ladrones y malos."* He nodded sagely. I started to chuckle. I'd developed a taste for straight-faced piss-taking through knocking around with Robbie Pryce. Then I looked hard at Guillermo, who was no mulatto but the colour of the ebony wood Chinese chairs at Atty Caladong's. Fuck, he wasn't being ironic. It was a straight-up caution.

"Gracias, hombre," I said.

I don't think Guillermo was being mean-spirited, generous rather, but then it was a culture that was in love with extravagance. Latin wasn't really a good tag for them, that precise, interlocking, balanced language of calculating engineers and dispassionate law-givers, who believed above all in proportion.

Holguin was a pretty small place, about a quarter the size of Cebu. You could look on their great Plaza as their equivalent of another small place's monumental ambition, Singapore's Changi airport. But it was startlingly easy to become lost, even as you refused to countenance the possibility that you had achieved this predicament in such a small town. That was because of the uniformity of the side streets but, less insidiously yet more confusingly, also because the main square had a smaller twin a couple of hundred metres away. Once you got off the main drag and looked back for reference, you saw the open space and colonnades but it could be the wrong square you were regarding. There were also several fifty-foot conifers set in the suburbs, each so impressive one supposed it was the only one of its kind in town. You'd take your bearings on them, advance confidently for twenty minutes, arrive, and find yourself someplace you'd never been. It wasn't just me being a large, direction-less lummox (which I often was). Out of town Cubans had the same problem, too. Disputative little groups or disconsolate, tight-lipped individuals could be seen at all times of day and night wandering the more affluent suburbs. I stayed with an elderly paediatrician and his dentist wife and two dentist daughters in a pleasant, leafy street reminiscent of a Philippine sub-division. They were glad to have me as an income supplement. *"Usted no es Negro, señor Rey,"* Doctor Roldan assured me. *"No, no."*

The Roldans had a few quality pieces of furniture, a handsome dinner-table and chairs, which were a trousseau from their pre-revolutionary wedding and the girls had also brought back some nice porcelain from Prague where they'd studied but otherwise the house was, as Fr. Paul remarked of the Pentecostal Church down the road from San Ignatio, "bare as Mother Hubbard's cupboard." I had a bedroom, toilet and cold shower-faucet upstairs with a set of rickety wooden stairs leading to a beautiful but perilously unfenced balcony.

I got hopelessly lost my first time out and had to approach the only person in sight, a moustached white guy with a leery-looking barkada of chums who would not have looked out of place in a Greek focsle. I knew it was a mistake as soon as I'd asked the way to Doctor Roldan's.

"Roldan?" repeated the only girl with the group in puzzlement. *"No. No hay nadie con ese nombre aqui."*

"Si," the moustached dude contradicted her vehemently in the no-holds barred Cuban patois where they amputated the ends of words at will and which would have surprised Fr. Paul with its difficulty. "I know where the doctor lives."

"Dr *Roldan?*" I said, not wanting to be taken to any doctor in his or her professional capacity but also not wanting to say I lodged with the Roldans as it was technically still illegal.

"Si, si. Roldan," my would-be guide said with some impatience. If I was going to repay Antillean white folks for the pains they took to measure blackness on a minutely detailed scale of gradations with an equally scrupulous and discriminating assessment of whiteness, he was an off-white guy. No African in him but he was a swarthy, olive sort of guy.

"I," he said, with a sneer that took in all detractors, "Hector, will show you the way, *señor.*"

"There is no need for that," I said. "Just tell me."

"Come. You like cigars?"

"No."

"Ron?"

"No. We got all the rum and cigars in the Philippines. Enough to ruin our lungs and livers ten times over. Dirt cheap. OK?"

"I have Cohibas, *señor.* I can show you in the box. The best. Oye, you come and eat with me, friend. Fresh fish. And you pay nothing. It's all free for you, man."

"Where is Dr Roldan's house?"

"So, so, Dr Roldan. I know. Not far. *No esta lejos.*"

None of the goddamned streets and houses looked familiar. Ten minutes later as we came out on to a grass field full of grazing burros, I knew we were nowhere near the Roldans. Probably as far from their house as it was geometrically possible to be in Holguin.

"Man, you're lost," I remarked evenly in a Spanish which at the very least could not have been worse than courteous. I might as well have told him I was going to shit in the milk of the whore who was his mother. "No, *señor*. No. I am your friend but do not say that. With care. It is not possible. I, Hector, I know all the roads of this city. Every *calle* in every *barrio*. Every grain of sand in the river, every crack in the sidewalk. I know them like the creases in my palm." He beat his chest with the said palm. "Every house and the people living in them, I know them all. There is nothing, nothing, Hector does not know in Holguin and I will dispute with the *maricon* who denies that."

"You don't know how big a fool you are," I said in Cebuano and made sure I smiled my most brilliant smile.

"I am Hector. There is no one in Holguin who does not know me, the celebrated Hector. Ask anyone. You have trouble from someone, tell them you are the friend of Hector. No problem. Lost? No, is not possible, friend. You know why? Because I am Hector. *Si, soy Hector* and I know the world and it knows me." By now he was way out of it, man, like I was waiting for him to start frothing at the mouth. It wasn't so much a question of his succeeding in finding the Roldans, more like him making a success of soft-landing in the real world again.

I edged away. He was really getting going on the breast-beating now. As I got to the corner Hector was still ranting and raving to the tolerant burros.

Over time, I was to discover that Hector wasn't a particularly extreme case. The Cubans were crackers in a typically Hispanic way in which they wanted nothing to do with anything that was ordinary or real-scale. It had to be super-special, gigantic, like Fidel was El Maximum Jefe hectoring the millions on TV for eight hour marathon-sessions and my Hector was the best guide in Holguin shouting at the burros. That was an aspect of machismo but *las chicas* had the affliction, too, as you'll see.

I got home that day by the simple but drastic expedient of climbing the big conifer and having a look-see, impelled not so much by experience of the nautical life as recollection of a farcical turn of the century English novel read to us at San Ignatio where people lost in a riverside maze – I think – were rescued by a man on a ladder.

Cuban girls, *las muchachas Cubanas, las Guantanameras, las Santiagueras, las Habaneras,* what can I say? Where do I begin? How can I conceivably do justice to the species? But as I think of it I can best describe them by what they were *not*. For me they were an especial paradox. They were the exact total opposite of the Filipina but they dressed just like them. Sartorially, they were twins. It was bizarre. White girls, lily-white *guerritas*, rasta-locked black chicks, slim mulattas, wobbling mamas, and negresses with their short wool peroxided blonde, all wearing rubber thongs, shorts, and denim cut-offs like our back home *dalagas*. As always, one application of the Fr. Paul method supplied the solution. What you wore depended on two things: the weather and your wallet. You dressed according to climate and what you could afford. It was damn hot in both Cebu and Cuba and times were hard in both places, so girls dressed skimpily to be cool and to economise. OK, they were bigger throughout Cuba on their trainers than our girls were, whether that was because trainers were what the state factories were churning out in Byelorussia that summer or because of Fidel's mania for sport, but that was the extent of the difference. It could have been the photographic negative of a Mactan street, with the Cuban negroes coming out as our white tourists or as Mormon missionaries. Yet, had I been blindfolded, I could have told you the difference between a Cubana and a Cebuana just with my nose or my tongue. Cuban girls bore the same curse as most girls who weren't East Asians – they stank under the armpits, black or white, like men. The cute black chicitas and the blancitas might as well have been shot-putters or power-lifters. They exuded that acrid smell of burning rubber from under their *kilikili* that I could never get used to. And when the trainers came off, Jeez, it was the gas-chamber as penalty for your lasciviousness. I never met the Asian girl whose shoes were a death trap.

Telling the difference with my tongue? That was when a Cubana kissed you. Those girls had fire in them. Brazen jezebels they mostly were, like I said, and even bigger gold-diggers than our girls but, man, they fucked you with conviction whether you were Peter Pan or the Hunchback of Notre Dame. I used to hang out at a traditional salsa hall in Holguin – all wood-panelling and photographs of the greats yellowed in smoke – and in Havana at a state of the art flashing discotheque but in both joints you'd see whippet-thin *negras* with their tongues deep in some grey-haired Italian or Canadian's throat, their trainer hooked round the knee of the green grandad's grey paints and their loins ardent against his. They were whole-hearted trollops, those gals.

I wasn't as much in demand as even an *ex*-basketball star might expect. "You needed me, vig voy," I can hear Danton saying. "I da bearer of da good tidings in your fanties, mans." I remembered all the Caucasian matrons – and one sari-clad Indian – who had ever swished their buttocks, soft as peeled eggs, and the harder ridge of their pantihose-elastic, against my monster in the District Line rush-hour. In Cuba, alas, I was a much less widely desired commodity. Some black girls shot sidelong street glances at me but *las blancitas* on the whole chiefly desired my dollars. "If you have no mohny, you're a dog, frien'," one partner said to me reflectively in a respite from sucking my dick. She was a student of agronomy, which I initially misheard as astronomy. The same lady, on the second occasion I encountered her, sitting swinging her trainers on the Malecon sea-wall, crossed the forty metres of tarmac between us like the athletic *negra* she wasn't and hissed, *"Te echo de menos, tesoro,"* into my sceptical ear. I could be pardoned my cynicism because on our first meeting, while I'd been spraying my dick in the CR, she'd dipped me of ten bucks from my hung trousers.

"Si, si, my paraiso," she'd insisted, *"mi cielo,* I never meet the man like you. *Vamo', chico.* Make my ecstasy that will come." Her tongue was the more eloquent part of her when her mouth was full but her fingers on my flies were the persuasive part of her at that moment. She took me round the corner to a genial old widow's ground floor tenement where she proposed marriage as she tried to sneak a finger up my ass. Her nails were too long for the latter and life too short for the former. While she douched I took ten bucks from her purse, added ten of my own to it, and gave her the twenty when she returned. That was theft that was no theft. An eye for an eye and a tooth for a tooth. Perhaps that was what Babyjane thought.

"No soy puta," she said as she slipped the greenbacks under her instep.

"And I'm not the Third Murderer, either," I said.

THE NATURAL GRAVITATION of the talented *Probinsyano* is to the metropolis and just as I had proceeded from the Visayas to Manila, so I was drawn ineluctably to Havana. I said goodbyes to my doctor hosts, the tears of the dentist daughters quite disinterested and not in the least feigned, reminding me not to generalise too much from my experience which, when I reviewed it, seemed to be exclusively of the gutter. They helped me secure one of the coveted places on the bus – the combination of their revolutionary bourgeois respectability and my robust frame, simulated intransigence, and eventual admission of foreignness an irresistibly potent combination on the black *jefe de estacion*. If it had been London Transport, I reflected, it would have been free but I decided not to look a gift horse in the mouth.

The confusion of the station ended on the vehicle. No standing was allowed. That was one reason why the wait-lists were so full. We fortunates smiled at each other with quiet satisfaction as we pulled out of the bus-bay. You would have thought we were on a one-way flight to Miami. Then we paid a call to the garage with its black, polluted earth, for an air-fill one mile down the road, before setting off to the ring-road and the highway. This went, Roman-or Russian-straight, for hundreds of kilometres. It reminded me, strangely enough, of Bohaiden: it was nearly completely deserted, eerily empty of vehicles. This was for quite opposed reasons. Bohaiden floated on a lake of oil, the sand the biscuit crumbs on a vast tub of mocca, while Cuba under the *bloqueo* and out from under the Soviet umbrella, had virtually no gasoline at all. But in both countries, you motored for miles without seeing another car or truck, the isolation most apparent at night, when your headlights tunnelled a mile ahead into realms of blackness that might have been outer space, without a single pair of twinkling red stars or the growing galactic glow of approaching headlamps to be seen for hours.

Unlike Pilipinos, Cubans didn't talk much on these bus-marathons and for sure no one was passing chicharon, with the vinegar and chilli dip floating in plastic bags, to their neighbours over the back of the seats. The non-athletes among them hadn't seen pork-crackling for years. I settled in to my surprisingly comfortable seat, next to a smartly-dressed old guy, bereft of shoelaces, in what must have been a Batista-era straw hat. We nodded at each other and then didn't exchange a single word for the next five hundred kilometres until as we lumbered through a tunnel into Habana he reached for his bag and said, *"Con permiso."* It was fine by me. I didn't want to be invited to stay as a guest of honour, free of charge (of course) and for as long as I liked, at his nephew/son/niece's house because I was such a lovable *señor*, only to be hit with a request for two hundred bucks at the end because haggling was beneath the consideration of such a grand and illustrious *señor* as myself. It was always, but always, a mistake to get friendly with Cubans. They had no shame at all. In the end, all the grandiloquence was for a penny hand-out. They were worse than us. They were haughty beggars. We knew what we were.

To live in Havana was to be beleaguered in a rococco stockade, defended with much noise but little conviction by its ageing and arbitrary chieftain.

Look, it's easy to kill a Yanqui, said the sign in the buses with diagrams of how to stab, impale, club, garotte, and in the last resort, shoot, an invader. The passengers in the "camel", the humped bus-trailer, gave it the same attention as Hong Kongers did the injunction to surrender seats to the handicapped. East to West, the encampment thudded with the beat of drums. And nowhere did they throb louder than in Old Havana. The signs and totems in the camp – *Venceremos, socialismo o muerte* (my thought was, *por favor la muerte*) – adjured puritanical revolutionary fervour, but in reality what was going on behind the palisade was a bacchanalian orgy.

Music filled the air, followed you from the Malecon with its outdoor speakers blaring free salsa at volumes that hurt the ear, to the lobbies of the five-stars, to back-street barrows selling dirty cane-juice, to the entrails of the ancient Spanish forts and casements, through echoing, ammoniac arcades and colonnades where beswörded gallants, hand on hilt, had swaggered two centuries ago, and from which the police, palm on Makarov-butt, now surveyed the *jiniteras*. When you thought you had escaped the drums and the brass and the strings in your own room, your landlord turned on the CD his Miami daughter had sent him. In the short-time hotel in the super-heated total blackout of your cubicle you thought you had given the slip to your ancient African inheritance until the obliging janitor turned on the system and filled your space with the brash melodies of Cuba. Once, entering a ten-mile cave system in Pinar del Rio, I congratulated myself on having found silence when, pow, from behind a stalagmite came three guys with guitars and a chick with maracas. Filipinos were just recreational music-users, Cubans were hard-core addicts.

It helped the monotonous, shitty food go down, *siguro*. I couldn't complain excessively because by not eating much I'd shed my flab but, to this day, I can't stand the sight of *moros y cristianos* or, more prosaically, beans and rice. Hot air from the mouths of the leaders and hot air from the trainers and the guts of the populace.

Doctor Roldan had given me an introduction to his anaesthetist nephew in Vedado, the more modern central area of Havana. Unfortunately the roof of his top-floor apartment was leaking so badly they'd had to evacuate to the floor of the family on the fourth. Cubans were good like that. They knew to help each other the best they could. This wasn't socialism; this was solidarity against the locos in the government bureaucracy. Young Dr Roldan was able to point me in the direction of a musician friend of his wife's brother with a room in Old Havana and, declining the offer of a ride in his economist friend's unofficial dollar taxi, I walked two miles along the sea-front, stopping en route for the first time at Engineer Javier's beer-counter.

As I arrived in the Calle Generalisimo Giap they were having a celebration. It would have been stretching it some to call it a fiesta, but there were a few light-bulbs and streamers above tables stocked with what I took initially to be small engineering bricks. Were they celebrating the circumstance that they actually had bricks? For lack of building materials a quarter of the district's venerable heritage had already collapsed as under foreign air-raids. On closer inspection these slate-grey 16x8x4cm slabs, flawed by the odd black spot of discoloration, perhaps leached mineral salts or the result of faulty temperature-control in the baking, turned out to be cakes and the black spots not adulterations but, wonder of wonders, raisins.

"*Pudim, señor,*" said a well-preserved middle-aged white woman. An interrogative emphasis would have constituted an invitation to partake in any one of the major European languages. What she was doing was conveying information in a level tone. E.g. you like-ee, you pay, Buster. Just about anywhere else in the world, Plaistow or Pasay, she'd have already retired from the sexual lists. Here in Havana, she had her dyed-auburn hair piled to expose her nape and was exhibiting midriff above and below the navel. Man, she was cocked, locked, and licensed to carry.

The pudding was the only kind of pudding available. *Pudim* meant but one thing: these dusky, compressed slabs of carbohydrate, manufactured out of the bread ration. I didn't get it. The Roldan daughters made a great guava paste from the tree in their garden. It resembled a brick of hash and I could have sold it as readily in any part of the world it tasted so good but, nope, it was *pudim* you saw exposed for sale in every other doorway of Old Havana. The first day I arrived in the district was also the last time I sampled the delicacy.

Sometimes unappetising-looking food startles with its flavour. I think of a particular grey stew I consumed driving up Malaysia with my freight of multi-national teenyboppers. Sometimes it lives down to your foreboding. *Pudim* was like having your mouth full of plasticine. I was given the opportunity to numb my palate subsequently by my midriff-baring white lady. Her sidekick was lacing ice-shavings with a choice of scarlet or yellow syrups, less dubious than the smeared bottles they were imprisoned in. The swish of the ice-razor sounded like cars in London slush and, although I liked the Spanish word for yellow, *amarillo*, the shade reminded me of the cold-induced piss-holes I'd made in the Plaistow snow. "*Rojo,*" I requested, immediately realising that colour was identical with the winter pavement outside the bar in France where Robbie Pryce had got himself bottled in the back on the night our friendship had begun.

If the viands on offer fell flat, there was no shortage of the food of love. The omnipresent music drowned the growling in my stomach. Rum was less than a US cent for a giant tumbler and on an empty stomach was doubly potent. Within half an hour of stumbling on the little barrio "fiesta" I was out of my head. I remember gyrating my hips a millimetre from those of my game old partner, then half a millimetre from her ass-cheeks in their brown cycling trunks – man, it was lewder than a fuck – before she swung her ten-year-old grand-daughter before me who proved no more inhibited in her steps. At two a.m. the ground shook with the clap of doom, followed by four or five claplets of doom and a resounding clattering, terminating in a sifting sound as might be made by the sands in a giant hour-glass.

"Ola," said my little partner.

"What was that?" I asked.

She shrugged. The adults weren't quite as cool as she was but still pretty nonchalant. Dancing resumed. The music had never stopped. My chicita showed me her tongue. It was amazingly furred and unhealthy-looking for someone her age, with a pronounced crease down the middle. I wondered if someone had marked the place.

"How old are you?" I asked. By way of answer she made the ubiquitous finger through hole sign. I figured she wasn't indicating that she was ten, *di ba*? Gradually, the dance throng thinned. Some went home, some collapsed on the pavement. My chicita gathered I wasn't interested. She gave me another finger-sign, the horns of the cuckold, spat and left.

Light came. Old Havana was as grey as Bombay but without the disturbing betel splashes and the other unmentionables. I sneezed. I rubbed my eyes. The dawn light was somewhat greyer than it should have been. I realised the air was full of very fine dust, not dirt or sand but snuff-like. I put my head round the corner. An entire nineteenth century block, still standing when I'd arrived, had collapsed, leaving only one wall standing, its pillars and decorative reliefs still intact, like the ruins of Rome in a San Ignatio textbook.

Cubans, mostly my fellow-blacks, were scavenging the rubble like Visi-Goths. The building appeared to have been used latterly as shoe-warehouse and, in smaller part, as antique book repository, for the looters were leaving with volumes and trainers. Both hide-bound, I thought. One lanky youth, in a pair of the ludicrously outgrown red school shorts he might have worn in early grade ten years ago scurried past me. From his overloaded arms dropped three shoes and a book. He picked up two shoes. I handed him the third with an *"Aqui esta, hombre,"* then as he got going, *"El libro."* He shook his head. An older black man came by with yet more athletic shoes and an ornate porcelain urn. Somehow the vase, with the unmistakable patina of venerability all over, had survived the collapse of the building about it – the initial deluge of bricks, masonry, and timber, and the aftermath of settling and collapsing – quite intact. I think Fr. Paul would not have chided me for using the word miraculous. The middle-aged guy holding the urn was also having trouble managing the entirety of his load. I could see him deciding to put some trainers into the vase and I didn't need a couple of seasons on the basketball court to see he was gonna butter-finger it. *"Voy a ayudarte,"* I called and I don't think the shock of my foreigner's Spanish had anything to do with him fumbling his grip on the handle. He was on the edge of an internal wall and the vase spun over and over ten feet down, a cornucopia cascading trainers. Well, the accident registered with him, I'd be a liar if I said it didn't, but it was history for him in a second. He jumped down and started to collect the trainers. I was already half-way over. His backside was in the air, I had the perfect amount of run-up. What else was there for me to do but follow the precept and example of my mentors? My kick lifted him in the air and then on to his hands and knees. There was absolutely no indignation in his face when he turned. I could see he thought I was another looter who happened to be bigger than he was. He settled for the shoes in his hands and made off. Further down the rubble-heap was the book the boy had dropped. I picked it up. It was the calf-bound Hakluyt's *Voyages* I still possess. I'd never even heard of the work until then, although I can recite whole passages of it now. That's serendipitous, man. I won't trouble you with the summary, *di ba*, but I recommend, I recommend, as the little Attorney used to exhort us.

ACTUALLY HABANEROS DIDN'T KNOW when they had it good. Robbie Pryce would have said "they made a meal of it". I'd say they made a meal of their hunger. They looked just great on the ration. People who eat too much die early. The Cubans weren't clogging their arteries with cholesterol. They needed a dose of Fr. Paul. The poor man's seed would have found soil even more barren than it did in Mactan. The Cubans wanted to indulge their starved senses: fucking a-plenty they already had but they wanted junk food and junk food of the soul, too. They wanted to be consumers of rubbish and trivia. High-minded self-denial of the Paulian kind was the last thing they wanted more of. Cubans lived for the gratifications of the present moment. They had the minds least advance-dirty of any people I ever met, including us. Their brains were wiped clean of anything except appetite and sensation. I saw us *pinoys* and our faults writ larger and darker in them, the flip-side of us Flips.

My landlord, Rodrigo, was the player of a stringed instrument in the second national orchestra. He was the fourth, or it might have been third, player. Before that he'd been top-player in a provincial orchestra. These guys seemed to get promotion in the way a ship's officers did.

Rodrigo was also a Cuban who didn't like Cubans. In short, he was a renegade. Being a *maricon* helped. It was him who put the idea in my head of them wanting the intellectual equivalent of the Big Mac. Rodrigo hated only one thing worse than machismo and that was pop music, in particular Swedish pop music. For the group Abba he reserved a scorn as deep as his contempt for Castro and the deceased Che. "But they are nothing, Rey," he exclaimed. "It is the veritable death of the mind." He expatiated on the simplicity of the rhythms and the predictable repetitions, the maudlin descants. "A–B–B–A, it's the perfect name for them. They never get beyond one–two, they never get beyond the first two letters of the alphabet."

"You know, Rodrigo, I never thought of it that way until now. Yeah, Fr. Paul used to break down Shakespeare's rhyme schemes for us like that on the blackboard. But you know what, *di ba*, his rhyme schemes – Shakespeare OK, not Fr. Paul – they were pretty basic variations on a theme, too, when you broke them down like that."

"Si, cabron, pero… mira, it's how you use the basic bricks. You have the pyramids or the adobe house, but the same basic blocks."

"O-o."

I really liked Rodrigo. I was able to have the kind of discussion with him I hadn't been able to have with anyone else since I'd gone on my travels, not with Robbie Pryce, not with Hubert, not even with Commander Smith on a good day.

Drigo was an auto-didact in despite of the excellent Cuban educational system. He'd taught himself English off cassettes and a Walkman that had been the property of a tourist until he'd found it in the back of a Panataxi. Grammar and vocabulary-building, one block at a time, *di ba*, were one thing but what Rodrigo possessed that was totally idiosyncratic was an ear which heard perfectly and a tongue that was slave to the ear's bidding. He sounded like a goddamned English duke, though he'd still to set foot in England. This shamed me who'd lived there and was identifiable as a Filipino as soon as I opened my mouth.

We all used to go in a pile, Drigo, me, and his *barkada*, to the Opera House at the top of the Prado of a summery evening. This was a band of the most outrageous fags in Havana and therefore of all Cuba. If you were a Cuban gay, you could go two ways.

Homosexuality was still a crime and the population was for once at one with its government in abhorring queers. *Maricones* went underground, pretended they were anything but, ridiculed their kind and practised their bent in secret, or they came screaming over the lip of the trench like Drigo and his mates. As we advanced in line abreast under the shady old trees of the Prado, sometimes halting to greet and absorb other rag-tag-and-bobtail units from the smooth-worn benches carved into the marble sides of the esplanade, I'd regard Drigo in his flaming-red shirt and white shorts with the degree of awe I used to reserve for a long-dead Cebu Cardinal in his purple eminence (also notoriously effete) and I'd think in Robbie Pryce's words, "Shit, these dudes are Grade-A poofters." Juan-Felix, Drigo's lieutenant, couldn't actually dress like a drag-queen and stay out of Castro's jail, but he came as close as he could in his voluminous-legged khaki shorts, with the huge leather belt nipping in his waist. *"Encantada,"* he'd boom in his virile voice as he was introduced, never using the masculine case. A troupe of gorillas processing up the Prado could not have gained a more vehement reaction from the Havana stage-army of *jiniteros*, whores, cigar-dealers, knowers of *habitaciones particulares*, police-informers, currency-traders, and assorted black-marketeers. At the end of the walkway, eight hundred metres away, past the top of the hill, you could receive over-the-curvature early-warning of Drigo's *barkada* in the form of the shrill, monotone Spanish whistling of disapproval, the nasal jeers of the whores and, to boot, the soprano insults of the primary school-children. It was all water off a duck's back for my companions. Nay, they courted it. *"Maricones,"* yelled the whores. *"Maricones,"* bellowed the construction-workers from their lorry heading to the site of the Canadian joint-venture five star hotel yet-to-be. *"Maricones, si, si, si,"* shrieked my team of perverts in retaliation as they pranced, pirouetted, and skipped their way up the venerable flagstones. All too plainly, I was one of them. With Rodrigo's arm through mine, there was no denying it. I think Drigo was using me as accessory, like the over-sized tan leather satchel he carried on his left shoulder. Still, I like to think I never flinched. I liked people who were out of context, the sore thumb of their societies, renegades as I say, and Drigo and his *barkada* stuck out like the proverbials.

Funny though – to be honest, not so passing strange – no one was in a great hurry to come up and shout the Spanish for "Fag!" in my face: not the burliest builder, not the sassiest schoolgirl. It was like being in a fraternity rumble all over again. My gay pals dragged me to the top of the Cuban Capitol like I was the prize catapult in some Roman siege. None of them cared what was showing at the Opera. That was beside the point. Theatre, modern or classical, a recital, an orchestra, the ballet comprising striated queens in cod-pieces hoisting tautly-drawn mulattas, all were impartially ignored by my boys as they patrolled the aisles and foyer. It was the interval they longed for, the opportunity to turn heads in the bar in outrage or amusement. As far as they were concerned, they were the performance.

Drigo hammed it up and camped with the best of them. He would be in a more sombre mood when he went cruising to the Coppelia ice-cream gardens and positively bleak when he discussed politics with me late-night in our easy-chairs on the roof. He'd start with a joke, then get bitter, just like our coffees when we'd used up the sugar-ration. Some of his jokes were good. "Why are Cubans so confused, Rey? Because, their island is in the Caribbean, the government is in Moscow, and the people are all in Miami." Or: "Rey, can you laugh at this? The people are queuing for potatoes. No, make it yams. An official comes outside: 'Not enough yams to go round. All the blacks fuck off. Come back tomorrow.' Five minutes pass. The official comes out again. 'Not enough. All mulattoes go away. Only Communist Party cadres can stay.' One hour later: 'Sorry, no potatoes. The truck ran out of gas at Tunas.' As they go away one cadre mutters to another: 'Those damn blacks, they have all the luck.'"

I used to play devil's advocate for his government, half out of sheer natural perversity, half to tease him. *"Mira, hombre,"* I'd put it to him. "The Maximum Leader pulled you all out of context. He didn't just unplug you from the United States. He took you right out of the Caribbean altogether. That was a good joke. The island isn't in the Caribbean at all, not morally. It's like Lee Kuan Yew took the Singaporeans out of the morass around *them.* They're a little oasis in a wilderness, man. You can't compare Cuba with Canada, or the US, or England, or even Costa Rica. You've got to compare it with Jamaica, with Haiti, the Dominican Republic, with what's around it.

And, fuck, man, it's a whole sight better here than in those places, *di ba*? You don't have gunmen roaming the streets at election time…"

"We don't have elections, they're a farce."

"But they're an orderly farce. You have universal free education, socialised health-care that's still some of the best in the world, literacy in the countryside, children free of skin and eye diseases…"

"Everyone being equally hungry and unfree."

"And major drug-abuse and violent street-crime are virtually unknown. World-class athletes. A real effort to deal with racial discrimination. The blacks respect Castro, don't tell me they don't."

"Rey, are you telling me the place is a paradise for blacks? That prejudice doesn't exist? That blacks aren't the poorest of the poor here?"

"No, Drigo. I may be impressionable but I'm not blind. On the other hand, the reason for that might be we aren't as good at turning the page as we are at jumping over fences."

"My friend, my friend, please…"

"I wasn't being sarcastic."

"I notice that, Rey. I always respect you for it."

Rodrigo had travelled plenty. Abroad was no mystery to him. He'd played with the orchestra in Berlin, Warsaw, Prague, and latterly Spain twice, France, and Italy. Playing the French horn or playing guard on the basketball team got you the same airline points in Fidel's Cuba. And much like the run of the mill cagers or baseball-players, it simply wasn't worth Drigo's while to give his minders the slip in Madrid or Bordeaux.

"To be candid, who would want me, Rey?" he asked, raising his eyebrows. "I'm not a genius, not even a maestro, not even a No 3 in the orchestra."

"O-o," I said, "You're there to make up the team numbers, man. And it isn't the dream team."

I didn't know who in that world of orchestras were the Chicago Bulls but Drigo was more of your token honkie than your actual Michael Jordan. Then his life was pretty comfortable for a Cuban. He travelled, he bought paperback books for himself, and packets of grey-rinse for his mother. He had access to the dollar economy. Even while he castigated the revolution as turned entirely corrupt, shorn of any idealism it might have possessed thirty years ago, he himself was part of its decadence.

Old Myte (pronounced "Mighty"), his moustached (female) housekeeper, couldn't stand the sight of me in the house. A nigger within those sacred portals! I did my best, man. I gave her one of my precious greenbacks – a single, but that was a bar of gold, better than a sackful of the *moneda nacional* – I gave her one of the Coronas I'd developed a taste for, I gave her a tiny flagon of scent I'd picked up at Dubai Duty Free to give to sister Bambi one day, hoping it would mature like a wine rather than lose its aroma. Shit, I even smiled at the old bag. I knew what it was to be a lackey, after all. I knew how Babyjane ticked; BJ was my basic blueprint to the Myte model. But it was to no avail at all. Myte snubbed me at every opportunity. Plates banged down in front of me at meal-times. No bedding-changes for days at a time in weather as sweltering as any in Cebu. Of course not. Dirty niggers didn't need clean sheets; they'd only defile the ancient, immaculately darned stock in her locked cupboard.

Finally, insignificant items started vanishing from my room. For instance, which might surprise, I have highly sensitive skin, literally if not in the figurative sense. I cannot shave simply by applying soap to my throat and cheeks. That leaves me with a blotchy rash that lasts hours. I require a particular brand of shaving-cream that contains balms. (Principally lanolin, a soother derived from sheep who all think and do alike and, so they say, promote sleep; perhaps I am also in need of people-emollient). Well, that canister de-materialised into the fourth dimension. I didn't think Myte was using it on her armpits and I had visible evidence that she hadn't shaved her moustache, so I could only presume it had gone on to, uh, *el mercado negro*. She'd always refused my offers of cigars. Now I'd see her on the balcony with a Corona jutting from her thin, wet lips. As it was still possible for a Cuban to enjoy one of the world's great smokes I couldn't actually point my finger in outrage, but I knew she'd purloined it from the way she rolled the chunky tube between her even fatter fingers and admired its colour and the perfection of its shape.

The biggest give-away was the brazen, amused insolence on her face. It was the first time I'd seen The Runt's Smile on an old person.

On Drigo Myte doted. How long she'd been with him I could never quite ascertain; he always returned evasive replies; asking her was out of the question. Maybe she'd wiped his ass in an influential way. She treated the queens like royalty when they came to dinner. I mean, she was still grumpy as fuck, nothing remotely approaching

497

a smile of welcome ever cracked her face, but she turned out stupendous black-market banquets for them. I wondered why Drigo didn't set up one of the ubiquitous private restaurants. She had a guy, as Robbie would have said, "straightened out" on the Malecon. This masked and be-flippered dude – his Italian snorkelling gear looked suspiciously new – gave her octopus fresher than Auntie Irish used to vend out of the bucket at rich folks' gates. From this she'd concoct a tarry and delicious stew that was the brother of *adobong nukos*. As it bubbled it filled every cubic foot of the apartment – its twenty-foot ceilings – with the odours of Triton's cave.

We'd sit round Drigo's Brazilian table – an item from his mother's trousseau even more handsome than that of my Holguin dentist landlord – and as I dipped my ration-roll in the gravy I'd think of the films of Luis Bunuel, a little season of which I'd attended with the fags at a clandestine art-house beyond Miramar. Surreal, man, was not the word for it. In Drigo's other spare room we'd have transient Dutch backpackers, Catalonian sex-tourists, Mexican drogados, and intrepid Swiss grandparents, to list but the run of the mill. They would always be invited to dinner, these *papa ricci con juanakikki*, mainly to provide straw-wrapped flasks of Chianti from the dollar-tienda.

There was one occasion which involved Alvaro, me, a fifty-year-old English female journalist, and her eighty-five-year-old mother. Alvaro was the most outrageous of the pathics who'd been in and out of prison as much as the other prisoners had been in and out of him. "Chico, it's true, the blacks have the biggest pistols. *No te enfadas conmigo, Rey.*"

"Hey, no offence, Alvaro."

Alvaro had rolled his napkin, put it through its silver hoop, and made for the john, bestowing a meaningful look on a new recruit to the band, a male nurse from Drigo's hospital. I helped myself to another glass of red wine, which I liked far more than white. The conversation at our table had gone its own way and split into different groups after half an hour of polite engagement. We were too variegated and while the queens were kamikaze non-conformists, I'd also learned many educated Caucasians of liberal tendency had rejected old-fashioned formal good manners along with religion. Suddenly I felt something on the inside fold of knee and thigh, rather like a hooked *molmol* flapping in the last phases of asphyxiation in the bottom of a pumpboat. The grey-haired lady journalist was looking at me with eyes as focussed as Cheech Chong when he was trying to psych me out before a game. I made a surreptitious eyes-down check. Yup, she was playing footsie with me. From the john drifted a low moaning. It was Alvaro's voice, getting louder by the moment. He was groaning *"Cogeme,"* at rhythmic intervals, I would surmise when the male nurse had it in to the hilt rather than on the out-stroke but I have no practical personal experience and, despite Fr. Paul, that's always worth volumes. *Di ba?*

"What's *Cogeme?*" the eighty-five-year old mother asked sharply. (She had been a Fabian. I had to look that up five months later in the USIS. It wasn't what I'd thought).

"It sounds like a mantra, mother," my molester answered.

"Oh, *yoga,*" the older lady said. "That's got here, too, has it."

BALLET-DANCERS TRAINED HARDER THAN CAGERS. I remember thinking so as I watched the Cuban national company going through their morning session. Alvaro was my entry here. He was after one of the juniors who, sadly, was one of the few heterosexuals in the troupe but so vain that he enjoyed Alvaro's adoration. "These straight boys are *much* more flirtatious than real gays," Alvaro observed to me. Then like the faithless butterfly he was, "But, *mira,* Rey, what I would love more than anything is a real, live, breathing… *torero!* Oh, can you imagine? What bliss!"

I laughed which made the vain, pirouetting boy scowl because he knew the attention was off him. Dutifully, Alvaro made calf eyes again.

One thing which gay and straight Cubans could agree on was the intrinsic fun and splendour of the beach. Both sexes cruised here and being a gay guy who was a fine swimmer with a great physique was the closest a fag could come to being patriotic.

Being called Castro took some living down, *siguro*. Even Rodrigo and Alvaro used to make sniggering references to the distaff, e.g. nigger, side of the family tree. I read this as directed against the Maximum Leader rather than me and I smiled my smile. I told them there was a Philippine plethora of Castros. "It must have been a common colonial name," I speculated. "Maybe they all came from a poor area or from large, well-to-do families with too many younger sons. Not everyone is equipped to go into the Church, believe me, guys." This caused more sniggering. Unknown to me then, though not by the time we'd finished the round of Hatueys I was buying in the Monserrate, one of Alvaro's kinks – failing *torero* – was being lashed to a makeshift wooden cross and sodomised, even though it had to be a back- to-front crucifixion.

Usually, we made our way to the Playas del Este, not the most promising of journeys: past the interminable Soviet-style housing blocks which I could not regard as improvements on Auntie Irish and Auntie Monalisa's nipa-theme, but there was nothing wrong with the beaches themselves. They went on for miles, a broad ribbon of the finest, white sand. A good back-drop, I thought as I lay on my back, for me. I stretched out there like an undeveloped photograph or *Moros y Cristianos*, or an exclamation mark on the front page of *Granma*, my head the dot. This was also one of the places where fish-steaks were cheap and, not only that, well-cooked. At a table in the shade of a tree with a ten-cents bottle of rum in front of you, it was easy to forget where you were. Florida was only ninety miles away. You could pretend you were already there. Reality returned soon enough when you were faced with the problem of getting back to the city on the sardine-tight *Gua-Gua*. I liked that word for the wallowing, exhaust-belching buses; it was almost Cebuano.

One time we got more ambitious and made for Mariel, via a little-known cove called Playa Hiradura. Our Lada had over-heated, much like Alvaro. There were five of us in the back and he was sitting in my lap, going "Oo-oo!" with simulated rapture every time we went over a pot-hole in the minor road. It had been Drigo's idea to take the scenic route. We took a cart-track off the small road to get water for the radiator which was steaming even more ominously than Alvaro. This turned out to be no problem – rural Cubans exhibited an even more commendable solidarity than that found in the cities – and within minutes a bucket of well-water was lowering the temperature but doing terrible invisible damage to the car's Russian innards.

As we passed the cove on the way back it was Alvaro's bright idea for us to go skinny-dipping – not under the cloak of darkness but at eleven a.m. There were two great sources of amusement for my companions here, one immediate, the other delayed. First, the sight of my organ – Alvaro pretending to wobble at the knees and secondly the fact that I as the only Negro in the party was the only one to get sun-burned. I got the burn on my shoulder-blades from watching the fish. I never saw so many in all my life. Lack of dynamite-fishing was the reason, I think. Fidel had every grain of gunpowder on the island accounted for. Among the rocks further out were so many lobsters one valued them as much as cockroaches in a kitchen. "Hubert, Hubert, where are you, man?" I murmured to myself.

I carried a rapturous, squeaking Alvaro up to the Lada so he wouldn't get his feet sandy, then announced I was driving. Which I did without incident; once again, it was as solitary as the Bohaiden Empty Quarter. A black-market gasoline top-up in an intervening township – the combination of black muscle and white respectability once again irresistible in provincial Cuba – and within a couple of hours we were at Mariel.

This was the port from which latterly the scum of the island had drifted across the Straits to Florida to make Miami even more unsafe than it already was. Drigo and his gay band, with me as Little John, had come to look across the ocean and pretend they had the balls to make the crossing. The big exodus was already over but there were still some rafters around. Many would end up travelling East, not North – to the US base at Guantanamo on the other end of Cuba. Some would die at sea. Some would deserve to die at sea.

Guys were still building their rafts on the shore and, considering the limited range of materials available, there was an amazing variety of what Hube would have called design solutions: monohulls, cats, tris, traditional log-rafts with cross-lashings. What they all had in common was oars to get the first mile offshore and then some rudimentary sails, though in truth it didn't need a Robbie Pryce to tell me current was going to be the chief factor in these waters.

"Take me, boys, take me," trilled Alvaro. This caused dark looks and mutterings amongst the surly, humour-less Cuban fuck-ups who comprised the majority of the *balseros*. No surprise. They'd have been low-lifers anywhere. They weren't so much anti-Castro as anti-everyone. I think they were the truly perverse type who fucked helpless heteros up the ass in jail and spurned the overtures of honest-to-God sodomites like Alvaro. Our queens made kissing noises and provocative wigglings of the hips. Now I heard the M-word, neighbour in the alphabet of the N-word, only infinitely more offensive. A couple of the *balseros* moved towards us but checked when I got in the way – much like the bull-elephant protecting his herd. They weren't to know I'd lost every street-fight of my life that involved my own interests. They went back to their lashings and hammerings while we continued along the sands. Passing by a glorified bath-tub with a single lateen-sail and a long steering-oar for the rudder, instead of the tiller most balseros seemed to prefer, I had a strange glance bestowed upon me by a refined-looking black guy. In fact, he'd done a double-take. There weren't that many black *balseros*, so he stuck out.

"Rey?" he asked, more of himself than me, in puzzlement. "Sugar?"

"*Si,*" I said hesitantly. He was familiar but I couldn't associate him with any Cuban context. I tried to bring him up from the layers of history but nothing swam up from the immediate past.

"*¿No me recuerdas?*" he inquired mournfully, but with a gentle humour that wasn't at all local. Much the way I might have chided a friend or expected another Flip or Thai to reproach me for my hurtful thoughtlessness. It wasn't Latin, it was Asian. It was like me.

"Michael!" I shouted. Black Michael. Vietnamese Michael, Hot Dang Man's friend and my contemporary, whom I'd met all those years ago, baking bread at the side of the airport road in Palawan with his sister Em. That was the day Atty Caladong had given the poor Viet marks in the refugee camp his spiel, then headed on back to the hotel in the trisikad with Skipper and Co, leaving me, Dant, and Lazares to hoof it.

"I shouldn't be dropping dead with the shock of it," I said. "Hot Dang Man filled me in but the visible fact of it is a kick in the ass."

From his eyes I could see the only word he'd understood had probably been the last one.

"Hey, still no spikka da English too good?" I asked.

He shook his head. "Speak better today Spanish."

Gee, I thought. Here were we soul-brothers doomed to communicate in a language completely alien to Michael and belonging to my own national yesterday. It was a conversation in the echo-chamber, man.

"Where's Em?" I asked.

"Ho Chi Minh. Saigon. What are *you* doing here?"

I explained. My presence in Cuba was completely accidental. It should've been Michael dropping dead of shock, not me. There was a predictable chain of events leading to him standing in that particular place at that particular time, whereas my ticket came straight out of the lottery.

Nguyen hadn't quite given me the full info. Perhaps he hadn't to the Americans at his debriefs, either. Michael had been given the choice of studying forestry in East Germany or veterinary science in Cuba. He'd gone for the trees rather than the ailing porkers. Plenty of opportunity for applying the lessons of *la silvicultura* in Vietnam: all that Agent Orange strewn over the jungle. But the re-afforestation programme was gonna have to manage without Michael. The East Germans had rejected him out of hand. I could guess why. A full-blooded Vietnamese was bad enough. Those East Germans had the quota imposed upon them by their government and ultimately Moscow but they hated foreigners (just like the Viets themselves, man). Anyone who looked Vietnamese had been beaten up twice already on the streets of the Democratic Republic and was agog for thrashing three. Slant-eyed gooks were sufficient provocation to the stolid squarehead citizenry, but a nigger and a nigger with slanty eyes and high cheek-bones at that!... oh, man! For his own good, they pulled him. I don't think Michael had a suspicion. I was the one with the mind belated-dirty piecing the jig-saw together. Uncle Ho's successors had sent him to Havana instead, where in place of the heavyweight grammatical certitudes of German he had to take aboard the elaborate yet simpler flourishes of Spanish. Poor Michael. He was as much a dunce at the sciences as I would have been. In that classroom of retentive Rumanians, know-all Nicaraguans, and bright Bulgarians, he had been the striking instance of the failure of affirmative socialist action. In short, the nigger in the woodpile. Then the fall of the Wall had left him high and dry.

"*No tengo exito, Rey,*" he grimaced. Then we laughed together. Whatever life had held and would hold in store for us, we were standing with the warm sunshine on our backs and the clean sand massaging our soles. I introduced him to Drigo and the gay band. Michael was either a perfect actor or simply didn't register that some of them were wearing eye-liner and lipstick. If I needed reminding of it, there were some very good things about Asian people.

As we sat on Michael's shirt – the *balseros* had angrily waved us off their rickety planks, quite correct I'd have done the same, too, it occurred to me to demand of my friend, "Michael, what the hell are you doing helping to build a boat on this beach?" He smiled brilliantly. "Just the same as everyone else, amigo. I want to go to America."

"Michael," I repeated incredulously, "Michael, are you telling me that you were one of the original boat-people in Asia, that you, shit, man..." I faltered under the burden of my own scornful disbelief, my hilarity despite the risks my alter ego was running, "Jeez, Michael. So you're telling me that the bad-ass pirates who raped your girls and banged you over the head with boat-irons, who drowned Vietnamese with less mercy than you or I would an unwanted cat, the fact that you nearly died, that your tongue swelled up blacker than your dick and hung out of your mouth... shit, all that, and now you're gonna brave the sharks and the currents and the sun all over again, and not with your own people but this goddamned jail carrion who'd suck your blood for refreshment without a second thought..."

"Si, amigo," he replied, and his teeth flashed even whiter in his face. I had to turn my own face away. Words failed me. Then I uttered in English one of Robbie Pryce's favourite expressions. "Well, fuck me backwards over a barge-pole."

"W-a-a-a-t?" inquired Alvaro hopefully, who had a smattering of English. Drigo translated. That Spanish-speaker's "W-a-a-a-t," quite normal said as an elongated *"Que?"* and so vulgar a sound in English it would have made Fr. Paul or Mrs Smith flinch. "Mm," said Alvaro.

"What do I have to lose, Sugar?" Michael asked "Florida currents is more predictable than any communist politician, no? And the sharks not so hungry. Yes, I made mistake not waiting for OD Programme in Vietnam *pero ahora...* I grab my chance."

"OK, second time lucky," I said. "But you've got to be setting a world-record here, buddy." I shook my head in bemusement again. OK, I wasn't being very supportive and I don't think the sensations in my breast – whatever they were, superiority, glee, ridicule – did me any credit, but sometimes we'd rather the boon buddies of our past stayed warm and glorious memories fixed in the briny solution of time rather than become living, changeable actualities in an awkward present. *Di ba?* And sometimes we don't want to be reminded of the history we have or what we once were. I don't know if Michael sensed my feelings – if what I had was a contagion, a disease of the soul – but if he was disappointed in me he never showed it. His friendship didn't falter, man, on the slopes of my indifference. He sat next to me on the beach, held my hand under the sand and asked about Danton. I considered lying. Then I told him the truth. The tears came to his eyes. He said, *"El era pequeño pero valiente."*

"Yeah," I said, "Dant the Ant."

Michael said, "You know what makes it worse? When you hid Nguyen and me on the ship to Zamboanga, it worked. We got away with it. You helped us, but you couldn't help yourselves."

"I never thought of it that way, Michael," I said. "But now you put it like that…"

To my surprise I found my own eyesight misting over. I told Michael a little of my life since then, not much because how could I make the Smiths, Faud, Hube, Robbie Pryce, Jock or that little imp Ali real to him?

Michael sensed this reluctance. He squeezed my hand and said, "Wherever you go, Sugar, think of me there, too. I have known you only a few hours of my life but it doesn't matter. They were worth years of knowing someone else. You look more like my brother than Em does my sister, and she is my real sister."

By the time I left Michael he'd made me feel a traitor's guilt. Yet I had never betrayed him in my life.

At the Lada the queens greeted me with jeers and catcalls about my new *"novio"*. I chased Alvaro up into a grove of palms. The seats of the car were baking-hot.

Ten days later we returned to see Michael and his fellow *balseros* off. These ruffians, stubbly already, as if they'd stepped off the raft after a week, rather than just embarking on their adventure, all had wives or sweethearts seeing them off. Tears, hugs, kisses, hysterics, we saw the full female gamut, as performed by that past-mistress of emotional display, the *chica Cubana*. Even the queens and I were impressed and, man, we knew those chicks would have their heels wrapped round another guy's butt that very night. What they were there for was to stake an anticipatory claim. Where we saw so many dishevelled fugitives from justice, they saw potential billionaires in top hats and spats, standing there like Scrooge McDuck with dollar-signs in their eyes. After all those years of Communist propaganda the Cubans still believed in the American dream. Probably more fervently than Fr. Boy did. It was the opposite of Filipinos lined up at the airport to greet the returning *balikbayan* – Ali Balikbayan and the Forty Relatives, man – all hot for a handout. That was a reception-committee. Avid Cuban relatives formed a despatch-committee.

I helped Michael lash a black plastic jerry-can of drinking water to the mast of the raft. Then I painted a white "M" on it. "That's yours, brother," I admonished him. "Don't let any of those wise-guys steal it from you." I slipped him the clasp-knife I'd brought.

I have to record that every single one of the *balseros*, except Michael, was drunk when they set sail and sat down to the oars. This was something of an anti-climax. The tide brought them back forty-five minutes later. Most of the girls had already gone. I could hear the guys cursing their luck from a hundred metres out. I figured a set of tide-tables would have been of more use than the Bible one dude had with him (entirely to impress the anti-Godless Commie Republican sects, I'm sure). They'd gone near high water when it was easy to launch but they needed the ebb to help pull them out to where the winds were. All the knowledge the early *balseros* had acquired had been lost in the interval. I was pointing this out as I helped push them in the shallows two hours later when one of the rafters, a guy with a long-healed cicatrix across his belly that did not look in the least surgical, said: "Since you know so much, *cabron*, why don't you hop aboard and help us?" He was just talking shit – he'd been pretending he knew how to use the Christmas-cracker compass they had with them – but Michael looked eagerly at me.

He held out his hand.

"You need asking twice? Take it *na lang*, Gorilla," said a voice in my ear.

I sprang. Not knowing if it was ladder's rung or serpent's coil, I sprang. I was the un-blond Prince Hamlet, regressing for his tribe.

CHAPTER XXII

Naples
November 20 1990

Dear Rey,

Hi it's me the one Vebegene *kumostaka* trusting it finds you well likewise concerning me just fine. Rey, I'm writing you from da Convent in Napoli that's Italy I'm *madre* now, you can believe? It's true. Maybe you don't recognise me under da wimple but it's still Bebegene. I like, I rilly-rilly like da life but more later.

Da most imfortant thing I know you like to hear is concerning Mrs Smith our late emfloyer. Gi-send to me by Myrlinda-Luz she's da one who is living next door us in Kowloon and she git it from Jennilyn she's da fat one friend of Erlinda used to be my friend walking Sunday but da snake going *mag-bori* da shopping mall until now with da guys *kada domingo* and she git it from Mary-Ann from General Santos City is Dadiangas City before and she now marry to da English guy name of Pete living in Harrow Ingland after they wait three year for da visa and da Inglands embassy ask her to her face she is *bori puta* or not when she is birgin almost. OK I'm now enclosing Zerox copy from da Feople newspaper.

You're welcome to keep it even da Zerox expensive here not like home:

Snobbish retired naval officer's wife Mrs Smith committed suicide from an overdose of sleeping pills after being exposed as a habitual thief.

The coroner's court recorded a verdict of suicide on Mrs Smith who had been convicted the previous month of shop-lifting when store-detectives stopped her outside Wilson's supermarket and found unpaid sweets and toiletries to the value of thirty five pounds in her shopping-bag. At the time of her arrest Mrs Smith had two credit-cards, a cheque-book, and one hundred and twenty three pounds in bank-

notes and assorted coins in her wallet. She had paid for twelve pounds eighty three pence worth of canned foods and toiletries at the check-out before proceeding into the street where she was challenged by the two store-detectives.

Mrs Smith entered a plea of not guilty to shop-lifting in the Magistrate's Court but later changed it to guilty. She received three months probation and a fine of one hundred pounds.

Neighbour Mrs Cohen in the posh suburb where the Smiths had retired after more than twenty years abroad, with a T-registration Jaguar in her own drive, said, "She was always going round with her nose in the air. She snubbed all my invitations to coffee-mornings and my Tupperware party. I was shocked at first but not when I think about it."

The manager of Wilson's, Mr Winston Greene, said that it was not usually the store's policy to prosecute offenders in Mrs Smith's circumstances but that it was the third time she had received a warning in as many months.

Store detective Mrs Michiko Johnson said she had noticed the defendant behaving in a suspicious manner by the dried fruit and nuts section, then observed her slip a 225mL bottle of liquid soap into her bag at toiletries. Mrs Smith's husband, a retired admiral, was unavailable for comment but her youngest daughter Jennifer, told our reporter to "Naff off. Mums would have never done anything like that."

Oldest daughter Nicola, 27, a mature student at Lavalle Polytechnic studying social work said, "My mother was in need of counselling for a mental and emotional disorder common in women of her age, not a barbaric persecution reminiscent of the middle ages. The system and we, her family, failed her."

Well, Rey, there is certainly a God in da Heaven and he move in mysterious ways to accomflish his will. So many time Satan rising in her heart insfire her to blame me for her money gone missing from her dresser or her focket – sometime I think she just da one to leave it there to tempt good people to sin and da Evil One he give her da cunning to leave it's like three hundred one dollars so easy to tell if someone tempt to take it. Now it's God who funish her and all da time it was her da one to be a big robber.

To be about me *balik-balik lang sa akong historia* I finish my contract with da *insik* Chineses in Aberdeen and find da family is Italian but before I go I sprinkle Holy Water on da head of da Chineses Buddha idol. They never know, hee-hee, I strike da blow for Jesus. Da Italians is real nice almost like da Filipinos themselves. Friendly, likes talk-talk, music, da singing, da vambini, and they also got spaghetti like we have in da Philippines but not so good coz chewy da noodles and bitter da sauce not like in home sweet home da RP da spags melt in da mouth. I got fat here already maybe you don't recognising me now.

Pretty soon time for my contract to exfire. I'm a little worried to go back home coz I not saved enough for old ages yet. Then every Sunday I going to Church and meet with da other hilfers afterward in da Fiazza. They said why you don't just joining da Convent. Full da convents already of da *pinay* runaways (da Thai girls is Bhuddist so cannot too bad for them *di ba*?). You tell me I remember that all da ships full already of Pilipinos sailors well all da convent of da madre da nun here is full of Filipinas more than da Irish ones!

By da way, we got scheme going here for relief of da unfortunate flight of da niggers peoples in Africa. Donation min of fifty thousand lira but given heartily even smaller is acceptable. You can send me here coz you is da nigger also. I can donate da money your behalf.

Hope to hear news soon use registered mails post here da same as Philippines.

PS Hear da *bori* frostie Erlinda committing already da mortal and detestable sin of abortion pray for her soul that's da *tsismis*.

In da vowels of Christ,

It's me Vebegene

c/o Ahmed's Halwa Shop and Juice-bar
Bohaiden
Undated

O Black One!

Thou who wert conceived as the spawn of a Kuwaiti sodomite and thy cross-eyed whore of an Ethiopian mother when thy lawful cuckolded father's back was turned, Ali greets you. *(Sir, Felicitation in the name of the Merciful, the Compassionate, forgive my trespasses, I am only the professional scribe and the little shaitan insists on the letter of his imprecations being conveyed to your distinguished self).*

The Fat One Al-Hubert hath vanished to America and thou also hath disappeared into the night in which thou wert conceived. But, O Wily One, thou hath not the wiles of Ali for I have discovered thee in thy artfulness! Thou gave instructions to the Lebanese whose coffee it was thy desire to imbibe and newspapers thy bent to peruse while Ali waited outside until the very heavens turned to stone without refreshment or even a coin to flip, to receive and convey thy mail onwards to thy situation. Do not deny it! Thou holds my letter even now as a soldier holds the pineapple before it explodes in his beard!

Faud would pay a ransom to hold thy eggs in his hand, Black One! The Lebanese hath satisfied my demands for silence and thou shalt too. The Lebanese knoweth not that I shall return as the bee to the flower as often as it pleaseth him and shall bear the sweetness of profit but thou I shalt milk but the once, for we are brothers. Accordingly send me dinars twenty thousand and my lips shall be sealed before Faud.

ALI

Southampton
January 1st 1991

Dear Rey,

Cor, that was a fucking fall and a half, shipmate. Don't think I'd have come out of it unless you and the French geezer (forgot his name, the hard-nut shirt-lifter anyway) hadn't got to me so quick. I remember I was sprawled across the girder and heading down again for a smash if you hadn't come along. Thanks, mate. The insurance paid up right enough, no complaints about the owners on that score. I had three busted ribs, a shiner, and the port-side leg you saw of course. What a mess. They patched me up good enough and I can still go to sea besides I got the dough by way of compensation which I used for the downpayment on a flat. I'll have my own ship yet, shipmate, and you can ship as the bosun. Don't know what else to tell you. My old lady kicked the bucket soon after I left hospital but as you didn't know her you won't be sorry. She was eighty-nine and deaf as a coot but otherwise sound and seaworthy. My old man dropped dead fucking years ago no loss to anyone. He was a professional gambler and a bookie's runner in the days when it was still illegal. Wouldn't have done bad at one of them cock-fights you used to tell me about in the Phillipines don't expect I've spelled that correct.

Rey, I'm writing to you care of your old pal Sparks, Gerry, the radio officer. Expect he might have your address or know someone who's got it. Maybe you'll get this in six months time but better late than never as the actress told the bishop. I heard you jumped ship after some ruckus. As I reckon what I heard was a pack of lies from beginning to end I won't bother you with the details. If you need my help with a character reference I'm always there, mate.

Best to you,
Robbie Pryce

Rey, I'm the one to write on the outside of Robbie's envelope at first. I first thought it would be easy to get a fix on you but it's not di ba? So I took the liberty, pare, to open and photocopy Robbie's letter. Then I'll send a general message broadcast on a different frequency hoping someone will pick it and relay it on to you e.g. I'm writing to you c/o all the addresses I got including

your Auntie's you gave me in RP. Over, pare. Let me have acknowledgement
hope it won't be a general Mayday. It's nice to know when you do get
through the static of life.

    Out,
    Gerry.

London E13
June 17 1991

Dear Rey,

Hope you didn't forget me already it's your landlady in Plaistow also your g-f Marites. Joke only. It's your dance-partner at Marcelino's by name of me.

Edwin mention your name other day when I'm visiting on a Sunday in Ladbroke Grove. Then I thought maybe you welcome a letter even it's only me. Things here not so good at the moment. Some trouble with black boys now you're gone but not so bad as before. Some kids come in and I say you're sleeping in back and they go away quickly so I think they can still remember you like hero of da revolution ba? I went up West last week again lost all money in Cromwell Mint too bad. I know I'm da stupid one but can't stop myself Rey it's a sickness like *adis-adis sa droga* rilly I can't help myself. Edwin wife put me in touch with Gamblers Anonimus and I just going to try to reform myself already I need proper programme thats what. I know your life now must be hard too but if you have any money to spare God know I can really need it and I fromise to Almighty God I never going to use it to gamble. I just buy foods and pay electricity bill *na lang* they already cut it off since one week and cold and dark here and especially no TV I miss Dallas.

My nephew no help at all. In fact I think he took forty-five pee from my purse as soon as my back turned yesterday. He always smell of glue I know what he's doing with his friends so *maldito* he not affreciate opportunity he have here different from Philippines.

Still, Rey, I try to be happy, sing, and smile coz we have life now and one day we be dead and then it's too late to wish you already enjoyed yourself. Long face no good to anyone. You tell me before, if you can laugh when life's hard, that's brave and I always remember that. You say "Humour is da antiseptic of life's ills," and I think Rey's a big tall guy but he got a brain good as da little Chinese guy or da Jewish is here. So guwapo bagets brainy I send you best wishes all da co-workers friends here don't forget us and rimimber – distance no hindrance of forgetfulness. Hugs and kisses from Marites in Plaistow still.

Mactan
February 6th 1992

My Son,

Many things have happened since I last wrote you and I am happy to say that between us your friends here have been able to secure a result as satisfactory as anything in this life can be said to be. In this country a dictatorship is forgotten and its cronies rehabilitated in six years, so well may ordinary misdemeanors be purged in less. Not that you have been anything other than an innocent party.

Before I bring you up to date with all this, I confirm I have received your two letters, the one from the British isles and the last from the United States. How strange to think of you setting foot on the shores of the New World though you have at least as much connection in essence with America as you do with the Philippines where you have still spent the majority of your years. I was amused by your account of your experiences with the representatives of the Immigration and Naturalisation Service and at your expectation, ironic I assume, that the Afro-American officer who interviewed you was going to admit you to the country "without a ticket" like the collectors at the ticket-barriers of the London Municipal Transportational system. I was sorry to hear all but two of you on the raft were washed overboard. How did that happen? I was delighted to hear your Vietnamese friend found sanctuary this time. You did not mention if he was a Roman Catholic. If so he would have been doubly discriminated against by his own government in Vietnam. No, I don't think the INS officer was kidding when he said he would try to locate your natural father but these things take a matter of years rather than months.

And, no, I am also not in the least surprised at your relative incuriosity as to your "spiritual homecoming" to your (unfortunately, unknown) father's country. Rather, I am only surprised that you should term the United States a spiritual home. I am aware that the other young men and women who find themselves by birth in your position – surely not so unusual in the environs of Mactan Field – may have thought in such terms, but then I have never thought of you as anything but a highly unusual person. Certainly the most unusual I have ever taught in all my years at San Ignatio. I thought we did our work better, I thought Paul did his work better than that. Your spiritual home is in the Roman Catholic Church and that, my son, is the Church Universal. The fifty years Filipinos are said to have spent in Hollywood were preceded by the three hundred in the Spanish Convent. You are not one of life's gum-chewers. I am only surprised Paul did not make a cricket-player of you.

Now, at last, in reply to your kind inquiry Fr. Paul is no longer connected with our mission here. He is best situated to explain the exact circumstances to you. I have known Paul for half a century. I could know him another fifty years and still feel it was presumptuous in me to think I knew him totally. He said he looked forward to hearing your voice again. It would probably please the Monsignor and the Bishop too if I were to cease all contact with Fr. Paul but I justify my continued – though much slighter – connection with him by the thought that I might alter his mind. Despair is of course a sin but I have noticed over-confidence may be a vaulter's downfall. Be wary of Fr. Paul. Consult me if he sows unease or doubt in your heart. In fact I do not believe Paul would wish to do this.

To turn to particular matters. I am no expert in Philippine law – the enumerated Republic Acts cover everything but seem to be enforced with as much will by our contemporary judges as the liberation theologians would Leviticus. However, I understand some witnesses and complainants signed affidavits of desistance, some have died of natural causes and some, I regret to say, as the result of violence which I trust was unconnected to their involvement in this particular case, while I am also informed some matters were judicially struck out because the issues had failed to prosper. Fr. Paul would no doubt say the entire country should be struck out because it had failed to prosper. Forgive my levity. I attach a letter from Mr Tan Sy couched wholly in Visayan (I absolve that gentleman of any desire to conceal secrets from me as we have enjoyed many conversations about you, our absent protege, in what Fr. Paul used to call "the pithiest vernacular". He goes into explanations in greater detail than myself and perhaps, after all, it is best that confidential communications in the foreign post should be in a language few outside the locality will understand (including our Tagalog friends in Manila!). Mr Tan Sy was trying to persuade me to use the electronic-mail system to which he has recently become connected but as I still have to avail of the facsimile machine I have had to disappoint him. It is somewhat more secure than the line of post: at least half my mail has been opened at the post office. There are few secrets in this country but many mysteries.

So here is Butch's letter and his account of his "rule-meeting" with your Atty Caladong, a gentleman I have yet to meet although Mr Tan Sy described him memorably to me as "the best professional fouler in the business". I know you will make up your own mind, if it is not already determined. Finally, I know you well enough to know you will not be offended by the trifling gift of money enclosed. It is from Fr. Paul and myself, but principally Fr. Paul. It will aid in defraying the expense of your return. It is not a loan and should not be mistaken as such. One should only feel grateful for a loan, timely extended. A gift is different for friends do not feel grateful to each other.

Ever truly yours,

Fr. "Boy"

CHAPTER XXIII

Yellow Ribbon Day – I meet Cheech Chong – Who tells me about Butch – Home Again – I give directions – Repairing a Crack Toothache – Fr. Paul's Soles – Lazarus13@hotmail.com Eye of Newt – All smiles stop

---

JUST AS A PAIR OF BEST PANTS left in the cupboard against the eventuality of a day for smart-wear – be it graduation or date – seem that bit tighter, that inch more restrictive when eventually we don them, so the places of our youth (remembered so momentously, bulking so large in their significance) disappoint in their shrunkenness when at last we revisit them. We can always reduce our waistline, we can never shrink our mental horizons again. I came back to Cebu to find myself busting out in all the wrong places. It wasn't Auntie Irish's shack which seemed small or Auntie Lovely-Anne who appeared mean. It was San Ignatio which struck me as provincial and its ambitions as petty.

Auntie Irish and Auntie Lovely-Anne had tied a yellow ribbon round the old jack-fruit tree and banana palms that stood at the entrance to our compound. On closer inspection it was revealed as the earth-wire of a non-Philippine electric-flex system. God knows where they had got it from but I surely appreciated the thought. Welcome Home, Blondel! said placards. Our Frodigal is Nigh said another I cared less for in what turned out to be the juvenile hand of Auntie Monalisa's fifth, a mestiza girl not yet a twinkle in her unknown – but physical evidence suggested fair-haired – father's eye when I'd left. "Tourist akong papa," she told me in the same reverential tone as one might have said Frog Prince. "*Di ba, 'be?*" I said consolingly.

"Vambi!" someone called. Bambi who had been purposely lurking in our old hooch gave a shriek of simulated surprise, nevertheless appreciated by one and all, and raced over to fling her arms round my neck. My own shock was unsimulated. I didn't recognise my kid sister. She'd ballooned, man. From sixty-five she'd hit one hundred pounds plus, easy. She had a butt rivalling Faud's first wife's and her face had filled out commensurately. I shouldn't say it, but I preferred the tubercular famine-victim to the picture of health before me now.

"Sis," I said weakly.

"Vlondel, I da fat one already," she confessed.

"That's good, '*be*," I lied.

"Work da medicines already, Brudder Blondel. I cured."

"Yeah, you told me in your letters. Did you get mine?"

"*Wala*. Not coming." She gave me our ingenuous bug-eyed look, the one Babyjane used to bestow on Mrs Smith. Even if you happened to be telling the truth it made you look dishonest.

"Shit, Bambi, not even the money I remitted, *koan*, OK you don't know that word…"

"Yes I know. Remittance is money sending."

"OK. Did you get the money I sent from Hong Kong and Bohaiden?"

"Ah, da money come."

"OK." I left it at that.

"I got job now assembly at Timex factory."

"Hey! Congrats, Sis!"

Auntie Irish pinched my butt. "Wow legs still, Blondel."

"Wow *sampot* also," said Auntie Lovely-Anne. I swatted these attacks off tolerantly. I would be riding Auntie Irish that night, drunk, and Auntie Lovely-Anne, Thursday, sober, both unsought episodes that I could regard as belated rites of passage.

"Ma dead," said Bambi.

"I got your letter, Sis," I told her. "*Nakadawat ka ba sa akong mga flowers ug wreath?*"

Bambi shook her head. I believed in her unfeigned simplicity this time. "Oh God, Fauper Funeral," she wailed and a tear came out of her eye and ran fatly down her plump cheek.

"I've seen and heard worse," I said. "Ma didn't know about it anyhow."

"Oh, Lord," shrieked Bambi, "Vlondel come back atheist."

"Uy, Uy, Sis," I said. "You're looking at a True Believer. I'm the Original Avenging Angel, Honeybunch." What you said to another Filipino wasn't so important as how you said it, much like the words of a pop song being inconsequential to the melody, and Bambi was

518

soon soothed, especially when I pulled out a fistful of pesos for the snacks everyone would have liked to offer but no one could afford to give me. So I bought a whole roast pig for lechon, threw the fistful of rock salt into its stitched belly myself to sweat out of the pores to crisp up the crackling, plucked lemon-grass from the garden; laid in cup gelatines and chocolate Yan Yan sticks for the kids; and finally ingratiated myself with Auntie Irish by purchasing her entire stock of soft drinks. It was a long time since I'd lit a BBQ pyre but I hadn't lost my hand from the days when Dant had us grilling live cats. We were little monsters.

I did my best to be the perfect host. All my life I'd been on the receiving-end. I strove to exhort without being domineering, to provide amply without showing off, to make one and all feel welcome in their own yard without giving the impression I'd invaded and usurped. I tried to be Faud in a tweed jacket, Commander Smith with a chilli down his briefs, Hubert sucking on a hookah, Slash n' Crap in Fred Astaire's tails. And, you know what, all those complicated mental gyrations and substitutions came down to the simplest of results: I just had to be me, man. I mean, we Filipinos had our faults but, rich or poor, we were the most open and hospitable of folks, even the worst among us. Ferdy and Melda, the two of them, threw great parties.

So, after the *lechon* I got in violet-yam ice-cream – I'd nearly forgotten what that tasted like: a scream gone gelid and its gritty texture like the earth confected with stratosphere (I was on Cloud Nine anyhow). After that, some flat flasks of Tanduay rum and then I gave everyone my interpretation of Enfermera Julaidis's Tex-Mex ballad, followed by a Bohaidenese desert love song accompanied by Auntie Irish on her genuine jack-fruit wood guitar. They all asked for an encore of the Arabo lament and were politely indifferent about the Spanish song. My inept rendition, I hope. After that, drunk as Captain Mac-Mac, I crept away to piss behind the banana palms. This was where Auntie Irish was able to catch up with me. I was full enough of rum 'n' Coke to have been pissing for over a minute already, with half a minute's worth still under pressure in my bladder. Not quite the fire-hose intensity of cold climes but alcohol had nearly the same effect as a radical drop in temperature. After I'd succeeded in dousing a couple of mating lizards I imagined myself a gasoline pump with the digits flashing up on the meter. This was when I heard rustling on the other side of the banana palm that was not my own pattering. Already in the squat, Auntie Irish waddled through the fronds like a duck. She'd obviously decided to change situations, having already started to pee. Now she let herself go right by my side, an amazing sizzling on the desiccated earth that was typically female in both its brevity and its intensity. If I'd had my eyes closed in bliss I'd still have known it was a woman. "Ah," I sighed, as my stream started to droop at the same moment Auntie Irish ceased scalding the dust and chickens' droppings. "Yikes, Vlondel!" she exclaimed. "Also you is here."

I grinned to myself. She was fifty-eight if she was a day, the mother of six living and two dead and, bless her for the *pinay* she was, still as maidenly a bull-shitter as any blushing fifteen-year-old. "O-o. What a coincidence, *na lang*, Auntie Irish."

"Could not see you, Vlondel, coz it's dark and you is so black, *pod*."

"When out tonight, wear something light."

"Hah?"

"Private joke only, Auntie Irish. No disrespect." I shook my pecker, confident it was invisible but it obviously wasn't so black that she couldn't see it, for I was rewarded with her low, old woman's chuckle.

"What's dat? Banana?"

"O. *Saging*," I replied. "Giant one."

"Hilaw, ba?"

"Dili. Hinug na kay itum kaayo. It's ripe because it's black."

Without another word Auntie Irish grabbed it and put it in her toothless mouth.

Oh, man. If I was to say I'd entered the portals of paradise I'd be a liar as well as a stylistic disappointment to Fr. Paul. But part of me sure had entered the realms of joy. Auntie Irish in fact had two teeth. I checked the complement the next morning when I told her a Robbie Pryce joke just to make her open her mouth again. (I knew she was as coarse as Robbie). They looked pretty much as I'd have imagined the fangs of Hubert's elderly female baboons – brown, broken, and still capable of inflicting a dangerous wound – but I didn't withdraw from her mouth just the same. It could have been a maiden half Auntie Irish's age with a full set of molars and incisors Colgate-pearly, and I wouldn't have enjoyed it so much. Auntie Irish gave a truly expert blow-job. Too expert. She had me on the brink rather more quickly than I wanted. With the same concentration as I'd find my way out of the ruck of players under the net, I gently held the ball that was Auntie Irish's bobbing head with both hands and steered it away from my important part.

"Dili ka gusto?" the old dear inquired anxiously. *"Gusto ko,"* I replied with the huskiness that should have been hers, "but team-work, *dili* solo," and with that I tipped her gently on her back as one might roll a tyre half a revolution. It was the work of a moment, as they used to say in Fr. Paul's children's classics, for me to have her holed duster up over her navel and her snowy panties round one ankle. *"Uga ko,"* were her only words to me, half-inquiry, half-apology for what she already knew. And she was right, man, she was as dry as an El Nino summer. It was the first time I'd never had to worry about hurting a Filipina but loose as she was, never stitched after any of the births, it was me who felt the discomfort of inadequate lubrication the most. I imagined Hubert having wise counsel on the subject which I would never hear. It was quick — unbeatable friction, man — but neither of us minded. As I lay there with it still in, Auntie Irish said, "Your Ma my best friend. I never have again like her."

"O-o, Auntie Irish," I said, and I said it with respect as Ma's son.

I was about to steal back, in advance of Auntie Irish to avoid embarrassing her, but she led me by the hand to the stand-pipe and pump. There she would brook no contradiction or remonstrance of mine but pulled down my Bermuda shorts and then my jockeys before she tenderly washed what had been inside her. Then she turned me round and washed my butt. Her hands were very hard but very smooth — a poor woman who had done an entire army's laundry over a lifetime. "I wash you here, hilf your Mama when you're just a Bebe. This bery spot."

"Yes, Auntie Irish," I replied. I thought back to those days. But Auntie Irish wasn't one to waste too much time on sentiment. She cuffed me on the butt and wandered back to my party. I was left with my hand on the tap, my tear-ducts as dry as the faucet.

I'D COME IN VIA METRO MANILA and Ma's was the second grave I'd visited of someone who'd been close to me. I couldn't exactly say I'd loved Butch Tan Sy but he'd been as formative an influence as any Jesuit. And my eyes had misted over as I stood by his headstone where they wouldn't over Ma's cross in the perfectly respectable cemetery Bambi had found for her.

It wasn't so much unfilial as that Butch Tan Sy's death was that much more recent. I don't care to say fresher. Butch got whacked eleven days before I landed at Ninoy Aquino International. They timed his death at 11.43 p.m. He'd been in the karaoke singing one of the only two songs he knew, *My Way*, when a guy no one could subsequently describe walked in as if to a table and shot him in the back of the head. I don't think Butch could have known anything about it. Just instant night for him. Funnily enough, my old adversary Cheech Chong, now a coach himself of course, was one of the guys drinking with Butch. And, no, it wasn't a set-up involving Cheech. He and Butch had become good pals, cronies almost. Cheech told me as much. He was an OK guy. "Ah, yeah, Castro," he said to me. "I remember. Nothing personal, man."

"Hey, nothing personal, Cheech," I reassured him and we shook on it. A little later he told me about the match-fixing syndicate that had been leaning on the coaches. Butch had told them what they could do with their envelope.

"I take it, man, to be honest you," Cheech said. "I ain't no heroes. Butch, he was different."

"O-o, Cheech," I said, "he was never a player, remember. It wasn't just a game for him. It was more of a religion with Butch."

"Siguro," said Cheech. "Hey, how come you never paid me back for what I did? There were other games we met after. I was sweating, man."

I laughed. "Nah, that would be petty, *di ba*, like revenge? I took out your Number 17 instead, Wenceslao I think his name was, after he clobbered our pointguard. So long as it's not for yourself, it's OK."

"Whatever you say, *pare*."

I bought Cheech a few beers and when his tongue grew loose, he mentioned a few names he shouldn't have which I duly committed to memory. I'd honour Butch my own way. I was under an obligation to him, which I had no intention of allowing to become an eternal obligation.

Manila lived down to my recollections. The dump hadn't changed except to get worse. We'd got rid of a dictator – rather my fellow-countrymen had – only to see a proliferation of crime on the streets. That was no accident; there was a connection. Drigo would see it when Fidel went. In my Artheneum days it had been the Wild

East, but the town surpassed itself in the three days I was there. I personally got to witness two shootings. The first was no mystery but a simple heist. I was walking down United Nations on the Luneta side when I saw a guy on a motor-bike come up behind another motor-cyclist at the red light and put two rounds straight into the other guy's helmet. Then he divested the body of its shoulder-bag and was roaring off as the light turned amber. I even had the crime explained to me in the next day's newspaper. The biker had been carrying pesos to an Ermita money-changer.

The next shooting was more enigmatic. I'd just come out of Robinson's with a few belated *pasalubong* for the Cebu crowd, being careful to buy stuff with foreign-made marks, when I noticed a young man of unmistakably Middle Eastern appearance standing by the kerbside waiting for an opportunity to cross the road. He was in white pants, white shoes, and white jacket through which his curly chest hairs poked and, absolute clincher that he was a medical stude, he clutched a stack of anatomy text-books. I was just congratulating myself on the fact that our med schools were famously cheap and not a hundred times worse than the Cuban ones when a Filipino in smart-casual attire (phrase Fr. Paul would surely find a contradiction in terms) came up behind him.

I was already a little uneasy. When I look back on it now it was that he was carrying a filthy, greasy towel of the kind more likely to be used by a jeepney-conductor. Something didn't fit about this accessory, and most of all his focussed eyes to go with his oh-so-random put-on walk. When a cager did that it was a signal a smart move was about to come off. Sure enough, a .38 came out from beneath the towel and I was once again reminded what a stupendously loud noise even small-calibre guns made. Nothing like the subdued and polite reports of firearms in the movies. Even I jumped out of my skin and I'd seen what was coming. Everyone else must have thought the heavens had fallen in. The Filipino fired three times. All the shots hit. The Arabo could have certified himself dead before he hit the sidewalk. Within two seconds there was blood everywhere. White couldn't have been a worse choice of clothing. He looked like the two halves of the Indonesian flag, man. He looked like the two sides of me. The dude who'd shot him headed in my direction. I did my best not to look at him. "Sister! Baby darling sister!" he shouted. He was still brandishing the gun, a particularly rusty piece of *paltik* workmanship that would never have passed muster with us kids in the old days, so I guessed on the two counts of the inferior weapon and the lack of emotional control that he was no pro, despite the careful stalking. "Now you pay! You pay!"

After he'd rounded the corner, I joined the throng around the body. I read the medical school ID tag. He was a Jordanian. No surprise. Most of them were. Poor fuck. I'd have saved him if I could, I really would. What was the Filipino but a quack dentist who'd pulled the wrong tooth. And in that line of prophylactic Philippine life-dentistry I saw myself as no bloody-handed quack but as meticulous a professional as Commander Smith.

Skipper and Atty Caladong didn't return my calls. On Skip's answering-machine I left a message. "I'll be back," I said. I wasn't paraphrasing MacArthur, but Arnold.

ALL THAT CAME THE WEEK BEFORE THE ROAST PIG and my carnality with Auntie Irish in the banana-grove. I was in no danger of turning vegetarian, *di ba*?

If I'd been accounting to myself, I'd have flown down home from Manila and to hell with the expense, but I was disbursing holy funds and I felt I owed it to my benefactors to be as miserly as an old Singaporean or a young Australian. I embarked on the ferry out of Tondo. The twenty-six hours passed without incident, other than the trips to the head. Even with Jean-Claude and Jock as ship-mates I'd never had to endure squalor of that order but then I guessed sailors were hardy but neat and passengers finicky but filthy. As I stood at the boat-deck railings while we passed under the gantries of the bridge connecting Mactan and Cebu islands I became conscious of a pair of blond backpackers. They were consulting a guide-book. "Good morning," I said.

Now I knew from my brief stay in Britain and my even briefer sojourn in the land of my father that mere sight of me could strike fear in the hearts of white people. At the very least it could cause unease the worse for being unacknowledged at source. Such feelings were absent from the pair of fair young faces turned towards me. "Good morning," said the friendly Finns straight back to me. If I was special blend, the ultimate in *Halo*[2], they were uncomplicated, unadulterated, homogeneous essence. They had no racial animosities, man, because they had no races.

"First time in Cebu?"

"Yes. You, sir?"

"No. I had the bad luck to be born here."

"Ah," laughed the girl, "we thought you were an American."

"A lot of people do. Can I be of any assistance to you?"

"Thank you. We're just looking for the Ruftan pension house here on this map."

Well, that was no problem. I knew where that particular flop-house was of old. I ushered the Finns down the gang-plank, carried the girl's back-pack with the aplomb of a bygone era, shoved obstructions and obstructers aside, and those locals who did not yield to my bulk were demolished by the vernacular eloquence issuing from completely the wrong face. In the RP if I spoke before I pulled a trigger, assuming the necessity, I'd always have the advantage of a moment's surprise. I figured sending strangers in the right direction was the obverse to handing out the *halo*es to those worthy of ruthless despatch. Negotiating the ancient grid of Spanish streets, past triangular Fort San Pedro, past Magallanes, past Juan Luna, I deposited them at their destination and was off before they could start to worry whether to tip me. Funnily enough, they'd changed the jeepney departure station to Opon while I'd been gone and I spent forty-five minutes finding it.

FR. BOY WAS OCCUPIED IN REPAIRING THE SCHOOL'S WATER-TANK when I paid him my call of duty and pleasure. The tank, a green toughened-polythene ball on its own four-metre tower, resembled nothing so much as a bean from Jack's magic-stalk and Fr. Boy our intrepid eponymous hero. I was steered his way by the janitor. What was remarkable, to me at least, was not that the janitor remembered me, the only six-foot two inches tall black man ever to attend the institution – which he thought was worth a tip – so much as he'd stayed so long in his job. Fr. Boy had his back to me as he stood on the service-ladder at nearly the height of a basketball-net. As I looked at his broad shoulders and the latissimus dorsi swelling under his *sando* I was reminded of an old Western I'd seen: Fr. Boy as Jesse James, me as the fink who shot him in the back while he was hanging a picture.

"Father," I said softly.

"Rey," he replied, without turning to see who it might be.

I waited.

"I'll be with you momentarily. This sealant needs me more than you do."

"O-o, Father. That's a nasty crack even from here."

"Crack? That's a six by six piece I'm glueing back in. It broke two days ago and there's no replacement tank available until next week."

"Hoy! Let me lend you a hand."

I jumped for a rung of the service-ladder three feet above my head, just under Fr. Boy's sneakers. To my unpleasant surprise I was unable to reach it. There was not so much a lack of strength in my quads as insufficient elasticity in the knee ligaments. I caught half-hold of the rung beneath as I dropped, wrenching my shoulder. Fr. Boy's thumb and forefinger instantly closed round my wrist, steadying me with the same reassurance as when I'd first vaulted a horse at age thirteen.

"A drop of oil on those knees, Rey," he said.

"Make it consecrated oil, Father."

"Just hold the glue-tube, *na lang*. I'll press the fragment on until it sticks."

We stayed companionably in that position without speaking for a while, me and Fr. Boy riding *habal-habal* into the sunset like Pancho and Cisco. After he'd got the shard to stick – I was able to read the small-print with my younger eyes and tell him it would take forty-eight hours to cure fully – we went to the refectory for a snack of *puto ug sikwate*. I dipped the springy rice-flour and coconut flake bun, which had the consistency of a teenager's tit, into the hot chocolate, sucked it, and was instantly rewarded with a sharp prong of pain in the left molar. I experimented with the other side. No problem. Another piece of ancient Spanish treat gave me an even sharper spike in the left side again. Shit.

"Toothache?" Fr. Boy asked solicitously. "I often think we have the worst teeth in the world here."

"I used to think I had the best, Father. I guess something happened to me while I was away."

"Well, it was a long time, Rey."

"And the wench is dead," I restrained myself from saying.

We spoke about some of my old classmates, nearly all successful in whatever their sphere was, be it humble or elevated (like gunnery-sergeants, the Jesuits encouraged you to aim low if you weren't quite up to the mark, for achievement was relative). I kept quiet when Fr. Boy confused my class with another one and he mentioned a boy I'd never heard of, who was now an air-con maintenance-mechanic, specialising in the National brand. Good luck to the poor fuck.

At last we got round to the apparently delicate subject of Fr. Paul.

"Has he, uh, been in regular correspondence with you?"

"Twice. But, Jeez, half my mail used to go astray. Sorry about my profanity, Father. I wasn't thinking."

"Did Fr. Paul say anything to which you or your spiritual adviser might take exception?"

"With respect, Father, I thought he *was* one of my spiritual advisers."

"Paul is sorely in need of guidance himself."

"Where is he now, Father? Did he return to England?"

"No. He's still here."

"Asa man gyud?"

"I'm not sure I should tell you."

"Why on earth not, Father? You don't trust me, *ba*? I'm no longer the child you knew."

"You don't have to tell me that, Rey. OK. He's at the SC Retreat House up past Talamban."

"Is he going to offer me the Kingdoms of the World?"

"He may well pull them all down and blind you with the dust." Fr. Boy stirred the thick chocolate in the jug and poured me another cup. I drank gingerly in a silence which was not at all uncomfortable. I realised why he had appeared so uninterested in my experiences when he invited me to make a confession just as I announced my departure. Fr. Boy – so bluff and so straightforward, but a Jesuit in essence under the singlet. His face seemed so frank I could not forebear smiling to myself. I was the unwily one but it was me who looked sly.

Yet after all, why not? It was high time I was shriven. Fr. Boy said by way of rebuttal, though the thought had not occurred to me, "Paul cannot hear your confession."

"Very well, Father," I said in all meekness. "Here?"

"No. We shall use the box. I believe this to be a rite hedged with formality for very good reasons. We shall not have the dubious benefit of anonymity but I can give you formality."

I bowed my head.

We entered the San Ignatio chapel. I knelt on the other side of the partition from my old mentor, my invigilator of character, if not intellect, and in the same place and in the same position as I had admitted to masturbation and shop-lifting, I attempted to classify my misdemeanors first into order of gravity, then to put them into order of chronology.

"When did you make your last confession?" the good, strong Father asked me in the time-honoured fashion. I told him and we proceeded. It was 11.49 when we went in and 12.37 when we emerged. Fr. Boy was sweating, I was cool. I would be, *di ba*? It wasn't exactly breaking news to me. I'd been living with it, more I'd been comfortable with it, for years rather than months.

Fr. Boy refused to absolve me. He said he had detected no sign of contrition. "Come back when you're ready." He spoke curtly. His face was set like the Mactan stone-facings on the school-wall. He was, as usual, right. So far from repenting I was thinking of all that I still had left to do – on behalf of the permanently absent and enjoying it the more for being the only one in the know, the other gagged by a vow of silence. I thought of Skipper's surprise, Lazares's shock. I thought I'd go down to Port Isabel, too, and see what ships were in to load grey bird-shit for Ukraine. Pride was the grand theological word. But what I felt was jaunty.

The old steel mirror in the bend outside the school, that we used to joke was a *fung shui* mirror, was still there. No one ever took care of it but it was burnished good as glass. I caught sight of my reflection. The smile froze on my face. What I had on was the Runt's Smile.

I FOUND FR. PAUL DISCUSSING AZALEAS with Fr. Alarico, the ex-priest from East Timor who ran the retreat. "Father" Alarico now had a Philippine wife, three bonny kids even darker than himself, and a glow of happiness which surrounded everything in his vicinity. Fr. Paul was of course in earshot of Fr. Alarico and therefore in his immediate vicinity but he was not happy. He was laughing but laughter and a smile, I do not need to assure anyone, are not always the concomitants of felicity or friendship. The most accomplished assassins serve death with a smile.

"Castro, dear boy!" he said. He already looked a bit glazed but my arrival left him dizzier. Of course. Fr. Boy hadn't warned him about it.

If I'd arrived in a puff of violet smoke it wouldn't have been that much stranger and possibly less surprising. Fr. Paul's brilliant smile didn't falter as he regarded me for some twenty seconds as he might a colourful and rare butterfly settling on the dense vegetation of the Retreat House garden. I also favoured him with my best smile. Best, but also genuine, while his was a mask. It was one of those rare occasions where I, part-Filipino, part-African, got out-smiled. My own head started to spin. I wondered if I looked as giddy as Fr. Paul.

"Do you know the name of this fruit?" he asked suddenly.

"What fruit?"

"This," he said impatiently, pointing at a tree thirty yards away.

"That?"

"Yes," he said with greater asperity, the benevolence gone. That was good. This was the Fr. Paul I knew.

I looked hard. The tree was *tambis*, like I'd seen in the Antilles. You saw the roseate or pale-jade fruits in piles on the sidewalks of Cebu. The flesh was crisp, white, tasteless as paper and usually eaten with salt. Funnily enough, I'd never seen the fruits on their tree before but it was a perfectly nondescript, medium-sized tree, maybe somewhat more gnarled than the run. "Yes, Father. *Tambis*."

It was as if my intervention had never been. "It is," mused Fr. Paul, "botanically speaking, *eugenia malaccensis*. Known also in the Antilles, to which it was transplanted – like the Pacific breadfruit – as Pomerac. Colloquially called in some parts the Java Apple."

Man, this was like old times. I'd often wondered if Fr. Paul had seemed so knowledgeable simply because I was young and impressionable. Either he was spectacularly erudite – or, on the other hand, I was still *tabula rasa*, waiting for impress. Most certainly he prepared for our school lessons, came forearmed. The allusions and background references, as carelessly strewn as banana-leaf sweet-meat wrappers at a cockfight, were assiduously collected. And maybe he'd boned up on the Retreat House botany, too.

We strolled towards the hardy upland specimen of *eugenia malaccensis*. Fr. Paul flicked a dangling *tambis* fruit with his forefinger in just the same way as he did our painstakingly crafted Christmas tree decorations: poor aids to our intrinsically heathen beliefs that were originally pagan props themselves. A giant two foot tikki flicked its forked tongue at him from the branch where it was waiting for mosquitoes. I fought an urge to giggle when quite unconsciously Fr. Paul repeated the same mannerism himself. "Well," he said, cocking an ear to a bird's sweet, seductive melody, "You could think yourself in Eden. Or Never Never Land."

I was beginning to think it was more like Alice in Wonderland.

"Have a Java Apple?"

"No, thank you, Father. Uh, Father, you must forgive my apparent gormlessness. This is a moment I have waited for over so many years. I want you to clarify the questionable things I have done…"

"Then don't call me Father," he said stiffly. "You are not my son." When he saw my genuine bafflement and hurt, he unbent and said less harshly, "I am no longer a priest."

"Pather Faul!" This time his smile was genuine and it prompted mine. I think we were amused by the same thing but I didn't check. There are some things in life that are on their surface too trifling to articulate but which you find subsequently have become an important definer of your friends, *di ba*? And then you think it's a shame you weren't crass enough at the time to ask, for instance, "Why were you laughing?", for your defining moment with your lifelong friend might be nothing more than a private solipsism.

"You're, uh, going to get married?" I faltered, thinking that for most failed priests the vow of celibacy was the hardest cross to bear. Even as I said it, I thought how ridiculous it was to apply this cliche of behaviour to Fr. Paul.

He, too, was amused. "A lot worse than that, Castro. That would be just a detail, wouldn't it? No. I've lost all belief, the whole shooting-match fails to hold any credibility for me these days. Trinity, saints, canon, all of it."

"You don't believe in Our Lord? Jesus, Father Paul."

"Well quite, Castro."

"But how did it happen? How *could* it happen?"

"Just say I saw the light on the road to Danao."

"Father, this is terrible. It's like an earthquake hit me. I mean, like everything I thought solid came toppling down."

"In that case I'm sorry. I wouldn't like to wish my mental condition on anyone. So foreign parts didn't make an atheist of you?"

"Foreign parts made Frankenstein's Monster, Father. But they strengthened my beliefs."

"I'm glad to hear it, I truly am, but for the last time I'm no longer *in loco parentis* to you. You may, if you so desire, call me Paul. If your hierarchical Philippine soul baulks at that, you could try Mr Paul. Failing that, the respectful 'sir' one extends to schoolmaster or adult stranger will be perfectly acceptable."

"Aye, aye, sir."

"I didn't give you a licence to be impertinent, Castro."

"Ah, *diay*! No, Father. It was a reflex – OK *na lang*. I'll call you," and I gulped, "Paul *lang*."

"Good. Now, if I can't prevail upon you to sample this most attractive fruit, would you care for some coffee?"

"*Salamat*. If we get Filipinos to drink more coffee we can raise the average national IQ."

"I fail to see a connection."

"We will all sleep less on our backs and get more oxygen."

"Saints alive! You remember. I am afraid I may have abused my position as your teacher."

"Never, Fr. Paul! I owe everything I am to you – nearly everything I am, but certainly everything I know. I've put it into practice the best I can, all the principles I learned from you."

"Well, I'm deeply flattered again. Sugar? No? A drop of milk? Good. Now tell me a little of your rich experience in the world."

Fr. Paul kicked off his sandals and put his feet on a stool, exposing the soles to me. I gulped. Then I spilled the beans. I told him pretty well most of it, *siguro*. Fr. Paul, as I will always think of him, listened without interrupting. I respected him the more for that because I know from my own experience how difficult it is not to make interjections. It takes more discipline to be a listener than it does to be the most accomplished raconteur. My confession to Fr. Boy had been punctuated by his exclamations, requests for amplifications and his highly unprofessional scolding. Doesn't a good psychiatrist let the patient do all the work?

My accounting to Fr. Paul lasted far longer than any tale I had heard on my travels. At length I fell silent. My eyes were fixed on my hands. Life at sea had not been all that kind to them. I stole a glance at Fr. Paul. His expression was, if anything, blander than when I had commenced.

"Hm," he commented.

"Yes?" I asked eagerly. He shook his head, smiling quizzically, an eyebrow raised. Fr. Paul was difficult to shock; more he prided himself on this English imperturbability. "Fr. Boy said I was as mad as I was bad."

"Did he, I wonder, use 'mad' in the English sense of insane or the American one of 'angry'."

"I think the English sense."

"One respects his opinion, conventional as it may be. On the other hand there is a good deal more violence, directed to less constructive ends, in the *Odyssey*. Have you castrated anyone since your restoration to us?"

"There's a kid in Manila deserves it but, no, I haven't yet."

"Good. Refrain from so doing."

At that moment the telephone rang.

"I'll just retire to the garden, sir."

Fr. Paul waved me down as he picked the receiver up. The telephone system had evidently improved in my more than seven years away. Prior to my departure, fully half the calls I fielded would be wrong numbers and you'd be lucky to get through on the third dial from any of the conveniently placed shop-front phones wrongly marked one peso minimum three minutes instead of maximum three minutes.

"Paul, speaking. Mark, how good to hear your dulcet tones. Yes, he is, as a matter of fact. Have you your barefoot spies out?"

I listened to Fr. Boy's voice on the other end. Unfortunately, while I could readily identify his distinctive drawl I couldn't make out the individual words. Fr. Paul's expression of mild amusement never left him but I don't think I was mistaken in believing Fr. Boy to have got madder since I'd last seen him.

"Frankenstein, Mark," said Fr. Paul evenly, "was the creator-scientist, not the monster, so your rather dramatic analogy is not quite correct. Furthermore, one supposes from his name he was Jewish which neither I nor what you like to term my monster are. Golem was the Jewish monster, of course."

There were more angry but unintelligible words from Fr. Boy at San Ignatio.

"I can see it's no use conversing with you in your present state, Mark," Fr. Paul said. "However, feel free to visit, as Americans say, with me when you so desire." He hung up and beamed at me. "The saint, Castro, moves in the world, not outside it. He is not some ethereal creature but flesh and blood. Rather more blood than flesh, I sometimes fear. Yes, dear boy. The saint sees the world with a clarity the impure would call ruthlessness. Do you see clearly, Castro?"

"I think so, sir," I said cautiously. I had an uneasy feeling Fr. Paul had lost his reason with his vestments.

"Why don't you join Opus Dei or the staff of General Lim?" he suggested. "You were saying, if I interpret you correctly, that ends justified means, particularly if no self-interest was involved. A strong medicine is best for prophylaxis if a stronger is not to be used for cure later." It was difficult to know if he was being serious or sarcastic or, knowing my man, both simultaneously.

"On the other hand," he continued, "to pursue a perhaps specious analogy, side-effects on the general population might mean cure was worse than disease which is in contravention of general medical practice as well as common-sense."

"You've lost me, sir," I said.

"I don't think so, Castro."

We were silent a while. I turned the focus on Fr. Paul. Of course I had known what he was talking about. "But what are your plans?" I inquired. "Surely you don't mean to stay here indefinitely."

"No, I don't. As a matter of fact I shall take the traditional course of those who have failed to find firm footing on land. I shall follow the sea."

"What?" I did my best to imagine Fr. Paul mixing with the likes of Jock or even Robbie.

"Yes, not quite a career before the mast, however. I am taking a position as lecturer on the SS Cicero, a vessel cruising the Eastern Mediterranean. Are you familiar with that part of the world?"

"Really through your classes, Fr. Paul. I was pulling ropes most of the time."

"Only Asia Minor, of course. Nothing to compare with the real intellectual glories but possibly more interesting from the archaeological point of view."

"You were always more a Roman than you were a Catholic, sir. By the way, you won't have escaped us, Father. All the stewards will be Filipinos."

"Bayot to boot, I don't doubt." This was possibly the nearest to a salacious conversation one could come with him.

"But what about you? Is there anything I can do to help, sir?"

"I rather think not. But here's my new card. There's my own Harrogate address on one side and my brother's apartment, they're called Chambers actually, interesting English archaism, near

Piccadilly. You might have trouble with the porter, I fear, but if you do come by, persistence will in the end prevail."

"I'm not sure I'd let myself in."

We both laughed together.

"Well, I won't detain you from your prodigal's round. Is there any way I can be of pecuniary assistance again?"

"Definitely not, Fr. Paul. I'm OK. And thanks for all the help before I didn't know about. I'm grateful, really grateful, but I'm most grateful for your teaching. Money is only money, *di ba*? But knowledge is the real treasure."

"Then I can consider I have taught you something useful after all."

"No, Father. It was beautiful because it was not useful. I applied it, then maybe it became something ugly in the application."

"You're talking in riddles."

"I think you know the solution to anything I set, sir."

Another silence fell upon us. Fr. Paul was before me now, he whom I had needed so many times during my helter-skelter scrambles up the ladders and down the snakes. Now my head was, of course, as empty as it had been of expedients before the Jocks and Nikitas of the world. Fr. Paul drummed his fingers on the table and followed a gecko's inverted passage across the ceiling. I understood my audience was over.

As I was at the door, he said, "Write."

CABLE HAD COME TO CEBU. Nobody was interested in traveller's tales. You didn't have to move two feet from your set or your more affluent neighbour's to see either a pageant of the world's great cities or its seamier spots.

"Uncivilised feoples," commented Auntie Irish complacently as she switched from Amerindians with wooden discs in their lower lips to her favourite Mexican soap-opera dubbed into Tagalog. (She thought the fair-skinned Mexicans were an upper-class family from Manila). Babelisation was to be had at the press of the channel-shift on the remote control nestling in one's palm: French, Chinese, Spanish, German, Italian, and Thai mingled with the snarl of the trisikads and the tootings of the jeepneys outside.

One afternoon I got two surprises. I liked to keep my finger on the arrow-down button rather than hitting on a specific channel-number. More like the fluidity of the court, man, more like the scenes of my life flashing before me as I drowned. So I got marmosets on Disney channel, the American President on CNN, a black buck beating on a plump pink guy penned in a corner of a boxing-ring on ESPN – high on comedy, albeit low on the surprise factor, over-niggering once again – a flash flood in Italy reported in staccato Latin American Spanish, BBC World Service doing their best with a fuzzy picture, and then sandwiched between Scooby Doo the Dog on Cartoon Network and the Asian stockmarket round-up, my expectations took a twist. Zip, down the coils of the snake. Prap, back up the rungs of the ladder.

I hadn't imagined it. There was Becky, yessir, Nicola Smith's teeny-bopper Singaporean friend, talking ten to the dozen in front of an alternating twinkling montage of pop-group, napalm bloom, starving children, girls licking strawberry cone (why didn't they just make it dick and have done?), and then back to strumming pop-group. You get the picture. Becky was prating in her perfect American-English and in mid-sentence she went into Mandarin which, to me at least, sounded as 100 per cent as her English, before she switched from birdy North Chinese burr into nasal cheer-leaderese again, followed for good measure by hard-palate Malay. If you shut your eyes it would have been difficult to assign a body to that American voice. Becky was a VJ. Shutting my eyes took my attention off the rapid-fire images, seven hundred a minute, the same as a machine-gun's rate of fire, and forced me to concentrate on what Becky was saying. And here was a wonder. She was addressing me and the millions in the perfection of idiom and pitch and I couldn't understand what the fuck she was talking about. I mean, if you'd asked me to do a Fr. Paul precis one minute after, I'd have been at a loss to remember what she'd said. The gist of it was that there wasn't a gist. She was the vampire in the mirror – no trace.

Next moment she had, indeed, disappeared and I got another kick up memory's butt: Sonika Narayan, the other teeny I'd driven up Malaysia into Thailand. Since I'd last seen her she'd lost twenty pounds of puppy-fat, lasered the moustache already incipient at fifteen, but acquired a diamond nose-stud which was both Indian and the height of teenage cool. She did the Becky mid-sentence trick but with Hindi and English-type English. Man, I was as awe-struck as when I saw Michael Jordan or Magic work a combination of moves. More so, for I'd had the prowess of physical fluency myself and, while I'd read stuff Becky would never in all her life trouble her little head with, as soon as I opened my mouth I was branded a Flip.

Jeez, I thought, with a warm glow of congratulation, I can claim acquaintance with these starlets. I wonder how much they get, was my next thought. Probably more than a dentist or the first mate of a tanker and certainly more than a Cardinal. You have not lived in vain, Castro, I imagined Fr. Paul telling me. What next? I turned to CNN, wondering if I'd see Slash 'n' Crap, no longer in sequined waistcoats but in the grimy white of the convinced, marching with placards on some embassy or other, but it was only the show-biz hour.

There was no need to leave the discomfort of your own hooch to see the world; the world would come to you at the touch of a button. I tried to impress Auntie Irish with an account of the waxworks in Madame Tussaud's, but "I already see dat," she informed me with icy dignity. Those who lived within the mighty span of the information-bearing cable did not care to be thought hicks. I was reading a book I'd picked up on Fr. Paul's desk which he, with typical generosity where the treasures of the mind were concerned, had pressed upon me. It was a history of human emotions, an encyclopaedia of sensibility. Sense it didn't possess too much of; it was way too idealistic for the humanity I'd seen, but it was an inspirational read. The author spoke of invisible filaments linking kindred spirits across space and time. But what, I thought, of the tendrils linking enemies? Incandescent wire gossamers which could shed eternal light on the perplexities of the moment. I imagined wrapping them around the necks of those so deserving; I imagined myself at the centre of a spider's web, cognisant of the vibration down my threads which would betray the whereabouts of the hostile and the unredeemed.

But for the moment it was a humbler kind of hands-on, while I awaited my party-invitation to the US of A. Cheech Chong dropped me a line. He wanted me to come up to Manila to be his team's physio, maybe also to help out a little with the coaching. Putting people on ice I knew about, so putting ice on people was no big deal. While up there I could give a couple of people the full *Halo*[2] treatment, for Haydee and Dant, for Butch.

I e-mailed my acceptance to Cheech at Chong@ slamdunk.speed.ph.com from the cybernet café in the brand-new mall in Cebu Uptown. What next, man? Would we be employing Bohaidenese maids and stubbing cigarettes out on their cheeks as casually as I punched the keys on the board? Would we be teaching music to Cubans? Accountancy to the Singaporeans? Time-tabling to the Germans? Ethics to Jenny Smith?

I looked at the transfigured young faces at the computer-screens around me. This was tomorrow and I was living in its glow. The off-duty pre-dentistry stude next to me in the Cebu Doctor's College uniform was clicking her way through the menus and the sites the way I would high-step across Butch's tyres in my prime. She didn't, to be objective, look like she'd suffered from anoxic slumbering at any time in her life. I read some indecipherable chat-room shorthand on her screen – *RU ^^ wid Ronagirl?* – and thought she held in the electronic mouse a priceless crystal and silver-filigree jug into which she was pouring a tooth-rotting soft-drink instead of ambrosia. I wished I'd brought Fr. Paul. I wished he'd open a Ciceronian chat-room, a *halo*[2] of classic and contemporary, inanity cloaked in the obscurity of a learned language no longer foolishness but crazed pedantry.

I thought how Dant would have been a jockey of the keyboard, the Lothario of the chat-room. I thought how it had all come too late for me, too: all the precautions I'd had to take with the post, the third parties, the forwarding when I was long gone. I always got the mail months late, the datelines mocking me like they must have Marryat's post-captains. I could have been a phoney e-mail number, getting my letters fresh as they were written whether I was in Bombay one week and Ebbiola the next. Dead letter boxes were no longer holes in trees but swivel-seats in an air-conditioned room perfumed with the scent of percolating coffee. You could be as anonymous or as accessible as you wanted, as devious or as brazen.

I opened an account in the name of Danton Zarcal, Lazarus13@hotmail.com. On a whim I tried the directory for Skipper. He was there. No surprise. The whole Frat and their relatives down to the fifth degree of consanguinity probably were. I clicked him a line from Dant: *I vack for you, mans.*

I found Brab on Yahoo! the stupid fuck. I clicked him a line from deadchick@daemon.com.ph: *this dish tastes best cold.* Then I walked into the dusk.

IT IS THE EVENING OF THE DAY, a poetical or at least a songwriter's expression which would offend the Fr. Pauls of this world with its grammatical redundancy. I sit on a bollard in my rubber slippers and shorts, my old team shorts that I haven't worn in more than seven years. I'm free of mosquito bites, the itchy dots that appear to be plaguing everybody else, judging by the scratching of ankles and slapping of ears going on, because I've applied OFF! lotion to my appendages and extremities. I'd like to rub that on a few skins. Oh, for Life lotion, that magic potion applied with the thoroughness that failed Achilles to the Huberts and Commander Smiths of this world from birth that preserves them from the indignities, inconveniences, and dangers presented by life's little bloodsuckers, those agents and vectors of lethal diseases, terrible out of all proportion to the tiny sting and itch which is their harbinger.

My team shorts. I think of how much I hate and fear teams: the congregation and the gang, the crew and the tribe.

The sun starts to set over Olango island to the west of my native Mactan, as it must have set the day Magellan got chopped to pieces by Lapu-Lapu's homeboys in the gory froth of the reef shallows. Magellan and my bad-self, finding a quietus after our globe-trottings.

I think of Brabazon and Nikita, of Dr Al-Elvis, of the last Cuban bully cringing on the raft as Michael and I watched him bleed and we got our breath back. I wonder if one day Nikita's face will loom up at my windscreen as I draw up at the pedestrian-crossing and how I will let my foot come off the clutch accidentally on purpose. I hear Dant's voice again. It says, "Never say die, Gorilla. Don't forget who your real friends are," and I want to reply, "It's not my friends I think of most."

Some girls are giggling over my size and blackness over by the pier-legs. I smile at them, kick off my slippers and show them the soles of my feet, a sickly colour paler than their faces.

I think of how I'd like to make a sundae-confection of all the bests I know, the surmounting glace-cherry at the apex of every civilisation. Then I think I might as well go and use eye of newt and tail of toad because too many bests would cancel each other out. Bests, man, are the flip-side of worsts. You don't have the one without the other.

I hear a voice again. It chides me, "Live and let live. You think too much, Gorilla." And I smile as I answer, "It takes two, Brod, it takes two. And didn't Fr. Paul teach you anything? Stopping thinking is a crime. That's a crime of omission, Brod."

I try to smile my millionth smile but it's frozen stiff on my face. My legs have gone to sleep under me. I can feel the pins and needles coming, bristling on me like I'm a voodoo doll. I check my watch, my Bambi-purloined, my Bambi-bestowed Timex. It's already 23:00. It's my eleventh hour, Brod, but I don't think the US Cavalry will be coming, more like the Horsemen of the Apocalypse.

I stand, I lurch.

ABOUT THE AUTHOR

Timothy Mo was born in Hong Kong in 1950 and educated there and at St John's College, Oxford. His novels have won the Geoffrey Faber Memorial Prize, the Hawthornden Prize, the E.M. Forster Award from the American Academy of Arts and Letters, and the James Tait Black Memorial Prize.

He is now based in South East Asia after more than twenty years in London.